PICK

C000245034

PICK-UP

Charles Willeford

Pick-Up

The Burnt Orange Heresy

Cockfighter

No Exit Press

1995

No Exit Press

18 Coleswood Rd

Harpenden, Herts, AL5 1EQ

This omnibus edition copyright   © Charles Willeford 1991

Pick-Up - First published 1967 - Copyright 1967

The Burnt Orange Heresy - First published 1987 - Copyright 1971

Cockfighter - First published 1987 - Copyright 1972

The right of Charles Willeford to be identified as author of this work has been asserted by him in accordance with the Copyright, Designs & Patents Act 1988.

All rights reserved. No part of this book may be reproduced, stored in a retrieval system, or transmitted, in any form, or by any means, electronic, mechanical, photocopying, recording or otherwise, without the written permission of the publishers

A CIP catalogue record for this book is available from the British Library.

 I S B N 1 - 874061 - 39 - 4   A Charles Willeford Omnibus

 9 8 7 6 5 4 3 2 1

Printed by The Guernsey Press

Chapter One

ENTER MADAME

It must have been around a quarter to eleven. A sailor came in and ordered a chilli dog and coffee. I sliced a bun, jerked a frank out of the boiling water, nested it, poured a half-dipper of chilli over the frank and sprinkled it liberally with chopped onions. I scribbled a check and put it by his plate. I wouldn't have recommended the unpalatable mess to a starving animal. The sailor was the only customer, and after he ate his dog he left.

That was the exact moment she entered.

A small woman, hardly more than five feet.

She had the figure of a teenage girl. Her suit was a blue tweed, smartly cut, and over her thin shoulders she wore a fur jacket, bolero length. Tiny gold circular earrings clung to her small pierced ears. Her hands and feet were small, and when she seated herself at the counter I noticed she wasn't wearing any rings. She was pretty drunk.

'What'll it be?' I asked her.

'I believe I need coffee.' She steadied herself on the stool by bracing her hands against the edge of the counter.

'Yes, you do,' I agreed, 'and you need it black.'

I drew a cupful and set it before her. The coffee was too hot for her to drink and she bent her head down and blew on it with comical little puffs. I stood behind the counter watching her. I couldn't help it; she was beautiful. Even Benny, from his seat behind the cash register, was staring at her, and his only real interest is money. She wasn't nearly as young as I had first thought her to be. She was about twenty-six or -seven. Her fine blonde hair was combed straight back. Slightly to the right of a well-defined widow's-peak, an inch-wide strip of silver hair glistened, like a moonlit river flowing through night fields. Her oval face was unlined and very white. The only make-up she had on was lipstick; a dark shade of red, so dark it was almost black. She looked up from her coffee and noticed that I was staring at her. Her eyes were a charred sienna-brown, flecked with dancing particles of shining gold.

'This coffee is too hot.' She smiled good-humoredly.

'Sure it is,' I replied, 'but if you want to sober up you should drink it hot as you can.'

'My goodness! Who wants to sober up?'

Benny was signaling me from the cash register. I dropped my conversation with the girl to see what he wanted. Benny was a fat, bald, hook-nosed little man with a shaggy horseshoe of gray hair circling his head. I didn't particularly like him, but he never pushed or tried to boss me and I'd stuck it out as his counterman for more than two months. For me, this was a record. His dirty eyes were gleaming behind his gold-rimmed glasses.

'There's your chance, Harry!' He laughed a throaty, phlegmy laugh.

I knew exactly what he meant. About two weeks before a girl had entered the café at closing time and she had been pretty well down on her luck. She'd been actually hungry and Benny had had me fix her up with a steak and french fries. Afterwards, he had made her pay him for the meal by letting him take it out in trade in the kitchen.

'I don't need any advice from you,' I said angrily.

He laughed again, deep in his chest. 'It's quitting time. Better take advantage.' He climbed down from his stool and walked stiffly to the door. He shot the bolt and hung the CLOSED sign from the hook. I started toward the kitchen and as I passed the woman she shook her empty cup at me.

'See? All finished. May I have another?'

I filled her cup, set it in front of her and went into the back room and slipped into my tweed jacket. The jacket was getting ratty. It was my only outer garment with the exception of my trenchcoat and I'd worn it for more than two years. The elbows were thin and the buttons, except one, were missing. The gold button was the top one and a coat looks funny buttoned at the top. I resolved to move it to the middle in the morning. My blue gabardine trousers hadn't been cleaned for three weeks and they were spotted here and there with grease. I had another pair of trousers in my room, but they were tuxedo trousers, and I used them on waiter and busboy jobs. Sober, I was always embarrassed about my appearance, but I didn't intend to stay sober very long. I combed my hair and I was ready for the street, a bar and a drink.

She was still sitting at the counter and her cup was empty again.

'Just one more and I'll go,' she said with a drunken little laugh. 'I promise.'

For the third time I gave her a cup of coffee. Benny was counting on his fingers and busily going over his receipts for the day. I tapped him on the shoulder.

'Benny, I need a ten until payday,' I told him.

'Not again? I let you have ten last night and today's only Tuesday. By Saturday you won't have nothing coming.'

'You don't have to worry about it.'

He took his copy-book from under the counter and turned to my page. After he entered the advance in the book he reluctantly gave me a ten dollar bill. I folded the bill and put it in my watch pocket. I felt a hand timidly tugging at my sleeve and I turned around. The little woman was looking up at me with her big brown innocent eyes.

'I haven't any money,' she said bitterly.

'Is that right?'

'Not a penny. Are you going to call a policeman?'

'Ask Mr. Freeman. He's the owner; I just work here.'

'What's that?' Benny asked, at the mention of his name. He was in the middle of his count and didn't like being disturbed.

'This young lady is unable to pay for her coffee.'

'Coffee is ten cents,' he said firmly.

'I'll tell you what, Benny. Just take it out of my pay.'

'Don't think I won't!' He returned to his counting.

I unlocked the door, and the woman and I went outside.

'You're a free woman,' I said to the girl. 'You're lucky that Benny didn't notice you were without a purse when you came in. Where is your purse, by the way?'

'I think it's in my suitcase.'

'All right. Where's your suitcase?'

'It's in a locker. I've got the key.' She took a numbered key out of the pocket of her fur jacket. 'The main trouble is that I can't seem to remember whether the locker's in the railroad station or the bus station.' She was genuinely puzzled.

'If I were you I'd look in the bus station first. You're quite a way from the railroad station. Do you know where it is?'

'The bus station?'

'Yes. It's seven blocks that way and one block that way.' I pointed down Market Street. 'You can't miss it. I'm going to have a drink.'

'Would you mind buying me one too?'

'Sure. Come on.'

She took my arm and we walked down Market. It was rather pleasant having a beautiful woman in tow and I was glad she had asked me to buy her a drink. I would never have asked her, but as long as she didn't mind, I certainly didn't mind. I shortened my stride so she could keep up with me and from time to time I looked down at her. Gin was my weakness, not women, but with a creature like her ... well, it was enough to make a man think. We were nearing the bar where I always had my first drink after work and my mind returned to more practical things. We entered, found seats at the end of the bar.

'Say,' she said brightly. 'I remember being in here tonight!'

'That's fine. It's a cinch you were in some bar.' The bartender knew me well, but his eyebrows lifted when he saw the girl with me.

'What'll you have, Harry?' he asked.

'Double gin and tonic.' I turned to the girl.

'I'd better not have a double. Give me a little shot of bourbon and a beer chaser.' She smiled at me. 'I'm being smart, aren't I?'

'You bet.' I lit two cigarettes and passed her one. She sucked it deeply.

'My name is Harry Jordan,' I said solemnly. 'I'm thirty-two years of age and when I'm not working, I drink.'

Her laugh closely resembled a tinkling bell. 'My name is Helen Meredith. I'm thirty-three years old and I don't work at all. I drink all of the time.'

'You're not thirty-three, are you? I took you for about twenty-six, maybe less.'

'I'm thirty-three all right, and I can't forget it.'

'Well, you've got an advantage on me then. Married?'

'Uh huh. I'm married, but I don't work at that either.' She shrugged comically. I stared at her delicate fingers as she handled the cigarette.

The bartender arrived with our drinks. Mine was good and cold and the gin taste was strong. The way I like it. I love the first drink best of all.

'Two more of the same,' I told the bartender, 'and see if Mrs. Meredith's purse was left here, will you?'

'I haven't seen a purse lying around. Are you sure you left it in here, miss?' he asked Helen worriedly.

'I'm not sure of anything,' she replied.

'Well, I'll take a look around. Maybe you left it in a booth.'

'Helen Meredith,' I said when the bartender left. 'Here's to you!' We clicked our glasses together and drained them down. Helen choked a bit and followed her shot down with the short beer chaser.

'Ahhh,' she sighed. 'Harry, I'm going to tell you something while I'm still able to tell you. I haven't lived with my husband for more than ten years, and even though I don't wear a ring, I'm still married.'

'You don't have to convince me.'

'But I want to tell you. I live with my mother in San

Sienna. Do you know where that is?'

'Sure. It's a couple of hundred miles down the coast. Noted for tourists, beaches, a mission and money. Nothing else.'

'That's right. Well as I told you, I drink. In the past two years I've managed to embarrass Mother many times. It's a small community and we're both well-known so I decided the best thing to do was get out. This morning I was half-drunk, half-hungover, and I bought a bottle and I left. For good. But I hit the bottle so hard I'm not sure whether I came to San Francisco on the bus or on the train.'

'I'm willing to lay odds of two to one it was the bus.'

'You're probably right. I really don't remember.'

The bartender brought us our second drink. He shook his head emphatically. 'You didn't leave no purse in here, miss. You might've thought you did, but you didn't.'

'Thanks for looking,' I told him. 'After we finish this one,' I said to Helen, 'we'll go back down to the bus station and I'll find your purse for you. Then you'd better head back for San Sienna and Mother.'

Helen shook her head back and forth slowly. 'No. I'm not going back. Never.'

'That's your business. Not mine.'

We finished our second drink and left the bar. It was a long walk to the bus station. Market Street blocks are long and crowded. Helen hung on to my arm possessively, and by the time we reached the station she had sobered considerably. The place was jampacked with servicemen of all kinds and a liberal sprinkling of civilians. The Greyhound station is the jumping-off place for servicemen. San Francisco is the hub for all the spokes leading to air bases, navy bases and army posts that dot the bay area.

'Does the bus station look familiar to you?'

'Of course!' She laughed. 'I've been to San Francisco many times. I always come up on the bus for my Christmas shopping.'

I felt a little foolish. 'Let's start looking then.' She handed me the numbered key. There are a lot of parcel lockers inside the Greyhound station and many more out on the waiting ramp, but in a few minutes we were able to locate the locker. It was the first row to the left of the Ladies' Room. I inserted the key and opened the locker.

I took the suitcase out of the locker and handed it to Helen. She unsnapped the two catches on the aluminum over-nighter and raised the lid. Her tiny hands ruffled deftly through the clothing. There wasn't any purse. I looked. No purse. I felt around inside the locker.

No purse.

'Do you suppose I could have left it in some other bar, Harry?' she asked me worriedly. 'Somewhere between here and the café?'

'That's probably what you did, all right. And if you did, you can kiss it goodbye. How much money did you have?'

'I don't know, but drunk or sober I wouldn't have left San Sienna broke. I know I had some traveler's checks.'

I took my money out of my watch pocket. There were eight dollars and seventy cents. I gave the five dollar bill to Helen. 'This five'll get you a ticket back to San Sienna. You'd better get one.'

Helen shook her head vigorously this time and firmly set her mouth. 'I'm not going back, Harry. I told you I wasn't and I meant it.' She held the bill out to me. 'Take it back; I don't want it.'

'No, you go ahead and keep it. We'll consider it a loan. But I'm going to take you to a hotel. If I turned you loose you'd drink it up.'

'It didn't take you long to get to know me, did it?' She giggled.

'I don't know you. It's just that I know what I'd do. Come on, we'll find a hotel.'

I picked up the light suitcase and we left the station. We crossed Market Street and at Powell we turned and entered the first hotel that looked satisfactory to me. There are more than a dozen hotels on Powell Street, all of them adequate, and it was our best bet to find a vacancy. The hotel we entered was furnished in cheap modern furniture and the floor was covered with a rose wall-to-wall carpet. There were several green plants scattered

about, all of them set in white pots with wrought-iron legs,
and by each foam-cushioned lobby chair there were
skinny, black wrought-iron ash-stands. We crossed the
empty lobby to the desk and I set the bag on the floor.
The desk clerk was a fairly young man with sleek black
hair. He looked up from his comic book with surly gray
eyes.

'Sorry,' he said flatly. 'No doubles left. Just singles.'

'That's fine,' I said. 'That's what I want.'

Helen signed the register card. Her handwriting was
cramped and it slanted to the left, almost microscopic in
size. She put the pen back into the holder and folded her
arms across her chest.

'The lady will pay in advance,' I said to the clerk,
without looking at Helen. She frowned fiercely for a
second then in spite of herself, she giggled and gave the
clerk the five dollar bill. He gave her two ones in return.
The night clerk also doubled as a bell boy and he came
out from behind the desk with Helen's key in his hand.

'You want to go up now?' he asked Helen, pointedly
ignoring me.

'I've still got two dollars,' Helen said to me. 'I'll buy you
a drink!'

'No. You go to bed. You've had enough for one day.'

'I'll buy you one tomorrow then.'

'Tomorrow will be time enough,' I said.

Helen's eyes were glassy and her eyelids were heavy. It
was difficult for her to hold them open. In the warmth of
the lobby she was beginning to stagger a little bit. The
night clerk opened the door to the self-operated elevator
and helped her in, holding her by the arm. I selected a
comfortable chair near the desk and waited in the lobby
until he returned. He didn't like it when he saw me sitting
there.

'Do you think she'll manage all right?' I asked him.

'She managed to lock the door after I left,' he replied
dryly.

'Fine. Good night.'

I left the hotel and walked up Powell as far as Lefty's,

ordered a drink at the bar. It was dull, drinking alone, after drinking with Helen. She was the most attractive woman I had met in years. There was a quality about her that appealed to me. The fact that she was an alcoholic didn't make any difference to me. In a way, I was an alcoholic myself. She wasn't afraid to admit that she was a drunk; she was well aware of it, and she didn't have any intention to stop drinking. It wasn't necessary for her to tell me she was a drunk. I can spot an alcoholic in two minutes. Helen was still a good-looking woman, and she'd been drinking for a long time. I never expected to see her again. If I wanted to, I suppose it would have been easy enough. All I had to do was go down to her hotel in the morning, and ...

I finished my drink quickly and left the bar. I didn't feel like drinking any more. I crossed the street and waited for my cable car. In a few minutes it dragged up the hill, slowed down at the corner, and I jumped on. I gave the conductor my fare and went inside where it was warmer. Usually, I sat in the outside section where I could smoke, but I was cold that night, my entire body was chilled.

On the long ride home I decided it would be best to steer clear of a woman like Helen.

Chapter Two

FINDERS KEEPERS

I got out of bed the next morning at ten, and still half-asleep, put the coffee pot on the two-ring gas burner. I padded next door to the bathroom, stood under the hot water of the shower for fifteen minutes, shaved, and returned to my room. It was the last one on the left, downstairs in Mrs. Frances McQuade's rooming house. The house was on a fairly quiet street and my room was well separated from the other rooms and roomers. This enabled me to drink in my room without bothering anybody, and nobody could bother me.

I sat down at the table, poured a cup of black coffee and let my mind think about Helen. I tried to define what there was about her that attracted me. Class. That was it. I didn't intend to do anything about the way I felt, but it was pleasant to let my mind explore the possibilities. I finished my coffee and looked around the room. Not only was it an ugly room; it was a filthy room. The walls were covered with a dull gray paper spotted with small crimson flowers. There was a sink in one corner, and next to it the gas burner in a small alcove. My bed was a double, and the head and footboard were made of brass rods ornately twisted and tortured into circular designs. The dresser was metal, painted to look like maple or walnut, some kind of wood, and each leg rested in a small can of water. I kept my food in the bottom drawer and the cans of water kept the ants away. There were no pictures on the walls and no rug upon the floor, just a square piece of tangerine lino-leum under the sink.

The room was in foul shape. Dirty shirts and dirty socks were scattered around, the dresser was messy with newspapers, book matches, my set of oil paints; and the floor was covered with gently moving dust motes. Lined up beneath the sink were seven empty gin bottles and an overflowing paper sack full of empty beer cans. The window was dirty and the sleazy cotton curtains were dusty. Dust was on everything ...

Suppose, by some chance, I had brought Helen home with me the night before? I sadly shook my head. Here was a project for me; I'd clean my room. A momentous decision.

I slipped into my shoes and blue gabardine slacks and walked down the hall to Mrs. McQuade's room.

'Good morning,' I said when she opened the door. 'I want to borrow your broom and mop.'

'The broom and mop are in the closet,' she said, and closed the door again.

Mrs. McQuade had a few eccentricities, but she was a kind, motherly type of woman. Her hair was always freshly blued and whenever I thought about it I would comment on how nice it looked. Why women with beautiful white hair doctor it with bluing has always been a mystery to me.

I found the broom and a rag mop and returned to my room.

I spent the rest of the morning cleaning the room, even going so far as to wash my window inside and out. The curtains needed washing but I shook the dust out of them and hung them back on the rod. Dusted and cleaned, the room looked fairly presentable, even with its ancient, battered furniture. I was dirty again so I took another shower before I dressed. I put my bundle of laundry under my arm, dragged the mop and broom behind me, and leaned them up against Mrs. McQuade's door.

I left the house and dumped my dirty laundry off at the Spotless Cleaner on my way to the corner and Big Mike's Bar and Grill. This was my real home, Big Mike's, and I spent more time in this bar than anywhere else. It was a friendly place, old-fashioned, with sawdust on the floor, and the walls paneled in dark oak. The bar was long and narrow, extending the length of the room, and it had a section with cushioned stools and another section with a rail for those who preferred to stand. There were a few booths along the wall, but there was also a dining-room next door that could be entered either from the street outside or from the bar-room. The food was good, reasonable, and there was plenty of it. I seldom ate anything at Mike's. Food costs money and money spent for food is money wasted. When I got hungry, which was seldom, I ate at Benny's.

I took my regular seat at the end of the bar and ordered a draught beer. It was lunch hour and very busy, but both of the bartenders knew me well and when my stein was emptied one of them would quickly fill it again. After one-thirty, the bar was clear of the lunch crowd and Big Mike joined me in a beer.

'You're a little late today, Harry,' Mike said jokingly. He had a deep pleasant voice.

'Couldn't be helped.'

Mike was an enormous man; everything about him was large, especially his head and hands. The habitual white shirt and full-sized apron he wore added to his look of massiveness. His face was badly scarred, but it didn't make him look hard or tough; it gave him a kindly, mellowed expression. He could be tough when it was necessary, however, and he was his own bouncer. The bar and grill belonged to him alone, and it had been purchased by his savings after ten years of professional football — all of it on the line, as a right tackle.

'How does my tab stand these days, Mike?' I asked him.

'I'll check.' He looked in the credit book hanging by a string next to the cash register. 'Not too bad,' he smiled. 'Twelve twenty-five. Worried about it?'

'When it gets to fifteen, cut me off, will you, Mike?'

'If I do you'll give me an argument.'

'Don't pay any attention to me. Cut me off just the same.'

PICK-UP

13

'Okay.' He shrugged his heavy shoulders. 'We've gone through this before, we might as well go through it again.'

'I'm not that bad, Mike.'

'I honestly believe you don't know how bad you really are when you're loaded.' He laughed to show he was joking, finished his beer, and lumbered back to the kitchen. I drank several beers, nursing them along, and at two-thirty I left the bar to go to work.

We picked up a little business from the theatre crowd when the afternoon show at the Bijou got out at three-thirty, and after that the café was fairly quiet until five. When things were busy, there was too much work for only one counterman, and I met myself coming and going. Benny was of no help at all. He never stirred all day from his seat behind the register. I don't know how he had the patience to sit like that from seven in the morning until eleven at night. His only enjoyment in life was obtained by eating orange gum-drops and counting his money at night. Once that day, during a lull, when no one was in the café, he tried to kid me about Helen. I didn't like it.

'Come on, Harry, where'd you take her last night?'

'Just forget about it, Benny. There's nothing to tell.' I went into the kitchen to get away from him. I don't like that kind of talk. It's dirty. All of a sudden, all ten seats at the counter were filled, and I was too busy to think of anything except what I was doing. In addition to taking the orders, I had to prepare the food and serve it myself. It was quite a job to handle alone, even though Benny didn't run a regular lunch or dinner menu. Just when things are running well and the orders are simple things like sand-wiches, bowls of chilli, and coffee, a damned aesthete will come in and order soft-boiled eggs wanting them two-and-one-half minutes in the water or something like that. But I like to work, and the busier I am the better I like it. When I'm busy I don't have time to think about when I'll get my next drink.

Ten o'clock rolled around at last, the hour I liked best of all. The traffic was always thin about this time and I only had another hour to go before I could have a drink. I felt a little hungry — I hadn't eaten anything all day — and I made myself a bacon and tomato sandwich. I walked around the counter and sat down to eat it. Benny eyed my sandwich hungrily.

'How about fixing me one of those, Harry?' he asked.

'Sure. Soon as I finish.'

'Fix me one too,' a feminine voice said lightly. I glanced to the left and there was Helen, standing in the doorway.

'You came back.' My voice sounded flat and strained. No longer interested in food, I pushed my sandwich away from me.

'I told you I would. I owe you a drink. Remember?' She had a black patent leather purse in her hand. 'See?' She shook the purse in the air. 'I found it.'

'Do you really want a sandwich?' I asked her, getting to my feet.

'No.' She shook her head. 'I was just talking.'

'Wait right there,' I said firmly, pointing my finger at Helen. 'I'll be back in one second.'

I went into the back room, and feverishly removed the dirty white jacket and leather tie. I changed into my own tie and sport jacket. Benny was ringing up thirty-one cents on the register when I came back. Helen had paid him for the coffee she had drunk the night before. Trust Benny to get his money.

I took Helen's arm, and Benny looked at us both with some surprise.

'Now just where in the hell do you think you're going?' he asked acidly.

'I quit. Come on, Helen.' We walked through the open door.

'Hey!' He shouted after us, and I know that he said something else, but by that time we were walking down the street and well out of range.

Chapter Three

FIRST NIGHT

'Did you really quit just like that?' Helen asked me as we walked down the street. Her voice was more amused than incredulous.

'Sure. You said you were going to buy me a drink. That's much more important than working.'

'Here we are then.' Helen pointed to the entrance door of the bar where we'd had our drinks the night before. 'Is this all right?'

I smiled. 'It's the nearest.' We went inside and sat down at the bar. The bartender recognized Helen right away. He nodded pleasantly to me and then asked Helen: 'Find your purse all right?'

'Sure did,' Helen said happily.

'Now I'm glad to hear that,' the bartender said. 'I was afraid somebody might have picked it up and gone south with it. You know how these things happen sometimes. What'll you have?'

'Double gin and tonic for me,' I said.

'Don't change it,' Helen ordered, stringing along.

As soon as the bartender left to fix our drinks I took a sideways look at Helen. She wasn't tight, not even mellow, but barely under the influence; just enough under to give her a warm, rosy-cheeked color.

'Where did you find your purse, by the way?' I asked Helen.

'It was easy,' she laughed merrily. 'But I didn't think so this morning.' She opened her purse, put enough change down on the bar to pay for the check and handed me a five dollar bill. 'Now we're even, Harry.'

'Thanks,' I said folding the bill and shoving it into my watch pocket, 'I can use it.'

'This morning,' she began slowly, 'I woke up in that miserable little hotel room with a hangover to end them all. God, I felt rotten! I could remember everything pretty well — you going down to the bus station with me, getting the room and so on, but the rest of the day was nothing. Did you ever get like that?'

'I recall a similar experience,' I admitted.

'All I had was two dollars, as you know, so after I showered and dressed I checked out of the hotel, leaving my bag at the desk. I was hungry, so I ate breakfast and had four cups of coffee, black, and tried to figure out what to do next.

'Without money, I was in a bad way —' She quickly finished her drink and shook the ice in her glass at the bartender for another. I downed mine fast in order to join her for the next round.

'So I returned to the bus station after breakfast and started from there.' She smiled slyly and sipped her drink. 'Now where would you have looked for the purse, Harry?'

I thought the question over for a moment. 'The nearest bar?'

'Correct!' She laughed appreciatively. 'That's where I found it. The first bar to the left of the station. There was a different bartender on duty — about eleven this morning — and he didn't know me, of course, but I described my bag and it was there, under the shelf by the cash register. At first he wouldn't give it to me because there wasn't any identification inside. Like a driver's license, something like that, but my traveler's checks were in the bag and after I wrote my name on a piece of paper and he compared the signatures on the checks he gave it to me. The first thing I did was cash a check and buy him a drink, joining him, of course.'

'No money at all?'

'Just the traveler's checks. I'm satisfied. Two hundred dollars in traveler's checks is better than money.'

'Cash a couple then and let's get out of here,' I said

happily. 'This isn't the only bar in San Francisco.'

We went to several places that night and knowing where to go is a mighty tricky business. Having lived in San Francisco for more than a year I could just about tell and I was very careful about the places I took her to. I didn't want to embarrass Helen any — not that she would have given a damn — but I wanted to have a good time, and I wanted her to have a good time too.

The last night club we were in was The Dolphin. I had been there once before, when I was in the chips, and I knew Helen would like it. It's a club you have to know about or you can't find it. It's down an alley off Divisadero Street and I had to explain to the taxicab driver how to get there. There isn't any lettered sign over the door; just a large, blue neon fish blinking intermittently, and the fish itself doesn't look like a dolphin. But once inside you know you're in The Dolphin, because the name is in blue letters on the menu, and the prices won't let you forget where you are. We entered and luckily found a booth well away from the bar. The club is designed with a South Seas effect, and the drinks are served in tall, thick glasses, the size and shape of a vase. The booth we sat in was very soft, padded thickly with foam rubber, and both of us had had enough to drink to appreciate the atmosphere and the deep, gloomy lighting that made it almost impossible to see across the room. The waiter appeared at our table out of the darkness and handed each of us a menu. He was a Mexican, naked except for a grass skirt, and made up to look like an islander of some sort: there were blue and yellow streaks of paint on his brown face, and he wore a shark's-tooth necklace.

'Do you still have the Dolphin Special?' I asked him.

'Certainly,' he said politely. 'And something to eat? Poi, dried squid, bird's-nest soup, breadfruit au gratin, sago palm salad —'

Helen's laugh startled the waiter. 'No thanks,' she said. 'I guess I'm not hungry.'

'Just bring us two of the Dolphin Specials,' I told him. He nodded solemnly and left for the bar. The Special is a good drink; it contains five varieties of rum, mint, plenty of snow-ice, and it's decorated with orange slices, pineapple slices and cherries with a sprinkling of sugar cane gratings floating on top. I needed at least two of them. I had to build up my nerve.

After the waiter brought our drinks I lit cigarettes and we smoked silently, dumping the ashes into the large abalone shell on the table that served as an ash-tray. The trio hummed into action and the music floating our way gave me a wistful feeling of nostalgia. The trio consisted of chimes, theremin and electric guitar and the unusual quality of the theremin prevented me from recognizing the melody of the song although I was certain I knew what it was.

With sudden impulsive boldness I put my hand on Helen's knee. Her knee jumped under the touch of my hand, quivered and was still again. She didn't knock my hand away. I drank my drink, outwardly calm, bringing my glass up to my lips with my free hand, and wondering vaguely what to do next.

'Helen,' I said, my voice a little hoarse, 'I've been hoping and dreading to see you all day. I didn't really expect to see you, and yet, when I thought I wouldn't, my heart would sort of knot up.'

'Why, Harry, you're a poet!'

'No, I'm serious. I'm trying to tell you how I feel about you,'

'I didn't mean to be rude or flippant, Harry. I feel very close to you, and trying to talk about it isn't any good.'

'I've had terrible luck with women, Helen,' I said, 'and for the last two years I've kept away from them. I didn't want to go through it all again — you know, the bickering, the jealousy, nagging, that sort of thing. Am I scaring you off?'

'You couldn't if you tried, Harry. You're my kind of man and it isn't hard to say so. What I mean is — you're somebody, underneath, a person, and not just another man. See?' She shook her head impatiently. 'I told you I couldn't talk about it.'

'One thing I want to get straight is this,' I said. 'I'll never tell you that I love you.'

'That word doesn't mean anything anyway.'

'I never thought I'd hear a woman say that. But it's the truth. Love is in what you do, not in what you say. Couples work themselves into a hypnotic state daily by repeating to each other over and over again that they love each other. And they don't know the meaning of the word. They also say they love a certain brand of tooth paste and a certain brand of cereal in the same tone of voice.'

Cautiously, I gathered the material of her skirt with my fingers until the hem was above her knee. My hand squeezed the warm flesh above her stocking. It was soft as only a woman's thigh is soft. She spread her legs at the touch of my hand and calmly sipped her drink. I tried to go a little higher and she clamped her legs on my hand.

'After all, Harry,' she chided me, 'we're not alone, you know.'

I took my hand away from the softness of her thigh and she pulled her skirt down, smiling at me sympathetically. With trembling hands I lit a cigarette. I didn't know what to do or what to say next. I felt as immature and inept as a teenager on the first date. And Helen wasn't helping me at all. I couldn't imagine what she was thinking about my crude and foolish passes.

'Helen,' I blurted out like a schoolboy, 'will you sleep with me tonight?' I felt like I had staked my life on the turn of a card.

'Why, Harry! What a thing to say.' Her eyes didn't twinkle, that is impossible, but they came close to it. Very close. 'Where else did you think I was going if I didn't go home with you?'

'I don't know,' I said honestly.

'You didn't have to ask me like that. I thought there was an understanding between us, that it was understood.'

'I don't like to take people for granted.'

'In that case then, I'll tell you. I'm going home with you.'

'I hope we're compatible,' I said. 'Then everything will be perfect.'

'We are. I know it.'

'I'm pretty much of a failure in life, Helen. Does it matter to you?'

'No. Nothing matters to me.' Her voice had a resigned quality and yet it was quietly confident. There was a tragic look in her brown eyes, but her mouth was smiling. It was the smile of a little girl who knows a secret and isn't going to tell it. I held her hand in mine. It was a tiny, almost pudgy hand, soft and warm and trusting. We finished our drinks.

'Do you want another?' I asked her.

'Not really. After I go to the potty I want you to take me home.' I helped her out of the booth. It wasn't easy for her to hold her feet, and she had had more to drink than I'd had. I watched her affectionately as she picked her way across the dimly lit room. She was everything I ever wanted in a woman.

When she returned to the table I took the twenty she gave me and paid for the drinks. We walked to the mouth of the alley and I hailed a taxi. I gave my address to the driver and we settled back on the seat. I took Helen in my arms and kissed her.

'It makes me dizzy,' she said. 'Roll the windows down.'

I had to laugh, but I rolled the windows down. The night air was cold and it was a long ride to my neighborhood. By the time we reached the rooming house I knew she would be all right. I lit two cigarettes, passed one to Helen. She took one deep drag, tossed it out the window.

'I'm a little nervous, Harry.'

'Why?'

'It's been a long time. Years, in fact.'

'It doesn't change.'

'Please don't say that! Be gentle with me, Harry.'

'How could I be otherwise? You're just a little girl.'

'I trust you, Harry.'

The taxi pulled up in front of my roominghouse and we got out. We climbed the stairs quietly and walked down the long, dark hall to my room. There was only a single 40-watt bulb above the bathroom door to light the entire length of the hall. I unlocked my door and guided Helen inside. It took me a while to find the dangling string to the overhead light in the ceiling. Finding it at last, I flooded the room with light. I pulled the shade down and Helen looked the shabby room over with an amused smile.

'You're a good housekeeper,' she said.

'Today anyway. I must have expected company,' I said nervously.

Slowly, we started to undress. The more clothes we took off, the slower we got.

'Hadn't you better turn the light off?' Helen asked, timidly.

'No,' I said firmly, 'I don't want it that way.'

We didn't hesitate any longer. Both of us undressed hurriedly. Helen crawled to the center of the bed, rolled over on her back and put her hands behind her head. She kept her eyes on the ceiling. Her breasts were small and the slenderness of her hips made her legs look longer than they were. Her skin was pale, almost like living mother-of-pearl, except for the flush that lay on her face like a delicately tinted rose. I stood in the center of the room and I could have watched her forever. I pulled the light cord and got into bed.

At first I just held her hot body against mine, she was trembling so hard. I covered her face with soft little kisses, her throat, her breasts. When my lips touched the tiny nipples of her breasts she sighed and relaxed somewhat. Her body still trembled, but it wasn't from fear. As soon as the nipples hardened I kissed her roughly on the mouth and she whimpered, dug her fingernails into my shoulders. She bit my lower lip with her sharp little teeth and I felt the blood spurt into my mouth.

'Now, Harry! Now!' She murmured softly.

It was even better than I'd thought it would be.

Chapter Four

NUDE MODEL

When I awoke the next morning Helen was curled up beside me. Her face was flushed with sleep and her nice hair curled all over her head. If it hadn't been for the single strand of pure silver hair she wouldn't have looked more than thirteen years old. I kissed her on the mouth and she opened her eyes. She sat up and stretched luxuriously, immediately awake, like a cat.

'I've never slept better in my entire life,' she said.

'I'll fix some coffee. Then while you're in the bathroom, I'd better go down the hall and tell Mrs. McQuade you're here.'

'Who is she?'

'The landlady. You'll meet her later on.'

'Oh. What're you going to tell her?'

'I'll tell her we're married. We had a long trial separation and now we've decided to try it again. It's a pretty thin story, but it'll hold.'

'I feel married to you, Harry.'

'For all practical purposes, we are married.'

I got out of bed, crossed to the dresser, and tossed a clean, white shirt to Helen. She put it on and the shirt tail came to her knees. After she rolled up the sleeves she left the room. I put on my slacks and a T-shirt, fixed the coffee and lit the gas burner under it, walked down the hall and knocked on Mrs. McQuade's door.

'Good morning, Mrs. McQuade,' I said, when she opened the door.

'You're not going to clean your room again?' she asked

with mock surprise in her voice.

'No.' I laughed. 'Two days in a row would be overdoing it. I just wanted to tell you my wife was back.'

'I didn't even know you were married!' She raised her eyebrows.

'Oh, yes! I've been married a good many years. We were separated, but we've decided to try it again. I'll bring Helen down after a while. I want you to meet her.'

'I'm very happy for you, Mr. Jordan.'

'I think it'll work this time.'

'Would you like a larger room?' she asked eagerly. 'The front upstairs room is vacant, and if you want me to —'

'No, thanks,' I said quickly, 'we'll be all right where we are.'

I knew Mrs. McQuade didn't believe me, but a woman running a rooming house doesn't get surprised at anything. She didn't mention it right then, but by the end of the week I could expect an increase in rent. That is the way those things go.

The coffee was ready, and when Helen returned I finished my cup quickly and poured one for her.

'We've only got one cup,' I said apologetically.

'We'll have to get another one.'

After I shaved, and both of us were dressed, we finished the pot of coffee, taking turns with the cup. Helen borrowed my comb, painted her dark lipstick on with a tiny brush, and she was ready for the street.

'Don't you even use powder?' I asked her curiously.

'Uh uh. Just lipstick.'

'We'd better go down and get your suitcase.'

'I'm ready.'

Mrs. McQuade and Miss Foxhall, a retired school-teacher, were standing by the front door when we came down the hall. Mrs. McQuade had a broom in her hand, and Miss Foxhall held an armful of books; she was either going to or returning from the neighborhood public library. They both eyed Helen curiously, Mrs. McQuade with a smile, Miss Foxhall with hostility. I introduced Helen to the two older women. Mrs. McQuade wiped

her hands on her apron and shook Helen's hand. Miss
Foxhall snorted audibly, pushed roughly between us
and hurried up the stairs without a word. I noticed that the
top book in the stack she carried was *Ivanhoe,* by Sir
Walter Scott.

'You're a very pretty girl, Mrs. Jordan,' Mrs. McQuade
said sincerely. All three of us pretended to ignore the
rudeness of Miss Foxhall.

We walked down the block to Big Mike's, Helen
holding my arm. The sun was shining and despite a slight
persisting hangover I was a proud and happy man.
Everyone who passed stared at Helen, and to know that
she was mine made me straighten my back and hold my
head erect. We entered Mike's and sat down at the bar.
Big Mike joined us at once.

'You're on time today, Harry.' He smiled.

'Mike, I want you to meet my wife. Helen Jordan, Big
Mike.'

'How do you do, Mrs. Jordan? This calls for one on the
house. Now what'll it be?'

'Since it's on the house, Mike,' Helen smiled, 'I'll have a
double bourbon and water.'

'Double gin and tonic for me,' I added.

Mike set up our drinks, drew a short beer for himself,
and we raised our glasses in salute. He returned to his
work table where he was slicing oranges, sticking tooth-
picks into cherries, and preparing generally for the noon-
hour rush period. It was quite early to be drinking and
Helen and I were the only people sitting at the bar.
Rodney, the crippled newsboy, was eating breakfast in one
of the booths along the wall. He waved to me with his fork
and I winked at him.

After we finished our drinks we caught the cable car to
the hotel on Powell Street and picked up Helen's suitcase.
It only took a minute and we were able to catch the same
car back, after it was ready to climb the hill again and
turned on the Market Street turnaround. The round trip
took more than an hour.

'I'm disgustingly sober,' Helen said, as we stood on the

curb, waiting for the light to change.

'What do you want to do? I'll give you two choices. We can drink in Big Mike's or we can get a bottle and go back to the room.'

'Let's get a bottle, by all means.'

At Mr. Watson's delicatessen I bought a fifth of gin, a fifth of whiskey and a cardboard carrier of six small bottles of soda. To nibble on, in case we happened to get hungry, I added a box of cheese crackers to the stack. We returned to our room and I removed my jacket and shirt. Helen took off her suit and hung it carefully in the closet. While I fixed the drinks Helen explored the room, digging into everything. She pulled out all the dresser drawers, then examined the accumulation of junk above the sink. It was pleasant to watch her walking around the room in her slip. She discovered my box of oil paints on the shelf, brought it to the table and opened it.

'Do you paint, Harry?'

'At one time I did. That's the first time that box has been opened in three years.' I handed her a drink. 'There isn't any ice.'

'All ice does is take up room. Why don't you paint any more?'

I looked into the opened paint box. The caps were tightly screwed on all of the tubes and most of the colors were there, all except yellow ochre and zinc white. I fingered the brushes, ran a finger over the edges of the bristles. They were in good shape, still usable, and there was a full package of charcoal sticks.

'I discovered I couldn't paint, that's why. It took me a long time to accept it, but after I found out I gave it up.'

'Who told you you couldn't paint?'

'Did you ever do any painting?'

'Some. I graduated from Mills College, where they taught us something about everything. I even learned how to shoot a bow and arrow.'

'I'll tell you how it is about painting, Helen, the way it was with me. It was a love affair. I used painting as a substitute for love. All painters do; it's their nature. When you're painting, the pain in your stomach drives you on to a climax of pure feeling, and if you're any good the feeling is transmitted to the canvas. In color, in form, in line and they blend together in a perfect design that delights your eye and makes your heart beat a little faster. That's what painting meant to me, and then it turned into an unsuccessful love affair, and we broke it off. I'm over it now, as much as I'll ever be, and certainly the world of art hasn't suffered.'

'Who told you to give it up? Some critic?'

'Nobody had to tell me. I found it out for myself, the hard way. Before the war I went to the Art Institute in Chicago for two years, and after the war I took advantage of the GI Bill and studied another year in Los Angeles.'

'Wouldn't anybody buy your work? Was that it?'

'No, that isn't it. I never could finish anything I started. I'd get an idea, block it out, start on it, and then when I'd get about halfway through I'd discover the idea was terrible. And I couldn't finish a picture when I knew it wasn't going to be any good. I taught for a while, but that wasn't any good either.'

Helen wasn't looking at me. She had walked to the window and appeared to be studying the littered backyard next door with great interest. I knew exactly what she had on her mind. The Great American Tradition: *You* can do anything you think you can do! All Americans believe in it. What a joke that is! Can a jockey last ten rounds with Rocky Marciano? Can Marciano ride in the Kentucky Derby? Can a poet make his living by writing poetry? The entire premise was so false it was stupid to contemplate. Helen finished her drink, turned around, and set the empty glass on the table.

'Harry,' she said seriously, 'I want you to do something for me.'

'I'll do anything for you.'

'No, not just like that. I want you to hear what it is first.'

'It sounds serious.'

'It is. I want you to paint my portrait.'

'I don't think I could do it.' I shrugged, looked into my

empty glass. 'It's been more than three years since I tried
to paint anything, and portraits are hard. To do a good
one, anyway, and if I were to paint you, I'd want it to be
perfect. It would have to be, and I'm not capable of it.'

'I want you to paint it anyway.'

'How about a sketch? If you want a picture of yourself,
I can draw a charcoal likeness in five minutes.'

'No. I want you to paint an honest-to-God oil painting
of me.'

'You really want me to; this isn't just a whim?'

'I really want you to.' Her face was as deadly serious as
her voice.

I thought it over and it made me feel a little sick to my
stomach. The mere thought of painting again made me
tremble. It was like asking a pilot to take an airplane up
again after a bad crash; a crash that has left him horribly
disfigured and frightened. Helen meant well. She wanted
me to prove to myself that I was wrong ... that I could do
anything I really wanted to do. That is, as long as she was
there to help me along by her inspiration and encourage-
ment. More than anything else in the world, I wanted to
please her.

'It takes time to paint a portrait,' I said.

'We've got the time. We've got forever.'

'Give me some money then.'

'How much do you need?'

'I don't know. I'll need a canvas, an easel, linseed oil,
turpentine, I don't know what all. I'll have to look around
when I get to the art store.'

'I'm going with you.' She began to dress.

Once again, we made the long trip downtown by cable
car. We went to an art store on Polk Street and I picked
out a cheap metal easel, in addition to the regular
supplies, and a large canvas, thirty by thirty-four inches.
As long as I had decided to paint Helen's portrait, I was
going to do it right. We left the store, both of us loaded
down with bundles and I searched the streets for a taxi.
Helen didn't want to return home immediately.

'You're doing something for me,' she said, 'and I want

to do something for you. Before we go home I'm going to buy you a new pair of pants and a new sport coat.'

'You can't do it, Helen,' I protested. 'We've spent too much already.'

She had her way, but I didn't let her spend too much money on my new clothes. I insisted on buying a pair of gray corduroy trousers, and a dark blue corduroy jacket at the nearest Army and Navy surplus store. These were cheap clothes, but they satisfied Helen's desire to do something nice for me. I certainly needed them. Wearing my new clothes in the taxi, on the way home, and looking at all the new art supplies piled on the floor, gave me a warm feeling inside and a pleasant tingling of anticipation.

The minute we entered our room I removed my new jacket and set up the easel. While I opened the paints and arranged the materials on a straight-backed chair next to the easel, Helen fixed fresh drinks. She held up her glass and posed, a haughty expression on her face.

'Look, Harry. Woman of Distinction.' We both laughed. 'Do you want me to pose like this?'

The pose I wanted Helen to take wasn't difficult. The hard part was to paint her in the way I wanted to express my feelings for her. I wanted to capture the mother-of-pearl of her body, the secret of her smile, the strand of silver in her hair, the jet, arched brows, the tragedy in her brown, gold-flecked eyes. I wasn't capable of it; I knew that in advance. I placed two pillows on the floor, close to the bed, so she could lean back against the bed to support her back. The light from the window would fall across her body and create sharp and difficult shadows. The hard way, like always. I took the hard way.

'Take off your clothes, Helen, and sit down on the pillows.'

After Helen had removed her clothes and settled herself comfortably I rearranged her arms, her right hand in her lap, her left arm stretched full length on the bed. Her legs were straight out, with the right ankle crossed over the other. The similarity between Helen and the woman in the

Olympia almost took my breath away with the awesomeness of it.

'Is that comfortable?' I asked her.

'It feels all right. How long do you want me to stay like this?'

'Just remember it, that's all. When I tell you to pose, get into it, otherwise, sit anyway you like. As I told you, this is going to take a long time. Drink your drink, talk, or smile that smile of yours. Okay?'

'I'm ready.'

I started with the charcoal, blocking in Helen's figure. She was sitting *too* stiffly, eyes straight ahead, tense. To me, the drawing is everything and I wanted her to talk, to get animation in her face.

'Talk to me, Helen,' I told her.

'Is it all right?'

'Sure. I want you to talk. Tell me about Mills College. What did you major in?'

'Geology.'

'That's a strange subject for a woman to take. What made you major in geology?'

'I was romantic in those days, Harry. I liked rocks and I thought geology was fascinating, but secretly, I thought if I could learn geology I could get away from Mother. I used to dream about going to Tibet or South America with some archeological expedition. Mother was never in the dream, but she was with me all the way through college. I had a miserable college education. She came with me and we took an apartment together. While the other girls lived in sororities and had a good time, I studied. She stood right over me, just like she did all the way through high school. My grades were fine, the highest in my class. Not that I was a brilliant student, but because I didn't do anything except study.

'In the summers we went back to San Sienna. One summer we went to Honolulu, and once to Mexico City so I could look at ruins. The trips weren't any fun, because Mother came along. No night life, no dates, no romance.'

'It sounds terrible.'

'It was, believe me.' She lapsed into silence, brooding.

It was a pleasant day. Helen made a drink for herself once in a while, but I didn't join her; I was much too busy. The outline shaped well and I was satisfied with the progress I had made. By the time the light failed Helen had finished the bottle of whiskey and was more than a little tight. We were both extremely tired from the unaccustomed activity. Helen would find that modeling was one of the toughest professions in the world before we were through.

We dressed and walked down the street to Big Mike's for dinner. I ordered steaks from Tommy the waiter, and while we waited we sat at the end of the bar and had a drink. There were three workmen in overalls occupying the booth opposite from where we were sitting and their table was completely covered with beer cans. They made a few choice nasty remarks about Helen and me, but I ignored them. Big Mike was a friend of mine and I didn't want to cause any trouble in his bar.

'Look at that,' the man wearing white overalls said. 'Ain't that the limit?' His voice was loud, coarse, and it carried the length of the bar-room.

'By God,' the man on the inside said, 'I believe I've seen it *all* now!' He nodded his head solemnly. 'Yes, sir, I've seen it *all*!' His voice had a forced quality of comic seriousness and his companions laughed.

Helen's face had changed from pale to chalky white. She quickly finished her drink, set the glass on the bar and took my arm. 'Come on Harry,' she said anxiously, 'let's go inside the dining-room and find a table.'

'All right.' My voice sounded as though it belonged to someone else.

We climbed down from the stools and crossed to the dining-room entrance. We paused in the doorway and I searched the room for a table. One of the men shouldered us apart and stared insolently at Helen.

'Why don't you try me for size, baby?'

His two friends were standing behind me and they snickered.

Without a word I viciously kicked the man in front of me in the crotch. The insolent smile left his face in a hurry. His puffy red face lost its color and he clutched his groin with both hands and sank to his knees. I kicked him in the mouth and blood bubbled out of his ripped cheek from the corner of his torn mouth all the way to his ear. I whirled around quickly, expecting an attack from the two men behind me, but Big Mike was holding both of them by the collar. There was a wide grin on his multi-scarred face.

'Go ahead, Harry,' he said gruffly, 'finish the job. These lice won't interfere.'

The man was on his feet again; some of the color was back in his mutilated face. He snatched a bread knife from the waiter's work table and backed slowly across the room.

Many of the diners had left their tables and were crowded against the far wall near the kitchen. I advanced on the man cautiously, my arms widely spread. He lunged forward in a desperate attempt to disembowel me, bringing the knife up fast, aiming for my stomach. At the last moment I twisted sideways and brought my right fist up from below my knee. His jaw was wide open and my blow caught him flush below the chin. He fell forward on the floor, like a slugged ox.

My entire body was shaking with fear and excitement. I looked wildly around the room for Helen. She was standing, back to the wall, frozen with fear. She ran to my side, hugged me around the waist.

'Come on, Harry.' She said tearfully. 'Let's get out of here!'

'Nothing doing,' I said stubbornly. 'We ordered steaks and we're going to eat them.'

I guided Helen to an empty table against the wall. Big Mike had bounced the other two workmen out and now he was back in the dining-room. Two waiters, at his nod, dragged the unconscious man out of the room through the kitchen exit. Tommy came over to our table.

'I saw the whole thing, Harry,' Tommy said, 'and if it goes to court or anything like that, I'll swear that he started the fight by pulling a knife on you!' He was so sincere I found it difficult to keep from laughing.

'Thanks, Tommy,' I told him, 'but I think that's the end of it.'

I couldn't eat my steak and neither could Helen although both of us made a valiant try.

'The hell with it, Harry,' Helen smiled. 'Let's get a bottle and go home.'

We left the grill, bought another fifth of whiskey at the delicatessen and returned to our room. My bottle of gin was scarcely tapped. I held it up to my lips, and drinking in short swallows, I drank until I almost passed out.

Helen had to undress me and put me to bed.

Chapter Five

CELEBRATION

If there was anything I didn't want to do the next morning, it was paint. My head was vibrating like a struck gong and my stomach was full of fluttering, little winged creatures. Every muscle of my body ached and all I wanted to do was stay in bed and quietly nurse my hangover.

Helen was one of those rare persons who seldom get a hangover. She felt fine. She showered, dressed, left the house and returned with a fifth of whiskey and a paper sack filled with cold bottles of beer.

'Drink this beer,' she ordered, 'and let's get started. You can't let a little thing like a fight and a hangover stop you.' She handed me an opened bottle of beer. I sat up in bed, groaning, and let the icy beer flow down my throat. It tasted marvelous, tangy, refreshing, and I could feel its coldness all the way down. I drank some coffee, two more beers and started to work.

I had to draw slowly at first. There was still a slight tremor in my fingers, caused partly by the hangover, but the unexpected fight the night before had a lot to do with it. I've never been a fighter and when I thought about my vicious assault on the man in Mike's, I could hardly believe it had happened. Within a short time, Helen's beauty pushed the ugly memory out of my head and I was more interested in the development of her picture.

Painting or drawing from a nude model had never been an exciting experience before, but Helen was something

33

else ... I didn't have the feeling of detachment an artist is supposed to have toward his model. I was definitely aware of Helen's body as an instrument of love, and as my hangover gradually disappeared I couldn't work any longer unless I did something about it ...

Helen talked about the dullness of San Sienna as I worked and from time to time she would take a shot from the bottle of whiskey resting on the floor, following it down with a sip of water. As she began to feel the drinks her voice became animated. And so did I. Unable to stand it any longer I tossed my charcoal stick down, scooped Helen from the floor and dropped her sideways on the bed. She laughed softly.

'It's about time,' she said.

I dropped to my knees beside the bed, pressed my face into her warm, soft belly and kissed her navel. She clutched my hair with both hands and shoved my head down hard.

'Oh, yes, Harry! Make love to me! Make love to me ...'

And I did. She didn't have to coax me.

It took all of the willpower I could muster to work on the picture again, but I managed, and surprisingly enough it was much easier than it had been. With my body relaxed I could now approach my work with the proper, necessary detachment an artist must have if he is to get anywhere. The drawing was beginning to look very well, and by four in the afternoon when I couldn't stick it out any longer and quit for the day, I was exhilarated by my efforts and Helen was pleasantly tight from the whiskey.

After we were dressed I took a last look at the picture before leaving for Mike's.

'This is my first portrait,' I told Helen as I opened the door for her. 'And probably my last.'

'I didn't know that, Harry,' she said, somewhat surprised. 'What kind of painting did you do? Land-scapes?'

'No,' I laughed. 'Non-objective, or as you understand it, abstract.'

'You mean these weird things with the lines going every

which way, and the limp watches and stuff —'

'That's close enough.' I couldn't explain what is impossible to explain. We went to Big Mike's, had dinner, and drank at the bar until closing time.

This was the pattern of our days for the next week and a half, except for one thing: I quit drinking. Not completely; I still drank beer, but I laid off whiskey and gin completely. I didn't need it any more. Painting and love were all I needed to make me happy. Helen continued to drink, and during the day, whether drunk or sober, if I told her to pose she assumed it without any trouble, and held it until I told her to relax.

For me, this was a fairly happy period. I hadn't realized how much I had missed painting. And with Helen for a model it was pure enjoyment. I seldom said anything. I was contented to merely paint and look at Helen. Often there were long silences between us when all we did was look at each other. These long periods usually ended up in bed without a word being spoken. It was as though our bodies had their own methods of communication. More relaxed, more sure of myself, I would take up my brush again and Helen would sit very much at ease, on the two pillows beside the bed and assume the pose I had given her. My Helen! My *Olympia*!

When I finished the drawing in charcoal I made a complete underpainting in tints and shades of burt sienna, lightening the browns carefully with white and turpentine. The underpainting always makes me nervous. The all-important drawing which takes so many tedious hours is destroyed with the first stroke of the brush and replaced with shades of brown oil paint. The completed drawing, which is a picture worthy of framing by itself, is now a memory as the turpentine and oil soaks up the charcoal and replaces it with a tone in a different medium. But it is a base that will last through the years when the colors are applied over it. I had Helen look at the completed brown-tone painting.

'It looks wonderful, Harry! Is my figure that perfect?'

'It's the way it looks to me. Don't worry about your

face. It's just drawn in a general way ... the effects of the shadows.'

'I'm not worried. It looks like me already.'

'When I'm finished, it will be you,' I said determinedly.

I started with the colors, boldly but slowly, in my old style. I didn't pay any attention to background, but concentrated on Helen's figure. At the time I felt that I shouldn't neglect the background, but no ideas came to me and I let it go. The painting was turning out far better than I had expected it to; it was good, very good. My confidence in my ability soared. I could paint, really paint. All I had to do was work at it, boldly but slowly.

Along with the ninth day, Helen, cramped by a long session got up and walked around the room shaking her arms and kicking her legs. I lit two cigarettes and handed her one. She put an arm around my waist and studied the painting for several minutes.

'This is me, Harry, only it looks like me when I was a little girl.'

'I'm not finished yet. I've been working on the hands. I figure a good two days to finish your face. If possible I want to paint your lips the same shade as your lipstick, but if I do I'm afraid it'll look out of place. It's a tricky business.'

'What about the background?'

'I'm letting that go. It isn't important.'

'But the picture won't be complete without a background.'

'I'm not going to fill the empty places with that gray wallpaper and its weird pattern of pink flowers!'

'You don't have to. Can't you paint in an open sky, or the ocean and clouds behind me?'

'No. That would look lousy. Wrong light, anyway.'

'You can't leave it blank!'

'I can until I get an idea. If I have to fill it with something I can paint it orange with black spots.'

'You can't do that! That would ruin it!'

'Then let's not discuss it any more.'

It made me a little sore. A man who's painting a picture

doesn't want a layman's advice. At least I didn't. This was the best thing of its kind I had ever done and I was going to do it my way.

That night when we went down to Mike's for dinner I started to drink again. Both of us were well-loaded when we got home and for the first time we went to sleep without making love.

I slept until noon. Helen didn't wake me when she went to the delicatessen for beer and whiskey. The coffee was perking in the pot and the wonderful odor woke me. I drank two cups of it black and had one shot of whiskey followed by a beer chaser. I felt fine.

'Today and tomorrow and I'll be finished,' I told Helen confidently.

'I'm sure tired of that pose.'

'You don't have to hold it any longer, baby. All I have to finish is your face.'

I had overestimated the time it would take me. By three-thirty there was nothing more to do. Anything else I did to the painting would be plain fiddling. Maybe I hadn't put in a proper background, but I had captured Helen and that was what I had set out to do. Enough of the bed and the two pillows were showing to lend form and solidity to the composition. The girl in the portrait was Helen, a much younger Helen, and if possible, a much prettier and delicate Helen, but it was Helen as she appeared to me. Despite my attempts to create the faint, tiny lines around her eyes and the streak of silver hair, it was the portrait of a young girl.

'It's beautiful,' Helen said sincerely and self-consciously.

'It's the best I can do.'

'How much could you sell this for, Harry?'

'I wouldn't sell it. It belongs to you.'

'But what would it be worth to an art gallery?'

'It's hard to tell. Whatever you could get, I suppose. Twenty dollars, maybe.'

'Surely, more than that!'

'It all depends upon how much somebody wants it. That's the way art works. The artist has his asking price, of course, and if a buyer wants the painting he pays the price. If they don't want it he couldn't give the picture away. My price for this picture is one hundred thousand dollars.'

'I'd pay that much for it, Harry.'

'And so would I.' There was a drink apiece left in the bottle of whiskey. We divided it equally and toasted the portrait.

'If I never paint another,' I bragged, 'I've painted one picture.'

'It doesn't really need a background, Harry,' Helen said loyally, 'it looks better the way it is.'

'You're wrong, but the hell with it. Get dressed and we'll go out and celebrate.'

'Let's stay in instead,' Helen said quietly.

'Why? If you're tired of drinking at Big Mike's we can go some place else. We don't have to go there.'

'No, that isn't it,' she said hesitantly. 'We're all out of money, Harry.' The corners of her mouth turned down wryly. 'I spent the last cent I had for that bottle.'

'Okay. So we're out of money. You didn't expect two hundred dollars to last forever did you? Our room rent's paid, anyway.'

'Do you have any money, Harry?'

After searching through my wallet and my trousers I came up with two dollars and a half dollar in change. Not a large sum, but enough for a few drinks.

'This is enough for a couple at Mike's,' I said, 'or we can let the drinks go and I can look around for a job. It's up to you.'

'I would like to have a drink ... but while you're looking for work, and even after you find it, there'll still be several days before you get paid.'

'We'll worry about that when we come to it. I've got fifteen dollars credit with Mike and it's all paid up. I paid him the other night when you cashed a traveler's check.'

'We don't have a worry in the world then, do we?' Helen said brightly.

'Not one.' I said it firmly, but with a confidence I didn't

feel inside. I had a lot of things to worry about. The smile was back on Helen's lips. She gave me a quick ardent kiss and dressed hurriedly, so fast I had to laugh.

When we got to Mike's we sat down in an empty booth and ordered hamburgers instead of our usual club steak. It was the only thing we had eaten all day, but it was still too much for me. After two bites I pushed my hamburger aside, left Helen in the booth, and signaled Mike to come down to the end of the bar.

'Mike,' I said apprehensively, 'I'm back on credit again.'

'Okay.' He nodded his massive head slowly. 'I'm not surprised, though, the way you two been hitting it lately.'

'I'm going to find a job tomorrow.'

'You've always paid up, Harry. I'm not worried.'

'Thanks, Mike.' I turned to leave.

'Just a minute, Harry,' he said seriously. 'That guy you had a fight with the other night was in here earlier and I think he's looking for you. I ran him the hell out, but you'd better be on the lookout for him. His face looks pretty bad. There's about thirty stitches in his face and the way it's sewed up makes him look like he's smiling. Only he ain't smiling.'

'I feel sorry for the guy, Mike. I don't know what got into me the other night.'

'Well, I thought I'd better mention it.'

'Thanks, Mike.' I rejoined Helen in the booth. She had finished her hamburger and mine too.

'You didn't want it, did you?' she asked me.

I shook my head. We ordered whiskey with water chasers and stayed where we were, in the last booth against the wall, drinking until ten o'clock. I was in a mighty depressed mood and I unconsciously transmitted it to Helen. I should never have let her talk me into painting her portrait. I should never have tried any type of painting again. There was no use trying to kid myself that I could paint. Of course, the portrait was all right, but any artist with any academic background at all could have done as well. And my temerity in posing Helen as *Olympia* was the crowning height to my folly. Who in the hell did I think I was, anyway? What was I trying to prove? Liquor never helped me when I was in a depressed state of mind; it only made me feel worse. Helen broke the long, dead silence between us.

'This isn't much of a celebration, is it?'

'No. I guess not.'

'Do you want to go home, Harry?'

'What do you want to do?'

'If I sit here much longer looking at you, I'll start crying.'

'Let's go home, then.'

I signed the tab that Tommy the waiter brought and we left. It was a dark, forbidding block to the rooming house at night. Except for Big Mike's bar and grill on the corner, the light from Mr. Watson's delicatessen across the street was the only bright spot on the way home. We walked slowly, Helen holding onto my arm. Half-way up the street I stopped, fished two cigarettes out of my almost empty package and turned into the wind to light them. Helen accepted the lighted cigarette I handed her and inhaled deeply. We didn't know what to do with ourselves.

'What's ever to become of us, Harry?' Helen sighed.

'I don't know.'

'Nothing seems to have much purpose, does it?'

'No, it doesn't.'

A man I hadn't noticed in the darkness of the street, detached himself from the shadows of the Spotless Cleaner's storefront and walked toward us. His hat was pulled well down over his eyes and he was wearing a dark-brown topcoat. The faint light from the street lamp on the corner barely revealed a long red scar on his face and neat row of stitches. Like Mike had told me, the left corner of his mouth was pulled up unnaturally, and it made the man look like he was smiling.

With a quick movement he jerked a shiny, nickel-plated pistol out of his topcoat pocket and covered us with it. His hand was shaking violently and the muzzle of the pistol jerked up and down rapidly, as though it was keeping time to wild music.

'I've been waiting for you!' His voice was thick and muffled. His jaws were probably wired together and he was forced to talk through his teeth. I dropped my cigarette to the pavement and put my left arm protectingly around Helen's waist. She stared at the man with a dazed, fixed expression.

'I'm going to kill you,' he said through his clenched teeth. 'Both of you!'

'I don't blame you,' I answered calmly. I felt no fear or anxiety at all, just a morbid feeling of detachment. Helen's body trembled beneath my arm, but it couldn't have been from fear, because the trembling stopped abruptly, and she took another deep drag on her cigarette.

'You may shoot me first, if you prefer,' she said quietly.

'God damn the both of you!' the man said through his closed mouth. 'Get down on your knees! Beg me! Beg for your lives!'

I shook my head. 'No. We don't do that for anybody. Our lives aren't that important.'

He stepped forward and jammed the muzzle into my stomach with a hard, vicious thrust.

'Pray, you son-of-a-bitch! Pray!'

I should have been frightened, but I wasn't. I knew that I should have been afraid and I even wondered why I wasn't.

'Go ahead,' I told him. 'Pull the trigger. I'm ready.'

He hesitated and this hesitation, I believe, is what cost him his nerve. He backed slowly away from us, the pistol dancing in his hand, as though it had an independent movement of its own.

'You don't think I'll shoot you, do you?' It was the kind of a question for which there is no answer. We didn't reply.

'All right, bastard,' he said softly, 'start walking.'

We started walking slowly up the sidewalk and he dodged to one side and fell in behind us. He jammed the pistol into the small of my back. I felt its pressure for ten or more steps and then it was withdrawn. Helen held my left arm with a tight grip, but neither one of us looked back as we marched up the hill. At any moment I expected a slug to tear through my body. We didn't look behind us until we reached the steps of the rooming house, and then I turned and looked over my shoulder while Helen kept her eyes straight to the front. There was no one in sight.

We entered the house, walked quietly down the dimly lit hallway, and went into our room. I closed the door, turned on the light, and Helen sat down on the edge of the bed. Conscious of Helen's eyes on me, I walked across to the painting and examined it for a long time.

'Did you feel sorry for him, Harry? I did.'

'Yes, I did,' I replied sincerely. 'The poor bastard.'

'I don't believe I'd have really cared if he'd killed us both ...' Helen's voice was reflective, sombre.

'Cared?' I forced a tight smile. 'It would have been a favor.'

Chapter Six

SUICIDE PACT

There was something bothering me when I got out of bed the next morning. I had a queasy, uneasy feeling in the pit of my stomach and it took me a few minutes to figure out what caused it. It was early in the morning, much too early to be getting out of bed. The sun was just coming up and the light filtering through the window was gray and cold. The sky was matted with low clouds, but an occasional bright spear broke through to stab at the messy backyards and the littered alley extending up the hill. I turned away from the window and the dismal view that looked worse by sunlight than it did by night.

I filled the coffee pot with water and put it on the burner. I took the coffee can down from the shelf above the sink and opened it. The coffee can was empty. I turned the fire out under the pot. No coffee this morning. I searched through my pockets before I put my trousers on and didn't find a dime. I didn't expect to, but I looked anyway. Not only had I spent the two and a half dollars in change, I had signed a chit besides for the drinks we had at Mike's. I opened Helen's purse and searched it thoroughly. There wasn't any money, but the purse contained a fresh, unopened package of cigarettes. After I finished dressing I sat in the straight chair by the window, smoking until Helen awoke.

Helen awoke after three cigarettes, sat up in bed and stretched her arms widely. She never yawned or appeared drowsy when she awoke in the mornings, but always appeared to be alert and fresh, as though she didn't need the sleep at all.

'Good morning, darling,' she said. 'How about lighting me one of those?'

I lit a fresh cigarette from the end of mine, put it between her lips, and sat down on the edge of the bed.

'No kiss?' she said petulantly, taking the cigarette out of her mouth. I kissed her and then returned to my chair by the window.

'We're out of coffee,' I said glumly.

'That isn't such a great calamity, is it?'

'We're out of money too. Remember?'

'We've got credit, haven't we? Let's go down to Big Mike's for coffee. He might put a shot of bourbon in it if we ask him real nice.'

'You really feel good, don't you?' I said bitterly.

Helen got out of bed and padded barefoot over to my chair. She put her arms around my neck, sat in my lap and kissed me on the neck.

'Look out,' I said. 'You'll burn me with your cigarette.'

'No, I won't. And I don't feel a bit good. I feel rotten.'

She bit me sharply on the ear, dropped her slip over her head and departed for the bathroom next door. I left my chair to examine my painting in the cold light of early morning. I twisted the easel around so the picture would face the window. A good amateur or Sunday painter would be proud of that portrait, I decided. Why wasn't I the one artist in a thousand who could earn his living by painting? Of course, I could always go back to teaching. Few men in the painting world knew as much as I did about color. The coarse thought of teaching made me shudder with revulsion. If you can't do it yourself you tell someone else how to do it. You stand behind them in the role of peer and mentor and watch them get better and better. You watch them overshadow you until you are nothing except a shadow within a shadow and then lost altogether in the unequal merger. Perhaps that was my main trouble? I could bring out talent where there wasn't any talent. Where there wasn't any ability I could bring

out the semblance of ability. A fine quality for a man born
to teach, but a heartbreaking quality for a man born to be
an artist. No, I would never teach again. There were too
many art students who thought they were artists who
should have been mechanics. But a teacher was never
allowed to be honest and tell them to quit. The art schools
would have very few students if the teachers were allowed
to be honest. But then, didn't the same thing hold true for
all schools?

I threw myself across the bed and covered my ears with
my hands. I didn't want to think about it any more. I
didn't want to think about anything. Helen returned from
the bathroom and curled up beside me on the bed.

'What's the matter, darling?' she asked solicitously.
'Have you got a headache?'

'No. I was just thinking what a rotten, stinking world
this is we live in. This isn't our kind of world, Helen. And
we don't have to answer to it either. We aren't going to
beat it by drinking and yet, the only way we can possibly
face it is by drinking!'

'You're worried because we don't have any money,
aren't you?'

'Not particularly.'

'I could wire my mother for money if you want me to.'

'Do you think she'd send it?'

'She'd probably bring it! She doesn't know where I am
and I don't want her to know. But we're going to have to
get money someplace.'

'Why?'

'You need a cup of coffee and I need a drink. That's
why.'

'I don't give a damn about the coffee. Why do you have
to have a drink? You don't really need it.'

'Sure I do. I'm an alcoholic. Alcoholics drink.'

'Suppose you were dead? You'd never need another
drink. You wouldn't need anything. Everything would be
blah. It doesn't make you happy to drink, and when I
drink it only makes me unhappier than I am already. All it
does in the long run is bring us oblivion.'

'I need you when I come out of that oblivion, Harry.' Her voice was solemn and barely under control.

'I need you too, Helen.' This was as true a statement as I had ever made. Without Helen I was worse than nothing, a dark, faceless shadow, alone in the darkness. I had to take her with me.

'I haven't thought about suicide in a long time, Helen,' I said. 'Not once since we've been together. I used to think about it all of the time, but I never had the nerve. Together, maybe we could do it. I know I couldn't do it alone.'

'I used to think about suicide too.' Helen accepted my mood and took it for her own. 'Down in San Sienna. It was such a tight, hateful little town. My bedroom overlooked the ocean, and I'd sit there all day, with the door locked, curled up on the window-seat, hiding my empty bottles in my dirty clothes hamper. Sitting there like that, looking at the golden sunshine glistening on the water, watching the breakers as they crashed on the beach ... It made me depressed as hell. It was all so purposeless!'

'Did you ever attempt it?'

'Suicide?'

'That's what we're considering. Suicide.'

'Yes, I tried it once.' She smiled wryly. 'On my wedding night, Harry. I was still a virgin, believe it or not. Oh, I wasn't ignorant; I knew what was expected of me and I thought I was ready for it. But I wasn't. Not for what happened, anyway. It was a virtual onslaught! My husband was a real estate man, and I'd never seen him in anything except a suit — all dressed up you know, with a clean, respectable look.

'But all of a sudden — I was in bed first, wearing my new nightgown, and shivering with apprehension — he flew out of the bathroom without a stitch on and rushed across the room. He was actually gibbering and drooling at the mouth. He tore the covers off me. He ripped my new, nice nightgown to shreds ...' Helen's voice broke as she relived this experience and she talked with difficulty. 'I fought him. I tore at his face with my nails; I bit him, hit at him, but it didn't make any difference. I'm positive now, that that's what he wanted me to do, you see. He over-powered me easily and completely. Then, in a second, it was all over. I was raped. He walked casually into the bathroom, doctored his scratches with iodine, put his pajamas on and climbed into bed as though nothing had happened.'

Helen smiled grimly, crushed her cigarette in the ashtray.

'It was his first and last chance at me,' she continued. 'I never gave him another. Lying there beside him in the darkness I vowed that he'd never touch me again. After he was asleep I got out of bed and took the bottle of aspirins out of my overnight bag and went into the bathroom. There were twenty-six tablets. I counted them, because I didn't know for sure whether that was enough or not. But I decided it was and I took them three at a time until they were gone, washing each bunch down with a glass of water. Then I climbed back into bed —'

'That wasn't nearly enough,' I said, interested in her story.

'No, it wasn't. But I fell asleep though, and I probably wouldn't have otherwise. They must have had some kind of psychological effect. But I awoke the next morning the same as ever, except for a loud ringing in my ears. The ringing lasted all day.'

'What about your husband? Did he know you attempted suicide?'

'I didn't give him that satisfaction. We were staying at a beach motel in Santa Barbara, and after breakfast he went out to the country club to play golf. I begged off — told him I wanted to do some shopping — and as soon as he drove away I packed my bag and caught a bus for San Sienna and Mother. Mother was glad to have me back.'

'And you never went back to him?'

'Never. I told Mother what happened. It was foolish of me, maybe, but she was determined to find out so I told her about it. Later on, when he begged me to come back to him, I was going to, but she wouldn't let me. He didn't know any better, the poor guy, and he told me so, after he found out the reason I left him. But it was too late then. I was safe in Mother's arms.'

She finished her story bitterly, and her features assumed the tragic look I knew so well, the look that entered her face whenever she mentioned her mother. I kissed her tenderly on the mouth, got out of bed, and paced the floor restlessly.

'I'm glad you told me about this, Helen. That's when you started to drink, isn't it?'

'Yes, that's when I started to drink. It was as good an excuse an any other.'

We were silent then, deep in our own thoughts. Helen lay on her back with her eyes closed while I paced the floor. I understood Helen a little better now. Thanks to me, and I don't know how many others, she didn't feel the same way about sex now, but she was so fixed in her drinking habits she could never change them. Not without some fierce drive from within, and she wasn't made that way. Before she could ever stop drinking she would have to have some purpose to her life, and I couldn't furnish it. Not when I didn't even have a purpose for my own life. If we continued on, in the direction we were traveling, the only thing that could possibly happen would be a gradual lowering of standards and they were low enough already. If something happened to me she would end up on the streets of San Francisco. The very thought of this sent a cold chill down my back. And I couldn't take care of her properly. It was too much of an effort to take care of myself ...

'It takes a lot of nerve to commit suicide, Harry,' Helen said suddenly, sitting up in bed, and swinging her feet to the floor.

'If we did it together I think we could do it,' I said confidently. 'Right now, we're on the bottom rung of the ladder. We're dead broke. I haven't got a job, and there's no one we can turn to for help. No whiskey, no religion, nothing.'

'Do you think we'd be together afterwards?'

'Are you talking about the hereafter?'

'That's what I mean. I wouldn't care whether I went to Heaven or Hell as long as I was with you.'

'I don't know anything about those things, Helen. But here's the way I look at it. If we went together, we'd be together. I'm positive of that.'

The thought of death was very attractive to me. I could tell by the fixed expression in Helen's eyes that she was in the same mood I was in. She got the cigarettes from the table and sat down again on the edge of the bed. After she lit the cigarettes, I took mine and sat down beside her.

'How would we go about it, Harry?' Helen was in earnest, but her voice quavered at her voiced thought.

'There are lots of ways.'

'But how, though? I can't stand being hurt. If it was all over with like that —' she snapped her fingers — 'and I didn't feel anything, I think I could do it.'

'We could cut our wrists with a razor blade.'

'Oh, no!' She shuddered. 'That would hurt terribly!'

'No it wouldn't,' I assured her. 'Just for one second, maybe, and then it would be all over.'

'I couldn't do it, Harry!' She shook her head emphatically. 'If you did it for me I could shut my eyes and —'

'No!' I said sharply. 'You'll have to do it yourself. If I cut your wrists, well, then it would be murder. That's what it would be.'

'Not if I asked you to.'

'No. We'll have to do it together.'

When we finished our cigarettes I put the ashtray back on the table. I was serious about committing suicide and determined to go through with it. There wasn't any fight left in me. As far as I was concerned the world we existed in was an overly-large, stinking cinder; a spinning, useless clinker. I didn't want any part of it. My life meant nothing to me and I wanted to go to sleep forever and forget about it. I got my shaving kit down from the shelf above the sink and took the package of razor blades, out of it. I unwrapped the waxed paper from two shiny single-edged blades and laid them on the table. Helen joined me at the table and held out her left arm dramatically.

'Go ahead,' she said tearfully. 'Cut it!'

Her eyes were tightly squeezed shut and she was breathing rapidly. I took her hand in mine and looked at her thin little wrist. I almost broke down and it was an effort to fight back the tears.

'No, sweetheart,' I said to her gently, 'you'll have to do it yourself. I can't do it for you.'

'Which one is mine?' she asked nervously.

'Either one. It doesn't make any difference.'

'Are you going to give a signal?' She picked up a blade awkwardly.

'I'll count to three.' I picked up the remaining blade.

'I'm ready!' she said bravely, raising her chin.

'One. Two. Three!'

We didn't do anything. We just stood there, looking at each other.

'It's no use, Harry. I can't do it to myself.' She threw the blade down angrily on the table and turned away. She covered her face with her hands and sobbed. Her back shook convulsively.

'Do you want me to do it?' I asked her.

She nodded her head almost imperceptibly, but she didn't say anything. I jerked her left hand away from her face and with one quick decisive motion I cut blindly into her wrist. She screamed sharply, then compressed her lips, and held out her other arm. I cut it quickly, close to the heel of her hand, picked her up and carried her to the bed. I arranged a pillow under her head.

'Do they hurt much?'

She shook her head. 'They burn a little bit. That's all.'

Her eyes were closed, but she was still crying noise-lessly. The bright blood gushed from her wrists, making crimson pools on the white sheets. I retrieved the bloody blade from the table where I'd dropped it, returned to the bed and sat down. It was much more difficult to cut my own wrists. The skin was tougher, somehow, and I had to saw with the blade to cut through. My heart was beating so loud I could feel it throb through my body. I was afraid to go through with it and afraid not to go through with it. The blood frothed finally, out of my left wrist and I transferred the blade to my other hand. It was easier to cut my right wrist, even though I was right-handed. It didn't hurt nearly as much as I had expected it to, but there was a searing, burning sensation, as though I had inadvertently touched my wrists to a hot poker. I threw the blade to the floor and got into bed beside Helen. She kissed me passionately. I could feel the life running out of my wrists and it made me happy and excited.

'Harry?'

'Yes?'

'As a woman I'd like to have the last word. Is it all right?'

'Sure it's all right.'

'I. Love. You.'

It was the first time she had said the word since we had been living together. I kissed each of her closed eyes tenderly, then buried my face in her neck. I was overwhelmed with emotion and exhaustion.

Chapter Seven

RETURN TO LIFE

My head was like a huge bubble perched on top of my shoulders, and ready for instant flight. I was afraid to move my head or open my eyes for fear it would float away into nothingness. Gradually, as I lay there fearfully, a feeling of solidity returned to my head and I opened my eyes. My arms were entwined around Helen, and she was lying on her side, facing me, her breathing soft and regular, in deep, restful sleep — but she was breathing! We were still alive, very much so! I disentangled my arms and raised my wrists so that I could see them. The blood was coagulated into little black ridges along the lengths of the shallow cuts. The bleeding had completely stopped. Oddly enough, I felt highly exhilarated and happy to be alive. It was as though I was experiencing a 'cheap' drink; I felt the way I had when I had taken a lower lip full of snuff many years before. My head was light and I was a trifle dizzy even though I was still in bed. I awakened Helen by kissing her partly open mouth. For a moment her eyes were startled and then they brightened into alertness the way they always did when she first awakened. She smiled shyly.

'I guess I didn't cut deep enough,' I said ruefully. 'I must have missed the arteries altogether.'

'How do you feel, Harry?' Helen asked me. 'I feel kind of wonderful, sort of giddy.'

'I feel a little foolish. And at the same time I feel better than I have in months. I'm light-headed as hell and I feel drunk. Not gin-drunk, but drunk with life.'

'I feel the same way. I've never been as drunk as I am

now and I haven't had a drink. I never expected to wake up at all — not here, anyway.'

'Neither did I,' I said quietly.

'Are you sorry, Harry?'

'No. I'm not exactly sorry. It's too easy to quit and yet it took me a long time to reach the point when I was ready. But now that I've tried it once I guess I can face things again. It's still a lousy world, but maybe we owe it something.'

'Light us a cigarette, Harry.'

I got out of bed carefully and staggered dizzily to the table. I picked up the package of cigarettes and a folder of book matches and then noticed the bloody razor blade on the floor. It was unreal and cruel-looking and somehow offended me. I scooped it off the floor with the edge of the cardboard match folder and dropped it into the paper sack where we kept our trash and garbage. I couldn't bear to touch it with my hands. I was so giddy by this time it was difficult to keep my feet. Tumbling back onto the bed I lit Helen's cigarette, then mine.

'You've got a surprise coming when you try to walk,' I said.

'You were actually staggering,' Helen said, dragging the smoke deeply into her lungs.

'This bed is certainly a mess. Take a look at it.'

'We'd better burn these sheets. I don't think the laundry would take them like this.' Helen giggled.

'That is, if we could afford to take them to the laundry.'

Both of us were in a strange mood, caused mostly by the blood we had lost. It wasn't a gay mood, not exactly, but it wasn't depressed either. All of our problems were still with us, but for a brief moment, out of mind. There was still no money, no job, no liquor and no prospects. I was still a bit light-headed and it was hard for me to think about our many problems. I wished, vaguely, that I had a religion or a God of some sort. It would have been so wonderful and easy to have gone to a priest or a minister and let him solve our problems for us. We could have gone anyway, religious or not, but without faith, any advice we listened to would have been worthless. The pat, standard homilies dished out by the boys in black were easy to predict.

Accept Jesus Christ as your personal Lord and Saviour and you are saved!

Any premise which bases its salvation on blind belief alone is bound to be wrong, I felt. It isn't fair to those who find it impossible to believe, those who have to be convinced, shown, who believe in nothing but the truth. But, all the same, suppose we did go to a church somewhere? What could we lose?

I rejected that false line of reasoning in a hurry.

'Let's bandage each other's wrists,' I said quickly to Helen. It would at least be something to do. I left the bed and sat down for a moment in the straight chair by the easel.

'I suppose we'd better,' Helen agreed, 'before they get infected. If we're going to burn these sheets anyway, why don't you tear a few strips from the edge? They'll make fine bandages.' Helen got out of bed wearily, and walked in tight circles, trying her legs. 'Boy, am I dizzy!' she exclaimed, and sat down on the foot of the bed.

I tore several strips of sheeting from the top sheet. Helen did some more circles and then sat down in a chair and fanned herself with her hands. I patted her bare shoulder reassuringly on my way to the dresser. My giddiness had all but disappeared, but my feeling of exhilaration remained. I had to dig through every drawer in the dresser before I could find the package of band-aids.

'Hold out your arms,' I told Helen. The gashes in her wrists hurt me to look at them. They were much deeper than my own and the tiny blue veins in her thin wrists were closer to the surface than they had been before. I was deeply ashamed, and bound her wrists rapidly with the sheeting. I used the band-aids to hold the improvised bandages in place and then we changed places. She bandaged my wrists while I sat in the chair, but did a much neater job of it.

Without warning Helen rushed into my arms and began

to sob uncontrollably. Her slender back was racked with violent, shuddering sobs and her hot flush of tears burned on my bare chest. I tried my best to comfort her.

'There, there, old girl,' I said crooningly, 'this won't do at all. Don't cry, baby, everything's going to be all right. There, there ...'

She continued to sob piteously for a long time and all I could do was hold her. I was helpless, confused. It wasn't like Helen to cry about anything. At last she calmed down, smiled weakly, and wiped her streaming eyes with her fingers, like a little girl.

'I know it's childish of me, Harry, to cry like that, but I couldn't help it. The thought exploded inside my head and caught me when I wasn't expecting it.'

'What did, honey?'

'Well, suppose you had died and I hadn't? And I woke up, and there you were — dead, and there I'd be, alone, still alive, without you, without anything ...' Her tears started to flow again, but with better restraint. I held her on my lap like a frightened child; her face against my shoulder. I made no attempts to prevent her silent crying. I just patted her gently on her bare back, letting her cry it out. I knew precisely how she felt, because my feelings were exactly the same. Within a few minutes she was calm again and smiling her secret, tragic smile.

'If you'd kept up much longer I'd have joined you,' I said, attempting a smile.

'Do you know what's the matter with us, Harry?'

'Everything. Just name it.'

'No.' She shook her head. 'We've lost our perspective. What we need is help, psychiatric help.'

'At fifty bucks an hour, we can't afford one second of help.'

'We can go to a hospital.'

'That costs even more.'

'Not a public hospital.'

'Well, there's Saint Paul's, but I'm leery of it.'

'Why? Is it free?' she asked eagerly.

'Sure, it's free all right, but what if they decide we're

nuts and lock us up in a state institution for a few years? You in a woman's ward, me in a men's ward?'

'Oh, they wouldn't do that, Harry. We aren't crazy. This wholesale depression we're experiencing is caused strictly by alcohol. If we can get a few drugs and a little conversation from a psychiatrist, we'll be just fine again. I'll bet they wouldn't keep us more than a week at the longest.'

'That isn't the way it works, baby,' I told her. 'A psychiatrist isn't a witch doctor with a speedy cure for driving out the devils. It's a long process, as I understand it, and the patient really cures himself. All the psychiatrist can do is help him along by guiding the thinking a little bit. He listens and says nothing. He doesn't even give the patient any sympathy. All he does is listen.'

'That doesn't make any sense to me.'

'But that's the way it works.'

'Well ...' She thought for a few moments. 'They could get us off the liquor, couldn't they?'

'If we didn't have any, and couldn't get any, yes. But even there, you have to have a genuine desire to quit drinking.'

'I don't want to drink anymore, Harry. Let's take a chance on it, to see what happens. We can't lose anything, and I know they aren't going to lock us up anywhere, because it costs the state too much money for that. Both of us need some kind of help right now, and you know it!'

I caught some of Helen's enthusiasm, but for a different reason. The prospect of a good rest, a chance to sleep at night, some proper food in my stomach appealed to me. It was a place to start from ...

'A week wouldn't be so bad at that,' I said. 'I could get straightened around some, maybe do a little thinking. I might come up with an idea.'

'I could too, Harry. There are lots of things we could do together! You know all about art. Why, I'll bet we could start an art gallery and make a fortune right here in San Francisco! Did you ever get your G.I. loan?'

'No.'

'A veteran can borrow all kinds of money! I think they

loan as high as four thousand dollars.'

'Maybe so, but an art gallery isn't any good. The dealers are all starving to death, even the well-established ones. People don't buy decent pictures for their homes any more. They buy pictures in the same place they get their new furniture. If the frame matches the davenport, they buy the picture, no matter what it is. No art gallery for me.'

'They give business loans too.'

'They may not take us in at the hospital.' I brought the subject back to the business at hand.

'If we show them our wrists, I'll bet they'll take us in!'

I knew that Helen was right and yet I was afraid to turn in to Saint Paul's Hospital. But I could think of nothing better to do. Maybe a few days of peace and quiet were all we needed. I could use a new outlook on life. It was the smart thing to do, and for once in my life, why couldn't I do the smart thing?

'All right, Helen. Get dressed. We'll try it. If they take us in, fine! If they don't, they can go to hell.'

After we were dressed, Helen began to roll up the bloody sheets to take them out to the incinerator. 'Just a second,' I said, and I tossed my box of oil paints and the rest of my painting equipment into the middle of the pile of sheets. 'Burn that junk, too,' I told her.

'You don't want to burn your paints!'

'Just do what I tell you. I know what I'm doing!'

While Helen took the bundle out to the backyard to burn it in the incinerator, I walked down the hall to Mrs. McQuade's room and knocked on her door.

'Mrs. McQuade,' I said, when she answered my insistent rapping. 'My wife and I are going out of town for a few days. We're going to visit her mother down in San Sienna.'

'How many days will you be gone, Mr. Jordan?' she asked suspiciously.

'I'm not sure yet. About a week, maybe not that long.'

'I can't give you any refund, Mr. Jordan. You didn't give me any advance notice.'

'I didn't ask for a refund, Mrs. McQuade.'

'I know you didn't, but I thought it best to mention it.' She fluttered her apron and smiled pleasantly. 'Now you go ahead and have a nice time. Your room'll still be here when you get back.'

'We will,' I said grimly. 'We expect to have a grand old time.'

I returned to the room. Helen was packing her suitcase with her night things, cold cream, and toothbrush. All I took was my shaving kit. As we left the room she handed me the suitcase and locked the door with her key. At the bottom of the steps, outside in the street, I gave her my leather shaving kit to carry so I could have one hand free.

'How do you feel, baby?' I asked Helen as we paused in front of the house.

'A wee bit dizzy still, but otherwise I'm all right. Why?'

'We've got a long way ahead of us, that's why.' I grinned. 'We don't have enough change for carfare.'

'Oh!' She lifted her chin bravely. 'Then let's get started,' she said resolutely, looking into my eyes.

I shrugged my shoulders, Helen took my arm, and we started walking up the hill.

Chapter Eight

HOSPITAL CASE

S an Francisco is an old city with old buildings, and it is built on seven ancient hills. And long before Helen and I reached the grounds of Saint Paul's Hospital it seemed as though we had climbed every one of them. The narrow, twisted streets, the weathered, brown and crumbling façades of the rotted, huddled buildings frowning upon us as we labored up and down the hills, gave me poignant, bitter memories of my neighborhood in early childhood days: Chicago's sprawling South Side. There was no particular resemblance between the two cities I could put my finger on, but the feeling of similarity persisted. Pausing at the crest of a long, steep hill for rest and breath, I saw the magnificent panorama of the great harbor spreading below us. Angel Island, Alcatraz, several rusty, vagrant ships, a portion of the Golden Gate, and the land mass of Marin County, San Francisco's bedroom, were all within my vision at one time. The water at the bay, a dark and Prussian blue, was the only link with Chicago and my past.

The long walk was good for me. I saw a great many things I had been merely looking at for a long time. It was as though I was seeing the city through new eyes, for the first time.

The late, slanting afternoon sun made long, fuzzy shadows; dark-colored shadows that dragged from the tops of the buildings like old-fashioned cloaks.

Noisy children were playing in the streets, shouting,

screaming, laughing; all of them unaware of money and security and death.

Bright, shiny new automobiles, chromium-trimmed, two-toned and silent, crept bug-like up and down the steep street. How long had it been since I had owned an automobile? I couldn't remember.

Housewives in house-dresses, their arms loaded with groceries in brown-paper sacks, on their way home to prepare dinner for their working husbands. How long had it been since I had had a home? I had never had a home.

I saw non-objective designs created with charm and simplicity on every wall, every fence, every puddle of water we passed; the designs of unconscious forms and colors, patterns waiting to be untrapped by an artist's hand. The many-hued spots of oil and water surrounded by blue-black macadam. The tattered, blistered, peeling ochre paint, stripping limply from a redwood wall of an untenanted house. The clean, black spikes of ornamental iron-work fronting a narrow stucco beauty-shop. Arranged for composition and drawn in soft pastels, what delicate pictures these would be for a young girl's bedroom. For Helen's bedroom. For our bedroom. If we had a house and a bedroom and a kitchen and a living-room and a dining-room and maybe another bedroom and I had a job and I was among the living once again and I was painting again and neither one of us was drinking ...

In a dim corner of my room for longer than my fancy
    thinks
A beautiful and silent Sphinx has watched me through
    the shifting gloom.

'Let's sit down for a while, Harry,' Helen said wearily. There was a bus passenger's waiting bench nearby, and we both sat down. I took the shaving kit out of Helen's lap and put it inside the suitcase. No reason for her to carry it when there was room inside the suitcase. She was more tired than I was. She smiled wanly and patted my hand.

'Do you know what I've been thinking about, Harry?'

'No, but I've been thinking all kinds of things.'

'It may be too early to make plans, Harry, but after we get out of the hospital and get some money again I'm going to get a divorce. It didn't make any difference before and it still doesn't — not the way I feel about you, I mean, but I'd like to be married to you. Legally, I mean.'

'Why legally?'

'There isn't any real reason. I feel that I'd like it better and so would you.'

'I like things better the way they are,' I said, trying to discourage her. 'Marriage wouldn't make me feel any different. But if it would make you any happier, that's what we'll do. But now is no time to talk about it.'

'I know. First off, I'll have to get a divorce.'

'That isn't hard. Where's your husband now?'

'Somewhere in San Diego, I think. I could find him. His parents are still living in San Sienna.'

'Well, let's not talk about it now, baby. We've got plenty of time. Right now I'm concerned with getting hospital treatment for whatever's the matter with me, if there is such a thing, and there's anything the matter with me. What do you say?'

'I'm rested.' Helen got to her feet. 'Want me to carry the suitcase a while?'

'Of course not.'

Saint Paul's hospital is a six-story building set well back from the street and surrounded by an eight-foot cyclone wire fence. In front of the hospital a small park of unkempt grass, several rows of geraniums, and a few antlered, unpruned elms are the only greenery to be seen for several blocks. The hospital stands like a red, sore finger in the center of a residential district; a section devoted to four-unit duplexes and a fringe of new ranch-style apartment hotels. Across the street from the entrance-way a new shopping-center and parking lot stretches half-way down the block. As we entered the unraked gravel path leading across the park to the receiving entrance, Helen's tired feet lagged. When we reached the thick, glass double-doors leading into the lobby, she stopped and squeezed my hand.

'Are you sure you want to go through with this, Harry?' she asked me anxiously. 'We didn't really have a chance to talk it over much. It was a kind of a spur-of-the-moment decision and we don't have to go through with it. Not if you don't want to,' she finished lamely.

'I'm not going to walk the three miles back to the rooming house,' I said. I could see the tiny cylinders clicking inside her head. 'You're scared aren't you?'

'A little bit,' she admitted. Her voice was husky. 'Sure I am.'

'They won't hurt us. It'll be a nice week's vacation,' I assured her.

'Well ... we've come this far ...'

I pushed open the door and we timidly entered. The lobby was large and deep and the air was filled with a sharp, antiseptic odor that made my nose burn. There were many well-worn leather chairs scattered over the brown linoleum floor, most of them occupied with incoming and out-going patients, with their poverty showing in their faces and eyes. In the left corner of the room there was a waist-high circular counter encircling two green, steel desks. Standing behind the desk, instead of the usual bald hotel clerk, was a gray-faced nurse in a white uniform so stiff with starch she couldn't have bent down to tie her shoe-laces. The austere expression on her face was so stern, a man with a broken leg would have denied having it; he would have been afraid she might want to minister to it. We crossed the room to the counter.

'Hello,' I said tentatively to her unsmiling face, as I set the suitcase on the floor. 'We'd like to see a doctor about admittance to the hospital ... a psychiatrist, if possible.'

'Been here before?'

'No, ma'am.'

'Which one of you is entering the hospital?'

'Both of us.' I took another look at her gray face. 'Maybe we are, I mean. We don't have a dime.'

'The money isn't the important thing. If you can pay, we charge, naturally, but if you can't, that's something else again. What seems to be the trouble?'

I looked at Helen, but she looked away and examined the yellowing leaves of a sickly potted plant with great interest. I was embarrassed. It was such a silly thing we had done that I hated to blurt it out to the nurse, especially such a practical-minded nurse. I was afraid to tell her for fear she would deliver a lecture of some sort. I forced myself to say it.

'We attempted suicide. We cut our wrists.' I stretched my arms over the counter so she could see my bandaged wrists.

'And now you want to see a psychiatrist? Is that right?'

'Yes, ma'am. We thought we would. We need help.'

'Come here, dear,' the nurse said to Helen, with a sudden change in manner. 'Let me see your wrists.'

Helen, blushing furiously, pulled the sleeves of her jacket back and held out her wrists to the nurse. At that moment I didn't like myself very well. It was my fault Helen was going through this degrading experience. I had practically forced her into the stupid suicide pact. The nurse deftly unwrapped the clumsy bandages I had affixed to Helen's wrists. She gave me an amused, professional smile.

'Did you fix these?'

'Yes, ma'am. You see, we were in a hurry to get here and I wrapped them rather hastily,' I explained.

The nurse puckered her lips and examined the raw wounds on Helen's slender wrists. She clucked sympathetically and handed each of us a three-by-five card and pencils. 'Suppose you two sit over there and fill in these cards,' she waved us to a decrepit lounge, 'and we'll see what we shall see.'

We sat down with the cards and Helen asked me in a whisper whether we should use our right names or not. I nodded and we filled in the cards with our names, addresses, etc. The nurse talked on her telephone, so quietly we couldn't hear the conversation from where we were sitting. In a few minutes a young, earnest-faced man, wearing white trousers and a short-sleeved white jacket got out of the elevator and walked directly to the desk. His feet, much too large for his short, squat body, looked larger than they were in heavy white shoes. He held a whispered conversation with the nurse, nodding his head gravely up and down in agreement. He crossed to our seats and pulled a straight chair around so it faced us. He sat down on the edge of the chair.

'I am Doctor Davidson,' he said briskly, unsmilingly. 'We're going to admit you both to the hospital. But first of all you will have to sign some papers. The nurse tells me you have no money. Is that correct?'

'Yes, that is correct,' I said. Helen said nothing. She kept her eyes averted from the doctor's face.

'The papers will be a mere formality, then.' His face was quite expressionless. I had a hunch that he practiced his blank expression in the mirror whenever he had the chance. He held out his hand for our filled-in cards. 'Come with me, please,' he ordered. He rose from his chair, dropped the cards on the counter, and marched quickly to the elevator without looking back. We trailed in his wake. At the sixth floor we got out of the elevator, walked to the end of the corridor, and he told us to sit down in two metal folding chairs against the wall. We sat for a solid hour, not talking, and afraid to smoke because there weren't any ashtrays. A young, dark-haired nurse came to Helen, crooked her finger.

'I want you to come with me, dear,' she said to Helen.

'Where am I going?' Helen asked nervously.

'To the women's ward.' The nurse smiled pleasantly.

'I thought we were going to be together —' Helen tried to protest.

'I'm sorry, dear, but that's impossible.'

'What'll I do, Harry?' Helen turned to me helplessly.

'You'd better go with her, I guess. Let me get my shaving kit out of the bag.' I opened the suitcase, retrieved my shaving kit, snapped the bag shut. 'Go on with her, sweetheart, we've come this far, we might as well go through with it.'

The nurse picked up the light over-nighter and Helen

followed reluctantly, looking back at me all the way down the corridor. They turned a corner, disappeared from view, and I was alone on my metal folding chair.

In a few minutes Dr. Davidson returned for me and we went down the hall in the opposite direction. We entered his office and he handed me a printed form and told me to sign it. I glanced through the fine print perfunctorily, without reading it in detail. It was a form declaring that I was a pauper. There was no denying that. I signed the paper and shoved it across the desk. 'You're entering the hospital voluntarily, aren't you?' he asked.

'That's about it.'

'Fill out these forms then.' He handed me three different forms in three different colors. 'You can use my office to fill them out.' He left the office and I looked at the printed forms. There were questions about everything; my life's history, my health, my relative's health, my schooling, and anything else the hospital would never need to know. For a moment I considered filling them in, but not seriously. I took the desk pen and made a check mark beside each of the numbered questions on all of the forms. That would show that I had read the questions, and if they didn't like it the hell with them. I didn't want to enter the hospital anyway. The doctor returned in about a half an hour and I signed the forms in his presence. Without looking at them he shoved them into a brown manila folder.

'I'm going to be your doctor while you're here,' he told me in his well-rehearsed impersonal manner, 'but it'll be a couple of days before I can get to you. Let me see your wrists.'

I extended my arms and he snipped the bandages loose with a pair of scissors, dropped the soiled sheeting into the waste-basket by his desk.

'What exactly brought this on, Jordan, or do you know?'

'We've been drinking for quite a while and we ran out of money. I suppose that's the main reason. Not that I'm an alcoholic or anything like that, but I'm out of work at present and I got depressed. Helen, more or less —'

'You mean, Mrs. Jordan?'

'No. Mrs. Meredith. Helen Meredith. We don't happen to be married, we're just living together, but we're going to be married later on. As I was saying, Helen takes my moods as hard as I do. If it hadn't been for me — well, this is all strictly my fault.'

'We aren't concerned with whose fault it is, Jordan. Our job is to make you well. Do you want a drink now?'

'I could stand one all right.'

'Do you feel like you need one?'

'No. I guess not.'

'We'll let the drink go then. Hungry?'

'No. Not a bit.'

He stood up, patted me on the shoulder, trying to be friendly. 'After we take care of those cuts we'll give you some soup, and I'll have the nurse give you a little something that'll make you sleep.'

We left his office and I followed him down the corridor to Ward 3-C. There was a heavy, mesh-wire entrance door and a buzzer set into the wall at the right. Dr. Davidson pressed the buzzer and turned me over to an orderly he addressed as Conrad. Conrad dressed my wrists and assigned me to a bed. He issued me a pair of gray flannel pajamas, a blue corduroy robe, and a pair of skivvy slippers. The skivvy slippers were too large for me and the only way I could keep them on was to shuffle my feet without lifting them from the floor. He kept my shaving kit, locked it in a metal cupboard by his desk, which was at the end of the ward.

I sat down on the edge of my bed and looked around the ward. There were twenty-six beds and eleven men including myself. They all looked normal enough to me; none of them looked or acted crazy. The windows were all barred, however, with one-inch bars. I knew I was locked in, but I didn't feel like a prisoner. It was more frightening than jail. A man in jail knows what to expect. Here, I didn't.

Conrad brought me a bowl of weak vegetable soup, a

piece of bread and an apple on a tray. He set the tray on my bedside stand.

'See what you can do to this,' he said.

I spooned the soup down, not wanting it, but because I thought the doctor wanted me to have it. I ignored the apple and the piece of bread. When he came for the tray, he brought me some foul-tasting lavender medicine in a shot glass and I drank it. He took the tray, and said over his shoulder as he left, 'You'd better hop into bed, boy. That stuff'll hit you fast. It's a legitimate Mickey.'

I removed my skivvy slippers and robe and climbed into bed. It was soft and high and the sheets were like warm snow. The sun was going down and its softly fading glow came through the windows like a warm good-night kiss. The light bulbs in the ceiling, covered with heavy wire shields, glowed dully, without brightness. I fell asleep almost at once, my head falling down and down into the depths of my pillow.

It was three days before I talked to Dr. Davidson again.

Chapter Nine

SHOCK TREATMENT

After getting used to it, and it is easy, a neuro-psychiatric ward can be in its own fashion a rather satisfying world within a world. It is the security. Not the security of being locked in, but the security of having everything locked out. The security that comes from the sense of no responsibility for anything. In a way, it is kind of wonderful.

And there is the silence, the peace and the quiet of the ward. The other patients kept to themselves and so did I. One of the orderlies, Conrad or Jones, brought our razors in the morning and watched us while we shaved. I would take a long, hot shower and then make my bed. That left nothing to do but sit in my chair by the side of my bed and wait for breakfast. Breakfast on a cart, was wheeled in and eaten. After breakfast we were left alone until lunch time. Then lunch would be wheeled in.

Near the door to the latrine there was a huge oak table. Spaced around the table there were shiny chromium chairs with colorful comfortable cushions that whooshed when you first sat down. Along the wall behind the table were stack after stack of old magazines. Except for the brief interruptions for meals and blood-tests I killed the entire first day by going through them. I considered it a pleasant day. I didn't have to think about anything. I didn't have to do anything, and I didn't have anything to worry about. The first night following my admittance I slept like a dead man.

The next morning, after a plain but filling breakfast of

mush, buttered toast, orange juice and coffee, I proceeded
to the stacks of magazines again. I had a fresh package of
king-sized cigarettes furnished by the Red Cross and I was
set for another pleasant day. We were not allowed to keep
matches and it was inconvenient to get a light from the
orderly every time I wanted to smoke, but I knew I
couldn't have everything.

Digging deeply into the stacks of magazines I ran across
old copies of *Art Digest, The American Artist* and *The
Modern Painter.* This was a find that pleased me. It had
been a long time since I had done any reading and
although the magazines were old, I hadn't read any of
them. One at a time I read them through, cover to cover. I
skipped nothing. I read the how-to-do's, the criticism, the
personality sketches and the advertisements. It all interested me. I spent considerable time studying the illustrations of the pictures in the recent one man shows,
dissecting pictures in my mind and putting them together
again. It was all very nice until after lunch. I was jolted
into reality. Really jolted.

There was an article in *The Modern Artist* by one of my
oldest teachers at the Chicago Art Institute. It wasn't an
exceptional article: he was deploring at length the plight
of the creative artist in America and filling in with the old
standby solution — *Art must have subsidy to survive* —
when I read my name in the pages flat before me. It
leaped off the pages filling my eyes. Me. Harry Jordan. A
would-be suicide, a resident of a free NP ward, and here
was my name in a national magazine! Not that there was
so much:

'*... and what caused Harry Jordan to give up
painting? Jordan was an artist who could do more
with orange and brown than many painters can do
with a full palette ...*'

Just that much, but it was enough to dissolve my
detached feelings and bring me back to a solid awareness
of my true situation. My old teacher was wrong, of course.

I hadn't given up painting for economic reasons. No real artist ever does. Van Gogh, Gauguin, Modigliani and a thousand others are the answer to that. But the mention of my name made me realize how far I had dropped from sight, from what I had been, and from what I might have been in my Chicago days. My depression returned full force. A nagging shred of doubt dangled in front of me. Maybe I could paint after all? Didn't my portrait of Helen prove that to me? Certainly, no painter could have captured her as well as I had done. Was I wrong? Had I wasted the years I could have been painting? Wouldn't it have been better to stay close to art, even as a teacher, where at least I would have had the urge to work from time to time? Maybe I would have overcome the block? The four early paintings I had done in orange-and-brown, the non-objective abstractions were still remembered by my old teacher — after all the elapsed time. It shook my convictions. Rocked me. My ruminations were rudely disturbed. My magazine was rudely jerked out of my hands.

'That's my magazine!' I turned in the direction of the high, reedy voice, verging on hysteria. A slight blond man stood by the table, clutching *The Modern Artist* to his pigeon breast. His face was flushed an angry red and his watery blue eyes were tortured with an inner pain.

'Sure,' I said noncommittally, 'I was just looking at it.'

'I'll stick your arm in boiling water!' He informed me shrilly.

'No you won't.' I didn't know what else to say to the man.

'I'll stick your arm in boiling water! I'll stick your arm in boiling water! I'll stick your arm in —' He kept repeating it over and over, his voice growing louder and higher, until Conrad was attracted from the end of the ward. Conrad covered the floor in quick strides, took the little man by the arm and led him away from the table.

'I want to show you something,' Conrad told the man secretly.

'What are you going to show me?' The feverish face

relaxed somewhat and he followed Conrad down the ward to his bed. Conrad showed him his chair and the man sat down wearily and buried his face in his hands. On the walk to his bed and chair, the magazine was forgotten, and it fell to the floor. On his way back to the table, Conrad picked up the magazine, slapped it on the table in front of me, and returned to his desk without a word of explanation. A man who had been watching the scene from the door of the latrine, crossed to the table and sat down opposite me.

'Don't worry about him,' he said. 'He's a Schizo.'

'A what?'

'Schizo. That's short for schizophrenic. In addition to that, he's a paranoid.'

I carefully looked over the patient who was talking to me. Unlike the rest of us he wore a pair of yellow silk pajamas, and an expensive vermillion brocade robe. His face was lined with crinkly crescents about his eyes and mouth, and a lightning blaze of white shot through his russet hair above each ear. He was smiling broadly; the little scene had amused him.

'My name is Mr. Haas,' he told me, reaching out to shake hands.

'Harry Jordan,' I said, shaking his hand.

'After a few years,' he offered, 'you get so you can tell. I've been in and out of these places ever since the war. I'm a Schizo myself and also paranoid. What's the matter with you?'

'Nothing,' I said defensively.

'You're lucky then. Why are your wrists bandaged?'

'I tried suicide, but it didn't work.'

'You're a manic-depressive then.'

'No, I'm not,' I said indignantly. 'I'm nothing at all.'

'Don't fight it, Jordan.' Mr. Haas had a kind, pleasant voice. 'It's only a label. It doesn't mean anything. Take my case for instance. I tried to kill my wife this time, and she had me committed. I won't be in here long, I'm being transferred to a V.A. hospital, and this time for good. It isn't so bad being a Schizo; there are many compensations. Did you ever have hallucinations?'

'No. Never.'

'I have them all the time, and the best kind. Most of us hear voices, but my little hallucination comes to me in the night and I can hear him, smell him and feel him. He feels like a rubber balloon filled with warm water, and he smells like Chanel Number Five. We carry on some of the damndest conversations you've ever heard.'

'What does he look like?' I was interested.

'The hell with you, Jordan. Get your own hallucination. How about some chess?'

'I haven't played in a long time,' I said.

'Neither have I. I'll get my board and chessmen.'

For the rest of the day I played chess with Mr. Haas. I didn't win a game.

By supper that night I was my old self again. Playing chess had made me forget the magazine article temporarily. After a supper of liver and new potatoes I crawled into bed. I was a failure and I knew it. The false hopes of the early afternoon were gone. The portrait of Helen was nothing but a lucky accident. My old orange-and-brown abstracts were nothing but experiments. Picasso's *Blue* period. Jordan's *Orange-and-Brown* period. They hadn't sold at my asking price and I'd destroyed them years ago. My name being mentioned, along with a dozen other painters, was no cause for emotion or elation. It was all padding. The prof. had to pad his article some way, and he had probably wracked his brain for enough names to make his point. But seeing my name in *The Modern Artist* had ruined my day.

It took me a long time to fall asleep.

The next morning I awoke with a slight headache and a sharp pain behind my eyeballs. I wasn't hungry, my hands were trembling slightly and my heart had a dull, dead ache. I felt terrible and even the hot water of the shower didn't relieve my depression.

I was back to normal.

At nine-thirty Conrad told me the doctor wanted to see me. He led the way and I sluffed along behind him in my slippers. Dr. Davidson's office was a small bare room, without a window, lit by fluorescent tubing the length of the ceiling. Two wooden chairs and a metal desk filled the room. The desk was stacked with patients' charts in aluminium covers. I sat down across from Dr. Davidson and Conrad closed the door, leaving us alone.

'Did you think I'd forgotten about you, Jordan?' The doctor tried a thin-lipped smile.

'No, sir.' My fists were tightly clenched and I kept my eyes on my bandaged wrists.

'You forgot to fill in the forms I gave you.'

'No, I didn't. I read the questions and that was enough.'

'We need that information in order to admit you, Jordan.'

'You won't get it from me. I'm ready to leave anyway.' I got to my feet and half-way to the door.

'Sit down, Jordan.' I sat down again. 'What's the matter? Don't you want to tell me about it?'

'Not particularly. It all seems silly now. Although it seemed like a good idea at the time.'

'Nothing is silly here,' he said convincingly, 'or strange, or secret. I'd like to hear about it.'

'There's nothing really to tell. I was depressed, as I usually am, and I passed my depression on to Helen — Mrs. Meredith. We cut our wrists.'

'But why are you depressed?'

'Because I'm a failure. I don't know how else to say it.'

'How long had you been drinking?'

'Off and on. Mostly on. Helen drinks more than I do. I don't consider myself an alcoholic, but I suppose she is, or close to it.'

'How long have you been drinking?'

'About five years.'

'I mean you and Mrs. Meredith.'

'Since we've been together. Three weeks, a month. Something like that.'

'What have you used for money? Are you employed?'

'Not now. She had a couple of hundred dollars. It's gone now. That's part of this.' I held up my arms. 'No money.'

'What kind of work do you do when you work?'

'Counterman, fry cook, dishwasher.'

'Is that all?'

'I used to teach. Painting, drawing and so on. Fine arts.'

'Why did you give it up?'

'I don't know.'

'By that you mean you won't say.'

'Take it any way you want.'

'How were your carnal relations with Mrs. Meredith?'

'Carnal? That's a hell of a word to use, and it's none of your business!' I was as high-keyed and ill-strung as a Chinese musical instrument.

'Perhaps the word was unfortunate. How was your sex life, then?'

'How is any sex life? What kind of an answer do you want?'

'As a painter — you did paint, didn't you?' I nodded. 'You should have a sharp notice for sensation, then. Where did it feel the best? The tip, the shaft, where?' He held his pencil poised over a sheet of yellow paper.

'I don't remember and it's none of your business!'

'You aren't making it easy for me to help you, Jordan,' he said patiently.

'I don't need any help.'

'You asked for help when you entered the hospital.'

'That was my mistake. I don't need any help. I'm sorry I wasted your time. Just let me out and I'll be all right.'

'All right, Jordan. I'll have you released in the morning.'

I stood up, anxious to get away from him. 'Thanks, Doctor. I'm sorry —'

'Sit down!' I sat down again. 'I've already talked to Mrs. Meredith, but I wanted to check with you. Is Mrs. Meredith colored?'

'Helen?' My laugh was hard and brittle. 'Of course not. What made you ask that?'

He hesitated for a moment before he answered. 'Her expression and eyes, the bone structure of her face. She denied it too, but I thought I'd check with you.'

'No,' I said emphatically. 'She definitely isn't colored.'

'I'm going to tell you something, Jordan. I think you need help. As a rule, I don't give advice; people don't take it and it's a waste of time. But in your case I want to mention a thing or two. My own personal opinion. I don't think you and Mrs. Meredith are good for each other. All I can see ahead for you both is tragedy. That is, if you continue to live together.'

'Thanks for your opinion. Can I go now?'

'Yes, you can go.'

'Will you release Helen tomorrow too?'

'In a few more days.'

'Can I see her?'

'No, I don't think so. It would be best for her not to have any visitors for the next few days.'

'If you'll call Big Mike's Bar and Grill and ask for me, I'll pick her up when you release her.'

'All right.' He wrote the address on the sheet of yellow paper. 'You can go back to your ward.'

Conrad met me outside the office and took me back to the ward. For the rest of the day I played chess with Mr. Haas. I didn't win any games, but my skill improved. I couldn't sleep that night, and finally I got out of bed at eleven and asked the nurse to give me something. She gave me a sleeping pill that worked and I didn't awaken until morning. As soon as breakfast was over with my clothes were brought to me and I put them on. Mr. Haas talked with me while I was dressing.

'I'm sorry to see you leave so soon, Jordan. In another day or so you might have won a game.' He laughed pleasantly. 'And then I would have killed you.' I didn't know whether he was kidding or not. 'Makes you think, doesn't it?' he added. We shook hands and I started toward the door. 'I'll be seeing you!' He called after me, and laughed again. This time rather unpleasantly, I thought. Conrad took me to the elevator and told me to stop at the desk in the lobby. At the desk downstairs, the nurse on duty gave me three pieces of paper to sign, and in a moment I was out on the street.

There wasn't any sun and the fog had closed down

heavily over the city. I walked through the damp mist, up and down the hills, alone in my own little pocket of isolation. I walked slowly, but in what seemed like a short length of time I found myself in front of Big Mike's. I pushed through the swinging doors, sat down at the bar and put my shaving kit on the seat beside me.

'Hello, Harry,' Mike said jovially. 'Where you been keeping yourself?'

'Little trip.'

'Drink?'

I shook my head. 'Mike, I need some money. No, I don't want a loan,' I said when he reached for his hip pocket. 'I want a job. Can you use me for a few days as a busboy or dishwasher?'

'I've got a dishwasher,' Mike rubbed his chin thoughtfully. 'But I don't have a busboy. Maybe the waiters would appreciate a man hustling dishes at noon and dinner. That's a busy time. But I can't pay you anything, Harry — dollar an hour.'

'That's plenty. It would really help out while I look for a job.'

'Want to start now?'

'Sure.'

'Pick up a white jacket in the kitchen.'

I started to work, grateful for the opportunity. The waiters were glad to have me clearing dishes and carrying them to the kitchen. I'm a fast worker and I kept the tables cleared for them all through the lunch hour, hotfooting it back and forth to the kitchen with a tray in each hand. By two-thirty the lunch crowd had slowed to a dribble and I was off until five. I took the time to go to my rooming house for a shower. I straightened the room, dumped trash and beer bottles into the can in the backyard, returned to Mike's. I worked until ten that evening, then returned to my room.

I found it was impossible to get to sleep. I quit trying to force it, dressed and went outside. I walked for a while and suddenly started to run. I ran around the block three times and was soon gasping for breath. I kept running. My heart thumped so hard I could feel it beating through my shirt. Bright stars danced in front of my eyes, turned gray, black. I had to stop. I leaned against a building, gasping until I got my breath back. My muscles twitched and ached as I slowly made my way back home. I took a shower and threw myself across the bed. Now I could sleep, and I did until ten the next morning.

It was three days before Dr. Davidson called me. It was in the middle of the noon rush and I was dripping wet when Mike called me to the telephone at the end of the bar. I didn't say anything, but held my hand over the mouthpiece until he walked away.

'Jordan here,' I said into the phone.

'This is Doctor Davidson, Jordan. We've decided to release Mrs. Meredith in your custody. As her common-law husband you'll be responsible for her. Do you understand that?'

'What time?' I asked impatiently.

'About three this afternoon. You'll have to sign for her to take her out. Sure you want to do it?'

'Yes, sir. I'll be there.' I racked the phone.

Big Mike was in the kitchen eating a salami sandwich and talking with the chef. The chef was complaining about the quality of the pork loin he was getting lately. I broke into the monologue.

'Mike, I have to quit.'

'Okay.'

'Can I have my money?'

'Okay.' He took a roll of bills out of his hip pocket, peeled six ones and handed them to me.

'Only six bucks?'

'I took out for your tab, Harry, but I didn't charge your meals.'

'Thanks, Mike. I don't like to leave you in the middle of a rush like this —' I began to apologize.

He waved me away impatiently, bit into his sandwich. 'Forget it.'

I hung the white mess jacket in the closet and slipped

into my corduroy jacket. At the rooming house I showered
and shaved for the second time that day. I rubbed my
worn shoes with a towel but they were in such bad shape
they didn't shine a bit. I caught a trolley, transferred to a
bus, transferred to another trolley. It was one-thirty when
I reached the entrance to the hospital. I sat down on a
bench in the little park and watched the minute hand in
the electric clock bounce to each mark, rarely taking my
eyes away from it. The clock was set into the center of a
Coca-Cola sign above the door of a drug store in the
shopping center across the street. At three, on the head, I
entered the hospital lobby. Helen was waiting for me by
the circular counter, her lower lip quivering. As soon as
she saw me she began to cry. I held her tight and kissed
her, to the annoyance of the nurse.

'Hey,' I said softly. 'Cut that out. Everything's going to
be all right.' Her crying stopped as suddenly as it started. I
signed the papers the nurse had ready, picked up Helen's
bag and we went outside. We sat down on the bench in
the little park.

'How'd they treat you, sweetheart?' I asked her.

'Terrible.' Helen shuddered. 'Simply terrible, and it was
boring as hell.'

'What did Dr. Davidson say to you? Anything?'

'He said I should quit drinking. That's about all.'

'Anything else?'

'A lot of personal questions. He's got a filthy mind.'

'Are you going to quit drinking?'

'Why should I? For him? That bastard!'

'Do you want a drink now?'

'It's all I've thought about all week, Harry,' she said
sincerely.

'Come on,' I took her arm, helping her to her feet.
'Let's go across the street.'

A few doors down the street from the shopping center
we found a small neighborhood bar. We entered and sat
down in the last booth. I saved out enough money for
carfare and we drank the rest of the six dollars. Helen was
unusually quiet and drank nothing but straight shots,

holding the glass in both hands, like a child holding a mug. Once in awhile she would almost cry, and then she would smile instead. We didn't talk; there was nothing to talk about. We left the bar and made the long, wearisome trip back to Big Mike's. We sat down in our old seats at the bar and started to drink on a new tab. Mike was glad to see Helen again and he saw that we always had a fresh, full glass in front of us. By midnight Helen was glassy-eyed drunk and I took her home and put her to bed. Despite the many drinks I had had, I was comparatively sober. Before going to bed myself I smoked a cigarette, crushed it savagely in the ashtray.

As far as I could tell, we were no better off than before.

Chapter Ten

MOTHER LOVE

Next morning I got out of bed early, and without waking Helen, took a long hot shower and dressed. Helen slept soundly, her lips slightly parted. I raised the blind and the room flooded with bright sunlight. A beautiful day. I shook Helen gently by the shoulder and she opened her eyes quickly, blinked them against the brightness. She was wide awake.

'I hated to wake you out of a sound sleep,' I said, 'but I'm leaving.'

Helen sat up in bed immediately. 'Leaving? Where?'

'Job hunting.' I grinned at her alarm. 'Not a drop of whiskey in the house.'

'No money at all, huh?'

'No money, no coffee, nothing at all.'

'What time will you be back?'

'I don't know. Depends on whether I can get a job, and if I do, when I get through. But I'll be back as soon as I can.'

Helen got out of bed, slid her arms around my neck and kissed me hard on the mouth. 'You shouldn't have to work, Harry,' she said sincerely and impractically. 'You shouldn't have to do anything except paint.'

'Yeah,' I said, disengaging her arms from my neck, 'and make love to you. I'd better get going.' I left the room, closing the door behind me.

There was a little change in my pocket, more than enough for carfare, and I caught the cable car downtown to Market Street. I had always been lucky finding jobs on

Market, maybe I could again. There are a thousand and one cafes. One of them needed a man like me. From Turk Street I walked toward the Civic Center, looking for signs in windows. I wasn't particular. Waiter, dishwasher, anything. I didn't care. I tried two cafes without success. At last I saw a sign: FRY COOK WANTED, hanging against the inside of a window, of a small café, attached with scotch tape. I entered the café. It was a dark, dingy place with an overpowering smell of fried onions. I reached over the shoulder of the peroxide blonde sitting behind the cash register and jerked the sign out of the window.

'What do you think you're doing?' she said indifferently.

'I'm the new fry cook. Where's the boss?'

'In the kitchen.' She jerked her thumb toward the rear of the café, appraising me with blue, vacant eyes.

I made my way toward the kitchen. The counter was filled, all twelve stools, and the majority of customers sitting on them were waiting for their food. There wasn't even a counterman working to give a glass of water or pass out a menu. The boss, a perspiring, overweight Italian, wearing suit pants and a white shirt, was gingerly dishing chilli beans into a bowl. Except for the old, slow-moving dishwasher, he was the only one in the kitchen.

'Need a fry cook?' I grinned ingratiatingly, holding up the sign.

'Need one? You from the Alliance?'

'No, but I'm a fry cook.'

'I been trying to get a cook from the Alliance for two days, and my waitress quit twenty minutes ago. The hell with the Alliance. Get busy.'

'I'm your man.' I removed my coat and hung it on a nail.

He wore a greasy, happy smile. 'Sixty-five a week, meals and laundry.'

'You don't have to convince me,' I told him, 'I'm working.'

I wrapped an apron around my waist and took a look at

the stove. The boss left the kitchen, rubbing his hands together, and started to take the orders. Although I was busy I could handle things easily enough. I can take four or five orders in my head and have four or more working on the stove at the same time. When I try to go over that I sometimes run into trouble. But there was nothing elaborate to prepare. The menu offered nothing but plain food, nothing complicated. The boss was well pleased with my work. I could tell that by the way he smiled at me when he barked in his orders. And I had taken him out of a hole.

At one my relief cook came on duty, a fellow by the name of Tiny Sanders. I told him what was working and he nodded his head and started to break eggs for a Denver with one hand. I put my jacket on, found a brown paper sack and filled it with food out of the icebox. I don't believe in buying food when I'm working in a café. The boss came into the kitchen and I hit him up for a five spot. He opened his wallet and gave me the five without hesitation.

'I'm giving you the morning shift, Jordan. Five a.m. to one.'

'That's the shift I want.' I told him. 'See you in the morning.' It was the best shift to have. It would give me every afternoon and evening with Helen.

I left the café and on the corner I bought a dozen red carnations for a dollar from a sidewalk vendor. They were old flowers and I knew they wouldn't last for twenty-four hours, but they would brighten up our room. On the long ride home I sniffed the fragrance of the carnations and felt well pleased with myself, revelling in my good fortune.

I was humming to myself as I ran up the stairs and down the hall to our room.

I opened my door and jagged tendrils of perfume clawed at my nostrils. Tweed. It was good perfume, but there was too much of a good thing. Helen, fully dressed in her best suit, was sitting nervously on the edge of the unmade bed. Across from her in the strongest chair was a formidable woman in her late fifties. Her hair was a streaked slate-gray and she was at least fifty pounds over-weight for her height — about five-nine. Her sharp blue eyes examined me like a bug through a pair of eight-sided gold-rimmed glasses. The glasses were on a thin gold chain that led to a shiny black button pinned to the breast of a rather severe blue taffeta dress.

'Harry,' there was a catch in Helen's throat, 'this is my mother, Mrs. Mathews.'

'How do you do?' I said. I put the carnations and sack of food on the table. 'This is a pleasant surprise.'

'Is it?' Mrs. Mathews sniffed.

'Well, I didn't expect you —'

'I'll bet you didn't!' She jerked her head to the right.

'The hospital notified Mother I was ill,' Helen explained.

'That was very thoughtful of them,' I said.

'Yes,' Mrs. Mathews said sarcastically, 'wasn't it? Yes, it was very thoughtful indeed. They also were thoughtful enough to inform me that my daughter was released from the hospital in the custody of her common-law husband. That was a nice pleasant surprise!'

For a full minute there was a strained silence. I inter-rupted it. 'Helen is all right now,' I said, trying a cheery note.

'Is she?' Mrs. Mathews asked.

'Yes, she is.'

'Well, I don't think so,' Mrs. Mathews jerked her head to the right. 'I think she's out of her mind!'

'Please, Mother!' Helen was very close to tears.

'I'm taking good care of Helen,' I said.

'Are you?' Mrs. Mathews hefted herself to her feet, clomped heavily across the room to the portrait. 'Is this what you call taking good care of her? Forcing her to pose for a filthy, obscene picture?' Her words were like vitriolic drops of acid wrapped in cellophane, and they fell apart when they left her lips, filling the room with poison.

'It's only a portrait,' I said defensively. 'It isn't for public viewing.'

'You bet it isn't! Only a depraved mind could have

conceived it; only a depraved beast could execute it; and only a leering, concupiscant goat would look at it.'

'You're too hard on me, Mrs. Mathews. It isn't that bad,' I said.

'Where have you been so long, Harry?' Helen asked me, trying to change the subject.

'I got a job, and that sack's full of groceries,' I said, pointing.

'What kind of job?' Mrs. Mathews asked. 'Sweeping streets?'

'No. I'm a cook.'

'I don't doubt it. Listen, er, ah, Mr. Jordan, if you think anything of Helen at all, you'll take some sense into her. I want her to come home with me, where she belongs. Look at her eyes! They look terrible.'

'Now that I've got a job she'll be all right, Mrs. Mathews. Would you like a salami sandwich, Helen?'

'No thanks, Harry,' Helen said politely. 'Not right now.'

'Why not?' Mrs. Mathews asked with mock surprise. 'That's exactly what you should eat! Not fresh eggs, milk, orange juice and fruit. That stuff isn't any good for a person right out of a sick bed. Go head. Eat a salami sandwich. With pickles!'

'I'm not hungry, Mother!'

'Maybe it's a drink of whiskey you want? Have you got whiskey in that sack, Mr. Jordan, or is it all salami?'

'Just food,' I said truthfully. 'No whiskey.'

'That's something. Are you aware that Helen shouldn't drink anything with alcohol in it? Do you know of her bad heart? Did she tell you she was sick in bed with rheumatic fever for three years when she was a little girl? Did she tell you she couldn't smoke?'

'I'm all right, Mother!' Helen said angrily. 'Leave Harry alone!'

Again we suffered a full minute of silence. 'I brought you some carnations,' I said to Helen; 'you'd better put them in water.' I crossed to the table, unwrapped the green paper, and gave the flowers to Helen.

'They're lovely, Harry!' Helen exclaimed. She placed

the carnations in the water pitcher on the dresser, arranged them quickly, inexpertly, sat down again on the edge of the bed, and stared at her mother. I sat beside her, reached over and took her hand. It was warm, almost feverish.

'Now listen to me, both of you.' Mrs. Mathews spoke slowly, as though she were addressing a pair of idiots. 'I can perceive that neither one of you has got enough sense to come in out of the rain. Helen has, evidently, made up what little mind she has, to remain under your roof instead of mine. All right. She's over twenty-one and there's nothing I can do about it. If you don't dissuade her and I can see you won't — not that I blame you — will you at least let me in on your plans?'

'We're going to be married soon.' Helen said.

'Do you mind if I call to your attention that you're already married?' Mrs. Mathews jerked her head to the right as though Helen's husband was standing outside the door waiting for her.

'I mean, after I get a divorce,' Helen said.

'And meanwhile, while you're waiting, you intend to continue to live here in sin? Is that right?'

Helen didn't answer for a moment and I held my breath. 'Yes, Mother, that's what I'm going to do. Only it isn't sin.'

'I won't quibble.' Mrs. Mathews sniffed, jerked her head to the right and turned her cold blue eyes on me. 'How much money do you make per week, Mr. Jordan? Now that you have a job.' The way she said it, I don't believe she thought I had a job.

'Sixty-five dollars a week. And I get my meals and laundry.'

'That isn't enough. And I doubt in here —' she touched her mammoth left breast with her hand — 'whether you can hold a position paying that much for any length of time. Here's what I intend to do. As long as my daughter won't listen to reason, I'll send her a check for twenty-five dollars a week. But under one condition: both of you stay out of San Sienna!'

'We don't need any money from you, Mother!' Helen said fiercely. 'Harry makes more than enough to support me.'

'I'm not concerned with that,' Mrs. Mathews said self-righteously. 'I know where my duty lies. You can save the money if you don't need it, or tear up the check, I don't care. But starting right now, I'm giving you twenty-five dollars a week!'

'You're very generous,' I said.

'I'm not doing it for you,' Mrs. Mathews jerked her head to the right. 'I'm doing it for Helen.'

Mrs. Mathews removed a checkbook and ballpoint pen from the depths of a cavernous saddle-leather bag and wrote a check. She crossed the room to the dresser, drying the ink by waving the check in the air, and put the filled-in check beside the pitcher of carnations. She sniffed.

'That's all I have to say, but to repeat it one more time so there'll be no mistake: Stay out of San Sienna!'

'It was nice meeting you, Mrs. Mathews,' I said. Helen remained silent.

Mrs. Mathews jerked her head to the right so hard her glasses were pulled off her nose. The little chain spring caught them up and they whirred up to the black button pinned to her dress. She closed the shirred beaver over the glasses, sniffed, and slammed the door in my face.

But the memory lingered on, in the form of a cloud of Tweed perfume.

Helen's face was pale and her upper lip was beaded with tiny drops of perspiration. She wound her arms around my waist tightly and pressed her face into my chest. I patted her on the back, kissed the top of her head.

'Oh, Harry, it was terrible!' Her voice was low and muffled against my chest. 'She's been here since ten o'clock this morning. Arguing, arguing, arguing! Trying to break me down. And I almost lost! I was within that much' — she pulled away from me, held thumb and forefinger an inch apart — of going with her.' She looked at me accusingly; her face wore an almost pitiful expression. 'Where were you? When I needed you the most, you weren't here!'

'I wasn't lying about the job, Helen. I found a job as a fry cook and had to go to work to get it.'

'Why do you have to work? It isn't fair to leave me here all alone.'

'We have to have money, sweetheart,' I explained patiently. 'We were flat broke when I went out this morning, if you remember.'

'Can't we live on what money Mother sends us?'

'We could barely exist on twenty-five dollars a week. The room rent's ten dollars, and we'd have to buy food and liquor out of the rest. We just can't do it.'

'What are we going to do, Harry? It's so unfair of Mother!' she said angrily. 'She could just as easily give us two hundred and fifty a week!'

'Can't you see what she's up to, Helen? She's got it all planned out, she thinks. She doesn't want you to go hungry, but if she gave us more money, she knows damned well you'd never go back to her. This way, she figures she has a chance —'

'Well, she's wrong! I'm never going back to San Sienna!'

'That leaves it up to me then, where it belongs. I'll work this week out, anyway. Maybe another. We'll pay some room rent in advance that way, and the tab at Mike's. And maybe we can get a few loose dollars ahead. Then I'll look for some kind of part time work that'll give me more time with you.'

We left it at that.

Helen picked the check up from the dresser and left for the delicatessen. She returned in a few minutes with a bottle of whiskey and a six-pack carton of canned beer. I had one drink with her and I made it last. I didn't want to drink that one. I felt that the situation was getting to be too much for me to handle. Helen drank steadily, pouring them down, one after the other, chasing the raw whiskey with sips of beer. Her mother's visit had upset her badly, and she faced it typically, the way she faced every situation.

By six that evening she sat numbly in the chair by the window. She was in a paralyzed stupor. I undressed her and put her to bed. She lay on her back, breathing with difficulty. Her eyes were like dark bruises, her face a mask of fragile, white tissue paper.

I didn't leave the room; I felt like a sentry standing guard duty. I made a salami sandwich, took one bite, and threw it down on the table. I sat in the chair staring at the wall until well past midnight.

After I went to bed, it was a long time before I fell asleep.

Chapter Eleven

BOTTLE BABY

The little built-in, automatic alarm clock inside my head waked me at four a.m. and I hadn't even taken the trouble to set it. I tried to fight against it and go back to sleep, but I couldn't. The alarm was too persistent. I reluctantly got out of the warm bed, shiveringly grabbed a towel, and rushed next door to the bathroom. Standing beneath the hot water of the shower almost put me back to sleep. With an involuntary yelp I twisted the faucet to cold and remained under the pelting needles of ice for three minutes. On the way back to my room I dried myself, and then dressed hurriedly against the background of my chattering teeth. The room was much too cold to hang around for coffee to boil and I decided to wait and get a cup when I reached Vitale's Café. I got my trench-coat out of the closet and put it on over my corduroy jacket. The trenchcoat was so filthy dirty I only wore it when I had to, but it was so cold inside the house I knew I would freeze on the street without something to break the wind.

Helen was sleeping on her side, facing the wall, and I couldn't see her face. Her hip made a minor mountain out of the covers and a long ski slope down to her bare round shoulder. I envied Helen's warmness but I pulled the blanket up a little higher and tucked it in all around her neck.

Helen had been so far under the night before when I put her to bed I thought it best to leave a note. I tore a strip of paper from the top of a brown sack and wrote in charcoal:

Dearest Angel,
Your slave has departed for the salt mine. Will be
home by one-thirty at latest. All my love,
                                                    Harry

Helen's bottle of whiskey was still a quarter full. I put the note in the center of the table and weighted it with the bottle where I knew she would find it easily when she first got out of bed. I turned out the overhead light and closed the door softly on my way out.

It was colder outside than I had anticipated it to be. A strong, steady wind huffed in from the bay, loaded heavily with salt and mist, and I couldn't make myself stand still on the corner to wait for my car. Cable cars are few and far between at four-twenty in the morning and it was far warmer to run a block, wait, run a block and wait until one came into view. I covered four blocks this way and the exertion warmed me enough to wait on the fourth corner until a car came along and slowed down enough for me to catch it. I paid my fare to the conductor and went inside. I was the only passenger for several blocks and then business picked up for the cable car when several hungry-looking long-shoremen boarded it with neatly-lettered placards on their way to the docks to picket. I dismounted at the Powell Street turnaround and walked briskly down Market with my hands shoved deep in my pockets. The wide street was as nearly deserted as it can ever be. There were a few early-cruising cabs and some middle-aged paper boys on the corners waiting for the first morning editions. There was an ugly mechanical monster hugging the curbs and sploshing water and brushing it up behind as it noisily cleaned at the streets. Later on there would be the regular street cleaners with brooms and trash-cans on wheels to pick up what the monster missed. I entered Vitale's Café.

'Morning, Mr. Vitale,' I said.

'It don't work for me,' the boss said ruefully. 'I poured hot water through ten times already and it won't turn dark. I have to use fresh coffee grounds after all.'

'Did you dry the old grounds on the stove first?'

'No, I've been adding hot water.'

'That's what's the matter then. If you want to use coffee grounds two days in a row you have to dry them out on the stove in a shallow pan. Add a couple of handfuls of fresh coffee to the dried grounds and the coffee'll be as dark as cheap coffee ever gets.'

I took off my jacket and lit the stove and checked on the groceries for breakfast. I wrapped an apron around my waist and stoned the grill while I waited for the coffee to be made, making a mental note to fix my own coffee the next morning before I left my room. By five a.m. I was ready for work and nobody had entered the café. I wondered why Vitale opened so early. I soon found out. All of a sudden the counter was jammed with breakfast eaters from the various office buildings and street, most of them ordering the Open Eye Breakfast Special: two ounces of tomato juice, one egg, one strip of bacon, one piece of toast and coffee extra. This breakfast was served for thirty-five cents and although it was meager fare it attracted the low income group. The night elevator operators, the cleaning women, the newsboys, the all-night movie crowd, and some of the policemen going off duty all seemed to go for it. Breakfast was served all day at Vitale's, but at ten-thirty I checked the pale blue menu and began to get ready for the lunch crowd. I was so busy during the noon rush I hated to look up from my fry grill when Tiny, my relief, tapped me on the shoulder at one on the head. I told Tiny what was working, wrapped up two one-pound T-bones to take home with me, and left the café with a wave at the boss.

On the long ride home I tried to think of ways to bring Helen out of the doldrums, but every idea I thought of was an idea calling for money. By the time I reached my corner my immediate conclusion was that all Helen needed was one of my T-bone steaks, fried medium rare

as only I could fry a steak and topped with a pile of french
fried onion rings. I bought a dime's worth of onions at the
delicatessen and hurried home with my surprise. I opened
the door to my room and Helen wasn't there. My note was
still under the whiskey bottle, but now the bottle was
empty. There was a message from Helen written under
mine and I picked it up and studied it.

> *Dear Harry,*
> *I can't sit here all day waiting for you. If I don't talk to*
> *somebody I'll go nuts. I love you.*
> > *Helen*

The message was in Helen's unmistakable microscopic
handwriting and it was written with the same piece of
charcoal I had used and left on the table. It took me
several minutes to decipher what she said and I still didn't
know what she really meant. Was she leaving me for
good? I opened the closet and checked her clothes, the
few she had. They were all in the closet and so was her
suitcase. That made me feel a little better, knowing she
wasn't leaving me. I still didn't like the idea of her running
around loose, half-drunk, and with nothing solid in her
stomach. She had killed the rest of the whiskey, which was
more than a half-pint, and she had the remainder of the
twenty-five bucks her mother had given her. She could be
anywhere in San Francisco — with anybody. I had to find
her before she got into trouble.

I opened the window, put the steaks outside on the sill,
and closed the window again. If the sun didn't break
through the fog they would keep until that evening before
they spoiled. I left the rooming house and walked down
the street to Big Mike's Bar and Grill. After I entered the
grill I made my way directly to the cash register where Big
Mike was standing. By the look in his eyes I could tell he
didn't want to talk to me.

'Have you seen Helen, Mike?' I asked him.

'Yeah, I saw her all right. She was in here earlier.'

'She left, huh?'

'That's right, Harry. She left.' His voice was surly, his expression sour. There was no use to question him any further. How was he supposed to know where she went? It was obvious something was bothering him and I waited for him to tell me about it.

'Listen, Harry,' Mike said, after I waited a full minute. 'I like you fine, and I suppose Helen's okay too, but from now on I don't want her in here when you ain't with her.'

'What happened, Mike. I've been working since five this morning.'

'I don't like to say nothing, Harry, but, you might as well know. She was in about eleven and drunker than hell. I wouldn't sell her another drink even, and when I won't sell another drink, they're drunk. She had her load on when she came in, and it was plenty. Anyway, she got nasty with me and I told her to leave. She wouldn't go and I didn't want to toss her out on her ear so I shoved her in a booth and had Tommy take her some coffee. She poured it on the floor, cussing Tommy out and after awhile three Marines took up with her. They sat down in her booth and she quieted down so I let it go. After a while they all left and that was it. I'm sorry as hell, Harry, but that's the way it was. I ain't got time to look after every drunk comes in here.'

'I know it, Mike. You don't know where they went, do you?'

'As I said, after a while I looked and they were gone.'

'Well, thanks, Mike.' I left the bar and went out on the sidewalk. If the Marines and Helen had taken the cable car downtown I'd never find them. But if they took a cab from the hack-stand in the middle of the block, maybe I would be all right. I turned toward the hack-stand. Bud, the young Korean veteran driver for the Vet's Cab Company was leaning against a telephone pole waiting for his phone to ring, a cigarette glued to the corner of his mouth, when I reached his stand. He had a pinched, fresh face with light beige-colored eyes, and wore his chauffeur's cap so far back on his head it looked like it would fall off. I knew him enough to nod to him, and saw him often around the corner and in Big Mike's, but I had never spoken to him before.

'I guess you're lookin' for your wife, huh, Jordan?' Bud made a flat statement and it seemed to give him great satisfaction.

'Yes, I am, Bud. Have you seen her?'

'Sure did.' He ripped the cigarette out of his mouth, leaving a powdering of flaked white paper on his lower lip, and snapped the butt into the street. 'She was with three Marines.' This statement gave him greater satisfaction.

'Did you take them any place?'

'Sure did.'

'Where?'

'Get in.' Bud opened the back door of his cab.

'What's the tariff, Bud?' I was thinking of the three one dollar bills in my watch pocket and my small jingle of change.

'It'll run you about a buck and a half.' He smiled with the left side of his face. 'If you want to go. She was with three Marines.' He held up three fingers. 'Three,' he repeated, 'and you are one.' He held up one finger. 'One.'

'We'll see,' I said noncommittally and climbed into the back seat.

Bud drove me to The Green Lobster, a bar and grill near Fisherman's Wharf. The bar was too far away from the Wharf for the heavy tourist trade, but it was close enough to catch the overflow on busy days and there was enough fish stink in the air to provide an atmosphere for those who felt they needed it. On the way, Bud gave me a sucker ride in order to run up his buck and a half on the meter. At most the fare should have been six-bits, but I didn't complain. I rode the unnecessary blocks out of the way and paid the fare in full when he stopped at The Green Lobster.

'This is where I left 'em,' he said. I waited on the curb until he pulled away. I couldn't understand Bud's attitude. He might have been a friend of the guy I had a fight with in Big Mike's or he might have resented me having a beautiful girl like Helen. I didn't know, but I resented his manner. I like everybody and it's always disconcerting when someone doesn't like me. I entered The Green Lobster and sat down at the end of the bar near the door.

A long, narrow bar hugged the right side of the room for the full length of the dimly lit room. There were high, wrinkled red-leather stools for the patrons and I perched on one, my feet on the chromium rungs. The left wall had a row of green-curtained booths, and between the booths and the narrow bar, there were many small tables for two covering the rest of the floorspace. Each small table was covered with a green oilcloth cover and held a bud vase with an unidentifiable artificial flower. I surveyed the room in the bar mirror and spotted Helen and the three Marines in the second booth. The four of them leaned across their table their heads together, and then they sat back and laughed boisterously. I couldn't hear them but supposed they were taking turns telling dirty jokes. Helen's laugh was loud, clear, and carried across the room above the laughter of the Marines. I hadn't heard her laugh like that since the night I first brought her home with me. After the bartender finished with two other customers at the bar he got around to me.

'Straight shot,' I told him.

'It's a dollar a shot,' he said quietly, half-apologetically.

'I've got a dollar,' and I fished one out of my watch pocket and slapped it on the bar.

He set an empty glass before me and filled it to the brim with bar whiskey. I sipped a little off the top, put the glass back down on the bar. At a dollar a clip the shot would have to last me. I didn't have a plan or course of action, so I sat stupidly, watching Helen and the Marines in the bar mirror, trying to think of what to do next.

If I tried a direct approach and merely asked Helen to leave with me, there would be a little trouble. Not knowing what to do, I did nothing. There was one sergeant and two corporals, all three of them bigger than me. They wore neat, bright-blue Marine uniforms and all had the fresh, well-scrubbed look that servicemen have on the first few hours of leave or pass. But in my mind I didn't see them in uniform. I saw them naked, Helen naked, and all of them cavorting obscenely in a hotel room somewhere, and as this picture formed in my mind my face began to perspire.

Helen inadvertantly settled the action for me. She was in the seat against the wall, the sergeant on the outside, with the two corporals facing them across the table. After a while, Helen started out of the booth to go to the ladies' room. The sergeant goosed her as she squeezed by him and she squealed, giggled, and broke clear of the table. As she looked drunkenly around the room for the door to the ladies' room she saw me sitting at the bar.

'Harry!' She screamed joyfully across the room. 'Come on over!'

I half-faced her, remaining on my stool, shaking my head. Helen crossed to the bar, weaving recklessly between the tables, and as soon as she reached me, threw her arms around my neck and kissed me wetly on the mouth. The action was swift and blurred from that moment on. An attack of Marines landed on me and I was hit a glancing blow on the jaw, my right arm was twisted cruelly behind my back, and in less than a minute I was next door on the asphalt of the parking lot. A corporal held my arms behind me and another was rounding the building. The sergeant, his white belt wrapped around his fist, the buckle dangling free, waved the man back. 'Go back inside, Adams, and watch that bitch! We'll take care of this bastard. She might try and get away and I spent eight bucks on her already.' The oncoming corporal nodded grimly and re-entered the bar. Under the circumstances I tried to be as calm as possible.

'Before you hit me with that buckle, Sergeant,' I said, 'why don't you let me explain?'

Businesslike, the sergeant motioned the Marine holding my arms behind my back to stand clear, so he could get a good swing at me with the belt.

'You don't have to hold me,' I said over my shoulder. 'If you want to beat up a man for kissing his wife, go ahead!'

I jerked away and dropped to my knees in front of the sergeant. Hopefully, I prayed loudly, trying to make my voice sound sincere:

'Oh, God above! Let no man tear asunder what You have joined in holy matrimony! Dear sweet God! Deliver this poor sinner from evil, and show these young Christian gentlemen the light of Your love and Your mercy! Sweet Son of the Holy Cross and —' That was as far as I got.

'Are you and her really married?' The sergeant asked gruffly.

'Yes, sir,' I said humbly, remaining on my knees and staring intently at my steepled fingers.

I glanced at the two Marines out of the corner of my eye. The youngest had a disgusted expression on his face, and was tugging at the sergeant's arm.

'Let it go, Sarge,' he said, 'we were took and the hell with it. I wouldn't get any fun out of hitting him now.'

'Neither would I.' The sergeant unwrapped the belt from his hand and buckled it around his waist. 'I'm not even mad any more.' There was a faint gleam of pity in his eyes as he looked at me. 'If she's your wife, how come you let her run loose in the bars?'

'I was working, sir,' I said, 'and I thought she was home with the children.' I hung my head lower, kept my eyes on the ground.

'Then it's your tough luck,' the sergeant finished grimly. 'Both of you got what you deserved.' They left the parking lot and re-entered the bar. I got off my knees, walked to the curb and waited. The sergeant brought Helen to the door, opened it for her politely, guided her outside, and as he released her arm, he cuffed her roughly across the face. Bright red marks leaped to the surface of her cheek and she reeled across the sidewalk. I caught her under the arms before she fell.

'That evens us up for the eight bucks.' The sergeant grinned and shut the door.

Helen spluttered and cursed and then her body went limp in my arms. I lifted her sagging body and carried her down to the corner and the hack-stand. She hadn't really passed out; she was pretending so she wouldn't have to talk to me. I put her into the cab without help from the driver and gave him my address. I paid the eighty-cent fare when he reached my house, and hoped he didn't see the large, wet spot on the back seat until after he pulled away. Helen leaned weakly against me and I half carried her into our room and undressed her. She fell asleep immediately. Looking inside her purse. I found ninety cents in change. No bills.

I thought things over and came to a decision. I couldn't work any more and leave her by herself. Either I'd have to get money from some other source, or do without it. Left to herself, all alone, Helen would only get into serious trouble. Already I noticed things about her that had changed. She let her hair go uncombed. She skipped wearing her stockings. Her voice was slightly louder and she seemed to be getting deaf in one ear.

We never made love any more.

Chapter Twelve

THE DREGS

I didn't sleep all night. I sat in the chair by the dark window with the lights out while Helen slept. I didn't try to think about anything, but kept my mind as blank as possible. When I did have a thought it was disquieting and ugly and I would get rid of it by pushing it to the back of my mind like a pack rat trading a rock for a gold nugget.

Vitale would be stuck again for a fry cook when I didn't show up, but it couldn't be helped. To leave Helen to her own devices would be foolish. When I thought about how close I came to losing her my heart would hesitate, skip like a rock on water and then beat faster than ever. I had a day's pay coming from Vitale that I would never collect. It would take more nerve than I possessed to ask him for it. I decided to let it go.

The night passed, somehow, and as soon as the gray light hit the window I left the room and walked down the block to the delicatessen. It wasn't quite six and I had to wait for almost ten minutes before Mr. Watson opened up. I had enough money with some left over for a half-pint of whiskey and Mr. Watson pursed his lips when he put it in a sack for me.

'Most of my customers this early buy milk and eggs, Harry,' he said.

'Breakfast is breakfast.' I said lightly and the bells above the door tinkled as I closed it behind me.

When I got back to the room, I brought the T-bone inside from the window sill, opened the package and smelled them. They seemed to be all right and I lit the burner and dropped one in the frying pan and sprinkled it with salt. I made coffee on the other burner and watched the steak for the exact moment to turn it. To fry a steak properly it should only be turned one time. Helen awoke after awhile, got out of bed without a word or a glance in my direction and went to the bathroom. The steak was ready when she got back and I had it on a plate at the table.

'How'd you like a nice T-bone for breakfast?' I asked her.

'Ugh!' She put her feet into slippers and wrapped a flowered robe around her shoulders. 'I'll settle for coffee.'

I poured two cups of coffee and Helen joined me at the table. I shoved the half-pint across the table and she poured a quarter of the bottle into her coffee. I started in on the steak. We both carefully avoided any reference to the Marines or the afternoon before.

'This a day off, Harry?' Helen asked after she downed half of her laced coffee.

'No. I quit.'

'Good.'

'But I'm a little worried.'

'What about?' she asked cautiously.

'Damned near everything. Money, for one thing, and I'm worried about you, too.'

'I'm all right.'

'You're drinking more than you did before, and you aren't eating.'

'I'm not hungry.'

'Even so, you've got to eat.'

'I'm not hungry.'

'Suppose ...' I spoke slowly, choosing my words with care, 'all of a sudden, just like that,' and I snapped my fingers, 'we quit drinking? I can pour what's left of that little bottle down the drain and we can start from there. We make a resolution and stick to it, see, stay sober from now on, make a fresh start.'

Helen quickly poured another shot into her coffee. 'No,

Harry. I know what you mean, but I couldn't quit if I wanted to.'

'Why not? We aren't getting any place the way we're going.'

'Who wants to get any place?' she said sardonically. 'Do you? What great pinnacle have you set your eyes on?' She rubbed her cheek gently. It was swollen from the slap the Marine had given her.

'It was just an idea.' Helen was right and I was wrong. We were too far down the ladder to climb up now. I was letting my worry about money and Helen lead me into dangerous thinking. The only thing to do was keep the same level without going down any further. If I could do that, we would be all right. 'Pass me the bottle,' I said.

I took a good swig and I felt better immediately. From now on I wouldn't let worry get me down. I would take things as they came and with any luck at all everything would be all right.

It didn't take much to mellow Helen. After two laced cups of coffee she was feeling the drinks and listening with intent interest to my story about Van Gogh and Gauguin and their partnership at Arles. Fingernails scratched at the door. Irritated by the interruption I jerked the door open. Mrs. McQuade stood in the doorway with a large package in her arms.

'This package came for you, Mrs. Jordan,' she said, looking around me at Helen. 'I signed for it. It was delivered by American Express.'

'Thanks, Mrs. McQuade,' I said. 'I'll take it.' I took the package.

'That's all right. I —' She wanted to talk some more but I closed the door with my shoulder and tossed the package on the bed. Helen untied the package and opened it. It was full of women's clothing.

'It's from Mother,' she said happily, 'she's sent me some of my things.'

'That's fine,' I said. Helen started through the package, holding up various items of clothing to show me how they looked. This didn't satisfy her, and she slipped a dress on to show me how well it looked on her, removed it and started to put another one on. I was bored. But this pre-occupation with a fresh wardrobe would occupy her for quite a while. Long enough for me to look around town for a way to make a few dollars. The half-pint was almost empty.

'Look, sweetheart,' I said, 'why don't you take your time and go through these things, and I'll go out for a while and look for a part-time job.'

'But I want to show them to you —'

'And I've got to pick up a few bucks or we'll be all out of whiskey.'

'Oh. How long will you be gone?'

'Not long. An hour or so at the most.' I kissed her goodbye and left the house. I caught the cable car down-town and got off at Polk Street. There wasn't any parti-cular plan or idea in my mind and I walked aimlessly down the street. I passed the Continental Garage. It was a five-story building designed solely for the parking of auto-mobiles. At the back of the building I could see two latticed elevators that took the cars up and down to the rest of the building. On impulse, I entered the side office. There were three men in white overalls sitting around on top of the desks. They stopped talking when I entered and I smiled at the man who had MANAGER embroidered in red above the left breast pocket of his spotless overalls. He was a peppery little man with a small red moustache clipped close to his lip. He looked at me for a moment, then closed his eyes. His eyelids were as freckled as the rest of his face.

'What I'm looking for, sir,' I said, 'is a part-time job. Do you have a rush period from about four to six when you could use another man to park cars?'

He opened his eyes and there was suspicion in them. 'Yes and no. How come you aren't looking for an eight-hour day?'

'I am.' I smiled. 'I'm expecting an overseas job in Iraq,' I lied. 'It should come through any day now and I have to hang around the union hall all day. That's why I can't take anything permanent. But the job I'm expecting is taking a lot longer to come through than I expected and I'm running short on cash.'

'I see.' He nodded, compressed his lips. 'You a mechanic?'

'No, sir. Petroleum engineer.'

'College man, huh?' I nodded, but I didn't say anything. 'Can you drive a car?'

I laughed politely. 'Of course I can.'

'Okay, I'll help you out. You can start this evening from four to six, parking and bringing them down. Buck and a half an hour. Take it or leave it. It's all the same to me.'

'I'll take it,' I said gratefully, 'and thanks.'

'Pete,' the manager said to a loosed-jointed man with big knobby hands, 'show him how to run the elevator and tell him about the tickets.'

Pete left the office for the elevators and I followed him. A push button worked the elevator, but parking the cars was more complicated. The tickets were stamped with a time-stamp and parked in time groups in accordance with time of entry. When the patron brought in his stub, it was checked for the time it was brought in and the serial number of the ticket. Cars brought in early to stay all day were on the top floor and so on down to the main floor. Patrons who said they would only be gone an hour or so had their cars parked downstairs on the main floor. Five minutes after I left Pete I was on the cable car and on my way home. The fears I had in the morning were gone and I was elated. By a lucky break my part time job was solved. With the twenty-five a week coming in from Helen's mother, plus another three dollars a day from the garage, we should be able to get along fine. And counting the half-hour each way to downtown and my two hours of work, Helen would only be alone three hours.

I opened the door to our room and Helen was back in bed fast asleep. Her new clothes were scattered and thrown about the floor. Without waking her I picked them up and hung them in the closet. I wanted a shot but the little half-pint bottle was empty. I pulled the covers over

Helen and lay down beside her on top of the bed. I
napped fitfully till three and then I left. I started to wake
her before I left, but she was sleeping so peacefully I didn't
have the heart to do it.

Right after four the rush started and I hustled the cars
out until six. It wasn't difficult and after a few minutes I
could find the cars easily. I looked up the red-haired
manager at six and he gave me three dollars and I left the
garage. Going down the hallway I spread the three dollars
like a fan before I opened the door to our room.

Helen was gone.

There wasn't any note so I assumed she was at Big
Mike's. She had probably forgotten about the ruckus with
him the day before and he was the logical man to give her
a free drink, or let her sign for one. I left the rooming
house for Big Mike's. He hadn't seen her.

'If you haven't found her by now,' he said, 'you might as
well forget about it, Harry.'

'I did find her yesterday, Mike. I was with her till three
this afternoon, and then I had to go to work.'

'This isn't the only bar in the neighborhood.' He
grinned. 'I wish it was.'

I made the rounds of all the neighborhood bars. She
wasn't in any of them and I didn't ask any of the bartenders if she had been in them. I didn't know any of the
bartenders that well. At eight-thirty I went back to the
rooming house and checked to see whether she had
returned. I didn't want to miss her in case she came back
on her own accord. She wasn't there and I started to check
the bars outside the neighborhood. I was hoping she
hadn't gone downtown, and I knew she didn't have
enough carfare to go.

It was ten-thirty before I found her. She was in a little
bar on Peacock Street. It was so dark inside I had to stand
still for a full minute before my eyes became accustomed
to the darkness. There was one customer at the bar and he
and the bartender were watching a TV wrestling match.
There were two shallow booths opposite the bar and
Helen was in the second. A sailor was with her and she

was wearing his white sailor hat on the back of her head. His left arm was about her waist, his hand cupping a breast, and his right hand was up under her dress, working furiously. Her legs were spread widely and he was kissing her on the mouth.

I ran directly to the booth, grabbed the sailor by his curly yellow hair and jerked his head back, pulling his mouth away from Helen's. Still keeping a tight grip on his hair I dragged him across her lap to the center of the floor. His body was too heavy to be supported by his hair alone and he slipped heavily to the floor, leaving me with a thick wad of curls in each hand. He mumbled something unintelligible and attempted to sit up. His slack mouth was open and there was a drunken, stupified expression in his eyes. I wanted to hurt him; not kill him, hurt him, mutilate his pasty, slack-jawed face. Looking for a handy weapon, I took a beer bottle from the bar and smashed it over his head. The neck of the bottle was still in my hand and the broken section ended in a long, jagged splinter. I carved his face with it, moving the sharp, glass dagger back and forth across his white face with a whipping wrist motion. Each slash opened a spurting channel of bright red blood that ran down his face and neck and splashed on the floor between his knees. My first blow with the bottle had partially stunned him but the pain brought him out of it and the high screams coming from deep inside his throat were what brought me to my senses. I dropped the piece of broken bottle, and in a way, I felt that I had made up somehow for the degradation I had suffered at the hands of the Marines.

Helen had sobered considerably and her eyes were round as saucers as she sat in the booth. I lifted her to her feet and she started for the door, making a wide detour around the screaming sailor. I opened the door for her and looked over my shoulder. The bartender was nowhere in sight, probably flat on the floor behind the bar. The solitary drinker was peering at me nervously from the safety of the doorway to the men's room. The sailor had managed to get to his knees and was crawling under the table to the first booth, the screams still pouring from his throat. I let the door swing shut behind us.

Helen was able to stand by herself, but both of her hands were pressed over her mouth. I released her arm and she staggered to the curb and vomited into the gutter. When she finished I put my arm around her waist and we walked up the hill. A taxi, coming down the hill on the opposite side of the street, made a U-turn when I signaled him and rolled to a stop beside us. I helped Helen into the cab. A block away from our rooming house I told the driver to stop. When I opened the door to get out I noticed my hand was cut. I wrapped my handkerchief around my bleeding hand and gave a dollar to the hackie. The cold night air had revived Helen considerably and she scarcely staggered as we walked the block to the house. As soon as we entered our room she made for the bed and curled up on her knees, pressed her arms to her sides, and ducked her head down. In this position it was difficult for me to remove her clothes, but before I finished taking them off she was asleep.

By that time I could have used a drink myself. I heated the leftover coffee and smoked a cigarette to control my uneasy stomach. I looked through Helen's purse and all I found was a crumpled package of cigarettes and a book of paper matches. Not a penny.

What was the use? I couldn't keep her. How could I work and stay home and watch her at the same time? I couldn't make enough money to meet expenses and keep Helen in liquor if I parked a million cars or fried a million eggs or waited on a million tables. I was so beaten down and disgusted with myself my mind wouldn't cope with it any longer. Sitting awake in the chair I had a dream, a strange, merging dream, where everything was unreal and the ordinary turned into the extraordinary. Nothing like it had ever happened to me before. The coffeepot, the cup, and the can of condensed milk on the table turned into a graphic composition, a depth study. It was beautiful. Everything I turned my eyes upon in the room was perfectly grouped. A professional photographer couldn't have arranged the room any better. The unshaded light in the ceiling was like a light above Van Gogh's pool table. Helen's clothing massed upon the chair swirled gracefully to the floor like drapes in a Titian drawing. The faded gray wallpaper with its unknown red flower pattern was suddenly quaint and charming. The gray background fell away from the flowers with a three-dimensional effect. Everything was lovely, lovely ...

I don't know how long this spell lasted, but it seemed to be a long time and I didn't want it to end. I had no thought at all during this period. I merely sensed the new delights of my quiet, ordinary room. Only Helen's gentle, open-mouthed snoring furnished the hum of life to my introspection. And then like a blinding flash of headlights striking my eyes, everything was clear to me. Simple. Plain. Clear.

I didn't have to fight any more.

For instance, a man is crossing the street and an automobile almost runs him down. He shakes his fist and curses and says to himself: 'That Buick almost hit me!' But it wasn't the Buick that almost hit him; the Buick was merely a vehicle. It was the man or woman driving the Buick who almost hit him. Not the Buick. And that was me. I was the automobile, a machine, a well-oiled vehicle now matured to my early thirties. A machine without a driver. The driver was gone. The machine could now relax and run wherever it might, even into a smash. So what? It could function by itself, by habit, reflex, or whatever it was that made it run. Not only didn't I know, I didn't care any more. It might be interesting for that part of me that used to think things out, to sit somewhere and watch Harry Jordan, the machine, go through the motions. The getting up in the morning, the shaving, the shower, walking, talking, drinking. I. Me. Whatever I was, didn't give a damn any more. Let the body function and the senses sense. The body felt elation. The eyes enjoyed the sudden beauty of the horrible little back bedroom. My mind felt nothing. Nothing at all.

Helen sat up suddenly in bed. She retched, a green

streak of fluid burst from her lips and spread over her white breasts. I got a towel from the dresser and wiped her face and chest.

'Use this,' and I handed her the towel, 'if it hits you again.'

'I think I'm all right now,' she gasped. I brought her a glass of water and held it to her lips. She shook her head to move her lips away from the glass.

'Oh, Harry. I'm so sick, so sick, so sick ...'

'You'll be all right.' I set the glass on the table.

'Are you mad at me, Harry?'

'What for?' I was surprised at the question.

'For going out and getting drunk the way I did.'

'You were fairly drunk when I left.'

'I know, but I shouldn't have gone out like that. That sailor ... the sailor who was with me didn't mean a thing —'

'Forget it. Go back to sleep.'

'Harry, you're the only one I've ever loved. I've never loved anyone but you. And if you got sore at me I don't know what I'd do.'

'I'm not angry. Go to sleep.'

'You get in bed too.'

'Not right now. I'm busy.'

'Please, Harry. Please?'

'I'm thinking. You know I'm not going to live very long, Helen. No driver. There isn't any driver, Helen, and the controls are set. And I don't know how long they're going to last.'

'What are you talking about?'

'Just that I'm not going to live very long. I quit.'

Helen threw the covers back, got out of bed and rushed over to me. I was standing flat-footed by the table. My feet could feel the world pushing up at me from below. Black old cinder. I laughed. Cooling on the outside, fire on the inside and nothing in between. It was easy to feel the world turn beneath my feet. Helen was on her knees, her arms were clasped about my legs. She was talking feverishly, and I put my hand on her head.

'What's the matter, Harry!' She cried. 'Are you going to try to kill yourself again? Are you angry with me? Please talk to me! Don't look away like that ...'

'Yes, Helen,' I said calmly. 'I'm going to kill myself.'

Helen pulled herself up, climbing my body, using my clothes as handholds, pressing her naked body against mine. 'Oh, darling, darling,' she whimpered. 'Let me go first! Don't go away and leave me all alone!'

'All right,' I said. I picked her up and carried her to the bed. 'I won't leave you behind. I wouldn't do that.' I kissed her, stroked her hair. 'Go on to sleep, now.' Helen closed her eyes and in a moment she was asleep. The tear-streaked lines on her face were drying. I undressed and got into bed beside her. Now I could sleep. The machine would sleep, it would wake, it would do things, and then it would crash, out of control and destroy itself. But first it must run over the little body that slept by its side. The small, pitiful creature with the big sienna eyes and the silver streak in its hair.

As I fell asleep I heard music. I didn't have a radio, but it wasn't the type of music played over the radio anyway. It was wild, cacophonous, and there was an off-beat of drums pounding. My laugh was harsh, rasping. I continued to laugh and the salty taste in my mouth came from the unchecked tears running down my cheeks.

Chapter Thirteen

DREAM WORLD

In my dream I was running rapidly down an enormous piano keyboard. The white keys made music beneath my hurried feet as I stepped on them, but the black keys were stuck together with glue and didn't play. Trying to escape the discordant music of the white keys I tried to run on the black keys, slipping and sliding to keep my balance. Although I couldn't see the end of the keyboard I felt that I must reach the end and that it was possible if I could only run fast enough and hard enough. My foot slipped on a rounded black key and I fell heavily, sideways, and my sprawled body covered three of the large white keys with a sharp, harsh discord. The notes were loud and ugly. I rolled away from the piano keyboard, unable to stand, and fell into a great mass of silent, swirling, billowing yellow fog and floated down, down, down. The light surrounding my head was like bright, luminous gold. The gloves on my hand were lemon yellow chamois with three black stitches on the back of each hand. I disliked the gloves, but I couldn't take them off no matter how hard I tried. They were glued to my hands; the bright orange glue oozed out of the glove around my wrists.

I opened my eyes and I was wide awake. My body was drenched with perspiration. I got out of bed without waking Helen, found and lit a cigarette. My mouth was so dry the smoke choked me and tasted terrible. The perspiration drying on my body made me shiver with cold, and I put my shirt and trousers on.

What a weird, mixed-up dream to have! I recalled each sequence of the dream vividly and it didn't make any sense at all. Helen, still asleep, turned and squirmed under the covers. She missed the warmth of my body and was trying to get close to me in her sleep. I crushed my foul-tasting cigarette in the ash-tray and tucked the covers in around Helen. I turned on the overhead light and sat down.

I felt calm and contented. It was time for Harry Jordan to have another cigarette. As though I sat in a dark theatre as a spectator somewhere I observed the quiet, studied actions of Harry Jordan. The exacting, unconscious ritual of putting the cigarette in his mouth, the striking of the match on his thumbnail, the slow withdrawal of smoke, the sensuous exhalation and the obvious enjoyment. The man, Harry Jordan, was a very collected individual, a man of the world. Nothing bothered him now. He was about to withdraw his presence from the world and depart on a journey into space, into nothingness. Somewhere, a womb was waiting for him, a dark, warm place where the living was easy, where it was effortless to get by. A wonderful place where a man didn't have to work or think or talk or listen or dream or cavort or play or use artificial stimulation. A kind old gentleman with a long dark cloak was waiting for him. Death. Never had Death appeared so attractive...

I looked at Helen's beautiful face. She slept peacefully, her mouth slightly parted, her pretty hair tousled. I would take Helen with me. This unfeeling world was too much for Helen too, and without me, who would care for her, look after her? And hadn't I promised to take her with me?

I crushed my cigarette decisively and crossed to the bed.

'Helen, baby,' I said, shaking her gently by the shoulder. 'Wake up.'

She stirred under my hand, snapped her eyes open, awake instantly, the perfect animal. She wore a sweet, sleepy smile.

'What time is it?'

'I don't know,' I said, 'but it's time.' My face was as stiff as cardboard and it felt as expressionless as uncarved stone. I didn't know and didn't want to explain what I was going to do and I hoped Helen wouldn't ask me any questions. She didn't question me. Somehow, she knew instinctively. Perhaps she read the thoughts in my eyes, maybe she could see my intentions in the stiffness of my smile.

'We're going away, aren't we, Harry?' Helen's voice was small, childlike, yet completely unafraid.

Not daring to trust my voice, I nodded. Helen's trust affected me deeply. In that instant I loved her more than I had ever loved her before. Such faith and trust were almost enough to take the curse out of the world. Almost.

'All right, Harry. I'm ready.' She closed her eyes and the sleepy winsome smile remained on her lips.

I put my hands around her slender neck. My long fingers interlaced behind her neck and my thumbs dug deeply into her throat, probing for a place to stop her breathing. I gradually increased the pressure, choking her with unrelenting firmness of purpose, concentrating. She didn't have an opportunity to make a sound. At first she thrashed about and then her body went limp. Her dark sienna eyes, flecked with tiny spots of gold, stared guilelessly at me and then they didn't see me any more. I closed her eyelids with my thumb, pulled the covers down and put my ear to her chest. No sound came from her heart. I straightened her legs and folded her arms across her chest. They wouldn't stay folded and I had to place a pillow on top of them before they would stay. Later on, I supposed, when her body stiffened with cold, her arms would stay in place without the benefit of the pillow.

My legs were weak at the knees and I had to sit down to stop their trembling. My fingers were cramped and I opened and closed my hands several times to release the tension. I had taken the irrevocable step and had met Death half-way. I could feel his presence in the room. It was now my turn and, with the last tugs of primitive self-preservation, I hesitated, my conscious mind casting about for a way to renege. But I knew that I wouldn't renege; it was unthinkable. It was too late to back out now. However, I didn't have the courage and trust that Helen had possessed. There was no one kind enough to take charge of the operation or do it for me. I had to do it myself, without help from anyone. But I had to have a little something to help me along ...

I omitted the socks and slipped into my shoes. I couldn't control my hands well enough to tie the laces and I let them hang loose. I put my jacket on and left my room, locked the door, and left for the street. It was dismally cold outside; there were little patches of fog swirling in groups like lost ghosts exploring the night streets. The traffic signals at the corner were turned off for the night; only the intermittent blinking of the yellow caution lights at the four corners of the intersection lit the lost, drifting tufts of fog. Although it was after one, Mr. Watson's delicatessen was still open. Its brightly colored window was a warm spot on the dark line of buildings. I crossed the street and entered and the tinkling bell above the door announced my entrance. Mrs. Watson was sitting in a comfortable chair by the counter reading a magazine. She was a heavy woman with orange-tinted hair and a faint chestnut moustache. She smiled at me in recognition.

'Hello Harry,' she said, 'How are you this evening?'

'Fine, Mrs. Watson, just fine,' I replied. I was glad that it was Mrs. Watson instead of her husband in the shop that morning. I wanted to talk to somebody and she was much easier to talk to than her husband. He was a German immigrant and it always seemed to me like he considered it a favor when he waited on me. I fished the two one dollar bills out of my watch pocket and smoothed them out flat on the counter.

'I think I'm getting a slight cold, Mrs. Watson,' I said, coughing into my curled fist, 'and I thought if I made a little hot gin punch before I went to bed it might cut the phlegm a little bit.'

'Nothing like hot gin for colds,' Mrs. Watson smiled and

got out of the chair to cross to the liquor shelves. 'What kind?'

'Gilbey's is fine — I'd like a pint, but I don't think I have enough here ...' I pointed to the two one dollar bills.

'I think I can trust you for the rest, Harry. It wouldn't be the first time.' She dropped a pint of Gilbey's into a sack, twisted the top and handed it to me. I slipped the bottle into my jacket pocket. My errand was over and I could leave, but I was reluctant to leave the warm room and the friendly, familiar delicatessen smells. Death was waiting for me in my room. I had an appointment with him and I meant to keep it, but he could wait a few minutes longer.

'What are you reading, Mrs. Watson?' I asked politely, when she had returned to her chair after ringing a No Sale on the cash register and putting my money into the drawer.

'*Cosmopolitan.*' Her pleasant laugh was tinged with irony. 'Boy meets girl, loses girl, gets girl. They're all the same, but they pass the time.'

'That's a mighty fine magazine, Mrs. Watson. I read it all the time; and so does my wife. Why, Helen can hardly wait for it to come out and we always argue over who gets to read it first and all that. Yes, I guess it's my favorite magazine and I wish it was published every week instead of every month! What month is that, Mrs. Watson? Maybe I haven't read it yet.'

'Do you feel all right, Harry?' She looked at me suspiciously.

'Yes, I do.' My voice had changed pitch and was much too high.

'You aren't drunk, are you ?'

'No, I get a little talkative sometimes. Well, that's a good magazine.'

'It's all right.' Mrs. Watson's voice was impatient; she wanted to get back to her story.

'Well, good night, Mrs. Watson, and thanks a lot.' I opened the door.

'That's all right, Harry. Good night.' She had found her place and was reading before I closed the door.

As soon as I was clear of the lit window I jerked the gin out of the sack, tossed the sack in the gutter, and unscrewed the cap from the bottle. I took a long pull from the bottle, gulping the raw gin down until I choked on it and hot tears leaped to my eyes. It warmed me through and my head cleared immediately. I crossed the street and walked back to the house. Sitting on the outside steps I drank the rest of the gin in little sips, controlling my impulse to down it all at once. I knew that if I tried to let it all go down my throat at once it would be right back up and the effects would be gone. I finished the bottle and tossed it into the hedge by the porch. My stomach had a fire inside it, but I was sorry I hadn't charged a fifth instead of only getting a pint.

I walked down the dimly lit hall, unlocked my door and entered my room. It rather startled me, in a way, to see Helen in the same position I had left her in. Not that I had expected her to move; I hadn't expected anything, but to see her lying so still, and uncovered in the cold room, unnerved me. Again I wished I had another pint of gin. I started to work.

I locked the door and locked the window. There were three old newspapers under the sink and I tore them into strips and stuffed the paper under the crack at the bottom of the door. I opened both keys on the two-ring burner and they hissed full blast. I sniffed the odor and it wasn't unpleasant at all. It was sweet and purifying. By this time the gin had hit me hard, and I found myself humming a little tune. I undressed carefully and hung my clothes neatly in the closet. I lined my shoes up at the end of the bed. Tomorrow we would be found dead and that was that. But there wasn't any note. I staggered to the table and with a piece of charcoal I composed a brief note of farewell. There was no one in particular to address it to, so I headed it:

To Who Finds This:
We did this on purpose. It isn't accidental.

I couldn't think of anything else to put in the note and I didn't sign it because the charcoal broke between my fingers. Leaving the note on the table I crawled into bed beside Helen and pulled the covers up over us both. I had left the overhead light on purposely and the room seemed gay and cheerful. I took Helen in my arms and kissed her. Her lips were like cold rubber. When I closed my eyes the image of the light bulb remained. I tried to concentrate on other things to induce sleep. The black darkness of the outside street, the inky San Francisco bay, outside space and starless skies. There were other thoughts that tried to force their way into my mind but I fought them off successfully.

The faint hissing of the gas jets grew louder. It filled the room like a faraway waterfall.

I was riding in a barrel and I could hear the falls far away. It was a comfortable barrel, well-padded, and it rocked gently to and fro, comforting me. It floated on a broad stream, drifting along with the current. The roar of the falls was louder in my ears. The barrel was drifting closer to the falls, moving ever faster toward the boiling steam above the lips of the overhang. I wondered how far the drop would be. The barrel hesitated for a second, plunged downward with a sickening drop.

A big black pair of jaws opened and I dropped inside. They snapped shut.

Chapter Fourteen

AWAKENING

There was a lot of knocking and some shouting. I don't know whether it was the knocking or the shouting that aroused me from my deep, restful slumbers, but I awoke, and printed in large, wavering red letters on the surface of my returning consciousness was the word for Harry Jordan: *FAILURE*. Somehow, I wasn't surprised. Harry Jordan was a failure in everything he tried. Even suicide.

The sharp little raps still pounded on the door and I could hear Mrs. McQuade's anxious voice calling, 'Mr. Jordan! Mr. Jordan! Open the door.'

'All right!' I shouted from the bed. 'Wait a minute.'

I painfully got out of bed, crossed to the window, unlocked it and threw it open. The cold, damp air that rushed in from the alley smelled like old laundry. The gas continued to hiss from the two open burners and I turned them off. Again the rapping and the call from Mrs. McQuade: 'Open the door!'

'In a minute!' I replied. The persistent knocking and shouting irritated me. I slipped into my corduroy trousers, buckled my belt as I crossed the room, unlocked and opened the door. Mrs McQuade and her other two star roomers, Yoshu Endo and Miss Foxhall, were framed in the doorway. It's a composition by Paul Klee, I thought.

I had always thought of Mrs. McQuade as a garrulous old lady with her hand held out, but she took charge of the situation like a television director.

'I smelled the gas,' Mrs. McQuade said quietly. 'Are you all right?'

'I guess so.'

'Go stand by the window and breathe some fresh air.'

'Maybe I'd better.' I walked to the window and took a few deep breaths which made me cough. After the coughing fit I was giddier than before. I turned and looked at Endo and Miss Foxhall. 'Won't you please come in?' I asked them stupidly.

Little Endo, his dark eyes bulging like a toad's in his flat Oriental face, stared solemnly at Helen's naked figure on the bed. Miss Foxhall had covered her face with both hands and was peering through the lattice-work of her fingers. Mrs. McQuade examined Helen for a moment at the bedside and then she pulled the covers over the body and face. Pursing her lips, she turned and made a flat, quiet statement: 'She's dead.'

'Yes,' I said. Just to be doing something, anything, I put my shirt on, sat down in the straight chair and pulled on my socks. A shrill scream escaped Miss Foxhall and then she stopped herself by shoving all her fingers into her mouth. Her short involuntary scream brought Endo out of his trance-like state and he grabbed the old spinster's arm and began to shake her, saying over and over again in a high, squeaky voice, 'No, no! No, no!'

'Leave her alone,' Mrs. McQuade ordered sharply. 'I'll take care of her.' She put an arm around Mrs Foxhall's waist. 'You go get a policeman.' Endo turned and ran down the hall. I heard the outside door slam. As Mrs. McQuade led Miss Foxhall away, she said over her shoulder: 'You'd better get dressed, Mr. Jordan.'

'Yes, Ma'am.' I was alone with Helen and the room was suddenly, unnaturally quiet. Automatically, I finished dressing, but my hands trembled so much I wasn't able to tie my necktie. I let it hang loosely around my neck, sat down in the straight chair after I donned my jacket.

Why had I failed?

I sat facing the door and I looked up and saw the transom. It was open. It wasn't funny but I smiled grimly. No wonder the gas hadn't killed me. The escaping gas was too busy going out over the transom and creeping through the house calling attention to Harry Jordan in the back bedroom. How did I let it happen? To hold the gas in the room I had shoved newspaper under the bottom of the door and yet I had left the transom wide open. Was it a primeval desire to live? Plain stupidity? Or the effects of the gin? I'll never know.

In a few minutes Endo returned to the room with a policeman. The policeman was a slim, nervous young man and he stood in the doorway covering me with his revolver. More than a little startled by the weapon I raised my arms over my head. The policeman bit his lips while his sharp eyes roved the room, sizing up the situation. He holstered the pistol and nodded his head.

'Put your arms down,' he ordered. 'Little suicide pact, huh?'

'No,' I replied. 'I killed her. Choked her to death.' I folded my hands in my lap.

The young policeman uncovered Helen's head and throat and looked carefully at her neck. Endo was at his side and the proximity of the little Japanese bothered him. He pushed Endo roughly toward the door. 'Get the hell out of here,' he told Endo. Leaving the room reluctantly, Endo hovered in the doorway. Muttering under his breath, the policeman shut the door in Endo's face and seated himself on the foot of the bed.

'What's your name?' he asked me, taking a small, black notebook out of his hip pocket.

'Harry Jordan.'

'Her name?' He jerked his thumb over his shoulder.

'Mrs. Helen Meredith.'

'You choked her. Right?'

'Yes.'

'And then you turned on the gas to kill yourself?'

'Yes.'

'She doesn't looked choked.'

'There's the note I left,' I said, pointing to the table. He crossed to the table and read my charcoaled note without touching it. He made another notation in his little black book, returned it to his hip pocket.

'Okay, okay, okay,' he said meaninglessly. There was uncertainty in his eyes. 'I've got to get my partner,' he informed me. Evidently he didn't know whether to take me along or leave me in the room by myself. He decided on the latter and handcuffed me to the radiator and hurried out of the room, closing the door behind him. The radiator was too low for me to stand and I had to squat down. Squatting nauseated me, and I got down on my knees on the floor. There was a queasy feeling in the pit of my stomach and it rumbled, but I didn't get sick enough to throw up.

In a few minutes he was back with his partner. He was a much older, heavier policeman, with a buff-colored, neatly trimmed mustache and a pair of bright, alert hazel eyes. The older man grinned when he saw me handcuffed to the radiator.

'Take the cuffs off him for Christ sake!' he told the younger policeman. 'He won't get away.'

After the first policeman uncuffed me and returned the heavy bracelets to his belt, I sat down in the chair again. By leaning over and sucking in my stomach I could keep the nausea under control. It was much better sitting down. The younger policeman left the room to make a telephone call and the older man took his place at the foot of the bed. He crossed his legs and after he got his cigarettes out he offered me one. He displayed no interest in Helen's body at all. He lit our cigarettes and then smiled kindly at me.

'You're in trouble, boy,' he said, letting smoke trickle out through his nose. 'Do you know that?'

'I guess I am.' I took a long drag and it eased my stomach.

'Relax, boy. I'm not going to ask you any questions. I couldn't care less.'

'Would it be all right with you if I kissed her goodbye?' That question slipped out in a rush, but he seemed to be easy-going, and I knew that after the police arrived in force I wouldn't be able to kiss her goodbye. This would be my last chance. He scratched his mustache, got up from the bed and strolled across the room to the window.

'I suppose it's all right' he said thoughtfully. 'What do you want to kiss her for?'

'Just kiss her goodbye. That's all.' I couldn't explain because I didn't know myself.

'Okay.' He shrugged his shoulders and looked out the window. 'Go ahead.'

Walking bent over I crossed to the bed and kissed Helen's cold lips, her forehead, and on the lips again. 'Goodbye, sweetheart,' I whispered low enough so the policeman couldn't hear me, 'I'll see you soon.' I returned to the chair.

For a long time we sat quietly in the silent room. The door opened and the room was filled with people. It was hard to believe so many people could crowd into such a small room. There were the two original uniformed policemen, two more in plainclothes, a couple of hospital attendants or doctors in white — Endo got back into the room somehow — Mrs. McQuade, and a spectator who had crowded in from the group in front of the house. A small man entered the room and removed his hat. He was almost bald and wore a pair of dark glasses. At his entrance the room was quiet again and the noise and activity halted. The young policeman saluted smartly and pointed to me.

'He confessed, Lieutenant,' the young man said. 'Harry Jordan is his name and she isn't his wife —'

'I'll talk to him,' the little man said, holding up a white, manicured hand. He removed the dark glasses and put them in the breast pocket of his jacket, crooked his finger at me and left the room. I followed him out and nobody tried to stop me. We walked down the hall and he paused at the stairway leading to the top floor.

'Want a cigarette, Jordan?'

'No, sir.'

'Want to tell me about it, Jordan?' He asked with his quiet voice. 'I'm always a little leery of confessions unless I hear them myself.'

'Yes, sir. There isn't much to tell. I choked her last

night, and then I turned on the gas. It was a suicide pact, in a way, but actually I killed Helen because she didn't have the nerve to do it herself.'

'I see. About what time did it happen?'

'Around one, or after. I don't know. By this time I would have been dead myself if I hadn't left the transom open.'

'You willing to put all this on paper, Jordan, or are you going to get a shyster and deny everything, or what?'

'I'm guilty, Lieutenant, and I want to die. I'll cooperate in every way I can. I don't want to see a lawyer, I just want to be executed. It'll be easier that way all around.'

'Then that's the way it'll be.' He raised his hand and a plainclothesman came down the hall, handcuffed me to his wrist, and we left the rooming house. A sizeable crowd had gathered on the sidewalk and they stared at us curiously as we came down the outside steps and entered the waiting police car. A uniformed policeman drove us to the city jail.

At the desk I was treated impersonally by the booking sergeant. He filled in my name, address, age and height and then asked me to dump my stuff on the desk and remove my belt and shoelaces. There wasn't much to put on the desk. A piece of string, a thin, empty wallet, a parking stub left over from the Continental Garage, a button and a dirty handkerchief were all I had to offer. I put them on the desk and removed my belt and shoelaces, added them to the little pile. The sergeant wrote my name on a large brown manila envelope and started to fill it with my possessions.

'I'd like to keep the wallet, Sergeant,' I said. He went through it carefully. All it contained was a small snapshot of Helen taken when she was seven years old. The little snapshot showed a girl in a white dress and Mary Jane slippers standing in the sunlight in front of a concrete bird-bath. Her eyes were squinted against the sun and she stood pigeontoed, with her hands behind her back. Once in while, I liked to look at it. The sergeant tossed me the wallet with the picture and I shoved it into my pocket.

I was fingerprinted, pictures were taken of my face, profile and full-face, and then I was turned over to the jailer. He was quite old, and walked with an agonized limp. We entered the elevator, were whisked up several floors, and then he led me down a long corridor to the shower room.

After I undressed and folded my clothes neatly on the wooden bench I got under the shower and adjusted the water as hot as I could stand it. The water felt wonderful. I let the needle streams beat into my upturned face. It sluiced down over my body, warming me through and through. I soaped myself roughly with the one-pound cake of dark-brown laundry soap, stood under the hot water again.

I toweled myself with a drab olive towel and dressed in the blue pants and blue work shirt that were laid out on the bench. The trousers were too large around the waist and I had to hold them up with one hand. I followed Mr. Benson the jailer to the special block and he opened the steel door and locked it behind us. We walked down the narrow corridor to the last cell. He unlocked the door, pointed, and I entered. He clanged the door to, locked it with his key. As he turned to leave I hit him up for a smoke. He passed a cigarette through the bars, lighted it for me with his Zippo lighter.

'I suppose you've had breakfast already,' he said gruffly.

'No, but I'm not hungry anyway.'

'You mean you couldn't stand a cup of coffee?'

'I suppose I could drink a cup of coffee all right.'

'I'll get you one then. No use playing coy with me. When you want something you gotta speak up. I ain't no mind-reader.'

He limped away and I could hear the slap-and-drag of his feet all the way down the corridor. While I waited for the coffee I investigated my cell. The walls were gray, freshly-painted, but the paint didn't cover all of the obscene drawings and initials beneath the paint where former occupants had scratched their records. I read some of the inscriptions: FRISCO KID '38, H.E., J.D.,

KILROY WAS HERE, Smoe, DENVER JACK, and others. Along the length of the entire wall, chest high, in two inch letters, someone had cut deeply into the plaster:
UP YOUR RUSTY DUSTY WITH A FLOY FLOY
This was very carefully carved. It must have taken the prisoner a long time to complete it.

A porcelain toilet, without a wooden seat, a washbowl with one spigot of cold water, and a tier of three steel beds with thin cotton pads for mattresses completed the inventory of the cell. No window. I unfastened the chains and let the bottom bunk down. I sat down on it and finished half my cigarette. Instead of throwing the butt away I put it into my shirt pocket. It was all I had. Presently, Mr. Benson came back with my coffee and passed the gray enameled cup through the bars.

'I didn't know whether you liked it with sugar and cream so I brought it black,' he said.

'That's fine.' I took the cup gratefully and sipped it. It was almost boiling hot and I had to let it cool some before I could finish it, but Mr. Benson waited patiently. When I passed him the empty cup he gave me a fresh sack of tobacco and a sheaf of brown cigarette papers.

'Know how to roll 'em, Jordan?'

'Sure. Thanks a lot.' I made a cigarette.

'You get issued a sack every day, but no matches. If you want a light you gotta holler. Okay?'

'Sure.' Mr. Benson lit my cigarette and limped away again down the hollow-sounding corridor. The heavy end door clanged and locked.

The reaction set in quickly, the reaction to Helen's death, my attempt at suicide, the effects of the liquor, all of it. It was the overall cumulation of events that hit me all at once. My knees, my legs, my entire body began to shake violently and I couldn't control any part of it. The wet cigarette fell apart in my hand and I dropped to my knees in a praying position. I started to weep, at first soundlessly, then blubbering, the tears rolled down my cheeks, streamed onto my shirt. Perspiration poured from my body. I prayed:

'Dear God up there! Put me through to Helen! I'm still here, baby! Do you hear me! Please hang on a little while and wait for me! I'll be with you as soon as they send me! I'm all alone now, and it's hard, hard, hard! I'll be with you soon, soon, soon! I love you! Do you hear me, sweetheart? I love you! I LOVE YOU!'

From one of the cells down the corridor a thick gutteral voice answered mine: 'And I love you, too!' The voice paused, added disgustedly: 'Why don't you take a goddam break for Christ's sake!'

I stopped praying, or talking to Helen, whatever I was doing, and stretched out full length on the concrete floor. I stretched my arms out in front of me and pressed my mouth against the cold floor. In that prone position I cried myself out, silently, and it took a long time. I didn't try to pull myself together, because I knew that I would never cry again.

Afterwards, I washed my face with the cold tap water at the washbowl and dried my wet face with my shirt tail. I sat down on the edge of my bunk and carefully tailored another cigarette. It was a good one, nice and fat and round. Getting to my feet I crossed to the barred door.

'Hey! Mr. Benson!' I shouted. 'How's about a light?'

Chapter Fifteen

CONFESSION

Lunch consisted of beef stew, rice, stewed apricots and coffee. After the delayed-action emotional ordeal I had undergone I was weak physically and I ate every scrap of food on my aluminum tray. With my stomach full, for the first time in weeks, I lay down on the bottom bunk, covered myself with the clean gray blanket and fell asleep immediately.

Mr. Benson aroused me at four-thirty by rattling an empty cup along the bars of my cell. It was time to eat again. The supper was a light one; fried mush, molasses and coffee with a skimpy dessert of three stewed prunes. Again I cleaned the tray, surprised at my hunger. I felt rested, contented, better than I had felt in months. My headache had all but disappeared and the peaceful solitude of my cell was wonderful. Mr. Benson picked up the tray and gave me a book of paper matches before he left. He was tired of walking the length of the corridor to light my cigarettes. I lay on my back on the hard bunk and enjoyed my cigarette. After I stubbed it out on the floor I closed my eyes. When I opened them again it was morning and Mr. Benson was at the bars with my breakfast. Two pieces of bread, a thimble-sized paper cupful of strawberry jam and a cup of coffee.

About an hour after breakfast the old jailer brought a razor and watched me shave with the cold water and the brown laundry soap. In another hour he brought my clothes to the cell. My corduroy slacks and jacket had been sponged and pressed and were fairly presentable.

'Your shirt's in the laundry,' he said, 'but you can wear your tie with the blue shirt.'

'Where am I going?' I asked as I changed clothes.

'The D.A. wants to talk to you. Just leave them blue work pants on the bunk. You gotta change when you get back anyways.'

'Okay,' I agreed. I tied my necktie as well as I could without a mirror, just as I had shaved without a mirror. I followed Mr. Benson's limping drag down the corridor and this time I took an interest in the other prisoners in the special block, looking into each cell as I passed. There were eight cells, all of them along one side facing the passage wall, but only two others in addition to mine were occupied with prisoners. One held a sober-looking middle-aged man sitting on his bunk staring at his steepled fingers, and the other held a spiky-haired, blond youth with a broken nose and one cocked violet eye. He cocked it at me as I passed the cell and his sullen face was without expression. I quickly concluded that he was the one who had mocked me the day before and I had an overwhelming desire to kick his teeth in.

A plainclothes detective, wearing his hat, met us at the end of the corridor, signed for me, cuffed me to his wrist and we walked down the hall to the elevator. We silently rode the elevator down to the third floor, got out, and walked down a carpeted hallway to a milk-glass door with a block-lettered inscription: *Asst District Atty San Francisco*. We entered the office and the detective removed the cuff and left the room. The office was small and shabbily furnished. There was a battered oak desk, a shelf of heavy law books, four straight chairs and a row of hunting prints on a sepia-tinted wall across from the bookshelf. The prints were all of gentlewomen, sitting impossibly on their horses and following hounds over a field-stone wall. All four prints were exactly the same. I sat down in one of the chairs and a moment later two men entered. The first through the door was a young man with a very white skin and a blue-black beard hovering close to the surface of his chin. It was the kind of beard that shows, because I could tell by the scraped skin on his jaws that he had shaved that morning. He wore a shiny blue gabardine suit and oversized glasses with imitation tortoise-shell rims. Business-like, he sat behind the desk and studied some papers in a folder. The other man was quite old. He had lank white hair drooping down over his ears and there was a definite tremor in his long, talon-like fingers. His suit coat and trousers didn't match and he carried a short-hand pad and several sharpened pencils. It seemed unusual to me that the city would employ such an old man as a stenographer. His white head nodded rapidly up and down and it never stopped its meaningless bobbing throughout the interview, but his deepset eyes were bright and alert and without glasses.

The younger man closed the folder and shoved it into the top drawer of his desk. His eyes fastened on mine and without taking them away he extracted a king-sized cigarette from the package on the desk, flipped the desk lighter and the flame found the end of the cigarette perfectly. He did this little business without looking away from my eyes at all. A movie gangster couldn't have done it better. After three contemplative drags on the cigarette he crushed it out in the glass ash-tray, rested his elbows on the desk, cradled his square chin in his hands and leaned forward.

'My name is Robert Seely.' His voice was deep and resonant with a lot of college speech training behind it. 'I'm one of the assistant district attorneys and your case has been assigned to me.' He hesitated, and for a moment I thought he was going to shake hands with me, but he didn't make such an offer. He changed his steady gaze to the old man.

'Are you ready, Timmy?'

The old man, Timmy, held up his pencils and notebook in reply.

'I want to ask you a few questions,' Robert Seely said. 'Your name is ...?'

'Harry Jordan.'

'And your residence?'

I gave him my rooming house address.

'Occupation?'

'Art teacher.'

'Place of employment?'

'Unemployed.'

'What was the name of the woman you murdered?'

'Helen Meredith. Mrs. Helen Meredith.'

'What was she doing in your room?'

'She lived there ... the past few weeks.'

'Where is her husband, Mr. Meredith?'

'I don't know. She said something once about him living in San Diego, but she wasn't sure of it.'

'Did Mrs. Meredith have another address here in the city?'

'No. Before she moved to San Francisco she lived with her mother in San Sienna. I don't know that address either, but her mother's name is Mrs. Matthews. I don't know the first name.'

'All right. Take one.' He pushed the package of cigarettes across the desk and I removed one and lit it with the desk lighter. Mr. Seely held the open package out to the ancient stenographer.

'How can I smoke and take this down too?' The old man squeaked peevishly.

'Why did you kill Mrs. Meredith?' Mr. Seely asked me.

'Well, I ...' I hesitated.

'Before we go any further, Jordan, I think I'd better tell you that anything you say may be held against you. Do you understand that?'

'You should've told him that before,' the old man said sarcastically.

'I'm handling this interview, Timmy,' Mr. Seely said coldly. 'Your job is to take it down. Now, Jordan, are you aware that what you say may be held against you?'

'Of course. I don't care about that.'

'Why then, did you kill Mrs. Meredith?'

'In a way, it's a long story.'

'Just tell it in your own words.'

'Well, we'd been drinking, and once before we'd tried suicide and it didn't work so we went to the hospital and asked for psychiatric help.'

'What hospital was that?'

'Saint Paul's. We stayed for a week, that is, Helen was in a week. I was only kept for three days.'

'How did you attempt suicide?'

'With a razor blade.' I held my arms over the desk, showing him the thin red scars on my wrists. 'The psychiatric help we received was negligible. We started to drink as soon as we were released from the hospital. Anyway, I couldn't work very well and drink too. The small amount of money I made wouldn't stretch and I was despondent all the time.'

'And was Mrs. Meredith despondent, too?'

'She always took my moods as her own. If I was happy, she was happy. We were perfectly compatible in every respect — counterparts, rather. So that's how I happened to kill her, you see. She knew all along I was going to kill myself sooner or later and she made me promise to kill her first. So I did. Afterwards I turned on the gas. The next thing I knew, Mrs. McQuade — that's my landlady — was hollering and pounding on the door. My — Helen was dead and I wasn't.' With food in my stomach and a good night's sleep and a cigarette in my hand it was easy for me to talk about it.

'I have your suicide note, Jordan, and I notice it's written in charcoal. In the back of your mind, did you have an idea you could rub the charcoal away in case the suicide didn't work? Why did you use charcoal?'

'I didn't have a pencil.'

Timmy chuckled at my reply, avoided Mr. Seely's icy stare and bent over his notebook.

'Then the death of Mrs. Meredith was definitely premeditated?'

'Yes, definitely. I plead guilty to everything, anything.'

'Approximately what time was it when you choked her?'

'I don't know exactly. Somewhere between one and two a.m. Right afterwards I went out and got a pint of gin at the delicatessen down the street. It must have been before two or it wouldn't have been open.'

'What delicatessen?'

'Mr. Watson's. Mrs. Watson sold me the gin, though. I still owe her forty-three cents.'

'All right. We'll check the time with her. The police arrested you at ten minutes after eight. If you actually intended to commit suicide, why did you leave your transom open?'

'I don't know. I must have forgot about it, I guess.'

'Did you drink the pint of gin?'

'It was a cold night, and I needed something to warm me up.'

'I see. Where did you teach art last? You said you were an —'

'Lately I've been working around town as a counterman or fry cook.'

'Do you have a particular lawyer in mind? I can get in touch with one for you.'

'No. I don't need a lawyer. I'm guilty and that's the way I plead. I don't like to go through all this red tape. I expected to be dead by now and all these questions are inconvenient. The sooner I get it over with in the gas chamber the happier I'll be.'

'Are you willing to sign a confession to that effect?'

'Certainly. I'll sign anything that'll speed things up.'

'How did you and Mrs. Meredith get together in the first place?'

I thought the question over and decided it was none of his business.

Timmy's head stopped bobbing up and down and wagged back and forth from side to side for a change. 'He doesn't have to answer questions like that, Mr. Seely,' he said in his weak, whining voice. The two men stared at each other distastefully and Timmy won the battle of the eyes.

'Have you got enough for a confession, Timmy?' Mr. Seely asked the old man, at last.

'Plenty.' Timmy nodded his white head up and down.

'That's all I have then, Jordan,' Mr. Seely said. 'No. One more question. Do you want to complain you were mentally unstable at the time? Or do you think you're mentally ill now?'

'Of course not. I'm perfectly sane and I knew what I was doing at the time. I'd planned it for several weeks.'

'You'd better put that in the confession, Timmy.' Mr. Seely left the desk and opened the door. The detective was waiting in the hall. 'You can return Jordan to his cell now,' Mr. Seely told the detective.

I was handcuffed and taken back to the special block and turned over to Mr. Benson. Back into my cell I changed back to my jail clothes and Mr. Benson took my own clothes away on a wire coat hanger. I was alone in my quiet cell.

My mind was much more at ease than it had been before. Thinking back over the interview I felt quite satisfied that the initial step was taken and the ball had started rolling. Blind justice would filter in and get me sooner or later. It was pleasant to look forward to the gas chamber. What a nice, easy way to die! So painless. Silent and practically odorless and clean! I would sit in a chair, wearing a pair of new black trunks, and stare back at a few rows of spectators staring at me. I would hear nothing and smell nothing. Then I would be dead. When I writhed on the floor and went into convulsions I wouldn't even know about it. Actually, it would be a much more horrible experience for the witnesses than it would be for me. This knowledge gave me a feeling of morbid satisfaction. I had to laugh.

Soon it was time for lunch. Mr. Benson brought a tray to my cell containing boiled cabbage, white meat, bread and margarine, raspberry jello and black coffee. I attacked the food with relish. Food had never tasted better. My mind was relieved now that things were underway and I wasn't eating in a greasy café and I hadn't to cook the food myself. I suppose that is why it all tasted so good. After wiping up the cabbage pot-licker with the last of my bread I rolled and smoked a cigarette. Mr. Benson took the tray away and was back in a few minutes with Old Timmy.

'I've got your confession ready, boy,' the old man said.

Timmy signed for me and we left the block for the
elevator. After Timmy pushed the button for the third
floor, he turned and smiled at me, bobbing his head up
and down.

'You aren't sensitive, are you, Jordan?'

'How do you mean?' I asked, puzzled.

'Well, it isn't really necessary for me to take you downstairs to sign your confession, and when you aren't in the
block you're supposed to wear regular clothes instead of
these ...' He plucked at my blue jail shirt. 'And I'm
supposed to have a police officer along too.' He laughed
thinly. 'But some of the girls in the office wanted to get a
look at you. Funny, the way these young girls go for the
crime passionel. I didn't think you'd mind.'

We walked down the carpeted hallway of the third floor
and entered a large office that held five desks, each with
telephone and typewriter. Old Timmy winked at me as I
nervously looked at the nine women who had crowded
into the office. They were all ages, but were still considered girls by Old Timmy.

'This is the steno pool,' Timmy said as we crossed to his
desk.

'I see it is,' I replied.

'I been in charge of this office for thirty-one years.' He
had seven neatly typed copies of my confession on his
desk and I signed them all with a ballpoint pen. He called
two of the girls over to sign on the witness lines and they
came forward timidly and signed where he held his talon-
like finger. I had the feeling if I said 'boo' the girls would
jump through the window. After they signed their names
they rejoined the other women, and the silent group stared
at me boldly as we left the office. As Timmy shut the door
behind us I heard the foolish giggling begin and so did the
old man.

'I hope it didn't bother you, boy,' he said, 'They're just
women.'

'Yes, I know,' I replied meaninglessly.

We entered the elevator again and Timmy pushed the
button and looked at me friendlily.

'What do you think of our brilliant Assistant District Attorney, the eminent Mr. Seely?' There were sharp overtones of sarcasm in his thin, whining voice.

'I don't think anything of him,' I said. 'That is, one way or the other,' I amended.

'He's an ass!' Timmy said convincingly. 'I'd like to assign him a case.'

'It doesn't make any difference to me,' I said.

'You should have read your confession, boy. It's iron-tight, you can bet on that. It's a good habit to get into, reading what you sign.'

'I'm not making any more habits, good or bad,' I said.

Timmy chuckled deep in his throat. 'You're right about that!'

We reached the special block and I returned to the custody of Mr. Benson. He opened the heavy end door and Old Timmy shook hands with me before he left, bobbed his head up and down.

He turned away, head bobbing, hands jerking, and tottered down the corridor, his feet silent on the concrete floor.

I settled down in my cell to wait. I would be tried as a matter of course, convicted, and go to wait some more in the death row at San Quentin. There, after a prescribed period and on a specified date, I would be executed. And that was that.

I wondered how long it all would take.

Chapter Sixteen

SANITY TEST

I don't know how long I waited in my quiet cell before I was taken out of it again. It might have been three days, four days or five days. There was no outside light, just the refulgent electric bulbs in my cell and in the corridor. If it hadn't been for the meals, I wouldn't have known the time of day. I didn't worry about the time; I let it slip by unnoticed. I was fed and I was allowed to take a shower every day. And the forty slim cigarettes that can be rolled from a sack of Bull Durham were just enough to last me one full day. Mr. Benson let me have matches when I ran out, and I got by very well. After breakfast one morning, Mr. Benson brought my clothes down to my cell.

'Get dressed, Jordan,' he told me, 'you're going on a little trip.'

'Where to?'

'Get dressed, I said.'

My white shirt, stiffly starched, was back from the laundry. I tore off the cellophane wrapping, put it on, my slacks, tied my necktie. The jailer gave me my belt and shoelaces and I put the laces in my shoes, the belt through the trouser loops, slipped into my sports jacket.

'Don't you know where I'm going?' I asked.

'Of course I know. Hospital. Observation.'

I hesitated at the door of my cell. 'Hell, I'm all right. I don't want to go to any hospital for observation. I signed a confession; what more do they want?'

'Don't worry about it,' Mr. Benson reassured me. 'It's routine. They always send murder suspects to the hospital nowadays. It's one of the rules.'

'It isn't just me then?'

'No. It's routine. Come on, I ain't got all day.'

I followed him down the corridor, but my mind didn't accept his glib explanation. I didn't believe my stay in the hospital would be very long, but I didn't want them to get any ideas that I was insane. That would certainly delay my case and I wanted to get it over with as soon as possible. Right then, I made up my mind to cooperate with the psychiatrist, no matter what it cost me in embarrassment. It wouldn't do at all to be found criminally insane and to spend the rest of my life in an institution.

The detective was the same one who had taken me downstairs for my interview with Mr. Seely. He still had his hat on, and after he signed for me, and we were riding down in the elevator, I took a closer look at him. He was big and tough looking, with the inscrutable look that old-time criminals and old-time policemen have in common. To be friendly, I tried to start a little conversation with the man.

'Those other two guys, the ones on the special block with me; what are they in for?' I asked him.

'What do you want to know for?'

'Just curious, I suppose.'

'You prisoners are all alike. You get in trouble and you want to hear about others in the same fix. If it makes you feel any better, I'll tell you this: they're in a lot worse shape than you are.'

We got out of the elevator into the basement and climbed into the back of a white ambulance that was waiting at the loading ramp. The window in the back was covered with drawn gray curtains and I couldn't see anything on the way to the hospital. But on the way, the detective told me about the other two prisoners, and like he said, they were in worse shape than I was in. The blond young man had killed his mother with an axe in an argument over the car keys, and the middle-aged man had killed his wife and three children with a shotgun and then had lost his nerve and failed to kill himself. It made me ill to hear about the two men and I was sorry I had asked about them.

A white-jacketed orderly met us at the hospital's receiving entrance and signed the slip the detective gave him. He was a husky young man in his early thirties and there was a broad smile on his face. His reddish hair was closely cropped in a fresh crew-cut and there was a humorous expression in his blue eyes. The detective uncuffed me, put the slip of paper in his pocket and winked at the orderly.

'He's your baby, Hank,' he said.

'We'll take good care of him, don't worry,' the orderly said good-naturedly and I followed him inside the hospital. We entered the elevator and rode it up to the sixth floor. Hank had to unlock the elevator door with a key before we could leave the elevator. As soon as we were in the hallway he locked the elevator door again and we left the hallway for a long narrow corridor with locked cells on both sides of it. He unlocked the door marked Number 3, and motioned for me to enter. It was a small, windowless room and the walls were of unpainted wood instead of gray plaster. There were no bunks, just a matt-ress on the floor without sheets, and a white, neatly folded blanket at the foot. The door was made of thick, heavy wood, several layers thick with a small spy-hole at eye-level, about the size of a silver dollar. Hank started to close the door on me and I was terrified, irrationally so.

'Don't!' I said quickly. 'Don't shut me up, please! Leave it open, I won't try to run away.'

He nodded, smiling. 'All right, I'll leave it open a crack. I'm going to get you some pajamas and I'll be back in a few minutes. You start undressing.' He closed the door partially and walked away.

I removed my jacket, shirt and pants, and standing naked except for my shoes I waited apprehensively for Hank's return. It wasn't exactly a padded cell, but it was the next thing to it. I was really frightened. For the first time I knew actual terror. There is a great difference between being locked in a jail cell and being locked in a madman's cell. At the jail I was still an ordinary human being, a murderer, yes, but a normal man locked up in jail with other normal men. Here, in addition to being a murderer, I was under serious suspicion, like a dangerous lunatic, under observation from a tiny spy-hole, not to be trusted. Mr. Benson must have lied to me. Evidently, they thought I was crazy. Why would they lock me away in such a room if they didn't think so? I wanted a cigarette to calm my fears, but I didn't dare call out for one or rap on the door. I was even afraid to look out the open door, afraid they would think I was trying to escape, and then I would be put into a padded cell for sure. From now on I would have to watch out for everything I did, everything I said. Full cooperation. That is what they would get from me. From now on.

The orderly returned with a pair of blue broadcloth pajamas, a thin white cotton robe and a pair of skivvy slippers.

'Shoes too, Harry,' he said.

I sat down on the mattress, removed my shoes and socks and slid my feet into the skivvy slippers. He dropped my clothes into a blue sack and pulled the cords tight at the top. He had a kind face and he winked at me.

'Just take it easy, Harry,' he said, 'I'll be back in a minute.'

It was a little better having something to cover my nakedness. Still, there is a psychological effect to hospital pajamas. Wearing them, a man is automatically a patient, and a patient is a sick man or he wouldn't be in a hospital. That was the way I saw it, the only way I could see it. Hank returned with a syringe and needle and took a blood sample from my right arm. When he turned to leave I asked him timidly for a cigarette.

'Why, sure', he said and reached into his jacket pocket. He handed me a fresh package of king-sized Chesterfields and I opened it quickly, stuck a cigarette in my mouth. He flipped his lighter for me and said: 'Keep the pack.' I was pleased to note that my hands had stopped shaking. 'I can't give you any matches,' Hank continued, 'but anytime

you want a light or want to go to the can, just holler. My
name is Hank, and I'm at the end of the hall.'

'Thanks, Hank,' I said appreciatively. 'It's nice to smoke
tailor-mades again. I've been rolling them at the jail.'

'They don't cost me nothing. And when you run out let
me know. I can get all I want from the Red Cross.' He
started to leave with the blood sample, turned and smiled.
'Don't worry about the door. I know it's a little rough at
first, but I'm right down the hall and if you holler I can
hear you. I'll shut the door but I won't latch it. Knowing
you aren't locked in is sometimes as good as an open
door.'

'Will you do that for me?' I asked eagerly.

'Why, sure. This maximum security business is a lotta
crap anyway. The elevator's locked, there's no stairs, and
the windows are all barred, and the door to the roof's
locked. No reason to lock your cell.' He closed the door
behind him, and he didn't lock it.

I sat down on the mattress, my back to the pine wall
and chain-smoked three cigarettes. It gave me something
to do. If the rest of the staff were as nice to me as Hank I
would be able to survive the ordeal and I knew it would be
an ordeal. My short stay at Saint Paul's had given me a
sample, but now I would be put through the real thing. At
noon, Frank brought me my lunch on a tray. There was no
knife or fork and I had to eat the lunch with a spoon. The
food was better than the jail food, pork chops, french fries
and ice cream, but it almost gagged me to eat it. I forced
myself to clean the tray and saved the milk for the last. I
gulped the milk down with one long swallow, hoping it
would clear away the food that felt caught in my throat.
When Hank returned for the tray he gave me a light for
my smoke. He was pleased when he saw the empty tray.

'That's the way, Harry,' he nodded and smiled good-
naturedly. 'Eat all you can. A man feels better with a full gut.
The doctor'll be back after a while and he'll talk to you
then. Don't let him worry you. He's a weirdie. All these
psychiatrists are a little nuts themselves.'

'I'll try not to let it bother me,' I said. 'How long are

they going to keep me here, anyway?'

'I don't know.' He grinned. 'That all depends.'

'You mean it all depends on me?'

'That's right. And the doctor.' He left with the tray, closing the door.

About one-thirty or two Hank returned for me and we left the cell and corridor and entered a small office off the main hallway. The office wasn't much larger than my cell, but it contained a barred window that let in a little sunlight. Through the window I could observe the blue sky and the bright green plot of grass in the park outside the hospital. The doctor was seated behind his desk and he pointed to the chair across from it.

'Sit down, Jordan,' he said. 'Hank, you can wait outside.'

There was a trace of accent in his voice. German, maybe Austrian. It was cultivated, but definitely foreign. That is the way it is in the United States. A native-born American can't make a decent living and here was a foreigner all set to tell me what was wrong with me. He had a swarthy sunlamp tan and his black beard was so dark it looked dyed. It was an Imperial beard and it made him resemble the early photographs of Lenin.

'Your beard makes you look like Lenin,' I said.

'Why thank you, thank you!' He took it as a compliment. I distrusted the man. There is something about a man with a beard I cannot stand. No particular reason for it. Prejudice, I suppose. I feel the same way about cats.

'I'm Doctor Fischbach,' the doctor said unsmilingly. 'You're to be here under my observation for a few days.' He studied a sheaf of papers, clipped together with large-sized paper clips, for a full five minutes while I sat there under pressure feeling the perspiration rolling freely down my back and under my arms to the elbows. He wagged his bearded chin from side to side, clucked sympathetically.

'Too bad you entered Saint Paul's for help, Jordan.' He continued to shake his head. 'If you and Mrs. Meredith had come to me in the first place you would have been all right.'

'Yeah,' I said noncommittally. 'You may be right.'

'Did Saint Paul's give you any tests of any kind? If so, we could obtain them and save the time of taking them over.'

'No, I didn't get any tests — just blood tests.'

'Then let us begin with the Rorschach.' Dr. Fischbach opened his untidy top desk drawer, dug around in its depths and brought out a stack of cards about six inches by six inches and set them before me, number one on top. 'These are ink blots, Jordan, as you can see. We'll go through the cards one by one and you tell me what they remind you of. Now, how about this one?' He shoved the first card across the desk and I studied it for a moment or so. It looked like nothing.

'It looks like an art student's groping for an idea.' I suggested.

'Yes?' He encouraged me.

'It isn't much of anything. Sometimes, Doctor, when an artist is stuck for an idea, he'll doodle around with charcoal to see if he can come up with something. The meaningless lines and mass forms sometimes suggest an idea, and he can develop it into a picture. That's what these ink blots look like to me.'

'How about right here?' He pointed with his pencil to one of the larger blots. 'Does this look like a butterfly to you?'

'Not to me. No.'

'What does it look like?'

'It looks like some artist has been doodling around with black ink trying to get an idea.' How many times did he want me to tell him?

'You don't see a butterfly?' He seemed to be disappointed.

'No butterfly.' I wanted to cooperate, but I couldn't see any point in lying to the man. It was some kind of trick he was trying to pull on me. I stared hard at the card again, trying to see something, some shape, but I couldn't. None of the blots made a recognizable shape. I shook my head as he went on to the next card which also had four strangely shaped blots.

'Do these suggest anything?' He asked hopefully.

'Yeah,' I said. If he wanted to trick me I would play one on him. 'I see a chicken in a sack with a man on its back; a bottle of rum and I'll have some; a red-winged leek, and an oversized beak; a pail of water and a farmer's daughter; a bottle of gin and a pound of tin; a false-faced friend and days without end; a big brown bear and he's going everywhere; a big banjo and a —'

He jerked the cards from the desk and shoved them into the drawer. He looked at me seriously without any expression on his dark face and twisted the point of his beard with thumb and forefinger. My thin cotton robe was oppressively warm. I smiled, hoping it was ingratiating enough to please the doctor. Like all doctors, I knew, he didn't have a sense of humor.

'I really want to cooperate with you, Doctor,' I said meekly, 'but I actually can't see anything in those ink blots. I'm an artist, or at least I used to be, and as an artist I can see anything I want to see in anything.'

'That's quite all right, Jordan,' he said quietly. 'There are other tests.' When he got to his feet I noticed he was slightly humpbacked and I had a strong desire to rub his hump for good luck. 'Come on with me.' I followed him down the hall, Hank trailing us behind. We entered another small room that was furnished with a small folding table, typing paper and a battered, standard Underwood typewriter.

'Do you know how to type, Jordan?' The doctor asked me.

'Some. I haven't typed since I left high school though.'

'Sit down.'

I sat down at the folding table and the doctor left the room. Hank lit a cigarette for me and before I finished it the doctor was back with another stack of cards. These were about eight by ten inches. He put the stack on the table and picked up the first card to show it to me. 'You'll have fun with these.'

The first picture was a reproduction of an oil painting in

black and white. It was a portrait of a young boy in white blouse and black knickers. His hair was long, with a Dutch bob, and he had a delicate, wistful face. He held a book in his hand. From the side of the portrait a large hand reached out from an unseen body and rested lightly on the boy's shoulder. The background was an ordinary living room with ordinary, old-fashioned furniture. Table, chairs, potted plants and two vases full of flowers made the picture a bit cluttered.

'What I want you to do is this,' Dr. Fischbach explained. 'Examine each picture carefully and then write a little story about it. Anything at all, but write a story. You've got plenty of paper and all the time in the world. After you finish with each one, put the story and picture together and start on the next one. Number the story at the top with the same number the picture has and they won't get mixed up. Any questions?'

'No, but I'm not much of a story teller. I don't hardly know the difference between syntax and grammar.'

'Don't let that bother you. I'm not looking for polished prose, I merely want to read the stories. Get started now, and if you want to smoke, Hank'll be right outside the door to give you a light. Right Hank?'

'Yes, sir,' Hank replied with his customary smile.

They left the room and I examined the little print for a while and then put a piece of paper into the machine. It wasn't fun, as Dr. Fischbach had suggested, but it passed the time away and I would rather have something to do, anything, rather than sit in the bleak cell they had assigned me. I wrote that the young boy was sitting for his portrait and during the long period of posing he got tired and fidgety. The hand resting on his shoulder was that of his father and it was merely comforting the boy and telling him the portrait would soon be over. In a few lines I finished the dull tale.

Each picture I tackled was progressively impressionistic and it did become fun after all, once I got interested. The last three reproductions were in color, in a surrealistic vein, and they bordered on the uncanny and weird.

However, I made up stories on them all, pecking them out on the old machine, even though some of the stories were quite senseless. When I finished, I racked stories and cards together and called Hank. He was down at the end of the hall talking to a nurse. He dropped the cards and stories off at the doctor's office and we started back to my cell. I stopped him.

'Just a second, Hank,' I said. 'Didn't you say something about a roof?'

'I don't know. We've got a roof,' and he pointed toward a set of stairs leading up, right next to the elevator.

'After being cooped up so long,' I said, 'I'd like to get some fresh air. Do you suppose the doc would let me go up on the roof for a smoke before I go back to that little tomb? That is, if you go along.'

'I'll ask him.' Hank left me in the hall and entered the little office. He was smiling when he came out a moment later. 'Come on,' he said, taking my arm. We climbed the short flight of stairs and Hank unlocked the door to the roof.

The roof was black tar-paper, but near the little building that housed the elevator machinery and short stairwell to the sixth floor, there were about twenty feet of duckboards scattered around and a small green bench. It was late in the afternoon and a little chilly that high above the ground, but we sat and smoked on the bench for about an hour. Hank didn't mind sitting up there with me, because, as he said, if he was sitting around he wasn't working. He was an interesting man to talk to.

'How come you stay with this line of work, Hank?' I asked him.

'I drifted into it and I haven't drifted out. But it isn't as bad as it looks. There are a lot of compensations.' He winked. 'As a hot-shot male nurse, I rank somewhere between a doctor and an interne. I have to take order from internes, but my pay check is about ten times as big as theirs, almost as big as some of the resident doctors. So the nurses, the lovely frustrated nurses, come flocking around, and I mean the female nurses. An interne doesn't make the dough to take them out and the doctors are married, or else they're too careful to get mixed up with fellow workers, you know, so I do all right. I get my own room right here, my meals, laundry and my money too. Funny thing about these nurses. They all look good in clean white uniforms and nice white shoes, but they look like hell when they dress up to go out. I've never known one yet who knew how to wear clothes on a date. They seem to be self-conscious about it too. But when the clothes come off, they're women, and that's the main thing with me. Did you see that nurse I was talking to in the hall?'

'I caught a glimpse of her.'

'She'll be in my room tonight at eleven. So you see, Harry, taking care of nuts like you has it's compensations.' He slapped me on the knee. 'Come on, let's go.' He laughed happily and I followed him down the stairs.

For supper that night I ate hamburger patties and boiled potatoes, lime jello and coffee. The mental work of thinking up stories had tired me and I fell asleep easily. As Hank said, having the door unlocked was almost like not being locked in.

The next morning I had another session with Dr. Fischbach. It was an easy one and didn't last very long. He gave me a written intelligence test. The questions were all fairly simple; questions like: 'Who wrote *Faust?*', 'How do you find the circumference of a circle?', 'Who was the thirty-second president?' and so on. In the early afternoon I was given a brainwave test. It was rather painful, but interesting. After I was stretched out on a low operating table, fifty or more needles were stuck into my scalp, each needle attached with a wire to a machine. A man pushed gadgets on the machine and it made flip-flop sounds. It didn't hurt me and I didn't feel any electric shocks, but it was a little painful when the needles were inserted under the skin of my scalp. All of this procedure seemed like a great waste of time and I hated the ascetic loneliness of my wooden cell. Sleeping on the mattress without any springs made my back ache.

The next few boring days were all taken up with more tests.

X-Rays were taken of my chest, head and back.

Urine and feces specimens were taken.

More blood from my arm and from the end of my forefinger.

My eyes, ears, nose and throat were examined.

My teeth were checked.

At last I began my series of interviews with Dr. Fischbach and these were the most painful experiences of all.

Chapter Seventeen

FLASHBACK

Doctor Leo Fischbach sat humped behind his desk twirling the point of his beard with thumb and forefinger. I often wondered if his beard was perfumed. It seemed to be the only link or concession between the rest of the world and his personality. If he had a personality. His large brown eyes, fixed and staring, were two dark mirrors that seemed to hold my image without interest, without curiosity, or at most, with an impersonal interest, the way one is interested in a dead, dry starfish, found on the beach. I was tense in my chair as I chain-smoked my free cigarettes and the longer I looked at Dr. Fischbach, the more I hated him. My efforts at total recollection, and he was never satisfied with less, had exhausted me. I began to speak again, my voice harsh and grating to my ears.

'The war, if anything, Doctor, was only another incident in my life. A nice long incident, but all the same, just another. I don't think it affected me at all. I was painting before I was drafted and that's all I did after I got in.'

'Tell me about this, er, incident.'

'Well, after I was drafted I was assigned to Fort Benning, Georgia. And after basic training I was pulled out of the group to paint murals in the mess-halls there. I was quite happy about this and I was given a free hand. Not literally, but for the army it was a good deal. Naturally, I knew the type of pictures they wanted and that's what I gave them. If I'd attempted a few non-objective pictures I'd have been handed a rifle in a hurry. So I painted army scenes. Stuff like paratroopers dropping out of the sky, a thin line of infantrymen in the field, guns, tank columns and so on.'

'Did this type of thing satisfy you? Did you feel you were sacrificing your artistic principles by painting this way?'

'Not particularly. If I thought of it at all I knew I had a damned good deal. I was painting while other soldiers were drilling, running obstacle courses and getting shot at somewhere or other. I missed all that, you see. As a special duty man I was excused from everything except painting.'

'You didn't paint murals for the duration of the war, did you?'

'Not at Fort Benning, no. After a year I was transferred to Camp Gordon — that's in Georgia too, at Augusta.'

'What did you do there?'

'I painted murals in mess-halls.'

'Didn't you have any desire for promotion?'

'No. None at all. But they promoted me anyway. I was made a T/5. Same pay as corporal but no rank or responsibilities.'

'How was your reaction to the army? Did you like it?'

'I don't know.'

'Did you dislike it then?'

'I don't know. I was in the army. Everybody was in the army.'

'How were you treated?'

'In the army everybody is the same. Nobody bothered me, because I was on special duty. Many times the officers would come around and inspect the murals I was working on. They were well pleased, very happy about them. Knowing nothing at all about art was to their advantage. On two different occasions I was given letters of commendation for my murals. Of course, they didn't mean anything. Officers like to give letters like that; they believe it is good for morale. Maybe it is, I don't know.'

'What did you do in your off-duty time in Georgia?'

Again I had to think back. What had I done? All I

could remember was a blur of days, distant and hazy days. Pine trees, sand and cobalt skies. And on pay-days, gin and a girl. The rest of the month — days on a scaffolding in a hot wooden building, painting, doing the best I could with regular house paint, finishing up at the end of the day, tired but satisfied, grateful there was no sergeant to make me change what I had done. A shower, a trip to the first movie, bed by nine. Was there nothing else?

'Well, I slept a lot. It was hot in Georgia and I slept. I worked and then I hit the sack.'

'When did you get discharged?'

'November, 1945. And then instead of returning to Chicago I decided to come out to California and finish art school out here.'

'Why?'

'I must have forgotten to tell you about it. I had a wife and child in Chicago.'

'Yes, you did.' He made a note on his pad. He made his notes in a bastard mixture of loose German script and speedwriting. 'This is the first time you've mentioned a wife and child.'

'It must have slipped my mind. It was some girl I married while I was attending the Chicago Art Institute. She has a child, a boy, that's right, a boy. She named him John after her father. John Jordan is his name. I've never seen him.'

'Why didn't you return to your wife and child? Didn't you want to see your son? Sometimes a son is considered a great event in a man's life.'

'Is that right? I considered it an unnecessary expense. I came to California because it was the practical thing to do. If I'd gone to Chicago I wouldn't have been able to continue with my painting. It would have been necessary for me to go to work and support Leonie and the child. And I didn't want to do it.'

'Didn't you feel any responsibility for your wife? Or to the child?'

'Of course I did. That's why I didn't go back. I didn't want to live up to the responsibility. It was more important to paint instead. An artist paints and a husband works.'

'Where's your family now?'

'I imagine they're still in Chicago. After I left the army I didn't write to her any more.'

'Do you have any curiosity about how they're faring?'

'Not particularly.'

Curiosity. That was an ill-chosen word for him to use. I could remember my wife well. She was a strong, intelligent, capable young woman. She thought she was a sculptor, but she had as much feeling for form as a steel worker. She didn't like Epstein and her middle-western mind couldn't grasp his purported intentions. If a statue wasn't pretty she didn't like it. But she was good on the pointing-apparatus and a fair copyist. Her drawings were rough but solid, workmanlike. She would get by, anywhere. And my son was only an accident anyway. I certainly didn't want a child, and she hadn't either. But she had one and as long as he was with his mother, as he should be, he was eating. I had no doubt about that, and no curiosity.

'And then you entered the L.A. Art Center.' Dr. Fischbach prodded.

'That's right. I attended the Center for almost a year, under the G.I. Bill.'

'Did you obtain a degree?'

'Just an A.A. Things didn't go so well for me after the war. I had difficulty returning to my non-objective style and I was unable to finish any picture I started. I still can't understand it. I could visualize, to a certain extent, what my picture would look like on canvas, but I couldn't achieve it. I began and tossed aside painting after painting. The rest of my academic work was way above the average. It was easy to paint academically and I could draw as well as anybody, but that wasn't my purpose in painting.'

'So you quit.'

'You might say I quit. But actually, I was offered a teaching job at a private school. I weighed things over in my mind and decided to accept it. I thought I'd have more free time to paint and a place to work as an art teacher.

The Center was only a place to paint and as a teacher I'd
get more money than the G.I. Bill paid.'

'What school did you teach at?'

'Mansfield. It's between Oceanside and San Diego. It's a
rather conservative little school. There isn't much money
in the endowment and the regents wouldn't accept state
aid. There were about a hundred and thirty students and
most of them were working their way through. It wasn't
accredited under the G.I. Bill.'

'How did you like teaching?'

'Painting can't be taught, Doctor. Either a man can
paint or he can't. I felt that most of the students were
being duped, cheated out of their money. It's one thing to
study art with money furnished by a grateful government,
but it's something else to pay out of your own pocket for
something you aren't getting. And every day I was more
convinced that I wasn't a painter and never would be one.
After a while I quit painting altogether. But I hung onto
my job at Mansfield because I didn't know what else to do
with myself. Without art as an emotional outlet I turned to
drinking as a substitute and I've been drinking ever since.'

'Why did you leave Mansfield then?'

'I was fired. After I started to drink I missed a lot of
classes. And I never offered any excuses when I didn't
show up. In my spare time I talked to some of the more
inept students and persuaded them to quit painting and go
into something else. Somehow, the school didn't like that.
But I was only being honest. I was merely balancing the
praise I gave to the students who were good.'

'After you were fired, did you come directly to San
Francisco?'

'Not directly. It kind of took me by surprise, getting
fired, I mean. They thought they had every reason to fire
me, but I didn't expect it. I was one of the most popular
teachers at the school, that is, with the students. But I
suppose drinking had dulled my rational mind to the
situation.'

'And you felt persecuted?'

'Oh, no, nothing like that. After I got my terminal pay I

thought things out. I wanted to get away from the city and things connected with culture, back to the land. Well, not back to it, because I'd never been a farmer or field hand, always in cities you know. But at the time I felt if I could work in the open using my muscles, doing really hard labor, I'd be able to sleep again. So that's what I did. I picked grapes in Fresno, and around Merced. I hit the sugar beet harvests in Chico, drifted in season, over to Utah, and I spent an entire summer in the Soledad lettuce fields.'

'Were you happier doing that type of work?'

'I was completely miserable. All my life I had only wanted to paint. There isn't any substitute for painting. Coming to a sudden, brutal stop left me without anything to look forward to. I had nothing. I drank more and more and finally I couldn't hold a field hand's job, not even in the lettuce fields. That's when I came to San Francisco. It was a city and it was close. In a city a man can always live.'

'And you've been here ever since?'

'That's right. I've gone from job to job, drinking when I've had the money, working for more when I ran out.'

I dropped my head and sat quietly, my hands inert in my lap. I was drained. What possible good did it do the doctor to know these things about me? How could this refugee from Aachen analyze my actions for the drifting into nothingness when I didn't know myself? I was bored with my dull life. I didn't want to remember anything; all I wanted was peace and quiet. The silence that Death brings, an all-enveloping white cloak of everlasting darkness. By my withdrawal from the world I had made my own little niche and it was a dreary little place I didn't want to live in or tell about. But so was Doctor Fischbach's and his world was worse than mine. I wouldn't have traded places with him for anything. He sat across from me silently, fiddling with his idiotic beard, his dark eyes on the ceiling, evaluating my story, probing with his trained mind. I pitied him. The poor bastard thought he was a god.

Did I? This nasty thought hit me below the belt. How else could I have taken Helen's life if I didn't think so?

What other justification was there for my brutal murder? I
had no right or reason to take her with me into my
nothingness. Harry Jordan had played the part of God
too. It didn't matter that she had wanted to go with me. I
still didn't have the right to kill her. But I had killed her
and I had done it as though it was my right, merely
because I loved her. Well, it was done now. No use
brooding about it. At least I had done it unconsciously
and I had been under the influence of gin. Doctor Fischbach was a different case. He was playing God deliberately.
This strange, bearded individual had gone to medical
school for years, deliberately studied psychiatry for
another couple of years. He had been psychoanalyzed
himself by some other foreigner who thought he was a god
— and now satisfied, with an ego as large as Canada he sat
behind a desk digging for filth into other people's minds.
What a miserable bastard he must be behind his implacable beard and face!

'During your employment as a field hand, Jordan, did
you have any periods which you felt highly elated,
followed by acute depression?'

'No,' I said sullenly.

'Did you ever hear voices in the night, a voice talking to
you?'

'No.'

'As you go about the city; have you ever had the feeling
you were being followed?'

'Only once. A man followed me with a gun in his hand,
but he didn't shoot me.'

'You saw this man with the gun?'

'That's right, but when I looked over my shoulder he
was gone.'

He made some rapid, scribbling notes on his pad.

'Did you ever see him again?'

'No.'

'So far, you've been reluctant to tell me about your
sexual relations with Mrs. Meredith. I need this information. It's important that I know about it.'

'Not to me it isn't.'

'I can't see why you object to telling me about it.'

'Naturally, you can't. You think you're above human relationship. To tell you about my intimate life with Helen is indecent. She's dead now, and I have too much respect for her.'

'Suppose we talk then about other women in your life. Your wife, for instance. You don't seem to have any attachment for her, of any great strength. Did you enjoy a normal marital relationship?'

'I always enjoy it, but not half as much as you do secondhand.'

'How do you mean that?'

I got to my feet. 'I'd like to go back to my cell, Doctor,' I said, forcing the words through my compressed lips. 'I don't feel like talking any more.'

'Very well, Jordan. We'll talk some more tomorrow.'

'I'd rather not.'

'Why not?'

'I don't like to waste time. I'm not crazy and you know it as well as I do. And I resent your vicarious enjoyment of my life's history and your dirty probing mind.'

'You don't really think I enjoy this, Jordan?' he said with surprise.

'You must. If you didn't, you'd go into some other kind of work. I can't believe anybody would sink so low just for money. I've gone down the ladder myself, but I haven't hit your level yet.'

'I'm trying to help you, Jordan.'

'You can help somebody that needs it then. I don't want your help.' I turned abruptly and left his office. Hank got up from the bench outside the door and accompanied me to my cell.

My cell didn't frighten me any longer. It was a haven, an escape from Dr. Fischbach. I liked its bareness, the hard mattress on the floor. It no longer mattered that I didn't have a chair to sit down upon. After a while I forced my churning mind into pleasant, happier channels. I wondered what they would have for supper.

I was hungry as hell.

Chapter Eighteen

THE BIG FIXATION

When I was about seven or eight years old, somebody gave me a map of the United States that was cut up into a jigsaw puzzle. Whether I could read or not at the time I don't remember, but I had sense enough to start with the water surrounding the United States. These were the pieces with the square edges and I realized if I got the outline all around I could build toward the center a state at a time. This is the way I worked it and when I came to Kansas it was the last piece and it fitted into the center in the last remaining space. This was using my native intelligence and it was the logical method to put a jigsaw puzzle together. Evidently, Doctor Fischbach did not possess my native intelligence. He skipped around with his questions as he daily dug for more revelations from my past and he reminded me of a door-to-door salesman avoiding the houses with the BEWARE OF THE DOG signs. Having started with my relationship with Helen, dropping back to my art school days, returning to my childhood, then back to Helen, we were back to my childhood again. I no longer looked him in the eyes as we talked together, but focused my eyes on my hands or on the floor. I didn't want to let him see the hate in my eyes.

'Did your mother love you?' he asked me. 'Did you feel that you got all of the attention you had coming to you?'

'Considering the fact that I had two brothers and five sisters I got my share. More than I deserved anyway, and I'm not counting two other brothers that were stillborn.'

'Did you feel left out in any way?'

'Left out of what?'

'Outside of the family. Were you always fairly treated?'

'Well, Doctor, money was always short during the depression, naturally, what with the large family and all, but I always got my share. More, if anything. My father showed partiality to me; I know that now. He thought I was more gifted than my brothers and sisters.'

'How did your father support the family? What type of work did he do? Was he a professional man?'

'No. He didn't have a profession, not even a trade. He contributed little, if anything, to our support. He worked once in a while, but never steady. He always said that his boss, whoever it happened to be at the time, was giving him the dirty end of the stick. He had a very strong sense of justice and he'd quit his job at the first sign of what he termed unfairness or prejudice. Even though the unfairness happened to someone else, he'd quit in protest.'

'How about drinking? Did your father drink?'

'I don't know.'

'Please try to remember. There might be some incidents. Surely you know whether he drank or not.'

'Listen, Doctor, it was still prohibition when he was alive. I don't remember ever seeing him take a drink. And when he went out at night I was too small to go with him. So if he drank I don't know about it.'

'If he didn't support your family, who did?'

'Mother. She was a beauty operator and she must have been a good one, because she always had a job. Ever since I can remember. She had some kind of new system, and women used to come to our house on Sundays, her off-day, for treatments. It seemed to me that she never had any free time.'

'What are your brothers and sisters doing now?'

'I suppose they're working. Father died first and then about a year later my mother died. From that time on we were on our own.'

'How old were you then, when your mother died?'

'Sixteen.'

'Weren't there any relatives to take you in with them?'

'We had relatives, yes. My mother's brother, Uncle Ralph, gathered us all together in his house about a week after her funeral. He had the insurance money by that time and it was divided equally between us. My share was two hundred and fifty dollars, which was quite a fortune in the depression. My uncle and aunt took my smallest sister to live with them, probably to get her two-fifty, but the rest of us were on our own. I got a room on the South Side, a part-time job, and finished high school. I entered the Art Institute as soon as I finished high school. Luckily, I was able to snag a razor-blade-and-condom concession and this supported me and paid my tuition. I studied at the institute until I was drafted, and I've told you about my experiences in the army already.'

'Sketchily.'

'I told you all I could remember. I wasn't a hero. I was an ordinary soldier like all the draftees. I had a pretty good break, yes, but that was only because I had the skill to paint and also because the army gave me the opportunity to use my skill. Many other soldiers, a hell of a lot more talented than I was, were never given the same breaks.'

'Do you have any desire to see your brothers and sisters again?'

'They all live in Chicago, Doctor. We used to have a saying when we were students in L.A. — "A lousy artist doesn't go to heaven or hell when he dies; his soul goes to Chicago." If that saying turns out to be true, I'll be seeing them soon enough.'

'How about sexual experiences? Did you ever engage in sex-play with your brothers and sisters?' His well-trained words marched like slugs into the cemetery of my brain. He asked this monstrous question as casually as he asked them all. Appalled, I stared at him unbelievingly.

'You must have a hell of a lot of guts to ask me a filthy question like that!' I said angrily. 'What kind of a person do you think I am, anyway? I've confessed to a brutal murder — I'm guilty — I've said I was guilty! Why don't you kill me? Why can't I go to the gas chamber? What you've been doing to me can be classified as cruel and inhuman treatment, and as a citizen I don't have to take it! How much do you think I can stand?' I was on my feet by this time and pounding the doctor's desk with my fists. 'You've got everything out of me you're going to get!' I finished decisively. 'From now on I'll tell you nothing!'

'What is it you don't want to tell me, Jordan?' He asked quietly, as he calmly twisted the point of his beard.

'Nothing. I've told you everything that ever happened to me. Not once, but time and time again. Why do you insist in asking the same things over and over?'

'Please sit down, Jordan.' I sat down. 'The reason I ask you these questions is because I haven't much time. I have to return you to the jail tomorrow —'

'Thank God for small favors!' I cut him off.

'So I've taken some unethical short cuts. I know it's most unfair to you and I'm sorry. Now. Tell me about your sex-play with your brothers and sisters.'

'My brothers and I all married each other and all my sisters are lesbians. We all slept together in the same bed, including my mother and father and all of us took turns with each other. The relationship was so complicated and the experiences were so varied, all you have to do is attach a medical book of abnormal sex deviations to my file and you'll have it all. Does that satisfy your morbid curiosity?' This falsehood made me feel ashamed.

'You're evading my question. Why? Everything you tell me is strictly confidential. I only ask you these things to enable me to give a correct report —'

'From now on I'm evading you,' I said. I got up from my chair and opened the door. Hank, as usual, was waiting for me outside, sitting on the bench. As I started briskly, happily, toward my cell Hank fell in behind me. My mind was relieved, my step was airy, because I never intended to talk to Dr. Fischbach again. I didn't look back and I've never seen the doctor since.

That afternoon I was so ashamed of myself and so irri- table I slammed my fists into the pine wall over and over again. I kept it up until my knuckles hurt me badly enough to get my mind on them instead of the other thoughts that boiled and churned inside my head. After a while, Hank opened the door and looked in on me. There was a wide smile on his lips.

'There's a lot of noise in here. What's going on, Harry?'

'It's that damned doctor, Hank,' I said. I smiled in spite of myself. Hank had the most infectious smile I've ever seen.

'Let me tell you something, Harry,' Hank said seriously, and he came as close to not smiling as he was able to do. 'You've got to keep a cool stool. It don't go for a man to get emotionally disturbed in a place like this. Speaking for myself, I'll tell you this much; you'll be one hell of a lot better off in the gas chamber than you'd ever be in a state institution. Have you ever thought of that?'

I snorted. 'Of course I've thought of it. But I'm not insane. You know it and so does the doctor.'

'That's right, Harry. But besides working here, I've worked in three different state institutions. And I've seen guys a hell of a lot saner than you in all three of them.' This remark made him laugh.

'I'm all right,' I told him.

'The way to prove it is to keep a cool stool.'

'I guess you're right. Dr. Fischbach says I can go back to jail tomorrow. And if he's halfway fair he'll turn in a favorable report on me, Hank. Up till today, anyway, I've cooperated with him all the way.'

'I know you have, Harry. Don't spoil it. It must be pretty rough, isn't it?'

'I've never had it any rougher.'

He winked at me conspiratorily. 'How'd you like to have a drink?' He held up his thumb and forefinger an inch apart.

'Man, I'd love one,' I replied sincerely.

Hank reached into his hip-pocket and brought out a half-pint of gin. He unscrewed the cap and offered me the bottle. I didn't take it. Was this some kind of trap? After all, Hank was a hospital employee, when all was said and done. Sure, he had been more than nice to me so far, but maybe there had been a purpose to it, and this might be it. How did I know it was gin in the bottle? It might be some kind of dope, maybe a truth serum of some kind? It might possibly be Fischbach's way of getting me into some kind of a jam. I knew he didn't like me.

'No thanks, Hank,' I said. 'Maybe I'd better not.'

Hank shrugged indifferently. 'Suit yourself.' He took a long swig, screwed the cap back on and returned the bottle to his hip pocket. He left my cell and slammed and locked the door. I was sorry I hadn't taken the drink. It might have made me feel better, and by refusing, I had hurt Hank's feelings. But it didn't make any difference. My problems were almost over. Tomorrow I would be back in jail. It would be almost like going home again.

That night I couldn't sleep. After twisting and turning on the uncomfortable mattress until eleven, I gave up the battle and banged on the door for the nurse. The night nurse gave me a sleeping pill without any argument, but even then it was a long time before I got to sleep. The next morning Hank brought me my breakfast on a tray. If he was still sore at me he didn't give any indication of it.

'This'll be your last meal here, Harry,' he said, smiling.

'That's the best news I've had since I got here,' I said. 'Hank, I'm really sorry about not taking that drink you offered me yesterday. I was upset, nervous, and —'

'It doesn't bother me, Harry. I just thought you'd like a little shot.'

'After a man's been in this place a while, he gets so he doesn't trust anybody.'

'You're telling me!' He opened the door and looked down the corridor, turned and smiled broadly. 'I found out something for you, Harry. Last night I managed to get a look at your chart, and Dr. Fischbach is reporting you as absolutely sane. In his report he stated that you were completely in possession of your faculties when you croaked your girlfriend.'

'That's really good news. Maybe Dr. Fischbach's got

a few human qualities after all.'

'I thought it would make you happy,' Hank said pleasantly.

'What about the Sanity Board you were telling me about the other day? Won't I have to meet that?'

'Not as long as Fischbach says you're okay. He classified you as a neurotic depressive, which doesn't mean a damn thing. The Sanity Board is for those guys who have a reasonable doubt. You're all right.'

I tore into my breakfast with satisfaction. Now I could go back to the special block safe in the knowledge I would go to the gas chamber instead of the asylum. Hank was in a talkative mood and he chatted about hospital politics while I finished my breakfast, and brought me another cup of coffee when I asked for it.

'Now that I'm leaving, Hank,' I said 'tell me something. Why is it that I never get a hot cup of coffee? This is barely lukewarm.'

He laughed. 'I never give patients hot coffee. About two years ago I was taking a pot of hot coffee around the ward giving refills and I asked this guy if he wanted a second cup. "No," he says, so I said, "Not even a half a cup?" and he says, "Okay." So I pours about a half-cup and he says, "A little more." I pours a little more, and he says, "More yet." This time I filled his cup all the way. He reached out then, grabbed my waistband and dumped the whole cupful of hot coffee inside my pants! Liked to have ruined me. I was in bed for three days with second degree burns!'

I joined Hank in laughter, not because it was a funny story, but he told it so well. He finished with the punch line:

'Ever since then I've never given out with hot coffee.'

Hank lit my cigarette and we shook hands. He picked up my tray.

'I want to wish you the best of luck Harry,' he said at the door. 'You're one of the nicest guys we've had in here in a long time.'

'The same goes for you, Hank,' I said sincerely. 'You've

made it bearable for me and I want you to know I appreciate it.'

More than a little embarrassed, he turned away with the tray and walked out, leaving the door open. Smitty, another orderly, brought me my clothes and I changed into them quickly. Smitty unlocked the elevator and we rode down to the receiving entrance and I was turned over to a detective in a dark gray suit. I was handcuffed and returned to the jail in a police car instead of an ambulance. I was signed in at the jail and Mr. Benson returned me to my cell, my old cell.

Wearing my blue jail clothes again and stretched out on my bunk, I sighed with contentment. I speculated on how long it would be before the trial. It couldn't be too long, now that the returns were in; all I needed now, I supposed, was an open date on the court calendar. If I could occupy myself somehow, it would make the time pass faster. Maybe, if I asked Mr. Benson, he would get me a drawing pad and some charcoal sticks. I could do a few sketches to pass away the time. It was a better pastime than reading and it would be something to do.

That afternoon, right after lunch, I talked to Mr. Benson, and he said he would see what he could do ...

Chapter Nineteen

PORTRAIT OF A KILLER

It must have been about an hour after breakfast. The daily breakfast of two thick slices of bread and the big cup of black coffee didn't always set so well. Scrambled eggs, toast, and a glass of orange juice would have been better. No question about it; I had eaten better at the hospital. The two lumps of dough had absorbed the coffee and the mess felt like a full sponge in my stomach. Somebody was at my door and I looked up. It was Mr. Benson. He had a large drawing pad and a box of colored pencils in his hand. The old man was smiling and it revealed his worn down teeth, uppers and lowers. He stopped smiling the moment I looked at him.

'I bought you this stuff outta my own pocket,' he said gruffly. 'You can't lay around in here forever doin' nothin'.' He passed the pad and pencil box through the bars and I took them.

'Thanks a lot, Mr. Benson,' I said. 'How'd you think to have me do your portrait? That is, after I practice up a little.'

'You pretty good?'

'I used to be, and you've got an interesting face.'

'What do you mean by that!' He bridled.

'I mean I'd enjoy trying to draw you.'

'Oh.' His face flushed. 'I guess I wouldn't mind you doin' a picture of me. Maybe some time this afternoon?'

'Any time.'

I practiced and experimented with the colored pencils all morning, drawing cones, blocks, trying for perspective.

I would rather have had charcoal instead of colored pencils, I like it much better, but maybe the colored pencils gave me more things to do. The morning passed like a shot. I hadn't lost my touch; if anything, my hand was steadier than it had been before.

Mr. Benson held out until mid-afternoon, and then he brought a stool down the corridor and seated himself outside my cell. For some reason, a portrait, whether a plain drawing or a full-scale painting, is the most flattering thing you can do for a person. I've never met a person yet who didn't want an artist to paint his portrait. It is one of the holdovers from the nineteenth century that enables artists who go for that sort of thing to eat. A simple drawing, or a painting should always be done from life to be worthwhile. But this doesn't prevent an organization in New York from making thousands of dollars weekly by having well-known artists paint portraits from photographs that are sent in from all over the United States. If the person has enough money, all he has to do is state what artist he wants and send in his photographs. The artists who do this type of work are a hell of a lot hungrier for money than I ever was.

I didn't spend much time with Mr. Benson. I did a profile view and by doing a profile it is almost impossible not to get a good likeness. By using black, coral, and a white pencil for the highlights, I got the little drawing turned out well and Mr. Benson was more than pleased.

'What do I owe you, Harry?' he asked, after I tore the drawing from the pad and gave it to him.

'Nothing.' I laughed. 'You're helping me kill time, and besides, you bought me the pad and pencils.'

'How about a dollar?'

'No.' I shook my head. 'Nothing.'

'Suit yourself.' He picked up his stool and left happily with his picture.

Mr. Benson must have spread the word or showed his picture around. In the next three days I did several more drawings. Detectives came up to see me and they would sit belligerently, trying to cover their embarrassment while

I whipped out a fast profile. They all offered me money, which I didn't accept, but I never refused a pack of cigarettes. The last portrait I did was that of a young girl. She was one of the stenos from the filing department, well-liked by Mr. Benson, and he let her in. She was very nervous and twitched on the stool while I did a three-quarter view. I suppose she was curious to see what I looked like, more than anything else, but it didn't matter to me. Drawing was a time-killer to me. I gave her a completed drawing and she hesitated outside my cell.

'You haven't been reading the papers have you, ah, Mr. Jordan?' she asked nervously.

'No.'

She was about twenty-one or -two with thin blonde hair, glasses, and a green faille suit. Her figure was slim, almost slight, and she twisted her long, slender fingers nervously. 'I don't know whether to tell you or not, but seeing you don't read the papers, maybe I'd better ...'

'Tell me what?' I asked gently.

'Oh, it just makes me sore, that's all!' She said spiritedly. 'These detectives! Here you've been decent enough to draw their pictures for nothing, and they've been selling them to the newshawks in the building. All of the papers have been running cuts, and these detectives have been getting ten dollars or more from the reporters.'

'The reporters have been getting gypped then,' I said, controlling my sudden anger.

'Well I think it's dirty, Mr. Jordan, and I just wanted you to know that I'm going to keep my picture.'

'That's fine. Just tell Mr. Benson I'm not doing any more portraits. Tell him on your way out, will you please?'

'All right. Don't tell anybody I told you ... huh?'

'No, I won't say anything. I'm not sore about them selling the pictures,' I told her. 'It's just that they aren't good enough for publication.'

'*I* think they are.' She gave me two packages of Camels and tripped away down the corridor. At first I was angry and then I had to laugh at the irony of the situation. Ten dollars. Nobody had ever paid me ten dollars for a picture. Of course, I had never priced a painting that low. The few I had exhibited, in the Chicago student shows, had all been priced at three hundred or more dollars, and none of them had sold. But anyway, no more portraits from Harry Jordan. The cheap Harry Jordan integrity would be upheld until the last sniff of cyanide gas ... Again I laughed.

The following afternoon, Mr. Benson opened the cell door and beckoned to me. He led me through a couple of corridors and into a small room sparsely furnished with a bare scratched desk, a couple of wooden chairs and, surprisingly, a leather couch without arms, but hinged at one end so that the head of it could be raised. It was the kind of couch you sometimes see in psychiatrists' offices and doctors' examining rooms.

'What's this?' I said.

'Examining room,' he said, as I'd expected. I started to get angry. He left the room, moving rather furtively, I thought, and he shut the door, locking it on the outside. After a couple of minutes the door opened again. It was that stenographer.

She walked in, her arms full of the drawing stuff I had left in my cell. The door closed behind her and I heard the lock click again, shutting us in. I couldn't figure it out.

She was looking at me, kind of breathlessly. She put the colored pencils and stuff down on the desk. 'I want you to draw me again,' she said.

'I don't know as I want to do any more drawing.'

'Please.'

'Why in here?'

'You don't understand. I want you to draw me in the nude.'

I looked at her. It was warm in the room, and there was plenty of light streaming in from the high, barred windows. The bars threw interesting shadows across her body. It was a good place to draw or paint, all right. But that wasn't what she wanted. I knew that much.

I sat woodenly. She laughed, kicked off her shoes, lay back on the couch. I could tell she was a little scared of me, but liking it. 'I'll be pretty in the nude,' she said. 'I'll be wonderful to draw.' She lifted a long and delicately formed leg and drew off the stocking. She did the same for her other leg. I could see that her thighs were a trifle plump. They were creamy-white, soft-looking, but the rest of her legs, especially around the knees, were faintly rosy.

She flicked a glance at me, to see what my response was. I had not moved. I was just standing there, watching. She stood up, made an eager, ungraceful gesture that unloosed a clasp, or a zipper or something. Her skimpy green skirt fell to the floor. She hesitated then, like a girl about to plunge into a cold shower, but took a deep breath, then quickly undid her blouse. It fell to the floor with the skirt. Another moment and her slip was off, and the wisps of nylon that were her underthings. I smelled their faint perfume in the warm room. She lifted her arms over her head and pirouetted proudly. 'See?' she said. 'See?'

I had not noticed before, even when I had been drawing her, how pretty she was. Maybe she was the kind of girl whose beauty only awakes when her clothes are off. I examined her thoughtfully, trying to think of her as a problem in art. Long legs. Plump around the hips and thighs. Narrow, long waist. Jutting bosom, a trifle too soft, too immature. Her face was narrow and bony, but attractive enough. The lips were full and red. Her corn-colored hair fell in a graceful line to her shoulders.

'You fixed this up?' I said.

She was tense and excited. 'Me and Mr. Benson,' she said. 'Nobody will bother us here.' She giggled.

This would be the last time, I was thinking. I would never have another chance at a woman. Not on this earth.

'Don't look so surprised,' she said. 'All kinds of things go on in a place like this. It's just a question of how much money and influence a person has. You don't have money, and neither do I — but I've got the influence —' She giggled again. Like a high school kid. Was this her first adventure with a man, I wondered.

I sat down on the hard leather couch.

'Come here,' I said.

She sat down on my lap.

I started by kissing her. First her silky hair. Then her soft parted lips. Then her neck, her shoulders, lower ...
'Harry,' she said. 'Harry!'

My arm was around her waist, and her skin felt creamy and smooth. I tilted her back, swinging her off my knees so that she lay supine on the couch. I stroked and kissed and fondled, slowly and easily at first, then faster and harder. Much harder. She began to breathe deeply. She was scared. I kissed her neck, at the same time taking her by the hair and drawing her head back.

'Harry,' she said. 'What are you going to do to me?'

'You're frightened, aren't you? That's part of the thrill. That's what you want, isn't it? To do it with a freak. A dangerous freak. And a murderer!'

'I want you, Harry!'

She was panting. She threw her arms around me, and her nails clawed my shoulders. It was my head that was pulled down now, and she was smothering me with lipstick and feverish kisses. This was the moment I had been waiting for. The moment when she would be craving ecstasy. I lifted my hand and, as hard as I could, slapped her in the face.

But instead of looking at me with consternation and fear and disappointment, she giggled. Damn her, in her eyes I was just living up to expectations. This was what she had come for!

In cold disgust, I hit her with my fist, splitting her lip so that the blood ran. The blow rolled her from the couch to the floor. For a moment I pitied her bare, crumpled body, but as soon as the breath got back into her she sprang to her feet. I was standing now, too. She flung her arms around me in a desperate embrace. 'I can't bear it. Please, Harry!'

I knocked her down again.

'Please, Harry! Now ... Now ...!'

'You slut. I loved a real woman. To her, I was no strange, freakish creature. She didn't come to me for cheap thrills. Get your clothes on!'

I picked up one of the chairs and swung at the door with it.

'Let me out of here,' I shouted, pounding the door. 'God damn it, let me out!'

Mr. Benson came, and shamefacedly opened the door. The girl, her clothes on, ran sobbing down the corridor. Mr. Benson looked at me.

'I'm sorry, Harry. I thought I was doing you a favor.'

I never did find out the girl's name.

The next day was Sunday. After a heavy lunch of baked swordfish and boiled potatoes I fell asleep on my bunk for a little afternoon nap. The jailer aroused me by reaching through the bars and jerking on my foot. It wasn't Mr. Benson; it was the Sunday man, Mr. Paige.

'Come on, Jordan,' he said, 'wake up. You gotta visitor.' Mr. Paige sold men's suits during the week, but he was a member of the Police Reserve, and managed to pick up extra money during the month by getting an active duty day of pay for Sunday work. At least, that is what Mr. Benson told me.

'I'm too sleepy for visitors,' I grumbled, still partly asleep. 'Who is it anyway?'

'It's a woman,' he said softly, 'a Mrs. Mathews.' I could tell by the expression on his face and his tone of voice he knew Mrs. Mathews was Helen's mother. 'Do you want to see her?'

I got off the bed in a hurry. No. Of course I didn't want to see her. But that wasn't the point. She wanted to see me and I couldn't very well refuse. She had every right to see the murderer of her daughter.

'Do you know what she wants to see me about?' I asked Mr. Paige.

He shook his head. 'All I know, she's got a pass from the D.A. Even so, if you don't want, you don't have to talk to her.'

'I guess it's all right. Give me a light.' He lit my cigarette for me and I took several fast drags, hoping the smoke would dissipate my drowsiness. Smoking, I stood close to

the barred doors, listening nervously for the sound of Mrs.
Mathews' footsteps in the corridor. And I heard her long
before I saw her. Her step was strong, resolute,
purposeful. And she appeared in front of the door, Mr.
Paige, the jailer, behind her and slightly to one side.

'Here's Harry Jordan, ma'am. You can't go inside the
cell, but you can talk to him for five minutes.' I was
grateful for the time limit Mr. Paige arbitrarily imposed.
He turned away, walked a few steps down the corridor,
out of earshot, beyond my range of vision.

Mrs. Mathews was wearing that same beaver coat, black
walking shoes, and a green felt, off-the-face hat. Her gray
hair was gathered and piled in a knot on the back of her
neck. She glared at me through her gold-rimmed glasses.
Her full lips curled back, showing her teeth, in a scornful,
sneering grimace of disgust. There was a bright gleam of
hatred in her eyes, the unreasoning kind of hate one
reserves for a dangerous animal, or a loose snake. She
made me extremely nervous, looking at me that way. My
hands were damp and I took them away from the bars,
wiped my palms on my shirt. As tightly as I could, I
gripped the bars again.

'It was nice of you to come and visit me, Mrs. Mathews...'
I said haltingly. She didn't reply to my opening remark
and I didn't know what else to say. But I tried.

'I'm sorry things turned out the way they did,' I said
humbly, 'but I want you to know that Helen was in full
accord with what I did. It was the way Helen wanted it ...'
My throat was tight, like somebody was holding my wind-
pipe, and I had to force the words out of my mouth. 'If we
had it all to do over again, maybe things would have
worked out differently ...'

Mrs. Mathews worked her mouth in and out, pursed
her lips.

'I've pleaded guilty, and —' I didn't get to finish my
sentence.

Without warning, Mrs. Mathews spat into my face.
Involuntarily, I jerked back from the bars. Ordinarily, a
woman is quite awkward when she tries to spit. Mrs.

Mathews was not. The wet, disgusting spittle struck my forehead, right above my eyebrows. I made no attempt to wipe it off, but came forward again, and tightly gripped the bars. I waited patiently for a stream of invective to follow, but it didn't come. Mrs. Mathews glared at me for another long moment, sniffed, jerked her head to the right, turned and lumbered away.

I sat down on my bunk, wiped off my face with the back of my hand. My legs and hands were trembling and I was as weak as if I had climbed out of a hot Turkish bath.

My mind didn't function very well. Maybe I had it coming to me. At least in her eyes, I did. I didn't know what to think. The viciousness and sudden fury of her pointless action had taken me completely by surprise. But how many times must I be punished before I was put to death? I don't believe I was angry, not even bitter. There was a certain turmoil inside my chest, but it was caused mostly by my reaction to her intense hatred of me. In addition to my disgust and loathing for the woman I also managed to feel sorry for her and I suspected she would suffer later for her impulsive action. After she reflected, perhaps shame would come and she would regret her impulsiveness. It was like kicking an unconscious man in the face. But on the other hand, she had probably planned what she would do for several days. I didn't want to think about it. Mr. Paige was outside the door and there was a contrite expression on his face.

'She didn't stay long,' he said.

'No. She didn't.'

'I saw what she did,' Mr. Paige said indignantly. 'If I'd have known what she was up to I wouldn't have let her in, even if she did have a pass from the D.A.'

'That's all right, Mr. Paige. I don't blame you; I don't blame anybody. But if she comes back, don't let her in again. I don't want to see her any more. My life is too short.'

'Don't worry, Jordan. She won't get in again!' He said this positively. He walked away and I was alone. I washed my face with the brown soap and cold water in my wash basin a dozen times, but my face still felt dirty.

The next day my appetite was off. I tried to draw something, anything, to pass the time away, but I couldn't keep my mind on it. Mr. Paige had told Mr. Benson what had happened and he had tried to talk to me about it, and I cut him off quickly. I didn't feel like talking. I lay on my back all day long, smoking cigarettes, one after another, and looking at the ceiling.

On Tuesday, I had another visitor. Mr. Benson appeared outside my cell with a well-fed man wearing a brown gabardine Brooks Brothers suit and a blue satin vest. His face was lobster red and his larynx gave him trouble when he talked. Mr. Benson opened the door and let the man into my cell.

'This is Mr. Dorrell, Jordan,' the old jailer said. 'He's an editor from *He-Men Magazine* and he's got an okay from the D.A.'s office so I gotta let him in for ten minutes.'

'All right,' I said, and I didn't move from my reclining position. There were no stools or chairs and Mr. Dorrell had to stand. 'What can I do for you, Mr. Dorrell?' I asked.

'I'm from *He-Men*, Mr. Jordan,' he began in his throaty voice. 'And our entire editorial staff is interested in your case. To get directly to the point — we want an "as-told-to" story from you, starting right at the beginning of your, ah, relationship with Mrs. Meredith.'

'No. That's impossible.'

'No,' he smiled, 'it isn't impossible. There is a lot of interest for people when a woman as prominent in society as Mrs. Meredith, gets, shall we say, involved?'

'Helen wasn't prominent in society.'

'Maybe not, not as you and I know it, Mr. Jordan. But certain places, like Biarritz, for instance, Venice, and in California, San Sienna, are very romantic watering places. And the doings of their inhabitants interests our readers very much.'

'My answer is no.'

'We'll pay you one thousand dollars for such an article.'

'I don't want a thousand dollars.'

'You might need it.'

'What for?'

'Money comes in handy sometimes,' he croaked, 'and the public has a right to know about your case.'

'Why do they?' I asked belligerently. 'It's nobody's business but my own!'

'Suppose you consider the offer and let us know later?'

'No. I won't even consider it. I don't blame you, Mr. Dorrell. You've got a job to do. And I suppose your readers would get a certain amount of morbid enjoyment from my unhappy plight, and possibly more copies of your magazine would be bought. But I can't allow myself to sell such a story. It's impossible.'

'Well, I won't say anything more.' Mr. Dorrell took a card out of his wallet, and handed it to me. 'If you happen to change your mind, send me a wire. Send it collect, and I'll send a feature writer to see you and he'll bring you a check, in advance.'

At the door he called for Mr. Benson. The jailer let him out of the cell and locked the door again. The two of them chatted as they walked down the corridor and I tore the business card into several small pieces and threw them on the floor. If Mr. Dorrell had been disappointed by my refusal he certainly didn't show it. What kind of a world did I live in, anyway? Everybody seemed to believe that money was everything, that it could buy integrity, brains, art, and now a man's soul. I had never had a thousand dollars at one time in my entire life. And now, when I had an opportunity to have that much money, I was in a position to turn it down. It made me feel better and I derived a certain satisfaction from the fact that I could turn it down. In my present position, I could afford to turn down ten thousand, a million ...

I didn't eat any supper that evening. After drinking the black coffee I tried to sleep but all night long I rolled and tossed on my narrow bunk. From time to time I dozed, but I always awakened with a start, and my heart would violently pound. There was a dream after me, a bad dream, and my sleeping mind wouldn't accept it. I was

grateful when morning came at last. I knew it was
morning, because Mr. Benson brought my breakfast.

After breakfast, when I took my daily shower, I noticed
the half-smile on the old jailer's face. He gave me my
razor, handing it in to me as I stood under the hot water,
and not only did I get a few extra minutes in the shower, I
got a better shave with the hot water. As I toweled myself
I wondered what was behind the old man's smile.

'What's the joke, Mr. Benson?' I asked.

'I've got news for you, Jordan, but I don't know whether
it's good or bad.' His smile broadened.

'What news?'

'You're being tried today.'

'It's good news.'

He brought me my own clothes and I put them on, tied
my necktie as carefully as I could without a mirror. I had
to wait in my cell for about a half-hour and then I was
handcuffed and taken down to the receiving office and
checked out. My stuff was returned and I signed the envelope to show that I had gotten it back. All of it. Button,
piece of string, handkerchief, and parking stub from the
Continental Garage. As the detective and I started toward
the parking ramp the desk sergeant called out to the
officer. We paused.

'He's minimum security, Jeff.'

Jeff removed the handcuffs and we climbed into the
waiting police car for the short drive to the Court House.

Chapter Twenty

TRIAL

I was in a small room adjacent to the courtroom. It was sparsely furnished; just a small chipped wooden table against the wall and four metal chairs. I stood by the window, looking down three stories at the gray haze of fog that palled down over the civic center. A middle-aged uniformed policeman was stationed in the room to stand guard over me, and he leaned against the wall by the door, picking at the loose threads of the buttonholes in his shiny navy blue serge uniform. There was nothing much to see out of the window, only the fog, the dim outlines of automobiles with their lights on, and in the street below, a few walking figures, their sex indistinguishable, but I looked out because it was a window and I hadn't been in a room with a window for a long time. One at a time I pulled at my fingers, cracking the joints. The middle finger of my left hand made the loudest crack.

'Don't do that,' the policeman said. 'I can't stand it. And besides, cracking your knuckles makes them swell.'

I stopped popping my fingers and put my hands in my trousers pockets. That didn't feel right, so I put my hands in my jacket pockets. This was worse. I let my arms hang, swinging them back and forth like useless pendula. I didn't want to smoke because my mouth and throat were too dry, but I got a light from the policeman and inhaled the smoke into my lungs, even though it tasted like scraped bone dust. Before I finished the cigarette there was a hard rapping on the door and the policeman opened it.

A round, overweight man with a shiny bald head

bounced into the room. He didn't come into the room, he 'came on,' like a TV master of ceremonies. There was a hearty falseness to the broad smile on his round face and his eyes were black and glittering, almost hidden by thick, sagging folds of flesh. His white hands were short, white, and puffy, and the scattering of paprika freckles made them look unhealthily pale. I almost expected him to say, 'A funny thing happened to me on the way over to the court house today,' but instead of saying anything he burst into a contagious, raucous, guffawing laugh that reverberated in the silence of the little room. It was the type of laughter that is usually infectious, but in my solemn frame of mind I didn't feel like joining him. After a moment he stopped abruptly, wiped his dry face with a white handkerchief.

'You are Harry Jordan!' He pointed a blunt fat finger at me.

'Yes, sir,' I said.

'I'm Larry Hingen-Bergen.' He unbuttoned his double-breasted tweed coat and sat down at the little table. He threw his battered briefcase on the table before him and indicated, by pointing to another chair that he wanted me to sit down. I pulled up a chair, sat down and faced him diagonally. 'I'm your defense counsel, Jordan, appointed by the court. I suppose you wonder why I haven't been to see you before this?' he closed his eyes, while he waited for my answer.

'No. Not particularly, Mr. Hingen-Bergen. After I told the District Attorney I was guilty, I didn't think I'd need a defense counsel.'

His eyes snapped open, glittering. 'And you don't!' He guffawed loudly, with false heartiness. 'And you don't!' He let the laugh loose again, slapped his heavy thigh with his hand. 'You!' He pointed his finger at my nose, 'are a very lucky boy! In fact,' his expression sobered, 'I don't know how to tell you how lucky you are. You're going to be a free man, Jordan.'

'What's that?' I asked stupidly.

'Free. Here's the story.' He related it in a sober, business-like manner. 'I was assigned to your case about two weeks ago, Jordan. Naturally, the first thing I did was have a little talk with Mr. Seely. You remember him?'

I nodded. 'The Assistant D.A.'

'My visit happened to coincide with the day the medical report came in. Now get a grip on yourself, boy. Helen Meredith was not choked to death, as you claimed; she died a natural death!' He took a small notebook out of his pocket. It was a long and narrow notebook, fastened at the top, covered with green imitation snakeskin, the kind insurance salesmen give away whether you buy any insurance or not. I sat dazed, tense, leaning forward slightly while he leafed through the little book. 'Here it is,' he said, smiling. 'Coronary thrombosis. Know what that is?'

'It isn't true!' I exclaimed.

He gripped my arm with his right hand, his voice softened. 'I'm afraid it is true, Jordan. Of course, there were bruises on her neck and throat where your hands had been, but that's all they were. Bruises. She actually died from a heart attack. Did she ever tell you she had a bad heart?'

I shook my head, scarcely hearing the question. 'No. No, she didn't. Her mother said something about it once, but I didn't pay much attention at the time. And I can't believe this, Mr. Hingen-Bergen. She was always real healthy; why she didn't hardly get a hangover when she drank.'

'I'm not making this up, Jordan.' He tapped the notebook with the back of his fat fingers. 'This was the Medical Examiner's report. Right from the M.E.'s autopsy. There's no case against you at all. Now, the reason the D.A. didn't tell you about this was because he wanted to get a full psychiatrist's report first.' Mr. Hingen-Bergen laughed, but it was a softer laugh, kind. 'You *might* have been insane, you know. He had to find out before he could release you.'

My mind still wouldn't accept the situation. 'But if I didn't actually kill her, Mr. Hingen-Bergen, I must have at least hastened her death! And if so, that makes me guilty, doesn't it?'

'No,' he replied flatly. 'She'd have died anyway. I read the full M.E. report. She was in pretty bad shape. Malnutrition, I don't remember what all. You didn't have anything to do with her death.'

The middle-aged policeman had been attentively following the conversation. 'By God,' he remarked, 'this is an interesting case, Mr. Hingen-Bergen!'

'Isn't it?' The fat lawyer smiled at him. He turned to me again. 'Now, Jordan, we're going into the court room and Mr. Seely will present the facts to the judge. He'll move for a dismissal of the charges and you'll be free to go.'

'Go where?' My mind was in a turmoil.

'Why, anywhere you want to go, naturally. You'll be a free man! Why, this is the easiest case I've ever had. Usually my clients go to jail!' He laughed boisterously and the policeman joined him. 'You just sit tight, Jordan, and the bailiff'll call you in a few minutes.' He picked his briefcase up from the table and left the room.

I remained in my chair, my mind numb. If this was true, and evidently it was — the lawyer wouldn't lie to me right before the trial — I hadn't done anything! Not only had I fumbled my own suicide, I'd fumbled Helen's death too. I could remember the scene so vividly. I could remember the feel of her throat beneath my thumbs, and the anguish I had undergone ... and all of it for nothing. Nothing. I covered my face with my hands. I felt a hand on my shoulder. It was the policeman's hand and he tried to cheer me up.

'Why, hell, boy,' he said friendly, 'don't take it so hard. You're lucky as hell. Here ...' I dropped my hands to my lap. The policeman held out a package of cigarettes. 'Take one.' I took one and he lighted it for me. 'You don't want to let this prey on your mind. You've got a chance to start your life all over again. Take it. Be grateful for it.'

'It was quite a shock. I wasn't ready for it.'

'So what? You're out of it, forget it. Better pull yourself together. You'll be seeing the judge pretty soon.'

The bailiff and Mr. Hingen-Bergen came for me and took me into the court room. I'd never seen a regular trial before. All I knew about court room procedure was what I had seen in movies; and movie trials are highly dramatic, loud voices, screaming accusations, bawling witnesses, things like that. This was unlike anything I'd ever seen before. Mr. Hingen-Bergen and I joined the group at the long table. The judge sat at the end wearing his dark robes. And he was a young man, not too many years past thirty; he didn't look as old as Mr. Seely. Mr. Seely sat next to the judge, his face incompliant behind his glasses. It was a large room, not a regular courtroom, and there were no spectators. A male stenographer, in his early twenties, made a fifth at the table. The bailiff leaned against the door, smoking a pipe.

Mr. Seely and the judge carried on what seemed to be a friendly conversation. I didn't pay any attention to what they were saying; I was waiting for the trial to get started.

'The Medical Examiner couldn't make it, Your Honor,' Mr. Seely said quietly to the judge, 'but here's his report, if that's satisfactory.'

There was a long period of silence while the judge studied the typewritten sheets. The judge slid the report across the desk to Mr. Seely, and the Assistant District Attorney put it back inside his new cowhide briefcase. The judge pursed his lips and looked at me for a moment, nodding his head up and down soberly.

'I believe you're right, Mr. Seely,' he said softly. 'There's really no point in holding the defendant any longer. The case is dismissed.' He got to his feet, rested his knuckles on the desk and stared at me. I thought he was going to say something to me, but he didn't. He gathered his robes about him, lifting the hems clear of the floor, and Mr. Hingen-Bergen and I stood up. He left the courtroom by a side door. Mr. Seely walked around the table and shook hands with me.

'I've got some advice for you, Jordan,' Mr. Seely said brusquely. 'Keep away from liquor, and see if you can find another city to live in.'

'Yes, sir,' I said.

'That's good advice,' Mr. Hingen-Bergen added.

'Of course,' Mr. Seely amended gravely, 'you don't *have* to leave San Francisco. Larry can tell you that.' He looked sideways at my fat defense counsel. 'You're free to live any place you want to, but I believe my advice is sound.'

'You bet!' Mr. Hingen-Bergen agreed. 'Especially, not drinking. You might end up in jail again if you go on a bat.'

'Thanks a lot,' I said vaguely.

I didn't know what to do with myself. Mr. Seely and the bailiff followed the young stenographer out of the room and I was still standing behind the table with Mr. Hingen-Bergen. He was stuffing some papers into various compartments of his briefcase. I had been told what to do and when to do it for so long I suppose I was waiting for somebody to tell me when to leave.

'Ready to go, Jordan?' Mr. Hingen-Bergen asked me, as he hooked the last strap on his worn leather bag.

'Don't I have to sign something?' It all seemed too unreal to me.

'Nope. That's it. You've had it.'

'Then I guess I'm ready to go.'

'Fine. I'll buy you a cup of coffee.'

I shook my head. 'No thanks. I don't believe I want one.'

'Suit yourself. What are your plans?'

Again I shook my head bewilderedly. 'I don't know. This thing's too much of a surprise. I still can't grasp it or accept it, much less formulate plans.'

'You'll be all right.' He laughed his coarse hearty laugh. 'Come on.'

Mr. Hingen-Bergen took my arm and we left the court room, rode the elevator down to the main floor. We stood on the marble floor of the large entrance way and he pointed to the outside door, the steep flight of stairs leading down to the street level.

'There you are, Jordan,' the lawyer smiled. 'The city.'

I nodded, turned away and started down the steps. Because of the heavy fog I could only see a few feet ahead of me. I heard footsteps behind me and turned as Mr.

Hingen-Bergen called out my name.

'Have you got any money?' the lawyer asked me kindly.

'No, sir.'

'Here.' He handed me a five dollar bill. 'This'll help you get started maybe.'

I accepted the bill, folded it, put it into my watch pocket.

'I don't know when I'll be able to pay you back ...' I said lamely.

'Forget it! Next time you get in jail, just look me up!' He laughed boisterously, clapped me on the shoulder and puffed up the stairs into the court house.

I continued slowly down the steps and when I reached the sidewalk, turned left toward Market. I was a free man.

Or was I?

Chapter Twenty-One

FROM HERE TO ETERNITY

After I left the Court House I walked for several blocks before I realized I was walking aimlessly and without a destination in mind. So much had happened unexpectedly I was in a daze. The ugly word, 'Freedom' overlapped and crowded out any nearly rational thoughts that tried to cope with it. Freedom meant nothing to me. After the time I had spent in jail and in the hospital, not only was I reconciled to the prospect of death, I had eagerly looked forward to it. I wanted to die and I deserved to die. But I was an innocent man. I was free. I was free to wash dishes again, free to smash baggage, carry a waiter's tray, dish up chilli beans as a counterman. Free.

The lights on the marquee up ahead advertised two surefire movies. Two old Humphrey Bogart pictures. It was the Bijou Theatre and I had reached Benny's Bijou Beanery. This was where it had started. I looked through the dirty glass of the window. Benny sat in his customary seat behind the cash register and as I watched him he reached into the large jar of orange gum drops on the counter and popped one into his mouth. The café was well-filled, most of the stools taken and two countermen were working behind the counter. Just to see the café brought back a vivid memory of Helen and the way she looked and laughed the night she first entered. I turned away and a tear escaped my right eye and rolled down my cheek. A passerby gave me a sharp look. I wiped my eyes with the back of my hand and entered the next bar I came to. Tears in a bar are not unusual.

The clock next to the mouldy deer antlers over the mirror read ten-fifty-five. Except for two soldiers and a B-girl between them, the bar was deserted. I went to the far end and sat down.

'Two ounces of gin and a slice of lemon,' I told the bartender.

'No chaser?'

'Better give me a little ice water.'

I was in better physical condition than I had enjoyed in two or three years, but after my layoff I expected the first drink to hit me like a sledge hammer. There was no effect. The gin rolled down my throat like a sweet cough syrup with a codeine base. I didn't need the lemon or the water.

'Give me another just like it,' I said to the bartender.

After three more my numb feeling disappeared. I wasn't drunk, but my head was clear and I was able to think again. Not that it made any difference, because nothing mattered anymore. I unfolded the five dollar bill Mr. Hingen-Bergen had given me, paid for the drinks and returned to the street. There was a cable car dragging up the hill and it slowed down at my signal. I leaped aboard for the familiar ride to my old neighborhood and the rooming house. I could no longer think of the ride as going home. Although the trip took a long while it seemed much too short. At my corner, I jumped down.

The well-remembered sign, BIG MIKE'S BAR & GRILL, the twisted red neon tubing, glowed and hummed above the double doors of the saloon. This was really my home, mine and Helen's. This was where we had spent our only really happy hours; hours of plain sitting, drinking, with our shoulders touching. Hours of looking into each other's eyes in the bar mirror. As I stood there, looking at the entrance, the image of Helen's loveliness was vivid in my mind.

Rodney, the crippled newsboy, left his pile of papers and limped toward me. There was surprise in his tired face and eyes.

'Hello Harry,' he said, stretching out his arm. I shook his hand.

'Hello, Rodney.'

'You got out of it, huh?'

'Yes.'

'Congratulations, Harry. None of us around here really expected you — I mean, well ...' His voice trailed off.

'That's all right, Rodney. It was all a mistake and I don't want to talk about it.'

'Sure, Harry. I'm glad you aren't guilty.' Self-conscious, he bobbed his head a couple of times and returned to his newspapers. I pushed through the swinging doors and took the first empty seat at the bar. It was lunch hour and the bar and café were both busy; most of the stools were taken and all of the booths. As soon as he saw me, Big Mike left the cash register and waddled toward me.

'The usual, Harry?' he asked me quietly.

'No. I don't want a drink.'

Mike's face was unfathomable and I didn't know how he would take the news.

'I didn't kill her, Mike. Helen died a natural death. It was a mistake. That's all.'

'I'm glad.' His broad face was almost stern. 'Let's have one last drink together, Harry,' he said, 'and then, I think it would be better if you did your drinking somewhere else.'

'Sure, Mike. I understand.'

He poured a jigger of gin for me and a short draught beer for himself. I downed the shot quickly, nodded briefly and left the bar. So Big Mike was glad. Everybody was glad, everybody was happy, everybody except me.

The overcast had yarded down thickly and now was a dark billowing fog. Soon it would drizzle, and then it would rain. I turned up my coat collar and put my head down. I didn't want to talk to anybody else. On my way to Mrs. McQuade's I had to pass several familiar places. The A & P, the Spotless Cleaners, Mr. Watson's delicatessen; all of those stores held people who knew me well. I pulled my collar up higher and put my head down lower.

When I reached the rooming house I climbed the front outside steps and walked down the hall to Mrs.

McQuade's door. I tapped twice and waited. As soon as she opened the door, Mrs. McQuade recognized me and clapped her hand to her mouth.

'It's quite all right, Mrs. McQuade,' I said, 'I'm a free man.'

'Please come in, Mr. Jordan.'

Her room was much too warm for me. I removed my jacket, sat down in a rocker and lit one of my cigarettes to detract from the musty, close smell of the hot room. The old lady with blue hair sat down across from me in a straight-backed chair and folded her hands in her lap.

'It'll probably be in tonight's paper, Mrs. McQuade, but I didn't kill Helen. She died from a heart attack. A quite natural death. I didn't have anything to do with it.'

'I'm not surprised.' She nodded knowingly. 'You both loved each other too much.'

'Yes. We did.'

Mrs. McQuade began to cry soundlessly. Her eyes searched the room, found her purse. She opened it and removed a Kleenex and blew her nose with a gentle, refined honk.

'How about Helen's things?' I asked. 'Are they still here?'

'No. Her mother, Mrs. Mathews, took them. If I'd known that you ... well, I didn't know, and she's Helen's mother, so when she wanted them, I helped her pack the things and she took them with her. There wasn't much, you know. That suitcase, now; I didn't know whether it was yours or Helen's so I let Mrs. Mathews take it.'

'How about the portrait?'

'Mr. Endo was keeping it in his room. He wasn't here, but when she asked for it, I got it out of his room. She burned it up ... in the incinerator. As I say, I didn't —'

'That's all right. I'd have liked to have had it, but it doesn't matter. Is there anything of hers at all?'

'Not a thing, Mr. Jordan. Just a minute.' The old lady got out of her chair and opened the closet. She rummaged around in the small dark room. 'These are yours.' She brought forth my old trenchcoat and a gray laundry bag. I spread the trenchcoat on the floor and dumped the contents of the bag onto it. There were two dirty white shirts, four dirty T-shirts, four pairs of dirty drawers, six pairs of black socks and two soiled handkerchiefs.

At the bottom of the bag I saw my brushes and tubes of paint, and I could feel the tears coming into my eyes. She hadn't thrown them out after all; she still had had faith in me as an artist!

Mrs. McQuade pretended not to notice my choked emotion.

'If I'd known you were going to be released I'd have had these things laundered, Mr. Jordan.'

'That's not important, Mrs. McQuade. I owe you some money, don't I?'

'Not a thing. Mrs. Mathews paid the room rent, and if you want the room you can have it back.'

'No, thanks. I'm leaving San Francisco, I think it's best.'

'Where are you going?'

'I don't know yet.'

'Well, when you get settled, you'd better write me so I can forward your mail.'

'There won't be any mail.' I got out of the chair, slipped my jacket on, then the trenchcoat.

'You can keep that laundry bag, Mr. Jordan. Seeing I gave away your suitcase I can give you that much, at least.'

'Thank you.'

'Would you like a cup of coffee? I can make some in a second.'

'No, thanks.'

I threw the light bag over my shoulder and Mrs. McQuade opened the door for me. We shook hands and she led the way down the hall to the outside door. It was raining.

'Don't you have a hat, Mr. Jordan?'

'No. I never wear a hat.'

'That's right. Come to think of it, I've never seen you with a hat.'

I walked down the steps to the street and into the rain.

A wind came up and the rain slanted sideways, coming down at an angle of almost thirty degrees. Two blocks away I got under the awning of a drug store. It wasn't letting up any; if anything, it was coming down harder. I left the shelter of the awning and walked up the hill in the rain.

Just a tall, lonely Negro.

Walking in the rain.

The End

THE BURNT ORANGE
HERESY

For the late, great Jacques Debierue c. 1886–1970
Memoria in aeterna

Nothing exists,
If anything exists, it is incomprehensible,
If anything was comprehensible,
it would be incommunicable.

Gorgias

Part One

Nothing exists.

Chapter One

Two hours ago the Railway Expressman delivered the crated, newly published *International Encyclopedia of Fine Arts* to my Palm Beach apartment. I signed for the set, turned the thermostat of the air-conditioner up three degrees, found a clawhammer in the kitchen, and broke open the crate. Twenty-four beautiful buckram-bound volumes, eggshell paper, deckle edged. Six laborious years in preparation, more than twenty-five hundred illustrations — 436 in full-color plates — and each thoroughly researched article written and signed by a noted authority in his specific field of art history.

Two articles were mine. And my name, James Figueras, was also referred to by other critics in three more articles. By quoting me, they gained authoritative support for their own opinions.

In my limited visionary world, the world of art criticism, where there are fewer than twenty-five men — and no women — earning their bread as full-time art critics (art reviewers for newspapers don't count), my name as an authority in this definitive encyclopedia means Success with an uppercase S. I thought about it for a moment. Only twenty-five full-time art critics in America, out of a population of more than two hundred million? This is a small number, indeed, of men who are able to look at art and understand it, and then interpret it in writing in such a way that those who care can share the aesthetic experience.

Clive Bell claimed that art was 'significant form.' I have no quarrel with that, but he never carried his thesis out to its obvious conclusion. It is the critic who makes the form(s) significant to the viewer! In seven more months I will reach my thirty-fifth birthday. I am the youngest authority with signed articles in the new *Encyclopedia,* and, I realized at that moment, if I lived long enough I had every opportunity of becoming the greatest art critic in America — and perhaps the world. With tenderness, I removed the heavy volumes from the crate and lined them up on my desk.

The complete set, if ordered by subscribers in advance of the announced publication date — and most universities, colleges, and larger public libraries would take advantage of the prepublication offer — sold for $350, plus shipping charges. After publication date, the *Encyclopedia* would sell for $500, with the option of buying an annual volume on the art of that year for only $10 (same good paper, same attractive binding).

It goes without saying, inasmuch as my field is contemporary art, that my name will appear in all of those yearbooks.

I had read the page proofs months before, of course, but I slowly reread my 1,600-word piece on art and the preschool child with the kind of satisfaction that any well-done professional job provides a reader. It was a tightly summarized condensation of my book, *Art and the Preschool Child,* which, in turn, was a rewritten revision of my Columbia Master's thesis. This book had launched me as an art critic, and, at the same time, the book was a failure. I say that the book was a failure because two colleges of education in two major universities adopted the book as a text for courses in child psychology, thereby indicating a failure on the part of the educators concerned to understand the thesis of the book, children, and psychology. Nevertheless, the book had enabled me to escape from the teaching of art history and had put me into full-time writing as an art critic.

Thomas Wyatt Russell, managing editor of *Fine Arts: The Americas,* who had read and understood the book, offered me a position on the magazine as a columnist and contributing editor, with a stipend of four hundred dollars a month. And *Fine Arts: The Americas*, which loses more than fifty thousand dollars a year for the foundation that supports it, is easily the most successful art magazine published in America — or anywhere else, for that matter. Admittedly, $400 a month is a niggardly sum, but my name on the masthead of this prestigious magazine was the wedge I needed at the time to sell freelance articles to other art magazines. My income from the latter source was uneven, of course, but with my assured monthly pittance it was enough — so long as I remained single, which was my avowed intention — to avoid teaching, which I despised, and enough to avoid the chilly confinement of museum work — the only other alternative open to those who selected art history as graduate degrees. There is always advertising, of course, but one does not deliberately devote one's time to the in-depth study of art history needed for a graduate degree to enter advertising, regardless of the money to be made in that field.

I closed the book, pushed it to one side, and then reached for Volume III. My fingers trembled — a little — as I lit a cigarette. I knew why I had lingered so long over the preschool child piece, even though I hated to admit it to myself. For a long time (I said to myself that I was only waiting to finish my cigarette first), I was physically unable to open the book to my article on Jacques Debierue. Every evil thing Dorian Gray did appeared on the face of his closeted portrait, but in my case, I wonder sometimes if there is a movie projector in a closet somewhere whirring away, showing the events of those two days of my life over and over. Evil, like everything else, should keep pace with the times, and I'm not a turn-of-the-century dilettante like Dorian Gray. I'm a professional, and as contemporary as the glaring Florida sun outside my window.

Despite the air-conditioning I perspired so heavily that my thick sideburns were matted and damp. Here, in this beautiful volume, was the bitter truth about myself at last. Did I owe my present reputation and success to Debierue, or did Debierue owe his success and reputation to me?

'Wherever you find ache,' John Heywood wrote, 'thou shalt not like him.' The thought of Debierue made me ache all right — and I did not like the ache, nor did I like myself. But nothing, nothing in this world, could prevent me from reading my article on Jacques Debierue ...

Chapter Two

Gloria Bentham didn't know a damned thing about art, but that singularity did not prevent her from becoming a successful dealer and gallery owner in Palm Beach. To hold her own, and a little more, where there were thirty full-time galleries open during the 'season', was more than a minor achievement, although the burgeoning art movement in recent years has made it possible to sell almost any artifact for some kind of sum. Nevertheless, it is more important for a dealer to understand people than it is to understand art. And Gloria, skinny, self-effacing, plain, had the patient ability to listen to people — a characteristic that often passes for understanding.

As I drove north toward Palm Beach on A1A from Miami, I thought about Gloria to avoid thinking about other things, but without much satisfaction. I had taken the longer slower route instead of the Sunshine parkway because I had wanted the extra hour or so it would take to sort out my thoughts about what I would write about Miami art, and to avoid, for an additional hour, the problem — if it was still a problem — of Berenice Hollis. Nothing is simple, and the reason I am a good critic is that I have learned the deep, dark secret of criticism. Thinking, the process of thinking, and the man thinking are all one and the same. And if this is true, and I live as though it is, then the man painting, the painting, and the process of painting are also one and the same. No one, and nothing, is ever simple, and Gloria had been anxious, too anxious, for me to get back to Palm Beach to attend the preview of her new show. The show was not important, nor was the idea unique. It was merely logical.

She was having a tandem showing of naive Haitian art and the work of a young Cleveland painter named Herb Westcott, who had spent a couple of months in Pétionville, Haiti, painting the local scene. The contrast would make Westcott look bad, because he was a professional, and it would make the primitives look good, because they were naively unprofessional. She would sell the primitives for a 600 percent markup over what she paid for them and, although most of the buyers would bring them back after a week or so (not many people can live with Haitian primitives), she would still make a profit. And, for those collectors who could not stand naive art, Westcott's craftsmanship would look so superior to the Haitians that he would undoubtedly sell a few more pictures in a tandem exhibit than he would in a one-man show without the advantage of the comparison.

By thinking about Gloria I had avoided, for a short while, thinking about Berenice Hollis. My solution to the problem of Berenice was one of mild overkill, and I half-hoped it had worked and half-hoped that it had not. She was a high school English teacher (eleventh grade) from Duluth, Minnesota, who had flown down to Palm Beach for a few weeks of sun-shiny convalescence after having a cyst removed from the base of her spine. Not a serious operation, but she had sick leave accumulated, and she took it. Her pale pink skin had turned gradually to saffron, and then to golden maple. The coccyx scar had changed from an angry red to gray and finally to slightly puckered grisaille.

Our romance had passed through similar shades and tints. I met Berenice at the Four Arts Gallery, where I was covering a traveling Toulouse-Lautrec exhibit, and she refused to go back to Duluth. That would have been all right with me (I could not, in all honesty, encourage anyone to return to Duluth), but I had made the mistake of letting her move in with me, a foolish decision which had seemed like a great idea at the time. She was a large — strapping is a better word — country girl with a ripe figure, cornflower-blue eyes, and a tangle of wheat-colored hair flowing down her back. Except for the thumb-tack scar on her coccyx, which was hardly noticeable, her sun-warmed sweet-smelling hide was flawless. Her blue eyes looked velvety, thanks to her contact lenses. But she wasn't really good natured, as I had thought at first, she was merely lazy. My efficiency apartment was too damned small for one person, let alone two, and she loomed in all directions. Seeing her dressed for the street or a party, no one would believe that Berenice was such a mess to live with — clothes strewn over every chair, wet bath towels, bikinis on the floor, the bathroom reeking of bath salts, powder, perfume, and unguents, a tangy mixture of smells so overpowering I had to hold my nose when I shaved. The state of the pullman kitchen was worse. She never washed a cup, dish, pot, or pan, and once I caught her pouring bacon grease into the sink.

I could live with messiness. The major problem in having Berenice around all the time was that I had to do my writing in the apartment.

It had taken all of my persuasive abilities to talk Tom Russell into letting me cover the Gold Coast for the season. (The official 'season' in Palm Beach begins on New Year's Eve with a dull dinner-dance at the Everglades Club, and it ends fuzzily on April 15). When Tom agreed, finally, he refused to add expenses to my salary. I had to survive in Palm Beach on my monthly stipend, and pay my air fare down out of my small savings (the remainder of my savings bought me a $250 car). By sub-letting my rent-controlled Village pad for almost twice as much as I was paying for it myself, I could get by. Barely.

I worked twice as hard, writing much better copy than I had in New York, to prove to Tom Russell that the Gold Coast was an incipient American art center that had been neglected far too long by serious art journals. Such was not truly the case, as yet, but there were scattered signs of progress. Most of the native painters of Florida were still dabbing out impressionistic palms and seascapes, but enough reputable painters from New York and Europe had discovered Florida for themselves, and the latter were exhibiting in galleries from Jupiter Beach to Miami. Enough painters, then, were exhibiting during the season to fill my *Notes* column on new shows, and at least one major artist exhibited long enough for me to honour him with one of my full-length treatments. There is money in Florida during the season, and artists will show anywhere there is enough money to purchase their work.

With Berenice around the tiny apartment all the time, I couldn't write. She would pad about barefooted, as quiet and as stealthy as a 140-pound mouse — until I complained. She would then sit quietly, placidly, not reading, not doing anything, except to stare lovingly at my back as I sat at my Hermes. I couldn't stand it.

'What are you thinking about, Berenice?'

'Nothing.'

'Yes, you are, you're thinking about me.'

'No, I'm not. Go ahead and write. I'm not bothering you.'

But she did bother me, and I couldn't write. I couldn't hear her breathing, she was so quiet, but I would catch myself listening to see if I *could* hear her. It took some mental preparation (I am, basically, a kind sonofabitch), but I finally, in a nice way, asked Berenice to leave. She wouldn't go. Later I asked her to leave in a harsh and nasty way. She wouldn't fight with me, but she wouldn't leave. On these occasions she couldn't even talk back. She merely looked at me, earnestly, with her welkin eyes wide open — the lenses sliding around — tears torrenting, suppressing, or making an effort to hold back, big, blubbery, gasping sobs — she was destroying me. I would leave the apartment, forever, and come back a few hours later for a reconciliation replay and a wild hour in the sack.

But I wasn't getting my work done. Work is important to a man. Not even a Helen of Troy can compete with a Hermes. No matter how wonderful she is, a woman is only a woman, whereas 2,500 words is an article. In desperation I issued Berenice an ultimatum. I told her that I was leaving for Miami, and that when I came back twenty-four hours later I wanted her the hell out of my apartment and out of my life.

And now I was returning seventy-two hours later, having added two extra days as insurance. I expected her to be in the apartment. I wanted her to be there and, paradoxically, I wanted her to be gone forever.

I parked in the street, put the canvas top up on the Chevy — a seven-year-old convertible — and started across the flagged patio to the stuccoed outside staircase. Halfway up the stairs I could hear the phone ringing in my apartment on the second floor. I stopped and waited while it rang three more times. Berenice would be incapable of letting a phone ring four times without answering it, and I knew that she was gone. Before I got the door unlocked the ringing stopped.

Berenice was gone and the apartment was clean. It wasn't spotless, of course, but she had made a noble effort to put things in order. The dishes had been washed and put away and the linoleum floor had been mopped in a half-assed way.

There was a sealed envelope, with 'James' scribbled on the outside, propped against my typewriter on the card table by the window.

Dearest dearest James —
You are a bastard but I think you know that. I still love you but I will forget you — I hope I never forget the good things. I'm going back to Duluth — don't follow me there.
B.

If she didn't want me to follow her, why tell me where she was going?

There were three crumpled pieces of paper in the wastebasket. Rough drafts for the final note. I considered reading them, but changed my mind. I would let the final version stand. I crumpled the note and the envelope and added them to the wastebasket.

I felt a profound sense of loss, together with an unreasonable surge of anger. I could still smell Berenice in the apartment, and knew that her feminine compound of musk, sweat, perfume, pungent powder, lavender soap, bacon breath, Nose-cote, padded sachet coat hangers, vinegar, and everything else nice about her would linger on in the apartment forever. I felt sorry for myself and sorry for Berenice and, at the same time, a kind of bubbling elation that I was rid of her, even though I knew that I was going to miss her like crazy during the next few terrible weeks.

There was plenty of time before the preview at Gloria's Gallery. I removed my sport shirt, kicked off my loafers, and sat at the card table, which served as my desk, to go over my Miami notes. My three days in Dade County hadn't been wasted.

I had stayed with Larry Levine, in Coconut Grove. Larry was a printmaker I had known in New York, and his wife Paula was a superb cook. I would reimburse Larry with a brief comment about his new animal prints in my *Notes* column.

I had enough notes for a 2,500-word article on a 'Southern Gothic' environmental exhibit I had attended in North Miami, and an item on Harry Truman's glasses was a good lead-off piece for my back-of-the-book column. Larry had steered me to the latter.

A mechanic in South Miami, a Truman lover, had written to Lincoln Borglum, who had finished the monumental heads on Mount Rushmore after his father's death, and had asked the sculptor when he was going to add Harry Truman's head to the others. Lincoln Borglum, who apparently had a better sense of humor than his late father, Gutzon, claimed, in a facetious reply, that he was unable to do so because it was too difficult to duplicate Harry Truman's glasses. The mechanic, a man named Jack Wade, took Borglum at his word, and made the glasses himself.

They were enormous spectacles, more than twenty-five feet across, steel frames covered with thickly enameled ormolu. The lenses were fashioned from twindex windows, the kind with a vacuum to separate the two panes of glass.

'The vacuum inside will help keep the lenses from fogging up on cold days,' Wade explained.

I had taken three black-and-white Polaroid snapshots of Wade and the glasses, and one of the photos was sharp enough to illustrate the item in my column. The spectacles were a superior job of craftsmanship, and I had suggested to Mr. Wade that he might sell them to an optician for advertising purposes. The suggestion made him angry.

'No, by God,' he said adamantly. 'These glasses were made for Mr. Truman, when his bust is finished on Mount Rushmore!'

The phone rang.

'Where have you been?' Gloria's voice asked shrilly. 'I've been calling you all afternoon. Berenice said you left and that you might never come back.'

'When did you talk to Berenice?'

'This morning, about ten-thirty.'

This news hit me hard. If I had returned in twenty-four hours, in forty-eight, or sixty — I'd still have Berenice. My timing had been perfect, but a pang was there.

'I've been in Miami, working. But Berenice has left and won't be back.'

'Lovers' quarrel? Tell Gloria all about it.'

'I don't want to talk about it, Gloria.'

She laughed. 'You're coming to the preview?'

'I told you I would. What's so important about second-hand Haitian art that you've had to call me all day?'

'Westcott's a good painter, James, he really is, you know. A first-rate draughtsman.'

'Sure.'

'You sound funny. Are you all right?'

'I'm fine. And I'll be there.'

'That's what I wanted to talk to you about. Joseph Cassidy will be there, and he's coming because he wants to meet you. He told me so. You know who Mr. Cassidy is, don't you?'

'Doesn't everybody?'

'No, not everybody. Not everybody needs him!' She laughed. 'But he's invited us — you and me and a few others — to supper at his place after the preview. He has a penthouse at the Royal Palm Towers.'

'I know where he lives. Why does he want to meet me?'

'He didn't say. But he's the biggest collector to ever visit *my* little gallery, and if I could land him as a patron I wouldn't need any others —'

'Don't sell him any primitives, then, or Westcotts.'

'Why not?'

'He isn't interested in conventional art. Don't try to sell him anything. Wait until I talk to him, and then I'll suggest something to you.'

'I appreciate this, James.'

'It's nothing.'

'Are you bringing, Berenice?'

'I don't want to *talk* about it, Gloria.'

She was laughing as I racked the phone.

Chapter Three

As much as I dislike the term 'freeloader,' no other word fits what I had become during my sojourn on the Gold Coast. There are several seasonal societal levels in Palm Beach, and they are all quite different from the social groups, divided uneasily by the Waspish and Jewish groupings found in Miami and Miami Beach. In Lauderdale, of course, the monied class is squarely WASP.

I belonged to none of the 'groups,' but I was on the periphery of all of them by virtue of my calling. I met people at art show previews, where cocktails are usually served, and because I was young, single, and had an acceptable profession, I was frequently invited to dinners, cocktail parties, polo games, boat rides, late supper, and barbecues. These invitations, which led to introductions to other guests, usually produced additional dinner invitations. And a few of the Gold Coast artists, like Larry Levine, for example, were people I had known in New York.

After two months in Florida I had many acquaintances, or connections, but no friends. I did not return any of the dinner invitations, and I had to avoid bars, night clubs, and restaurants where I might get stuck with a check. The man who never picks up a check does not acquire friends.

Nevertheless, I felt that my various hosts and hostesses were recompensed for my presence at their homes. I put up genially with bores, I was an extra man at dinners where single, heterosexual young men were at a premium, and when I was in a good mood, I could tell stories or carry conversation over dead spots.

I had two dinner jackets, a red silk brocade and a standard white linen. There were lipstick mouthings on the white jacket, where a tipsy Berenice had bitten me on the shoulder while I was driving back from a party. I was forced, then, to wear the red brocade.

As I walked the six blocks from my apartment to Gloria's gallery, I speculated on Joseph Cassidy's invitation to supper. A social invitation wasn't unusual, but she had said that he wanted to meet me, and I wondered why. Cassidy was not only famous as a collector, he was famous as a criminal lawyer. It was the huge income from his practice in Chicago that had enabled him to build his art collection.

He had one of the finest private collections of contemporary art in America, and the conclusion I came to, which seemed reasonable at the time, was that he might want to hire me to write a catalogue for it. And if he did not want to see me about that (to my knowledge, no catalogue had been published on his collection), I had a good mind to suggest it to him. The task would pay off for me, as well as for Cassidy, in several ways. I could make some additional money, spend a few months in Chicago, do some writing on midwestern art and artists, and my name on the published catalogue would enhance my career.

The more I thought about the idea the more enthusiastic I became, but by the time I reached the gallery my enthusiasm was tempered by the knowledge that I could not broach the suggestion to him. If he suggested it, fine, but I could not ask a man for employment at a social affair without a loss of dignity.

And what else did I have to offer a man in Cassidy's position? My pride (call it *machismo*) in myself, which I overrated and which I knew was often phony, was innate, I supposed — a part of my heritage from my Puerto Rican father. But the pride was there, all the same, and I had passed up many opportunities to push myself by considering first, inside my head, what my father would have done in similar circumstances.

By the time I reached the gallery, I had pushed the idea out of my mind.

Gloria forced her thin lips over her buck teeth, brushed my right sideburn with her mouth, and, capturing my right arm in a painful armlock, led me to the bar.

'Do you know this man, Eddy?' she said to the bartender.

'No,' Eddy shook his head solemnly, 'but his drink is familiar.' He poured two ounces of Cutty Sark over two ice cubes and handed me the Dixie cup.

'Thanks, Eddy.'

Eddy worked the day shift at Hiram's Hideaway in South Palm Beach, but he was a popular bartender and was hired by many hostesses during the season for parties at night. I usually ran into him once or twice a week at various places. Everybody, I thought, needs something extra nowadays. A regular job, and something else. Gloria, for example, wouldn't have been able to pay the high seasonal rent on her gallery if she didn't occasionally rent it out in the evenings for poetry readings and encounter-group therapy sessions. She detested these groups, too. The people who needed to listen to poetry, or tortured themselves in encounter-group sessions were all chain smokers, she claimed, who didn't use the ashtrays she provided.

Eddy worked at a sheet-covered card table. There was scotch, bourbon, gin and vermouth for martinis, and a plastic container of ice cubes behind the table. I moved back to give someone else a chance, and picked up a mimeographed catalogue from the table in the foyer. Gloria was greeting newcomers at the door, bringing them to the table to sign her guest book, and then to the bar.

Her previews were not exclusive by any means. In addition to her regular guest list for previews, she gave invitations to Palm Beach hotel P.R. directors to hand out to guests who might be potential buyers. The square hotel guests, 'honoured' by being given printed preview invitations to a private show, and thrilled by the idea that they were seeing 'real' Palm Beach society at an art show preview, occasionally purchased a painting. And when they did, the publicity director of the hotel they came from received a sports jacket or a new pair of Daks from Gloria. As a consequence, the preview crowd at Gloria's gallery was often a weird group. There were even a couple of teenage girls from Palm Beach Junior College peering anxiously at the primitives and writing notes with ballpoints in Blue Horse notebooks.

Herbert Westcott, I learned from the catalogue, was twenty-seven years old, a graduate of Western Reserve who had also studied at the Art Students League in New York. He had exhibited in Cleveland, the Art Students League, and Toronto, Canada. A Mr. Theodore L. Canavin of Philadelphia had collected some of his work. This exhibit, recent work done in Haiti during the past three months, was Westcott's first one-man show. I looked up from the catalogue and spotted the artist easily. He was short — about five seven — well-tanned, with a skimpy, light brown beard. He wore a six-button, powder blue Palm Beach suit, white shoes, and a pale pink body shirt without a tie. He was eavesdropping on a middle-aged couple examining his largest painting — a Port-au-Prince market scene that was two-thirds lemon sky.

He drew well, as Gloria had said, but he had let his colors overlap by dripping to give the effect of fortuitous accident to his compositions. The drips — a messy heritage from Jackson Pollock — were injudicious. He had talent, of course, but talent is where a painter starts. His Haitian men and women were in tints and shades of chocolate instead of black, something I might not have noticed if it had not been for the Haitian paintings on the opposite wall, where the figures were black indeed.

The dozen Haitian paintings Gloria had rounded up were all suprisingly good. She even had an early Marcel, circa 1900, so modestly different from the contemporary primitives, with their bold reds and yellows, it riveted one's attention. The scene was typically Haitian, some thirty people engaged in voodoo rites, with a bored, comical goat as a central focusing point, but the picture was painted in gray, black, and white — no primary colors at all. Marcel, as I recalled, was an early primitive who had painted his canvases with chicken feathers because he could not afford brushes. It was priced at only fifteen hundred dollars, and someone would get a bargain if he purchased the Marcel ...

'James,' Gloria clutched my elbow, 'I want you to meet Herb Westcott. Herb, this is Mr. Figueras.'

'How do you do?' I said, 'Gloria, where did you get the Marcel?'

'Later,' she said. 'Talk to Herb.' She turned away, with her long freckled right arm outstretched to a tottering old man with rouged cheeks.

Westcott fingered his skimpy beard. 'I'm sorry I didn't recognize you before, Mr. Figueras — Gloria told me you were coming — but I thought you wore a beard ...'

'It's the picture in my column. I should replace the photo, I suppose, but it's a good one and I haven't got another one yet. I had my beard for about a year before I shaved it. You shouldn't tug at your beard, Mr. Westcott ...'

He dropped his hand quickly and shuffled his feet.

'I worked it all out, Mr. Westcott, and found that a beard would add about six weeks to my life, that is, six full weeks of shaving time saved in a lifetime, seven weeks if one uses an electric razor. But it wasn't worth it. Like you, I could hardly keep my fingers off the damned thing, and my neck itched all the time. The secret, they say, is never to touch your beard. And if you've already got that habit, Mr. Westcott, your beard is doomed.'

'I see,' he said shyly. 'Thanks for the advice.'

'Don't worry,' I added, 'you probably look handsomer without one.'

'That's what Gloria said. Here,' he took my empty Dixie cup — 'let me get you a fresh drink. What are you drinking?'

'Eddy knows.'

I turned back to examine the Marcel again. I wanted to leave. The small high-ceilinged room, which seemed smaller now as it began to get crowded, was jammed with loud-voiced people, and I did not want to talk to Westcott about his paintings. That's why I got off onto the beard gambit. They were all derivative, which he knew without my telling him. The entire show, including the Marcel, wasn't worth more than one column inch (I folded the catalogue and shoved it into my hip pocket), unless I got desperate for more filler to make the column come out to an even two thousand words.

Gloria was standing by the bar, together with a dozen other thirsty guests. Poor Westcott, who was paying for the liquor, hovered on the outskirts trying to get Eddy's attention. I took the opportunity to slip into the foyer and then out the door. I was on Worth Avenue in the late twilight, and heading for home. If Mr. Cassidy wanted to meet me, he could get my telephone number from Gloria and call for an appointment.

Twilight doesn't last very long in Florida. By the time I reached my ocherous predepression stucco apartment house — a mansion in the twenties, now cut up into small apartments — my depression was so bad I had a headache. I took off my jacket and sat on a concrete bench beneath a tamarisk tree in the patio and smoked a cigarette. The ocean wind was warm and soft. A few late birds twittered angrily as they tried to find roosting places in the crowded tree above my head. I was filling with emptiness up to my eyes, but not to the point of overflowing. Old Mrs. Weissberg, who lived in No. 2, was limping down the flagstone path toward my bench. To avoid talking to her I got up abruptly, climbed the stairs, heated a Patio Mexican Dinner for thirty minutes in the oven, ate half of it, and went to bed. I fell asleep at once and slept without dreams.

Chapter Four

Gloria shook me awake and switched on the lamp beside the Murphy bed. She had let herself in with the extra key I kept hidden in the potted geranium on the porch. She had either witnessed Berenice using the key or heard her mention that one was there. I blinked at Gloria in the sudden light, trying to pull myself together. My heart was still fluttering, but the burbling fear of being wakened in the dark was gradually going away.

'I'm sorry, James,' Gloria said briskly, 'but I knocked and you didn't answer. You really ought to get a doorbell, you know.'

'Try phoning next time. I almost always get up to answer the phone, in case it might be something un-important.' I didn't try to conceal the irritation in my voice.

My cigarettes were in my trousers, which were hanging over the back of the straight chair by the coffee table. I slept nude, with just a sheet over me, but because I was angry as well as in need of a smoke, I threw the sheet off, got up and fumbled in the pockets of my trousers for my cigarettes. I lit one and tossed the match into the stone-ware ashtray on the coffee table.

'This is important to me, James. Mr. Cassidy came and you weren't there. He asked about you and I told you had a headache and left early —'

'True.'

Gloria wasn't embarrassed by my nakedness, but now I felt self-conscious, standing bare-assed in the center of the room, smoking and carrying on a moronic conversation. Gloria was in her late forties, and had been married for about six months to a hardware-store owner in Atlanta, so it wasn't her first time to see a man without any clothes on. Nevertheless, I took a terry-cloth robe out of the closet and slipped into it.

'He wants you to come to supper, James. And here I am, ready to take you.'

'What time is it, anyway?'

'About ten-forty.' She squinted at the tiny hands on her platinum wristwatch. 'Not quite ten forty-five.'

I felt refreshed and wide-awake, although I had only slept two hours. Being awakened that way, so unexpectedly, had stirred up my adrenalin.

'I think you're overstating the case, Gloria. What, precisely, did Mr. Cassidy say to make you so positive he wanted me — in particular — to come to his little gathering?'

She rubbed her beaky nose with a skinny forefinger and frowned. 'He said, "I hope that Mr. Figueras' headache won't keep him from coming over this evening for a drink." And I said, "Oh, no. He asked me to pick him up later at his apartment. James is very anxious to meet you." '

'I see. You turned a lukewarm chunk of small talk into a big deal. And now I have to go with you to get you off the hook.'

'I wouldn't put it that way. He bought a picture from me, James, one of the primitives — the big one with the huge pile of different kinds of fruit. For his colored cook to hang in the kitchen.'

'No Westcotts?'

'He didn't like Herb's pictures very much. I could tell, although he didn't say anything one way or another.'

'I think he did. Buying a Haitian primitive for his cook says something, don't you think? Do I need another shave?'

She felt my chin with the tips of her fingers. 'I don't think so. Brush your teeth, though. Your breath is simply awful.'

'That's from the Mexican dinner I had earlier.'

I dressed in gray slacks, a white shirt, and brown leather tie, dark brown loafers, and a gray-and-white striped seersucker jacket, resolving to take my soiled dinner jacket to the cleaner's in the morning. I remember how calm I was, and how well my mind seemed to be functioning after only two hours of sleep. All of my muscles were loose and stretchy. There was a spring to my step, as though I were wearing cushioned soles. I was in a pleasant mood, so much so that I pinched old Gloria through her girdle as we left the apartment.

'Oh, for God's sake, James!'

As we drove toward the Royal Palm Towers, a seven-story horror of poured concrete, in Gloria's white Pontiac, I found myself looking forward to meeting Mr. Cassidy and to seeing his paintings. He was bound to have a few pictures in his apartment, although his famous collection was safe in Chicago. I wondered, as well, why he had elected to live in the Royal Palm Towers, which over-looked Lake Worth instead of the Atlantic. He would be able to see the Atlantic from his rooftop patio, but only from a distance, and that wasn't the same as being on the beach.

The Towers was a formless mixture of rental apartments, condominium apartments, hotel rooms, and rental suites. The corporation that owned the building had over-looked very little in the way of income-producing cells. There were rental offices on the mezzanine (Cassidy also had a suite of offices there), and on the ground floor the corporation leased space for shops of all kinds, including a small art gallery. The coffee shop, the lounge-bar, and the dining room were all leased to various entrepreneurs. The corporation itself invested nothing in services and took from everybody. Cassidy probably maintained the pent-house, I decided, because the Royal Palm Towers was one of the few apartment hotels in Palm Beach that remained open all year round.

Many New Yorkers, who didn't like Florida for its climate, loved the state because there was no state income tax. By maintaining a residence for six months and one day in Florida they could beat New York's state income tax. An ignoble but practical motive for moving one's residence and business headquarters to Florida.

'Where,' I asked Gloria, 'did you get the Haitian primitives?'

'A widow in Lauderdale sold them to me,' she giggled. 'For a song. Her husband just died, and she sold everything — house, furniture, collection, and all. She was moving back to Indiana to live with her daughter and grandchildren.'

'You priced the Marcel too low, baby. You can get more than fifteen hundred for it.'

'I doubt it, and I can't lose anything — not when I only paid twenty-five dollars for it.'

'You're a thief and a bitch.'

Gloria giggled. 'You're a blackguard. What have you done with Berenice?'

'She went back to Minnesota. I don't want to talk about her, Gloria.'

'She's an awfully nice girl, James.'

'I said I don't want to talk about her, Gloria.'

We took the elevator to the penthouse, but the door didn't open automatically. There was a small one-way window on the steel door (a mirror on our side), and the Filipino houseboy checked us out before pressing the door release from his side. There was probably a release button concealed somewhere within the elevator cage. There had to be. Cassidy couldn't keep someone in his penthouse at all times, just to push a button and let him in — or could he? The very rich do a lot of strange things.

The party was not a large one. Seven people counting Mr. Cassidy. Gloria and I brought the total to nine. It was the kind of party where it was assumed that everyone knows one another and therefore no one is introduced. There are many parties like that in Palm Beach. The main idea is to eat first, and then drink as much as possible before the bar is closed or the liquor runs out. If one feels the need to talk to someone, he introduces himself or starts talking to someone without giving his name. It makes very little difference. Mr. Cassidy had to know everyone there — at least slightly — to brief the Filipino houseboy on the person's credentials for admittance.

Sloan, the bartender (he wore a name tag on his white jacket), poured us Cutty Sarks over ice cubes. I trailed Gloria toward the terrace, where Mr. Cassidy was talking to a grayhaired man who was probably a senior officer in some branch of the armed forces. He wore an Oxford gray suit with deeply pleated trousers. The suit was new, indicating that he didn't wear it often. This meant that he wore a uniform most of the time. A suit lasts army and navy officers for eight or nine years. Pleats were long out of fashion and Oxford gray is the favorite suit color for high-ranking officers. They lead dark, gray lives.

'I appreciate that, Tom,' Cassidy said, sticking out his hand, and the gray-haired man was dismissed.

I watched the old-timer head for the elevator. I could have confirmed, easily enough, whether the man was in the service by asking, 'Isn't that General Smith?' In this case, however, I believed that I was right and didn't feel the need of confirmation.

Joseph Cassidy was short, barely missing squatness, with wide meaty shoulders and a barrel chest. His tattersall vest was a size to small and looked incongruous with his red velvet smoking jacket. He needed the vest for its pockets — pockets for his watch and chain, and the thin gold chain for his Phi Beta Kappa key. He had a tough Irish face, tiny blue eyes, with fully a sixteenth of an inch of white exposed beneath the irises, and square white teeth. His large upper front teeth overlapped, slightly, his full lower lip. His high forehead was flaking from sunburn. He wore a close-cropped black moustache, and his black hair, which was graying at the sides, was combed straight back and slicked down with water. Cassidy was a formidable man in his early fifties. He carried himself with an air of authority, and his confident manner was reinforced by his rich, resonant bass voice. And his gold-rimmed glasses — the same kind that Robert McNamara wore when he was Secretary of Defense — were beautifully suitable for his face.

Gloria introduced us and started toward the indoor fountain to look at the carp. The pool was crowded with these big fish, and I could see their backs, pied with gold and vermilion splotches, from where I stood, some fifteen feet away from the pool. A concrete griffin, on a pedestal in the center of the pool, dribbled water from its eagle beak into the carp-filled pool. It was a poorly designed griffin. The sculptor, who probably knew too much about anatomy, had been unable to come to terms with the idea of a cross between an eagle and a lion. Medieval sculptors, who knew nothing about anatomy, had no trouble at all in visualizing griffins and gargoyles. Cassidy took my arm, grasping my left elbow with a thumb and forefinger.

'Come on, Jim,' he said, 'I'll show you a couple of pictures. They call you "Jim," don't they?'

'No,' I replied, hiding my irritation. 'I prefer James. My father named me Jaime, but no one ever seemed to pronounce it right, so I changed it to James. Not legally,' I added.

'It's the same name,' He shrugged his meaty shoulders. 'No need for a legal change, James.'

I smiled. 'I didn't ask for that advice, Mr. Cassidy, so please don't bill be for it.'

'I don't intend to. I was just going to say that you don't look like a man named Jaime Figueras.'

'Like the stereotype Puerto Rican, you mean? The peculiar thing is that my blond hair and blue eyes come from my father, not my mother. My mother was Scottish-Irish, with black hair and hazel eyes.'

'You don't have a Spanish accent, either. How long have you lived in the States?'

'Since I was twelve. My father died, and my mother moved back to New York. She never liked Puerto Rico, anyway. She was a milliner, a creative designer of hats for women. You can't sell original hats to Puerto Rican women. All they need is a mantilla — or a piece of pink Kleenex pinned to their hair — to attend mass.'

'I've never met a milliner.'

'There aren't many left. My mother's dead now, and very few women wear originals nowadays, even when they happen to buy a hat.'

'Are hats worth collecting?' he asked suddenly, moistening his upper lip with the tip of his pink tongue. 'Original hats, I mean?'

I knew then that Mr. Cassidy was a true collector, and, knowing that, I knew a lot more about him than he thought I knew. In general, collectors can be divided into three categories.

First, the rare patron-collectors who know what they want and order it from artists and artisans. This first category, in the historical past, helped to establish styles. Without the huge demand for portraits in the sixteenth and seventeenth centuries, for example, there would have been no great school of portrait painters.

Second, the middle-ground people, who buy what is fashionable, but collect fashionable art because they either like it without knowing why (it reflects their times is why) or have been taught to like it.

In the third category are the collectors for economic reasons. They buy and sell to make a profit. That is, in a tautological sense, they are collectors because they are collectors, but they enjoy the works of art they possess at the moment for their present and future value.

The one trait that all three types of collectors have in common is miserliness. They write small, seldom dotting 'i's' or crossing 't's' and they are frequently costive. Once they own something, *anything*, they don't want to give it up.

The collector's role is almost as important to world culture as the critic's. Without collectors there would be precious little art produced in this world, and without critics, collectors would wonder what to collect. Even those few collectors who are knowledgeable about art will not go out on a limb without critical confirmation. Collectors and critics live within this uneasy symbiotic relationship. And artists — the poor bastards — who are caught in the middle, would starve to death without us.

'No.' I shook my head. As we crossed through the living room toward his study I explained why. 'Hats are too easy to copy. Original hats, during the twenties and thirties, were expensive because they were made specifically for one person and for one occasion. As soon as a new hat was seen on Norma Shearer's head, it was copied and mass produced. The copy, except perhaps for the materials, looked about the same. Some of the hats worn during the Gilded Age, when egret feathers were popular, might be worth collecting, but I doubt if restoration, storage, and upkeep costs would make it worthwhile to collect even those.'

'I see. You have looked into it then?'

'Not exhaustively. Fashion isn't my field — as you know.'

We entered his study, which was furnished in black leather, glass, and chrome. Cassidy sank into an audibly cushioned chair while I looked at the three pictures on the apple-green wall. There was an early Lichtenstein (a blown-up Dick Tracy panel), an airbrush Marilyn Monroe, in pale blue, from the Warhol series, and a black-and-white drawing of a girl's head by Matisse. The latter was over the ebony desk, in quiet isolation. The drawing was so bad Matisse must have signed it under duress. I sat across from Cassidy and put my empty glass on the rose-wood coffee table. The Filipino house-boy appeared with a fresh drink on a tray, picked up my empty glass, and handed me the drink and a cocktail napkin.

'You wish something to eat, sir?'

'I think so. A turkey sandwich, all white meat, on white toast. With mayonnaise and cranberry sauce, and cut off the crusts, please.'

He nodded and left.

'You don't like the drawing, do you?'

I shrugged, and sipped from my glass. 'Matisse had a streak of meanness in him that many Americans associate with the French. When he went out to a café — after he became well known — he would often sketch on a pad, or sometimes on a napkin. Then, instead of paying his tab in cash, he'd leave the drawing on the table and walk out. The proprietor, knowing that the drawing was worth a good deal more than the dinner, was always delighted. A man full of rich food and a couple of bottles of wine doesn't always draw very well, Mr. Cassidy.'

He nodded, relishing the story, and looked fondly at his Matisse. A bad drawing is a bad drawing, no matter who has drawn it. But my little story — and it was a true one — had merely enhanced the value of the Matisse for Cassidy. An ordinary person, if he had purchased a bad Matisse, would have felt gypped. But Cassidy wasn't an ordinary person. He was a collector, and not an ordinary collector.

'An interesting story.' He smiled. 'I don't have much here, and I haven't decided what to bring down from Chicago.'

Here was a natural opening, and I took it. 'I'd like to see the catalogue of your collection some time, Mr. Cassidy.'

'Don't have one yet, but I've got a good man at the University of Chicago working on it. Dr. G. B. Lang. D'you know him?'

'Yes, but not personally. He wrote an excellent monograph on Rothko.'

'That's Dr. Lang. It isn't costing me a dime, either — except for the printing costs. Dr. Lang teaches at the university, and one of my clients is on the Board of Trustees. Through him, my client, I managed to get Lang a reduced teaching schedule. He teaches two courses, and the rest of his load is research, the research being my catalogue. Dr. Lang's happy because he'll get another publication under his belt and, if he does a bang-up job, the University of Chicago Press will probably publish it.'

When Cassidy smiled, exposing his teeth, his canines made little dents in his bottom lip. He stared at me for two long beats. His eyes, behind the gold-rimmed glasses, were flat and slightly magnified. He leaned forward slightly. 'When men of good will get together, some sort of deal can be worked out to everyone's satisfaction. Isn't that right, James?'

'If they're "men of good will," yes. But my own experience has led me to believe that there aren't many of them around.'

He laughed, as though I had said something funny. The houseboy brought my sandwich. I took a bite and called him back before he got out the door. 'Just a minute! This isn't mayonnaise, this is salad dressing.'

'Yes, sir.'

'Don't you have any mayonnaise?'

'No, sir. May I bring you something else, sir?'

'Never mind.'

In his own way, Joseph Cassidy was as famous as Lee Bailey. In court Cassidy was certainly as good a lawyer, but he wasn't as flamboyant with reporters outside of court as Bailey, nor did he take cases for sheer publicity value. He was a cash-in-advance, on-the-line lawyer. No one had written a biography on Cassidy yet, but he had socked away a lot more money than Bailey. His shrewdness in buying the right painters at the right time and at rock-bottom prices had made him another fortune — if he ever decided to put his collection on the market.

The houseboy still hovered about, wanting but unwilling to leave. He was upset because I didn't eat the sandwich.

'Close the bar, Rizal,' Cassidy ordered quietly, 'and tell Mrs. Bentham that I'll see that Mr. Figueras gets home all right.' He exposed his toothy smile. 'You don't mind sticking around for a while, do you, James?'

'Of course not, Mr. Cassidy.'

Because of my upbringing, which has been on the formal side — insofar as observing the amenities was concerned — I resented the easy use of my first name by Mr. Cassidy without my permission or invitation. But I knew that he wasn't trying to patronize me. He was attempting to put me at my ease. Nevertheless, although I considered the idea, I couldn't drop to his level and call him Joe. There's too much informality in America as it is, and in Palm Beach, during the season, it is often carried to ridiculous lengths.

Rizal left to close the bar, which meant that the party was over. The guests would depart without saying good-bye to their host, and that would be that. Not out of rude-ness, but out of deference. If Cassidy had gone out for a series of formal good-nights they would have adjusted to that kind of leave-taking just as easily.

After Rizal closed the door, Cassidy took a cigar out of his desk humidor, lighted it, and sat down again. He didn't offer me one.

'James,' Cassidy said earnestly, 'I know a lot more about you than you think I do. I rarely miss one of your critical articles, and I think you write about art with a good deal of insight and perception.'

'Thank you.'

'This is all straight talk, James. I'm not in the habit of handing out fulsome praise. A second-rate critic doesn't deserve it, and a first-rate critic doesn't need it. In my opinion, you're well on the way to becoming one of our best young American critics. And, according to my invest-igations, you're ambitious enough to be *the* best.'

'By investigations, if you mean you've been talking to Gloria about me, she isn't the most reliable witness, you know. We've been friends for several years now, and she's prejudiced in my favor.'

'No, not only Gloria, James, although I've talked to her, too. I've talked to dealers, to some of my fellow collectors, and even to Dr. Lang. You might be interested to know that Dr. Lang's highly impressed with your work, and he knows more about art history and criticism than I'll ever know.'

'I'm not sure about that, Mr. Cassidy.'

'He should. That's his business — and yours. I'm an attorney, not an art historian. I don't even intend to write a foreword to my catalogue — although Lang suggested it to me.'

'Most collectors do.'

He nodded, and waved his right hand slowly so the ash wouldn't fall off the end of his cigar. 'In the art world, you happen to have a reputation for integrity. And I've been informed that you're incorruptible.'

'I'm not getting rich as an art critic, if that's what you mean.'

'I know. I also know how to make inquiries. That's my business. The law is ninety-five percent preparation, and if a man does his homework, it's easy to look good in the courtroom. To return to corruption for a moment, let me say that I respect your so-called incorruptibility.'

'The way you say it makes me feel as if I've missed some opportunity to make a pile of dough or something and turned it down. If I have missed out on something, I sure don't know about it.'

'If you want to play dumb, I'll spell it out for you. Number one — free pictures. That kid's show this evening, ah, Westcott. Suppose you had said to Gloria that you would give Westcott a nice buildup in return for a couple of free pictures, what would have happened?'

'In Westcott's case, she'd have given *all* of them to me.' I grinned. 'But you aren't talking about integrity now, Mr. Cassidy, you're talking about my profession. I've never taken a free picture. The walls of my apartment in the Village are bare except for chance patterns of flaking paint. But if I ever took one picture, just one, that I could resell for two or three hundred bucks, the word would be out that I was on the take. From that moment on I would be dead as a critic. And a good review for pay, which is still being done in Paris, has damned near ruined serious art criticism in France.

'There are some exceptions, naturally, and those of us in the trade know who they are. So the way things are, I can't even afford to take legitimate art gifts from friends, even when I know that there are no strings attached. The strings would be there inadvertently. The mere fact that I took the gift might influence my opinion if I ever had to cover the man's show. By the same token, I don't buy anything either. And I've had some chances to buy some things that even I could afford. But if I owned a painting, you see, there might be a temptation on my part to push the artist beyond his worth — *possibly* — I don't know that

I would — in order to increase the value of my own painting. I don't mean that I am completely objective either. That's impossible. I merely try to be most of the time, and that allows me to go overboard and be subjective as hell when I see something I really flip over.'

I finished the last of my drink and set the glass down a little harder than I had intended. When I looked up, there was a smile on Cassidy's Irish face. Perhaps he had been baiting me, but I had been through this kind of probing before. It was natural, in America, for people to think that a critic had been paid off when he gave some artist a rave write-up, especially when they didn't know anything about art. But Cassidy knew better.

'You know all this, Mr. Cassidy, so don't give me any undeserved credit for integrity. I like money as much as anyone, and I made more money when I taught art history at CCNY than I do now. I'm ambitious, yes, but for a reputation, not for money. When I have a big enough reputation as a critic, then I'll make more money, but never a huge amount. That isn't the game. The trick — and it's a hard one — is to earn a living as an art critic, or, if you prefer, art expert. If you want me to authenticate a painting for you, I'll charge you a fee. Gladly. If you want to ask my advice on what to buy next for your collection, I'll give you suggestions free of charge.' I held up my empty glass. 'Except for another drink. Or is the bar closed for me, too?'

'I'll get the bottle.' Cassidy left the room and returned almost immediately with an open bottle of Cutty Sark and a plastic bucket of cubes. I poured a double shot over two ice cubes and lit a cigarette. Cassidy picked up a yellow legal pad from his desk, sat down with it, and unscrewed the top from a fountain pen.

'I don't have any pictures for you to authenticate, James. And I didn't intend to ask you for any advice on collecting, but since you made the offer, what do you have in mind?'

I decided to tell him about my pet project.

'*Entartete Kunst.* Degenerate art.'

'How do you spell that?'

I told him and he wrote it on the pad.

'It's a term that was used by Hitler's party to condemn modern art. At the time, Hitler was on an ethnic kick, and the official line was folk, or people's, art. Modern art, with its subjective individualistic viewpoint, was considered political and cultural anarchy, and Hitler ordered it suppressed. Even ruthlessly. Then, as now, no one was quite sure what modern art was, and it became necessary to make up a show of "degenerate art" so that party men throughout Germany would know what in the hell they were supposed to prevent. So, in July 1937, they opened an exhibit of modern art in Munich. It was for adults only, so no children would be corrupted, and the exhibit was called *Entartete Kunst.* It was supposed to be an example, a warning to artists, and to people who might find such art attractive. After the Munich showing, it traveled all over Germany.'

I leaned forward. 'Listen to the names of the painters represented — Otto Dix, Emil Nolde, Franz Marc, Paul Klee, Kandinsky, Max Beckmann, and many more. I have a copy of the original catalogue in New York, locked away in the bottom drawer of my desk at the office.'

'Those paintings would be worth a fortune today.'

'The paintings are all a part of art history now — and any of, say, Marc's paintings are expensive. But suppose you had every painting in this particular show? Every German museum was "purified". That was the term they used, "purified". And the painters represented by the show, if the museum happened to have any of their work, were removed. Some were destroyed, some were hidden, and some were smuggled out of the country. But to have the *original* traveling exhibit, and it would be *possible* to obtain these pictures . . .'

Cassidy drew a line through the two words on his pad and shook his head. 'No, I could never swing anything like that by myself. I'd have to get a group together to raise the money, and — no, it wouldn't be worth it to me. Any more ideas?'

'Sure, but you didn't ask me here for my ideas on collecting.'

'That's right. Basically, James, you and I are honest men, and, in our own ways, we are equally ambitious. One dishonest act doesn't make a person dishonest, not when it's the only one he ever performs. That is, a *slightly* dishonest act. A little thing, really. Suppose, James, that you were given the opportunity to interview' — he hesitated, moistened his lips with his tongue — 'Jacques Debierue?'

'It would merely set me up with the greatest exclusive there is! But Debierue is in France, and he's only given three interviews in forty years — no, four — and none since his home burned down a year or so ago.'

'In other words,' he chuckled, 'you would be somewhat elated if you could look at his new work and talk to him about it personally?'

'Elated isn't the word. *Ecstatic* isn't strong enough. Now that Duchamp is dead, Debierue is Mr. Grand Old Man of Modern Art.'

'Don't go on, I know. Just listen. Suppose I told you that I could make arrangements for you to see and talk with Debierue?'

'I wouldn't believe you.'

'But if it was true — and I am now telling you that it *is* true — what would you do for me in return?'

My throat and mouth were suddenly dry. I tipped the plastic ice bucket and poured some ice water into my empty glass. I sipped it, and it tasted almost warm. 'You have something dishonest in mind. Isn't that what you implied a moment ago?'

'No. Not dishonest for you, dishonest for me. But even so, Debierue is in debt to me, if I want to look at it that way, and I do. I don't want money from him, I want one of his paintings.'

I laughed. 'Who doesn't? No individual, and not a single museum, has a Debierue. If you had one, you'd be the only collector in the world to have one! As far as I know, only four critics have been privileged to see any of his work. A servant or two has seen his paintings, probably, I don't know — maybe some of his mistresses a few years back, when he was still young enough to have them. But no one else —'

'I know. And I want one. In return for the interview, I want you to steal a picture for me.'

I laughed. 'And then, after I steal it, all I have to do is smuggle it back here from France. Right?'

'Wrong. And that's all I'll tell you now until I get a commitment from you. Yes or no. In return for the interview, you will steal a picture from Debierue and give it to me. No picture, no interview. Think about it.'

'Hypothetically?'

'Not hypothetical. Actual.'

'I'd do it. I *will* do it. That is, I'll steal one if he has any paintings to steal. Everything he had went up in smoke with his house, according to the reports. And if he hasn't painted anything since, well ...'

'He has. I know that he has.'

'You've got a deal. But I don't have the money for a round-trip air fare to France, not even for a slow freighter.'

'Let's shake hands on it.'

We got to our feet and shook hands solemnly. The palms of my hands were damp, and so were his, but we both gripped as hard as we could. He got the humidor and offered me a cigar. I shook my head and sat down. I started to pour another drink, but decided I didn't need it. My head was light and close to swimming. My heart was fluttering away as if I had swallowed a half-dozen butterflies.

'Debierue,' Cassidy laughed, a snort rather than an actual laugh, 'is here in Florida, thirty-odd miles south, via State Road Seven. And that is my so-called dishonest act, my friend. I have just betrayed a client's confidence. A counselor isn't supposed to do that, you know. But now that I have, I'll tell you the rest of it.

'Arrangements were made for Debierue to come to Florida more than eight months ago, and I was the inter-mediary here. The emigration was set up by a Paris law firm, who contacted me, and I handled the matter on a no fee basis, which I was glad to do. I rented the house — a one year lease — hired a black woman to come in and clean it for him once a week, bought his art supplies at Rex Art in Coral Gables, and picked him up at the airport. The whole thing. He's a poor man, as you know.'

'And you're supporting him now?'

'No, no. The money comes from *Les Amis de Debierue.* You are —'

'I send them five bucks a year myself.' I grimaced. 'It's tax deductible, if I ever make enough money to list it among my many charities.'

'Right. That's it. The Paris *Amis*, through the law firm, send me small sums more or less regularly, and I see that the old man's bills are paid — such as they are — and keep him in pocket money. He doesn't need much. The house is cheap, because of the rotten location. It was built by a man who retired to raise chickens. After six months of trying, and not knowing anything about poultry, he went back to Detroit. He's been trying to sell the house for two years, and was happy as hell to get a year's rent in advance.' Cassidy smiled. 'I even selected the old man's phoney name for him — Eugene V. Debs. How do you like it?'

'Beautiful!'

'Better than beautiful. Debierue never heard of Gene Debs. And that's about it.'

'Not quite. How did he get into the States without reporters finding out?'

'No problem. Paris to Madrid, Madrid to Puerto Rico, through the customs at San Juan, then on to Miami — and he came in on a student visa. J. Debierue. Who's going to suspect a man in his nineties on a student visa? And Debierue is a common enough name in France. There are about sixty flights a day from the Caribbean coming into Miami International on Sundays. It's the busiest airport in the world.'

I nodded. 'And the ugliest, too. So he's been right here in Florida for eight months?'

'Not exactly. The negotiations started eight months ago, and it took some time to set everything up. The funny thing is, the old man will actually be a student. I mentioned my connections at the University of Chicago — well, starting in September, Debierue will be taking twelve hours of college credit, by correspondence, from Chicago.'

'What's his major?'

'Cost accounting and management. I've got a young man working for me who can whip through those correspondence courses with his left hand, and he'll probably get the old man an A average. On a student visa, you see, you have to carry twelve hours a semester to stay in the country. As long as you're making good grades with the college, you can stay as long as you like.'

'I know. But why me? Why don't *you* steal a picture from Debierue?'

'He'd know it was me, that's why. After I got him settled, he told me he didn't want me to visit him. For the sake of secrecy. I went down a couple of times anyway and pestered him for a painting. He got good and angry the last time, and his studio is kept padlocked. I want one of his paintings. I don't care what it is, or whether anyone knows that I have one. *I'll* know, and that's enough. For now. Of course, if you manage to get a successful interview — and that's your problem — and you write about his new work — he hasn't got *too* many years to live — then I can bring my painting out and show it. Can't I?'

'I understand. You'll have pulled off the collector's coup of this decade — but what happens to me?'

'You'll stand still for it, no matter what happens. I've checked you out, I told you. You're ambitious, and you'll be the first, as well as the *only*, American critic to have an exclusive interview with the great Jacques Debierue. After you steal one of his pictures, he sure as hell won't talk to anyone else.'

'What time is it set up for, and when?'

'It isn't. That's up to you.' He wrote the address on the yellow pad, and sketched in State Road Seven and the branch road leading into it from Boynton Beach. 'If you happen to drive past the turnoff, and you might miss Debierue's road because it's dirt and you can't see the house from the highway, you'll know you missed it when you spot the drive-in movie about a half mile farther on. Turn around and go back.'

'Does he know I'm coming?'

'No. That's your problem?'

'Why did he decide to come to Florida?'

'Ask him. You're the writer.'

'He might slam the door in my face, then?'

'Who knows? We made a deal, that's all, and we shook hands on it. I know my business, and you should know yours. Any more questions?'

'Not for you.'

'Good.' He got to his feet, an abrupt signal that the discussion was finished. 'When are you driving down?'

'That's my business.' I grinned, and stuck out my hand.

We shook hands again, and Cassidy asked kindly if he could telephone for a taxi. Sending me home in a cab at my own expense was his method of 'seeing that I got home all right.'

I declined, and rode down in the elevator. To clear my head, I preferred to walk the few blocks to my apartment. As I walked the quiet streets through the warm soft night, a Palm Beach police car, staying a discreet block behind, trailed me home. I wasn't suspected of anything. The cops were merely making certain that I would get home all right. Palm Beach is probably, together with Hobe Sound, the best-protected city in the United States.

Now that I was alone, I was so filled with excitement I could hardly think straight. Dada, first, and Surrealism, second, were my favourite periods in art history. And because of my interest in these movements when I had been in Paris, I knew the Paris art scene of the twenties better, in many respects, than most of the people who had participated in it. And Debierue — Jacques Debierue! Debierue was the key figure, the symbol of the dividing line, if a line could be delineated, in the split between Dada and Surrealism! In my exhilarated state, I knew I wouldn't be able to sleep. I was going to put on a pot of coffee and jot down notes on Debierue from memory in preparation for the interview. Tomorrow, I thought, *tomorrow*!

I turned the key in the door and opened it to unexpected light. The soft light streamed in from the bathroom. Silhouetted in the bathroom doorway, wearing a gray-blue shorty nightgown, was my tawny-maned schoolteacher. Her long, swordlike legs trembling at the knees.

'I — I came back, James,' Berenice said tearfully.

I nodded, dumbly, and lifted my arms so she could rush into them. After she calms down, I thought, I'll have her make the coffee. Berenice makes much better coffee than I do ...

Chapter Five

Debierue is a difficult artist to explain, I explained to Berenice over coffee:

'*No pido nunca a nadie* is a good summary of the code Debierue's lived by all his life. Translated, it means, "I never ask nobody for nothing."'

'I think that's the first time I've ever heard you talk in Spanish, James.'

'And it might be the last. It didn't take me long to quit speaking Spanish after we moved to New York from San Juan. And as soon as I wised up to how they felt about Puerto Ricans, I got rid of my Spanish accent, too. But the Spanish *No pido nuncia a nadie* sounds better because the reiterated double negatives don't cancel each other out as they do in English. And that's the story of Debierue's life, one double negative action after another until, by not trying to impress anybody, he ended up by impressing everybody.'

'But why did you give up speaking Spanish?'

'To prove to myself, I suppose, that a Puerto Rican's not only as good as anybody else, he's a damned sight better. Besides, that's what my father would've done.'

'But your father's dead, you told me —'

'That's right. He died when I was twelve, but technically I never had a father. He and my mother separated before I was a year old, you see. They didn't get divorced because they were Catholics, although my mother made semi-official arrangements with the church for them to live apart. There was no money problem. He supported us until he died, and then we came up to New York, Mother and I, with the insurance and the money from the sale of our house in San Juan.'

'But you saw him once in a while, didn't you?'

'No. Never. Not after their separation — except in photographs, of course. That's what made things so tough for me, Berenice. What I've had instead is an imaginary father, a father I've had to make up myself, and he's what you might call *un hombre duro* — a hard man.'

'What you mean, James, you've deliberately made things hard on yourself.'

'It isn't that simple. A boy who doesn't have a father around doesn't develop a superego, and if you don't get a superego naturally you've got to invent one —'

'That's silly. Superego is only a jargon word for "conscience," and everybody's got a conscience.'

'Have it your way, Berenice, although Fromm and Rollo May wouldn't agree with you.'

'But *you've* got a conscience.'

'Right. At least I've got one intellectually, if not emotionally, because I was smart enough to create an imaginary father.'

'Sometimes I don't understand you, James.'

'That's because you're like the little old lady in Hemingway's *Death in the Afternoon.*'

'I've never read it. That's his book on bullfighting, isn't it?'

'No. It's a book about Hemingway. By talking about bullfighting he tells us about himself. You can learn a lot about bullfighting in *Death in the Afternoon*, but what you learn about life and death is a matter of Hemingway.'

'And the little old lady ...?'

'The little old lady in *Death in the Afternoon* kept asking irrelevant questions. As a consequence, she didn't learn much about bullfighting or Earnest Hemingway and toward the end of the book Hemingway has to get rid of her.'

'I'm not a little old lady. I'm a young woman and I can learn. And if I want to understand you better, I should listen to what you have to say about art because it's a matter of life and death to you.'

'You might put it that way.'

'I am putting it that way.'

'Would you like to hear about Jacques Debierue?'

'I'd love to hear about Jacques Debierue!'

'In that case, I'll begin without the overall frame of reference and fill in the necessary background as I come to it. I said, I'll begin without the — I see, you don't have any relevant questions and you've decided to remain silent until you do? Fine. You'll understand my exhilaration about my opportunity to meet Jacques Debierue, then, when I tell you that I've read all, as far as I know, that's been written about him. The scope is wide, but the viewpoint is narrow.

'Only four other critics, all Europeans, have actually seen and written about his work at firsthand. I'll be the first American critic to examine his work, and it'll be new, original painting that no one else has ever seen before. For the first time in my critical career, I'll see the most recent Nihilistic Surrealistic paintings by the most famous artist in the world. It will also be possible, afterward, for me to evaluate and compare my opinions with the critiques of those critics who've written about his earlier work. I'll have a broad view of Debierue's growth — or possible retrogression — and historical support, or better yet, nonsupport, for my convictions.

'The incidental factors that led to Debierue's fame during the course of contemporary art history are marvelous. His silent, uphill fight against improbable odds appears, on the surface, to be effortless, but such was not the case. Mass hostility is always omnipresent toward the new, especially in art. Hundreds of books, as you know, have been filled with exegetical opinions about the Impressionists, Expressionists, Suprematists, Cubists, Futurists, Dadaists, and Surrealists of the early years of this century. All of the major innovators have been examined in detail, but there were many other painters who received no recognition at all. And there were smaller movements that were formed and then dissolved without being mentioned. How many, no one knows.

'But it was these minor movements that I was interested in during my year in Europe. It was a way to earn a reputation, you see. And if I could've pinned *one* of them down, one that got away, a movement that I could've written about and established as an important but overlooked movement in art history, I could've started my critical career immediately instead of teaching art survey courses to bored accountants at CCNY.

'Paris seethed with new developments in art before, during, and after the First World War. Hardly a day passed without a new group being formed, a new manifesto being drafted, followed by polemics, fistfights, dissolvements.

'Three painters would meet in a café, argue affably among themselves until midnight, and decide to form their own little splinter group. Then, as wine and arguments flowed for the remainder of the night as they scribbled away at a new manifesto, they detested each other by dawn.

'White-faced with anger and lack of sleep, they'd march off to their studios in the nacreous light of morning, their new movement junked before it was begun.

'A few of these lesser movements caught on, however, lasting for a few days or weeks after a scattered flurry of press publicity, but most of them died unheralded, unnoticed, for want of a second — or for no discernible reason. The fortunate, well-publicized movements lasted long enough to influence enough imitators to gain solid niches in art history. Cubism, for example, a term that pleased the reading public, was one of them.

'Paris, of course, was the center of the vortex during the early twenties, but forays into new and exciting art expressions were by no means confined to France.

'During my single year in France, as I tried to track down tangible evidence of these minor movements without success, my side trips to Brussels and Germany were even more tantalizing.

'In Brussels, the Grimm Brothers, Hal and Hans, who called themselves "The Grimmists," spent months in dark mines collecting expressive lumps of coal. These were exhibited as "natural" sculptures on white satin pillows. Within two days, however, shivering Belgians had pilfered these exposed lumps of coal, and the exhibit closed. The Belgians are a practical people, and 1919 was a cold winter. In their own way, the Brothers Grimm had originated "Found" art —'

'James — when you say that you have no superego, or conscience, does that mean that you've never done anything *bad*, anything you've ever been sorry for, later?'

'Yeah. Once. There was an assistant professor I knew at Columbia, an anthropologist, whose wife died. He had her cremated, and bought a beautiful five-hundred-dollar urn to keep her ashes in. He used to keep the urn on his desk at home, as a *memento mori*. Anthropologists, as you know, are pretty keen on ritual, burial ceremonies, and pottery — things of that nature. His wife died of tuberculosis.

'I never knew his first wife, but I met his second wife, who was one of his graduate students. Men, like women, are usually attracted to the same type of person when they remarry —'

'That isn't true! I've never known anyone like you before —'

'But then you've never been married, Berenice. And I'm talking about a widower who married again. His name doesn't matter to you, but it happened to be Dr. Hank Goldhagen. Anyway, his second wife, Claire, was *also* susceptible to respiratory infections. Sometimes, when they got into an argument, Hank would point to the urn of ashes, and say, "My first wife, in that urn, is a better woman and a better wife to me than you are, right now!"'

'What a terrible thing to say!'

'Isn't it? I sometimes wonder what she said to him to provoke it. But the marriage didn't last long. Following a weekend skiing trip to New Hampshire, Claire developed lumbar pneumonia and died. To save Hank money, I advised him to put Claire's ashes in the same expensive urn with his first wife.'

'But why ...?'

'There was ample room in the urn, and why not? Did it make any sense to buy a second expensive urn? And if he bought a cheaper one, that would've indicated to his friends that he thought less of Claire than he did of his first wife. But my practical suggestion backfired. Hank got so he was staring at the urn all the time brooding over and about the mixed ashes of these two women, and eventually he cracked up. And because it was my fault, I felt bad about it for weeks.'

'That isn't a true story, is it? Is it, James?'

'No, it isn't a true story. I made it up to please you, because, it seems, you're a little old lady who likes stories.'

'No, I'm not — and I don't like stories like that!'

'I'm leading up to Debierue, and I promise you that it's much more interesting than the story of Dr. Goldhagen's two wives.'

'I'm sorry I interrupted, James. May I pour you another cup of coffee?'

'Please. Let me tell you first about the *Scatölögieschul* that was formed by Willy Büttner in Berlin, during the post-war years of German political art. The *Scatölögieschul* probably holds the European record for short-livedness. It opened and closed in eight minutes flat. Herr Büttner and his three defiant fellow exhibitors, together with their cretin model — who denied her obvious presence in every painting — were carted off to jail. The paintings were confiscated, never to be seen by the public again. According to rumor, these ostensibly pornographic paintings wound up in General Goering's private collection. They're now believed to be in Russia, but no one really knows. I couldn't find a single eyewitness who had seen the pictures, although a lot of people knew about the exhibit. This was another frustrating experience for me in Europe.

'By the early sixties the trail was too cold for valid, documentary evidence. I was too late. The European Depression and World War Two had destroyed the evidence. I still feel that the critical neglect of these so-called minor movements may prove to be an incalculable loss to art history. Then, as now, critics only choose a very small number of painters to be *the* representatives of their times. And we only remember the names of those who come in first. Any sports writer can recall that Jesse Owens was the fastest runner in the 1936 Olympics, but he won't remember the names of the second and third place runners who were only split seconds behind him.

'Therefore, it's almost miraculous that Jacques Debierue was noticed at all. When you think about the peculiar mixture of hope and disillusionment of the twenties, he seems to be the most unlikely candidate of all the artists of the time to be singled out for fame. And he was studiously indifferent to the press.

'One painter, a true archetype, can hardly be said to constitute a movement, but Debierue rose above the Parisian art world like an extended middle finger. Paris critics found it embarrassing to admit that none of them knew the exact date his one-man show opened. The known details of the discovery of Debrierue, and the impact of his influence on other painters, has been examined at some length by August Hauptmann in his monograph entitled *Debierue.* This isn't a long book, not for the work of a German scholar, but it's a well-documented study of Debierue's original achievement.

'There isn't any mass of published work on Debierue, as there is on Pablo Picasso, but Debierue's name crops up all the time in the biographies and autobiographies of other famous modern painters — usually in strange circumstances. The frequent mention of his name isn't surprising. Before Debierue was in the art world, he was of it. Because he framed their paintings, he knew personally, and well, most of the other firsts of the war and postwar years.'

'He was a picture framer?'

'At first, yes. Miró, De Chirico, Man Ray, Pierre Roy, and many other painters found it expedient to visit him in his tiny framing shop. He gave them credit, and until they started to make money with their work, they sorely needed credit. Debierue's name is brought up in the studies published on every important postwar development because he was there — and because he knew all the artists involved. But his only commonality with other innovators is the fact that he was a first in his own right as the acknowledged father of Nihilistic Surrealism. Debierue, by the way didn't coin this term for his work.

'The Swiss essayist and art critic, Franz Moricand, was the first writer to use this term with reference to Debierue's art. And the label, once attached, stuck. The term appeared originally in Moricand's essay, '*Stellt er nur*?' in *Mercure de France*. The article wasn't penetrating, but other critics were quick to snatch the term "Nihilistic Surrealism" from the essay. An apt and descriptive bridge was needed, you see, to provide a clear dividing line between Dada and Surrealism. Both groups have attempted at various times to claim Debierue, but he was never in either camp. Dada and Sureralism both have strong philosophical underpinnings, but no one knows what Debierue's leanings are.

'Chance is an important factor in the discovery and recognition of every artist, but what many modern critics fail to accept is that Debierue's many artist-friends paid him off by sending people to see Debierue's one-man show. In his Montmartre hole-in-the-wall framing workshop he had mounted many paintings at cost, and others absolutely free, for poor young painters whose work sold a few months later for high prices. Those "crazy boatloads" of Americans, as Fitzgerald called them, coming to France during the boom period, always carried more than fifty dollars in cash on their person. They bought a lot of paintings, and the selling painters didn't forget their obligations to Debierue.

'Despite Hauptmann's book, an aura of mystery about Debierue's first and only one-man show remains. No invitations were issued, and there were no posters or newspaper ads. He didn't even mention the show to his friends. One day, and the exact date is still unknown, a small, hand-lettered card appeared in the display case behind the street window of his framing shop. "Jacques Debierue. *No. One.* Shown by request only." It was spelled Capital N-o-period. Capital O-n-e.'

'Why didn't he use the French *Nombre une*?'

'That's a good point, Berenice. But no one really knows. The fact that he used the English *No. One* instead of *Nombre une* may or may not have influenced Samuel Beckett to write in French instead of English, as the literary critic Leon Mindlin has claimed. But everyone concerned agrees that it was an astute move on Debierue's part when American tourists, with their limited French, began to arrive on the Paris scene. Using a number as a title for his picture, incidentally, was another first in art that has been indisputably credited to Debierue. Rothko, who uses numbers exclusively for his paintings, has admitted privately, if not in writing, his indebtedness to Debierue. The point's important because several art historians falsely attribute the numbering of paintings as a first for Rothko. Debierue hasn't said anything one way or another about the matter. He's never commented on his picture, either.

'This much is certain. *No. One* postdated Dada and predated Surrealism, thereby providing a one-man bridge between the two major art movements of this century. And Debierue's Nihilistic Surrealism may, in time, turn out to be the most important movement of the three. In retrospect, it's easy enough for us to see how Debierue captured the hearts and minds of the remaining Dadaists who were gradually, one by one, dropping out of Dada and losing their hard-earned recognition to the burgeoning Surrealists. And you can also realize, now, why the Surrealists were so anxious to claim Debierue. But Debierue stood alone. He neither admitted nor denied membership in either movement. His work spoke for him, as a work of art is supposed to do.

'*No. One* was exhibited in a small and otherwise empty room — once a maid's bedroom — one short flight of stairs above Debierue's downstairs workshop. An environment had been created deliberately for the picture. The

visitor who requested to see it — no fee was asked — was
escorted upstairs by the artist himself and left alone with
the picture.

'At first, as the viewer's eyes became adjusted to the
murky natural light coming into the room from a single
dirty window high on the opposite wall, all he could see
was what appeared to be an ornate frame, without a
picture in it, hanging on the wall. A closer inspection, with
the aid of a match or cigarette lighter, revealed that the
gilded frame with baroque scrollwork enclosed a fissure or
crack in the gray plaster wall. The exposed wire, and the
nail which had been driven into the wall to hold both the
wire and the frame, were also visible. Within the frame,
the wire, peaking to about twenty degrees at the apex — at
the nail — resembled, if the viewer stood well back from
the picture, a distant mountain range.'

Berenice sighed. 'I don't understand it. The whole thing
doesn't make any sense to me.'

'Exactly! No sense, but not nonsense. This was an irrational work in a rational setting. Debierue's Nihilistic
Surrealism, like Dada and Surrealism, is irrational. That's
the entire point of Dada, and of most of the other postwar
art movements. Distortion, irrationality, and unlikely
juxtaposition of objects.'

'What did the reviewers say about it?'

'What the reviewers said in the newspapers isn't
important, Berenice. There's a distinction between a
reviewer and a critic, as you should know. The reviewer
deals with art as a commodity. He's got three or four
shows a week to cover, and his treatment of them is super-
ficial, at best. But the critic is interested in aesthetics, and
in placing the work of art in the scheme of things — or
even as a pattern of behavior.'

'All right, then. What did the critics say about *No.
One*?'

'A great many things. But criticism begins with the structure, and often ends there, especially for those critics who
believe that every work of art is autotelic. Autotelic. That
means —'

'I know what autotelic means. I studied literary criticism in college, and I've got a degree in English.'

'Okay. What does it mean?'

'It means that a work of art is complete in itself.'

'Right! And what else does it mean, or imply?'

'Just that. That the poem, or whatever, should be considered by itself, without reference to anything else.'

'That's right, but there's more. It means that the artist himself should not be brought into the criticism of the work being considered. And although I'm a structuralist, I don't think that any work — poem, painting, novel — is autotelic. The personality of the artist is present in every work of art, and the critic has to dig it out as well as explicating the structure and form. Take pro football —'

'I'd love to. It's more interesting than painting.'

'To you, yes, but I want to make an analogy. A good critic's like a good football announcer on television. We see the same play that he does, but he breaks it down for us, reveals the structure and the pattern of the play. He explains what went wrong and what was right about the play. He can also tell us what is likely to come next. Also, because of the instant tape replay, he can even break down the play into its component parts for us to see again in slow motion. We do the same thing in art criticism sometimes, when we blow up details of a painting in slides.'

'Your analogy doesn't explain the "personality" in the football play.'

'Yes it does. This is the quarterback, who caused the play in the first place. That is, if the quarterback called the play. Sometimes the coach calls every play, sending in the new play every time with a substitute. If the announcer doesn't know what the coach is like, what he has done before, *or* the quarterback, I'll say, his explanation of the structure of the play is going to be shaky, and any prediction he makes won't be valid. Do you follow me?'

'I follow you.'

'Good. Then you shouldn't have any trouble in understanding the success of *No. One.* Only one person at a time was allowed to examine the picture. But there was no time limit set by the artist. Some visitors came downstairs immediately. Others remained for an hour or more, inconveniencing those waiting below. The average viewer was satisfied by a cursory inspection. But according to Hauptmann, there were a great many repeats.

'One old Spanish nobleman from Seville visited Paris a half-dozen times for the sole purpose of taking another look at *No. One.* No visitor's log was kept, but the fact that a vast number of people visited Debierue's shop to see the picture is a matter of public record. Every Parisian artist of the time made the pilgrimage, usually bringing along some friends. And *No. One* was widely discussed.

'Sporadic newspaper publicity, the critical attention Debierue provoked in European art reviews, and word-of-mouth discussion of the exhibit, brought a steady stream of visitors to his gallery until May 25, 1925, when he sold his shop for the purpose of painting full time.

'*No. One,* naturally, was a picture that lent itself to varied, conflicting opinions. The crack enclosed by the mount, for example, might've been on the wall before Debierue hung the frame over it — or else it was made on purpose by the artist. This was a basic, if subjective, decision each critic had to make for himself. The conclusions on this primary premise opened up two diametrically opposed lines of interpretive commentary. The explicit versus the implicit meaning caused angry fluctuations in the press. To hold any opinion meant that one had to see the picture for himself. And the tiny gallery became a "must see" for visiting foreign journalists and art scholars.

'Most of the commentators concentrated their remarks on the jagged crack within the frame. But there were a few who considered this point immaterial because the crack couldn't be moved if the frame were to be removed. They were wrong. A critic has to discuss what's there, not something that may be somewhere else. And he never exhibited it anywhere else after he sold his shop. The consensus, including the opinions of those who actually detested the picture, was an agreement that the crack represented the final and inevitable break between traditional academic art and the new art of the twentieth century. In other words, *No. One* ushered in what Harold Rosenberg has since called "the tradition of the new".

'Freudian interpretations were popular, with the usual sexual connotations, but the sharpest splits were between the Dadaists and the Surrealists concerning the irrational aspects of the picture. Most Surrealists (Buñuel was an exception) held the opinion that Debierue had gone too far, feeling that he had reached a point of no return. Dadaists, many of them angered over the use of a gilded baroque mounting, claimed that Debierue hadn't carried irrationality out far enough to make his point irrevocably meaningless. Neither group denied the powerful impact of *No. One* on the art of the times.

'By 1925 Surrealism was no longer a potent art force — although it was revived in the thirties and rejuvenated in the early fifties. And the remaining Dadaists in 1925, those who hadn't joined André Breton, were largely disorganized. Nevertheless, Debierue's exhibit was still a strong attraction right up until the day it closed. And it was popular enough with Americans to be included on two different guided tours of Paris offered by tourist agencies.

'Once Nihilistic Surrealism became established as an independent art movement, Debierue was in demand as a speaker. He turned these offers down, naturally —'

'Naturally? Doesn't a speaker usually get paid?'

'Yes, and he would've been well paid. But an artist doesn't put himself in a defensive position. And that's what happens to a speaker. A critic's supposed to speak. He welcomes questions, because his job is to explain what the artist does. The artist is untrained for this sort of thing, and all he does is weaken his position. Some painters go around the country on lecture tours today, carrying racks of slides of their work, and they're an embarrassed, inarticulate lot. The money's hard to turn down, I suppose, but in the end they defeat themselves and negate their work. A creative artist has no place on the lecture platform, and that goes for poets and novelists, as well as painters.'

'So much for the Letters section of *The New York Review of Books*.'

'That's right. At least for poets and novelists. The nonfiction writer is entitled to lecture. He started an argument on purpose when he wrote his book, and he has every right to defend it. But the painter's work says what it has to say, and the critic interprets it for those who can't read it.'

'In that case, you're responsible to the artist as well as to the public.'

'I know. That's what I've been talking about. But it's a challenge, too, and that's why I'm so excited about interviewing Debrierue. When Debierue was preparing to leave Paris, following the closing of his shop and exhibit, he granted an interview to a reporter from *Paris Soir*. He didn't say anything about his proposed work in progress, except to state that his painting was too private in meaning for either his intimate friends or the general public. He had decided, he said, not to show any of his future work to the general public, nor to any art critic he considered unqualified to write intelligently about his painting.

'For the "qualified" critic, in other words, if not for the general public, the door was left ajar.

'The villa on the Riviera had been an anonymous gift to the artist, and he had accepted it in the spirit in which it was offered. No strings attached. He wasn't well-to-do, but the sale of his Montmartre shop would take care of his expenses for several months. The *Paris Soir* reporter then asked the obvious question. "If you refuse to exhibit or to sell your paintings, how will you live?"

' "That," Debierue replied, "isn't my concern. An artist has too much work to do to worry about such matters." With his mistress clinging to his arm, Debierue climbed into a waiting taxi and was off to the railroad station.

'Perhaps it was the naiveté of his reply that agitated an immediate concern among the painters he had known and befriended. At any rate, an organization named *Les Amis de Debierue* was formed hastily, within the month following his departure from the city. It's never disbanded.'

'There was an organization like that formed for T. S. Eliot, but it disbanded. The purpose was to get Mr. Eliot out of his job at the bank.'

'I know. But Eliot took another job in publishing. Debierue, so far as we know, never made another picture frame, except for his own work. *Les Amis* held its first fund-raising banquet in Paris, and through this continuing activity enough money was collected to give the artist a small annual subsidy. Other donations are still solicited from art lovers annually. I've been giving *Les Amis de Debierue* at least five bucks a year since I left graduate school.

'During World War Two, the Germans let Debierue alone. Thanks to two critical articles that had linked his name with Nietzsche, he wasn't considered as a "degenerate" French artist. And apparently they didn't discover any of his current work to examine for "flaws."

'When the Riviera was liberated, it was immediately transformed into an R and R area for U.S. troops, and he was soon visited by art students, now in uniform, who'd read about him in college. They mentioned him in their letters home, and it didn't take long for American art groups to begin a fresh flow of clothing, food, art supplies, and money to his Riviera outpost.

'Debierue had survived two world wars, and a dozen ideological battles.

'The first three reviews of Debierue's Riviera works, with a nod to *symbolisme*, are self-explanatory. "Fantasy," "Oblique," and "Rain" are the names given to his first three "periods" — as assigned by the first three critics who were allowed to examine his paintings. The fourth period, "Chironesque," is so hermetic it requires some amplification.'

Berenice nodded in assent.

'A paucity of scholastic effort was put into the examination of these four important essays. Little has been published, either in book or monograph form as in-depth studies of each period — the way Picasso's Rose and Blue periods have been covered. This is understandable, because the public never saw any of these pictures.

'The established critic prefers to examine the original work, or at least colored slides of that work, before he reaches his own conclusions. To refute or to agree with the critic who's seen the work puts a man on shaky ground. Each new article, as it appeared, however, received considerable attention. But writers were chary of making any expanded judgements based upon the descriptions alone.'

'Yes, I can understand that.'

'This general tendency didn't hold true for Louis Galt's essay, "Debierue: The Chironesque Period," which appeared in the Summer 1958 edition of *The Nonobjectivist*. It was reprinted in more than a dozen languages and art journals.

'Galt, you see, was known as an avowed purist in his approach to nonobjective art, and that's why he published his article in *The Nonobjectivist* when he could've had it published by *Art News* for ten times as much money. Galt had once gone so far as to call Mondrian a "traitor" in print when the Dutchman gave up his black-and-white palette to experiment with color in his linear paintings. I didn't agree with him there, but he made some telling points. But with so many able critics available, all of them anxious to see Debierue's post-World War Two work, it was considered a damned shame that he'd chosen a purist who would only look at the new work from a prejudiced viewpoint.

'The appellation "Chironesque" was considered as a derogatory "literary" term. It was deeply resented by Susan Sontag, who said so in *The Partisan Review*. The Galt essay wasn't, in all fairness, disrespectful, but Galt stated bluntly that Debierue had retrogressed. He claimed that "bicephalous centaurlike creatures" were clearly visible in the dozen paintings Debierue had shown him. And this forced Galt to conclude that the "master" was now a "teacher", and that didacticism had no place in contemporary art. The "purist" view, of course.'

'Of course.' Berenice nodded.

'At any rate — and here he was reaching for it — because Chiron the centaur was the mythical teacher of Hercules, and other Greek heroes, Galt christened the period "Chironesque." This was a cunning allusion to the classicism Galt destested, elements Galt would've considered regressive in any modern painter.

'Debierue, of course, said nothing.'

Berenice nodded and closed her eyes.

'The controversial Galt essay was well timed. It rejuvenated interest in the old painter, and the "bicephalous centaur-like creatures," as described by Galt, made the new work resemble — or appear to resemble — Abstract Expressionism. Some wishful thinking was going on. Nineteen fifty-eight wasn't an exciting pictorial year. Except for a handful of New York painters, called the "Sidney Janis Painters", after their dealer, the so-called New York School was undergoing a transitional phase. And Debierue was news, of course, because he'd received so little public notice in recent years.'

Berenice dropped her chin. 'Uh huh.'

'One New York dealer cabled Debierue an offer of fifty thousand dollars for any one of the Chironesque paintings, sight unseen. Debierue acknowledged it by sending back a blank cablegram — with just his type signature. The dealer took advantage of the publicity by blowing up a copy of his offer and Debierue's reply and by placing the photo blow-ups in the window of his Fifty-seventh Street gallery. Other dealers, who aped and upped the original offer, didn't receive any replies.

'How I'll manage it, I don't know, Berenice. I know only that I'm determined to be the first critic to see Debierue's American paintings, and I've already decided to call it his "American Period"!'

But I was talking to myself. Berenice, I noticed, with some irritation, had fallen asleep.

Chapter Six

Despite her size, and she was a large woman, Berenice, curled and cramped up in sleep, looked vulnerable to the point of fragility. Her unreasonably long blond lashes swept round flushed cheeks, and her childish face, in repose and without makeup, took several years from her age. Her heavy breasts and big round ass, however, exposed now, as the short flimsy nightgown rode high above her hips, were incongruously mature in contrast with her innocent face and tangled Alice-in-Wonderland hair. As I examined her, with squinted-eyed, ambivalent interest, a delicate bubble of spit formed in the exact center of her bowed, slightly parted lips.

Oh, I had put Berenice to sleep all right, with my discursive discussion of Jacques Debierue. With an impatient, involuntary yawn of my own I wondered how much she had understood about Debierue before she had drifted off completely. She had been attentive, of course, as she always was when I talked to her, but she had never asked a serious question. Not that it made much difference. Berenice had a minimal interest in art — or in anything that bordered on abstract thought — and for some time I had suspected that the slight interest she was able to muster occasionally was largely feined. An effort to please me.

Except for her adhesive interest in me as a person, or personality, and in matching sexual frequencies, I wondered if anything else had ever stimulated her intellectually. For a woman who had majored in English, and taught the subject (granted, she taught on a high school level), she was surprisingly low on insight into the nature of literature.

No one could accuse her of being well read, either. Her insights into literature when I had, on occasion, attempted to draw her out, were either sophomoric or parroted generalities remembered from her college English courses. She had an excellent memory for plot lines and the names of characters, but for little else.

She was probably a poor classroom teacher, I decided. She had such a lazy, good-natured disposition she could not have been any great shakes as a disciplinarian. But she would have few disciplinary problems in a city like Duluth, where teenagers were polite incipient Republicans. New York high school students would have had a gentle woman like Berenice in tears within minutes.

But how did I know? I didn't. In a power situation, with children, she might inspire terror, fear, and trembling. She never talked about her work and, for all I knew, she might be an expert in grammar and a veritable hotshot in the classroom.

The persona of a woman in love is highly deceiving.

Did she feign sentimentality as well as other things? She cried real tears one night when Timmy Fraser sang 'My Funny Valentine' at the Red Pirate Lounge — stretching out the song in the mournful way that he does for fully ten minutes. Any woman who fails to recognize the inherent viciousness of Lorenz Hart's 1930s lyrics has a head filled with cornmeal stirabout instead of brains. She also mentioned once that she had cried for two days over Madame Bovary's suicide. Fair enough. Flaubert had earned those tears, but she had no insight into the style of the novel, nor did she analyze how Flaubert had maneuvered her emotionally into weeping over the death of that poor, sick woman.

Knowing this much, and after thinking about it, I realized that I knew very little about her, it was unreasonable of me to expect a wakeful interest from Berenice in Jacques Debierue. Berenice was a funny valentine, that is what she was, and her chin was a little weak, too. In a vague abstract way I loved her. At the same time, I wondered what to do with her. She had been a sounding board to diminish some of the excitement inside me, but now it was two a.m. and I was going to be busy today. Busy, busy. Perhaps if I used her right, she would be an asset. Wouldn't it help to have a beautiful woman in tow when I called on Debierue? He would hardly slam the door in the face of a strikingly attractive woman. A Frenchman? Never ...

The bubble of spit ballooned suddenly as she exhaled, and inaudibly popped. Berenice whimpered in her sleep and tried, wriggling, to find a more comfortable position in her chair. This was impossible. With her long legs cramped up under her rear and in a tight-fitting canvas officer's chair, it was miraculous that she could fall asleep in the first place.

I stopped rationalizing, recognizing what I was doing — rationalizing — and prodded Berenice's soft but rather flat belly with a stiff forefinger.

'Wake up, Audience,' I said, not unkindly.

'I wasn't asleep,' she lied. 'I just closed my eyes for a second to rest them.'

'I know. I forgot to ask, but where have you been the last couple of days?'

'Here.' Her eyes widened. 'Right here.'

'Not today you weren't.'

'Oh, you mean today?'

'Yes. Today.'

'I was at Gloria's apartment. Honestly, I got so blue just sitting around here all alone waiting for you to come back that I called her. She drove over for me and took me in.'

'I thought as much. Gloria tried to pump me on the phone when I got back. I thought something was odd about her phony laughter, but couldn't figure it out. If you didn't intend to go back to Duluth, why did you take your bags and leave that weird note for me?'

'I tried to go, I really did, but I just couldn't!' Her eyes moistened. 'I want to stay with you, James ... don't you want me to?'

I had to forestall her tears. Why can't women learn how to say 'Good-bye' like a man?

'We'll see, baby, we'll see. Let's go to bed now. We'll talk about it in the morning, much later *this* morning.'

Berenice rose obediently, crossed her arms, and with a sweeping graceful movement removed her shorty nightgown. No longer sleepy, she grinned wickedly and crawled into the tumbled Murphy bed, shaking her tremendous stern as she did so. I smiled. She was amusing when she tried to be coy because she was so big. I undressed slowly and crawled in beside her. The air-conditioner, without enough BTUs to cool the apartment adequately, labored away — uh uh, uh uh, uh uh.... As a rule I could shut the sound out, but now it bothered me.

I was tense, slightly high from drinking four cups of black coffee, and overstimulated by my ability to recall, with so little effort, the details of Debierue's career. Three, no, four days had passed since the last time, and yet, strangely, I wasn't interested in sex. To make love now would be to initiate a new beginning to a something I had written 'ending' to — perhaps that was the reason. That, or my unresolved feelings about Berenice now that I was on the verge of a future — if everything worked out all right — that held no place for a woman who was interested in me as a person. Any relationship between a man and a woman that is based upon bodies and personalities alone can lead only to disaster.

It was a premonition, or some kind of precognitive instinct for self-preservation, I should have heeded. But at two in the morning, with my mind still reeling with matters intellectual, I was physically unable to muster enough brute bellicosity to toss Berenice and her suitcase down the stairs. She was loving, too loving.

The inchoate premonition, or whatever it was, of some disaster, froze my body as well as my mind into a state of flaccid inaction. Berenice was puzzled, I know. When none of her usual tricks worked, she climbed over me suddenly, got out of bed, and switched off the floor lamp. Except for the tiny red light on the electric coffeepot, which was not a red, baleful staring eye, but merely an effective reminder that the coffee was hot if I was not, the room was as dark as my thoughts. We had never made love in the dark before. I didn't know about Berenice, but such a peculiar idea had never occurred to me in my lifetime. It is too impersonal to make love in the dark. Your partner could be *anyone*, anyone at all.

How she knew this I don't know, but the gimmick worked. As Berenice whipped her head back and forth, stinging first my chest and then my stomach with her long hair, my doubts disappeared. And because this unseen woman became any woman, and was no longer a problem named Berenice Hollis, I became rigid with the pain of need, and mounted her savagely. Savagely for me, because I am usually methodical in sexual relations, knowing what I like and dislike. Being flagellated with long hair was a new experience for me as well, and I favored Berenice with the best ride she had ever had. She climaxed as I entered, then twice, and we made the final one together. She bit my shoulder so hard to keep from mewing (knowing how irritated I get when she makes animal noises) she left the marks of her teeth in my skin.

Euphoric, my tenseness dissipated, the thought of sending this big, marvelous woman back to Minnesota became intolerable. She turned on the floorlamp and rummaged around in her suitcase for douching equipment.

'Hang up that yellow linen suit of yours, baby,' I told her, 'so the wrinkles will shake out.'

'Why?' she asked, doing as she was told. 'It isn't wrinkled.'

'Because I want you to wear it tomorrow. I'm taking you with me.'

'Where are we going? Are we going to have fun?'

'To call on M. Debierue.' I sighed. 'I'll try to explain it again tomorrow — in one-syllable words.' With the light on, Berenice Hollis was a problem again.

'We'll have fun, though, won't we?'

'Sure,' I replied glumly. 'Fun, fun, fun.'

I closed my eyes as she went into the bathroom. I remember dimly being washed with a warm washrag, but I was sound asleep before she finished.

Part Two

If anything exists, it is incomprehensible.

Chapter One

The apartment looked terrible, as if a small whirlwind had been turned loose for a few minutes, but Berenice, in her lemon linen suit, with its skimpy microskirt, was beautiful. At my request she wore stockings, sheer enough to enhance the sienna brown of her deeply tanned legs. The skirt was so short, when she sat or leaned over, the white metal snaps that held up her stockings were exposed slyly enough to make her as sexy as a Varga drawing.

Instead of a blouse she wore a filmy blue-and-red scarf around her neck. The two loose ends of the scarf were tucked crosswise beneath the lapels of the square-cut double-breasted jacket. Very few women would dare to wear such a severely cut suit, but the square straight lines of the jacket exaggerated the roundness of Berenice's lush figure. With the supplement of a rat she had put up her hair, and ample mound of tawny hair, sun-tinged with yellow streaks, piled on top of her head, together with her childish features, gave her an angelic expression.

There was, I think, too much orange in her lipstick, but perhaps this slight imperfection was the single needed touch that made her so lovely as a whole.

I had shaved and showered before Berenice took over the bathroom for an hour, and I had trimmed my Spanish Don sideburns neatly with scissors. Nevertheless, I looked incongruously raunchy beside Berenice in my faded blue denim, short-sleeved jumpsuit, especially when she slipped on a pair of white gloves. It was too hot outside for a jacket, and I needed the multiple pockets in the jumpsuit to carry all my paraphernalia.

I had three pens, a notebook, my wallet and keys, a handkerchief, two packs of Kools, and my ribbed-model Dunhill lighter (one of the few luxuries I had treated myself to when I had a regular teaching salary coming in), a tiny Kodak Bantam in my right trousers pocket, some loose change, a pocket magnifying glass in a leather case, finger-nail clippers, and a two-inch piece of clammy jade, with indentations for a finger grip. Except for the well-concealed Kodak Bantam, loaded with color film, I carried too much crap around with me, but I had gotten used to carrying it and could hardly do without it.

We had slept late and had a leisurely breakfast. After getting dressed, I had jotted down a few questions in my notebook. I would not refer to the questions, but the act of writing them down had set them in my mind. This was an old reporter's trick that worked, and I always took my Polaroid camera along, loaded with black-and-white, and extra film. Professionals sneer at Dr. Edwin H. Land's Polaroids, but I was an expert with them and rarely snapped more than two shots before getting what I wanted. I had learned, too, that people will okay without argument almost any picture that they have seen, but will refuse to allow photos to be published when they haven't seen everything on the roll.

By 1:30 p.m. we were ready to go. I preceded Berenice down the stairs into the glare of the breaktaking Florida sunlight. The humidity was close to ninety, although the temperature wasn't quite eighty-five. There were threatening nimbus clouds farther south, but the sky was clear and blue above Palm Beach. It doesn't always rain in South Florida when the humidity hits 100 percent, although technically it is supposed to, but inasmuch as we were heading toward the dark sky above Boynton Beach, I decided not to put the canvas top back. Inside the car, on burning leatherette seats, we sweltered.

We had hardly crossed the bridge into West Palm when Berenice pointed to a blazing orange roof and said, 'Let's stop at Howard Johnson's.'

'Why? We just finished breakfast an hour ago.'

'I have to widdle. That's why.'

'I told you to pee before we left.'

'I did, but I have to go again.'

It was partly the heat, but I jerked the car into the parking lot, thinking angrily that it wasn't too late. I could call a cab and send Berenice back to the apartment.

But once inside the cave-cold depths and booth-seated, I ordered two chocolate ice cream sodas, waited for them and Berenice, and smoked a Kool. Because the service was seasonal, Berenice joined me at the table long before the sodas arrived. She picked up my cigarette from the ashtray, took a long drag, replaced the cigarette exactly as she found it, held the inhaled smoke inside her lungs like a skin diver trying to break the hold-your-breath-underwater record, and finally let what was left of the smoke out. I had noticed, during the three days I was in Miami, when Berenice had not been with me, that her so-called efforts to quit smoking caused three packs a day to go up in smoke instead of my usual two. She had merely quit buying and carrying them. She smoked mine instead — or took long drags off the cigarette I happened to be smoking. She hated mentholated cigarettes, or so she claimed, but not enough, apparently, to give them up altogether.

'If you want a cigarette,' I said, pushing the pack toward her, 'take one. When you drag mine down a quarter of an inch that way, I finish the cigarette unsatisfied because I didn't have the exact ration of smoke I'm accustomed to. Then, because I feel gypped out of a quarter inch, I light another one, only to find that an entire cigarette, smoked too soon after the one I just finished, is too much. I butt it, replace it in the pack, and when I finally get around to lighting the butt the next time I want a smoke, it tastes too strong and it still isn't a regular-length smoke. If I throw the butt away, with only a couple of drags gone, it's a waste, and—'

Berenice put a cool hand over mine. There were faint crinkles in the corner of her guileless cornflower blue eyes. Her bowed lips narrowed as they flickered a rapid smile.

'What's bothering you, James?'

I shrugged. 'I don't know. I took an up with my third cup of coffee, and the combination of a benny with too much coffee makes me talk too much. As I told you last night, Berenice, this is a one-of-a-kind opportunity for me. And I'm apprehensive, that's all.'

She shook her head. The smile appeared and disappeared against so fast I almost missed it. 'No, James, you told me so much about this painter last night I got confused, bogged down in details so to speak. Something is either missing or you didn't tell me everything.'

'You fell asleep, for Christ's sake.'

'No, I didn't. Well, maybe toward the end. But what I don't understand is how this painter, this Debierue, can be such a famous painter when no one has ever seen any of his paintings. It doesn't make sense.'

'What do you mean, no one has seen his paintings? Thousands of people saw his first one-man show, and his subsequent work has been written about by Mazzeo, Charonne, Reinsberg, and Galt, who all studied his paintings. These are some of the most famous critics of this century, for God's sake!'

She shook her head and pursed her lips. 'I don't mean them, or even you — that is, if you get to see what he's painted since coming to Florida. I mean the public, the people who flock to museums when a traveling Van Gogh show comes in, and buy all kinds of Van Gogh reproductions and so on. I had seen dozens of Van Gogh paintings in books and magazines long before I ever saw one of his originals. That's what I mean by famous. How can I be impressed by Debrierue's fame when I've never seen any of his work and can't judge for myself how good he is?'

Our ice cream sodas arrived. I didn't want to hurt Berenice's feelings, but I was forced to because of her ignorance.

'Look, baby, you aren't qualified to judge for yourself. Now keep quiet, and drink your nice ice cream soda — there's a good girl — and I'll try and explain it to you. Did you ever study cetology?'

'I don't now. What is it?'

'The scientific study of whales. A cetologist is a man who studies whales, and he can spend an entire lifetime at it, just as I've spent my life, so far, studying art — as have the critics who wrote about Debierue. Now, let's suppose that you pick up a copy of *Scientific American* and read an article about whales written by a well-known cetologist —'

'Are there any well-known cetologists?'

'There are bound to be. I don't have any names to rattle off for you — that isn't my racket. But I haven't finished yet. All right, you're reading this article by a cetologist in *Scientific American* and he states that a baby sperm whale is a tail presentation.'

'What does that mean?'

'It means that a baby whale, unlike other mammals, is born tail first.'

'How do you know that?'

'I read a lot. But the same would hold true even if the cetologist said that it was a cephalic presentation. The point I'm making is this: The article is written by a cetologist and published in *Scientific American*, and you will accept an expert's word for it. You aren't going to get yourself a god-damned boat and sail around the seven fucking seas trying to find a pregnant whale, are you? Just so you can check on whether a baby whale is born head first or tail first?'

Berenice giggled. 'You're cute when you're stern. No ... I guess not, but art, it seems to me, is supposed to be for everybody, not just for those critics you mentioned ...'

I put down the spoon and wiped my lips on a paper napkin. '*Whales* are for everybody, too, sweetheart. But not everybody studies whales as a lifetime occupation. That's the big difference you don't seem to understand.'

'All right.' She shrugged. 'I still think there's something you haven't told me about all this.'

I grinned. 'There is. In return for Debierue's address I've got to do a favor for Mr. Cassidy —'

'The lawyer who told you about Debierue?'

'Yeah.' I nodded. 'And what I'm telling you is "privileged information", as Cassidy would put it. It's between you and Mr. Cassidy and these ice cream sodas.'

'You can trust me, James.' Her face softened. 'You can trust me with your life.'

'I know. And in a way if *is* my life. Anyway, Mr. Cassidy gave me privileged information — where Debierue is living — and all I have to do in return is to steal a picture for him.'

'Steal a picture? Why can't he buy one? He's rich enough.'

'Debierue doesn't sell his pictures. I explained all that. If Cassidy gets a picture, even one that's been stolen, he'll be the only collector in the world to have one, you see.'

'What good will it do him? If it's a stolen picture, Debierue can get it back by calling the police.'

'Debierue won't know he has it, and neither will anyone else — until after Debierue's dead, anyway. Then the picture will be even more valuable.

'How're you going to steal a picture without Debierue knowing it was you?'

'I don't know yet. I'm playing things by ear at the moment. It might not be a picture. If he's working with ceramics, I can slip a piece in my pocket while you distract him. Maybe there are some drawings around. Mr. Cassidy would be satisfied with a drawing. In fact he'd be delighted. But until I find out what Debierue has been doing, I won't know what to do myself.'

'But you want me to help you?'

'If you want to, yes. He can't watch both of us at the same time, and he's an old man. So when a chance comes, and it will, I'll give you the high sign and then I'll snatch something.'

'It's awfully haphazard, James, the way you say it. Besides, as soon as we leave, he'll know that you're the one who stole it — what*ever* it is.'

'No.' I shook my head. 'He won't know. He'll *suspect* that I took it, but he won't be able to prove it. I'll deny everything, if charged, and besides it'll never get that far.

Meanwhile, Mr. Cassidy will have the painting, chunk of sculpture, drawing, or whatever, hidden away where Jesus Christ couldn't find it. See?'

'Do you realize, James,' she said, rather primly, 'that if you ever got caught stealing a painting from anybody that your career would be over?'

'Not really, and not, certainly, from Debierue. His work, as you mentioned before about Van Gogh, belongs to the world — and if I were ever tried for something like that, which I wouldn't be — I'd have a defense fund from art lovers and art magainzes that would make me look like a White Panther. Anyway, that's the plan — in addition to somehow getting an interview, of course.'

'It isn't much of a plan.'

'True. But now that you know what I have to do, you might get an idea once we're on the scene. The important thing is this: don't take anything yourself. I'll take it when the time is propitious. I have to get the interview before anything else is done.'

'I understand.'

The rain caught us before we reached Lake Worth.

There were torrents of it, and I could hardly see to drive. Berenice, because of her suit, had to roll up her window, but it was too hot for me to roll up mine. My left shoulder and arm got soaked, but with the humidity I would have been just as wet inside the car with the window rolled up. The rain finally came down so hard I had to pull over to the curb in Lake Worth to wait for a letup.

Berenice was frowning. 'How much,' she asked, 'does a baby whale weight when it's first born?'

'One ton. And it's fourteen feet long.' I lit a cigarette and passed it to Berenice. She shook her head and handed it back. I took a long drag. 'One ton,' I said solemnly, 'is two thousand pounds.'

'I *know* how much a ton is!' she said angrily. 'You — you — you damned intellectual, you!'

I couldn't contain myself. I had to laugh and ruin my joke.

Chapter Two

I could have taken State Road Seven straight away by picking it up west of West Palm Beach, but because the old two-lane highway was used primarily by truck traffic barreling for Miami's back door, into Hialeah, I stayed on U.S.1 all the way to Boynton Beach before searching for a through road to make the cutover. I got lost for a few minutes and made several aimless circles where new blacktops had been crushed down for a subdivision called inappropriately Ocean Pine Terraces (miles from the ocean, no pines, no terraces), but when I finally reached the state highway, it was freshly paved, and the truck traffic wasn't nearly as bad as I had expected.

The rain, mercifully, had stopped.

My crude map was clear enough, but I had zipped past Debierue's turnoff to the Dixie Drive-in Movie Theater before I realized it. The mixed dirt-and-gravel private road leading to Debierue's home and studio was clearly visible from the highway, and on the right of the highway about three hundred yards before the drive-in entrance, but I had failed to notice it. I made a crimped circle in the deserted drive-in entrance and this time, from the other side of the highway, it was easy to spot the break.

Thick gama grass had reclaimed the deep wheel ruts of the road, and I crawled along in first gear. The bumpy, rarely used trail straight-lined through a stand of second-growth slash pine for about a half mile and then made a sigmoid loop to circumvent two stinking stagnant ponds of black swamp water. On the right of the road, abandoned chicken runs stretched into the jungly mass of greenery, and weeds had grown straight and tall along the sagging chicken-wire fences. The unpainted wooden chicken-houses had weathered to an unpatterned dirty gray, and most of the roofs had caved in. The narrow road petered out at an open peeled-pine gate. I eased into the fenced area, with its untended, thickly grassed yard, which resembled a huge, brown bathmat, and pulled up in front of the screened porch of the house.

Paradoxically, I was awed by my first sight of the old painter. I switched off the engine, and as it ticked heatedly away, I sat and stared. I say 'paradoxically' because Debierue in person was anything but awe-inspiring.

He resembled any one of a thousand, no literally tens of thousands, of those tanned Florida retirees one sees on bridges fishing, on golf courses tottering, and on the shuffleboard courts of rest homes and public parks shuffling. He even wore the uniform. Green-billed khaki baseball cap, white denim Bermuda shorts, low-cut Zayre tennis shoes in pale blue canvas, and the standard white, open-necked 'polo' shirt with short sleeves. The inevitable tiny green alligator was embroidered over the left pocket of the shirt, an emblem so common in Florida that any Miami Beach comedian could get a laugh by saying, 'They caught an alligator in the Glades the other day, and he was wearing a shirt with a little man sewn over the pocket ...'

But unlike those other thousands of old men who had retired to Florida in anticipation of a warm death, men who had earned their dubious retirement by running shoe stores, managing light-bulb plants in Amarillo, manufacturing condoms in Newark, hustling as harried sales managers in the ten western states, Debierue had served, and was still serving, the strictest master of them all — the self-discipline of the artist.

Debierue, apparently unperturbed by the arrival of a strange, beat-up convertible in his yard, sat limberly erect in a green-webbed aluminium patio chair beside the porch door, soaking up late afternoon sun. I was pleased to see that he was allowing his white beard to grow again (for several years he had been clean shaven), but it was not as long and Melvillean as it had been in photos of the old artist taken in the twenties.

Physically, Debierue was asthenic. Long-limbed, long-bodied, slight, with knobbly knees and elbows. Advanced age had caused his thin shoulders to droop, of course, and there was a melony potbelly below his belt. His sun-bronzed skin, although it was wrinkled, gave the old man a healthy, almost robust appearance. His keen blue eyes were alert and unclouded, and the great blade of his beaky French nose did not have those exposed, tiny red veins one usually associates with aged retirees in Florida. His full, sensuous lips formed a fat grape-colored 'O' — a dark, plump circle encircled by white hair. His blue stare, with which he returned mine, was incurious, polite, direct, and distant, but during the long uncomfortable moment we sat in silent confrontation, I detected an air of vigilance in his sharp old eyes.

As a critic I had learned early in the game how unwise it was to give too much weight or credence to first impressions, but under his steady, unwavering gaze I felt — I *knew* — that I was in the presence of a giant, which, in turn, made me feel like a violator, a criminal. And if, in that first moment, he had pointed to the gate silently — without even saying 'Get out!' — I would have departed without uttering a word.

But such was not the case.

Berenice, her hands folded in her lap over her chamois drawstring handbag, sat quietly, and there she would sit until I got out of the car, walked around it, and opened the door on her side.

I was uninvited, an unexpected visitor, and it was up to me to break the frozen sea that divided us. Apprehensively, and dangling the Land camera from its carrying strap on two fingers, I got out of the car and nodded politely.

'Good afternoon, M. Debierue,' I said in French, trying to keep my voice deep, like Jean Gabin, 'at long last we meet!'

Apparently he hadn't heard any French (and mine wasn't so bad) for a long time. Debierue smiled — and what a wonderful, warmhearted smile he had! His smile was so sweet, so sincere, so insinuating that my heart twisted with sudden pain. It was a smile to shatter the world. His age-ruined mouth, purple lips and all, was beautiful when he smiled. Several teeth were missing, both uppers and lowers, and those that remained gave a jack-o'-lantern effect to his generous mouth. But the swift transformation from mournful resignation to rejuvenated, unrestrained happiness changed his entire appearance. The grooved down-pointing lines in his face were twisted into swirling, upswept arabesques. He rose stiffly from his chair as I approached, and shook a long forefinger at me in mock reproach.

'Ah, Mr. Figueras! You have shaved your beard. You must grow it back quickly!'

His greeting me by name that way brought sudden moisture to my eyes. He pumped my hand, the single up-and-down European handshake. His long spatulate fingers were warm and dry.

'You — you *know* me?' I said, in unfeigned astonishment.

He treated me to the first in a series of bona fide Gallic shrugs. 'You, or another —' he said mysteriously, 'and it is well that it is you. I am familiar with your work, naturally, Mr. Figueras.

I gulped like a tongue-tied teenager, abashed, not knowing what to say, and then noticed that he was looking past my shoulder toward Berenice.

'Oh!' I said, running around the car, and helping Berenice out the door. 'This is my friend, M. Debierue, Mlle Hollis.'

Berenice glared at me when I pronounced her name 'Holee,' and said, 'Hollis, Mr. Debierue,' in English, 'Berenice Hollis. And it's a pleasure to meet you, sir.'

Debierue kissed her hand, and I thought (I was probably oversensitive) he was a little uneasy, or put off by her presence. He didn't know — and there was no unawkward way for me to enlighten him — whether she was truly just a friend, my mistress, my secretary, or a well-heeled art patron. I decided to say nothing more. He would be able to tell for himself by the way she looked at me and touched my arm from time to time that we were on intimate terms. It was best to let it go at that.

The old man's English was adequate, despite a heavy accent, and as we talked in French, that beautiful late April afternoon, he or I occasionally translated or made some comment to Berenice in English.

'I'm one of those obscure journalists who presume to criticize art,' I said modestly, with a nervous smile, but he stopped me by raising a hand.

'Non, no, no' — he shook his head — 'not obscure, Mr. Figueras. I know your work well. The article you wrote on the California painter ... ?' He frowned.

'Vint? Ray Vint, you mean?'

'Yes, that's the name. The little fly. That was so droll.' He chuckled reflectively. 'Do not feel guilty, Mr. Figueras.' He shrugged. 'The true artist cannot hide forever, and if not you, another would come. Now, come! Come inside! I will give you cold orange juice, fresh frozen Minute Maid.'

I was flattered that he knew my work as well as my name, or at least *one* article — I checked myself — written in English, at that, and not to my knowledge translated into French. But why did he mention this particular article on Vint? Ray Vint was an abstract painter whose paintings sold sparsely — for a dozen good reasons I won't go into here. Vint was an excellent craftsman, however, and could get all the portrait work he desired — more, in fact, than he wanted to paint. He needed the money he made from portraits to be able to work on the abstracts he preferred to paint. But because he hated to do portraits, he also hated the people who sat for them and provided him with large sums for flattering likenesses. He got 'revenge' on the sit.ers by painting a fly on them.

In medieval painting, and well into the Renaissance, a fly was painted on Jesus Christ's crucified body: the fly on Jesus' body was a symbol of redemption, because a fly represented sin and Jesus was without sin. A fly painted on the person of a layman, however, signified sin *without* redemption, or translated into 'This person is going to Hell!' Ray Vint painted a trompe-l'oeil fly on every portrait.

Sometimes his patrons didn't notice the fly for several days, and when they did they were unaware of its significance. They were usually delighted when they discovered it. The fly became a conversational gambit when they showed the portrait to their friends: 'Notice anything unusual there about my portrait?'

Artists, of course, when they saw the fly, laughed inwardly, but said nothing to the patrons about the meaning of the Vintian trademark. I had hesitated about whether to mention Vint's symbolic revenge when I wrote about him, not wanting to jeopardize his livelihood. But I had decided, in the end, to bring the matter up because it was a facet of Vint's personality that said something implicit about the emotionless nature of his abstracts.

As I guided Berenice into the house in Debierue's wake, holding her left elbow, I became apprehensive about the old painter's offhand remark and dry, brief chuckle. A chuckle, unlike a sudden smile or a sincere burst of laughter is difficult to interpret. Whether a chuckle is friendly or unfriendly, it merely serves as a nervous form of punctuation. But to mention one particular incident, or paragraph, out of the thousands I had written, and the 'fly' symbol at that, caused the knot of anxiety in the pit of my stomach to throb. The fact that he had read my piece on Vint (not a hack job, because I don't write hack pieces, but it certainly wasn't one of my best articles — Vint's work simply hadn't been good enough for a serious in-depth treatment) could be a hindrance to me.

No one knew, because Debierue had never commented, what the old man had thought about Galt's article, with its fanciful 'Chironesque' interpretations, but writers with reputations much greater than mine had been turned down subsequently when they had asked the painter for interviews. After the Galt article, Debierue had every right to distrust critics.

Damn Galt, anyway, I thought bitterly. Then I saw the

gilded baroque frame on the wall and pointed to it.

'That isn't the famous *No. One*, is it?'

Debierue pursed his lips, and shrugged. 'It was,' he answered lightly, and entered the kitchen.

The moment I examined the picture I knew what he meant, of course. There was no crack on the wall behind the mount. The frame, without the crack, and not hanging in its original environment, was no longer the fabled *No. One*. My exultation was great nevertheless. It was something I had never expected to see in my lifetime. Berenice, after a quick glance at the empty frame, seated herself in a Sears-Danish chair and asked me for a cigarette.

I shook my head impatiently. 'Not till we ask permission,' I told her.

There was a narrow bar-counter built into the wall. It separated the kitchen from the living-room. There was no dining room, and the living-room was furnished spartanly. The chicken farmer-tenant who had built the house had probably intended, like many Floridians, to use the large screened porch as a dining area. There was a square, confirming pass-through window from the kitchen to the porch.

There were no other pictures on the walls, and the living-room was furnished cheaply and austerely with Sears furniture. Mr. Cassidy had certainly spared expense in furnishing the house for the famous visitor. There wasn't a hi-fi stereo, a radio, or television set, and there were no drapes to mask the severe horizontal lines of the Venetian blinds covering the windows. Except for two Danish chairs, a Marfak-topped coffee table, a black Naugahyde two-seater couch and one floor lamp — all grouped in a tight oblong — the huge living room, with its carpetless terrazzo floor, was bare. A *Miami Herald* and a superclick copy of *Réalités* were on the coffee table. There were two tall black wrought-iron barstools at the counter. Debierue either had to have his meals at this bar-counter or take his food out to the porch and eat on a Samsonite card table.

Mr. Cassidy would not, I knew, tip Debierue off that I was coming, but if the old painter asked me how I had found him, what could I say? He didn't appear surprised by my sudden appearance. If he asked, I would say that my editor had told me and that he sent me down on an assignment. These thoughts nagged at my mind as Debierue prepared the frozen orange juice. He placed an aluminum pitcher on the table, opened the frozen can with an electric can opener, and then made three trips to the sink to fill the empty can with tap water.

He worked methodically, with great concentration, adding each canful of water to the pitcher like a chemist preparing an experiment. With a long-handled spoon he stirred the mixture, smiled, and beckoned for us to come and sit at the bar. Berenice and I climbed onto the stools, and he filled three plastic glasses to their brims.

Without touching his glass he looked beyond me to *No. One* on the wall. 'This is the new world, M. Figueras, and there are no cracks in the wall of the new world. Here the concrete, brick, and stucco walls are hurricane-proof. My insurance policy guarantees this.'

This might be a good opening or closing sentence for my article, I thought. I leaned forward, prepared to explore his thinking on the New World in more detail, but he shook his head as a signal for me to remain silent.

'I will not suggest to you that only M. Cassidy could have directed you here, M. Figueras. It is unimportant now that you are here, and we are both aware that M. Cassidy is, like all collectors, a most peculiar man.'

Grateful for the easy out, I asked for permission to smoke. Debierue took a saucer from the cabinet, set it between us, and waited until I lighted Berenice's cigarette and mine before he continued. He refused a cigarette by waving his hand.

'What can I say to you, M. Figueras, that would dissuade you from writing about me for your magazine?'

'Nothing, I'm afraid. You make me feel like a complete bastard, but —'

'I'm sorry for your feelings. But as a favor to me, do you have so much zeal that you must tell my address in your magazine? Much privacy is needed for my work, as it is for all artists. Every day I must work for at least four hours, and to have frequent interruptions —'

'That's no concession at all, sir. I'll dateline my piece "Somewhere in Florida." I know how you feel, of course. The Galt article was damned unfair to you, I know —'

'How do you know?' Again the sad, sweet smile.

'I know Galt's attitude toward art, that's how I know. He's got a one-track mental set. He invariably puts everything he sees into a highly subjective pattern — whether it fits or not.'

'Is not all art subjective?'

'Yes.' I grinned. 'But didn't Braque say that the subject was not the object?'

'Perhaps. I don't know whether Braque said this himself, or whether some clever young man — a man like yourself, M. Figueras — *said* that he said it.'

'I — I don't recall,' I replied lamely, 'where the quote originated, not at the moment, but he is supposed to have said it himself. And if not ... well ... the play on words has a subtle validity, for ... the art of our times. Don't you think?'

'The word "validity" cannot be used validly for the art of any time.'

I hesitated. He was testing me. By going into theoretical entelechy I could have answered him easily, but I didn't want to argue with him — I shrugged and smiled.

'By validity,' he smiled back, 'do you mean that the eye contains the incipient action?' The corners of his eyes wrinkled with amusement.

'Not exactly, sir. Cartesian dualism, as an approach to aesthetics, no longer has intrinsic value — and that's Galt's fault. He has never been able to transcend his early training. Not to be summational is the hardest task facing the contemporary critic. To see the present alone, blocking out the past and future, calls for optic mediation.' My face grew warm under the force of his steady blue eyes. 'I don't mean to run Galt down, sir, or to give you the impression that I'm a better critic than he is. It's just that I'm twenty-five years younger than Galt, and I've looked at more contemporary art than he has —'

'Do not be so nervous, M. Figueras. *(?)Debemos dar preferencia al hablar del español?'*

'No. I think in Spanish when I speak it, and I prefer to think in English and talk in French —'

'What are you talking about?' Berenice said, sipping from her glass.

'The difference between Spanish and English and French,' I said.

'I hate Spanish,' Berenice said, winking at me. 'It's got too many words for bravery, which makes a person wonder sometimes about the true bravery of the Spanish character.'

'And French, I think,' Debierue said in English, 'has too many words for love.' He reached over and touched my hair. 'You have nice curly yellow hair, and she should not tease you. Come now, drink your orange juice.'

The paternal touch of his hand unknotted my inner tenseness, and I realized that the old artist was trying to make things easier for me. At any rate, my guilty feelings had been dissipated by his casual acceptance of both me and my professionalism. My awe of the old painter was also going away. I was still mightily impressed by him, and I felt that our conversation was going well.

Any writer who is awed in the presence of the great or the near-great cannot function critically. I respected Debierue enough to be wary, however, knowing that he was not an ingenuous man, knowing that he had survived as an individual all of these years by maintaining an aloof, if not an arrogant, silence, and a studied indifference to journalists. Debierue realized, I think, that I was on his side, and that I would always take an artist's viewpoint before that of the insensitive public's. He had read my work and he remembered my name. I could therefore give him credit for knowing that I was as unbiased as any art critic can ever be. To see his paintings, which was the major reason for my odyssey, I now had to gain his complete confidence. I had to guard against my tendency to argue. Nor should I bait him merely to obtain a few sensational opinions about art as 'news'.

'I am curious about why you immigrated to Florida, M. Debierue.'

'I almost didn't. For my old bones, I wanted the sun. When more than fifty years of my work was burned in the fire — you knew about the fire?'

'Yes, sir.'

'A most fortunate accident. It gave me a chance to begin again. The artist who can begin again at my age is a very fortunate man. So it was to the new world I turned, the new world and a new start. Tahiti, I think at first, would be best, but my name would then be linked somehow to Gauguin.' He shook his head sadly. 'Unavoidable. Such comparisons would not be fair, but they would have been made. And on the small island, perhaps the bus would pass my studio every day with American tourists to stare at me. Tahiti, no. Then I think, South America? No, there is always trouble there. And then Florida seems exactly right. But I did not come right away. I knew about the war in Florida, and I have had enough war in my lifetime.'

'The war?' I said, puzzled. 'The war in Vietnam?'

'No, no. The Seminole War. It is well known in Europe that these, the Florida Seminole Indians, are at war with your United States. Is it not so?'

'Yes, I suppose so, but only in a technical sense. The Seminoles are actually a very small Indian nation. And it's not a real war. It's a failure on the part of the Indians to sign a peace treaty with the U.S., that's all. Once in a while there's a slight legal flare-up, when some Florida county tries to force an Indian kid to go to school when he doesn't want to go — although a lot of Indians go to school now voluntarily. But there hasn't been an incident with shots fired for many years. The Seminoles have learned that they're better off than other Indian nations, in a legal way, by not signing a treaty.'

'Yes.' He nodded. 'I learned this from M. Cassidy, but I wrote some letters first to be certain.' He pursed his lips solemnly and looked down at the countertop. 'I will die in Florida now. This much I know, and a Frenchman does not find it so easy to leave France when he knows he will never see it again. There are other countries in the world that would have welcomed me, M. Figueras. Greece, Italy. The world is too good to me. I have always had many good friends, friends that I have never met. They write me letters, very nice letters from all over the world.'

I nodded my understanding. It was perfectly natural for strangers in every country to write to Debierue, although it had never occurred to me to write him myself. The same thing had happened to Schopenhauer in his old age, and he had been as pleased as Debierue to receive the letters. Any truly radical artist with original ideas who lives long enough will not only be accepted by the world at large, he will be admired, if not revered, for his dogged persistence — even by people who detest everything he stands for.

But there was a major difference between the old German philosopher and this old French painter. Schopenhauer had accepted the flood of congratulations on his birthdays during his seventies as a well-deserved tribute, as a vindication. Debierue, on the other hand, while grateful, seemed bewildered and even humbled by the letters he received.

'But I am not sorry I came to Florida, M. Figueras. Your sun is good for me.'

'And your work? Has it gone well for you, too?'

'The artist' — he looked into my eyes — 'can work anywhere. Is it not so?'

I cleared my throat to make the pitch I had been putting off. 'M. Debierue, I respect your stand on art and privacy very much. In fact, just to sit here talking to you and drinking your fresh orange juice —'

'The fresh *frozen*,' he amended.

'... is an honor. A great honor. I'm well aware of your reluctance to show your work to the public and to critics, and I can't say that I blame you. You have, however, on occasion, permitted a few outstanding critics to examine and write about your work. You've only been in Florida for a few months, as I understand it, and I don't know if you've completed any paintings you'd be willing to show an American critic. But if you have, I would consider it a privilege —'

'Are you a painter, M. Figueras?'

'No, sir, I'm not. I had enough studio courses in college to know that I could never be a successful painter. My talent, such as it is, is writing, and I'm a craftsman rather than an artist, I regret to say. But I am truly a superior craftsman as a critic. To be frank, in addition to the personal pleasure I'd get from seeing your American paintings, an exclusive, in-depth article in my magazine would be a feather in my cap. The sales of the magazine would jump, and it would be the beginning for me of some very lucrative outside assignments from other art journals. As you know, only *one* photograph of any single one of your paintings would be art news big enough to get both of us international attention —'

'Do you sculpt? Or work with collage, ceramics?'

'No, sir.' I tried to keep the annoyance I felt out of my voice. 'Nothing like that. I'm quite inept when it comes to doing work with my hands.'

'But I do not understand, M. Figueras. Your critical articles are very sensitive. I do not understand why you do not paint, or —'

'At one time this was a rather sore point with me, but I got over it. I tried hard enough, but I simply couldn't draw well enough — too clumsy, I guess. If I didn't have a well-developed verbal sense I'd probably have a tough time making a living.'

'I've got to go to the restroom, Mr. Debierue,' Berenice said shyly.

'Certainly.' Debierue came around the bar and pointed down the hallway. 'The door at the far end.'

I climbed off the stool when she did and looked down the hallway past Debierue's shoulder. Berenice was undoubtedly bored, but she also undoubtedly had to go to the can. At the end of the short hallway there were two more doors *en face*, in addition to the door to the bathroom straight ahead. One door was padlocked, and one was not. The padlocked door, with its heavy hasp, was probably Debierue's studio and formerly the master bedroom of the original owner.

I took the Polaroid camera out of its leather case, and checked to see if there was an unused flash bulb in the bounce reflector.

'This camera,' I said, 'is so simple to operate that an eight-year-old child can get good results with it almost every time. It's that simple.' I laughed. 'But before I learned how to work the damned thing I ruined ten rolls of film. It's ridiculous, I know. And with typing, which I had to learn, I was equally clumsy. I took a typing course twice, but the touch system was too much for me to master.' I held up my index and second fingers. 'I have to type my stuff with these four fingers. So you can see why I quit trying to paint. It was too frustrating, so I quit trying before I suffered any emotional damage.'

He looked at me quizzically, and stroked his hooked nose with a long finger.

'I guest I sound a little stupid,' I said apologetically.

'No, no. The critic — all critics — arouses my curiosity, M. Figueras.'

'It's quite simple, really. I'm purported to be an expert, or at least an authority, on art and the preschool child. And what it boils down to is this. Most motor activity is learned before the age of five. A preschool child can only learn things by doing them. And if you have a mother who does everything for you — little things like tying shoelaces, brushing your teeth, feeding you, and so on, you don't do them yourself. After five or six, when you *have* to do them yourself, in school, for example, it's too late ever to master the dexterity and motor control a painter will need in later years. Overly solicitous mothers, that is, mothers who wait on their children hand and foot, inadvertently destroy incipient artists.'

'Have you ever written about this theory?'

I nodded. 'Yes. A short book entitled *Art and the Preschool Child*, and I'll mail you a copy. It explains, in part, why men who are psychologically suited to becoming painters turn out so much bad art. It isn't a theory, though, it's a fact. A neglected point that I made is that such people are not lost to the world as artists. If their problem is recognized, they can be rechanneled into other artistic activities that do not call for great manual dexterity.'

'Like what?' Debierue appeared to be genuinely interested.

'Writing poetry, composing electronic music. Or even architecture. The late Addison Mizner, who couldn't draw a straight line in the sand with a pointed stick, became an important South Florida architect. His buildings in Palm Beach — those that remain — are beautifully designed, and his influence on other Florida architecture has been considerable, especially here on the east coast.'

I stopped before I got wound up. Debierue was pulling on me — on *me*! — one of the oldest tricks not in the book, and here I was, falling for it, just like the rawest of cub reporters. It is a simple matter for the person who is wise with the experience of being interviewed to learn the interests of the interviewer. Then, all he has to do is to keep feeding questions to the interviewer and the interviewer will end up with an interview of himself! Naively happy with a long and pleasant conversation, the interviewer will leave the subject in a blithe mood, only to learn later, when he sits chagrined at his typewriter, that he has nothing to write about.

The toilet flushed. Debierue waited politely for me to continue, but I swirled the juice in my glass, sipped the rest of it slowly until Berenice rejoined us, and then excused myself on the pretense that I also had to use the facility.

I still carried my camera, of course, and I quickly opened the door on the left of the hall, across from the padlocked door. I closed it softly behind me and took the room in rapidly. If one of Debierue's paintings was on the wall, I was going to take a picture of it. But there was only one painting on the wall, a dime-store print in a cheap black frame of *Trail's End* — the ancient Indian sitting on his wornout horse. In the 1930s almost every lower middle class home in America contained a print of

Trail's End, but I hadn't expected to find one in Debierue's bedroom. Either Cassidy, in his meanness, had hung it on the wall, or it had been left there by the owner of the house. But I still couldn't fathom how Debierue could tolerate the corny picture, unless, perhaps, he was amused by the ironic idea behind the print. Of course, that was probably the reason.

The bedroom was austere. A Hollywood single bed, made up with apple green sheets — and no bedspread — an unpainted pine highboy, a wrought-iron bedside table with a slab of white tile for a top, and a red, plastic Charles Eames chair beside the bed made up the inventory. There was a ceiling light, but no lamp. Debierue was a nihilist and stoic in his everyday life as well as in his art, but I felt a wave of sympathy for the painter all the same. It was a shame, I felt, that this great man had so few creature comforts in his old age. There was no need for me to slide open the closet door, or to search the drawers of the highboy and paw through his clothing.

I took a nervous leak in the bathroom, and turned on the tap to wash my hands in the washbowl. I opened the mirrored cabinet to see what kind of medicines he kept there. If he had any diseases, or an illness of some kind, the medicines he used would furnish a valid clue, and that might be worth writing about. Except for Elixophyllin-K1 (an expectorant that eases the ability to breathe for persons with asthma, emphysema, and bronchitis) and three bars of Emulave (a kind of 'soapless' soap, or cleansing bar for people with very dry skin — and I had noted the dryness of the painter's hands already), there was nothing out of the ordinary in the cabinet. A pearl-handled straight razor, a cup with shaving soap and brush, a bottle of blue-green Scope, a half-used tube of Stripe toothpaste, a green plastic Dr. West toothbrush, a 100-tablet bottle of Bayer aspirin, with the cotton gone, and that was it. There wasn't even a comb, although Debierue, with a bald head as slick as a peeled almond, didn't need a comb. As bathroom medicine chests in America go, this was the barest cabinet — outside of a rented motel room — I had ever seen.

I returned to the living room in time to hear Berenice say, 'Don't you get lonely, Mr. Debierue, living way out here all alone?'

He smiled, patted her hand, and shook his head.

'It's the nature of the artist to be lonely,' I answered for him. 'But the painter has his work to do, which is ample compensation.'

'I know,' Berenice said, 'but this place is a million miles from nowhere. You ought to get a car, Mr. Debierue. Then you could drive over to Dania for jai-alai at night or something.'

'No, no,' he protested, still patting her hand, 'I am too old now to learn how to drive an automobile.'

'You could take some students,' Berenice said eagerly. 'There would be a lot of students who would like to work with you in your studio! And I bet they'd come with cars from all over' — she turned to me — 'wouldn't they, James?'

Debierue laughed, and I joined him, although I was laughing more at Berenice's droll expression — half anger and half bewilderment — because we were laughing at her. For any other painter of equal stature, Picasso, for instance, the suggestion of a student working with a master was valid enough. But for Debierue, who showed his work to no one, the idea was absurd. Debierue had sidetracked me neatly. It was time to get back to business.

I put an affectionate arm around Berenice's waist and squeezed her as a signal to keep quiet. 'You didn't answer my question a while ago, M. Debierue,' I said soberly. 'You have been very nice to me — to us both — even though we've invaded your privacy. But I would like to see your present work —'

He sighed. 'I'm sorry, M. Figueras. You have made your visit without reason. You see,' he shrugged, 'I have no work to show you.'

'Nothing at all? Not even a drawing?'

The corners of his mouth drooped morosely. 'Work I have, yes. But what things I have done in Florida are not deserving of your attention.'

'Why don't you let me be the judge of that?'

His strained half-smile was weary, but his features stiffened with a mask of discernible dignity. His voice dropped to a husky whisper. 'The artist alone is a final judge of his work, M. Figueras.'

I flushed. 'Please don't misunderstand me,' I said quickly. 'I didn't mean what I said to come out that way. What I meant was that I don't intend to criticize your work, or judge it in any way. I meant to say that I would prefer to be the judge of whether I'd like to *see* it or not. And I would. It would be an honor.'

'No. I am sorry but I must refuse. You are a critic and you cannot help yourself. For you, to see a picture is to make a judgment. I do not want your judgment. I paint for Debierue. I please myself and I displease myself. For a young man like you to say to me, "Ah, M. Debierue, here in this corner a touch of terracotta might strengthen the visual weight," or "I like the tactile texture, but I believe I see a hole in the overall composition ..."' He chuckled drily. 'I must say no, M. Figueras.'

'You are putting me down, sir,' I said. 'I know there are critics such as you describe, but I'm not one of them.' My face was flaming, but my voice was under control.

'With the art of Debierue, one man is a crowd. Me. Debierue. Two people are a noisy audience. But to have one spectator with a pen, the critic, is to have many thousands of spectators. Surrealism does not need your rationale, M. Figueras. And Debierue does not paint "bicephalous centaurs."'

'He won't let you see his pictures, will he?' Berenice guessed, looking at my face.

I shook my head.

'Maybe,' she turned and looked coyly at Debierue, 'you'll let me see them instead, Mr. Debierue?'

He stepped back a few feet and examined her figure admiringly. 'You have a wide pelvis, my dear, and it will be very easy for you to have many fine, beautiful babies.'

'By that he means no for me too, doesn't he?'

'What else?' I shrugged, and lit a cigarette.

As I had suspected, Debierue had disliked Galt's criticism. I could have begged, but that would have been abhorrent to me. If this was the way he felt there was no point in pursuing the matter anyway. In one way, he was right about me. It would have been impossible for me to look at his work without judging it. And although I would not have said anything derogatory about his work, no matter how I felt about it, there was bound to be some indication of how I felt — pro or con — reflected in my face. If he didn't actually believe that his paintings were worthy (although his faculty for criticism was certainly not as good as mine), all I could do now was take him at his word. I felt almost like crying. It was one of the greatest disappointments of my life.

'Perhaps another time, then, M. Debierue,' I said.

'Yes, perhaps.' He stroked his beaked nose pensively and studied my face. Not rudely, but earnestly. He glanced toward the hallway leading to his padlocked studio, looked back at me, smiled at Berenice, and tugged pensively at his lower lip. I suspected that he had expected me to put up a prolonged, involved argument, and now he didn't know whether to be grateful or disappointed by my failure to protest.

'Tell me something, M. Figueras. I am called *the* Nihilistic Surrealist, but I have never known why. Do you see much disorder here, in my little house?'

'No, sir.' I looked around. 'Far from it.'

For an artist, the lack of clutter was most unusual. Painters, as a 'class', are a messy lot. They collect things. An old board, with concentric swirls, a rock, with an intriguing shape, jumbles of wire, seashells, any and all kinds of things that have, to them, interesting shapes or colors. A chunk of wood, for example, may gather a heavy patina of dust for years before a sculptor finally detects the shape within the object and liberates it into a piece of sculpture.

Painters are even messier, in most instances, than sculptors. They stick drawings up here and there. Pads with sketches are scattered about haphazardly, and they clutter their quarters with all kinds of props and worthless junk.

Things are needed for visual stimulation and possible
ideas. This clutter is not confined to their studios either. It
generally spills over into their everyday habitat, including
the kitchen and bathroom.

And a Surrealist, like Debierue, dealing in the juxtaposition of the unlikely, would ordinarily require a great
many unrelated objects in his home and studio to nudge his
subconscious. But then, Debierue was an anomaly among
painters. My experience with the habits of other painters
could hardly apply to him. Besides, I had not, as yet, seen
the inside of his studio ...

'As you see, I am an orderly, clean old man. Always it
was so, even as a young man. So it may be, after all, that I
am not the Surrealist. Is it not so?' The grooved amusement lines crowding his blue eyes deepened as he smiled.

'It's a relative term,' I said politely. 'A convenient label.
"Surrealist" or "Subrealist" would both have served as
well. The term "Dada" itself was just a catchall word at
first, but the motto "Dada *hurts*," when it was truly
followed or lived up to in plastic expression, was quite
important to me. In fact it still is, but I've always considered "Surrealism" as a misnomer.'

'Debierue does not like any label. Debierue is Debierue.
Marcel Duchamp I admired very much, and he too did not
like labels. Do you remember what Duchamp did when a
young writer asked him for permission to write his biography?'

'No, sir.'

'When Duchamp was asked for the quite personal
information about himself he said nothing. He did not
have to think. He emptied all of the drawers from his desk
onto the floor and walked out of the room.'

'An existential act.' The story was one I hadn't heard.

'Another label, M. Figueras?' He clucked his tongue.
'So now on the floor are odds and ends, little things saved
in the desk for many years for no good reason. Snapshots,
little notes one receives or makes for himself. Old letters
from friends, enemies, ladies. And, what is it? — the *doodles*,
little pencil squigglings. And pretty canceled stamps saved

because they are exotic perhaps. Stubs from the theater.'
He shrugged.

'It sounds like my desk in New York.'

'But this was the Duchamp biography. The clever young
man picked up everything from the floor and went away.
He pasted all of the objects in a big book, entitled it *The
Biography of Marcel Duchamp* and sold it for a large sum
of dollars to a rich Texas Jew.'

'It's funny I never heard about it. I thought I knew pract-
cally everything about Duchamp there was to know ...'

'And so did the young man who "wrote" the biography
about Duchamp out of odds and ends from a desk.'

'Nevertheless,' I said, 'I'd like to take a look at that
book. Every scrap of information about Duchamp is
important because it helps us to understand his art.'

The artist shrugged. 'There is no such book. The story is
apochryphal — I made it up myself and spread it to a few
friends many years ago to see what would happen. And
because it is something Duchamp might do, many
believed it as you were prepared to do. The chance debris
of an artist's life does not explain the man, nor does it
explain the artist's work. The true artist's vision comes
from here.' He tapped his forehead.

Debierue's face was expressionless now, and I was
unable to tell whether he was serious, teasing me, or
getting hostile. He turned to Berenice and smiled. He took
her right hand in both of his and spoke in English.

'If a man had a wife and children, perhaps a short biography to leave his family, a record for them to remember
him ... but old Debierue has no wife, children, no relatives now living, to want such a book. The true artist, my
dear, is too responsible to marry and have a family.'

'Too responsible to fall in love?' Berenice asked softly.

'No. Love he must have.'

I cleared my throat. 'The entire world is the artist's
family, M. Debierue. There are thousands of art lovers all
over the world who would like to read your biography.
Those who write to you, I know, and those who —'

He patted my arm. 'Let us be the friends. It is not

friendly to talk about nothing with such seriousness on your face. It is getting late, and you will both stay to dinner with me, please.'

'Thank you very much. We would like very much to stay.' He had changed the subject abruptly, but the longer I stayed the better my chances became to gain information about the old man. Or did they?

'Good!' He rubbed his dry hands together and they made a rasping sound. 'First I will turn on my electric oven to four-two-five degrees. I do not have the printed menu, but you may decide. There is the television turkey dinner. Very good. There is the television Salisbury steak. Also very good. Or maybe, M. Figueras, you would most like the television patio dinner? Enchilada, tamale, Spanish rice, and refried beans.'

'No,' I said. 'I guess I'll have the turkey.'

'I'd rather have the Salisbury steak,' Berenice said. 'And let me help you —'

'No. Debierue will also have the turkey!' He smiled happily, and turned toward the stove. Relenting, he changed direction, went to the sideboard and got out a box of Piknik yellow plastic forks and spoons. There was a four-mat set of sticky rubber yellow place mats in the drawer. He handed the mats and the box of plastic utensils to Berenice and asked her to set the card table on the porch.

So far, I thought bitterly, as I glumly watched this bustling domestic activity, except for a few gossipy comments on a low curiosity level, I had picked up damned little information of any real interest from the old artist. If anything, he had learned more about me than I had about him. He had refused to let me see his work, and just as he had started to open up he had slammed the lid on what might have been an entire trunkful of fascinating material. He was a bewildering old man, all right, and I couldn't decide whether he was somewhat senile (no, not that), putting me down, with some mysterious purpose in mind, or what ...

Working away, stripping the cardboard outer covers

from the aluminum TV dinners he had taken from the freezer compartment of the purple Kentone refrigerator, Debierue sang a repetitious French song in a cracked falsetto.

No matter how he downgraded himself, false modesty or not, he was the world's outstanding Nihilistic Surrealist. That was the reason I wasn't getting anywhere with him. I was trying to talk to him as if he were a normal person. Any artist who has isolated himself from the world for three-fourths of his life either has to be a Surrealist or crazy. But Debierue was as sane as any other artist I had ever met. Even the fact that he denied being a Surrealist emphasized the fact that he was one. What else could he be? This was the rationale of the purposeful irrationality of Surrealism. The key. But the key to what?

How could a man live all alone as he did — without a phone, a TV, a radio — for months on end without going off his rocker? Even Schweitzer, when he exiled himself to Africa, took an organ along, and surrounded himself with sick, freeloading black men ...

From this desperate brooding, my pedestrian mind came up with one of the best original ideas I ever had, an idea so simple and direct I almost lost it. The thought was still formless, but I didn't let the idea get away from me. Berenice put three webbed chairs up to the table on the porch. She re-entered the living-room, and I clutched her wrist.

'I'm going to do something strange,' I whispered. 'But don't let on, no matter what happens. Understand?'

She nodded, and her blue eyes widened.

Debierue came out of the kitchen and tapped my wrist-watch. 'Sometimes I do not hear so well the timer on the oven, so you will please watch the time for us. And in thirty-five minutes when you say "Now," we will have the dinner all ready to eat!' He beamed his jack-o'-lantern smile at Berenice. 'So simple. The television dinner is the better invention for wives than the television itself. Is it not so, my dear?'

'Oh, absolutely,' Berenice said cheerfully.

'Look, M. Debierue,' I said, taking my Polaroid from the bar, 'I know it's a lot to ask, at least from your view-point, but I've got this Polaroid here, and you can see the results for yourself in about ten seconds. While we wait for dinner, let me take a few shots of you, and until we get one that you think is all right, you can just tear them up. Fair enough?'

'In only ten seconds? A picture?'

'That's all. Maybe fifteen seconds inside the house here, for a little extra snap and contrast.'

He frowned slightly, and fingered his white whiskers. 'My beard isn't trimmed . . .'

'In a photo, it doesn't matter. No one can tell from a black-and-white picture.' I promised recklessly.

He hesitated. His eyes were wary, but he was wavering. 'Should I put on a necktie?'

'No, not for an informal picture,' I said, before he could change his mind. Taking him by the arm, I guided him to a point in front of the coffee table. I picked up the *Miami Herald*, flipped through it to find the classified ad section, opened it and thrust the paper into his hands.

'There. Just spread the paper, and pretend to read it. You can smile if you feel like it, but you don't have to.'

A trifle self-consciously, he followed my simple direc-tions. After focusing the camera on him, and setting it for 'dark', I asked him to lower his arms slightly to make certain his face and beard would be in the picture. The flag of the *Miami Herald* and *Classified* could both be read through the viewfinder. I moved forward and touched his hand.

'No,' I admonished, 'please don't move or look up at me. I'll take the photo from back there.'

This was the last moment to take my premeditated chance, and one chance was all I could expect to get. I forced a loud cough to cover the slight click of my Dunhill, and ignited the paper at the bottom. A moment later, six feet back, I was squinting through the viewfinder. The timing was perfect. The bounce flash bulb worked, and it was only a split second after I snapped the shutter that the flames burst through the paper on his side and he dropped it with an astonished yelp. Berenice, who had been watching with bulging eyes and with her right hand clamped over her mouth, moved forward squealing, and began to stamp on the burning paper. I helped her, and it only took us moments to crush out the flames on the terrazzo floor.

I had expected an angry reaction from Debierue, but he was merely puzzled. 'Why,' he asked mildly, 'did you light the paper? I don't understand.' He looked about bewilderedly as the charred bits of newsprint, caught by the slight breeze coming through the jalousied door, fluttered over his clean floor.

I grinned and held up a forefinger. 'Wait. Give me ten seconds, and then you'll see the picture.'

I was all thumbs with excitement, but I took my time, being careful as I jerked out the strip of prepared paper that started the developing process and, instead of guessing, I watched the sweep-second hand on my watch, allowing exactly twelve seconds for the developer to work.

As curious as a child, the old artist was brushing my shoulder with his as I opened the back of the camera to remove the print. When I turned the photo face up on the bar, his jarring burst of jubilant laughter startled me.

'Don't touch it!' I said sharply, sliding the print out of the reach of his clutching fingers. 'I've got to coat it first.' I straightened the print on the edge of the counter and then gave it eight precise sweeps with the gooey print coater. It was the best photo, absolutely the finest, that I had ever taken.

Perfectly centered, the old man wore his wise, beautiful, infectious smile. He appeared to be reading the want ads in the *Herald* as if he didn't have a care in the world. His face was purely serene, and the deeply etched lines in his face were sharp, clear-cut, and as black as India ink. He had been completely unaware of the blazing newspaper when I snapped the picture, but no one who saw the paper would ever guess that. The entire lower half of the paper blazed furiously away. No professional model could have posed knowingly with a flaming newspaper without a slight twinge of anxiety showing in his face. But the old man, with his skinny legs exposed beneath the flames, with his bland innocent face and the wonderful smile flowing through his downy white beard, appeared as relaxed as a man who had spent a restful night in a Turkish bath.

Debierue watched me coat the print, but he kept reaching for it impatiently. I guarded it with my arm so it could dry.

'Let me see,' he said childishly.

'If you touch it now,' I explained patiently, 'it'll pick up your fingerprints and be ruined.'

'Very well, M. Figueras,' he said good-naturedly. 'I want this photo. It's the most formidable *surréalité* I've ever seen!'

His exuberance was as great as my own. 'You'll have it, all right,' I said happily. 'In fact, when I get back to New York, I'll send you fifty copies of the picture if you want them, and a copy to every friend on your mailing list.'

Chapter Three

When Debierue granted his permission for me to keep and publish the photograph, I hurried out to the car and got one of our magazine's standard release forms out of the glove compartment. The mimeographed form (large circulation magazines have them printed) is a simple agreement between subject and magazine to make publication legal, to protect one party from the other. There is nothing underhanded about a signed photo release. Debierue could read English, of course, but the involved legalese the form was couched in forced me to explain the damned thing at some length before he would sign it. Debierue wasn't stupid or willful. He believed naively that his oral okay was enough.

Because of this discussion, the dinners were ready before we knew it. I forgot to look at my watch, and it was Berenice who heard and recognized the faint buzzing in the kitchen as the oven timer.

It was almost pleasant on the screened porch. A light breeze came up, and although the wind was hot, it was relatively comfortable in the darkening twilight as we sat at the candlelit card tabletop to eat the miserable off-brand TV dinners.

The dinners had been purchased by the Negro maid who came every Wednesday to take care of the old man's laundry and to do his difficult cleaning. She also brought his other weekly food supplies. By buying these cheap TV dinners, she was probably knocking down on the food money. I didn't suggest this to him, but I discussed brand names, the brand-name fallacy, and wrote out a short list of worthwhile frozen food buys he could depend upon.

He had a delusion that frozen foods were better, somehow, than fresh. Berenice started halfheartedly to tell him otherwise, but when she saw me shake my head she changed the subject to domestic wines. Debierue distrusted California wines, but I added the brands of some Napa Valley wines to the frozen food list, and he said he would try them. Other than tap water, all he drank, because French wines were too dear, was frozen orange juice.

The Gold Coast for some twenty miles inland, from Jupiter downstate to Key Largo, is tropical — not *sub*-tropical, as so many people erroneously believe. The tropical weather is caused by the warmth of the Gulf Stream, less than six miles off the coast. There is little difference between the weather in Miami and that of Saigon. Debierue's house, on a hammock with a black swamp and the Everglades for a backyard, was depressingly humid. After eating the dry turkey dinner, my mouth felt as if it were dehydrated, and I couldn't drink enough fluid to unparch my throat. I poured another glass of orange juice (my fourth) and sensed, as I did so, a certain anxiety or impatience developing in the old man. As an experienced dinner guest, I have picked up an instinct about wearing out welcomes.

The sky had darkened from bruise blue to gentian violet, and it was only a few minutes after six thirty. It was much too early for him to go to bed, but even Berenice, who was not particularly observant, became aware of the old painter's restlessness. She winked across the table, tapped her wrist significantly, and gave me a brief, comical shrug. I nodded, and slid my chair back from the table.

'It's been delightful, M. Debierue, the dinner by candle-light,' I lied socially, 'but I have another appointment in Palm Beach tonight, and we have to drive back.'

'Of course,' he replied, standing, 'but please keep your seat a few moments more. Already, you see, it is past the time for me to get ready. I must go to the movies tonight. I must go to the movies every night,' he added, by way of fuller explanation, 'and I must now change my clothes.'

'The movies?' I asked stupidly.

His face brightened and he rubbed his hands together briskly. 'Oh, yes, perhaps you did not see it — the Dixie Drive-in Movie Theater ...' He pointed in the general direction of the drive-in. 'Tonight there are three long features, two films with the Bowery Boys and the film about a werewolf. And before these, the regular films, there are always two and sometimes three cartoons. The first long film tonight is *The Bowery Boys Meet Franken-stein*, a very special treat, no? And if you will kindly drive me —'

'Certainly, I said, eagerly, 'I'll be happy to take you in the car.'

'My ignorance,' Debierue chuckled reminiscently, 'it was the amusing thing. When I was first here and taking a walk one evening, I saw the automobiles driving inside the Dixie Drive-in Theater. I did not then know the American custom, and I thought that one must have the automobile to enter the movie. Never before had I seen the drive-in movies, and I said to myself, "Why not see if the permission to go from the manager can be arranged?" So I talked then to the Manager, M. Albert Price. He arranged for me to go, and gave me the Senior Citizen Golden Years' membership card.' Debierue fumbled his wallet out of his hip pocket, extracted the card, which entitled him to a 15 percent discount on movie tickets, and proudly showed it to us. It was made out to Eugene V. Debs.

'That's very nice,' Berenice said, smiling.

'M. Price is a very nice man,' Debierue said, carefully replacing the card in his thin, calfskin wallet. 'There are very good seats in front of the snack bar. The parents with the automobiles sometimes send their children to sit in these seats, and they are also for those patrons who do not have the automobile, as M. Price explained to me. Over to the right of these seats is the zinc slide and little swings, the Kiddyland for these, the children, who become tired of watching the movie screen. I *like* the children — I am a Frenchman — but the little children begin to make too much noise playing in the Kiddyland after the cartoons are finished. This arrangement is good for the parents inside the cars with speakers, but not for me. The noise becomes too loud for me. M. Price and I are now good friends, and he reserves for me each night a seat and special earphones. I hear only the movie with the earphones and no more the children.'

I smiled. 'Can you understand American English, the way the Bowery Boys speak it?'

'No, not always,' he replied seriously. 'But it is no matter. These Bowery Boys are too wonderful comedians — the Surrealist actors, no? I like M. Huntz Hall. He is very droll. Last week there were the three pictures one night with the bourgeois couple and their new house, Papa and Mama Kettle. I like them very much, and also John Wayne.' He shook his fingers as if he had burned them badly on a hot stove. 'Oh ho! *He* is the tough guy, no?'

'Yes, sir, he certainly is. But you've surprised me again, M. Debierue. I had no idea you were a movie fan.'

'It is pleasant to see the cinema in the evenings.' He shrugged. 'And I like also the grape snow cone. Do you like these, the grape snow cones, M. Figueras?'

'I haven't had one in a long time.'

'Very good. Fifteen cents at the snack bar.'

'That's quite a long walk down there and back every night, M. Debierue. And as long as you haven't seen these old movies anyway, why don't you buy a television? There are at least a half-dozen films on TV every night, and —'

'No,' he said loyally, 'this is not good advice. M. Price had already explained to me that the TV was harmful to the eyes. The little screen, he said, will give one bad head-aches after one or two hours of watching.'

I was going to refute this, but changed my mind and lit a cigarette instead. Debierue excused himself and left for his bedroom. I stubbed out the cigarette in the sticky remains of the imitation cranberry sauce well in the TV dinner plate. My mouth was too dry to smoke.

'Have you got any tranquilizers in your purse?'

'No, but I've got a Ritalin, I think.' Berenice untied the drawstring and searched for her pillbox.

'O.K., and give me two Excedrins while you're at it.'

'I've only got Bufferin —'

I took two Bufferin and the tiny Ritalin pill and chased them with the remainder of my orange juice.

'It looks as though things are going to break for us after all,' I said softly.

'What do you mean?'

'What do you think I mean?'

She looked at me with the blank vacant stare that always infuriated me. 'I don't know.'

'Never mind. We'll talk about it later.'

Within a few minutes Debierue returned, wearing his moviegoer's 'costume'. He had exchanged the short-sleeved polo shirt for a long-sleeved dress shirt, and it was buttoned at the neck and cuffs. He wore long white duck trousers instead of shorts, and had pulled his white socks up over the cuffs and secured them with bicycle clips. With his tennis shoes and Navy blue beret he resembled some exclusive tennis club's oldest living member. In his left hand he carried a pair of cotton Iron Boy work gloves. It was a peculiar getup, but it was a practical uniform for a man who was determined to sit for six hours in a mosquito-infested drive-in movie.

Debierue locked the front door and dropped the key into a red pottery pot containing a thirsty azalea, and trailed us to the car. Berenice sat in the middle, and as I drove cautiously down the grassy road toward the highway she and the old man discussed mosquitoes and mosquito control. His beloved M. Price had a huge smoke-spraying machine on a truck that made the circuit of the theater before the films began and again at intermission, but Debierue had to take the gloves along because the mosquitoes were so fierce on his walk home. She told him about, and recommended, a spray repellent called Festrol, and I was repelled by the banality of their conversation. But with his mind on the movies, it was too late for me to ask him any final questions about his art.

I pulled over in the driveway short of the ticket window and waved a car by. I gave the old man one of my business

cards with the magazine's New York address and telephone number, and wedged in a parting comment that if
he changed his mind about letting me see his pictures he
could call me collect at any time. He nodded impatiently
and, without looking at the card, dropped it into his shirt
pocket. We shook hands, the quick one-up-and-one-down
handshake, Berenice gave him a peck on his beard, and he
got out of the car. By the time I got the car turned around,
he had disappeared into the darkness of the theater. Music
and insane woodpecker laughter filled the night suddenly
as I turned onto the highway. Berenice sighed.

'What's the matter?'

'Oh, I was just thinking,' she said. 'We held him up too
long and now he'll have to wait until intermission to get
his grape snow cone.'

'Yeah. That's tough.'

Chapter Four

I drove into Debierue's private road, stopped, and switched off the headlights. Before she could say anything I turned to Berenice and said, 'Before you say anything I'm going to tell you. Then, if you have questions, ask them. I'm going down now to take a look a Debierue's pictures. He said he had painted a few, and now that I know there are pictures in his studio I can't go back without one for Mr. Cassidy.'

'Why not? He doesn't know that there are any.'

'I made a deal. And even if I decide not to take one back, which I doubt, I still have to see them for myself. If you don't understand that, you don't understand me very well.'

'I understand, but it's dangerous —'

'With Debierue in the movies, it's safer than houses. He dropped the door key into a potted plant on the porch. You saw him too, didn't you?'

'But the studio is still locked, and —'

'I don't want to get you involved any more than you are already. But I want you to stay here by the highway, just in case. Debierue might think about the key himself and come back for it. I don't believe he will, but if he does you can run down the road and warn me and we'll get the hell out. Okay?'

'I can't stand out here in the dark all by myself! I'm scared and there are all these mosquitoes and I want to go with you!'

'We're wasting time. It's one thing for me to be a house-breaker, but it's something else for you — as a school-teacher. There's nothing to be frightened about — I'm sorry about the mosquitoes — but if you're really afraid I'll take you down the highway to a gas station. You can lock yourself in the women's room till I come back for you.'

'I don't want to lock myself up in —'

'Get out of the car. I want to get this over with.'

'Let me have your cigarettes.'

I handed her my half-empty pack, not the full one, and she climbed resignedly out of the car. 'How long are you going to be?'

'I don't know. That depends upon how many paintings I have to look at.'

'Don't do it, James. Please don't do it!'

'Why, for God's sake?'

'Because Debierue doesn't want you to, that's why!'

'That's not a reason.'

'I — I may not be here when you get back, James.'

'Good! In that case, I can say you weren't with me at all tonight if I'm caught and you won't get into any trouble.'

Without lights I eased the car down the road, but turned them on again as soon as I was well into the pines and around the first bend. There was no good reason not to have taken Berenice with me except that I didn't want her along. That is, there was no rational reason. She had looked rather pitiful standing in the tall grass beside the road. Maybe I thought she would be in the way, or that she would talk all the time. Something ... It might have been something in my subconscious mind warning me about what I would find. As soon as I parked in front of the house I considered, for a brief moment, going back for her. I got out of the car instead, but left the headlights on.

Because of the rain-washed air the few visible stars seemed to be light years higher in the void than they usually were. There was no moon as yet, and the night was inky. In the black swamp beyond the house a lonesome bull alligator roared erotically. This was such a miserable, isolated location for an artist to live. I was grateful that the old painter had a place to go every night — and not only because the house was so easy to break into. If I had to live out here all alone, I too would have been looking forward to seeing the Bowery Boys and three color cartoons.

Debierue's 'hiding' of the key was evidently a habitual practice, a safeguard to prevent its loss as he walked to and from the theater each night. I doubted that the idea entered his head that I would return to his empty house to make an illegal use of the key. But I didn't really know. My guilt, if any, was light. I felt no more guilt that that of a professional burglar. A burglar must make a living, and to steal he must first invade the locked home where the items he wants to steal are safeguarded. I meant no harm to the old artist. Any picture I took, and I was only going to take one, Debierue, could paint again. And except for the visual impressions of his painting in my mind — and a few photos — I would take nothing else. There was no reason to feel guilty.

So I cannot account for the dryness of my mouth, the dull stasis of my blood, the tightness of the muscles surrounding my stomach, and the noticeable increase in my rate of breathing. These signs of anxiety were ridiculous. The old man was sitting in the drive-in with a pair of headphones clamped to his ears, and even if he caught me inside the house, the worst he could so would be to express dismay. He couldn't hurt me physically, and he would hardly report me to the police. But I was an amateur. I had never broken into anyone's house before, so I supposed that my anxiety stemmed from the melodramatic idea that I was engaged in a romantic adventure. But after I had unlocked the front door and let it swing inward, I had to muster a good deal of courage before I could force my hand to reach inside to flip on the living room lights.

The light coming through the window would be bright enough to see my way back from the car. I switched off the headlights, and returned hurriedly to the house with a tire iron and a hammer I got from the trunk. But as it turned out, these tools were unnecessary.

The only barrier to the studio was the hasp and the heavy Yale lock on the door. Once broken there would be no way to prevent Debierue from guessing that I had returned. But if the artist had been afraid he might lose his house key, it also seemed unlikely that he would take the studio padlock key to the theater.

Switching on the lights as I searched, I made a hasty, fruitless examination of the kitchen before moving on to the bedroom. Two keys together on a short twist of copper wire, both of them identical, were in plain view on top of the highboy dresser. I unlocked the padlock, opened the studio door, and flipped the row of toggles on the wall. The boxlike windowless room, after hesitant blue white flickers, brightened into an icy, intense brilliance. There were a dozen overhead fluorescent tubes in parallel sets of three (two blue white to one yellow) flush with the ceiling. Under this cold light I noticed first the patching of new brickwork that filled the spaces where two windows had been before, despite the new coat of white enamel that covered the walls.

Blinking my eyes to accustom them to the intense overhead light, I closed the door behind me. My thumping heart was prepared for the impact of the unusual, the unique, for the miraculous in visual art, but instead of wine and fish I didn't even find bread and water.

There were canvases, at least two dozen of them, and all of these pristine canvases were the same size, 24″ × 30″. They were stacked in white plastic racks against the western wall. The racks were the commercial kind one often finds in art supply stores. I checked every one of these glittering white canvases. None of them had been touched by paint or charcoal.

There was a new, gunmetal desk in the southwest corner of the studio, with a matching chair cushioned in light gray Naugahyde. On the desk there was a fruit jar filled with sharpened pencils and ballpoint pens, a square glass paperweight (slightly magnified) holding down some correspondence, and a beautiful desk calendar (an Almanacco Artistico Italiano product in brilliant colors, made by Alfieri & Lacroix, Milano). Without shame, I read the two letters that had been held down by the paperweight.

One was a letter from a Parisian clipping service, stating that Debierue's name had been mentioned twice in the foreword to a new art history pictorial collection, but inasmuch as the illustrated volume was quite expensive, the manager had written to the publisher and requested a courtesy copy for Debierue. He would send it along as soon as — or if — he received it. There was a news clipping from *Paris Soir*, an unsigned review of a Man Ray retrospective exhibit in Paris, and Debierue's name was mentioned, together with the names of a dozen other artists, in a listing of Dadaists who had known Man Ray during the 1920s.

Debierue had answered the manager of the clipping service in a crabbed, backhanded script with cursive letters so microscopic he must have written the letter with the aid of the magnified paperweight. He merely told the manager not to send the book if he got a free copy, and not to buy it if he did not. Except for Debierue's surname (the tiny lower-case letters 'e' through 'e' were all contained within a large capital 'D') there was no complimentary closing. Debierue had a unique signature. I folded the letter and put it into the breast pocket of my jumpsuit.

As I looked through the unlocked drawers of the desk, I found nothing else to hold my interest, except for a scrapbook of clippings. The scrapbook, 10″ × 12″, bound in gray cardboard covers, was less than half filled, and from the first clipping to the last one pasted in, covered an eighteen-month period. Most of the earlier clippings were reports of the fire that had burned down his villa, similar accounts from many different newspapers. The more recent clippings were shorter — like the mention of his name in the Man Ray art review. The items in the other drawers were what one expected to find. Stationery and supplies, stamps, glue, correspondence in manila folders — unusual perhaps because of the meticulous neatness one doesn't associate with desk drawers.

There was a two-shelf imitation walnut bookcase beside the desk that held about thirty books. Most of them were paperbacks, five *policiers* from the Série Noire, three Simenons and two by Chester Himes, Pascal's *Pensées, From Caligari to Hitler, Godard on Godard,* an autographed copy of Samuel Beckett's *Proust,* and several paperback novels by French authors I had never heard of before. The hardcover books were all well worn. A French-English dictionary and a French-German dictionary, library reference size, a tattered copy of *Heidi* (in German), a boxed two-volume edition of Schopenhauer's *The World as Will and Idea* (also in German), *Les Fleurs du Mal,* and an autographed copy of August Hauptmann's *Debierue.* I fought down my impulse to steal the autographed copy of Beckett's *Proust,* the only book in the small library I coveted, and scribbled the list of book titles into my notebook.

In addition to the books, there were several neat piles of art magazines, including *Fine Arts: The Americas,* all of them in chronological order, with the most recent issues on the top of each stack, arranged along the wall. I considered leafing through these magazines to look for drawings, but it would be absurd for Debierue, with his keen sense of order, to hide sketches in magazines.

In the center of the studio was a maple worktable (in furniture catalogues, they are called 'Early American Harvest' tables), and this table, in a rather finicky arrangement, held a terracotta jar with several new camel's-hair brushes in varying lengths and brush widths, four rubber-banded, faggoty bundles of charcoal drawing sticks, four one-quart cans of linseed oil and four one-quart cans of turpentine, all unopened, and a long row of king-sized tubes of oil paint in almost every shade and tint on the spectrum.

There were at least a hundred tubes of oil paint, in colors, and three of zinc white. None of the tubes had been opened or squeezed. There was a square piece of clear glass, about 12″ × 12″, a fumed oak artist's palette, a pair of white gloves (size 9/12), a twelve-inch brass ruler, a palette knife, an unopened box of assorted color pencils, and a heaped flat pile of clean white rags. There were

other unused art materials as well, but the crushing
impression of this neatly ordered table was that of a
commercial layout of art materials in an art supply show-
room.

Beside the table was an unpainted wooden A-frame
easel and a tall metal kitchen stool painted in white
enamel. There was an untouched 24″ × 30″ canvas on the
easel. Bewildered, and with a feeling of nausea in the pit
of my stomach, I climbed onto the high stool facing the
easel and lit a cigarette. A single silver filament, a spider's
let-down thread, shimmering in the brilliant light washing
the room from the overhead fluorescents, trailed from the
right-hand corner of the canvas to the floor. The spider
who had left this evidence of passage had disappeared.

Except for the pole-axed numbness of a steer, my mind
was too stunned for a contiguous reaction of any kind. I
neither laughed nor cried. For minutes I was unable to
formulate any coherent thoughts, not until the cigarette
burned my fingers, and even then I remember looking at it
stupidly for a second or so before dropping it to the floor.

Debierue's aseptically forlorn studio is as clear in my
mind now as if I were still sitting on that hard metal stool.

I had expected something, but not Nothing.

I had expected almost anything, but not Nothing.

Prepared for attendance and appreciation, my mind
could not undo its readiness for perception and accept the
unfulfilled *preparation* for painting it encountered.

Here was a qualified Nothing, a Nothing of such deep
despair, I could not be absolved of my aesthetic responsibility — a nonhope Nothing, a non-Nothing — and yet, also
before my eyes was the evidence of a dedication to artistic
expression so unyieldingly vast in its implications that my
mind — at least at first — bluntly refused to accept the
evidence.

I had to work it out.

The synecdochic relationship between the place and the
person was undeniable. An artist has a studio: Debierue
had a studio: Debierue was an artist.

Here, in deadly readiness, Debierue sat daily in fruitless

preparation for a painting that he would never paint, waiting for pictorial adventures that would never happen. *Waiting*, the incredibly patient waiting for an idea to materialize, for a single idea that could be transferred onto the ready canvas — but no ideas ever came to him. Never.

Debierue worked four hours a day, he claimed, which meant sitting on this stool staring at an empty canvas from eight until noon, every day, seven days a week, waiting for an idea to come — every single day! At that precise moment I *knew*, despite all of the published documentary evidence to the contrary, that he was not merely suffering a so-called dry period, a temporary inability to paint since moving to Florida. Without any other evidence (my own eyes were witness enough, together with my practiced critical intuition), I *knew* that Jacques Debierue had never had a plastic idea, nor had he painted a picture of any kind in his entire lifetime!

Debierue was a slave to hope. He had never accepted the fact that he couldn't paint a picture. But each day he faced the slavery of the attempt to paint, and the subsequent daily failure. After each day of failure he was destroyed, only to be reborn on the next day — each new day bringing with it a new chance, a new opportunity. How could be he so strong-willed to face this daily death, this vain slavery to hope? He had dedicated his life to Nothing.

The most primitive nescience in man cannot remain completely negative — or so I had always believed. Forms and the spectrum range of colors, the sounds a man makes with his mouth, the thousands of daily perceptions of sight and sound, invade our senses from moment to moment, consciously and subconsciously. And all of these sights and sounds — and touch, too, of course — demand an artistic interpretation. Knowing this basic natural truth, I knew that Debierue, an intelligent, sentient human being, must have had hundreds, no, literally thousands of ideas for paintings during the innumerable years he sat before an empty canvas. But these ideas were unexpressed, locked inside his head, withheld from graphic presentation because of his fear of releasing them. He was afraid to take a chance, he was unable to risk the possibility — a distinct possibility — of failure. His dread of failure was not a concern with what others might think of his work. It was a fear of what he, Debierue, the Artist, might think of his accomplished work. The moment an artist expresses himself and fails, or commits himself to an act of self-expression by action, and realizes that he did not, that he cannot, succeed, and that he will never be able to capture on canvas that which he sees so vividly in his mind's eye, he will know irrevocably that he is a failure as an artist.

So why should he paint? In fact, how can he paint?

How many times had Debierue leaned forward, reaching out timidly toward the shining canvas before him with a crumbling piece of charcoal in his trembling fingers? How many times? — and with the finished, varnished, luminous masterpiece glowing upon the museum wall of his febrile mind? — only to stay his hand at the last possible moment, the tip of the black charcoal a fraction of an inch away from the virgin canvas?

'Nonono! Not yet!'

The fear-crazed neural message would race down the full length of the motor neuron in his extended arm (vaulting synapse junctions), and in time, always in the nick of time, the quavery hand would be jerked back. The virgin canvas, safe for another day, would once again remain unviolated.

Another day, another morning of uncommitted, untested accomplishment had been hurdled, but what difference did it make? What did anything matter, at high noon, so long as he had delayed, put off until tomorrow, postponed the execution of the feeble idea he had today when there would be a much better idea tomorrow? If he did not prove to himself today that he could paint the image in his mind, or that he could *not* paint it, a tendril of comfort remained. And hope.

Faith in his untried skills provided a continuum.

Why not? Wasn't he trying? Yes. Was he not a dedicated artist? Yes. Did he ever fail to put in his scheduled work period every day? No. Was he not faithful to the sustained effort? — the devoted, painful, mental concentration? — the agony of creation? Yes, yes and yes again.

And who knew? Who knows? The day might arrive soon, perhaps tomorrow! That bright day when an idea for a painting would come to him that was so powerful, so tremendous in scope and conception, that his paint-loaded brush could no longer be withheld from the canvas! He would strike at last, and a pictorial masterpiece would be born, delivered, created, a painting that would live forever in the hearts of men!

All through life we protect ourselves from countless hurtful truths by being a little blind here — by ignoring the something trying to flag our attention on the outer edges of our peripheral vision, by being a little shortsighted there — by being a trifle too quick to accept the easiest answer, and by squinting our eyes against the bright, incoming light all of the time. Emerson wrote once that even a corpse is beautiful if you shine enough light on it.

But that is horseshit.

Too much light means unbearable truth, and too much truthful light sears a man's eyes into an unraging blindness. The blind man can only smell the crap of his life, and the sounds in his ears are cacophonous corruptions. Without vision, the terrible beauty of life is irrevocably gone. Gone!

And as I thought of all Debierue's lost visions, never to appear on canvas for the exhilaration of my eyes, scalding tears ran down my cheeks.

Part Three

*If anything was comprehensible,
it would be incommunicable.*

Chapter One

I took my time.

What I had to do had to be done right or not at all. Once I committed, although my concern for Berenice (frightened and waiting for me in the tall grass by the highway) did not diminish, it would have been foolhardy to rush. I might have overlooked something important.

I looked in the kitchen for string and wrapping paper, but there was neither. There was newspaper, but it would have been awkward to wrap a canvas in newspaper when there was no string to tie the bundle. There were several large brown paper grocery sacks under the sink, and I took one of these back to the studio to hold the art materials I would need. I took a clean sheet from the hall linen closet and wrapped one of the new canvases from the plastic rack in it. I then filled the brown sack with several camel's-hair brushes, a can of turpentine, one of linseed oil, and a half-dozen tubes of oil paint. With cadmium red, chrome yellow, Prussian blue, and zinc white I can mix almost any shade or tint of color I desire (this much I had learned in my first oil painting course because the tyrannical teacher had made us learn how to mix primary colors if he taught us nothing else). I added tubes of burnt sienna and lampblack to the others because they were useful for skin tones (there were no compositional ideas in my mind at the time, just nebulous multicolored swirls floating loosely about in my head) if some figures became involved in the composition. The palette knife was also useful and I dropped it into the sack, but I didn't take the expensive palette. It was too expensive and could be traced, and I wouldn't want to be caught with it in my possession.

These art materials could be purchased anywhere, of course, as could the prepared 30″ × 24″ canvas, but I needed Debierue's materials in the event the authenticity of the painting was ever questioned. Mr. Cassidy, who had purchased everything for Debierue, would have a bill from the art store listing these materials, their brands, and so would Rex Art. My mind was racing, but I was clear-headed enough to realize how close a scrutiny the painting would receive when and if it were ever painted and exhibited.

I put the wrapped canvas, the sackful of supplies, and the hammer and tire iron into the trunk of the car, and returned to the studio.

I ran into trouble with the fire. Turpentine is flammable, highly flammable, but I had difficulty in getting it lighted and in keeping it burning once it was lit. I finally had to take the remains of the *Miami Herald,* crumple each separate page into a ball, and partially soak each sheet with turpentine before I could get a roaring fire started beneath the Early American Harvest table.

Once it got started, however, the fire burned beautifully. I poured most of the last can on the studio door, and dribbled the rest to the blaze beneath the table. I then tossed the new canvases into the fire and backed out of the room. Because the fire would need a draft, I left the studio door and the front door standing open. Whether the house burned down or not was unimportant. The important thing was a charred and well-gutted studio. I wanted no evidence of any paintings left behind, and the crackling prepared canvases, sized with white lead, burned rapidly.

Satisfied, I turned out the living room and kitchen lights and got into the car. When I reached the highway and stopped, Berenice was gone. I shouted her name twice and panicked momentarily. Had she hitchhiked a ride back to Palm Beach? If she stuck out her thumb, any truck driver who saw it would stop and pick her up. But I calmed down by putting myself in her place, turned toward the drive-in theater instead of turning left for Palm Beach, and found her waiting for me in the gravel road of the driveway, standing near the well-lighted marquee.

'What took you so long?' Her voice wasn't angry. She was too relieved to see me, happy to be in the car again. 'I thought you were never coming back.'

'I'm sorry. It look longer than I expected.'

'Did you stea — take a picture?'

'Yeah.'

'What were they like? The pictures?'

'I'll turn over here U.S. One. There're too many trucks on Seven.'

'How long do you think it'll be, before he misses the picture?'

'I've got to go back to New York, Berenice. Tonight. So as soon as we get back to the apartment I'll pack — you're still packed, practically — and then I can drop you off at the airport. Or, if you'd rather, you can stay on for a few more days. The rent's paid till the end of the month, so ...'

'If you're going to New York so am I!'

'But what's the point? You've got your school year contract, and you have to go back to work, don't you? Besides, I'm going to be busy. I won't have any time for you at all. First, there's the Debierue article to write, and the deadline is tighter than hell now. I'll have to find a place to crash. The man in my pad has still got another month on the sub-lease, you see. I'm almost broke, and I'll have to borrow some money, and —'

'Money isn't a problem, James. I've got almost five hundred dollars in traveler's checks, and more than five thousand in savings in the credit union. I'm going to New York with you.'

'Okay,' I said bitterly, 'but you'll have to help me drive.'

'Watch out!' she shrilled. 'That car's only got one head-light!'

'I don't mean *that* way. I mean to spell me at the wheel on the way up, so we can make better time.'

'I know what you meant, but you might have thought it was a motorcycle. We can trade off every two hours.'

'No. When I get tired, we'll trade.'

'All right. How're you going to get your twenty dollars back?'

'What twenty dollars?'

'The deposit at the electric company. If we leave tonight, you won't be able to have them cut off the electricity or get your deposit back.'

'Jesus, I don't know. I can let the landlady handle it and send me the money later. They'll subtract what I owe anyway. Please, Berenice, I'm trying to think. I've got so much on my mind I don't want to hear any more domestic crap, and those damned non sequiturs of yours drive me up the goddamned tree.'

'I'm sorry.'

'So am I. We're both sorry, but just be quiet.'

'I will. I won't say anything else!'

'Nothing else! Please!'

Berenice gulped, closing her generous mouth, and puckered her lips into a prim pout. She looked straight ahead through the windshield and twisted her gloves, which she had removed, in her lap. I had shouted at her, but in my agitation, somehow, had consented to take her with me to New York. This was the last thing I wanted to do. It would take two days, perhaps three, to write the article on Debierue — and I had to do something about the painting for Mr. Cassidy. It wasn't a task I could have done for me, although I knew a dozen painters in New York who could have produced anything on canvas I asked them to put there, and the product would have been a professional job.

But no one could be trusted. It was something I had to do myself, to fit Debierue's 'American Period' — at that moment I coined the title for my article: 'Debierue: The American Harvest Period.' It was a major improvement over my previous title, and 'American Harvest' — the idea must have come to me from the worktable in his studio — would provide me with a springboard for generating associative ideas.

But there was still Berenice, and the problem of what to

do with her — but wasn't it better to have her with me than to simply turn her loose where she could learn about the fire by reading about it in a newspaper, or by hearing a newscast? How soon would the report go out? Would Debierue telephone Mr. Cassidy and tell him about it? That depended upon the extent of the fire, probably, but Cassidy would be the only person Debierue knew to contact, and I could certainly trust Cassidy to make the correct decision. He might inform the news media, and again he might not. Before doing anything, he would want to know whether I got a picture for him before the fire started. And although Cassidy might suspect me of setting the fire, he wouldn't know for sure, and he wouldn't give a damn about the other 'paintings' destroyed in the fire so long as he got his.

I still had about three hours, or perhaps closer to four, to contact Cassidy before Debierue learned about the fire and managed to telephone him.

And Berenice? It would be best to keep her with me. At least for now. Once we reached New York, I could settle her in a hotel for a few days until I finished doing the things I had to do, and then we could work out a compromise of some kind. The best compromise, and I could work out the details later, would be for her to return to Duluth and teach until the summer vacation. In this way, we could reflect upon how we *really* felt about each other — at a sane distance, without passion interfering — and, if we both felt as if we still loved each other, in truth, and our affair was not just a *physical* thing, well, we could then work out some kind of life arrangement together when we met in New York — or somewhere — during her two-month summer vacation.

This was an idea I could sell, I decided, but until I had time for it, she could stay with me for the ride. It would take hours of argument to get rid of her now, and I simply couldn't spare the time on polemics when I had to concentrate every faculty I possessed on Debierue, his 'American Harvest' period, his painting, and what I was going to write.

I took the Lake Worth bridge to pick up A1A, to enter Palm Beach from the southern end of the island, and Berenice shifted suddenly in her seat.

'Do you know that we've driven for more than forty-five minutes, and you haven't said a single word?'

'Crack your wind-wing a little, honey,' I said, 'and we'll get some more air.'

'Oh!' She cracked the window. 'You're the most exasperating man I've ever met in my life, and if I didn't love you so much I'd tell you so!'

By leaving the food in the refrigerator, and the canned food and staples on the shelves, it didn't take us long to pack. I put my clean clothes in my small suitcase, and the dirty clothes, which made up the bulk of my belongings, all went into the big valopack with my suits, slacks, and jackets. While Berenice looked around to see if we had forgotten anything, I took my bags and typewriter to the car and tossed them into the back seat.

On my way back for Berenice's luggage I stopped at the landlady's apartment, gave her the receipt for the power company's twenty-dollar deposit, and told her to take the money that remained to pay someone to clean the apartment. When she began to protest that this small sum wouldn't be enough to pay a cleaning woman, I told her to add the balance of the rent money I had paid her in advance instead of returning it to me and she said: 'I hope you have a pleasant trip back to New York, Mr. Figueras, and perhaps you'll drop me a card some time from Spanish Harlem.'

She was a real bitch, but I shrugged off her parting remark and returned to the apartment for Berenice and her things.

I stopped at the Western Union office in Riviera Beach and sent two telegrams. The first one, to my managing editor in New York, was easy:

HOLD MY SPACE 5000 WORDS PERSONAL ARTICLE ON DEBIERUE DRIVING WITH IT NOW TO NY FIGUERAS

This telegram would put Tom Russell into a frenzy, but he would hold the space, or rip out something else already set for a piece on Debierue. But he would be so astonished about my having an article written on Debierue he wouldn't know whether to believe me or not. And yet, he would be afraid not to believe me. I gave the operator his home address on Long Island, and the New York magazine address as well, with instructions to telephone the message to him before delivering it. The girl assured me that he would have it before midnight, which assured me that Tom would have a sleepless night. Well, so would I.

The wire to Joseph Cassidy at the Royal Palm Towers, only a twenty-minute drive from Riviera Beach at this time of evening, was more difficult to compose. I threw away the first three drafts, and then sent the following as a night letter, with instructions not to deliver it until at least eight a.m.:

EMERGENCY STOP URGENT I REPORT TO NY MAGA-
ZINE OFFICE STOP WILL WRITE AND SEND PICTURE
FROM THERE FIGUERAS

There was ambiguity in the wording, but I wanted it to read that way. He would not be able to ascertain from the way the wire was worded whether I would write and fill him in on the 'emergency,' or whether I would be sending Debierue's 'picture' from New York. If nothing else, the wire would make him cautious about what he would say to the press about Debierue and the fire, although I knew he would have to release something. Knowing that *he* didn't set the fire, and without knowing for sure that *I* had set it, Debierue would most certainly contact Cassidy. If he suspected that the fire had been set by vandals, Debierue would probably be afraid to stay at the isolated location even though the rest of the house was only slightly damaged.

Berenice, happy to have her way about going to New York, sat in the car while I sent the telegrams and, except for humming or singing snatches of Rodgers and Hart songs, confined her conversation to reminding me occasionally to dim my lights or to kick them to bright again. Brooding about what to write, and how to write it, especially after we got onto the straight, mind-dulling Sunshine Parkway, I needed frequent reminders about the headlights.

The rest-stop islands, with filling stations at each end, and Dobbs House concession restaurants sandwiched between the gas stations, are staggered at uneven distances along the Parkway. Because they are unevenly spaced, it wasn't possible to stop at every other one (sometimes it was only twenty-eight miles to a rest stop, whereas the next one would be sixty miles away), and a decision, usually to halt, had to be made every time. Berenice always went to the can twice, once upon debarking, and again after we had a cup of coffee. I said nothing about the delay (as a man I could have stopped anywhere along the highway, but I would have been insane to make such a suggestion to a middle-western schoolteacher), and besides, the rest stops soon became useful. Sitting at the counter over coffee with my notebook, I organized my vagrant thoughts about Debierue's 'American Harvest' Florida paintings, and by writing down my ideas at each stop, I retained the good ones, eliminated the poor ones, and gradually developed a complicated, but pyramiding, gestalt for the article.

I allowed Berenice to drive between the Fort Pierce and Yeehaw Junction rest stops, but, finding that I thought better at the wheel, persuaded her to put her head on my shoulder and go to sleep with the promise that she could drive all the next morning while I slept. Toward morning the air became nippy, but by nine a.m., with Berenice driving, as we entered the long wide thoroughfare leading into downtown Valdosta, I knew that we had to stop.

If I didn't write the piece on Debierue now, while my ideas were still fresh, the article would suffer a hundred metamorphoses in my mind during the long haul to New York. I would be bone tired by then, confused, and unable to write anything. There were some references, dates,

names, and so on, I would have to check in New York, but
I could write the piece now and leave those spaces blank.
Besides, Tom Russell would want to read the piece the
moment I got into the city. I also had to paint a picture
before I wrote the article. By looking at it (whatever it
turned out to be), it would be a simple matter to describe
the painting with it sitting in front of me, and I could tie
the other paintings to it somehow.

'Berenice,' I said, 'we're going to stop here in Valdosta,
not in a motel, but in the hotel downtown, if they have
one. In a hotel we can get room service, and two rooms,
one for you and —'

'Why two rooms? Why can't I —'

'I know you mean well, sweetheart, and you're awfully
quiet when I'm working, but you also know how it bugs
me to have you tiptoeing around while I'm trying to write.
I won't have time to talk to you while I'm working, and I
won't stop, once I start, until I've got at least a good rough
draft on paper. Take a long nap, a good tub bath — motels
only have showers, you know — and then go to a movie
this afternoon. And tonight, if I'm fairly well along with it,
we can have dinner together.'

'Shouldn't you sleep for a few hours first? I had some
catnaps, but you haven't closed your eyes.'

'I'll take a couple of bennies. I'm afraid if I go to sleep
I'll lose my ideas.'

Being reasonable with Berenice worked for once.
Downtown, we stopped at the tattered-awninged entrance
of a six-story brick hotel, The Valdosta Arms. I asked the
ancient black doorman if the hotel had a parking garage.

'Yes, sir,' he said. 'If you checking in, drive right aroun'
the corner there and under the buildin'. I'll have a bellman
waitin' there for your bags.'

I reached across Berenice and handed the old man two
quarters.

'If you want out here, I'll carry your car aroun' myself,'
he offered.

'No,' I shook my head. 'I like to know where my car is
parked.'

320 CHARLES WILLEFORD

He was limping for the house phone beside the revolving glass doors before Berenice got the car into gear.

I wanted to know where the car was parked because I intended to return for the canvas and art materials after getting Berenice settled in. The bellman had a luggage truck waiting, and we followed him into the service elevator and up to the lobby.

'Two singles, please,' I said to the desk clerk. A bored middle-aged man, his eyes didn't even light up when he looked at Berenice.

'Do you have a reservation, sir?'

'No.'

'All right. I can give you connecting rooms on three, if you like.'

'Fine,' Berenice said.

'No.' I smiled and shook my head. 'You'd better separate them. I have to do some typing, and we've been driving all night and it might disturb her sleep.'

'Five-ten, and Five-oh-five.' He shifted his weary deadpan to address Berenice. 'You'll be dreckly across the hall from him, Miss.'

I signed a register card, and while Berenice was signing hers, crossed to the newsstand and looked for her favorite magazine on the rack. Unable to find it, I asked the woman behind the glass display case if she had sold out of *Cosmopolitan.* Setting her lips in a prim line, she reached beneath the counter and silently placed a copy on the glass top. I handed her a dollar and she rang it up (a man who buys 'under the counter' magazines has to pay a little more). I joined Berenice and the bellman at the elevators and we went up to our rooms.

The first thing I did after tipping the bellman and closing the door was to change out of my jumpsuit. From the guarded but indignant looks I had received in the lobby from the newsstand woman, the bellman, and two blue-suited men with narrow ties (the desk clerk's face wouldn't have registered surprise if I had worn jockey shorts), gentlemen were not expected to wear jumpsuits in downtown Valdosta. And I didn't want people to stare at me when I went down to the basement garage for my art materials. I put on a pair of gray slacks, a white silk shirt, with a white-on-white brocade tie, and a lime sports jacket, the only unrumpled clothes I had.

By taking the service elevator down and up, I was back in my room in fewer than five minutes. The room was hot and close. I stripped to my underwear, turned the air-conditioner to 'Cool,' and put the canvas against the back of a straight laddered chair. There was a large, fairly flat, green ceramic ashtray on the coffee table. This ashtray served to steady the canvas upright against the back of the chair, and would perform double duty as a palette. I squeezed blobs of blue, yellow, red, and white paint onto the ashtray, opened the cans of turpentine and linseed oil, lined up the brushes on the coffee table, and stared at the canvas. After fifteen minutes, I brought the other straight-backed chair over from the desk, sat down on it, and stared at the blank canvas some more.

Twenty minutes later, still staring at the white canvas, I was shivering. I turned the reverse-cycle air-conditioner to 'Heat,' and fifteen minutes later I was roasting, with perspiration bursting out of my forehead and clammy streams of sweat rolling down my sides from my damp armpits. I turned off the air-conditioner and tried to raise the window. The huge air-conditioner occupied the bottom half of the window, and the top half of the window was nailed shut, with rusty red paint covering the nail-heads. But there was an overhead fan, and the switch still worked. The fan, with wobbly two-foot blades, turned lazily in the high ceiling. The room was still close, so I unlocked the door, and kept it ajar with an old-fashioned brass hook-and-eye attachment that held the door cracked open for approximately four inches. No one could seen in from the corridor and within minutes the room was perfectly comfortable with just enough fresh air coming in from the hallway to be gently wafted about by the slow and not unpleasantly creaking overhead fan.

An hour later I was still physically comfortable. I had smoked three Kools. I was still staring at the virgin canvas,

and realized, finally, that I was unable to paint an original
Debierue painting. Not even if I sat there for four straight
hours every day ...

Chapter Two

My eyes, bright and alert, stared at the blank, shining canvas, and my stout heart, stepped up slightly, if inaudibly, from the depressing uppityness of two nugatory bennies, pumped willing blood to my even more willing fingers. I had forgotten, for two wasted hours, the hard-learned lesson of our times. In this, the Age of Specialization, where we can only point to Hugh Hefner or, wilder yet, to the early Marlon Brando as our contemporary 'Renaissance Men,' I had tackled my problem ass-backwards.

I was a writer confined by choice but still confined to contemporary art — writing about it, not painting it. I could wield a paintbrush, of course, passably. I had learned to paint in college studio courses before going on to my higher calling, in the same way that a man who wants to become a brigadier general and command an Air Force wing must first learn how to fly an airplane. The general does not have to be a superior pilot to command a wing, but he attains his position because, as an ex- or now part-time pilot, he understands the daily flight problems of the pilots under his command. The system doesn't work very well, of course, because the man who wants to fly an Air Force jet, and plans his career accordingly, seldom enters that active occupation with the preconceived plan of ending up some day at a desk where he rarely files. The 'hot' pilot does not make a good paper-shuffling general because the makeup of a man who wants to fly does not include a love of administration, learning letters, and enforcing discipline.

I had learned how to paint because I had to learn the

problems confronting painters, and I had taught college
students because that was what I had to do to survive as
an art historian. But in my secret heart I had intended to
become an art critic from the very beginning. And
although my major passion was contemporary art, during
my year in Europe I had grimly made my rounds in the
Louvre, in Florence, in Rome, tramping dutifully through
ancient galleries because I knew that I had to examine the
art of the past to understand the art of the present.

I was a writer, not a painter, and a writer gets his ideas
from a blank piece of paper, not from a blank piece of
canvas. I moved my chair to the desk and my typewriter
and immediately started to write.

This is the way it works. The contemporary painter
approaches his canvas without an idea (in most cases),
fools around with charcoal, experimenting the lines and
forms, filling in here, using a shaping thumb, perhaps, to
add some depth to a form that is beginning to interest
him, and sooner or later he sees something. The painting
develops into a composition and he completes it. His
subconscious takes over, and the completed painting may
turn out well or, more often than not, like most writing,
turn out badly. Even when the painter begins with an idea
of some kind his subconscious takes over the painting
once he starts working on it. The same theory, essentially,
holds true for the writer. A man paints or writes both
consciously and subconsciously beginning with, at most, a
few relevant mental notes.

So once I sat at my typewriter, the article began to take
shape. One idea led quickly to another. It was an inspired
piece of work, because it was morally right to write it. My
honor and Debierue's were both at stake. And yet,
although it was in some respects easy to write, it was one
of the most difficult pieces I had ever written because of
the fictional elements it contained.

My creative talents flagged when it came to describing
the pictures Debierue had failed to paint, although, once
over this block, it was a simple matter to interpret the
paintings because I could visualize them perfectly in my

mind's eye. I was familiar enough with Debierue's background to summarize the historical details of his earlier accomplishments. It was also simple enough to record a tightly edited version of our conversation, with a few embellishments for clarity, and a few bits of profundity for reader interest. Perhaps there is a little something of the fiction writer inside every professional journalist.

My imaginative powers were strong enough to describe the paintings that I, myself, would have liked to paint if I had had the ability to paint them, but I ran into conceptual difficulties because, at first, I thought I had to describe the paintings that *Debierue* wanted to paint. But this was a futile path. I could not possibly see the world as Debierue did. And if I was unable to live in his arcane world, I could never verbalize it into visual art.

My predetermined term, 'American Harvest,' for Debierue's so-called American period, provided me with the correlative link I needed to visualize mental pictures I was capable of describing. I began with red, white and blue — the colors of France's noble tricolor and our own American flag. Seeing these three colors on three separate panels I began to rearrange the panels in my mind. Side by side, in a row, close together, well separated, overlapping, horizontal and vertical with the floor, and scattered throughout a room on three different walls. But there are four walls to a room. A fourth panel was required — not for symmetry, because that doesn't matter — but for variety, for the sake of an ordered environment. Florida, Sun. Orange. An autumnal sun for Debierue's declining years. Burnt orange. But not a panel of burnt orange in toto — that would be heresy, because Debierue, even at his great age, was still painting, still creating, still growing. So the ragged square of burnt orange required a lustrous border of blue to surround the dying sun and to overflow the edges of the rectangle. Bluebird sky? Sky blue? No, not sky nor Dufy blue, because that meant using cobalt oil paint, and cobalt blue, with the passage of years, gradually turns to bluish gray. Prussian blue, with a haughty whisper of zinc white added to make it bitterly cold. Besides, right here in this hotel room, I had a full tube of Prussian blue.

Texture? Tactile quality? Little, if any. Pure, smooth even colors.

The four paintings, 30″ × 24″, were the only paintings Debierue had painted since coming to Florida. The paintings were for his personal aesthetic satisfaction, to enjoy during the harvest years of his stay in American, and yet they were in keeping with his traditionally established principles of Nihilistic Surrealism.

Every morning when Debierue arose at six a.m., depending upon his waking mood, he hung one of the red, white, or blue panels next to the permanently centered burnt orange, blue-bordered panel, the painting representing the painter — the painter's 'self.' For the remainder of the day, when he was not engaged in the planning of another (undisclosed to the writer) work of art, he studied and contemplated the two bilateral paintings which reminded him of America's multiple 'manifest destinies,' the complexities of American life in general, and his personal artistic commitment to the new world.

Did he ever awaken in a mood buoyant enough to hang two or perhaps three panels at once alongside the burnt orange panel?

'No,' he said.

I had typed eighteen pages for a total of 4,347 words. Now that the concept was firmly established, I could have gone on to write another dozen pages of interpretive commentary, but I forced myself to stop with the negative. Wasn't it about time? Does every contemporary work of art have to end with an affirmative? Joyce, with his coda of yesses in *Ulysses*, Beckett, with the 'I will go on' of his trilogy, and those 1,001 phallically erected obelisks and church spires pointing optimistically toward the heavens — for once, just once, let a negative prevail.

My conclusion was not a lucky accident. It was a valid, pertinent statement of Debierue's life and art. Skipping two spaces, I put a '— 30 —' to the piece.

I was suddenly tired. My neck and shoulders were sore and my back ached. I looked at my watch. Six o'clock.

There was a plaintive rumble in my hollow stomach. Except for going into the can three times, I had been at the typewriter for almost six straight hours. I got up, stretched, rubbed the back of my neck, and walked around the coffee table shaking my hands and fingers above my head to get rid of the numb feeling in my arms.

I was tired but I wasn't sleepy. I was exhilarated by completing the article in such a short time. Every part had fallen neatly into place, and I knew that it was a good piece of writing. I had never felt better in my entire life.

I sighed, put the cover on the Hermes, moved the typewriter to the bed, and sat at the desk again to read and correct the article. I righted spelling errors, changed some diction, and penciled in a rough transitional sentence between two disparate paragraphs. It wasn't good enough, and I made a note in the margin to rewrite it. One long convoluted sentence with three semicolons and two colons made me laugh aloud. My mind had really been racing on that one. I reduced it, without any trouble, to four clear, separate sentences—

The phone rang, a loud, jangling ring designed to arouse traveling salesmen who had been drinking too much before going to bed. I almost jumped out of my chair.

Berenice's voice was husky. 'I'm hungry.'

'Who isn't?'

'I've been sleeping.'

'I've been working.'

'I've been awake for a half hour, but I'm too lazy to get out of bed. Why don't you come over and get in with me?'

'Jesus, Berenice, I've been working all day and I'm tired as hell.'

'If you eat something, you'll feel better.'

'All right. Give me an hour, and I'll be over.'

'Should I order dinner sent up?'

'No. I prefer to eat something hot, and I've never had a hot meal served in a hotel room. We'll go down to the dining room.'

'I'll do my nails.'

'In an hour.' I racked the phone.

I finished reading and proofing the typescript and put the manuscript in a manila envelope before tucking it safely away in my suitcase. There were only minimal changes to be made in New York. Only two pages would require rewriting. I put the canvas, ashtray palette, and other art materials into the closet. I could paint the picture after dinner.

The tub in the bathroom was huge, the old-fashioned kind with big claw feet clutching metal balls. The hot water came boiling out, and I shaved while the tub filled. The water was much too hot to get into, but I added a little cold water at a time until the temperature dropped to the level I could stand. Sliding down into the steaming, man-sized tub until I was fully submerged, except for my face, I soaked up the heat. The soreness gradually left my back and shoulders. I finished with a cold shower, and by the time I was dressed, I felt as if I had had eight hours' sleep. I called the bar, ordered two Gibsons to be sent to 510, Berenice's room, and studied the road maps I had picked up at the last Standard station.

After dinner, I figured I could paint the picture in an hour or at most an hour and a half. Now that the article was finished there was no point in staying overnight in an hotel. I wasn't sleepy, and with both of us driving we could make it to New York in about thirty hours. The front wheels of the old car started to shimmy if I tried to push it beyond fifty-five mph, but thirty hours from Valdosta was a fairly accurate estimate. I had forty dollars in my wallet and some loose change. My Standard credit card would get the car to New York, but I decided to save my cash. Berenice had traveler's checks, and she could use some of them to pay the hotel tab. Through the cracked door, I heard the bellman knock on 510 across the way. I waited until Berenice signed the chit and the waiter had caught the down elevator before I crossed the hallway and knocked on her door.

Berenice was willowy in a blue slack suit with lemon, quarter-inch lines forming windowpane checks, and the four tightly grouped buttons of the double-breasted jacket were genuine lapis lazuli. The bells of the slacks were fully sixteen inches in diameter, and only the toes of her white wedgies were exposed. There was a silk penny-colored scarf around her neck. She had done her nails in Chen Yu nail varnish, that peculiar decadent shade of red that resembles dried blood (the sexiest shade of red ever made, and so Germanic thirtiesish that Visconti made Ingrid Thulin wear it in *The Damned*), and she had painted her lips to match. During her six weeks in Palm Beach, Berenice had learned some peculiar things about fashion, but the schoolteacher from Duluth had not disappeared.

She giggled and pointed to the tray on the coffee table. 'These are supposed to be Gibsons!'

There were two miniatures of Gilbey's gin and another of Stock dry vermouth (two tenths of gin, an eighth of vermouth), a glass pitcher with chunks, not cubes, of ice, and a tiny glass bowl containing several cocktail onions.

I shrugged. 'I don't think they're allowed to serve mixed drinks in this Georgia county, although the waiter would've mixed them for you if you'd tipped him. Actually' — I twisted the metal caps off the two gin miniatures — 'it's better this way. Most bartenders overuse vermouth in Gibsons, and I'd rather make my own anyway.'

'It just struck me funny, that's all,' Berenice said.

While I mixed the Gibsons, I tried to work out a simple plan and a way of presenting it to Berenice to keep her away from my room until we were ready to leave.

'Did you go to a movie this afternoon?'

She shook her head, and sipped her cocktail. 'I wouldn't go to a movie alone back home, much less in a strange town. I'm not the scary type, you know that, James, but there are some things a woman shouldn't do alone, and that's one of them.'

'At any rate, you got through the day.'

'I slept like the dead. How's the article coming?'

'That's what I wanted to talk to you about. I finished it.'

'Already? That's wonderful, James!'

'It's a good rough draft,' I admitted, 'but it'll need a few things filled in up in New York —'

'Am I in it? Can I read it?'

'No. It's an article about Debierue and his art, not about you and me. When did you become interested in art criticism?' I grinned.

'When I met Mr. Debierue, that's when.' She smiled. 'He's the nicest, sweetest old gentleman I ever met.'

'I'd rather you'd wait till I have the final draft, if you don't mind. I want to get back to New York as soon as possible to finish it. So after dinner, I'll take a short nap until midnight, and then we can check out of here and get rolling. If we trade off on the driving, we can reach the city in about thirty hours.'

'You won't get much sleep if we leave at midnight ...'

'I don't need much, and you've already had enough. You wouldn't be able to sleep much tonight anyway, not after being in the sack all day.'

'I'm not arguing, James, I was just worried about you —'

'In that case, let's go downstairs to dinner, so I can come back up and get some sleep before midnight.'

During dinner, Berenice asked me if she could see Debierue's picture, but I put her off by telling her it was all wrapped up securely in the trunk of the car, and that it wouldn't be a good idea for anyone to see us looking at a painting in the basement garage. I reminded her conspiratorially that it was a 'hot' picture, and we didn't want anyone suspecting us and making enquiries. Because I half-whispered this explanation, she nodded solemnly and accepted it.

The food was excellent — medium-rare sirloins, corn on the cob, okra and tomatoes, creamed scalloped potatoes, a cucumber and onion salad, with a chocolate pudding dessert topped with real whipped cream, not sprayed from a can — and I ate every bit of it, including four hot biscuits with butter (my two, and Berenice's two). I felt somewhat lethargic following the heavy meal, but after drinking two cups of black coffee, although I was uncomfortably stuffed, I still wasn't sleepy.

I signed the check and penciled in my room number. 'After all that food, I'm sleepy.' I said.

Berenice took my arm as we left the dining room to cross the lobby to the elevators. 'Wouldn't you like a little nightcap,' she squeezed my arm, 'to make you sleep better — in my room?'

'No,' I replied, 'and when I say No to an offer like that you know I'm sleepy enough already.'

I took her room key, opened the door, and kissed her good night. 'I'll leave a call for eleven thirty, and then I'll knock on your door. Try and get some more sleep.'

'If I can,' she replied, 'and if not, I'll watch television. Let me have another one of those good-night kisses . . .'

My room was musty and close again, although I had not turned off the overhead fan. I didn't want to go through the too-hot–too-cold routine with the reverse-cycle air-conditioner — which had far too many BTUs for the size of the small room — so I cracked the door again and clamped it open with the brass hook-and-eye attachment. I stripped down to my shorts and T-shirt, took the art materials out of the closet, and got busy with the picture.

I mixed Prussian blue, adding zinc white a dollop at a time, until I had a color the shade of an Air Force uniform. I thinned it slightly with turpentine and brushed a patch on the bottom of the canvas. It was still too dark, and I added white until the blue became much bolder. I then mixed enough of the diluted blue to paint a slightly ragged border, not less than an inch in width, nor more than three inches, around the four sides of the rectangle. To fill the remaining white space with burnt orange was simple enough, once I was able to get the exact shade I wanted, but it took me much longer than I expected to mix it, because it wasn't easy to match a color that I could see in my mind, but not in front of me.

But the color was rich when I achieved it to my satisfaction. Not quite brown, not quite mustardy, but a kind of burnished burnt orange with a felt, rather than an observable, sense of yellow. I mixed more of the paint than I would need, to be sure that I would have enough, and thinned the glowing pile with enough linseed oil and turpentine to spread it smoothly on the canvas. Using the largest brush, I filled in the center of the canvas almost to the blue border, and then changed to a smaller brush to carefully fill in the narrow ring of white space that remained.

I backed to the wall for a long view of the completed painting, and decided that the blue border was not quite ragged enough. This was remedied in a few minutes, and the painting was as good as my description of it in my article. In fact, the picture was so bright and shining under the floor lamp, it looked even better than I had expected.

All it needed was Debierue's signature.

I had a sharp debate with myself whether to sign it or not, wondering whether it was in keeping with the philosophy of the 'American Harvest' period for him to put his name on one of the pictures. But inasmuch as the burnt orange, blue-bordered painting represented the 'self' of Debierue, I concluded that if he ever signed a painting, this was one he would *have* to sign. I made a mental note to add this information to my article — that this was the first real picture Debierue had ever signed (it would certainly raise the value for Mr. Cassidy to possess a signed painting!).

Debierue's letter to the manager of the French clipping service was still in my jumpsuit. I took it out and studied Debierue's cramped signature, sighing gratefully over the uniqueness of the design. Forgers love a tricky signature: it makes forgery much simpler for them because it is much easier to copy a complicated signature than it is a plain, straightforward signature. There are two ways to forge a signature. One is to practice writing it over and over again until it is perfected. That is the hard way. The easy way is to turn the signature upside down and draw it, not write it, but copy it the way one would imitate any other line drawing. And this is what I did. Actually, I didn't have to turn the canvas upside down. By copying Debierue's signature onto the upper left-hand side upside down, when the picture itself was turned upside down the top would then be the bottom, and the signature would be rightside up and in the lower right-hand corner where it belonged.

Nevertheless, it took me a long time to copy it, because I was trying to paint it as small as possible in keeping with Debierue's practice of writing tiny letters. To put *ebierue* inside the 'D' wasn't simple, and I had to remember to 'write' with my brushstrokes up instead of down, because that is the way the strokes would have to be when the painting was turned upside down.

'*James!*'

Berenice called out my name. I was so deeply engrossed in what I was doing I wasn't certain whether this was the first or the second time she had called it out. But it was too late to do anything about it. I was sitting in the straight-backed chair facing the canvas, and I barely had time to turn and look at her, much less get to my feet, before she lifted the brass hook, opened the door, and entered the room.

'James,' she repeated flatly, halting abruptly with her hand still on the doorknob. She had removed her makeup, and her pale pink lips made a round 'O' as she stared at me, the canvas, and the makeshift palette on the low coffee table. The sheet I had used to wrap the once-blank canvas was on the floor and gathered about the chair I was using as an easel. I had spread it there to prevent paint from dropping onto the rug.

'Yes?' I said quietly.

Berenice shut the door, and leaned against it. She supported herself with her hands flat against the door panels. 'Just now ... on TV,' she said, not looking at me, but with her rounded blue eyes staring at the canvas, '... on the ten thirty news, the newscaster said that Debierue's house had burned down.'

'Anything else?'

She nodded. 'Pending an investigation — something like that — Mr. Debierue will be the house guest of the famous criminal lawyer Joseph Cassidy, in Palm Beach.'

I swallowed, and nodded my head. I am a highly verbal individual, but for once in my life I was at a loss for words.

One lie after another struggled for expression in my mind, but each lie, in turn, was rejected before it could be voiced.

'Is that Debierue's painting?' Berenice said, as she crossed the room toward my chair.

'Yes. I needed to look at it again, you see, to check it against the description in my article. It was slightly damaged — Debierue's signature — so I thought I'd touch it up some.'

Berenice pressed her forefinger to the exact center of the painting. She examined the wet smear on her fingertip.

'Oh, James,' she said unhappily, 'you painted this awful picture ...!'

Chapter Three

Looking back (and faced with the same set of circumstances), I don't know that I would have handled the problem any differently — except for some minor changes from the way that I did solve it. Ignorant women have destroyed the careers, the ambitions, and the secret plans of a good many honorable men throughout history.

It would have been easy enough to blame myself for allowing Berenice to discover the painting. If I had locked the door, instead of being concerned with my physical discomfort in the hotel room, I could have hidden the painting from her before allowing her into the room. This one little slip on my part destroyed everything, if one wants to look at it that way. But the problem was greater than this — not a matter of just one little slip. There was an entire string of unfortunate coincidences, going back to the unwitting moment I had allowed Berenice to move in on me, and continuing through my fool-hardy decision to allow her to accompany me to Debierue's house.

And now of course, caught red handed — or burnt orange handed — Berenice was in possession of a lifelong hold over me if I carried my deception through — with the publication of the article, with the sending of the painting to Joseph Cassidy, to say nothing of the future, *my* future, and the subsequent furor that the publication of an article on Debierue would arouse in the art world.

Berenice loved me, or so she had declared again and again, and if I had married her, perhaps she would have kept her mouth shut, carrying her secret knowledge, and mine, to her grave. I don't know. I doubted it then, and I doubt it now. Love, according to my experience, is a fragile transitory emotion. Not only does love fall a good many years short of lasting forever, a long stretch for love to last is a few months, or even a few weeks. If I think about my friends and acquaintances in New York — and don't consider casual acquaintances I have known elsewhere, in Palm Beach, for example — I can't think of a single friend, male or female, who hasn't been divorced at least once. And most of them, *more* than once. The milieu I live in is that way. The art world is not only egocentric, it is ecoeccentric. The environment is not conducive to lasting friendships, let alone lasting marriages. And that was my world ...

My remaining choice, which was too stupid even to consider seriously, was a bitter one. I could have destroyed The Burnt Orange Heresy (such was the title I assigned to the painting), and torn up the article I had written, which would mean that the greatest opportunity I had ever had to make a name for myself as an art critic would be lost.

These thoughts were jumbled together in my mind as I confronted Berenice, but not in any particular order. Emotionally, I was only mildly annoyed at the time, knowing I had a major problem to solve, but bereft, at least for the moment, of any solution.

'You may believe that this is an "awful" picture,' I said coldly to Berenice, 'and it's your privilege to think so if, and the key word is *if*, if you can substantiate your opinion with valid reasons as to *why* it's an "awful" picture. Otherwise, you're not entitled to any value judgments concerning Debierue's work.'

'I — I just can't believe it!' Berenice said, shaking her head. 'You're not going to try to pass this off as a painting by Debierue, are you?'

'It *is* a painting by Debierue. Didn't I just tell you that I was touching it up a little because it was damaged slightly in transit?'

'I'm not *blind*, James.' She made a helpless, fluttering gesture with her hands, her big eyes taking in the evidence of the art materials and the painting itself. 'How do you expect to get away with something so *raw*? Don't you know that Mr. Cassidy will *show* this painting to Debierue, and that —'

'Berenice!' I brought her up sharply. 'You're sticking your mid-western nose into something that is none of your damned business! Now get the hell out of here, get packed, and if you aren't ready to leave in twenty minutes, you can damned well stay here in Valdosta!'

Her face flushed, and she took two steps backward. She nodded, nibbled her nether lip, and nodded again. 'All *right*! There is obviously something going on that I don't understand, but that isn't any reason to blow off at me like that. You can at least explain it to me. You can't blame me for being bewildered, can you? I can see that, well, the way it looks is *funny*, that's all!'

I got up from the chair, put my arm around her shoulders, and gave her a friendly hug. 'I'm sorry,' I said gently, 'I shouldn't have woofed at you like that. And don't worry. I'll explain everything to you in the car. There's a good girl. Just get packed, and we can get out of here and be on our way in a few minutes. Okay?'

I held open the door. Still nodding her head, Berenice crossed the hallway to her room.

The moment her door closed, I wrapped the art materials in the sheet, washed the ashtray palette under the bathtub hot water tap and dried it with a towel. I slipped on my trousers and a shirt, and took the painting and the small bundle of art materials down to the basement garage on the elevator. I dumped the bundle in a garbage can, and placed the painting carefully, wet side up, in the trunk of my car. It took another three minutes to unfasten the canvas convertible top, fold it back, and snap the fasteners of the plastic cover. It would be chilly riding with the top back at this time of night, but I could put it up again later. The night garage attendant, a young black man wearing white overalls, stood in the doorway of the small, lighted office, watching me silently as I struggled with the top. Finished, I crossed the garage, handed him a quarter, and told him I was checking out.

'Call the desk, please,' I said, 'and tell the clerk to send a bellman with a truck to get our baggage in five-ten and five-oh-five in about fifteen minutes. Tell the bellman to pile it on the back seat when he comes down. The trunk is already filled with other things.'

'Yes, sir,' he said.

I returned to my room, packed in less than five minutes, pulled a sleeveless sweater on over my shirt, and slipped into my sports coat. Berenice wasn't ready yet, but I helped her close her suitcases, and advised her to wear her warm polo coat over her slack suit. The bellman came with his truck, and when he got off at the lobby to check out, he continued on down to the basement to put our luggage in the car. Berenice paid the bill, which was surprisingly reasonable, by cashing two traveler's checks, and the bellman had the car out in front for us before we had finished checking out. The night deskman didn't ask questions about why we were leaving in the middle of the night, and I didn't volunteer any information.

The night air was chilly when we got into the car, and there was a light, misty fog hovering fifty feet or so above the deserted city streets. I lit two cigarettes, handed Berenice one of them, and pulled away from the curb. She shivered slightly and huddled down in her seat.

'You're probably wondering why I put the top back,' I said.

'Yes, I am. But after the way you barked at me last time, I'm almost afraid to ask any questions.'

I laughed and patted her leg. 'If it gets too cold, I'll put it up again. But I thought it would be best to get as much fresh air as possible to keep myself awake. It isn't really cold, and there won't be much traffic this time of night, so we should make fairly good time.'

Berenice accepted this moronic explanation, and I increased the speed the moment we got out of the downtown area and onto the new four-lane highway that was still bordered by residential streets containing two- and three-story houses.

From my examination of the map I knew that there were several small lakes between Valdosta and Tifton, and a few pine reserves as well, first- and second-growth forests to feed the Augusta paper mills. Most of the rich, red land was cultivated, however — tobacco, for the major crop, but also with melons, corn, peas, or anything else that a farmer wanted to grow, including flax. East of Valdosta was the Great Okefonokee Swamp, which filled a large section of southeast Georgia, and there were many small lakes, streams, and brooks that filtered well-silted water into the swamp.

I was unfamiliar with the highway and the countryside, and I didn't know precisely what I was looking for, other than a grove of pines, a finger of swamp, and a rarely used access road. I slowed down considerably a few miles north of Valdosta, as soon as I was in open country with only widely scattered farmhouses, and I began to keep my eyes open for side roads leading nowhere. Berenice, who had been as silent as a martyr, and suffering from my silence as well, finally had to open her mouth.

'Well?' she said.

'Well, what?'

'I'm waiting for the explanation, that's what. You said you'd explain, what are you waiting for?'

'I've been thinking things over, Berenice, and I'm beginning to come to my senses. You really don't think it would be a good idea, do you, to send that painting to Mr. Cassidy?'

'That's your business, James. It isn't up to me to tell you what to do, but if you're asking me for an opinion, I'd say no. But as you said, I don't know all there is to know about what it is you're trying to do — so until I do, I'll keep my long "mid-western nose" out of your business.'

'I apologized for that, sweetheart.'

'That's all right. I know that my nose fits my face. What does bother me though is that I've been more or less forced to think that you set fire to Debierue's house.'

'Me?' I laughed. 'What makes you think I'd do something like that?'

'Well, for one thing, you didn't show any surprise,' she said shrewdly, 'when I told you about the news of the fire on television.'

'Why should I be surprised? His villa in France burned down, too. It does surprise me, however, that you would think that I did it.'

'Then tell me that you didn't do it, and I'll believe you.'

'What would my motive be for doing such a thing?'

'Why not give me a simple yes or no?'

'There are no simple yes or no answers in this world, Big Girl — none that I've ever found. There are only qualified yes and no answers, and not many of them.'

'All right, James, I can't think of a valid motive, to use one of your favorite words, "valid," but I can think of a motive that *you* might consider valid. I think you've faked an article about some paintings that Debierue was supposed to paint, but didn't paint. You looked at the paintings he did paint and didn't like them, probably because they didn't meet your high standards of what you thought they should be, so you burned them by setting fire to the house. You then invented some nonexistent paintings of your own and wrote about them instead.'

'Jesus, do you realize how crazy that sounds?'

'Yes, I do. But you can show me how crazy it is by letting me read the article you wrote. If there's no mention of that weird orange —'

'Burnt orange —'

'All right, *burnt* orange painting in your article, then you can easily prove me wrong. I'll apologize, and that'll be that.'

'That'll be *that*, just like that? And then you'll expect me to forgive your wild accusation as if you'd never made it, right?'

'I said that I might be wrong, and I sincerely hope that I am. It's easy enough to prove me wrong, isn't it? What I *do* know, though, and there's nothing you can ever say to persuade me that I'm wrong, is that Debierue never painted that picture in your hotel room. *You* painted it. It was still wet when I touched it — including Debierue's signature. And the only reason I can possibly come up with for you to do such a thing is because you want to write about it, and pass it off as Debierue's work. I — I don't know what to think, James, the whole thing has given me a headache. And really — you may not believe this — I actually don't care! *Honestly*, I don't! But I don't want you to get into any trouble, either. Arson is a very serious offence, James.'

'No shit?'

'It isn't funny. I'll tell you that much. And if you did set fire to Debierue's house, you should tell me!'

'Why? So you can turn me in to the police for arson?'

'Oh, James,' she wailed. Berenice put her face into cupped hands and began to cry.

'All right, Berenice,' I said quietly, after I had let her cry for a minute or so. 'I'll tell you what I'm going to do.' I handed her my handkerchief.

She shook her head, took a Kleenex tissue out of her purse, and blew her nose with a refined honk.

'You're right, Berenice, on all counts,' I continued, 'and I might as well admit it. I guess I got carried away, but it isn't too late. Setting the fire was an accident. I didn't do it on purpose. The old man had spilled some turpentine, and I accidentally dropped my cigarette and it caught. I thought I'd put it out, but apparently it flared up again. Do you see?'

She nodded. 'I thought it was something like that.'

'That's the way it happened, I guess. But painting the picture was another matter. I don't now how I expected to get away with it, and the chances are I would've chickened out at the last minute anyway. What I'll do is throw the picture away, and then rewrite the article altogether, using the information I've actually got.'

'He told us lots of interesting things.'

'Sure he did.'

There was a dirt road on the right, leading into a thick stand of pines. I made the turn, shifted down to second gear, but kept up the engine speed because of the sand.

'Where are you going?'

'I'm going to drive back in here well off the highway and burn the painting.'

'You can wait until morning, can't you?'

'No. I think that the sooner I get rid of it the better. If I kept it I might change my mind again. It *would* be possible, you know, to get away with it —'

'No, it wouldn't, James,' she said crisply.

The sandy road, after more than a mile, ended in a small clearing. The clearing was filled with knee-high grass, and we were completely surrounded by second-growth slash pines. It would be another two years, at least, before these trees would be tall enough to cut. I left the lights on and cut the engine. Without another word I got out of the car, opened the trunk with the key, and picked up the tire iron. It was about ten inches long, quite hefty, and the flattened end, although it wasn't sharp, was thin enough to make a good cutting edge. Rounding the car on Berenice's side, I brought the heavy iron down on her head.

'Ooauh!' She expelled her breath, clasped both hands over her head, and turned her face toward me. Her eyes were wide and staring, but her face was expressionless. I hadn't hit her hard enough, or I had miscalculated the thickness of her hair, piled on top of her head, which had cushioned the blow. I hit her on top of the head again, much harder this time, and she slumped down in the seat.

I opened the door, grabbed the thick collar of her polo coat, and dragged her out of the car. She was inert, unbelievably heavy, and her left leg was still in the front seat. I was working one-handed, still clutching the tire iron in my right hand, and trying to free her leg from the car door, when she convulsed, rolled over, and came up off the ground, head down, butting me in the stomach like a goat.

Caught my surprise, I fell backward and my shoulder hit a splintered tree stump. At the same time my left elbow banged against the ground sharply, right on the ulna bone. My right shoulder felt as if it were on fire, and crazy prickles from my banged funny bone danced inside my forearm. I dropped the tire iron, rubbed my right shoulder with the fingers of my left hand, and the pain in my elbow and shoulder gradually subsided. Through the trees, and getting farther away every second, Berenice's voice screamed shrilly. I picked up the tire iron.

I turned off the headlights and started after her, judging direction by the sound of her screams, which were growing fainter, in the dark forest. Berenice ran awkwardly, like most women, and she was hampered by the knee-length coat. I didn't think she could run far, but I was unable to catch up with her. I tried to run myself, but after tripping over a stump and sprawling full length on the damp ground, I settled for a fast walk.

The screaming stopped, and so did I. The abrupt silence startled me and, for the first time, I was frightened. I had to find her. If she got away, everything was over for me — everything.

I moved ahead, walking slower now, searching every foot of ground, now that my eyes had become adjusted to the dim light. A light mist hovered a hundred feet above the trees, but there was a moon, and I could see a little better with every passing moment. The trees thinned out and the wet ground began to get mushy. I was on the edge of a swamp, and after another fifty yards or so, I came to the edge of a lake of black, stagnant water. I knew Berenice well enough to know that she wouldn't have plunged into that inky water. The way was easier going toward the left, and I took it, figuring that she would do the same.

I found her a few minutes later, catching sight of her light-colored coat. She was in a prone position, with her legs spread awkwardly, partially hidden under a spreading dogwood tree. Afraid to touch her, I rolled her over on her back. A pale shaft of moonlight filtered through the tree branches, lighting her bloody face and wide staring eyes.

I didn't know whether she was dead or not, but I had to make certain. There was one thing I did know. I wouldn't have been able to hit her again. As I knelt down beside her and opened her coat, an aroma of Patou's 'Joy' filled my nostrils with loss. I put my head down on her chest and listened for a heartbeat. Nothing. Berenice was dead, but my blows on her head hadn't killed her. She had died from shock. No one, mortally wounded, would have been able to run so far. On the other hand, both of us for a few moments had been gifted with superhuman strength. She was a big woman, stronger than hell, and she had been fighting for her life.

But so had I.

I dragged her to the edge of the water and wedged her body under a fallen tree that was half in and half out of the swamp. By leaning dead branches and by piling brush over the unsubmerged part of the tree, she was completely hidden from view. Debierue knew that she was with me, and if she were to be found, and if he learned that she had been killed, he would tell Cassidy immediately. That is, he would tell Cassidy if her body was found before he received the tear sheets of my article on his American Harvest period. He would be so delighted by my article he wouldn't risk mentioning Berenice's name to anyone. His reputation, as well as mine, depended upon that article. But there would be time, plenty of time. Months, perhaps years, would pass before her body was found.

Suddenly I was weak and dispirited. All of my strength disappeared. I leaned against the nearest tree and vomited my dinner — the corn, the tomatoes and okra, the stringy chunks of sirloin, the biscuits, everything. Panting and sobbing until I caught my breath, I returned to the dogwood tree and picked up my tire iron. It had my fingerprints on it, and in case I had a flat tire on my way to New York, I would need it again.

I started back toward the car, and after walking for five minutes or so I discovered that I was lost. I panicked and began to run. I tripped and fell, banging my head against a tree, scratching a painful gash in my forehead. As Freud said, there are no accidents. Fighting down my panic by taking long deep breaths, I calmed down further by forcing myself to sit quietly on the damp ground, with my back against a tree, and by smoking a cigarette down to the cork tip. I was all right. Everything was going to be all right.

Calmer now, although my hands were still trembling, I managed to retrace my path back to the swamp and Berenice. I now had a sense of direction. I started back in what I thought was the general direction of the car, and hit the sandy road, missing the clearing and the car by about fifty yards. My face was flushed with heat, and I was shivering at the same time with cold. Before setting out. I put up the canvas top, and then kicked over the engine.

Two weeks later, back in New York, when I was cleaning out the car in order to sell it, I found one of Berenice's fingers, or a part of one — the first two joints and the Chen Yu-ed fingernail. She must have got it lopped off when she had put her hands over her head in the car. I wrapped the finger in a handkerchief and put it safely away. Perhaps a day would come, I thought, when I would be able to look at this finger without fear, pain, or remorse.

Chapter Four

The photograph of Debierue 'reading' the flaming copy of the *Miami Herald*, which illustrated my article in *Fine Arts:The Americas* was republished in *Look* and *Newsweek*, and in the fine arts section of the *Sunday New York Times*. UPI, after dickering with my agent, finally bought the photo and sent it out on the wire to their subscribers. The money I made from this photo provided me with my first tailor-made suit. Coat and trousers, four hundred dollars.

I had made one side trip off the superhighway to Baltimore, on my way back to New York, where I checked Berenice's luggage in two lockers inside the Greyhouse bus station (including her handbag and traveler's checks, knowing that her mother could use this money someday, if and when the bags were ever claimed). Except for this brief stopover, I drove straight through to the city.

There were five message slips in my office telling me to telephone Joseph Cassidy, collect, immediately, so I called him before I did anything else.

'Did you get the picture?' he asked.

'Yes, of course.'

'Good! Good! Hold it for a few days before sending it down. I want to get Mr. Debierue settled in a good nursing home, you see — he doesn't know that you have the painting, does he?'

'No, and it'll be better if he doesn't. I've mentioned it in my article, although I won't run a photograph of it. Before sending it to Palm Beach I intend to take some good color plates of *The Burnt Orange Heresy* for *eventual* publication, if you get what I mean ...'

'Naturally — is that the title, *The Burnt Orange Heresy*? That's great!'

'Yeah. It'll probably have an additional title, too. *Self-portrait.*'

'Jesus-James, I can hardly wait to see it!'

'Just let me know when, Mr. Cassidy, and I'll send it down to you air express.'

'Don't worry, I'll call you. And listen, James, I'm not going to forget this. When the time comes to exhibit it, you've got an exclusive to cover the opening.'

'Thanks.'

'My problem right now is to persuade Debierue to enter a rest home. He's much too old to take care of himself. If he had been asleep when the fire started, he would've been killed you know. And when I think of those paintings that went up in smoke — Jesus!'

'Did he tell you anything about them?'

'Not a word. You know how he is. And nothing seems to faze him. He spends most of his time just sitting around watching old movies on TV and drinking orange juice. He can do that in a rest home. Well, you'll hear from me. This is a long distance call, you know.'

'Sure. Later.'

He didn't call me again, however. He sent me a special delivery letter after he had settled Debierue in the Regal Pines Nursing Home, near Melbourne, Florida. I sent Cassidy the painting, air express collect, although I had to pay the insurance fee, in advance, before they would agree to send it collect.

The critical reaction to my article, when it appeared in *Fine Arts: The Americas*, followed the pattern I had anticipated. Canaday in the *Times*, had reservations. Perreault, in *The Village Voice*, was enthusiastic, and there was a short two-paragraph item in *The L.A. Free Press* recommending the article to would-be revolutionary painters in Southern California. This was more newspaper coverage than I expected.

My real concern was with the concentric ripples in the art journals and critical quarterlies. This reaction was slow in coming, because a lot of thought had to be put into them. The best single article, which set off a long string of letters in the correspondence department, appeared in *Spectre*, and was written by Pierre Montrand. A French chauvinist, he saw Debierue's 'American Harvest' period as a socialistic rejection of DeGaullism. This was an absurd idea, but beautifully expressed, and controversial as hell.

With my photograph of Debierue, many newspapers printed sketchy accounts of Debierue's mysterious immigration to the United States, but I kept my promise to Cassidy and the old man. I never divulged Debierue's Florida address after Cassidy had him admitted under a false name to the Regal Pines Nursing Home, and Cassidy had covered his tracks so well the reporters never found him. I mailed Debierue the tearsheets of my article, a dozen 8″ × 10″ photographs of the burning newspaper shot, and an autographed copy of my book, *Art and the Preschool Child.* He didn't acknowledge the package, but I knew that he received it because I had mailed it Return Receipt Requested.

For the first week after my return to New York I bought a daily copy of the *Atlanta Journal-Constitution* (it 'covers Dixie like the dew'), and searched through the pages to see if there was any mention of a body being found near Valdosta. But I disliked the newspaper, and searching for such news every day was making me morbid. I quit buying the paper. If they found her, they found her, and there was nothing I could do about it. Inevitably, though, a reaction appeared in my psyche, caused, naturally enough, by the death of Berenice. It wasn't that my conscience bothered me, although that was a part of my reaction. It was a second-thought overlap of self-doubt, a feeling of ambivalence that vitiated my value judgments of the new work I witnessed. I overcame this feeling, or overreaction, by compartmentalizing Debierue in a corner of my mind. I was able to rid myself of my ambivalence by setting Debierue apart from other artists as a 'one-of-a-kind' painter, and by not considering him in connection with the mainstream of contemporary art. It didn't take too many weeks before I adjusted to this mental suggestion. I was able to function normally again on my regular critical assignments.

My reputation as a critic didn't soar, but my workload doubled and, with it, my income. Tom Russell gave me a fifty dollar raise, which brought me up to $450 a month at the magazine. My lecture fee was raised, and I gave more lectures, including a lecture at Columbia on 'New Trends in Contemporary Art' to the art majors — and the Fine Arts Department paid me a $600 lecture fee. To lecture in my old school, where I had once been a poverty-stricken graduate student, was perhaps the high point of the entire year.

My agent unloaded some older, unsold articles I had written months before — two of them to art magazines which had earlier rejected them.

I had always done a certain amount of jury work, judging art shows for 'expenses only,' and more often without any compensation at all. I now began to receive some decent cash offers to judge and hang important exhibits at major museums. On a jury show I served on at Hartford, there was a Herb Westcott painting entered in the show. Westcott had changed his style to Romantic Realism, and his fine, almost delicate draftsmanship was well suited to the new style. The Hartford show had an antipollution theme, and Westcott had painted an enormous blowup of a 1925 postcard view of Niagara Falls. The painting wasn't in the First Prize category, but I was able to persuade the other jury members (the museum director and Maury Katz, a hard-edge painter) to tag Westcott's painting with an honorable mention and a thousand-dollar purchase prize. I had treated Westcott rather shabbily in Palm Beach, running out on him and his show at Gloria's gallery, and it pleased me to give him a leg up — which he well deserved in any case.

Now included in my books to review were books that the managing editor used to reserve for himself — beautiful, expensive, handsomely illustrated, coffee-table art books — that retailed for $25, $35, and even $50. After being reviewed, these expensive books can be sold at half of their wholesale price to bookdealers. This pocketed cash is found money I.R.S. investigators cannot discover easily.

I no longer slept well. I didn't sleep well at all.

I knew that Debierue had read my article, and although I had made an educated guess that he would say nothing, I could not be positive that he would continue to say nothing. I had dared to assume that four important European art critics had also invented imaginary paintings by Debierue to write about. But *they* couldn't denounce me. Only Debierue could do that and, thanks to the fire I had set, he couldn't actually prove anything.

Nevertheless, late at night, I often awoke from a fitful sleep, covered with perspiration. Sitting in the dark on the edge of my bed, trying to keep my mind as blank as possible, I would light one cigarette after another, afraid to go back to sleep. In time, I would tell myself, all in good time, my nightmares would run their course and stop.

A year after, almost to the day that I returned to New York, Debierue died in Florida. Mr. Cassidy wired me, inviting me to the funeral, but I was tied up with other work and couldn't get away on such short notice. Bodies, in Florida, must be buried within twenty-four hours, according to the state law. I wrote the obituary — a black-bordered one-page tribute — for the magazine, of course, inasmuch as I was *the* authority on Debierue, and had already written the definitive piece on him for the forthcoming *International Encyclopedia of Fine Arts.*

Ten days after Debierue's death I received a long, bulky package at the office. When I unwrapped it at my desk I discovered the dismantled baroque frame that had once been Debierue's famous *No. One.* This unexpected gift from beyond the grave made me cry, the first time I had wept in several months. There was no personal note or card with the frame. Debierue had probably left word with someone at the nursing home to mail it to me after he died. But the fact that he sent me the frame meant exoneration. Not only a complete exoneration, it proved that he had been pleased by my critique of his 'American Harvest' period. From all of his many critics, Debierue had singled me out as his beneficiary for *No. One.*

The dismantled frame had no intrinsic value, of course. I probably could have sold it somewhere, or donated it to the Museum of Modern Art for its curiosity value, but I couldn't do that to the old man. His gesture deeply moved me.

I walked down the hall to throw the frame down the incinerator. As I opened the metal door, I noticed a small dead fly scotch-taped to one of the sides of the frame. The old man, despite his age, had a keen memory. After seeing the fly, I couldn't throw the parts down the chute. On my way home from the office I left the bundled frame under my seat in the subway instead.

I had some correspondence with Joseph Cassidy concerning *The Burnt Orange Heresy.* He wanted me to suggest the best place for unveiling it for the public, New York or Chicago. I advised him to wait and to exhibit the painting at Palm Beach instead, at the opening of the next season, to coincide, as nearly as possible, with the publication date of the *International Encyclopedia of Fine Arts,* which would have a full-page color plate of the painting facing my definitive article on the painter ...

... I opened the heavy volume and found my piece on Jacques Debierue. The color plate of *The Burnt Orange Heresy* was a beautiful reproduction of the painting. Reduced in size, color photographs often look better than the original oils. And this colored photo, on expensive, white-coated stock, shone like burnished gold.

I read my article carefully. There were no errors in spelling, and no typographical errors. My name was spelled correctly at the end of the article. A short bibliography of the books and major critical articles on Debierue followed my by-line, set in $5^{1}/_{2}$ point agate boldface. There were no typos in the bibliography either.

Satisfied, I began to leaf through some of the other

volumes of the Encyclopedia, here and there, to check the
writing and the quality of the work. I read pieces on some
of my favorites — Goya, El Greco, Piranesi, Michelangelo.

My stomach became queasy, and I had a peculiar
premonition. The articles I had read were well researched
and well written, particularly the piece on Piranesi, but my
stomach felt as it if had been filled with raw bread dough
that was beginning to rise and swell inside me. I opened
my desk drawer and took out my brass ruler. Taking my
time, to make certain there would be no mistakes, I
measured the column inches in the *Encyclopedia* to see
how many inches had been allotted to Goya, El Greco,
Piranesi, Michelangelo — and Debierue.

Goya had nine and one-half inches. El Greco had
twelve. Piranesi had eight. Michelangelo had fourteen.
But Debierue had *sixteen column inches*! The old man,
insofar as *space* was concerned, had topped the greatest
artists of all time.

I closed the books, all of them, and returned them to
the crate. I lit a cigarette and moved to the window. The
buttery sunlight of Palm Beach scattered gold coins
beneath the poinciana tree outside my window. The dark
green grass in the apartment-house courtyard was still wet
from the sprinklers the yardman had recently turned off.
The pale blue sky, without any clouds, unpolluted by
industrial smoke, was as clear as expensively bottled
water. I wasn't fooled by the air-conditioning of the room.
It was hotter than hell outside in the sun.

But my work was over. Debierue had triumphed over
everyone, and so had I. There would never be another
Jacques Debierue, not in my lifetime, and I would never
want to meet another one like him if one ever did come
along. There was no place else for me to go as an art critic.
How could I top myself? Not in *this* world.

But what about Berenice Hollis? Could I pass the test?
In a cigar box in the bottom drawer of my dresser,
together with a picture of my father, taken when he was
seven years old, and a dry, rough periwinkle shell (a

reminder, because I had picked it up on the beach as a kid, that I was born in Puerto Rico), was Berenice's dried finger, wrapped in a linen handkerchief. I unrolled the handkerchief and looked at the shriveled finger. The blood-red Chen Yu nail varnish was dull, and some of it had flaked off. I looked at the finger for a long time without feeling fear, pain or remorse.

Debierue, and his achievement, had been worth it, and there was nothing else left for me to do. Somebody else, another critic, could cover the unveiling of Cassidy's only signed Debierue at the Everglades Club. The time had come for me to pay my dues for the death of Berenice Hollis.

I showered, shaved, and put on my tailor-made suit, together with a white shirt, a wide red-white-and-blue striped tie, black silk socks, and polished cordovan shoes.

Taking my time, strolling, I walked through the late afternoon streets to the Spanish-style Palm Beach police station. No one else would ever know the truth about Debierue, and no one, other than myself, knew the truth about my part in his apotheosis. And I would never tell, never, but I had to pay for Berenice. The man who achieves success in America must pay for it. It's the American way, and no one knows this fact of life any better than I, a de-islanded Puerto Rican.

There were a sergeant and two patrolmen inside the station. One patrolman was going on duty and the other was going off, but they both looked so clean and well groomed it would have been impossible to tell them apart. All three policemen were looking at a copy of *Palm Beach Life*, the slick, seasonal magazine that covers Palm Beach society. The policeman going off duty had his picture in it — a shot of a group of women on a garden tour, and he was smiling in the background.

'Good afternoon, sir,' the sergeant said politely, getting to his feet, 'may I help you?'

I nodded. 'Good afternoon, Sergeant,' I replied. I unfolded the handkerchief on the table, and Berenice's finger rolled out. 'I want to confess to a crime of passion.'

COCKFIGHTER

For Mary Jo

What matters is not the idea a man holds, but the depth at which he holds it.

Ezra Pound

Chapter One

First, I closed the windows and bolted the flimsy aluminium door. Then I flicked on the overhead light and snapped the Venetian blinds shut. Without the cross ventilation, it was stifling inside the trailer. Outside, in the Florida sunlight, the temperature was in the high eighties, but inside, now that the door and the windows were locked, it must have been a hundred degrees. I wiped the sweat away from my streaming face and neck with a dishcloth, dried my hands, and tossed the cloth on the floor. After moving Sandspur's traveling coop onto the couch, I checked the items on the table one more time.

Leather thong. Cotton. Razor blade. Bowl of lukewarm soapy water. Pan of rubbing alcohol. Liquid lead ballpoint pencil. Sponge. All in order.

I lifted the lid of the coop, brought Sandspur out with both hands, turned the cock's head away from me, and then held him firmly with my left hand under his breast. I looped the noose of leather over his dangling yellow feet, slipped it tight above his sawed-off spur stumps, and made a couple of turns to hold it snug. Holding the chicken with both hands again, I lowered him between my legs and squeezed my knees together tight enough to hold him so he couldn't move his wings. Sandspur didn't like it. He hit back with both feet four times, making thumping sounds against the plastic couch, but he couldn't get away.

I pinched off a generous wad of cotton between my left thumb and forefinger and clamped my fingers over his lemon-yellow beak. There was just enough of a downward curve to his short beak so he couldn't jerk his head out of my fingers. He couldn't possibly hurt himself, as long as the cotton didn't slip.

Impatient knuckles rapped on the door. Dody again. A vein throbbed in my temple. At that moment I would have given anything to be able to curse.

'How long you gonna be, Frank?' Dody's petulant voice shrilled through the door. 'I gotta go to the bathroom!'

I didn't answer. I couldn't. She rapped impatiently a couple of more times and then she went away. At least she didn't holler anymore.

My right hand was damp again, and I wiped my fingers on my jeans, still holding Sandspur's beak with my left thumb and forefinger. I picked up the razor blade and cut a fine hairline groove across his bill as high up as possible. This was ticklish work and I cut a trifle too deep on the right side. I dropped the razor blade back on the table and released the cock's head. I picked up the ballpoint lead pencil with my left hand and rubbed the point across my right fingertip until it was smeared with liquid lead. Pinching off more cotton with my left hand, I caught Sandspur's beak again and rubbed the almost invisible groove with my lead-smeared forefinger. I took my time, and Sandspur glared at me malevolently with his shiny yellow eyes.

As soon as I was satisfied, I unloosened the thong around his feet and put the bird on the table, washed his legs with luke-warm soapy water, and rubbed his breast and thighs. I repeated the rubdown with alcohol. I was particularly careful with his head and bill, only using cotton dipped in the pan of alcohol.

Finished, I returned the items to my gaff case and dumped the used soapy water and alcohol into the sink. Sandspur was a fine-looking cock, and after his light rubdown he felt in fine feather. Holding his head high he strutted back and forth on the slick Masonite table. He was a Whitehackle cross in peak condition, a five-time winner, a real money bird. I knew he would win this afternoon, but I also knew he *had* to win.

I stepped in close to the table, made a feinting pinch for his doctored beak and he tried to peck me. I examined his beak, and even under close scrutiny the bill looked cracked. The liquid lead inside the hairline made the manufactured crack look authentic even to my expert eyes. As a longtime professional cocker I knew the crack would fool Mr. Ed Middleton, Jack Burke, and the accordion-necked fruit tramp bettors. I picked Sandspur up and lowered him gently into his coop.

I opened the door, but Dody was nowhere in sight. She was probably visiting inside one of the other trailers in the camp. After sliding up all the windows again I lit a cigarette and sat down. What I had done to Sandspur's bill wasn't exactly illegal, but I didn't feel too proud about it. I only wanted to boost the betting odds and my slender roll.

Although I knew I couldn't possibly lose, I was apprehensive about the fight coming up. Everything I had, including my old Caddy and my Love-Lee-Mobile Home, was down on this single cockfight. And Sandspur was the only cock I had left. In my mind, I reviewed my impulsive bet. I had been a damned fool to bet the car and trailer.

At four that morning I had slid out of bed without waking Dody and switched on the light. Dody slept like a child, mainly because she was a child. The girl was only sixteen. I had picked her up in Homestead, Florida, three weeks before at a juke joint near the trailer camp where I had been staying. Her parents had their trailer in the Homestead camp, and Dody was only one out of their five children. It was a family of fruit tramps, and I doubt very much if they even missed her when I took her away with me. I wasn't the first man to sleep with Dody, not by any means. There had been dozens before me, but seeing her asleep and vulnerable that morning made me feel uneasy about our relationship. She was awfully damned young. At thirty-two, I was exactly twice as old as Dody.

It was too hot in Belle Glade to have even a sheet over you, and Dody lay on her back wearing a flimsy cotton shorty nightgown. She slept with her mouth open, her long taffy-coloured braids stretched out on the pillow. Her face was flushed with sleep, and she didn't look twelve years old, much less sixteen. Her body was fully mature, however, with large, melon-heavy breasts, and long tapering legs. In her clumsy, uninhibited way she was surprisingly good in bed. She was as strong as a tractor, but not quite as intelligent.

I felt sorry for Dody. She didn't have much to show for her life so far. With her parents, she had followed crops all over the country — staying locked in a car by a field someplace until she was big enough to carry baskets — and this constant exposure to the itinerant agricultural worker's lackadaisical code of living had made her wise beyond her age. After spending the night with me in my trailer in Homestead, she had begged to be taken along, and I brought her with me to Belle Glade. Why I weakened I don't know, but at the time I had been depressed. I had lost four birds in the Homestead fighting, and if Sandspur hadn't won his fight, the Homestead meet would have been a major disaster. But three weeks is a long time to live with a young, demanding girl — and a stupid, irritating girl, at that.

Anyway, it was four a.m. I dressed and took Sandspur outside and around to the back of the trailer.

It was still dark and I wanted to flirt him for exercise. A cooped bird gets stale in a hurry. I sidestepped the chicken six times, gave him six rolls, and let him drink a half dip of water. He would get no more water until after the fight. When the sky began to lighten I released him. Sandspur lifted his head and crowed twice. I lit my first cigarette of the day. As I watched the cock scratch in the loose sand, a shadow fell across my face. I looked up and there was Jack Burke, a wide grin splitting his homely face. I scooped Sandspur up quickly, dropped him into the coop and closed the lid. Burke had seen him, but there still wasn't enough light for a close look.

'That the mighty Sandspur?' Burke said.

I nodded.

'He don't look like no five-time winner to me. Tell you what I'll do, Mr. Mansfield,' Burke said, as though he were doing me a big favor, 'I'll give you two to one.'

When Burke made this offer, I had just started to get to my feet. But now I decided to remain in my squatting position. Burke is a man of average height, but I am a full head taller than he is, and my eyes are bluer. My blond hair is curly, and his lank blond hair is straight. Looking down on me that way gave him a psychological advantage, a feeling of power, and I wanted him to have it — hoping that his overconfidence would help me get even better odds that afternoon.

Burke had written me a postcard to Homestead, challenging Sandspur to the fight at even money. I had accepted by return mail, glad to get a chance at his Ace cock, Little David. Little David wasn't so little in his reputation. He was an eight-time winner and had had a lot of publicity. When my Sandspur beat Burke's Little David, his value would be doubled, and my chances for taking the Southern Conference championship would be improved.

On the drive from Homestead to Belle Glade, I had thought of the crack-on-the-bill plan, and now I didn't want even money or two to one either. After the bettors looked at the birds before the pitting, I expected to get odds of four to one, at least. I had eight hundred and fifty dollars in my wallet and I didn't want to take Burke's offer, but after accepting an even-money fight by mail, I couldn't legitimately turn down the new odds.

I snapped my fingers out four times, folded in my thumb, and held up four fingers. I nodded twice.

'You mean you've only got a hundred dollars to bet?' Burke said, with a short angry laugh. 'I figured on taking you for at least a thousand!'

I pointed to the coop and lifted a forefinger to show Burke I only had the one cock. He knew very well I had lost four birds at Homestead. By this time, everybody in Florida and half of Georgia knew it.

Jack Burke followed the Cocker's Code of Conduct, and he was honest, but he disliked me. Although my luck had been mostly bad for the last three years, four years before at Biloxi my novice stag, Pinky, had killed his Ace,

Pepperpot. He would never be able to forgive or forget that beating. Pinky had won only one fight against five for his cock, and Burke had taken a terrific loss at five-to-one odds. More than the money he had lost, he had resented my winning. A columnist in *The Southern Cockfighter* had unfairly blamed his conditioning methods for the loss. Actually, Pinky had only made a lucky hit. A man is foolish to fight stags, but I had needed the young bird to fill out my entry for the main — not expecting to clobber Pepperpot.

Burke studied the ground, rubbing his freshly shaven chin. He was in his middle forties, and he wore his pale, yellow hair much too long. He paid considerable attention to his clothes. Even at daybreak he was wearing a blue seersucker suit, white shirt and necktie, and black-and-white shoes. Two-toned shoes indicate an ambivalent personality, a man who can't make up his mind.

'Okay, Mr. Mansfield,' Burke said at last, slapping his leg. 'I'll take your hundred dollars and give you a two-to-one. I know damned well Sandspur can't beat Little David, but your cock always has a chance of getting in a lucky hit ... the way Pinky did in Biloxi, for instance. So let's say you really get lucky — what do you have? Two hundred dollars. To give you a fighting chance to get on your feet again after Homestead, I'll put up eight hundred bucks against your car and trailer. Even money.'

I chewed my lower lip, but the bet was fair. My battered Caddy was worth at least eight hundred, but I didn't know what the trailer was worth. Secondhand trailers bring in peculiar prices, and mine was fairly small, with only one bedroom and one door. If I unloaded the car and trailer through a newspaper advertisement, I could've probably sold them both together for at least a thousand. Burke wanted to beat me so bad he could taste it. And if Little David won, I'd be out on the highway with my thumb out.

I stuck out my right hand and Burke grabbed it eagerly. The bet was made.

'Too bad you haven't got anything else to lose,' Burke laughed gleefully. 'I'd like to make another bet that you just made a bad bet!'

My lips curved into a broad smile as I thought of Dody sleeping peacefully inside the trailer. In the unlikely event that Burke's cock did win the fight, he would also be stuck with Dody. When I pictured Burke in my mind stopping at every gas station on the road to buy Dody ice cream and Coca-Colas it was impossible to suppress my smile. On the way up from Homestead she had damned near driven me crazy.

But now the bet was made.

I consulted my wristwatch. Two thirty. It was time to go. Bill Sanders was going to meet me outside the pit at three to pick up my betting money. I stashed a hundred dollars in the utensil cupboard to cover my two-to-one bet with Burke, counted the rest of my money, and it came out to an even seven hundred and fifty dollars. That was everything, except for a folded ten-dollar bill in my watch pocket. This was my getaway bread — just in case.

I put my straw cowboy hat on my head to protect my face from the Florida sun, picked up the aluminium coop and my gaff case, and stepped outside. There were fourteen trailers in Captain Mack's Trailer Camp, including mine, and if you had touched any one of them, you would have burned your hand. In the distance, across the flat, desolate country, I could see Belle Glade, three miles away. The heat waves rising off the sandy land resembled great sheets of quivering cellophane. I turned away from the trailers and started toward the hammock clump a mile away where the pit had been set up. As hot as it was, I was in no mood to unhitch my car from the trailer and work up a worse sweat than I had, and the walk was only a mile.

There was a wire gate behind the camp, with an old-timer collecting an entrance fee of three dollars. I raised my coop to show him I was an entrant, and he let me through without collecting a fee. As I passed through the gate, Dody came flying up the trail, pigtails bouncing on her shoulders. She was barefooted, wearing a pair of red silk hotpants and a white sleeveless blouse. Her big unhampered breasts jounced up and down as she ran.

'Frank!' she called out before she reached the gate. 'Take me with you! Please, Frank!'

The gateman, a grizzled old man in blue overalls, raised his white brows. I shook my head. He closed and latched the gate as Dody reached it.

'Damn you, Frank!' Dody shouted angrily. 'You don't let me do nothin'. You know I've never seen you cockfight. Please let me go!'

I ignored her and continued up the trail. I had enough to worry about, without her yammering around the pit and asking questions.

Captain Mack, who had made all the arrangements for the Belle Glade pitting, was talking earnestly to a Florida trooper when I reached the parking area. The trooper's state patrol car was parked directly behind a new convertible with a Dade County plate. The right door of the convertible was open, and a pretty blonde woman sat in the front seat. Her face was pale, and she had her eyes closed, breathing deeply through her open mouth. There was a wet spot in the sand outside the door. I supposed the girl had watched a couple of fights inside the pit and got sick as a consequence. Not many city women have the stomach for watching cockfights.

The pit was surrounded on four sides by a green canvas panorama made from army surplus latrine screens. There were about thirty cars in the parking area, not counting the trucks. I set down my gaff case and coop in the sparse shade of a melaleuca tree, and leaned against a parked Plymouth, watching Captain Mack argue with the trooper. Captain Mack shrugged wearily, took his wallet out of his hip pocket, and handed two bills to the trooper. Through a gap in the canvas wall, they went inside the pit. Although cockfighting is legal in Florida, betting is not, so Captain Mack had been forced to pay out some protection money.

There was excited shouting from inside the pit, followed by several coarse curses, and then the voices subsided. Mr. Ed Middleton's baritone carried well as he announced the winning cock.

'The winner is the Madigan! One minute and thirty-one seconds in the third pitting!'

Again there were curses, followed by the derisive sound of laughter. I lit a cigarette, took my notebook out of my shirt pocket, and wrote the essential information concerning Sandspur on a fresh sheet of paper. A few minutes later Bill Sanders came outside and joined me beneath the tree. I handed him my roll of seven hundred and fifty dollars and he counted it. Bill put the money in his trousers and watched my fingers. I held up four fingers on my left hand and my right forefinger.

'I doubt if I can get you four to one, Frank.' Bill shook his head dubiously. 'Your reputation is too damn good. You could show up with a battered dunghill, and if these red-neckers thought you fed it, they'd bet on it. But I'll try.'

If anybody could get good odds for me, Sanders could, and I knew he would certainly try. When I was discharged from the Army, I had spent two months in Puerto Rico with Sanders, living in the same hotel; and we had attended mains at all the best game clubs — San Juan, Mayagüez, Ponce, Arecibo, and Aibonito. I had steered Sanders right on the betting, after I had gotten accustomed to the fighting techniques of the Spanish slashers, and both of us had returned to Miami with our wallets full of winnings. Bill Sanders was not a professional cockfighter like myself, he was a professional gambler. He had lost his share of the money he won in Puerto Rico at the Miami horse and dog tracks. A little bald guy with a passion for high living, he lived very well when he had money and even better when he had none. He was that kind of a man, and a good friend.

I took Sandspur out of his coop and pointed out the 'cracked' beak. Bill whistled softly and his blue eyes widened.

'If that bill breaks off, you've had it, Frank.' He shrugged. 'But that mutilated boko should get me the four-to-one odds.'

Sanders hit me lightly on the shoulder with his fist and returned to the pit.

I held Sandspur with my left hand, filled my mouth with smoke, and blew the smoke at his head. He clucked angrily, shaking his head. Blowing tobacco smoke at a cock's head irritates it to a fighting pitch, and I was smoking a mild, mentholated cigarette. I enveloped the cock's head with one more cloud of smoke and returned him to his coop. Too much smoke could make a cock dizzy.

I opened my gaff case and removed two sets of heels. I put a pair of short spurs in my left shirt pocket and a pair of long jaggers in my right shirt pocket. After shutting my gaff case, I picked up the coop and case and entered the pit.

There were only about sixty spectators inside, but this was a fairly good crowd for September. The Florida cockfighting season didn't start officially until Thanksgiving Day, when an opening derby was held in Lake Worth. And Belle Glade isn't the most accessible town in Florida. The canvas walls successfully prevented any breeze from getting into the pit, and it was as hot inside as a barbecue grill.

I recognized a couple of Dade County fanciers and nodded acknowledgments to them when they greeted me by name. There was a scattering of Belle Glade townspeople, two gamblers from Miami who probably owned the blonde and the convertible, Burke and his two handlers, and two pregnant women I had seen around the trailer camp. The remainder of the crowd was made up from the migrant agricultural workers' camp on the other side of town.

The cockpit was made of rough boards, sixteen inches high, and about eighteen feet in diameter. The pit was surrounded on three sides by bleachers, four tiers high. Under an open beach umbrella on the fourth side of the pit, Mr. Middleton sat at a card table with Captain Mack. Behind the table there was a blackboard. I noted that Jack Burke had won both of the short-entry derbies, the first, four-one, and the second, three-two. That accounted for the glum expressions on the faces of the two Dade County breeders. Not only had they made a poor showing, their one-hundred-dollar entry fees, less Captain Mack's ten percent, had wound up in Burke's pocket as prize money.

Two men in the bleachers I didn't know called out my name and wished me good luck. I waved an acknowledgment to them, and joined Ed Middleton and Captain Mack. I removed Sandspur from the coop and handed the slip of paper to Mr. Middleton. Jack Burke and his handler, Ralph Hansen, came over. The handler was carrying Little David. Mr. Middleton produced a coin.

'Name it, gentlemen,' he said.

'Let Mr. Mansfield call it,' Burke said indifferently.

I tapped my forehead to indicate 'heads.' Mr. Middleton tossed the half dollar into the air and let it land with a thump on the card table. Heads, I reached into my left shirt pocket, pulled out the short gaffs, and held them out in my open palm. They were hand-forged steel gaffs, an inch and a quarter in length. Burke nodded grimly and turned to his handler.

'All right, Ralph,' he said bitterly. 'Short spurs, but set'em low.'

Burke was a long gaff man, but I preferred the short heels. Sandspur was a cutter and fought best with short gaffs. Little David was used to long three-inch heels. Winning the toss had given Sandspur a slight advantage over Little David.

The cockfight between Sandspur and Little David was an extra hack, and I had not, of course, been required to post any entry fee. However, Mr. Middleton examined both cocks with minute attention. He was acting as judge and referee and had received at least a minimum fee of one hundred and fifty dollars, plus expenses, from Captain Mack. The judge of a cockfight has to be good, and Ed Middleton was one of the best referees in the entire South. His word in the pit was law. There is no appeal from a cockfight judge's decision. As sole judge-referee, Ed Middleton's jurisdiction encompassed spectator betting as well. The referee's job has always been the most important at a cockfight. As every cocker knows, for

example, honest Abe Lincoln was once a cockpit referee
during his lawyer days in Illinois. Hard and fair in his decisions, and as impersonal as doom, Ed Middleton was fully
aware of the traditional responsibilities of the cockpit
referee.

After completing his examination of the cocks to see
that they were not soaped, peppered or greased and that
they were trimmed fairly, Mr. Middleton stepped back to
the table.

'Southern Conference rules, gentlemen?' he asked.

'What else?' Burke said.

I nodded my head in agreement.

'Forty-minute time limit, or kill?'

I closed my fist, jerked my thumb toward the ground.

'What else?' Burke said.

Captain Mack held Sandspur while Jack Burke
examined him, and I took a close look at Little David.
Burke's chicken was a purebred O'Neal Red and as arrogant as a sergeant-major in the Foreign Legion. Although
I had never seen Little David fight before, I had followed
his previous pittings in *The Southern Cockfighter*, and I
knew that he liked aerial fighting. But so did Sandspur
fight high in the air, and my cock was used to short gaffs.
The three additional wins Little David had over Sandspur
didn't worry me when I had such an advantage.

Burke tapped me on the shoulder and grinned. 'If I'd
known your chicken had him a cracked bill, I'd have given
you better odds.'

I shrugged indifferently and sat down on the edge of the
pit to arm my cock. I opened my gaff case, removed a
bottle of typewriter cleaning solvent and cleaned Sandspur's spur stumps. Most cockers use plain alcohol to
clean spurs, but typewriter solvent is fast-drying and, in
my opinion, removes the dirt easier. After fitting tight
chamois-skin-coverings over both spurs, I slipped the
metal sockets of the short heels over the covered stumps
and tied them with waxed string, setting them low and a
trifle to the outside. The points of the tapered heels were
as sharp as needles, and a man has to be careful when he

arms a cock. I had a puckered puncture scar on my right forearm caused by a moment of carelessness seven years before, and I didn't want another one.

The betting had already started, but the crowd quieted down when Mr. Middleton stepped into the pit. They listened attentively to his announcement.

'This is an extra hack, gentlemen,' he said loudly. 'Little David versus Sandspur. Southern Conference rules will prevail. No time limit, and short gaffs. Little David is owned by Mr. Jack Burke of Burke Farms, Kissimmee, Florida. He's an Ace cock, with eight wins and will be two years old in November. Little David will be handled by Mr. Ralph Hansen of Burke Farms.'

The crowd gave Little David a nice hand, and Mr. Middleton continued.

'Sandspur is owned by Mr. Frank Mansfield of Mansfield Farms, Ocala, Florida, and he will handle his own chicken. Sandspur is a five-time winner and a year-and-a-half old. Both cocks will fight at four pounds even.'

Sandspur got a better hand than Little David, and the applause was sustained by the two Dade County breeders who wanted him to beat Burke's cock. Mr. Middleton examined Sandspur's heels and patted me on the shoulder. Many cockers resent the referee's examination of a cock's heels, but I never have. A conscientious referee can help you by making this final check. Once the fight has started and your cock loses a metal spur, it cannot be replaced.

As Mr. Middleton crossed the pit to examine Little David, I watched the flying fingers of the bettors. The majority of the betting at cockfights is done by fingers — one finger for one dollar, five for five dollars, and then on up into the multiples of five — and I was an expert in this type of betting. I had learned finger betting in the Philippines when I was in the army and didn't understand Tagalog, and I had also used the same system in Puerto Rico, where I didn't understand Spanish very well. Little David was the favorite, getting two-to-one, and in some cases three-to-one odds.

Bill Sanders, Jack Burke and the two Miami gamblers were in a huddle next to the canvas wall. Both gamblers were staring across the pit at Sandspur while Sanders and Burke talked at the same time. Sanders had a roll of money in his hand and was talking fast, although I couldn't hear his voice from where I was sitting beside the pit.

A fistfight broke out on the top tier of seats between two fruit tramps, and one of them was knocked off backward and fell heavily to the ground. Before he could climb back into the stands, the state trooper had an armlock on him and made him sit down on the other side of the pit. When I looked back to Bill Sanders, he was smiling and holding up three fingers.

So Bill had got three-to-one. That was good enough for me. When Sandspur won, I'd be $2,250 ahead from the Miami gamblers, plus $1,500 more from Jack Burke. $3,250. This would be more than enough money to see me through the Southern Conference season, and enough to purchase six badly needed fighting cocks besides.

'Get ready!' Mr. Middleton yelled. I stood up, stepped over the edge of the pit, and put my toes on the back score. The backscore lines placed us eight feet away from each other. Ralph Hansen, holding Little David under the chest with one hand, called impatiently to the referee.

'How about letting us bill them first, Mr. Middleton?'

Billing is an essential prelude to pitting. Ed Middleton didn't need the reminder. 'Bill your cocks,' he growled.

We cradled our fighters over our left arms, holding their feet, and stood sideways on our center scores, two feet apart, so the cocks could peck at each other. These cocks had never seen each other before, but they were mortal enemies. Ed allowed us about thirty seconds for the teasing and then told us to get ready. Ralph backed to his score and I returned to mine. I squatted on my heels and set the straining Sandspur with his feet on the score. The cocks were exactly eight feet apart.

I watched Mr. Middleton's lips. This was a trick I had practiced for hours on end and I was good at it. Before a man can say the letter 'P' he must first compress his lips. There isn't any other way he can say it. The signal to release the cocks is when the referee shouts 'Pit' or 'Pit your cocks!' The handler who releases the tail of his cock first on the utterance of the letter 'P' has a split-second advantage over his rival. And in the South, where 'Pit' is often a two-syllable word, 'Pee-it', my timing was perfect.

'Pit!' Mr. Middleton announced, and before the word was out of his mouth Sandspur was in the air and halfway to Little David. The cocks met in midair, both of them shuffling with blurred yellow feet, and then they dropped to the ground. Neither cock had managed to get above the other.

With new respect for each other, the two birds circled, heads held low, watching each other warily. Little David feinted cleverly with a short rush, but Sandspur wasn't fooled. He held his ground, and Burke's cock retreated with his wings fluttering at the tips.

As he dropped back, Sandspur rose with a short flight and savagely hooked the gaff of his right leg into Little David's wing. The point of the heel was banged solidly into the bone and Sandspur couldn't get it dislodged. He pecked savagely at Little David's head, and hit the top of the downed cock's dubbed head hard with his bill open ... too hard.

The upper section of Sandspur's bill broke off cleanly at the doctored crack I had made. A bubble of blood formed, and Sandspur stopped pecking. Both cocks struggled to break away from each other, but the right spur was still stuck and all Sandspur could do was hop up and down in place on his free leg. I looked at Mr. Middleton.

'Handle!' the judged shouted. 'Thirty seconds!'

A moment later I disentangled the gaff from Little David's wing and retreated to my starting line. I put Sandspur's head in my mouth and sucked the blood from his broken beak. I licked the feathers of his head back into place and spat as much saliva as I could into his open mouth. For the remaining seconds I had left I sucked life into his clipped comb. The comb was much too pale ...

'Get ready!' I held Sandspur by the tail on the line. 'Pit your cocks!'

Instead of flying into the air, Sandspur circled for the right wall. Little David turned in midair, landed running, and chased my cock into the far corner. Sandspur turned to fight, and the cocks met head on, but my injured bird was forced back by the fierceness of Little David's rush.

On his back, Sandspur hit his opponent twice in the chest, drawing blood both times, and then Little David was above him in the air and cutting at his head with both spurs. A sharp gaff entered Sandspur's right eye, and he died as the needle point pierced his central nervous system. Little David strutted back and forth, pecked twice at my lifeless cock, and then crowed his victory.

'The winner is Mr. Burke's Ace,' Mr. Middleton announced, as a formality. 'Twenty-eight seconds in the second pitting.'

All I had left was a folded ten-dollar bill in my watch pocket and one dead chicken.

Chapter Two

There was a burial hole in the marshy ground, about four feet square and three feet deep, on the far side of the parking area. Water was seeping visibly into the mucky pit, and the dead roosters in the bottom had begun to float.

I removed the gaffs from my dead cock's spurs and added his body to the floating pile of dead chickens. As I put the heels away in my gaff case, Bill Sanders joined me at the edge of the communal burying pit.

'I just wanted to let you know that I got all your dough down, Frank,' he said. 'Every dollar at three-to-one, and there's nothing left.'

I nodded.

'Tough, Frank, but my money was riding on Sandspur with yours.'

I shrugged and emptied the peat moss out of the aluminium coop into the hole on top of the dead chickens.

'You're going to be all right, aren't you? I mean, you'll be on the Southern Conference circuit this year, and all?'

I nodded and shook hands with Sanders. As I looked down at Bill's bald head, I noticed that the top was badly sunburned and starting to peel. The little gambler never wore a hat.

'Okay, Frank. I'll probably see you in Biloxi.'

I clapped Bill on the shoulder to squeeze out a farewell. He went over to the blue Chrysler convertible and started talking to the blonde. She had evidently recovered from her upset stomach. She had remade her face, and she now listened with absorbed attention to whatever it was Bill Sanders was telling her.

I removed the bamboo handle from the aluminium coop, collapsed the sides, and made a fairly flat, compact square out of the six frames. After locking them together with the clamps, I attached the handle again so I could carry the coop folded. A machinist in Valdosta had made two of the traveling coops for me to my own specifications and design. At one time I had considered having several made, and putting them up for sale to chicken men traveling around the country, too, but the construction costs were prohibitive to make any profit out of them. My other traveling coop was at my farm in Ocala.

Carrying my gaff case and coop, I walked back to the trailer camp. Dody met me at the door of the Love-Lee-Mobile Home with a bright lopsided smile. Her lipstick was on crooked, and there was too much rouge on her cheeks. She wanted to look older, but makeup made her look younger instead.

'Did you win, Frank?'

I leaned the folded coop against the side of the trailer and pointed to it with a gesture of exasperation.

'Oh!' she said. Her red lips were fixed in a fat, crooked 'O' for an instant. 'I'm real sorry, Frank.'

I placed my gaff case beside the coop and entered the trailer. There was a dusty leather suitcase under the bed, and I wiped the scuffed surfaces clean with a dirty T-shirt I found on top of the built-in dresser. I unstrapped the suitcase, opened it on the bed, and began to pack. There wasn't too much to put into it. Most of my clothes were on the farm. I packed my clean underwear, two clean white shirts, and then searched the trailer for my dirty shirts. I found them in a bucket of cold water beneath the sink. Dody had been promising to wash and iron them for the past three days, but just like everything else, she hadn't gotten around to doing it. I couldn't very well pack wet shirts in the suitcase on top of clean dry clothing, so I left the dirty shirts in the bucket.

In the tiny bathroom I gathered up my toilet articles and zipped them into a blue nylon Dropkit. When I packed the Dropkit into the suitcase, Dody began to evidence an avid interest in my actions.

'What are you packing for, Frank?' she asked.

Despite the fact that I had never said as much as a single word to her in the three weeks we had been living together, she persisted in asking questions that couldn't be answered by an affirmative nod, a negative waggle of my head, or an explanatory gesture of some kind. If I had answered every foolish question she put to me in writing, I could have filled up two notebooks a day.

I tossed two pairs of clean blue jeans into the open suitcase, and then undressed as far as my shorts. I pulled on a pair of gray-green corduroy trousers, and put on my best shirt, a black oxford cloth Western shirt with white pearl buttons. The jodhpur boots I was wearing were black and comfortable, and they were fastened with buckles and straps. I had ordered them by mail from a bootmaker in El Paso, Texas, and had paid forty-five dollars for them. They were the only shoes I had with me. I untied the red bandana from around my neck and exchanged it for a square of red silk, tying a loose knot and tucking the ends inside my collar before I buttoned the top shirt button. It was much too hot to wear the matching corduroy coat to my trousers, so I added it to the suitcase. The coat would come in handy in northern Florida.

'You aren't leaving, are you, Frank?' Dody asked worriedly. 'I mean, are we leaving the trailer?'

I nodded impatiently, and searched through a dozen drawers and compartments before I found my clean socks. There were only three pairs, white cotton with elastic tops. I usually wear white socks. Colored socks make my feet sweat. I put the socks into the suitcase.

'Where're we going, Frank? I can get ready in a second,' the girl lied.

There were five packages of Kools left, a half can of lighter fluid and a package of flints. I put a fresh pack of Kools in my pocket, and tossed the remaining packs, fluid and flints into the suitcase. After one last look around I closed the lid and buckled the straps. To get my guitar from under the bed I had to lie flat on the floor and reach

for it. The guitar was now the substitute for my voice, and
my ability to play it was what had attracted Dody to me in
the first place. When I needed a woman again, the guitar
would help me get one.

I carried the guitar case and suitcase into the combination kitchen-living-dining room.

'Why don't you answer me!' Dody yelled, pounding me
on the back with her doubled fists. 'You drive me almost
crazy sometimes. You pretend like you can't talk, but I
know damned well you can! I've heard you talking in your
sleep. Now answer me, damn you! Where're we going?'

I drank a glass of water at the sink, set the glass down
on the sideboard, and pointed in a northerly direction.

'I don't consider that an answer! North could be
anywhere. Do you mean your farm in Ocala?'

Dody had an irritating voice. It was high and twangy,
and there was a built-in nasal whine. I certainly was sick of
listening to her voice.

The pink slips for the Caddy and the mobile home were
in the drawer of the end table by the two-seater plastic
couch. I opened the drawer, removed the pink slips and
insurance papers and put them on the Masonite dinette
table. In the linen cupboard of the narrow hallway I found
a ruled writing pad and a dirty, large brown Manila envelope. I took the five twenty-dollar bills out of the utensil
cupboard and sat down at the table. Now that I had lost, I
was happy about having had the foresight to hide the
money from Dody to cover my bet with Burke.

Standing at the sink, her arms folded across her breasts,
Dody glared at me with narrowed eyes. Her lips were
poked out sullenly and drawn down at the corners. I put
the insurance policies, pink slips and money into the envelope. With my ballpoint lead pencil I wrote out a bill of
sale on the top sheet of the ruled pad.

To Whom It May Concern
  I, Frank Mansfield, hereby transfer the ownership
of a 1963 Cadillac sedan, and one Love-Lee-Mobile

Home to Jack Burke, in full payment of a just and honorable gambling debt.
                                                    (Signed) Frank Mansfield

That would do it, I decided. If Burke wanted to transfer the pink slips and insurance to his own name, the home-made bill of sale would be sufficient proof of ownership.

'Is that note for me?' Dody asked sharply.

Although I answered with a short, negative shake of my head, Dody rushed across the narrow space, snatched the pad from the table and read it anyway. Her flushed face paled as her lips moved perceptibly with each word she read.

'Oh, you didn't lose the trailer?' she exclaimed.

I nodded, curiously watching her face. The girl was too young to have control over her features. Every emotion she felt was transmitted to her pretty, mobile face. Her facial expressions underwent a rapid exchange of dismay, anger, frustration and fear, settling finally on a fixed look of righteous indignation.

'And, of course,' she said, with an effort at sarcasm, 'you lost all your money, too?'

I nodded again and held out a hand for the pad. She handed it to me, and I ripped off the top sheet and added it to the contents of the bulging envelope.

'You don't give a damn what happens to me, do you?'

I shook my head. I felt sorry for her, in a way, but I didn't worry about her. She was pretty, young and a good lay. She could get by anywhere. Twisting in the seat, I reached into my pocket for my key ring. I unsnapped the two car keys and the door key for the trailer. After dropping them into the envelope, I licked the flap, sealed it and squared it in the center of the table.

There was a rap on the door. I jerked my head toward the door, and Dody opened it, standing to one side as Jack Burke came inside.

'Afternoon, ma'am,' Burke said politely, removing his hat. He turned to me. 'I'm sorry, Mr. Mansfield, but I made the bet in good faith and sure didn't know Sandspur had him a cracked hill. But if you'd won, I know damned well you'd've come around for eight hundred dollars from me. So I'm here for the car and trailer.'

Still seated, I shoved the envelope toward him. Burke unfastened the flap, which hadn't quite dried, and pawed through the contents. He put the hundred dollars into his wallet before he read the bill of sale. His face reddened, and he returned the bill of sale to the envelope.

'Please accept my apology, Mr. Mansfield. I don't know why, but I guess I expected an argument.'

Either he was plain ignorant or he was trying to make me angry. A handshake by two cockfighters is as binding as a sworn statement witnessed by a notary public, and he knew this as well as I did. For a long moment I studied his red face and then concluded that he was merely ill-at-ease on account of Dody's presence and didn't know what he was implying.

Dody leaned against the sink, glaring angrily at Burke. 'I never heard of nobody so low-down mean to take a family's home away from them!' she said scathingly.

Her remark was uncalled for, but it caused Burke a deeper flush of embarrassment. 'I reckon you don't know Mr. Mansfield, little lady,' he said defensively, 'and not overmuch about cockfighting neither. But a bet is a bet.'

'For men, yes! But what about me?' Dody patted her big breasts several times with both hands and looked beseechingly into Burke's eyes. He was troubled and he scratched his head, slanting his wary eyes in my direction.

I stood up, smiled grimly, and holding out my hands with the palms up, I made an exaggerated gesture of presentation of Dody to Jack Burke. There could be no mistake about the meaning.

'Well, I don't rightly know about that, Mr. Mansfield.' Burke scratched his head. 'I already got me a lady friend up Kissimmee way.'

I stepped out from behind the table and put on my cowboy hat. Dody came flying toward me with clawing nails. The space was cramped, but I sidestepped her rush and planted a jolting six-inch jab into her midriff. Dody sat down heavily on the linoleum floor and stayed there, gasping for breath and staring up at me round-eyed with astonished disbelief.

There are three good ways to win a fight: A blow to the solar plexus, *first,* an inscrutable expression on your face, or displaying a sharp knife blade to your opponent. Any of these three methods, singly or in combination, will usually take the bellicosity out of a man, woman or child.

The swift right to her belly and the sight of my impassive face were enough to take the fight out of Dody. Burke tried to help her to her feet, but she shrugged his hands away from her shoulders as she regained her lost breath.

'You — can — go — to — hell, Frank Mansfield!' Dody said in gasps. 'I can take care of myself!' However, she prudently remained seated, supporting herself with her arms behind her back.

Burke said nothing. He ran his fingers nervously through his long hair, looking first at me and then at Dody and back to me again. He wanted to say something but didn't know what he wanted to say. I sat down at the table again and scratched out a short note.

Mr. Burke — If your Little David is still around, I challenge you to a hack at the Southern Conference Tournament—

I pushed the straw cowboy hat back from my forehead and handed him the note. After reading the message, Burke crumpled the paper and looked at me thoughtfully.

'You don't have any fighting cocks left, do you, Mr. Mansfield?'

I shook my head, and moved my shoulders in a barely perceptible shrug.

'Do you honestly believe you can train a short-heeled stag to beat Little David, a nine-time winner' — he counted on his fingers — 'in only six-months' time?'

In reply, I pointed to the crumpled challenge in his hand.

'Sure, Mr. Mansfield. I accept, but it'll be your funeral.

And I expect you to put some money where your mouth is when the hack's held.'

We shook hands. I picked up my suitcase and guitar and went outside. As I collected my gaff case and coop together, trying to figure out how I could carry everything, Burke and Dody followed me outside. The four odd-sized pieces made an awkward double armload.

'I'll give you ten bucks for that coop,' Burke offered.

The suggestion was so stupid I didn't dignify it with so much as a shrug. If Burke wanted a coop like mine, he could have one made.

Ralph Hansen had Burke's Ford pickup parked on the road about twenty yards away from the trailer. Burke strolled over to his truck to say something to Ralph. The other handler was in the truck bed with Burke's fighting cocks. The truck bed had steel-mesh coops welded to the floor on both sides, with solid walls separating each coop so that none of the cocks could see each other. A nice setup for traveling, with plenty of space down the center to carry feed, luggage and sleeping bags. I walked down the sandy road toward the open gate and the highway.

A moment later Dody caught up with me and trotted along at my side.

'Please, Frank,' she pleaded, 'take me with you. I don't want to stay with Mr. Burke. He's an old man!'

Burke was only forty-five or -six and not nearly as old as Dody thought. I shook my head. Dody ran ahead of me then, and planted herself in my path, spreading her long bare legs, and holding her arms akimbo. I stopped.

'I'll be good to you, Frank,' she said tearfully. 'Real good! Honest, I will! I know you don't like them TV dinners I been fixin', but I'm really a good cook when I try. And I'll prove it to you if you'll take me with you. I'll wash your clothes and sew and everything!' She began to blubber in earnest. Juicy tears rolled out of her moist brown eyes and flowed over her smooth round cheeks, cutting furrows in her pancake makeup.

I jerked my head for her to get out of my way. Dody moved reluctantly to one side and let me pass. At the open gate to the highway I put my luggage down and lit a cigarette. Ralph stopped the white pickup at the gate.

'I can carry you up as far as Kissimmee, Mr. Mansfield,' he offered. 'Mr. Burke is going to bring your Caddy and trailer up tomorrow, he said.'

I shook my head friendlily, and waved him on his way. I didn't want any favors from Jack Burke. After Ralph made his turn onto the highway, I looked back toward my old trailer. Jack Burke and Dody had their heads together, and it looked like both of them were talking at the same time. A moment later, Burke held the trailer door open for Dody and then followed her inside.

It occurred to me that I didn't know Dody's last name. She had never volunteered the information and, of course, I had never asked her. I hate to write notes, and I only write them when it is absolutely necessary. What difference did it make whether I knew her last name or not? But it *did* make a difference, and I felt a sense of guilty shame.

The long blue convertible came gliding down the trail from the cockpit. The driver stopped at the gate. The blonde sat between the two Miami gamblers on the front seat, and Bill Sanders, puffing a cigar, was sitting alone in the back.

'Do you want to go to Miami, by any chance?' Sanders asked.

I shook my head and smiled.

'We've got plenty of room,' the driver added cheerfully. 'Glad to take you with us.'

I shook my head again and waved them on. Sanders raised a hand in a two-finger 'V' salute, and the big car soon passed out of sight.

I didn't want to go to Miami, and I had turned down a free ride to Kissimmee. Where did I want to go? The lease on my Ocala farm had two more years to run, and it was all paid up in advance. But without any game fowl, and without funds to buy any, there was no point in going there right now. The first thing on the agenda was to obtain some money. After I had some money, I could start worrying about game fowl.

Doc Riordan owed me eight hundred dollars. His office was in Jacksonville, and he was my best bet. My younger brother, Randall, owed me three hundred dollars, but the chances of getting any money from him were negligible. Doc Riordan was the man to see first. Even if Doc could only give me a partial payment of two or three hundred, it would be a start. With only a ten-dollar bill in my watch pocket, and a little loose change, I felt at loose ends. After collecting some money from Doc I could make a fast trip home to Georgia and see my brother. I couldn't go home completely broke. I never had before, and it was too late to start now.

As I thought of home I naturally thought of Mary Elizabeth. My last visit had been highly unsatisfactory, and I had left without telling her good-bye.

On my last trip home two years before, I had been driving a black Buick convertible, and I had worn an expensive white linen suit. Although I looked prosperous, most of it was front. My roll had only consisted of five hundred dollars. That was when Randall had nicked me for the loan of three hundred. In the rare letters I had received from him since — about one every four or five months — he had never once mentioned returning the money.

Jacksonville it would be then. If nothing else, I could pick up my mail at the Jacksonville post office.

Two ancient trucks rolled through the gate loaded down with fruit tramps. They were returning to the migrant camp on the other side of Belle Glade. A couple of the men shouted to me, and I waved to them. There was a maroon Cadillac sedan about two hundred yards behind the last truck, hanging well back out of the dust. This was Ed Middleton's car. As he came abreast of the gate, I grinned and stuck out my thumb. Mr. Middleton pressed a button, and the right front window slid down with an electronic click.

'Throw your stuff in the back seat, Frank,' Ed Middleton said. 'I don't want to lose this cold air.' The window shot up again.

I opened the back door, arranged my luggage on the floor so it would ride without shifting, slammed the door, and climbed into the front seat. A refreshing icy breeze filled the roomy interior from an air-conditioning system that actually worked.

I settled back comfortably, and Ed pointed the nose of the big car towards Orlando.

Chapter Three

Ed Middleton is one of my favorite people. He is in his early sixties, and if I happen to live long enough, I want to be exactly like him someday. He is a big man with a big voice and a big paunch. Except for a bumpy bulbous nose with a few broken blood vessels here and there on its bright red surface, his face is smooth and white, with the shiny licked look of a dog's favorite bone.

Against all the odds for a man his age, Mr. Middleton still has his hair. It is a shimmering silvery white, and he always wears it in a thick bushy crew cut. A ghost of a smile — as though he is thinking of some secret joke — usually hovers about the corners of his narrow lips. In southern cockfighting circles, or anywhere in the world where cockers get together for chicken talk, his name is respected as the man who bred the Middleton Gray. Properly conditioned, the purebred Middleton Gray is a true money bird.

Despite his amiable manner, Ed can get as hard as any man when the time to get tough presents itself, and he wears the coveted Cocker of the Year medal on his watch fob.

'Lost your car and trailer, eh Frank?'

I nodded. Bad news has a way of traveling faster than good news.

'Tough luck, Frank.' Mr. Middleton laughed aloud. 'But I don't worry about you landing on your feet. If I know you, you've probably got a rooster hidden away somewhere that'll give Jack Burke his lumps.'

I smiled ruefully, made an 'O' with the thumb and forefinger of my left hand and showed it to him.

'I sure didn't suspect that, Frank,' Mr. Middleton said sympathetically.

I opened a fresh package of cigarettes, offered them to Ed and he waved them away. He was silent for more than ten minutes, and then he fingered his lower lip and squirmed about slightly in the seat. The signs were easily recognized. He wanted to confess something; a problem of some kind was on his mind. Two or three times he opened his mouth, started to speak his mind, and then shook his head and clamped his lips together. But he would get it out sooner or later, whatever it was. Since my vow of silence I had become, unwillingly, a man who listened to confessions. Now that I couldn't talk, or wouldn't talk — no one, other than myself, knew the truth about my muteness — people often told me things they would hesitate to tell to a priest, or even to their wives. At first, it had bothered me, learning things about people I didn't want or need to know, but now I just listened — not liking it, of course, but accepting the confessions as an unwelcome part of the deal I had made with myself.

We sailed through the little town of Canal Point and hit Highway 441 bordering Lake Okeechobee.

From time to time, when the roadbed was higher than the dike, I got a glimpse of the calm mysterious lake, which was actually a huge inland sea. Small herds of Black Angus cattle were spotted every few miles between the lake and the highway, eating lush gama grass, but there were very few houses along the way. Lake Okeechobee, with its hundreds of fish and clear sweet water, is a sportsman's paradise, but the great flood of the early twenties, when thousands of people were drowned, had discouraged real-estate development, I supposed. No plush resort hotels or motels had ever been built near its banks.

'Frank,' Ed Middleton said at last, lowering his voice to conspiratorial tones, 'today's pitting at Belle Glade was my last appearance at a cockpit. Surprises you, doesn't it?'

It did indeed. I reached up and twisted the rear-view mirror into position so Ed could look at my face without taking his eyes off the highway too much. I looked seriously into the mirror and widened my eyes slightly.

'Nobody can keep a secret long in this business, Frank, but I've kept my plans to myself to avoid the usual arguments. I've argued the pros and cons of cockfighting thousands of times, and you know I've always been on the pro side. If there's a better way of life than raising and fighting game chickens, I haven't found it yet,' he said grimly. 'But I'm a married man, Frank, and you aren't. That's the difference. I'm happily married, and I have been for more than thirty years, but I can still envy a man like you. There aren't a dozen men in the United States who've devoted their lives solely to cockfighting like you have, that is, without earning their living in some other line of business.

'I suppose I've known you for ten years or more and, as a single man, you've got the best life in the world. You've earned the admiration and respect of all of us, Frank.'

I was embarrassed by the praise.

'That was a clever trick you pulled this afternoon, Frank!'

I started with surprise, and Mr. Middleton guffawed loudly.

'I haven't seen anyone pull that stunt with the cracked bill to raise the odds in about fifteen years. Don't blame yourself for losing the fight. Write it off to bad luck, or face up that Jack Burke had the better chicken. But that isn't what I wanted to talk about.

'Martha has been after me to quit for years, and I finally gave in. I'm not too old, but I certainly don't need the money. I've got enough orange trees in Orlando to take care of my wants for three lifetimes. If Martha shared my enthusiasm for the game, it would be different. But she won't go on the road with me. This business of living alone in motel rooms doesn't appeal to me anymore. The two months I spent refereeing in Clovis, New Mexico, last spring were the loneliest weeks of my entire life.

'Anyway, I've sold all my Grays. Made a deal for the lot with a breeder in Janitzio, Mexico, and shipped out the last crate of April trios last week. If he fights my Grays as slashers, he'll lose his damned *camisa,* but at any rate, they won't be fighting in the States.

'If you wonder why I refereed today's fight, it was because I promised Captain Mack a year ago. But that was my last appearance in the pit, and you won't see me in the pits again, either as a referee or spectator.' Ed sighed deeply, his confession completed. 'Like the lawyer feller says, Frank, "Further deponent sayeth not."'

Several dissuading arguments came immediately to my mind, but I remained silent, of course. As far as I was concerned, what Ed Middleton did was his business, not mine, but his loss to the game would be felt in the South. We needed men like him to keep the sport clean and honest. But I didn't say anything because of my self-imposed vow of silence.

Up to this moment I've never told anyone why I made the vow. What I do is my business, but the silver medal on Ed Middleton's watch fob held the answer. Money had nothing to do with my decision to keep my mouth shut.

All of us in America want money because we need it and cannot live without it, but we don't need as much money as most of us think we do. Money isn't enough. We must have something more, and my *something more* was the Cockfighter of the Year award.

The small silver coin on Ed's watch fob was only worth, in cash, about ten or fifteen dollars, but a lot of men have settled for lesser honors. A man may refuse a clerk's job with a loan company, for instance, for one hundred dollars a week. But if this same man is put in charge of three typists and is given the exalted title of office manager, the chances are that he will work for ninety dollars a week. In business, this is a well-known 'for instance.'

Unlike Great Britain, we don't have any peerages to hand out, or any annual Queen's Honour List, so most of us settle for less, a hell of a lot less. In large corporations, the businessman has reached his goal in life when he gets a title on his door and a corner office with two windows instead of one. But I'm not a businessman. I am a full-time cockfighter.

My goal in life was that little silver coin, not quite as large as a Kennedy half dollar. On one side of the medal there is an engraved statement: *Cockfighter of the Year.* In the center, the year the award is given is engraved in Arabic numerals. At the bottom of the coin are three capital letters: S.C.T. These letters stand for Southern Conference Tournament.

To a non-cocker, this desire might sound childish, but, to a cockfighter, this award is his ultimate achievement in one of the toughest sports in the world. The medal is awarded to the man Senator Jacob Foxhall decides to give it to at the completion of the annual S.C.T. held in Milledgeville, Georgia. However, Senator Foxhall doesn't always see fit to award the medal. In the last fifteen years he has only awarded the medal to four cockfighters. Ed Middleton was one of them.

In addition to the medal there is a cash award of one thousand dollars. In effect, the cocker who wins this award has the equivalent of a paid-up insurance policy. He can demand a minimum fee of one hundred and fifty dollars a day as a referee from any pit operator in the South, and the operator considers it an honor to pay him. To a cocker, this medal means as much as the Nobel Prize does to a scientist. If that doesn't convey an exact meaning of the award, I can state it simpler. The recipient is the best damned cockfighter in the South, and he has the medal to prove it.

For ten years this medal has been my goal. The S.C.T. is the toughest pit tourney in the United States, and a cockfighter can't enter his game fowl without an invitation. Only top men in the game receive invitations, and I had been getting mine for eight years — even during the two years I was in the army and stationed in the Philippine Islands.

A vow of silence, however, isn't necessary to compete for the award. That had been my own idea, and not a very bright idea either, but I was too damned stubborn to break it.

Three years before I had been riding high on the list of eligible S.C.T. cockfighters. In a hotel room in Biloxi, I had gotten drunk with a group of chicken men, and shot off my big mouth, boasting about my Ace cock, a Red Madigan named Freelance.

Another drunken breeder challenged me, and we staged the fight in the hotel room. Freelance killed the other cock easily, but in the fight he received a slight battering. The next day at the scheduled S.C.T. pitting, I had been forced to pit Freelance again because I had posted a two-hundred-dollar forfeit, and I had been too ashamed to withdraw. Freelance lost, and I had lost my chance for the award.

A few weeks later, while brooding about this lost fight, a fight that had been lost by my personal vanity and big mouth, I made my self-imposed vow of silence. I intended to keep the vow until I was awarded that little silver medal. No one, other than myself, knew about my vow, and I could have broken it at any time without losing face. But *I* would know, and I had to shave every day. At first it had been hell, especially when I had had a few drinks and wanted to get in on the chicken talk in a bar or around the cockhouses at a game club, but I had learned how to live with it.

On the day Mr. Middleton picked me up in his Cadillac at Captain Mack's Trailer Court in Belle Glade, I hadn't said a word to anyone in two years and seven months.

'You're a hard man to talk to since you lost your voice!' Ed Middleton boomed in his resonant baritone.

With a slight start, I turned and grinned at him.

'I mean it,' he said seriously. 'I feel like a radio announcer talking into a microphone in a soundproof room. I know I must be reaching somebody, but I'll be damned if I know who it is. You've changed a lot in the last two or three years, Frank. I know you're working as hard as you ever did, but you shouldn't take life too seriously. And don't let a run of bad luck get you down, do you hear?'

I nodded. Ed jabbed me in the ribs sharply with his elbow.

'You've still got a lot of friends, you big dumb bastard!' he finished gruffly. With a quick movement he snapped on the dash radio, twisted the volume on full and almost blasted me out of my seat. He turned the volume down again and said bitterly: 'And on top of everything else, there's nothing on the radio these days but rock 'n' roll!'

He left the radio on anyway, and said no more until we reached Saint Cloud. We pulled into the parking area of a garish drive-in restaurant and got out of the car. It was only six thirty, but the sun had dropped out of sight. There were just a few jagged streaks of orange in the western sky, an intermingling of nimbus clouds and smoke from runaway muck fires. As we admired these fiery fingers in the sky, Mr. Middleton smacked his lips.

'How does a steak sound, Frank?'

I certainly didn't intend to spend my remaining ten dollars on a steak. In reply, I emptied my pockets and showed him a double handful of junk, and some loose change.

'I didn't expect you to pay for it,' he said resentfully. 'Let's go inside.'

The sirloin was excellent. So was the baked potato and green salad and three cups of coffee that went with it. After three weeks of Dody's halfhearted cooking, I appreciated a good steak dinner. On regular fare, such as greens, pork chops, string beans, cornbread and so on, I'm a fairly good cook, and I enjoy the preparation of my own meals. But I never prepare food when I have a woman around to do it for me. As I ate, I wondered vaguely how Jack Burke was making out with the girl. Although I was broke, the steak restored my good spirits, and I felt a certain sense of new-found freedom now that I no longer had Dody to worry about.

We lingered over dinner for more than an hour and didn't arrive at Mr. Middleton's home until after nine. His ranch-style, concrete brick and stucco house was about three miles off the main highway on a private gravel road and completely surrounded by orange groves. An avid fisherman, Ed had built his home with the rear terrace overlooking a small pond. He parked in a double carport, set well away from the house, backing in beside a blue Chevy pickup.

Before we crossed the flagstone patio, Ed flipped a switch in the carport and flooded the patio and most of the small lake with light. The pond was about forty yards in diameter, and there was an aluminium fishing skiff tied to a concrete block pier at the edge of the gently sloping lawn.

'I've stocked the damned lake with fish four different times,' Ed said angrily, 'but they disappear someplace. Hide in the muck at the bottom, I suppose. Anyway, I've never been able to catch very many.'

When the lights were turned on, Mrs. Middleton opened the back door and peered out. Her dark hair, shot through with streaks of gray, was coiled in a heavy round bun at the nape of her neck.

'Who's that with you, Ed?' she asked.

We crossed the patio to the door and Ed kissed his wife on the mouth. He gripped my upper arm with his thick fingers and pulled me in front of him.

'Frank Mansfield, Martha. You remember him, I'm sure. He's going to spend the night with us.'

'Of course,' Martha said. 'Come on inside, Frank, before the mosquitoes eat you alive!'

We entered the kitchen and I blinked uncomfortably beneath the blue-and-yellow fluorescent lights. I shook hands with Mrs. Middleton after she wiped her hands unnecessarily on her clean white apron. She was a motherly woman, about ten or fifteen years younger than her husband, but without any children to 'mother.'

'Have you boys had your dinner?' she asked.

'We had a little something in Saint Cloud,' Ed admitted.

'Restaurants!' she said. 'Why didn't you bring Frank on home to dinner when you were that close?' she scolded. 'Sit *down*, Frank! How've you been? Could you eat a piece of key lime pie? Of course you can. I know you both want coffee.'

As we sat down at the breakfast nook together, Ed

winked at me. Mrs. Middleton bustled around in her bright and shiny kitchen, banging things together, just as busy as she could be.

'Force some pie down anyway, Frank,' Mr. Middleton said in a loud stage whisper. 'I'm going to eat a piece even though I hate it.'

'Ha!' Martha said from beside the stove. 'You hate it all right!'

After we were served and eating our pie, there was nothing else Mrs. Middleton could do for us. She stood beside the table with her hands clasped beneath her apron, working her pursed lips in and out. I had the feeling that she wanted to ask me questions, but out of consideration for my so-called affliction, she wanted to phrase her questions so that I could answer them yes or no, and yet she couldn't manage any questions of that kind. I hadn't seen Mrs. Middleton or talked to her for at least four years. As I recalled, the last time I had seen her was at a banquet held following the International Cockfighting Tournament in Saint Petersburg. My 'dumbness' had been a subject that she and her husband had undoubtedly discussed between them.

'Sit down, Martha,' Ed said. 'Have a cup of coffee with us.'

'And stay awake all night? No thanks.' She sat beside her husband, however, and smiled across the table. 'Do you like the pie, Frank?'

I kissed my fingertips and rolled my eyes toward the ceiling.

'Lime is Ed's favorite.' She put a hand on her husband's sleeve. 'How was the trip, Ed?'

Ed Middleton put his fork crosswise on his empty plate, wiped his lips with a napkin, and looked steadily at his wife. 'The trip doesn't matter, Martha,' he said, 'because it was the last, the very last.'

For a long time, a very long time it seemed to me, the elderly couple looked into each other's eyes. Mr. Middleton smiled and nodded his head, and Martha's lower lip began to tremble and her eyes were humid. An instant later she was crying. She hurriedly left the table, put her apron to her face and, still crying, ran out of the room.

Mr. Middleton crumpled the square of linen and tossed it toward the stove. The napkin fluttered to the floor, and he smiled and shook his head.

'She's crying because she's happy,' he said. 'Well, dammit, I promised to give up cockfighting, and a promise is a promise!' He got up from the table, doubled his right fist, and punched me hard on the shoulder. 'Pour yourself some more coffee, eat another piece of pie. I'll be back in a minute.'

He pushed through the swinging door and disappeared.

The lime pie was tart, tasty, with a wonderful two-inch topping of snow white, frothy meringue. I ate two more pieces, drank two more cups of coffee. I smoked two cigarettes. Just as I was beginning to wonder whether Ed was going to come back to the kitchen or not, he pushed through the door.

'Come on, Frank,' he snapped his fingers, 'Let's go get your suitcase.'

We went out to his Caddy, and after he unlocked the doors, I got my suitcase out of the back. When we returned to the kitchen, he switched off the patio lights. I followed him through the living-room and into his study.

'This was supposed to be a third bedroom,' he explained. 'Actually, it was designed as the master bedroom, and it's a lot larger than the other two bedrooms in the back. But Martha and I decided to each take a small bedroom apiece so our snoring wouldn't bother each other. And besides, I needed a large room like this as an office. A big man needs a big room.' He opened the door leading to the bathroom. 'Here's the can, Frank. Take a shower if you want to. There's always hot water, and these towels are all clean in here. I'll get you some sheets.'

Ed left the room and I could hear him clumping down the hallway, yelling to his wife and asking her where she kept the clean sheets hidden.

The Middletons' ranch-style home was so modern in

design and color that the old-fashioned furniture in the study was out of place. The walls were painted a bright warm blue, and there were matching floor-to-ceiling drapes over both windows. The floor was black-and-white pebbled terrazzo, and there the modernity stopped. The floor was covered with an oval-shaped hooked rag rug. There was an ugly, well-scratched, walnut rolltop desk against one wall, and there was an ancient horsehair-stuffed Victorian couch against the opposite wall. Beneath one window there was a scuffed cowhide easy chair, and a shiny black steamer trunk under the other window. A red-lacquered straight chair, with a circular cane seat, stood beside the desk. Three heavy wrought-iron smoking stands completed the furnishings.

I was attracted to the framed photographs on the walls. Each photo was framed in a cheap glass-covered black frame, the type sold in dime stores. Most of the glossy photos were of gamecocks, but there were several photos of Ed Middleton and his cronies. An old cover page of *The Southern Cockfighter*, with a four-color drawing of Ed Middleton's famous cock Freddy, held the place of honor above the desk. Freddy had won nineteen fights and had died in his coop ten years before. Anywhere chicken talk is held, Freddy's name comes up sooner or later.

Mr. Middleton re-entered the room, carrying sheets, a blanket and a pillow under his right arm, and a portable television set in his left hand. He tossed the bedcovers on the couch, placed the portable set on the seat of the red straight-backed chair, and plugged the cord into the wall socket.

'I told Martha you wouldn't need a blanket, but you know how women are.'

I nodded. I knew how women were. I began to make up the lumpy couch with the sheets.

'To give you something to do, I brought in the TV. It isn't much good but you can get Orlando, anyway. I'd stay up and keep you company for a while, but I'm pretty tired. This has been a long day for an old man.'

I soon had the couch made up, but Mr. Middleton lingered in the room. He studied a photograph of a framed cock on the wall, and beckoned to me as I started to sit down.

'Come here, Frank. Take a look at this cock. It's a phenomenon in breeding and you'll never see another like it. A bird called Bright Boy, one of the most courageous birds I ever owned. Yet it was bred from a father and a daughter. By all the rules, a cock bred that way usually runs every time, but this beauty never did. He was killed in his second fight in a drag pitting. Sorry now I didn't keep him for a brood cock to see what would have happened. I suppose there are similar cases, but this is the only one I really know is true. Did you ever hear of a real fighter bred of father and daughter?'

I shook my head. If true, and I doubted Ed's story, this was an unusual case. When it comes to cocks of the same blood, those bred from mother and son have the biggest heart for fighting to the death. Somebody had probably switched an egg on old Ed.

'Every time a man thinks he's got the answers on cock-breeding, something like this happens to teach him something new. I'm going to be pretty well lost without my chickens, Frank, but I've got a lot of stuff stored away in that trunk, old game-strain records and so on. Maybe I could write a useful book on breeding.' He shook his head sadly. 'I don't know. I suppose I'll find something to do with my time.'

To get rid of him, I clapped him on the shoulder, sat down, and unbuckled my jodhpur boots.

I was growing weary of always being on the receiving end of personal confidences and long sad stories. The man who is unable to talk back is at the mercy of these people. He is like an inexperienced priest who listens tolerantly to the first simple confessions of impure thoughts, and then listens with increasing horror as the sins mount, one outdoing the other until he is shocked into dumbness. And, of course, the sinner takes advantage of a man's credulousness, loading ever greater sins upon him to see how far he can really go now that he has found a trapped listener who is unable to stop him. My ears had been battered by the outpourings of troubles, tribulations, aspirations, and the affairs of broken hearts for two years and seven months. Only by being rude enough to leave the scene had I evaded some of my confessors.

But Ed Middleton was wise enough to take the hint.

'Good night, Frank,' he said finally, 'I'll see you in the morning,' and the door closed behind him.

After taking a needed shower I switched on the little television set and sat on the couch to watch the gray, shimmering images. There was a lot of snow, and jagged bars of black appeared much too often. In less than five minutes I was forced to turn it off. I'm not overly fond of television anyway. Traveling around so much I have never formed the habit of watching it. And I've never owned a set.

I was impressed by this pleasant room of Ed Middleton's. It was a man's room, and if he really wanted to write a book about cock-breeding, it was certainly quiet enough. I doubted, however, that he would ever write one. What Ed Middleton did with his remaining years was no concern of mine, and yet I found myself worried about him. He had been fighting game fowl and refereeing pit matches for thirty-odd years. Without any birds to fool around with, what could he possibly do with his time? I felt sorry for the old man.

He had a nice home, his wife was a wonderful woman, and the Citrus Syndicate took care of his orange groves. He had turned over the operation of his groves to the Central Citrus Syndicate some years back. In return, they paid him a good percentage on the crop each year, and now he didn't have to do anything with his trees except to watch them grow. By giving up cockfighting he was giving up his entire existence, and, like most elderly men who retire, he probably wouldn't live very long — with nothing to do. Martha was wrong, dead wrong, in forcing Ed to give up his game chickens.

Mary Elizabeth's opposition to the sport was the major

reason we had never gotten married. Why can't the American woman accept a man for what he is instead of trying to make him over into the idealized image of her father or someone else?

There was no use worrying about Ed Middleton. I had problems of my own that were more pressing. But with a little pushing from me, my problems would somehow take care of themselves. All I knew was that I had to do what I knew best how to do. Nothing else mattered.

I switched off the light and, despite the lumpiness of the beat-up old couch, fell asleep within minutes.

Chapter Four

It seemed as if I had only been asleep for about five minutes when the lights were switched on and Ed Middleton yelled at me to get up.

'Are you going to sleep all day?' he shouted gruffly. 'I've been up for more than an hour already. Come on out to the kitchen when you get dressed. I've got a pot of coffee on.'

Reluctantly, I sat up, kicked off the sheet, and swung my feet to the floor. The door banged shut and I looked at my wristwatch. Five thirty. It was pretty late to be sleeping. No wonder Ed had hollered at me. I stumbled into the bathroom. After a quick shave I dug some clean white socks out of my suitcase, and put on the same clothes I had worn the day before. I joined Ed in the kitchen, and sat at the breakfast nook.

'We can eat breakfast later, Frank,' he said, pouring two cups of coffee. 'Coffee'll hold us for a while. I want to show you something first.'

I drank the coffee black, and it was thick enough to slice with my knife.

'You want a glass of orange juice?'

I held up a hand to show that coffee was enough for now.

Ed refilled my cup, set the pot back on the stove, and paced up and down on the shiny terrazzo floor. He wore an old pair of blue bib overalls and an expensive, embroidered short-sleeved sport shirt. The bottoms of the overalls were tucked into a pair of ten-inch, well-oiled engineer boots. His great paunch stretched the middle of the overalls tight, but the bib on his chest flapped loosely as he walked.

The second cup of coffee seemed hotter than the first, and I was forced to sip it slowly. Ed snapped his fingers impatiently, pushed open the back door, and said over his shoulder, 'Come on, Frank. We can have breakfast later, like I told you already.'

I gulped down the remainder of the coffee and followed him outside to the patio. The sun was just rising, and the upper rim could be seen through the trees. The tops of the orange trees across the pond were dipped in molten, golden-green fire. The oranges on the darker green lower limbs of the trees looked as if they had been painted on. A mist rose from the tiny lake like steam rising from a pot of water just before it begins to boil. Ed Middleton sat down in the center of the little skiff tied to the concrete pier, and fitted the oars into the locks. I sat forward in the prow.

'Untie the line, Frank, and let's cast off.'

Mr. Middleton rowed across the lake — all forty yards of it. It would have been less trouble to take the path that circled the pond, but if he wanted to use the skiff, it didn't make any difference to me.

When we reached the other side of the pond, I jumped out, held the skiff steady for Mr. Middleton, and then both of us pulled the boat onto dry land. There was a narrow path through the grove, and I trailed the old man for about five hundred yards until we reached his chicken walks. There was a flat, well-hidden clearing in the grove, and about a dozen coop walks, each separated by approximately twenty yards. The walks were eight feet tall, about ten feet wide by thirty feet in length, with the tops and sides covered with chicken wire. The baseboards were two feet high, and painted with old motor oil to keep down the mite population.

Seeing the empty walks reminded me of my own farm in Ocala, although I had a better setup for coop-walked birds than Ed Middleton. At one time, many years before, long before he had converted his land to orange trees, he had had the ideal setup for a country-walked rooster. A pond, gently rolling terrain, and enough trees for the chickens to choose their own limbs for roosting. We walked down the row of walks to the end coop. As the rooster crowed, Ed turned around with a proud expression and pointed to the cock.

If there is anything more beautiful than the sight of a purebred gamecock in the light of early morning I do not know what it is. This fighting cock of Ed's was the most brilliantly colored chicken I had ever seen, and I've seen hundreds upon hundreds of chickens.

Middleton had devoted sixteen years and countless generations of game fowl to developing the famous Middleton Gray, and there were traces of the Gray in the cock's shawl and broad, flat chest. But the cock was a hybrid of some kind that I couldn't place or recognize. He walked proudly to the fence and tossed his head back and crowed, beating the tips of his long wings together. The tips of his wings were edged with vermilion. The crow of a fighting cock is strong and deep and makes the morning sounds of a common dunghill barnyard rooster sound puny in comparison.

The same flaming color that tipped his wings was repeated in his head feathers and thighs, but his remaining feathers, including the sweep of his high curving tail, were a luminous peacock blue. Ed was planning — or had planned — to keep him for a brood cock, because his comb and wattles hadn't been clipped for fighting. His lemon beak was strong, short and evenly met. His feet and legs were as orange and bright as a freshly painted bridge.

The floor of the cock's private walk was thickly covered with a mixture of finely ground oyster shells and well-grated charcoal, essential ingredients for a fighter's diet. The oyster shells were for lime content, and the charcoal for digestion, but against this salt-and-pepper background, the cock's colorful plumage was emphasized.

Unfortunately, coloring is not the essential factor for a winning gamecock. Good blood *first*, know-how in conditioning, and a good farm walk are the three essentials a pit bird needs to win. I knew that thirty years of cock-breeding knowledge had found its way into that cock. I could see it in every feather, and his good blood was assured by the pleased smile on Ed Middleton's thin lips.

'Except for a couple of battered Grays and an old Middleton hen I've kind of kept around for a pet, this is the only cock I've got left. I've never pitted him, and he's overdue, but I was afraid to lose him. Not really, Frank. I know damned well he can outhit any other cock in the South!'

I agreed with him, at least in theory. I spread my arms, grinned, and shook my head with admiration. Ed nodded sagely with self-satisfaction, and I didn't blame him. A flush slowly enveloped his features until his entire face was as red as his bulbous nose.

'He's got a pretty damned fancy handle, Frank,' Ed said. 'I call him Icarus. You probably remember the old legend from school. There was a guy named Daedalus, who had a son named Icarus. Anyway, these two — Greeks they were — got tossed into jail, and Daedalus made a pair of wings out of wax for his boy to escape. This kid, Icarus, put on the wings and flew so damned high he reached the sun and the wings melted on him. He fell to the ground and was killed. No man has ever flown so high before or since, but, anyway, that's the handle I hung on the chicken. Icarus.'

Ed Middleton cracked his knuckles and clomped away from the walk and entered the feed shack. I gripped the chicken wire with my fingers and turned my attention to Icarus. For a rugged character like Ed Middleton, the highbrow name and the story that went with it were fairly romantic, I thought. Most cockers who fight a lot of cocks don't get around to naming them in the first place. A metal leg band with the cock's weight and owner number usually suffices for identification. Of course, a favorite brood cock, or a bird that has won several battles, is frequently named. But I went along with Ed all the way. As far as looks were concerned the fancy name fitted the chicken to a T. However, if I had owned the bird, I would have called him Icky, and kept the private name to myself.

I entered the feed shed, dipped into the open sack of cracked corn in the corner, and picked out a dozen fat grains. I returned to the cock's walk, opened the gate and entered. As the cock watched me with his head to one side I lined up the grains of corn on the ground about six inches apart. The cock marched toward me boldly, eating as he came, and pecked the remaining grain of corn out of my outstretched palm. He wasn't a man fighter. Ed had probably spent a good many hours talking to the cock and gently handling him. I picked Icarus up with both hands, holding him underhanded, and examined the cock's legs and feet.

They hung down in perfect alignment with his body. If a cock's legs are out of line with the direction of his body, he is called a dry-heeled cock, because he can't hit and do much harm. But if the legs are in perfect direction, the cock stands erect, and he rises high. And usually he's a close hitter. This cock's legs were perfect.

I lowered the cock to the ground, released him and opened the gate. The cock tried to follow me out, and I liked that, for some reason. Ed came out of the feed shack, and showed me the bird's weight chart, which was attached to a clipboard.

Icarus was seventeen months old and weighed 4:03 pounds. He had maintained this weight fairly well for the past three months, within two ounces either way. For a cock that wasn't on a conditioning diet, this even weight indicated that the bird was healthy enough. He was fed cracked corn twice a day, barley water, and purged twice a week with a weak solution of one grain of calomel and one grain of bicarbonate of soda dissolved in water.

The flirting and exercising sections on the chart were empty. I tapped them with a forefinger and looked questioningly at Mr. Middleton.

'I haven't done any conditioning, Frank. But as you can see, I've watched his weight closely. He should go to 4:05, maybe, or 4:07 at most — under training. That's my opinion, anyway,' he qualified his estimate. For a full minute, Ed looked through the fence at the cock, and I returned the weight chart to the hook on the wall inside the shack.

'Do you want this cock, Frank?' Ed asked fiercely, when I rejoined him.

What could I say? I stretched out the fingers of my left hand and made a sawing gesture on my right forearm. I shook my head, then made the sawing motion higher up, at the shoulder.

'Okay, Frank. You can have him for five hundred dollars. I told Martha last night you'd come home with me to buy the last of my chickens. So that's the price. Pay me and take him!'

The old cock fancier dug his hands into his pockets and walked away from me, unable, for the moment, to look me in the face.

He knew perfectly well I didn't have five hundred dollars, and he also knew that the cock wasn't worth that much. For fifty dollars apiece I could purchase country-walked gamecocks, with authenticated bloodlines, from almost any top breeder in the United States. And fifty dollars was a good price. The average for a purebred cock was thirty-five, and I could buy stags for ten and fifteen dollars apiece. I've seen Ace cocks sell for a hundred, and sometimes for one hundred and fifty — but never for five hundred.

No breeder wants to sell any of his fighters to another cocker he may meet at the same pit someday. The cock he sells or gives away may possibly kill some of his own birds in a pitting. On the other hand, the breeders who raise game fowl to sell would be thought ridiculous if they attempted to peddle an untested cock for five hundred dollars!

The answer was simple. Ed Middleton didn't want to sell Icarus. He was looking for an out to keep his pet. After I left he could tell Martha I had made an offer and that he had promised to sell it to me. Anybody else who came around to buy it could be legitimately refused. 'I'd be glad to sell it,' he could truthfully say to a prospective buyer, 'but I've promised the cock to Frank Mansfield. Sorry...'

The old bastard was trying to renege on his promise to his wife. Knowing that I didn't have his price and was unlikely to pay it if I did, he planned on keeping his pet cock until it died of an old age. One thing I did know. If I showed up with the money, he would have to sell it. And I wanted that bird. I seemed to sense somehow that this was the turning point in my run of bad luck at the pits ... Little Icky.

Standing by an orange tree, Ed jerked a piece of fruit from a lower limb and threw it in a looping curve over the trees. I could hear the mushy thud of the orange as it landed deep in the grove. I crossed the space separating us with an outstretched right hand.

Ed grimly accepted my promise to buy his cock with a strong handshake.

While Mr. Middleton made a mixture of barley water, I leaned against the door of the feed shack and finished my cigarette. Somehow, I was going to get the money to buy that cock. Now my impending trip to Jacksonville had a sharpened point to it. If Doc Riordan had any money at all, I intended to get it.

Ed measured out the cracked corn and fed his pet, the two battered Gray roosters, and the old hen. Although I could feel some sympathy for Martha in not wanting her husband out traveling the cockfight circuits, I could not understand her desire to make him give up cock-breeding. If she considered cock-breeding morally wrong, she could have consoled herself with the idea that Ed was doing the breeding, not her. A man like Ed Middleton could never give up his love of the game. Perhaps she was going through her menopause and, as a consequence, was losing her mind.

'Let's go get us some breakfast, Frank,' Ed said, as he locked the feed shack door. Ed started down the path toward the lake, and I lingered for a last look at Icarus. He pecked away at his grain hungrily. I could see the fine breeding of the cock in his stance and proud bearing. The cock had shape, health, and an inborn stamina. Through proper conditioning I could teach him responsiveness, alertness, improve his speed, and sharpen his natural reflexes. Other than that, there wasn't much else I could do for the cock. His desire to fight was inherited. And the only way his gameness could be tested truly was in the pit.

I turned away from the walk and ran down the path to catch up with Ed.

When we entered the kitchen Martha greeted us cheerfully and began to prepare our breakfast. Ed and I sat down across from each other at the breakfast nook and I inhaled the delicious fragrance of the frying bacon. It was quite a breakfast: crisp bacon, fried eggs, hot biscuits, grits and melted butter, orange juice, and plenty of orange-blossom honey to coil onto the fluffy biscuits.

As I sat back with a full stomach to drink my after-breakfast coffee, Ed told his wife that I was going to buy his remaining chickens.

'That's wonderful, Ed,' Martha said happily. She smiled at me and bobbed her chin several times. 'You know Ed wouldn't sell those old birds to just anybody, Frank. But Ed has always had a lot of respect for you, and I know you'll take good care of them.'

I nodded, finished my coffee, and slid out of the booth.

'Frank isn't taking the cocks today, Martha,' Ed said, getting up from the table. 'He'll be back for them later on.'

'Oh, I didn't know that! I thought he was taking them now.'

'These deals aren't made in an instant, sweetheart,' Ed said sharply. 'But we've shaken hands on the deal, and Frank'll be back, all in good time.' He forced a smile and turned toward me. 'Come on, Frank. I'll drive you into Orlando.'

'Where're you going, Frank?' Martha asked.

I shrugged indifferently and returned her smile. This was the kind of question that could only be answered by writing it down, and I didn't feel that it required an answer. Where I was going or what I was going to do couldn't possibly have any real interest for the old lady.

'Frank can't answer questions like that without writing them down,' Ed reminded his wife. 'But you know we'll be reading about him in the trade magazines.'

'Well, I'll pack a lunch for you anyway. Wait out on the patio. Take some more coffee out there with you. It'll only take a minute and you can surely wait that long.'

While she fixed a lunch for me, I repacked my suitcase and took it out to the car. Ed unlocked the door, and I removed the coop and handed it to him before I tossed the suitcase on the floorboards.

'Sure, leave the coop with me if you like,' he said, leaning it against the concrete wall.

When I returned for Icky, I could use the coop to carry him, and I didn't feel like lugging it along to Jacksonville, not hitchhiking, anyway.

A few minutes later Martha joined us on the patio and handed me a heavy paper bag containing my lunch.

'I used the biscuits left from breakfast,' she said, 'and made a few ham sandwiches. There's a fat slice of tomato on each one and plenty of mayonnaise. There wasn't any pie left, but I put in a couple of apples for dessert.'

Rather than simply shake hands with her, I put an arm around her narrow shoulders and kissed her on the cheek. Mrs. Middleton broke away from me and returned to the safety of her kitchen. Ed called through the door that he would be back from Orlando when he got back.

We drove down Ed's private road to the highway. I didn't know where he was taking me, but I hoped he wouldn't drop me off in the center of town. With the baggage I was carrying, the best place to start hitchhiking was on the I-4 Throughway on the other side of Winter Park. Several years had passed since I had been forced to use my thumb, and I wasn't too happy about the prospect.

Orlando is a fairly large city and well spread out. The streets that morning were crowded with traffic. Ed drove his big car skillfully, and when he hit the center of town, he made several turns and then stopped in front of the Greyhound bus station. I took my baggage out of the back and started to close the door, but held it open when Ed heaved himself across the seat. He got out on my side, reached in his wallet, and handed me a twenty-dollar bill.

'You can't hitchhike with all that stuff, Frank. You'd better take a bus.'

I nodded, accepted the bill and buttoned it into my shirt pocket. That made five hundred and twenty dollars I owed him, but I was grateful for the loan.

We shook hands rather formally, and Ed plucked at his white chin with his puffy fingers. 'Now don't worry about Icarus, Frank,' he said with an attempt at levity. 'I'll take good care of him whether you come back for him or not.' His eyes were worried just the same.

I held up two spread fingers in the 'V' sign. It was a meaningless gesture in this instance, but Ed smiled, thinking I meant it for him. I remained at the curb and waved to him as he drove away.

I picked a folder out of the rack, circled Jacksonville on the timetable with my ballpoint pencil, shoved the folder and my twenty under the wicket, and paid for my ticket. After slipping the ticket into my hatband, I gathered my baggage around me and sat down on a bench to wait for the bus.

I thought about Icky. In reality, five hundred dollars wasn't even enough money to get started. I needed a bare minimum of one thousand five hundred dollars to have at least a thousand left over after paying for the cock. Two thousand was more like it.

Somehow, I had to get my hands on this money.

Chapter Five

I didn't arrive in Jacksonville until a little after three that afternoon. Instead of waiting for an express, I had taken the first bus that left Orlando, and it turned out to be the kind that stops at every filling station, general store and cow pasture along the way. A long, dull ride.

After getting my baggage out of the side of the bus from the driver I left the station and walked three blocks to the Jeff Davis Hotel, where I always stayed when I was in Jax. On the way to the hotel I stopped at a package store and bought a pint of gin.

Perhaps the Jeff Davis isn't the most desirable hotel in Jax, but it is downtown, handy to everything, the people know me there, and crowded or not I can always get a room. The Manager follows cockfighting, advertises in the game fowl magazines, and there is usually someone hanging around the lobby who knows me. The daily rate is attractive, as well — only three dollars a day for cockers, instead of the regular rate of five.

As soon as I checked in at the desk and got to my room, I opened my suitcase and dug out my corduroy coat. In September, Jacksonville turns chilly in the afternoons, and the temperature drops below seventy. Not that it gets cold, but the weather doesn't compare favorably with southern Florida. The long pull of gin I took before going out on the street again felt warm in my stomach.

I walked briskly through the streets to the post office, entered, and twirled the combination dial on my post-office box. It didn't open, but I could see that there was mail inside the box through the dirty brown glass window. I searched through my wallet, found my box receipt for the rental, and shoved it through the window to the clerk. He studied the slip for a moment, and called my attention to the date.

'You're almost ten days overdue on your quarterly box payment, Mr. Mansfield,' he said. 'Your box was closed out and rented to somebody else. I'm sorry, but there's a big demand for boxes these days and I don't have any more open at present. If you want me to, I'll put your name on the waiting list.'

I shook my head, pointed to the rack of mail behind him. This puzzled him for a moment, and then he said: 'Oh, you mean your mail?'

I nodded impatiently, drumming my fingers on the marble ledge.

'If you have any, it'll be at the general-delivery window.'

I picked up my receipt and gave it to the woman at the general-delivery window. She handed me two letters and my current *Southern Cockfigher* magazine. I shoved the letters and magazine into my coat pocket and filled in change-of-address cards to transfer the magazine and post-office-box letters to my Ocala address. After mailing one card to the magazine and turning in the other to the woman at the window I returned to my hotel room.

The first letter I opened was from a pit operator in Tallahassee inviting me to enter a four-cock derby he was holding in November. I tossed the letter into the waste-basket. The other letter was the one I had been expecting. It was from the Southern Conference Tournament committee, and contained my invitation, the rules, and the schedule for the S.C.T. season.

I studied the mimeographed schedule, but I wasn't too happy about it. There wasn't a whole lot of time to obtain and keep gamecocks for the tourney.

SCHEDULE
SOUTHERN CONFERENCE

Oct. 15	— Greenville, Mississippi
Nov. 10	— Tifton, Georgia
Nov. 30	— Plant City, Florida

Dec. 15   — Chattanooga, Tennessee
Jan. 10   — Biloxi, Mississippi
Jan. 28   — Auburn, Alabama
Feb. 24   — Ocala, Florida
Mar. 15–16   — S.C.T. — Milledgeville, Georgia

I was already too late for Greenville, Mississipi. The S.C.T. was unlike other invitational mains and derbies, both in rules and gamecock standards. When Senator Foxhall had organized the S.C.T. back in the early thirties, his primary purpose had been to improve the breeds and gameness in southern cockfighting. The hardest rule of the tourney was that all the cocks entered in the final round at Milledgeville had to be four-time winners. A cock can win one or sometimes two fights with flashy flies in the first pitting, and some good luck. But any cock that wins four in a row is dead game. Luck simply doesn't stretch through four wins. This single S.C.T. rule, more than any other, had certainly raised breeding standards in the South, and it kept out undesirables and fly-by-night cockers looking for a fast dollar. All the pit operators on the S.C.T. circuit were checked from time to time by members of the committee, and if their standards of operation dropped, they were dropped, in turn, by the senator.

Like the other big-time chicken men, I had fought cocks in the highly competitive six-day International Tournament in both Orlando and Saint Pete, and I intended to enter it again someday, but I preferred the more rigid policies of the S.C.T. It was possible to enter the annual International Tournament by posting a preliminary two-hundred-dollar forfeit, which was lost if you didn't show up and pay the three-hundred-dollar balance. The winning entries made big money at the International, but I could make just as much at S.C.T. pits and at the final Milledgeville meet. And the wins on the S.C.T. circuit really meant something to me.

At that moment, however, I didn't feel like a big-time cockfighter. I was at rock bottom and it was ironical to even think about fighting any cocks this season. All I had in my wallet was eighteen dollars, plus some loose change in my pockets. I owned a thirty-dollar guitar, a gaff case, a few clothes in a battered suitcase, and a lease on a farm.

Of course, the contents of my gaff case were worth a few hundred dollars, but I needed everything I had to fight cocks. I sat down on the edge of my bed, and opened my gaff case to search for the last letter Doc Riordan had sent me. I opened the letter, but before reading it again, I made a quick inventory of the gaff case to see if there was anything I could do without. There wasn't. I needed every item.

There were sixteen sets of gaffs, ranging from the short one-and-one-quarter-inch heels I preferred, up to a pair of three-inch Texas Twisters. I even had a set of slashers a Puerto Rican breeder had given me one afternoon in San Juan. With slashers, the bird is armed on one leg only. I don't believe in fighting slashers for one simple reason. When you fight slashers, the element of chance is too great, and the best cock doesn't always win. With a wicked sharp blade on a cock's left leg, the poorest cock can sometimes get in a lucky hit. Pointed gaffs, round from socket to point, are legitimate. Once a cock's natural spur points have been sawed off, the hand-forged heels fitted over the half-inch stumps are a clean substitute for his God-given spurs, and they make for humane fighting. Two cocks meeting anywhere in their natural state will fight to the death or until one of them runs away. Steel spurs merely speed up the killing process, and a cock doesn't have to punish himself unnecessarily by bruising his natural spurs.

Of course, I had fought slashers when I was a soldier in the Philippines because I had to, and I knew how to fight them. But I had never considered them altogether fair because of that slight element of chance. Cockfighting is the only sport that can't be fixed, perhaps the only fair contest left in America. A cock wouldn't throw a fight and couldn't if he knew how.

Every pair of my sixteen sets of heels was worth from twenty to thirty-five dollars, and I needed them all. The

correct length of heels is a common argument, but what
really determines the right length for any given cock is the
way it fights. And even though I favor short heels, like
they use in the North, or 'short-heel country' as the North
is called, I would never handicap a cock by arming him
with the wrong spurs out of vain, personal preference. It is
a crime not to arm a cock with the spurs which will allow
him to fight his very best.

In addition to my heel sets I had a spur saw, with a
dozen extra blades, moleskin heeling tape, blade
polishers, gaff pointers, a set of artificial stubs for heeling
slip-leg cocks, two pairs of dubbing shears, one curved
and the other straight, and two new heeling outfits, each
containing pads, tie strings and leather crosspieces. There
was also a brand new roll of Irish flax, waxed tie string,
some assorted salves and a few gland stimulation capsules.
To anybody except a cocker, this collection of expensive
equipment was worthless junk. If I pawned the entire
contents of my case, a pawnbroker wouldn't give me more
than forty dollars for the lot.

For a few thoughtful moments I clicked the dubbing
shears in my hand, and then picked up Doc's letter. I'd
been carrying it around in my case for more than three
months.

Dear Frank,

*I haven't written you for some time, but I wanted you
to know your investment is as good as gold. Don't be
surprised if you get a stock split one of these days soon
and double your eight hundred dollars. Next time you
get to Jax, drop in and see me and I'll give you the
details.*

Very truly yours,

Doc Riordon

To anyone who didn't know Doc Riordan, this letter
would have sounded encouraging indeed. But the letter
was more than three months old and, unfortunately, I

knew Doc too well. I liked the man for what he was and respected him for what he was trying to be. But unlike me, Doc lived with a big dream that was practically unattainable. All I wanted to be was the best cockfighter who ever lived. Doc, who had already reached his late fifties, wanted to be a big-time capitalist and financier.

He wasn't a real doctor, I knew that much. He was a pharmacist, and a good one, and somewhere along the years he had added Doc to his name. I had met him several years before at various Florida cockpits, and I had bought conditioning powder and ergot capsules from him when he still had his mail-order business. Conditioning powder can be made up by any pharmacist who is given the formula, but Doc was dependable, well liked by cockers, and he had also invented a salve that was a quick healer for battered cocks. However, there are a lot of businessmen who advertise the same types of items in the cocker journals. There wasn't enough big money in cocker medical supplies for Doc, and he dropped out of the field. However, he would still supply a few friends like myself when we wrote to him.

Some four years before, Doc had caught me in an amiable mood and with more than five thousand dollars in my pockets. I had put eight hundred dollars into his company — The Dixie Pharmaceutical Company — and I had never received a dividend. I had had several glowing letters from him, but not a cent in cash. In fact, I didn't even have any stock certificates to show for my investment. It was one of those word-of-mouth deals so many of us enter into in the South. A handshake is enough, and I knew my money would be returned on demand ... providing Doc had it. But whether he had it or not was something else altogether.

It was five o'clock and I decided to wait and see him in the morning. Feeling as low as I did, I didn't want to return to my room with a turndown that evening.

I left my room, walked down the street to a café and ate two hamburgers and drank two glasses of milk. When I returned to my room, I nipped at the gin and read my new

Southern Cockfighter magazine. The magazine had been published and mailed out before the Belle Glade derby, but there was a short item about the Homestead pitting, and my name was mentioned in Red Carey's column, 'On the Gaff.'

> *Looks like bad luck is still dogging Silent Frank Mansfield. His sad showing at Homestead makes us wonder if his keeping methods are off the beam. Another season like his last three, and we doubt if he'll still be on the S.C.T. rolls.*

The item should have irritated me, but it didn't. A columnist has to put something in his column, and I was fair game. There was nothing wrong with my conditioning methods. They had paid off too many times in the past. My problem was to get the right cocks, and when I got Icky from Mr. Middleton, I would be off to a good season. I finished the rest of the gin and went to bed.

As far back as 320 B.C. an old poet named Chanakya wrote that a man can learn four things from a cock: To fight, to get up early, to eat with his family, and to protect his spouse when she gets into trouble. I had learned how to fight and how to get up early, but I had never gotten along too well with my family and I didn't have any spouse to protect. Fighting was all very well, but getting up early was not the most desirable habit to have when living in a big city like Jacksonville.

The next morning I was up, dressed and shaved, and sitting in the lobby by five thirty. I bought a morning *Times-Union*, glanced at the headlines and then went out for breakfast because the hotel coffee shop didn't open until seven thirty. I lingered as long as I could over coffee, but it was still only six thirty when I returned to the hotel. I was too impatient just to sit around, and I soon left the dreary lobby and walked the early morning streets. The wind off the river was chilly and it felt good to be stirring about. A sickly sun rode the pale morning sky, but after an hour passed it began to get warm and promised to be a good day.

Promptly at eight I entered the Latham building to see if Doc Riordan had arrived at his office. The Latham building was an ancient red-brick structure of seven stories built in the early 1900s. Nothing had been done to it since. The entrance lobby was narrow, grimy and filled with trash blown in from the street. There was a crude, hand-lettered sign on the elevator stating that it was out of order. Doc's company was on the sixth floor.

The stairwell up was unlighted and without windows. I climbed the six flights only to discover that his office was closed. The office was two doors away from the far end of the hallway, and the frosted glass top half of the door had gold letters painted on it four inches high:

THE DIXIE PHARMACEUTICAL CO.
Dr. Onyx P. Riordan
PRESIDENT AND GENERAL MANAGR.

I tried the door and found it locked. Rather than descend the stairs and then climb up again I leaned against the wall and smoked cigarettes until Doc showed up.

The wait was less than twenty minutes and I heard Doc huffing up the stairs long before I could see him. He entered the hall, red-faced, carrying a large cardboard container of coffee. The container was too hot for him to hold comfortably, and as he recovered his breath, he kept shifting it from one hand to the other as he fumbled with his key in the door lock.

'Come on in, Frank,' Doc said, as he opened the door. 'Soon as I set this coffee on the desk I'll shake hands.'

I followed Doc into the tiny office, and we shook hands. Doc wiped his perspiring bald head and brow with a handkerchief and cursed angrily for two full minutes before he sat down behind his desk.

'I've told the superintendent before and I'm going to tell him one more time,' Doc said as he ran down, 'and if he don't get that damned elevator fixed, I'm moving out!

That's a fact, Frank, a fact!'

I sat down in a straight-backed chair in front of Doc's desk, and surveyed his ratty little office. A single dirty window afforded a close-up of the side of a red-brick movie theater less than three feet away, and the proximity of the building didn't allow much light into the room. Doc probably had to burn his desk and ceiling lights even at midday. Doc's desk was a great, wooden, square affair, and much too large for the size of the room. In front of the fluorescent desk lamp was his carved desk sign: *Dr. Onyx P. Riordan, Pres.* (and a beautifully carved ornate job it was, too). In addition to his desk there was a low two-drawer filing cabinet, the swivel executive chair he was sitting in, and two straight-backed chairs. These simple furnishings made the room overly crowded. On the wall behind his desk was a hand-lettered, professionally done poster in three primary colors praising the virtues of a product called Licarbo. After reading the poster I studied Doc's face. He had taken two green dime-store cups out of his desk and was filling them with black coffee.

With his bald head and tonsure of thin, fine gray hair, Doc looked his fifty some-odd years, all right, but there was a certain youthfulness about his face that denied those years. His features were all small, gathered together in the center of a round, bland face. His mouth and snubby nose were small. His blue eyes were ingenuously wide and revealed the full optic circle. With his round red cheeks and freshly scrubbed look, Doc could probably have passed for thirty if he wore a black toupee and dyed his eyebrows to match.

'It's been a long time, Frank,' Doc said sincerely, 'and I'm really glad to see you again.' He sat back with a pleased smile. 'I want to show you something!'

He began to rummage through his desk. I sipped some coffee and lit another cigarette from the butt of the one I was smoking. The sight of this little hole-in-the-wall office had dashed any hopes I might have had about getting even a portion of my money back from the old pharmacist.

'Read this, Frank!' Doc said eagerly, sliding a letter across the broad surface of the desk. I read the letter. It was from a drug laboratory in New York.

President
Dixie Pharmaceutical Co.
Latham Building
Jacksonville, Florida

Dear Dr. Riordan:

We have made exhaustive tests of your product, LI-CARBO, at your request, and we agree that it is nontoxic, and that it will provide nonharmful relief to certain types of indigestion, such as overeating, overindulgence, etc.

However, we are not in the market for such a product at this time. Thank you for letting us examine it. Best wishes.

Very truly yours,

The signature was indecipherable, but vice-president was typed beneath the inked scribble. I put the letter down on the desk.

'Do you realize what that letter means, Frank?' Doc said excitedly. 'They're interested, definitely interested! They couldn't find a single fault, and do you know why? Licarbo doesn't have any, that's why! I've dealt with companies like that before. They think I'll sell out for little or nothing, but if they want Licarbo, and you can read between the lines of the letter that they're dying to get it, it'll cost them plenty!'

Doc sat back in his big chair, steepled his fingers together, and attempted to look shrewd by narrowing his eyes. His narrowed eyes only made him look sleepy, however.

'Not only do I want a flat ten thousand for my rights, Frank, I'm also holding out for a percentage on every package sold. Now what do you think of that?'

I admired Doc's spirit, but, evidently, he refused to recognize a politely worded turndown when he saw it. I shrugged my shoulders noncommittally.

'By God, I forgot!' Doc snapped his fingers. 'You haven't tried Licarbo yet, have you?'

I shook my head. Doc opened the top right drawer of his desk and removed three flat packets approximately the size and shape of restaurant-size sugar packets. The name Licarbo was printed in red ink on each packet, including directions to take as needed, with or without water, following overindulgence, overeating or for mild stomach distress.

'Go ahead, Frank, open one up and taste it. There isn't a better relief for indigestion in the world than Licarbo! Take it with a glass of water and you'll belch every time. What more does a man want than a big healthy belch when his belly hurts him? Right? In the South we like our medicines in powder and liquid form. No self-respecting Southerner will take a fancy capsule for belly pains, no matter how many colors it's got.'

I ripped open a packet and spilled some of the mixture into my hand. Licarbo resembled gunpowder, or a mixture of salt and black pepper, heavy on the pepper. I put my tongue to the mixture. It tasted like licorice, not an unpleasant taste at all.

'Mix it in with your coffee, Frank. Licarbo will dissolve almost instantly.'

I shuddered at this suggestion, shook my head and smiled.

'Tastes good, don't it?' Doc beamed proudly, folding his short arms across his chest. 'All it is, Frank, is a mixture of licorice root, bicarbonate of soda, a few secret ingredients and some artificial coloring. But the formula will make me rich, and you too, Frank. It takes time, however, to invent and develop a new product and get it out to the waiting market. The New York company isn't my only prospect, not by any means. I've got feelers out all over the nation. This is the *big* one, Frank, the one I've been working up to through thirty years in practical pharmacy. I've invented other products and sold them too, but this time I'm holding out to the last breath. Why, if I only had the capital I could manufacture Licarbo myself and literally make a fortune. A fortune!'

Doc turned in his chair, sighed deeply, and looked out the window at the rusty wall of the theater.

'People just don't have faith no more, Frank. People today don't recognize a commercial drug when they see and taste it, damn them all, anyway! But this product has got to go over, it *has* to!' Doc dropped the level of his voice, and said softly, as if to convince himself, 'It's only a matter of time, Frank. Only a matter of time ...'

I slipped the two unopened packets of Licarbo into my jacket pocket. At least I had something to show for my eight-hundred-dollar investment. Doc swiveled his chair and faced me with a bright smile.

'I made this first batch up myself, Frank, and had the sample packages printed up here in town. It costs a lot of money to get started, but you've got to admit the product is good, don't you?'

I nodded, pursing my lips. As far as I was concerned, Licarbo was as good as any one of a hundred similar products on the market. Plain old bicarbonate of soda will make you belch if a belch is required, and that was Doc's main ingredient.

'You'd like to have your eight hundred dollars back just the same. Am I right?' Doc said hesitantly.

I spread my hands, palms up, and nodded.

'Well, I just don't have it right now, Frank.' Doc wet his thumb. 'I just don't have it. But you'll get it back one of these days soon, every damned dime, and with plenty of interest. To be honest, I'm just hanging on these days. Don't even have a phone anymore in the office, as you can see. I've got a part-time pharmacist's job at night in a drug-store near my rooming house, and every cent I make goes into office rent, promotion of Licarbo, and I'm barely getting by on what's left. I've dropped everything else to concentrate on Licarbo, but when it hits, and it's going to, it'll be big, really big!'

Old Doc Riordan was another man like myself, riding along on an inborn, overinflated self-confidence and a wide outward smile. Deep inside, I knew he was worried sick about being unable to write me a check for my money. Well, I could relieve him from that worry in a hurry. Whether his product ever went over big or not was no concern of mine. I wasn't about to ride another man's dream; I had a big dream of my own. It was time to get the hell off Doc's back.

There was a writing tablet on his desk. I reached for it, took my ballpoint lead pencil out of my coat pocket and wrote on the pad:

President, Dixie Pharm. Co.

In return for a ten-year supply of conditioning powder and other medicinal aids for poultry at the Mansfield Farms, the undersigned hereby turns over all his existing stock in the Dixie Pharm. Co. to the President.

After signing my name with a flourish, I smiled, and handed Doc the tablet. He read the note and frowned.

'Don't you have any faith in Licarbo, Frank?'

I looked at him expressionlessly and nodded slowly.

'Then why are you pulling out?'

I got to my feet, leaned over the desk and underlined 'ten-year supply' on the note I had written.

A knowing smile widened Doc's tiny mouth, and he nodded sagely.

'You're a mighty shrewd businessman, Frank. Why, if you ever expand your farms you'll double your eight hundred dollars in five years easily! But damn your eyes, anyway!' He laughed gleefully. 'I'm just going to take you up on this proposition! Whether Licarbo hits big or not, I'll either have my own lab or work in a pharmacy someplace where I can get wholesale prices on drugs. So on a deal like this, neither one of us can lose!'

We shook hands, and I turned to go. Doc stopped me at

the door by putting his hand on my arm. 'Just a minute, Frank. As soon as I can afford it, I'm moving to a better office. And, of course, when I get enough capital, I'm going to build my own laboratories. But meanwhile, here's the address of the drugstore where I work.' He handed me a card and I slipped it into my wallet. 'I'm on duty there every Friday, Saturday and Sunday night from six to midnight. And almost every Wednesday from noon till midnight. I relieve the owner, you see. So when you need anything, drop me a line there, or come by and see me yourself.'

I opened the door, and returned my wallet to my hip pocket.

'You going to put an entry in the Orlando tourney, Frank?'

I shook my head and pointed north.

'Southern Conference then?'

I nodded.

'Well, I'll probably see you in Milledgeville, then. I haven't missed an S.C.T. in ten years and I don't intend to now. And when you see any of the boys on the road, say hello for me, and tell them I still send out a few things when they write.'

I winked, clapped him on the shoulder, and we shook hands again. I started down the hallway toward the stairwell and Doc watched me all the way. When I reached the stairs, he called good-bye to me again. I waved an arm and descended the stairs. At the drugstore on the corner I had a cup of coffee at the counter and then returned to my room at the Jeff Davis Hotel. Fortunately, I had kept my morning newspaper.

I turned to the classified ads and looked under the Help Wanted, Male section to see what I could do about getting a job.

Chapter Six

It is a funny thing. A man can make a promise to his God, break it five minutes later and never think anything about it. With an idle shrug of his shoulders, a man can also break solemn promises to his mother, wife or sweetheart, and, except for a slight, momentary twinge of conscience, he still won't be bothered very much. But if a man ever breaks a promise he has made to himself he disintegrates. His entire personality and character crumble into tiny pieces, and he is never the same man again.

I remember very well a sergeant I knew in the army. Before a group of five men he swore off smoking forever. An hour later he sheepishly lit a cigarette and broke his vow to the five of us and to himself. He was never quite the same man again, not to me, and not to himself.

My vow of silence was much harder to maintain than a vow to quit smoking. It was a definite handicap in everything I did. I read through the want ads three times, studying them carefully, and there wasn't a single thing I could find to do. A man who can't, or won't, talk is in a difficult situation when it comes to finding a job in the city. Besides, I had never had a job in my life — except for my two years in the service.

Of course, during my year of college at Valdosta State I had waited tables in the co-op for my meals, but I didn't consider that as a job. Growing up in Georgia, I had done farm work for my father when I couldn't get out of it, such things as chopping cotton, milking a cow, and simple carpentry repair jobs around the farm. There were a good many things I was capable of doing around a farm without having to talk. But the want ads in the newspaper were no help to me at all. Unwilling to use my voice, I couldn't even ask for a job unless I wrote it down. The majority of the situations that were open in the agate columns were for salesmen. And a man who can't talk can't sell anything. I wadded the newspaper into a ball, and tossed it into the wastebasket.

One thing I could always do was walk and condition cocks for another breeder. There were plenty of chicken men in the South who would have jumped at the chance to pay me five dollars apiece for every game fowl I conditioned for them. But for a man who was still considered a big-time cockfighter throughout the South, it would be too much of a comedown to work for another cock breeder. I had never worked for anybody else in my thirty-two years on this earth, and it was too late to start now. By God, I wasn't that desperate!

Sitting in that hotel room, with only a few loose dollars in my pocket, I was beginning to feel sorry for myself. My eyes rested on my guitar case.

My guitar was an old friend. During the first few months of my self-enforced silence, the days and nights had almost doubled in length. It is surprising how much time is killed everyday in idle conversation. Just to have something to fill in time I had purchased a secondhand Gibson guitar for thirty dollars in a Miami pawnshop. The case wasn't so hot — cheap brown cardboard stamped to resemble alligator leather — but the guitar was a good one, and it had a strong, wonderful tone. The guitar served as a substitute for my lost voice, and I don't know what I would have done without it.

I opened the guitar case, removed the instrument and ran through a few exercises to limber my fingers. I hadn't played the guitar for five or six days, but the calluses on my fingers were still hard and tough. The Uncle who sold me the Gibson had also thrown in a free instruction booklet, but I had never learned how to play any regular songs. After learning most of the chords and how to tune and pick the strings, I had tossed the booklet away.

I only knew three songs, and they were tunes I had

made up myself, sitting around, picking them out until they sounded like the mental images I wanted them to resemble. One was 'Georgia Girl.' This was a portrait in sound of Mary Elizabeth, my fiancée. The second tune I had composed I called 'Empty Pockets.' My pockets had been empty many times in my life, and in making up this song I had discovered a way of getting a hollow sound effect by banging the box near the hole and playing a succession of fast triplets on the lower three strings at the same time. Despite the hollow sounds, this was a gay, fast tune and I was rather fond of it. The remaining song was merely my impression of an old patchwork quilt Grandma had made many years ago, and that's what I called it — 'Grandma's Quilt.' I had tried to duplicate the colors and designs of that old patchwork, faded quilt in chord patterns, and I had been fairly successful.

My repertoire, then, consisted of three highly personal songs. If it was music, it was reflective music made up for my own personal enjoyment, and not for the general public. But I had to get a few dollars together, and soon, and maybe my guitar was the way? I could have pawned the Gibson for twenty dollars or so, and this sum would pay a week's rent, but if I pawned the guitar, where would I be then?

I decided to take a chance and temporarily invade the world of music. As a last resort, when push came to shove, I could pawn the instrument. I removed my wristwatch, waited until the sweep hand hit twelve, picked up my guitar and played my three songs in succession all the way through. Time elapsed: seventeen minutes, fourteen seconds. Not a lot of time for a guitar concert, but I had nothing to lose by trying, and the songs were all different. Perhaps some bar owner would put me on for a few dollars in the evening.

I shucked out of my black cowboy shirt, which was getting dirty around the collar, even though it didn't show very much, and changed into a clean white shirt. I retied my red silk neckerchief, slipped into my corduroy suit and looked at myself in the dresser mirror. I looked clean and presentable. The red kerchief looked good with a white shirt and my gray-green corduroy suit. The cheap straw cowboy hat pushed back from my forehead was just the right touch for a would-be guitar player. I had burned my name into the yellow box of my guitar with a hot wire two years before, so all I had to do was write something simple on a piece of paper and get going.

I took a fresh sheet of paper out of my notebook, sat down at the desk and looked at it, trying to figure out a strong selling point for my slender abilities. At last it came to me, a simple straightforward statement of fact. In large capital letters I wrote JOB on the page, and put the slip of paper in my shirt pocket. If a prospective owner was interested in the word JOB he would give me an audition. If I got an audition, my guitar would have to talk for me.

I checked the little square felt-covered box inside the case, and there were plenty of extra plastic picks and two new strings wrapped in wax paper. As I started toward the door, carrying my guitar, I caught a glimpse of my grim, determined expression in the mirror. I almost laughed. I made an obscene gesture with my thumb at my grinning reflection and left the room.

The time was only ten thirty. There were dozens of bars, cabarets and beer-and-wine joints in Jacksonville, and I decided to cover them all, one by one, until I found a job.

I entered the first bar I came to down the street and handed the slip of paper to the bartender. He glanced at it, gave it back and pointed to the door.

At the bar on the next corner I tried a different tactic. I had learned a lesson in the first bar. Before presenting my slip of paper to the man in the white jacket, I made the sign of the tall one, and put change on the bar to pay for the beer. Beer is the easiest drink there is to order, whether you can talk or not. No matter how noisy a place is you can always get a bartender's attention by holding stiff hands out straight, the right hand approximately one foot above the left. This gesture will always produce a beer, draft if they have it, or a can of some brand if they do not.

'Sorry, buddy,' the bartender returned my slip of paper, 'but I don't have a music and dancing license. I couldn't hire you if I wanted to.'

I finished my glass of beer and returned to the sidewalk. A license for music and dancing had never occurred to me, but that simple requirement narrowed my search. I decided to become more selective. After bypassing several unlikely bars, and walking a half-dozen blocks, I came to a fairly nice-looking cabaret. There was a small blue winking neon sign in the window that stated Chez Vernon. The entrance-way was between a men's haberdashery and a closed movie theater. To the left of the bar entrance another door opened into the package store, which was also a part of the nightclub, and there was a sandwich board on the sidewalk announcing that the James Boys were featured inside every night except Sunday.

There were four eight-by-ten photos of the James Boys mounted on the board, and I studied them for a moment before I went inside. They wore their hair long, almost to the shoulder, but they had on Western-style clothes. They were evidently a country music group. In the smiling photos two of them had Spanish guitars like mine, one held an electric guitar and the remaining member peeped out from behind a bass. I entered the bar.

The bar was in a fairly narrow corridor — most of the space it should have had was crowded out by the partitioning for the package store — but there were approximately twenty-five stools, and a short service bar at the far end. Only one bartender was on duty, and there was only one customer sitting at the first stool. The customer sat with his arms locked behind his back glaring down distastefully at a double shot of whiskey. At night, with a fair-sized crowd, a bar this long would require at least two bartenders.

Beyond the bar there was a large square room with a small dance floor, a raised triangular platform in the corner for the musicians and two microphones. There were about thirty-five small circular tables, with twisted wire ice-cream parlor chairs stacked on top of them. The walls of the large room had been painted in navy blue. Silver cardboard stars had been pasted at random upon the wall and ceiling to simulate a night sky. The ceiling was black, and the scattered light fixtures on the ceiling were in various pastel colors.

Between the bar and the nightclub section there were two lavatories, with their doors recessed about a foot into the wall. A crude effort at humor had been attempted on the rest-room doors: One was labeled SETTERS and the other POINTERS. After sizing the place up, I sat down at the far end of the bar and made the sign of the tall one. As I reached for the stein with my left hand, I handed the bartender the slip of paper with my right.

'I only work here,' he said indifferently, eyeing my guitar. 'The James Boys are supposed to play out the month, but the boss is in the back.' He pointed to a curtain covering an arched doorway near the right corner of the bandstand. 'Go ahead and talk to him if you want to.' His face colored slightly as he realized I couldn't talk, but he smiled and shrugged his shoulders. 'His name is Mr. Vernon. Lee Vernon.'

As soon as I finished my beer, I picked up my guitar, dropped a half dollar on the bar and headed for the back, pushing the curtain to one side. The hallway was short. There was a door leading to an alley, and two doors on either side. I opened the first door on the right, but it was a small dressing room. I knocked at the door opposite the dressing room and didn't enter until I heard 'Come in.'

For a nightclub owner, Lee Vernon was a much younger man than I expected to meet. He was under thirty, with a mass of black curls, a smiling well-tanned face, and gleaming china-blue eyes. There were three open ledgers on his gray metal desk and a few thick Manila folders. He tapped his large white teeth with a pencil and raised his black eyebrows. I removed my guitar from the case before I handed him the slip of paper.

Lee Vernon laughed aloud when he saw the word JOB

and shook his head from side to side with genuine amusement. 'A nonsinging guitar player!' he exclaimed, still smiling. 'I never thought I'd see the day. Go ahead' — he looked at my name burned into the guitar box — 'Frank, is it?'

I nodded, and wiped my damp fingers on my jacket so the plastic pick wouldn't slip in my fingers. I put my left foot on a chair, and cradled the instrument over my knee.

'Play anything, Frank,' Vernon smiled. 'I don't care. I've never turned down an excuse to quit working in my life.'

I vamped a few chords and then played 'Empty Pockets' all the way through. Mr. Vernon listened attentively, tapping his pencil on the desk in time with the music. This was the shortest of my three songs, but it sounded good in the tiny office. The ceiling was low and there was a second listen effect reverberating in the room, especially during the thumping part.

'I like the sound, Frank,' Vernon said. 'You're all right. All right. But I don't think I can use you right now. I'm trying to build the Chez Vernon into a popular night spot, and the James Boys pretty well fill the bill. I pay them eight hundred a week and if I pay much more than that for music, I'll be working for them instead of myself. Do you belong to the union, Frank?'

I shook my head. The idea of any free American male paying gangsters money for the right to work has always struck me as one of the most proposterous customs we have.

'Tell you what,' Vernon said reflectively. 'Do you really need a job?'

I nodded seriously.

'Okay, then. The James Boys play a forty-minute set, and then they take a twenty-minute break. They play from nine till midnight, an extra hour if the crowd warrants it, and till two a.m. on Saturday nights. In my opinion, a twenty-minute break is too long, and I lose customers sometimes just because of it, but those were the terms I hired them under. If you want to sit in by yourself on the stand to fill the breaks I'm willing to try it for a few nights to see how it goes. I can give you ten bucks a night, but that's the limit.'

For a few moments I thought about it, but ten dollars was too much money to give me when I only knew three songs. I held up five fingers.

'You want fifty dollars?' Vernon asked incredulously.

I shook my head and snapped out five fingers.

'You're a pretty weird cat.' Vernon laughed. 'Not only do you not sing, you're honest. Five bucks a night it is, Frank. But I'll tell Dick James to clean out his kitty between his sets, and any tips you get on the breaks belong to you. You'll pick up a few extra bucks, anyway.'

I nodded, shook hands with my employer and returned my guitar to its case.

'Come in about eight thirty, Frank,' Vernon concluded the interview, 'and I'll introduce you to the James Boys.'

I returned to the hotel and stretched out on my bed for a nap. Although I had taken a lower figure than the ten he offered, I still felt a little uneasy. After Lee Vernon heard me playing the same songs all evening he wouldn't be too happy about it. But during the days, maybe I could make up a few more. If so, I could ask for a raise to ten. The immediate problem was remedied. I could pay my room rent of three dollars a day, and eat on the other two until I could work my way out of the hole with an ingenious plan of some kind.

A few minutes later I was asleep.

Chapter Seven

The James Boys were very good. If Lee Vernon was paying them eight hundred dollars a week, they were worth every cent of it.

I sat at the end of the bar where I could take in the entire room, enjoying the music and the singing, and the antics of the patrons at various tables. Not many of the couples danced. It wasn't the smallness of the floor that prevented them from getting to their feet, it was just that the James Boys were more amusing to watch than they were to dance to. They wore red Western shirts with white piping on the collars and cuffs, but they didn't restrict their playing to Western music. They seemed to be equally at home with calypso and rock 'n' roll. Each of the boys, in turn, sang into the microphone, and they all had good voices.

Dick James was at the microphone, and his face had a mournful expression. He said, 'It is now my sad duty to inform you, ladies and gentlemen, that for the next twenty minutes we will be absent from the stand.'

He held up a hand to silence the murmurs of disappointment. 'We don't want to go. Honest! It's just that we can't afford to drink here. We have to go down the street to a little place where the drinks are cheaper. And I might add,' he said disingenuously, 'unwatered!'

A very small ripple of laughter went through the room. Perhaps the patrons of the Chez Vernon thought their drinks were watered.

'But during our brief absence, the management has obtained for your listening pleasure, at *great* expense, one of the world's greatest guitarists! Ladies and gentlemen, I give you Frank Mansfield!'

I had been so engrossed in watching and listening, and drinking a steady procession of beers, I hadn't realized how quickly the time had passed. To a burst of enthusiastic applause, led by the four James Boys, I threaded my way through the close-packed tables to the stand. As I sat down in a chair on the stand and removed my guitar from its case, Dick James lowered the microphone level with my waist.

'Good luck, Frank,' he said, and followed the other members of the group into the hallway leading to the dressing room. I was in shirt sleeves, but wore my hat. I wished that I could have gone with them, picked up my coat in the dressing room, and made a getaway through the back door to the alley. In anticipation of fresh entertainment, the audience was fairly quiet. I felt like every eye was on me as I sat under the baby spot on the small, triangular stand.

I delayed as long as I could, well aware that I had twenty full minutes to fill before the James Boys returned, and not enough music to fill it with. I vamped a few chords, tuned the 'A' string a trifle higher, and then played 'Empty Pockets.' The moment I hit the last chord, I got to my feet and bowed from the waist to the thin, sporadic applause. Before playing 'Grandma's Quilt,' I went through the motions of tuning again, and slowed the tempo of the song as I picked through it. The applause was stronger when I finished. By this time the crowd realized that my music was unusual, or, at least, different. My last number was the best, my favorite, and my nervousness had disappeared completely. There was hardly a sound from the audience as I played 'Georgia Girl,' but when I finished and stood up to take a bow, the applause was definitely generous.

'I could take lessons from you,' Dick James said, as he climbed onto the stand. 'You make some mighty fine sounds, Frankerino.'

I nodded, smiled and wet my lips. The James Boys were also unaware that my repertoire only consisted of three homemade numbers. Lee Vernon, a tall drink in his hand, crossed the room and congratulated me. He whispered something to Dick, and readjusted the microphone. I had returned my guitar to the case and was halfway to the bar when Vernon's voice rasped out of the speakers in the ceiling.

'Ladies and gentlemen, there's something you don't know about Frank Mansfield!' His voice stopped me, and I looked down at the floor. 'In view of his great manual dexterity, it may be difficult to believe, but Frank Mansfield is the only deaf-and-dumb guitar player in the world! Let's give Frank another big hand? Let him feel the vibrations through the floor!'

As the drunken crowd applaused wildly and stomped their feet on the floor, I ran across the room, pushed aside the curtain to the hallway, and rushed blindly into the dressing room. I supposed Lee Vernon meant well, but I was angered by his announcement. Not only did I want to quit, I wanted to punch him in the nose. In view of his stupid announcement, he would be damned well embarrassed when I played the same three songs forty minutes later.

There was an open bottle of bourbon on the dressing table. I hit it a couple of times and smoked five cigarettes before my next appearance on the stand. Tiny James, the bass player, came and got me.

'You're on, Mansfield.' He jerked his thumb. 'Dick's announced you already.'

I returned to the stand and got out my guitar. The room had twice as many patrons and the air was blue with smoke. Vernon's announcement had created a morbid interest. The bar crowd had pushed their way in and standees blocked the way to the service bar. The moment I picked up my instrument and strummed a few riplets, there were shushing sounds from the tables and the room was silent.

Indifferently, expertly, I played through my three numbers without pause. The applause was generous. I put the guitar back in the case and made my exit to the dressing room. When the door closed on the last James Boy I took a pull out of the open bottle of whiskey. Lee Vernon entered the room. His face was flushed and he was laughing. He held out a hand for the bottle and, when I handed it to him, freshened the drink in his left hand.

Watching him sullenly, I took another drink out of the bottle. Vernon let loose with a wild peal of happy laughter.

'Those are the only three songs you know, aren't they?' he said.

I grinned and took another short drink.

'That's wonderful, Frank,' he said sincerely. 'Really wonderful!' He smiled broadly, showing his big white teeth. 'Did you make them up yourself?'

I nodded.

A frown creased Vernon's flushed face, and he placed his glass down carefully on the narrow ledge in front of the mirror. He's going to fire me, I thought. The moment I put the five-dollar bill in my pocket I'm going to knock his teeth out.

'I think that's terrific, Frank. I really do. Any fool can take a few lessons and play ordinary songs on a guitar. Hell, I can play a little bit myself, and if I sing while I'm playing, I can drown out the mistakes I make. But you ...' He shook his head comically. 'To deliberately master the damned guitar the way you have and compose your own songs — well, I can only admire you for it.' He picked up his glass and raised it. 'To Frank Mansfield! You've got a job at the Chez Vernon for as long as you want to keep it!'

He drained his glass and opened the door. His shoulder hit the side of the door as he left, and he staggered slightly as he walked down the hall.

I closed the door and sat down, facing the back of the chair. If a man accepts life logically, the unexpected is actually the expected. I should have known he wouldn't fire me. A nightclub owner, by the fact that he is a nightclub owner, must necessarily accept things as they are. Vernon had accepted the situation cheerfully, like a peacetime soldier who finds himself suddenly in a war. There was nothing else he could do.

I had wanted to quit, but now I was unable to quit. I was in an untenable position. I had only one alternative. Every time I played my twenty-minute stint, I would have to improvise something new. If I couldn't do it, I would have to walk away and not even stop to collect the five dollars I had coming to me. It was unfair to keep playing the same three songs over and over.

I took another drink, a short one this time. I was beginning to feel the effects of the whiskey on top of the beers I had had earlier. I made my decision. When my turn came to play again I would improvise music and play something truly wonderful.

After Dick James announced me, I sat quietly in my chair, the guitar across my lap, a multicolored pick gripped loosely between my right thumb and forefinger. The room was filled to capacity. Under the weak, colored ceiling lights I could make out most of the faces nearest the stand. There was a hint of nervous expectancy in the room. Here is a freak, their silence said, a talented, deaf-and-dumb freak who plays music he cannot hear, who plays for applause he can only feel. This was the atmosphere of the Chez Vernon, caused in part by Lee Vernon's earlier announcement, and by my last session on the stand when the listeners had heard a different kind of music. Vernon sat at a table close to the platform, his face flushed with liquor, a knowing smile on his lips. On his left was a young man with long blond hair, dressed in a red silk dinner jacket, white ruffled shirt, and plaid bow tie. On Vernon's right, a tall pink drink before her, was a woman in a low-cut Kelly green evening gown. She was in her early forties, but she was the type who could pass easily for thirty-nine for a few more years.

Her lips were wet and shiny, and her dark eyes were bright with excitement as I caught them with mine and held them. She nodded politely, put long tapering fingers to her coal black hair. The woman and the young man at Vernon's table stood out from the crowd. Most of the patrons were wearing short-sleeved sport shirts. Only the younger men with dates wore coats and ties. Lee Vernon raised his glass and winked at me.

The microphone was less than a foot away from my guitar. I tapped the pick on the box. The sound, amplified by six speakers, sounded like knocking on a wooden door. Scratching the wooden box of the Gibson produced a sound like the dry rasping of locusts. The locusts reminded me of the long summer evenings in Mansfield, Georgia, and I thought about the bright silvery moths circling the lamp on the corner, down the street from Grandma's house.

I played their sound, picking them up and flying and flickering with them about the streetlight, teasing them on the 'E' string.

Down the block, swinging to and fro on a lacy, metal porch swing, the chains creaking, complaining, a woman laughed, the joyful, contented laughter of a well-bred Southern woman, a mother perhaps, with two young children, a boy and a girl, and the little boy said something that amused her and she laughed and repeated what the child said to her husband sitting beside her.

I played that.

And I repeated the solid rumbling laugh of her husband, which complemented her own laughter, and then my fingers moved away from them, up the staff to pick out the solid swishing whispering smack of a lawn sprinkler and a man's tuneless humming a block away. And there came a boy in knickers down the sidewalk, walking and then running, dancing with awkward feet to avoid stepping on a crack, which would *surely* break his mother's back! He bent down and picked up a stick and scampered past a white picket fence, the stick bumping, rattling, drowning out a man's lecture to a teenage girl on the porch of that old white house two doors down from the corner, the house with the four white columns.

And I played these things, and

then the sounds of supper and the noises, the fine good clatter in the kitchen when Grandma was still alive, and

Randall and I sent to wash up before dinner in the dark downstairs bathroom where the sound of water in the pipes made the whiney, sharp, unbearable spine-tingling noise and kept it up until the other tap was turned on and modulated it, turning the groaning into the surreptitious scraping of a boy's finger on a blackboard, and sure enough, we had the schoolteacher for dinner that night and she was talking with Mother, monotonously, like always, and I hated her, and the dry, flat registers of her authoritative voice would put you to sleep in the middle of a lesson if you didn't keep pinching yourself, and Daddy pulled out his watch with the loud ticks and it was supper-time, the solid ring of the good sterling silver, the tingle-tinkle of the fine crystal that pinged with a fingernail and listen to the echo! and the rich dark laughter of Aimee, our Negro cook in the kitchen, and after supper I was allowed to go to the movie but Randall wasn't because he was three years younger and had to go to bed

so I played these things and

what a wonderful movie it was! Young Dick Powell, handsome, in his West Point uniform, and the solid ranks of straight tall men marching in the parade and only vaguely did the old songs filter through the story, *Flirta-tion Walk*, and the lovely girl under the Kissing Rock, and then the movie was over but I stayed to see it again, and repeated it very quickly because nothing is ever any good the second time and I was late, it was dark, and I was running down the black narrow streets, the crickets silenced ahead of my slapping feet, and the grim and heavy shadows of the great old pecan trees on our black, forbidding block. As I reached our yard, safe at last from whatever it was that chased me, Mother was on the front porch waiting with a switch in her hand, and she intended to use it, I know, but I began to cry and a moment later she pulled me in close to her warm, wonderful, never changing smell of powder, spicy lilac and cedar and sweet, sweet lips kissing me and chiding and kissing and scolding and

damned if the 'G' string didn't break.

The pick fell from my fingers and I looked numbly at the guitar. The room was as silent as death. A moment later, like an exploding dam, the room rocked with the sound of slapping hands and stomping feet. I fled into the dressing room with the guitar still clutched by the neck in my left hand. The James Boys, who had been listening by the arched, curtained doorway to the hall, followed me into the small room, and Dick handed me the bottle.

'I'll be a sonofabitch, Frank,' he said warmly. 'I never heard finer guitar in my life. You can be a James Boy anytime you want. Go ahead, take another snort!'

I sat down, lit a cigarette and studied my trembling fingers. My throat was dry and tight and for the first time in my life and I felt lonely, really lonely, and I didn't know why. I had buried all those memories for so many years, it was frightening to know that they were still in my head.

The James Boys returned to the stand, leaving the door open, and I could hear the heated strings of their first number, 'The Big D Rock.'

'Mr. Mansfield —' I looked up at the sound of Lee Vernon's voice, and got to my feet quickly as he ushered in ahead of him the young man and the woman who had been sitting at this table out front. 'I want to introduce you to Mrs. Bernice Hungerford and Tommy Hungerford.' He turned and smiled at the woman. 'Mr. Frank Mansfield.'

'Tommy is my nephew,' Bernice Hungerford said quickly, holding out her hand. I shook it briefly, and then shook hands with her nephew. His expression was studiedly bored, but he was slightly nervous.

Mrs. Hungerford was a truly striking woman, now that I could see her under the bright lights of the dressing room. A white cashmere stole was draped over her left arm, and she clutched a gold-mesh evening bag in her left hand. Her burnt sienna eyes never left my face. I was amused by the scattering of freckles on her straight nose. The freckles on her face and bare shoulders belied her age sure enough.

With a straight face, Vernon said: 'Mrs. Hungerford was very impressed by your concert, Mr. Mansfield. When I told her that you had studied under Segovia in Seville for ten years, she said she could tell that you had by your intricate fretwork.'

Bernice Hungerford bobbed her head up and down delightedly and shook a teasing forefinger at me. 'And I recognized the tone poem, too.' She winked and flashed a bright smile. Her teeth were small, but remarkably well matched and white. 'You see, Mr. Mansfield,' she continued, 'I know a few things about music. When I hear Bach, it doesn't make any difference if it's piano or guitar, I can recognize the style. That's what I told Mr. Vernon, didn't I, Lee?' The woman turned to the implacable Lee Vernon who was covering his drunkenness masterfully. Only the stiffness of his back gave him away.

'You certainly did, Bernice. But I had to tell her, Mr. Mansfield. She thought you were playing a Bach fugue, but it was a natural mistake. She didn't know that it was a special Albert Schweitzer composition written on a theme of Bach's. Quite a natural mistake, indeed.'

'If we don't get back to your guests, their throats will be dreadfully parched, Auntie dear,' Tommy said lazily. 'We've been gone, you know, for the better part of an hour, and that's a long time just to refurbish the liquor supply.' The careless elisions of his voice were practiced, it seemed to me.

'But if we take Mr. Mansfield back with us, we'll be forgiven.' Mrs. Hungerford patted her nephew's arm.

'I don't want to hold you up any longer, Mrs. Hungerford,' Vernon said. 'Why don't you and Tommy wait in the package store. Your liquor is ready, and I'll do my best to bring Mr. Mansfield along in a minute. All right?'

'But you will persuade him, won't you?' Mrs. Hungerford said.

'I'll certainly try,' he replied cheerfully.

As soon as they had gone, Vernon closed the door, leaned against it and buried his face in his arms. His shoulders shook convulsively, and for a moment I thought he was crying. Then he let out a whoop of laughter, turned away from the door and sat down. Recovering, he wiped his streaming eyes with a forefinger and said, 'I'm sorry,

Frank, but the gag was too good to resist. When she started that talk about Bach and Segovia at the table, I had to go her one better. But it's a break for you. She has a few guests at her house, and only stopped by here to pick up some Scotch. I told her that she mustn't miss your performance, and when you came out with that tricky, weird chording and impressed her so much, I thought it might be a break for you. Anyway, the upshot is that she wants you to go home with her and play for her guests. Should be worth a twenty-dollar bill to you, at least.'

I shrugged into my corduroy jacket. All through the talk about Bach and Segovia I had thought they were attempting some kind of joke at my expense, but apparently Mrs. Hungerford actually believed I had studied under the old guitarist. Vernon had gone along with the gag, which was a break for me, although I detested the condescending sonofabitch. If she wanted to pay me twenty dollars I would accept it, play my three songs, and then get out of her house. I had already made up my mind not to return to the Chez Vernon. A final concert for a group of rich people who could afford to pay for it and wouldn't miss the money would be a fitting end to my short, unhappy musical career.

'By the way, Frank,' Vernon said, as soon as I was ready to go, 'don't get the idea that I was trying to make fun of you by falling in with the gag. If I'd been strictly sober, I might have set her straight, but basically I poured it on so you could pick up a few extra bucks. No hard feelings?'

I ignored the outstretched hand, and brushed by him, carrying my instrument. Vernon followed me out into the club. As I stopped at the stand, to put the guitar in the case, be handed me a ten-dollar bill.

'Hell, don't be sore about it, Frank.'

There was a black silhouette cutout of a plyboard cat at the end of the stand. I wadded the bill in my fist and shoved it into the open mouth of the kitty before crossing the dance floor and entering the inside door to the package store. If Lee Vernon had followed me into the package store, I would have knocked his teeth out, even if he was drunk. Although I wasn't the butt of the joke, I didn't like to be patronized by a man I considered an inferior. But Vernon was wise enough not to come outside, and I've never seen him since.

Tommy drove the Olds and Mrs. Hungerford sat between us on the wide front seat. With the guitar case between my legs, my left leg was tight against her right leg, and I could feel the warmth of her body through my corduroy trousers.

'This isn't exactly a party, Mr. Mansfield,' she explained, as we drove through the light traffic of the after-midnight streets. 'We all attended the Jacksonville Little Theater to see *Liliom*, and I invited the bunch home for a cold supper and a few drinks. It was a real *faux pas* on my part. There's plenty of food, but I didn't realize I was out of Scotch. But bringing you home to play will more than make up for my oversight, I'm sure. Don't you think so, Tommy?'

'If they're still there,' he observed dryly.

'Don't worry,' Mrs. Hungerford laughed pleasantly, 'I know my brother!' She turned toward me and put her hand lightly on my knee. 'There are only two couples, Mr. Mansfield. Tommy's father and mother, and Dr. Luke McGuire and his wife. Not a very large audience, I'm afraid, after what you're accustomed to, is it?'

In reply, I spat out the window.

'But I know you'll find them appreciative of good music.'

A few minutes later we turned into a driveway guarded by two small concrete lions. Tommy parked behind a Buick on the semicircular gravel road that led back to the street. The two-story house was of red brick. Four fluted wooden columns supported a widow's walk directly above the wide, aluminium-screened front porch. The lawn slanted gradually to the street for almost a hundred yards, broken here and there with newly planted coconut palms. The feathery tips of the young trees rattled in the wind. She was wasting money and effort attempting to grow coconut trees as far north as Jax. The subtropics start at Daytona Beach, much farther downstate.

Mrs. Hungerford rushed ahead of us after we got out of the car. Tommy, carrying two sacked fifths of Scotch under his left arm and a six-pack of soda in his right hand, hurried after her. As I climbed the porch steps, Mrs. Hungerford switched on the overhead lights and opened the front doors. She held a finger to her lips, as she beckoned me into the foyer with her free hand.

'Now, you stay right here in the foyer,' Mrs. Hungerford whispered excitedly, 'so I can surprise them!'

Closing the front door softly, she followed her nephew into the living room. The voices greeting them contained a mixture of concern over the prolonged absence, and happiness at the prospect of a drink. Above the sound of their conversation, the clipped electronic voice of a newscaster rattled through his daily report of the late news.

The foyer was carpeted in a soft shade of rose nylon. The same carpeting climbed the stairway to the walnut-balustraded second floor. A giant split-leaved philodendron sat in a white pot behind the door. There was a spindly-legged, leather-covered table beneath a gilded wall mirror, and a brass dish on the table held about thirty calling cards. Out of long-forgotten habit I felt a few of the cards to see if they were engraved. They were. I turned my attention to a marble cherub mounted on a square ebony base. It was about three feet high, and the well-weathered cherub looked shyly with its dugout eyes through widespread stubby fingers. A lifted, twisted right knee hid its sex, and three fingers of the left hand were missing. I removed my cowboy hat and hung it on the thumb of the mutilated hand.

The bored announcer was clicked off in midsentence, and Mrs. Hungerford came after me a moment later.

'They're all tickled to death, Mr. Mansfield,' she said happily. 'Come on, they want to meet you!'

In one corner of the large living room, Tommy was engaged behind a small bar. Two middle-aged men got out of their chairs and crossed the room to greet me. Dr.

McGuire was a thick-set man without a neck, and his gray hair was badly in need of cutting. Mr. Hungerford, Sr., Tommy's father, was an older edition of his blond son, except that he no longer had his hair and the top of his head was bronzed by the Florida sun. Both of the men wore white dinner jackets and midnight blue tuxedo trousers. I acknowledged the introductions by nodding my head and shaking hands. The two wives remained seated on a long, curving white sofa, and didn't offer their hands to be shaken.

'I know you're all eager to hear Mr. Mansfield play,' Bernice announced to the room at large, 'but you'll have to wait until he has a drink first.'

Welcome news. After dropping my guitar case on the sofa I headed for the bar.

'There's plenty of gin if you don't want Scotch,' Tommy suggested.

I poured two ounces of Scotch into a tall glass in reply, and added ice cubes and soda. An uneasy silence settled over the room as I hooked my elbows over the bar and faced the group. Bernice, or Tommy, one, had evidently informed them about my inability to talk, and they were disturbed by my silence. The two matrons, bulging in strapless evening gowns, had difficulty in averting their eyes from my face. I doubt if they meant to be rude, but they couldn't keep from staring at me. Dr. McGuire, standing with his back to the fireplace, lit a cigar and studied the tip through his bifocals. Only Bernice was at ease, sitting comfortably on the long bench in front of the baby grand piano, apparently unaware of her guests' discomfort. Mr. Hungerford, Sr., cleared his throat and set his glass down on a low coffee table.

'Bernice tells us you studied under Segovia, Mr. Mansfield,' he said.

'Yes,' Bernice replied for me. 'That's what Mr. Vernon told us, didn't he, Tommy?'

'That's right. And he played a beautiful thing written by Dr. Albert Schweitzer. I hope he'll play it again for us.'

'African rock 'n' roll, I suppose,' Dr. McGuire chuckled

from the fireplace. 'That would be a treat!' When no one joined him in his laughter, he said quickly, 'We're very grateful you came out to play for us, Mr. Mansfield.'

I finished my drink lifted my eyebrows for Tommy Hungerford to mix me another. I took my guitar out of the case, and started to restring it with another 'G' string to replace the broken one. While I restrung the guitar, Mrs. Hungerford asked her brother and the doctor to move chairs into the center of the room and form a line. She then had her guests sit in the rearranged chairs facing me, as I stood with one foot on the piano bench. Tommy Hungerford, smiling at the new seating arrangements, remained standing at the bar. I plucked and tightened the new string, and Bernice hit the 'G' on the piano for me until I had the guitar in tune. Satisfied, I put the guitar on the bench and returned to the bar for my fresh drink. The small audience waited patiently, but Dr. McGuire glowered when Tommy insisted that I have another before I began. I shook my head, picked up my guitar and played through my three-song repertoire without pause.

The moment I hit the last chord I smiled, bowed from the waist and put the guitar back in the case. Bernice Hungerford, who had hovered anxiously behind the row of chairs during my short concert, led the applause.

'Is that all he's going to play, Bernice?' the doctor asked. 'I'd like to hear more.'

'I think we all would,' his fat wife echoed.

I shrugged, and joined Tommy at the bar for another drink.

'No, that's enough,' Bernice said. 'Mr. Mansfield has been playing all evening and he's tired. We shouldn't coax him. The concert is all over. Go on home. You've been fed, you've had your drinks, now go on home.'

Bernice herded the two wives out of the room to get their wraps, and their husbands joined Tommy and me at the bar for a nightcap.

'You play very well, young man,' Dr. McGuire said. 'Did you ever play on television?'

I shook my head, and added Scotch to my glass to cut the soda.

'I think you should consider television, don't you, Tommy?'

'Not really, sir,' Tommy wrinkled his brow. 'I'm not so sure that the mass audience is ready for classical guitar music. I'm trying to recall, but I can't remember ever hearing or seeing a string quartet on television. If I did, I can't remember it.'

'By God, I haven't either!' the doctor said strongly. 'And certainly the string quartet is the most civilized entertainment in the world! Don't you agree, Mr. Mansfield?'

I shrugged my shoulders inside my jacket, and lit a cigarette.

He didn't want a reply, anyway. 'But there's a definite need for serious music on TV,' he continued. 'And, by God, the public should be forced to listen! No matter how stupid people are today, they can be taught to appreciate good music.' He banged his fist on the bar.

The two middle-aged men drained their glasses quickly as Bernice came into the room, and turned to join their wives in the foyer. Bernice crossed the room, and placed a hand on my arm. So far, she had never missed a chance to touch me.

'Mrs. McGuire would like to know if you'd consent to play for her guests next Saturday night. She's giving a party, quite a large one, and she's willing to —'

I shook my head, and crushed out my cigarette in a white Cinzano ashtray.

'It's "no", then?'

I nodded. She smiled, turned away and returned to the foyer to say good night to her guests and break the news to Mrs. McGuire.

'Tell me something, Mr. Mansfield,' Tommy said hesitantly. 'Did you really study under Segovia?'

I grinned, and shook my head. After setting my glass down, I picked up my guitar case. Tommy laughed, throwing his head back.

'I didn't think you did, but I'll keep your secret till the day I die.'

Bernice Hungerford returned with a smile brightening

her jolly face. I didn't know why, but I was attracted to this graceful, pleasant woman. She appeared to be so happy, so eager to please, and yet, there were tiny, tragic lines tugging at the corners of her full lips.

'I'll drive Mr. Mansfield back into town, Auntie,' Tommy said.

'Oh, no you won't!' Bernice said cheerfully. She took the guitar case out of my hand and placed it on the couch. 'I'll drive him back myself. You can just run along, Tommy. I'm going to fix Mr. Mansfield something to eat — you could eat something, couldn't you?'

I shrugged, then smiled. She hadn't paid the twenty dollars yet, and I could always eat something. The cold buffet supper, however, didn't appeal to me. There were several choices of lunch meat, cold pork, three different cheese dips and pickles. I looked distastefully at the buffet table.

'Now, don't you worry,' Bernice said, patting my arm with her small, white hand. 'I won't make you eat the remains of the cold supper. I'll fix you some ham and eggs.'

'Me, too, Auntie dear?' Tommy grinned.

'No, not you. Don't you have a job of some kind to report to in the morning?'

Tommy groaned. 'Don't remind me. Well, good night, Mr. Mansfield.' He shook hands with me, brushed his lips against his aunt's cheek and made his departure from the room. A few moments later the lights of his Olds flashed on the picture window as he made the semicircle to the street.

Now that we were alone in the big house, Bernice's composure suddenly disappeared. She blushed furiously under my level stare, and then took my hand. 'Come on,' she said brightly. 'You can keep me company in the kitchen while I cook for you.'

I followed her into the kitchen, and sat down at a small dinette table covered with a blue-and-white tablecloth. There were louvred windows on all three sides of the small dining alcove, but the kitchen itself, like those of most depression-built homes, was a large one. The cooking facilities were up to date, however. In addition to a new yellow enameled electric stove, there was a built-in oven with a glass door, and a row of complicated-looking knobs beneath it.

'There's coffee left, but its been sitting on the warm burner so long it's probably bitter by now. I'd better make fresh coffee, if you don't mind waiting awhile, but by that time I'll have the other things ready. I think that coffee setting too long gets bitter, don't you? I've got some mashed potatoes left over from dinner, and I'll make some nice patties to go with your ham.'

Bernice kept a running patter of meaningless small talk going as she cooked, and I listened thoughtfully and smoked, watching her deft, efficient movements from my chair. She had tied a frilly, ruffled white apron about her waist, and it looked out of whack with her Kelly green evening gown. She kept talking about pleasant things to eat, and I got hungrier by the second.

She wanted to please me, even though she didn't now why. She knew she was a good cook, and by cooking a decent meal for me, she knew I would be pleased. If I was pleased with her, I'd take her to bed. These thoughts probably never entered her conscious mind, but I sensed this, and knew instinctively that she was mine if I wanted her. As she chattered away, gaily, cheerfully, I learned that I did want her, very much so. She was a damned attractive woman, a little heavy in the thighs, perhaps, but I didn't consider that a detriment. I like women a little on the fleshy side. Skinny, boyish-type figures may be admired by other women, but not by most men.

I smiled appreciatively, showing my teeth, when she set the huge platter before me. The aroma of the fried ham steak, four fried eggs, and fluffy potato pancakes all blended beautifully as they entered my nose. Bernice poured two steaming cups of fresh coffee and sat down across from me to watch me eat, her face flushed from recent exertion and pleasure as I stowed the food away.

'I should have made biscuits,' she said, 'but I could tell

you were too hungry to wait, so I made the toast instead. Would you like some guava jelly for your toast?' She started to get up, but I shook my head violently, and she remained seated.

A minute later she smiled. 'I like to see a man eat,' she said sincerely.

I've heard a lot of women make that trite remark: Grandma, Mother, when she was still alive, and a good many others. I believe women really do like to see men eat, especially when they're fond of the man concerned, and he's eating food they have prepared for him. I have never denied any woman the dubious pleasure of watching me eat. Outside of taking care of a man's needs, women don't get very much pleasure out of life anyway.

When I finished eating everything in sight, I pushed the empty platter to one side, and wiped my mouth with a square of white damask napkin. Smiling over the lip of her cup, Bernice nodded with satisfaction. I winked slowly, returned her smile, and she blushed and lowered her eyes.

'My husband's been dead for five years, Mr. Mansfield,' she said shyly. 'You don't know how nice it is to cook a meal for a man again. I'd almost forgotten myself. I loved my husband very much, and still do, I suppose. My brother's always telling me how foolish I am to keep this big house and live here all alone. An apartment would be easier to keep, I know, and give me more free time, but I don't know what I'd do with more free time if I had it. I don't know what to do with myself half the time as it is.

'This old house has a lot of pleasant memories for me, and I'd miss them if I ever sold it. I can see my husband in every room. Sometimes, during the day, I pretend he isn't dead at all. He's at the office, that's where he is, working, and when six o'clock comes he'll be coming home through the front door like always, and ...' Her voice trailed away, and two tears escaped into her long black eyelashes.

Bernice wiped them away, tossed her head impatiently and laughed.

'Morbid, aren't I? How about some more coffee?'

I nodded, took my cigarettes out of my shirt pocket,

and offered them to her. She put the cork tip in her mouth, and when I flipped my lighter, she held my hand with both of hers to get a light. This was unnecessary. My hand was perfectly steady. After refilling the cups she sat down again and described circles on the tablecloth with a long red fingernail.

'I know that you want to go, Mr. Mansfield,' she said at last, 'but I'm finding this a novel experience. It's a rare instance when a woman can pour her troubles into a man's receptive ear without being told to shut up!' She laughed, and shrugged comically.

'But I really don't have any troubles. As far as money goes, I'm fixed forever. My husband saw to that, God bless him. I own the house, and my trust fund is well guarded by the bank trustees. And I have a circle of friends I've known most of my adult life. So where are my troubles?' She sighed audibly and licked her lips with the point of her tongue like a cat.

'I should be the happiest woman in the world. But once in a while, just once in a while, mind you, Mr. Mansfield, I'd like to go into my bathroom and find the toilet seat up instead of down!' Color flooded into her face, and the freckles almost disappeared. She got up from the table hastily and pushed open the swinging door leading to the living room. 'I'll get your money for you, Mr. Mansfield.'

She had aroused my sympathy. I wondered what her husband had been like. An insurance executive probably. Every time he had gotten a promotion he had used the extra money for more protection, more insurance. It must have cost her plenty to keep up this big house. And it was a cinch she didn't have any children, or she would have talked about them instead of a man five years dead. If I could have talked, I would have been able to kid her out of her mood in no time. My sex life had really suffered since I gave up talking. Not completely, because money always talks when words fail, but a lot of women had gotten away during the last couple of years because of my stubborn vow of silence.

As I pondered the situation, how best to handle it, Bernice returned to the kitchen. She placed a fifty-dollar bill on the table. The fifty ruined everything for me.

I could have accepted a twenty, because Lee Vernon had set the fee, but I couldn't, with good conscience, accept *fifty* dollars. My concert wasn't worth that much. I knew it, and Bernice Hungerford knew it. She was trying to buy me and I resented it. I folded the bill into a small square, placed it on the edge of the table and flipped it to the floor with my forefinger. I got up from the table and left the room.

I picked up my guitar in the living room and had almost reached the foyer when Bernice caught up with me. She tugged on my arm, and when I stopped, got in front of me, looking up wistfully into my face. My jaws were tight and I looked over her head at the door.

'Please!' she said, stuffing the folded bill into my shirt pocket. 'I know what you're thinking, but it isn't true! The only reason I gave you a fifty was because I didn't have a twenty. I thought I had one, but I didn't. Please take it!'

I dropped my eyes to her face, looked at her steadily, and she turned away from me.

'All right. So I lied. Take it anyway. Fifty dollars doesn't mean anything to me. I'm sorry and I'm ashamed. And if you want to know the truth I'm more ashamed than sorry!'

I retrieved my hat from the marble angel's thumb and put it on my head. But I didn't leave. I reconsidered. Damn it all anyway, the woman was desirable! I removed my hat, replaced it on the angel's thumb and dropped my guitar case to the carpeted floor. Bernice had started up the stairs, but I caught up with her on the third step, lifted her into my arms and continued up the stairs. She buried her face in my neck and stifled a sob, clinging to me with both arms like a child. As I climbed I staggered beneath her weight — she must have weighed a solid one hundred and forty-five pounds — but I didn't drop her. When I reached the balcony I was puffing with my mouth open to regain my wind.

Bernice whispered softly into my ear, 'The bedroom's the first door on the right.'

The first time was for me. As nervous as Bernice was, at least at first, it could hardly have gone any other way. But I was gentle with her, and providing me with satisfaction apparently gave her the reassurance she needed. There was none of that foolishness about wanting to turn off the bedside lamps, for example, and when she returned from the bathroom, she still had her clothes off.

I had propped myself up on both pillows, and I smoked and watched her as she poured two small snifters of brandy. The cut-glass decanter was on a side table, beside a comfortable wing chair. It was unusual, I thought to keep a decanter of cognac in a bedroom, but having a drink afterward was probably a postcoital ritual that she and her late husband had practiced.

Although Bernice was a trifle on the chunky side, she had a good figure. Her heavy breasts had prolapsed slightly, but the prominent nipples were as pink as a roseate spoonbill. Her slim waist emphasized the beautiful swelling lines of her full hips, and her skin, except for a scattering of freckles on her shoulders, was as white as a peeled almond. With her thick black hair unloosened, and trailing down her back, Bernice was a very beautiful woman. To top it off, she had a sense of style. I wanted to talk to her so badly I could almost taste the words in my mouth, and it was all I could do to hold back the torrent that would become a flood if I ever let them go.

After Bernice handed me my glass, she sat cross-legged on the bed, facing me, swirling her brandy in the snifter she held with cupped hands. Her face was flushed slightly with excitement. She peered intently into her brandy glass, refusing to meet my level stare.

'I want to tell you something, Frank,' she said in a soft contralto, 'something important. I'm *not* promiscuous.'

She said this so primly I wanted to laugh. Instead, I grinned, wet a forefinger in my brandy and rubbed the nipple of her right breast.

'And no matter what you may think, you're the first man I've let make love to me since my husband died.'

I didn't believe her, of course, not for an instant. But that is the way women are. They always feel that a man will think less of them if they act like human beings. What did it matter to me whether she had slept with anyone or not for the last five years? What possible difference could it make at this moment? Now was now, and the past and the future were unimportant.

As the nipple gradually hardened beneath my circling finger she laughed, an abrupt, angry little laugh, and tossed off the remainder of her brandy. I took her glass, put both of them aside, pulled her down beside me, and kissed her.

The second time was better and lasted much longer. Although I was handicapped by being unable to issue instructions, Bernice was experienced, cooperative and so eager to please me that she anticipated practically everything I wanted to do. And at last, when I didn't believe I could hold out for another moment, she climaxed. I remained on my back, with Bernice on top of me, and she nibbled on my shoulder.

'I could fall in love with you, Frank Mansfield,' she said softly. 'If there were only some way I could prove it to you!'

Suddenly she got out of bed, grabbed my undershirt and shorts from the winged chair, and entered the bathroom. I raised myself on my elbows, and watched her through the open door as she washed my underwear in the washbowl. She hummed happily as she scrubbed away. My underwear wasn't dirty. I had put it on clean after a shower at the hotel before reporting in at the Chez Vernon at eight thirty that evening. Women, sometimes, have a peculiar way of demonstrating their affection.

Five o'clock finally rolled around, but I hadn't closed my eyes. Bernice slept soundly at my side, a warm heavy leg thrown over mine, an arm draped limply across my chest. She breathed heavily through her open mouth. I eased my leg out from beneath hers and got out of bed on my side. The sheet that had covered us was disarranged, kicked to the bottom of the bed. I pulled it over her shoulders, before taking my clothes from the chair into the bathroom. My underwear was still dripping wet and draped over the metal bar that held the shower curtain. I pulled on my clothes without underwear. As soon as I was dressed, I raised the toilet seat, switched off the bathroom light and tiptoed out of the bedroom, closing the door softly behind me.

At the foot of the stairs, I retrieved my hat and guitar, and made my exit into the dawn. The sky was just beginning to turn gray. I opened the guitar case, removed the instrument, and tried to scrape off my name with my knife. It was burned in too deeply, but Bernice would be able to see that I had tried to scrape it off. Then I put the neck of the guitar on the top step, and stomped on it until it broke. After cutting the strings with my knife, I placed the broken instrument on the welcome mat.

There was an oleander bush on the left side of the porch. I tossed the guitar case into the bush. Now I could keep the fifty-dollar bill in good conscience. The guitar had been worth at least thirty dollars, and the fee for the private concert was twenty dollars. We were even. The message was obscure, perhaps, but Bernice would be able to puzzle it out eventually.

I walked down the gravel driveway to the street, and noticed the number of the house on a stone marker at the bottom of the drive. 111. I grinned. I would always remember Bernice's number.

Carrying my wet underwear, I had to wander around in the strange neighborhood for almost five blocks before I could find a bus stop and catch a bus back to downtown Jacksonville.

Chapter Eight

All day long I stayed in my room. Ideas and plans circulated inside my head, but none of them were worthwhile. One dismal thought kept oozing to the top, and finally it lodged there.

I had been cheated out of my inheritance.

This wasn't a new thought by any means. I had thought about it often in the five years since Daddy died, but I had never considered seriously doing anything about it before. The telegram informing me of Daddy's death had reached me one day too late to allow me to attend the funeral. I had immediately wired Randall and given him the circumstances. Two weeks later I had received a letter from Judge Brantley Powell, the old lawyer who handled the estate, together with a check for one dollar. He had also included a carbon copy of Daddy's will. Randall, my younger brother, had inherited the four-hundred-acre farm, seven hundred dollars in bonds, and the bank account of two hundred and seventy dollars. The check for one dollar was my part of the inheritance.

With plenty of money in my pockets at the time, I had dismissed the will from my mind. After all, Randall had stayed home, and I had not. He had gone to college, earned a degree in law and passed the Georgia bar exams, returning home ostensibly to practice. I had attended Valdosta State College for one year only and had quit to go to the Southwestern Cocking Tourney in Oklahoma City. I had never returned to college and Daddy had never gotten over it. He had always wanted to keep both of us under his thumb, but no man can tell me what to do with my life.

What had happened to the lives we lived?

I had gone on to make a name for myself in cock-fighting.

Sure, I was broke now, but I had firmly established myself in one of the toughest sports in the world. And what did Randall have to show for his fine education? What had he done with his inheritance?

When he was accepted for the bar he went to work as a law clerk for Judge Brantley Powell. Six months later, claiming that he was doing most of the work anyway, he asked for a full partnership in the firm. When the judge turned him down, he had quit, and he hadn't done much of anything since. He hadn't even hung out his own shingle. All day long he sat in the big dining room at home, looking for obscure contradictions in his law books, occasionally having an article published on some intricate point of law in some legal quarterly nobody had ever heard of before. To get by, he sold off small sections of the farm to Wright Gaylord, my fiancée's brother. He had also married Frances Shelby, a dentist's daughter from Macon. I suppose she had some dowry money and a few dollars from her father once in a while, but Randall's total income from tobacco, pecans and land sales was probably less than three thousand dollars a year. He was also writing a book — or so Frances said.

By all rights, Daddy should have left the farm to me. There were no two ways about it. I was the oldest son, and there wasn't a jury in Georgia that wouldn't award the farm to me if I contested the will. They read the Bible in Georgia, and in the Holy Bible the eldest son always inherits the property.

By four that afternoon I had made up my mind. I would go home and press Randall for the three hundred dollars he owed me. If he paid me, I'd forget about the farm and never consider taking it away from him again. If he didn't, I'd see Judge Powell and do something about it. I needed money, and if I didn't get some soon I'd miss out on the cockfighting season.

I checked my bag and gaff case at the desk, wrote a

message for the desk clerk to hold any mail that came for me, paid my bill, and headed for the bus station. I only planned to stay overnight at home, so my shaving kit was enough baggage. If my black shirt got too dirty, I could have my sister-in-law wash and iron it for me.

The bus pulled out at 4:45. There was a one-hour layover in Lake City to change buses, and I arrived in Mansfield, Georgia, at 3:30 a.m. The farm was six miles out of town on the state highway. I could either wait for the rural route postman and ride out with him or I could walk. After being cramped up in the bus for such a long time, I decided to stretch my legs.

I enjoyed the walk to the farm. When I had attended school in town the county had been too poor to afford a school bus. I had walked both ways, winter and summer, over a deeply-rutted red dirt road, muddy when it rained, and dusty when it hadn't rained. The road was paved now, and had been since right after the Korean war. Soldiers from Fort Benning had used a lot of the county as a maneuver area. When the war was over the county had sued the United States Army for enough money to blacktop most of the county roads.

I reached the farm a little after six. I passed Charley Smith's house first, the only Negro tenant Randall had left, but I didn't stop to see the old man, even though a coil of black smoke was curling out of his chimney. Charley was much too old to do hard farm work any longer, but his wife, Aunt Leona, helped Frances around the house four or five days a week, and she was still a good worker.

The old homestead was a gray clapboard two-story structure set well back from the road. Randall hadn't done anything to improve the looks of the place in the five years he had owned it. The ten Van Deman pecan trees, planted between the house and the road some sixty years before, had been the deciding factor when Daddy first bought the place. In another month or so, Charley, Aunt Leona and Frances would be under the trees gathering nuts. If Randall hit a good market, he would realize three or four hundred dollars from the pecans before Christmas, but I couldn't wait that long to get the money he owed me.

Old Dusty was lying on the long front gallery near the front door, but he didn't bark or lift his head when I entered the yard through the fence gate. He could neither see nor hear me. The old dog was almost sixteen years old, blind and stone-deaf. When I reached the steps, however, he felt the vibration, snuffled, and began to bark feebly. His hind legs were partially paralysed. When he tried to struggle to his feet, I patted his head and made him lie down again. The hair of his great head was white now. Unable to hear himself, he would have continued to bark indefinitely, so I closed his mouth with my hand to shut him up. He recognized me, of course, and licked my hand, his huge tail thumping madly on the loose floor-boards of the gallery. He had been a good hunting dog once, and despite his infirmities, I was grateful to Randall for not putting him away. I hadn't expected to see Old Dusty again.

Instead of entering by the front door, I took the brick walk around the house to the back. I opened the screen door to the kitchen, leaned against the doorjamb, and grinned at the expression of surprise and chagrin on my sister-in-law's face.

But I believe I was more shocked than Frances. She had begun to put on weight the last time I had seen her, but in two years' time she had gained another forty pounds. She must have been close to one hundred and eighty pounds. Her rotund body was practically shapeless under the faded blue dressing gown she wore over her nightgown. Frances's face was still young and pretty, but it was as round and shiny as a full moon. Her short brown hair was done up tight with a dozen aluminium curlers. With a grimace of dismay, Frances put a chubby hand to her mouth.

'You would catch me looking like this!' she exclaimed. 'Why didn't you let us know you were coming?'

I put an arm about her thick waist and kissed her on the cheek.

'Well,' she said good-naturedly, 'you can stop grinning like an ape and sit down at the table. The coffee'll be ready in a minute. I was just fixing to start breakfast.'

I sat down at the oilcloth-covered kitchen table. Frances lifted the lid of the coffee pot to look inside, and clucked her tongue disapprovingly. 'You may have lost your voice, Frank,' she scolded, 'but you can still write! We haven't heard from you in more than six months.'

I spread my arms apologetically.

'I guess I'm a fine one to talk,' she said, smiling, 'I never write myself, but we do enjoy hearing from you once in a while.' Frances filled two white mugs with coffee, put the sugar and cream where I could reach it easily, and sat down across from me.

'Randy'll be down pretty soon. He was up late last night working on an article, and I didn't have the heart to wake him. He likes to work at night, he says, when it's quiet. But if it was any quieter in the daytime I don't know what I'd do. We never go anyplace or do anything anymore, it seems to me.' She sipped her hot coffee black and then fanned a dimpled hand in front of her pursed lips. 'This isn't getting your breakfast ready now, is it?'

Because Frances knew how fond I was of eating, or because she used my visit, as an excuse, she prepared a large and wonderful breakfast. Fried pork chops, fried eggs, grits, with plenty of good brown milk gravy to pour over the grits, and fresh hot biscuits. I ate heartily, hungry after walking out from town, listening with stolid patience to the steady flow of dull gossip concerning various kinfolk and townspeople. I was finishing my third cup of coffee when I heard Randall on the stairs. As he entered the room, I got up to greet him.

'Well, well,' he said with false heartiness, holding onto my hand and grinning, 'if it isn't the junior birdman!'

He patted his wife on her broad rump, crossed to the sideboard and poured a shot glass full of bourbon. He swiftly drank two neat shots before turning around.

'Welcome home, Bubba,' he said, 'how long are you going to stay?'

He sat at the table, and I dropped into my seat again. Randall looked well. He always did, whether he had a hangover or didn't have one. His face was a little puffy, but he was freshly shaven, and his curly russet hair had been cut recently. His starched white shirt, however, was frayed at the cuffs. The knot of his red-and-blue striped rep tie was a well-adjusted double windsor, and his black, well-worn oxford flannel trousers were sharply creased.

When I managed to catch his eyes with mine, I shrugged.

'I see,' he nodded, 'the enigmatic response. Before I came downstairs I looked outside, both in front and out back, and didn't see a car parked. Until I realized it was you, I thought Frances was merely talking to herself again. But if you're broke, you're welcome to stay home as long as you like and close ranks with me. I've never been any flatter.'

'I saved two pork chops for you, Randy,' Frances said quickly.

'No, thanks. Just coffee. Save the chops for my lunch.' Randall smiled abstractedly, clasped his fingers behind his head and studied the ceiling. 'It isn't difficult to divine the purpose of your visit, Bubba,' he continued. 'When you're flush, you wheel up in a convertible, your pockets stuffed with dollar cigars. When you're broke, you're completely broke, and on your uppers. But if the purpose of your visit is to collect the honest debt I owe you, you're out of luck. Three hundred dollars!' He shook his head and snorted. 'Frankly, Bubba, I'd have a hard time raising twenty!'

He leaned forward in his chair and said derisively, 'But you can live here as long as you like. We can still eat, and thanks to Daddy there's a wonderful roof over our heads. And whether we pay our bills in town or not, the Mansfield credit is still good.'

To drink the coffee Frances set before him, Randall gripped the large white mug with both hands. His fingers didn't tremble, but it must have taken a good deal of concentrated effort to hold them steady.

'Going to see Mary Elizabeth?' he asked suddenly.

I shrugged and lit a cigarette. I offered the pack to my brother. He held up a palm in refusal, changed his mind and took one out of the pack. He held both of his hands in his lap, after putting the cork tip in hs mouth, and I had to lean across the table to light it for him.

'You kind of believe in long engagements, don't you, Bubba?' he said, smiling sardonically. 'It's been about seven years now, hasn't it?'

'Eight,' Frances amended. 'Eight years come November.'

'Well, you can't say I haven't done my part to bring you together,' Randall said wryly, watching my face closely. 'Five years ago our farms were almost three miles apart. But thanks to selling land to Wright Gaylord, we're less than a mile away from them now!' He laughed with genuine amusement.

I was unable to listen to him any longer. He made me feel sick to my stomach. I rose from the table, and picked up my shaving kit from the sideboard.

'There's plenty of hot water upstairs if you want to shave, but not enough yet for a bath. Lately I've taken to turning the heater off at night and not lighting it again till I get up,' Frances said. 'Your room is dusty, too, but when Leona comes over this morning I'll have her do it up and put fresh sheets on the bed.'

I nodded at my sister-in-law and left the room. As I climbed the stairs to the second floor, Randall said, 'Maybe you'd better scramble me a couple of eggs, hon. But don't put any grease in the skillet, just a little salt ...'

Not only was Randall weak, he was a petty tyrant to his long-suffering wife. Before she could scramble eggs she would have to pour the good milk gravy into a bowl, and wash and dry the frying pan.

My old room was at the very end of the upstairs hallway, next to the bathroom. When Daddy bought the farm and moved us out from town, I had been elated about the move because it meant having a room to myself. And somehow, Daddy had made a go of the farm when many other good farmers were half starving in Georgia.

He had earned a fair sum by *not* planting things and by collecting checks from the government. But even when times were excellent, he had never made any real money out of the farm. He was a fair farmer, but a poor businessman. Daddy had only been good for giving Randall and me advice, cheap advice, and he had never found anything in either one of us except our faults.

My room was dusty all right, as Frances had said. It had also been used as a catchall storeroom during the two years I had been away. The stripped double bed had been stacked with some cardboard cartons full of books, two shadeless table lamps and two carelessly rolled carpets. Extra pieces of dilapidated furniture had been tossed haphazardly into the room, and the hand-painted portrait of Grandpa was lying flat on top of my desk. A thick layer of dust was scattered over everything. When I opened the window, dust puffs as large as tennis balls took out after each other across the floor.

For a moment or two I looked out the window at the familiar view, but it didn't seem the same. Something was missing. And then I noticed that the ten-acre stand or slash pine had disappeared — cut down and sold as firewood probably, and not replanted.

I lifted the stern-faced portrait of Grandpa off the desk and leaned it against the dresser. I wiped the surface of the desk with my handkerchief. After rummaging though the drawers, I found a cheap, lined tablet with curling edges. Sitting down at the desk, I took out my ballpoint.

It took approximately half an hour to write out a list of instructions for Judge Brantley Powell. I wanted to be sure that I covered everything completely so he wouldn't have any questions. After rereading the list, and making a few interlinear corrections, I folded the sheaf of papers and stuffed them into my hip pocket.

I went into the bathroom and shaved, planning on an immediate departure for town in order to catch the judge in his office before he went home for the day. After returning to my room, I was rebuttoning my shirt when a soft rap sounded at the door.

'Bubba,' Randall's voice called through the door. 'How long're you going to be?'

I opened the door and looked quizzically at my brother. He was smiling a sly, secretive smile. Whenever Mother had caught him smiling that way, she slapped his face on general principles, knowing instinctively that he had done something wrong, and also knowing that she would never find out what he had done.

'Come on downstairs,' he said mysteriously. 'I've got a surprise for you.' Still smiling, he turned away abruptly and descended the stairs.

I slipped into my corduroy jacket, put my hat on and followed him.

The surprise was Mary Elizabeth, the last person I wanted to see right then, standing at the bottom of the stairs, cool and crisp in a wide-necked white blouse, blue velvet pinafore and white sling pumps. Ordinarily, I would have stopped to see Mary Elizabeth first, before coming home, but I didn't want to see her at all when I was broke and without a car. My last visit home, when I had first made my vow of silence, had been a strained, miserable experience for both of us.

'Hello, Frank,' Mary Elizabeth said shyly, 'welcome home.'

She hadn't changed a fraction in two years. She was every bit as beautiful as I remembered. Mary Elizabeth had pale golden hair, and dark blue eyes — which often changed to emerald green in bright sunlight — a pink-and-white complexion, fair, thick, untouched pale brows, and long delicate hands. Her figure was more buxom than it had been ten years before, but that was to be expected. She was no longer a young girl. She was a mature woman of twenty-nine.

A moment later Mary Elizabeth was in my arms and I was kissing her, and it was as though I had never been away. There was a loud click as Randall closed the double doors to the dining-room and left us alone. At the sound, Mary Elizabeth twisted her face to one side. I released her reluctantly and stepped back.

'Your voice still hasn't come back.' It was a statement, not a question.

Slowly, regretfully, I shook my head.

'And you haven't been to a doctor, either, have you?' she said accusingly.

Again the negative headshake, but accompanied this time with a stubborn smile.

'I've had a lot of time to think about it, Frank,' she said eagerly, 'and I don't believe your sudden loss of speech is organic at all. There's something psychological about it.' She dropped her eyes demurely. 'We can discuss it later at The Place. Randall's telephone call caught me just as I was leaving for school, and I don't think Mr. Caldwell liked it very well when I called him at the last minute that way. When I take a day off without notice, or get sick or something, he has to take my classes.

'But I've packed a lunch, and it's still warm enough to go for a swim at The Place ...' She colored prettily. 'If you want to go?'

I opened the front door and took her arm. As we climbed into her yellow Nova, she was over her initial nervousness, and she began to scold me.

'Did it ever occur to you, Frank, that even a picture postcard mailed in advance would be helpful to everybody concerned?' I rather enjoyed the quality of Mary Elizabeth's voice. Like most schoolteachers of the female sex, she had an overtone of fretful impatience in her voice, and this note of controlled irascibility amused me.

I grinned and tweaked the nipple of her right breast gently through the thinness of her white cotton blouse.

'Don't!' The sharp expletive was delivered furiously, and her blue-green eyes blazed with sudden anger. She set her lips grimly and remained silent for the remainder of the short drive to her farm, where she lived with her brother. As she pulled into the yard and parked beneath a giant pepper tree, I noticed that she had cooled off. The moment she turned off the engine, I pulled her toward me and kissed her mouth softly, barely brushing her lips with mine.

'You *do* love me, don't you, Frank?' she asked softly, with her eyes glistening.

I nodded, and kissed her again, roughly this time the way she liked to be kissed. One day, when we had first started to go together, Mary Elizabeth had asked me thirty-seven times if I loved her. At each affirmative reply she had been as pleased as the first time. Women never seem to tire of being told, again and again and again.

'Here comes Wright,' Mary Elizabeth said quickly, looking past my shoulder. 'We'd better get out of the car.'

We got out of the car and waited beneath the tree, watching her brother approach us from the barn with his unhurried, shambling gait. Wright Gaylord hated me, and I was always uneasy in his presence because of his low boiling point. He worshipped his little sister and had put her through college. Now in his late forties, Wright was still unmarried. He had never found a woman he could love as much as he loved his sister. He hated me for two reasons. One, I could sleep with Mary Elizabeth and he couldn't. After all these years he was bound to know about us, or at least suspect the best. And two, when I married Mary Elizabeth, he knew that I would take her away and he would never see her again. When our engagement had been announced and published in the paper, he had locked himself in his bedroom for three days.

'I didn't get sick or anything,' Mary Elizabeth said as Wright came within earshot. 'Frank came home, so I took the day off for a picnic.'

Wright glared at me. His face reminded me of a chunk of red stone, roughly hewn by an amateur sculptor, and then left in the rain to weather.

'When are you leaving?' Wright asked rudely, shoving both hands into his overall pockets deliberately, to avoid shaking hands.

'Now, that's no way to talk, Wright,' Mary Elizabeth chided. 'Frank just got home this morning.' She patted her brother's meaty arm. 'We're going to The Place for our picnic. Why don't you come with us?'

'I ain't got time for picnics,' he said sullenly. 'I got too much work to do. Anyway, I've been meanin' to go to town all week. Give me the keys, and I'll take your car instead of the pickup.'

Mary Elizabeth handed him her keys. 'It might do you good to take a day off and come with us.'

Wright grunted something under his breath, got into the car, and slammed the door. We entered the house, picked up a quilt and the lunch basket to take with us, and then cut across the fields for The Place.

We had called it The Place for as long as I could remember. The tiny pool in the piney woods wasn't large enough to be called a swimming hole. Fed by an underground spring that bubbled into a narrow brook about fifty yards up the pine-covered slope, the pool was only big enough for two or three people to stand in comfortably, and the water was only chest deep. The clear water was very cold, even on the hottest days. On a cruel summer day, a man could stand in the pool, his head shaded by pines, and forget about the heat and humidity of Georgia.

The Place had other advantages. There was a wide flat rock to the right of the pool, with enough room for one person at a time to stretch out on it and get some dappled sunlight. To the left of the pool, facing up the steep hill, there was a clearing well matted with pine needles. For two people, the clearing was the perfect size for an opened quilt and a picnic. Best of all, The Place was secluded and private. Located on the eastern edge of the Gaylord farm, the wooded section merged with a Georgia state forest. The only direct access to The Place was across Wright Gaylord's property, and nobody in his right mind would have trespassed on Wright's land.

Two hours before, Mary Elizabeth and I had arrived at the pool, hot and dusty from trudging across the cultivated fields. We had stripped immediately and jumped into the water. After splashing each other and wrestling playfully in the icy water, we had allowed the sun to dry us thoroughly before we made love on the quilt stretched flat on the bed of pine needles. There had been no protest from Mary Elizabeth, despite my long absence. Her natural, animal-like approach to sex was really miraculous in view of her strong religious views. I sometimes wondered if she ever connected the physical act of love with her real life.

I don't believe she thought consciously of sex at all. If she did, she must have thought of it as 'something Frank and I do at The Place,' but not connected with conjugal love or as something out of keeping with her straitlaced Methodist beliefs. Perhaps it was only habit.

I had never managed to make love to Mary Elizabeth anywhere else. She had been seventeen the first time, with just the two of us at The Place. It had been an accident more than anything else. Afterward I had been ashamed of myself for taking advantage of her innocence. But the first time had led to the second, and all during that never-to-be-forgotten summer we had made daily pilgrimages to The Place.

I have never underrated Mary Elizabeth nor under-estimated her intelligence, but the situation was unusual. After all, Mary Elizabeth was a college graduate now, and a teacher of high school English — she surely must have known what we were doing. But we had never discussed sex. I had an idea that the subject would be distasteful to her, and she had never brought it up on her own. And yet, every time I came home we headed for The Place like homing pigeons long absent from their coop. I had a hunch, and I had never pressed my good fortune, that as long as Mary Elizabeth never thought about it, or discussed it, we could continue to make love at The Place forever.

Once, and only once, I had asked Mary Elizabeth to drive to Atlanta with me for a weekend. She had been shocked into tears by my reasonable proposition.

'What kind of girl do you think I am?' she had asked tearfully.

Completely bewildered by her reaction, I had been unable to come up with a ready reply. I had never brought up the subject again. And besides, there wasn't a better spot in the world for making love than The Place.

Mary Elizabeth sat up suddenly, swung her long bare legs gracefully around, and sat on the rock facing me, dangling her feet in the water. I was in the pool, chest deep, and I had been studying her body as she lay flat on her back. Spreading a towel across her lap, but leaving her breasts uncovered, Mary Elizabeth looked at me sternly, and then wet her lips.

'What about us, Frank?' she said at last. 'How long do we go on like this?' The tone of her voice had changed. It wasn't harsh, but it wasn't feminine either. It was more like the voice of a young boy, on the near verge of changing.

I raised my eyebrows, watching her intently.

She cupped her breasts and pointed the long pink nipples toward the sky. She narrowed her eyes, no longer greenish, but now a dark aquamarine, and caught mine levelly.

'Are they still beautiful, Frank?' she asked in this strange new voice.

I nodded, dumbly, trying to figure out what she was driving at.

'You're wrong.' She smiled wanly, dropped her hands, and her plump breasts bobbed beautifully from their own momentum. 'You haven't noticed, but they're beginning to droop. Not much, but how will they look in five years? Ten years? Nobody's ever seen them except you, Frank, but how much longer will you be interested? All I've ever asked you to do is quit cockfighting so we could get married. We've drifted along in a deadlock too long, Frank, and it's impossible for me to accept your way of life. I thought that as you got older, you would see how wrong it is, but now you seem to be entangled in a pattern. And cockfighting is wrong, morally wrong, legally wrong, and every other kind of wrong! You're a grown man now, Frank!'

I sloshed forward in the tiny pool, put my arms around her hips, warm from the sun, and buried my face in her lap.

'Yes, you big, dumb child,' she said softly, running her fingers through my damp hair, 'but I can't meet you halfway on an issue like cockfighting. My roots are here and so are yours. Give it up, please, give it up, and marry me. Can't you see that you're wrong, wrong, wrong!' She gripped my hair with both hands and tugged my head gently from side to side.

'I can't exist on postcards any longer, Frank. '*Dear M.E. I'm in Sarasota. Won the derby 4–3. I love you. Will write from Ocala. F.!*' In a few more weeks, I'll be thirty years old. I want to be married and have children! I'm tired of people snickering behind my back at our engagement. Nobody believes it any more. If you loved me only half as much as I love you, you'd give it up. Please, Frank, stay home, marry me —'

There was a catch in her voice, and I lifted my head to look at her face. She wasn't crying, far from it. She was trying to beat me down again with an emotional appeal to my 'reason'. I had explained patiently to Mary Elizabeth, a dozen times or more, that cockfighting was not a cruel sport, that it was a legitimate, honorable business, and I had asked her to witness one fight, just one fight, so she could see for herself instead of listening to fools who didn't know what they were talking about. She had always refused, falling back on misinformation learned from reformers, the narrow-minded Methodist minister, and the shortsighted laws prohibiting the sport that were pushed through by a minority group of do-gooders. If she wouldn't see for herself, how could I persuade her?

'You're a brilliant man, Frank,' Mary Elizabeth continued earnestly. 'You could make a success out of anything you went into in Mansfield. This farm is half mine, you know, and when we're married, it'll be half yours. If you don't want to farm with Wright, I've got enough money saved that you can open a business of some kind in town. I've saved almost everything I've earned. Wright doesn't let me spend a penny, and I've been teaching for six years. And I'll help you get your voice back. We'll work it out together, you and I, Frank.

We can get a book on phonetics and you —'

As she constructed these impossible feminine castles I got restless. I pulled away from her, clambered up the opposite bank and began to dress, without waiting to get dry.

'What are you doing?' she said sharply.

As she could see for herself, I was putting my clothes on.

'You haven't listened to a single word, have you?'

I grinned, and buckled the straps on my jodhpur boots.

'If you leave, now,' she shouted, 'you needn't come back! We're through, d'you hear? Through! I won't be treated this way!'

When a woman starts to scream unreasonably, it's time to leave. I snatched a cold fried chicken leg out of the basket, draped my coat over my arm and started down the trail. Mary Elizabeth didn't call after me. Too mad, I reckoned.

Mary Elizabeth was stubborn. That was her problem. Anytime she truly wanted to get married, all she had to do was say so. But it had to be on my terms. I loved her, and she was a respectable woman with a good family background. I knew she would make me a good wife, too, once she got over this foolishness of wanting me to give up cockfighting and settle down in some dull occupation in Mansfield. We had been over this ground too many times, and I had a new season of cockfighting to get through. Nothing would have pleased me more than to have Mary Elizabeth as a bride at my Ocala farm, preparing meals and keeping my clothes clean. And, until she became pregnant, what would keep her from teaching school in Ocala, if that was what she wanted to do? As soon as she came around to seeing things my way, and quit trying to tell me what I could and couldn't do, we'd be married quick enough. And she knew it.

I grinned to myself, and tossed the chicken bone in the general direction of an ant nest. Mary Elizabeth had a sore point on those postcards. I'd have to do better than that. When I got back to Ocala, I'd write her a nice, interesting letter, a long newsy one for a change.

When I crossed through Wright's yard to the state road, I looked about apprehensively to see if he had returned, but he hadn't come back from town. Every time Wright caught me alone, he attempted to goad me into a fight. For Mary Elizabeth's sake, I had always refused to fight him. It would have given me a good deal of pleasure to knock a little sense into his thick head, but I knew that as soon as we started fighting he would whip out his knife, and then I would have to kill him.

I walked down the asphalt road. My biggest problem now was how to retrieve my shaving kit from the dresser in my room. If I returned to the house to get it, Randall would be curious as to why I was leaving so soon. If I wrote a note informing him I was going to take my rightful property and have him and Frances tossed out, he would attempt, with his trained lawyer's logic, to argue me out of my convictions. As I remembered, I had never really bested him in an oral argument. The only way I had ever won an argument with Randall was by resorting to force. And besides, Frances would bawl and carry on like crazy.

By the time I was level with the house, I decided to hell with the shaving kit, and continued on down the road. It would be less trouble all the way round if I bought another razor and toothbrush when I got back to Jacksonville.

I walked about four miles before I was picked up by a kid in a hot rod and taken the rest of the way into Mansfield. When he let me out at a service station, I walked through the shady residential streets to Judge Brantley Powell's house on the upper side of town. He only went to his office in the mornings, and I was certain I could catch him at home. When I rapped with the wrought-iron knocker, I only had to wait a minute before Raymond, his white-wooled Negro servant, opened the door. Raymond peered at me blankly for a moment or so before he recognized me, and then he smiled.

'Mr. Frank,' he said cordially, 'come in, come in!'

It was dark in the musty hallway when he closed the door. Raymond took my hat, led the way into the dim living room and raised the shades to let in some light.

'The judge he takin' his nap now, Mr. Frank,' he said uneasily. 'I don't like to wake him 'less it's somethin' important.'

I considered. What was important to me probably wouldn't be considered important by the old judge. I waved my right hand with an indifferent gesture, and settled myself in a leather chair to wait.

'You goin' to wait, Mr. Frank?'

I nodded, picked up an old *Life* magazine from the table beside the chair and leafed through it. Raymond left the room silently, and returned a few minutes later with a glass of ice cubes and a pitcher of lemonade. A piece of vinegar pie accompanied the lemonade. Firm, tart and clear, with a flaky, crumbly crust, it was the best piece of vinegar pie I had ever eaten.

It was almost five before the judge came downstairs. Evidently Raymond had told him I was waiting on him because he addressed me by name when he entered the room and apologized for sleeping so late. Judge Powell had aged considerably in the four or five years that had gone by since I had last talked to him. He must have been close to eighty. His head wobbled and his hands trembled as he talked. I handed him the list of instructions I had written, and he sat down in a chair close to the window to read them. He looked through the papers a second time, as if he were searching for something, and then removed his glasses.

'All right, Frank,' he said grimly. 'I'll handle this for you. Your Daddy was a stubborn man, and I told him he was wrong when he changed his will.'

I picked up my hat from the table where Raymond had placed it.

'One more thing, Frank. How long do you expect to be at the Jeff Davis Hotel in Jax?'

I shrugged, mentally totaled my remaining money, and then held up four fingers.

'You'll hear from me before then. And when you get your money, Frank, I hope you'll settle down. A dog has fun chasing his own tail, but he never gets anywhere while he's doing it.'

I shook hands with the old man and he walked me to the front door. 'Can you stay for dinner, son?'

I shook my head and smiled my thanks, but when I opened the door he grasped my sleeve.

'There're all kinds of justice, Frank,' he said kindly, 'and I've seen most of them in fifty years of practice. But poetic justice is the best kind of all. To measure the night, a man must fill his day,' he finished cryptically.

I nodded knowingly, although I didn't know what he meant, and I doubt very much whether he did either. When a man manages to live as long as Judge Powell has, he always thinks he's a sage of some kind.

I cut across town to the U.S. Highway and ate dinner in a trucker's café about a mile outside the city limits. Two hours later I was riding in the cab of a diesel truck on my way back to Jacksonville. I had the feeling inside that I had finally burned every bridge, save one, to the past. But I didn't have any regrets. To survive in this world, a man has got to do what he has got to do.

Chapter Nine

I was tired when I reached Jacksonville, but I wasn't
sleepy. I had hoped to get some sleep in the cab of the
truck on the long drive down, but the driver had talked
continuously. As I listened to him, dumbly, my eyes
smarting from cigarette smoke and the desire to close
them, he poured out the dull, intimate details of his boring
life — his military service with the First Cavalry Division
in Vietnam, his courtship, his marriage and his plans for
the future (he wanted to be a truck dispatcher so he could
sit on his ass). He was still going strong when we reached
Jax. To finish his autobiography, he parked at a drive-in
and bought me ham and eggs for breakfast.

After shaking hands with the voluble truck driver, who
wasn't really a bad guy, I caught a bus downtown and
checked into the Jeff Davis Hotel. One look at the soft
double bed and I became wide awake. If my plan was
successful, I would know within three days, and I didn't
have time to sleep all day. I had to proceed with a confidence I didn't actually have, as though there could be no
doubt of the outcome.

After I shaved, I prepared a list for Doc Riordan. These
were supplies I would need, and I intended to take advantage of our agreement. It would take a long time to use
up eight hundred dollars' worth of cocker's supplies.

One. Conditioning powder. Doc made a reliable conditioning powder — a concoction containing iron for
vigor, and Vitamin B1. This powder, mixed with a gamecock's special diet, is a valuable aid to developing a bird's
muscles and reflexes. I put down an order for three
pounds.

Two. Dextrose capsules. A dextrose capsule, dropped down a gamecock's throat an hour before a fight, gives him the same kind of fresh energy a candy bar provides to a mountain climber halfway up a mountain. On my list I put down an order for a twenty-four-gamecock season supply.

Three. Doc Riordan's Blood Builder. For many years Doc had made and sold a blood coagulant that was as good as any on the market. If he didn't have any on hand he could make more. This was a blood builder in capsule form containing Vitamin K, the blood coagulating vitamin, whole liver and several other secret ingredients. Who can judge the effectiveness of a blood coagulant? I can't. But if any blood coagulants worked, and I don't leave any loopholes when it comes to conditioning, I preferred to use Doc Riordan's. Again I marked down enough for a twenty-four-gamecock supply.

Four. Disinfectants. Soda, formaldehyde, sulfur, carbolic acid, oil of tansy, sassafras, creosote, camphor and rubbing alcohol. Insects are a major problem for cockfighters. Lice are almost impossible to get rid of completely, but a continuous fight against them must be fought if a man wants to keep healthy game fowl. *Give me a plentiful supply of all these,* I wrote on my list.

Five. Turpentine. Five gallons. The one essential fluid a cocker must have for survival. God has seen fit to subject chickens to the most loathsome diseases in the world — pip, gapes, costiveness, diarrhea, distemper, asthma, catarrh, apoplexy, cholera, lime legs, canker and many others. Any one of these sicknesses can knock out a man's entire flock of game fowl before he knows what has happened to him. Fortunately, a feather dipped in turpentine and shoved into a cock's nostrils, or swabbed in his throat, or sometimes just a few drops of turpentine on a bird's drinking water, will prevent or cure many of these diseases. When turpentine fails, I destroy the sick chicken and bury him deep to prevent the spread of his disease.

When I completed my list I sealed it in a hotel envelope, wrote Doc Riordan's name on the outside, and headed for the drugstore where he had part-time work. Doc wasn't in, but the owner said he was expected at noon. Figuring that Doc would freely requisition most of the items on my list from the owner, I decided not to leave it, and to come back later.

I walked to the Western Union office and sent two straight wires. The first wire was to my neighbor and fellow cocker in Ocala, Omar Baradinsky:

HAVE LIGHTS AND WATER TURNED ON AT MY FARM. WILL REIMBURSE UPON ARRIVAL. F. MANSFIELD.

I knew Omar wouldn't mind attending to this chore for me in downtown Ocala and inasmuch as I didn't know what day or what time I would arrive at the farm, I wanted to be certain there was water and electricity when I got there.

The other wire was to Mr. Jake Mellhorn, Altamount, North Carolina. Jake Mellhorn bred and sold a game strain called the Mellhorn Black. It was a rugged breed, and I knew this from watching Blacks fight many times.

These chickens fought equally well in long and short heels, depending upon their conformation and conditioning, but they were unpredictable fighters — some were cutters and others were shufflers — and they had a tendency to alternate their tactics in the pit. As a general rule I prefer cutters over shufflers, but I needed a dozen Aces and a fair price. Jake Mellhorn had been after me for several years to try a season with his Blacks, and I knew that he would give me a fairly low price on a shipment of a dozen. If I won with his game strain at any of the major derbies, he would be able to jack the price up on the game fowl he sold the following season to other cockers. I could win with any hardy, farm-walked game strain that could stand up under my conditioning methods — Claret, Madigan, Whitehackle, Doms — but the excellent cocks I would need would cost too much, especially after putting out five hundred dollars for Icky. It wouldn't hurt anything to send a wire to Jake and find out what he had to offer anyway.

TO: JAKE MELLHORN, ALTAMOUNT, N.C.
NEED TWELVE FARM-WALKED COCKS. NO STAGS. NO
COOPWALKS WANTED. PUREBRED MELLHORNS ONLY. NO
CROSSES. SEND PRICE AND DETAILS C/O JEFF DAVIS
HOTEL, JACKSONVILLE, FLA. F. MANSFIELD.

If I knew Jake Mellhorn, and I knew the egotistic, self-centered old man well, I'd have a special delivery letter from him within a couple of days. And on my first order, at least, he would send me Aces.

I paid the girl for the wires, and then ate a hamburger at a little one-arm joint down the street before returning to Foster's Drugstore.

Now that the wires were on their way, I felt committed, even though they didn't mean anything in themselves. I felt like I was getting the dice rolling by forcing my luck.

I couldn't pay for the Mellhorns, no matter how good a price Jake gave me. I couldn't even repay Omar Baradinsky the utilities deposit money he would put up for me in Ocala — and yet I felt confident. Surely Judge Powell would come through with one thousand five hundred dollars now, because I had acted as though he would. It was a false feeling of confidence, and I knew that it was bogus in the same way a man riding in a transatlantic airplane knows that there cannot possibly be a crack-up because he bought one hundred dollars' worth of insurance at the airport before the plane took off.

Doc Riordan was sitting at the fountain counter, wearing a short white jacket, when I entered the drugstore. I eased onto the stool beside him and tapped him on the shoulder.

'Hello, Frank,' he said, smiling. In the cramped space, we shook hands awkwardly without getting up. 'Mr. Foster said there was a big man with a cowboy hat looking for me. Inasmuch as I don't know any bill collectors who don't talk, I figured it was you.'

I handed Doc the envelope. He studied the list, and whistled softly through closed teeth. 'That's a mighty big order on short notice, Frank,' he said, frowning. 'I don't have any conditioning powder made up, and there's been so much flu going around Jax lately, I've got sixty-three prescriptions to fill before I can do anything else.' He tapped the list with a forefinger. 'Can you let me have a couple of days?'

I had to smile. At that stage I could have let him have a couple of months. I clapped him on the shoulder and nodded understandingly.

'Good. Come in day after tomorrow and it'll be waiting for you. All of it.' He smiled. 'Kinda looks like you've got your chickens for the season, and I hope you'll have a good one. Anytime you need something fast, just drop me a card here at Foster's. I know damned well I'll make the Milledgeville Tourney, but that'll be the only one this year. I've got too many feelers out on Licarbo to go to chicken fights. But then, I might get a chance to run down to Plant City —'

He had work to do, so I slid off the stool and left abruptly while he was still talking.

For the rest of the afternoon I prowled used car lots as a tire-kicker, trying to locate a pickup truck of some kind that would hold together for four or five months. Around four o'clock I discovered an eight-year-old Ford half-ton pickup that looked suitable, and the salesman rode around the block with me when I tried it out. All afternoon my silence had unnerved talkative used car salesmen. After five minutes of my kind of silence, they usually gave up on their sales talks and let me look around in peace. This fellow was more persistent. After reparking the truck in its place on the fourth row of the lot, I looked at the salesman inquisitively.

'This is a real buy for one fifty,' he said sincerely. He was a young man in his early twenties, with a freckled earnest face. His flattop haircut, and wet-look black leather sports jacket, reminded me of a Marine captain wearing civilian clothes for the first time. For all I knew, he was an ex-Marine.

I looked steadily into his face and he blushed.

'But old pickups don't sell so well these days. Too many

rich farmers buying new ones. So I'll let you have it for a hundred-dollar bill.'

I studied him for a moment, maintaining my expressionless face, and then got out of the cab of the truck. I started toward the looping chain fence that bordered the sidewalk, and he caught up with me before I reached the first line of cars. He put a freckled hand on my arm, but when I dropped my eyes to his hand, he jerked it away as though my sleeve were on fire.

'I'll tell you what I'll do, sir,' he said quickly. 'Just to move the old Ford and get it off the lot, I'll give up my commission. You can have the truck for eighty-five bucks. Give me ten dollars down, and drive it away. Here're the keys.' He held out the keys, but I didn't look at them. I kept my eyes on his face.

'All right,' he said nervously. 'Seventy-five, and that's rock bottom.'

I nodded. A fair price. More than fair. The truck had had hard use, and most of the paint had been chipped off in preparation for a new paint job. But no one had ever gotten around to repainting it. I pointed to the low sun above the skyline, and he followed my pointing finger with his pale blue eyes. To catch his wandering attention again I snapped my fingers and then held up three fingers before his face.

'Three suns?' he asked. 'You mean three days?'

I nodded.

'Without a deposit, I can't promise to hold it for you, sir.'

I shrugged indifferently and left the lot. I had a hunch that the pickup would still be there when I came back for it.

When I got back to my hotel room I counted my money. Twenty-three dollars and eighty-one cents. Money just seems to evaporate. I had no idea where all of it had gone, but I had to nurse what was left like a miser. Twelve dollars would be needed to pay four days' rent on the hotel room, and I would have to eat and smoke on the remainder. If I didn't get a letter from Judge Powell within three days, or four at the most, I would have to make other plans of some kind.

I spent the next three days at the public library. There was a long narrow café near the hotel that featured an 'Eye-Opener Early-Bird Breakfast,' consisting of one egg, one slice of bacon, one slice of brushed margarine toast and a cup of coffee — all for forty-two cents. After eating this meager fare, I walked slowly to the library and sat outside on the steps until it opened, thinking forward to lunch. I read magazines until noon in the periodical room, and then returned to the hotel and checked the desk for my mail. I then returned to the library. By two o'clock I was ravenous, and I would eat a poor boy sandwich across the street, and drink a Coca-Cola. The poor boy sandwich had three varieties of meat, but not much meat. I then returned to the library and read books until it closed up at nine p.m.

My taste in reading is catholic. I can take Volume III of the *Encyclopedia Americana* out of the stacks and read it straight through from Corot to Deseronto with equal interest, or lack of interest, in each subject. *Roget's Thesaurus* or a dictionary can hold my attention for several hours. I don't own many books. There were only a few on poultry breeding at my Ocala farm and a first edition of *Histories of Game Strains* that I won as a prize one time at a cockfight. And I also owned a beat-up copy of *Huckleberry Finn*. I suppose I've drifted down the river with Huck Finn & Co. fifty times or more.

When the library closed at nine, I ate a hamburger, returned to the hotel and went to bed.

Three days passed quickly this way. On the morning of the fourth day, however, I didn't leave the hotel. My stomach was so upset I didn't even feel like eating the scanty 'Eye-Opener Early-Bird Breakfast', afraid I couldn't hold it. I sat in the lobby waiting apprehensively for the mail.

There were two letters for me, both of them special delivery. One was a thick brown envelope from Judge

Powell, and the other was a flimsier envelope from Jake Mellhorn. I didn't open either letter until I reached my room. My fingers were damp when I opened the thick envelope from Judge Powell first, but when I emptied the envelope onto my bed, the only thing I could see was the gray-green certified check from the Mansfield Farmer's Trust, made out to my name for one thousand five hundred dollars!

My reaction to the check surprised me. I hadn't realized how much I had counted on getting it. My knees began to shake first, and then my hands. A moment later my entire body was shivering as though I had malaria, and I had to sit down quickly. I was wet from my hair down to the soles of my feet with a cold, clammy perspiration that couldn't have been caused by anything else but cold, irrational fear. Of course, I hadn't allowed my mind to dwell on the possibility of failure, but now that I actually had the money, the suppressed doubts and fears made themselves felt. But my physical reaction didn't last very long. I stripped to the waist and bathed my upper body with a cold washrag, and dried myself thoroughly before reading Judge Powell's letter. It was a long letter, overly long, typed single spaced on his law firm's letterhead, water-marked stationery:

Mr. Frank Mansfield
c/o The Jeff Davis Hotel
Jacksonville, Florida

Dear Frank:

I handled this matter personally, following your desires throughout, feeling you knew your brother Randall better than me. You did. When I called on him and informed him that you intended to break the will of your father, he laughed. If it hadn't been for your copious notes, his laughter would have surprised me.

'Is Frank willing to fight this in court?' he asked
me.

'No,' I told him (again following your instructions).
'Your brother Frank said it wouldn't be necessary.
"When Randall sees that he is in an untenable position, he will sign a quitclaim deed immediately and
move out."'

Again your brother laughed as you predicted. 'Do
you think I'm in an untenable position, Judge?' he
then asked.

'Yes, you are,' I told him. 'That's why I brought a
quitclaim deed for you to sign.'

He laughed and signed the deed. 'In New York,' he
said, 'you wouldn't have a chance, Judge.' I remained
silent instead of reminding him that the case, if
brought to a trial, would be held in Georgia. 'When
does Frank want me to leave?'

'As soon as the property is sold.'

'Does Frank have a buyer in mind?'

'He recommended that I try Wright Gaylord first,' I
said.

This statement gave your brother additional cause
for merriment, because he laughed until the tears
rolled down his face.

'Frank only wants a profit of one thousand, five
hundred dollars,' I told your brother. 'He instructed
me to give you any amount over that, after deducting
my fee, of course.'

'That's generous of Frank,' he said, 'but there are
some taxes due, about seven hundred dollars.'

'I'm aware of the taxes,' I said.

'All right, Judge. You've got your quitclaim deed.
Continue on down the road and sell the property to
Wright Gaylord. I'll be ready to leave tomorrow
morning when you bring me my share, if there's
anything left over.'

Wright Gaylord gave me a check the same afternoon for three thousand five hundred dollars, which I
accepted reluctantly. Given more time I am positive

that your property would have sold for eight or possibly ten thousand dollars. But the sum adequately covered your required one thousand five hundred and my fee of five hundred dollars, so I closed the sale then and there. You didn't mention it in your notes, but I realize the astuteness of selling to Mr. Gaylord, although I doubt if he did. Upon your marriage to his sister you will automatically get half your farm back and half of his as well. Mr. Gaylord is also a client of mine, and this was a fine point of legal ethics, but inasmuch as he is certainly aware of your engagement to his sister, I did not deem it necessary to remind him.

Enclosed is a certified check for one thousand five hundred dollars. My fee of five hundred dollars has been deducted, the taxes have been paid, plus stamps, and miscellaneous expenses. I gave your brother a cheque for seven hundred and sixty-eight dollars and fifty cents. Randall and his wife left yesterday on the bus for Macon.

Mr. Gaylord has already begun to tear down your father's farmhouse and the outlying buildings. He hired a wrecking crew from Atlanta, and I saw some of their equipment moving through town yesterday. However, he agreed to keep your Negro tenant on the place if he wanted to stay, per your request. But he would not consent to keep him on shares because Charley Smith is too old. Your main concern, I believe, was to maintain a home for Charley and his family, so again, in lieu of instructions to the contrary, I agreed to this condition.

There are also some papers enclosed for you to sign on the places marked with a small X in red pencil. They have been predated, including the power of attorney, in order to send you the money without undue delay. Please return them (after you have signed them) as quickly as possible.

If your father were alive, I know he would want you to use your money wisely, so I can only say the same. 'A rolling stone gathers no moss' is an old saying but a

true one nevertheless. If I can help you further do not
hesitate to ask me.

Very truly yours,

BRANTLEY POWELL
Attorney-at-Law

BP/bj

I didn't mind the moralizing of the windy old man,
because he didn't know what I planned to use the money
for, but I was irritated because he had dictated the letter to
his big-mouthed old maid secretary, Miss Birdie Janes.
The small initials 'bj' in the lower left-hand corner of the
letter meant that my business would be spread all over the
county by now. I realized that it was a long letter, and I
appreciated the details, but the old man should have
written the letter personally. When I returned to Mansfield, eventually, sides would be taken — some for Randall
and some for me, but the majority would take Randall's
side, even though I was legally and morally right about
taking what rightfully belonged to me.

The letter from Jake Mellhorn was more pressing:

Dear Frank,

Glad to see you're getting sense enough to know that
the Mellhorn Black is the best gamecock in the world,
bar none!!! And you're lucky you wired me just when
you did. I just brought in twenty-two cocks, but if you
only want a dozen country-walked roosters, you can
have the best of the lot, which is plenty damned
good!!! I can ship you six Aces, two to three years old.
The other six are brothers, five months past staghood,
but all are guaranteed dead game, and they'll cut for
you or your money back. As you know, I ship them
wormed, in wooden coops, but they'll need watering
upon arrival. Don't trust the damned express company
to water birds en route — they'll steal the cracked corn
out of the coops and make popcorn out of it. As a
special price — TO YOU ONLY!!! One dozen Mell-

horn Blacks for only seven hundred dollars. That's much less than seventy-five apiece. Let me know by return wire, because I can sell them anywhere for one hundred to one hundred and twenty-five dollars each.

For a good season,
JAKE MELLHORN

An outlay of seven hundred dollars, although it was an exceptionally fair price for Ace Mellhorns, would make a deep dent in my one thousand five hundred dollars, but I had little choice. I had to have them, or others just as good. Another five hundred to Ed Middleton, seventy-five dollars for the truck, and I'd be down to only two hundred and twenty-five. Luckily, I had feed at Ocala left over from last year, and the older Flint corn is, the better it is for feeding. And within two weeks I could win some money at the Ocala cockpit. At least two, or possibly three birds could be conditioned for battle by that time.

After packing and checking out of the hotel, I cashed the check at the bank. I wired seven hundred dollars to Jake Mellhorn immediately with instructions to ship the cocks to my farm. I mailed the signed papers back to Judge Powell special delivery, and headed for the used car lot to buy the staked-out pickup truck.

Within two hours, I was driving out of Jacksonville. The cocker's supplies from Doc Riordan were in the truck bed, along with my suitcase and gaff case, covered by a tarp. The remainder of my money, in tens and twenties, was pinned inside my jacket pocket with a safety pin.

As I turned onto Highway 17 I thought suddenly of Bernice Hungerford. She had been in my thoughts several times during the last three days, especially late at night when I had been trying to sleep, with hunger pangs burning at my stomach. In fact, I had considered seriously going out to her house and chiseling a free meal. But I had felt too guilty to go. Leaving a broken guitar on her front porch hadn't been a brilliant idea

There was a filling station ahead, and I pulled onto the ramp and pointed to the regular pump.

'How many sir?'

I pulled a finger across my throat.

'Filler up? Yes, sir.'

While I was still looking at the large city map inside the station, the attendant interrupted me to ask if everything was all right under the hood. The question was so stupid I must have looked surprised, because he blushed with embarrassment and checked beneath the hood without waiting for a reply. How else can a man discover whether oil and water are needed unless he looks?

I traced the map and found Bernice's street. Her house was about three miles out of my way. I didn't really owe her anything, but I knew my conscience would be eased if I repaid the woman the thirty dollars she had advanced me when I had needed it. I turned around, and drove slowly until I reached a shopping center that had a florist's shop. I parked, entered the shop, and selected a dozen yellow roses out of the icebox. The stems were at least two feet long.

'These will make a beautiful arrangement,' the gray-haired saleswoman smiled. 'Do you want to include a card?'

When I nodded she gave me a small white card and a tiny envelope that went with it. I scrawled a short note:

Dear Bernice:

Drop me a line sometime. RFD # 1. Ocala, Fla.

Frank Mansfield

Whether Bernice would write to me or not I didn't know. I did feel, however, that the roses and thirty dollars in cash would make up for my abrupt leave-taking without saying good-bye. And I did like the woman. I tucked the money inside the little envelope, together with the card, and licked the flap.

'And where do you wish these delivered, sir?' the saleswoman asked, handing me a pink bill for twenty-five dollars and fifty cents. I put the money on the counter, and tugged at my lower lip. By having them delivered I could save time.

'We deliver free, of course,' the woman smiled.

That settled it. I had to deliver the roses and the note myself. The woman was too damned anxious. Her gray hair and kindly, crinkle-faced smile didn't fool me. I had selected the twelve yellow roses with care. If I had allowed them to be delivered she would have either switched them for older roses, or changed them for carnations or something. After pocketing my change, I pointed to the stack of green waxed paper and made a circular motion with my hand for the woman to wrap them up.

When I reached 111 Melrose Avenue, I rang the bell several times, but there was no one at home. I waited impatiently for five minutes, and then left the flowers at the door. I slipped the note containing the money under the door. Maybe it was better that way.

The next move, if any, would be up to Bernice. If she had been home, I probably would have stayed overnight with her and lost another day. There was too much work ahead of me to waste time romancing a wealthy widow.

The old pickup drove well on the highway, but I was afraid to drive more than forty miles an hour. When I revved it up to fifty, the front wheels shimmied. Long before reaching Orlando I was remorseful about the grand gesture of giving the roses and thirty bucks to Bernice Hungerford. It would have been wiser to wait until I was flush again. The damned money was dripping through my fingers like water, and I'd have to win some fights before any more came in. But when I pictured the delighted expression on Bernice's jolly face when she discovered the flowers at her front door, I felt better.

I reached Orlando before midnight. I saved eight dollars by driving through town to Ed Middleton's private road, and by sleeping in the back of the truck in his orange grove. The excitement had drifted out of my mind, and, as tired as I was, I slept as well in the truck as I would have slept in a motel bed.

The next morning, when I parked in his carport, and

knocked on his kitchen door at six a.m., Ed wasn't happy to see me. Martha Middleton, however, appeared to be overjoyed by my early morning appearance. She cracked four more eggs into the frying pan and decided to make biscuits after all.

'I didn't expect you back so soon,' Ed said gruffly, after he filled my cup with coffee.

I grinned at his discomfiture, took the money out of my jacket, and peeled off five hundred dollars on the breakfast-nook table. Ed glared at the stack of bills. Martha stayed close to her stove, pursing her lips. I drank half my coffee, and started in on my fried eggs before Ed Middleton said a word. In the back of my mind, I was more or less hoping he would change his mind and renege on the deal. Icarus was a mighty fine rooster, but five hundred dollars was a lot of money, and I needed every cent I could get at that moment.

'Well,' Ed said thoughtfully. He counted the money twice, removed the top five twenty-dollar bills and shoved the remaining four hundred dollars back across the table.

'Here!' he said angrily. 'I won't hold you to the ridiculous price we agreed on, Frank. I'll just take a hundred as a token payment. Besides, I'm sick of looking at game chickens. I'm tired of the whole business! Come on, let's go get your damned rooster!'

By the time Ed had finished talking, he was almost shouting and out of the nook and fumbling at the doorknob.

'Can't you wait until Frank finishes his breakfast?' Martha said, with quiet good humor.

'Sure, sure,' Ed managed to get the door open. 'Take your time, Frank,' he said contritely. 'I'll go on out to the runs and put Icarus in your aluminium coop. Also, those two battered Grays are in good shape again. You can have them and the game hen, too. I'll have them all in coops by the time you finish eating.' The door banged shut.

I wiped some egg yolk off the top twenty with a napkin and returned the money to my inside jacket pocket. The kitchen door opened up again, and Ed stuck his head in.

'Can you use some corn? Barley?'

I nodded.

'Good. There's about three or four partly used sacks of both in the feed shack. But if you want 'em, you'll have to carry 'em to the truck yourself. I'll be goddamned if *I'm* going to do it!' The door slammed again.

I wanted to follow him out the door but thought it best to finish my breakfast and let Ed cool off a little bit. He had never really expected me to show up with five hundred dollars for his pretty pet game cock. But his astonishment was in my favor. He had been shamed into returning four hundred dollars, and now I was way ahead of the game. The Middleton Gray game hen was valuable for breeding, and the two Gray game cocks were worth at least fifty dollars apiece.

'Don't you pay any mind to Ed's bluster, Frank,' Martha said gently. 'He's just upset and doesn't mean half of what he says. I know how much store he sets by those chickens. Someday, he'll thank me, Frank. You think I'm unreasonable, I know, making him give up his chickens and stopping him from following fights all over the country, but I'm not really. Ed's had two heart attacks in the last eighteen months. After the last one he was in bed for two weeks and the doctor told him not to do anything at all. Nothing.' She shook her head.

'He isn't supposed to pick so much as an orange up off the ground. Why, the last time the doctor came out and saw that the roosters were still out there he had a fit! Now go out and get your chickens, Frank, and don't let Ed help you lift anything.'

I slid out from the table and patted Martha on the shoulder. Ed Middleton certainly knew how to keep a secret. I hadn't known anything about his ailing heart.

'I know you won't say anything, Frank,' Martha said, smiling, 'but don't *look* anything, either!' Despite her smile and the humor in her voice, there were sparks of terror in her eyes. 'Ed hasn't told a soul about his bad heart, and I know he wouldn't want me to tell you. He tries to pretend he's as strong as he ever was.'

I wanted to say something, anything that would comfort the woman, but I couldn't. He was going to die soon. I could tell by her eyes.

I smiled, nodded and left the kitchen. The moment I was outside, I lit out around the little lake at a dead run to get my prize rooster before Ed Middleton could change his mind.

Chapter Ten

The scarlet cock, my lord likes best,
*   And next to him, the gray with thistle-breast.*
This knight is for the pile, or else the Black.
A third cries no cock like the dun, yellow back.
The milk-white cock with golden legs and bill.
Or else the Spangle, choose as you will.
The King he swears (of all), these are the best.
They heel, says he, more true than all the rest.
But this is all mere fancy, and no more,
The color's nothing, as I've said before!

This anonymous English cocking poem was thumbtacked to the wall beside my bed. I had copied it in longhand and stuck it there as a reminder that experience, rather than experiment, would be my best teacher. This poem must have been more than two hundred years old, and yet it still held a sobering truth. The best gamecock has to be of a proven game strain. Crossed and recrossed, until the color of the feathers resemble mud, if a cock can be traced to a legitimate game strain on both sides, he will fight when he is pitted and face when he is hurt. This old poem contained a particularly worthwhile truth to remember, now that I possessed Icky, the most gaily plumaged cock I had ever owned. The bettors at every pit on the circuit would be anxious to back him because of his bright blue color, and he would have to be good, because of the odds I'd be forced to give on him.

While I poured coffee into cups at the gate-legged table, Omar Baradinsky, his hairy fingers clasped behind his back, studied the poem on the wall. He must have read it three or four times, but if he moved his lips when he read, I wouldn't have known about it. Omar's pale face, which no amount of exposure to the Florida sun could tan, was almost completely covered by a thick, black, unmanageable beard. This ragged hirsute growth, wild and tangled, began immediately below his circular, heavily pouched brown eyes, and ended in tattered shreds halfway down his chest. A thick, untrimmed moustache, intermingled with his beard, covered his mouth completely. When he talked, and Omar liked to talk, his mouth was only a slightly darker hole in the center of the jet-black tangle of face hair. Out of curiosity, I had asked Omar once why he wore the beard, and his answer had been typical of his new way of life.

'I'll tell you, Frank,' he had boomed. 'Did you ever eat baked ham with a slice of glazed pineapple decorating the platter?'

When I admitted that I had, he had pulled his fingers through his beard fondly and continued. 'Well, that's what my face looked like when I went to the office every day in New York. Like a slab of glazed, fried, reddish pineapple! For me, shaving once a day wasn't enough. The whiskers grew too fast. I shaved before leaving home in the morning, again at noon, and if I went out again at night, I had to scrape my jowls again. For as long as I can remember, my face was sore, raw in fact, and even after a fresh shave people told me I needed another. So, I no longer have to shave and I no longer shave, and I'll never shave again!'

To see Omar Baradinsky now, standing in my one-and-a-half-room shack near Ocala, wearing a pair of faded blue denim bib overalls, a khaki work shirt with the sleeves cut off at the shoulders, scuffed, acid-eaten, high-topped work shoes, and that awe-inspiring growth of black hair covering his face — no one in his right mind would have taken him for a once successful advertising executive in New York City. A closer look at his clothes, however, would reveal that Omar's bib overalls and shirt were expensive and tailored — which they were. He ordered his clothes from Abercrombie & Fitch up in New York, and they would wash and dry without needing to be ironed. In the beginning, I suspect that he had probably started to wear bib overalls as a kind of uniform, to fit some imaginary role he had made up in the back of his mind. But now they had become a part of him, and I couldn't picture Omar wearing anything else.

But Omar had been an advertising man four years before. Not only had he been a successful executive with a salary of thirty-five thousand dollars a year, he had also owned a twenty-unit luxury apartment house in Brooklyn. He was now a breeder and handler of game cocks in Florida, keeping Claret crosses and Allen Roundheads, and after four experimental years, slowly beginning to pull ahead. The one remaining tie Omar had with New York was his wife. She visited him annually, for one week, when she passed through central Florida on her way to Miami Beach for the winter season. So far, she had been unable to make him change his mind and return to New York. Omar's wife wasn't the type to bury herself on an isolated Florida chicken farm, so they were stalemated.

Unlike most American sportsmen, the cockfighting fan has an overwhelming tendency to become an active participant. There is no such thing as a passive interest in cockfighting. Beginning as a casual onlooker, a man soon finds the action of two game cocks battling to the death a fascinating spectacle. He either likes it or he doesn't. If he doesn't like it, he doesn't return to watch another fight. If he does like it, he accepts, sooner or later, everything about the sport — the good with the bad.

As the fan gradually learns to tell one game strain from another, he admires the vain beauty of a game rooster. Admiration leads to the desire to possess one of these beautiful creatures for his very own, and pride of ownership leads to the pitting of his pet against another game cock. Whether he wins or loses, once the fan has got as far as pitting, he is as hooked as a ghetto mainliner.

Of course, not every beginner embraces the sport like Omar Baradinsky — to the point of quitting a thirty-five-thousand dollar-a-year position, and leaving wife, family and friends to raise and fight game cocks in Florida. The majority of fans are content to participate on a smaller scale — as a handler, perhaps, or as an owner of one or two game cocks, or as a lowly assistant holding a bird for a handler while he lashes on the heels. Many spectators, unfortunately, are interested in the gambling aspects of cockfighting to the exclusion of everything else. But even gamblers must learn a lot of information about game fowl to win consistently. Whether he wins or loses, the gambler still has the satisfaction of knowing that a cockfight cannot be fixed, and not another sport in the United States will give him as fair a chance for his money.

Omar Baradinsky, however, had gone all the way, caught up in the sport at the dangerous age of fifty, the age when a man begins to wonder just what in the hell he has got out of his life so far, anyway? Omar was still as bewildered by his decision to enter full-time cockfighting now as he had been when he started.

'I can't really explain it, Frank,' he had told me one idle morning, after we got to know each other fairly well, right after he had first moved to Florida. 'I had done a better than average job on one of my smaller advertising accounts, and the owner invited me to his home in Saratoga Springs for a weekend. Smelling a little bonus money in the deal, you see, something my firm wouldn't know anything about, I accepted and drove to this fellow's place early on a Saturday morning.

'Just as I anticipated, he presented me with a bonus check for a thousand clams. And we sat around his swimming pool all afternoon — which was empty by the way — drinking Scotch and water and talking business. Out of nothing, he asked me if I'd like to see a cockfight that night.

'"Cockfight!" I said. "They're illegal, aren't they?" "Sure, they are!" he laughed. "But so was sleeping with that blonde you fixed me up with in New York. If you've never seen a cockfight, I think you might get a kick out of it."

'So I went to my first cockfight. I'll never forget it, Frank. The sight of those beautiful roosters fighting to the death, the gameness, even when mortally wounded, was an exciting, unforgettable experience. Before the evening was over, I knew that that's what I wanted to do with my life: breed and fight game fowl. It was infantile, crazy maybe, I don't know. My wife thought I'd lost my mind and wouldn't even listen to my reasons. Probably because I couldn't give her any, not valid reasons. I *wanted* to do it and that was my sole reason!

'I was fed up to the teeth with advertising, and I had saved enough money to quit. I was only fifty, and although my future still glimmered on Madison Avenue, I didn't really need any more money than I already had. Still, I played it pretty cagy with the firm. I made a secret deal with one of the other vice-presidents to feed him my accounts in return for supporting my resignation on the grounds of ill health. That way, I picked up twenty-five thousand dollars in severance pay. I sold my apartment house and set up a trust fund for my wife to take care of her needs in New York. Besides, she has money of her own. Her father was a proctologist, and he left her plenty when he died. And for the first time in my life, I'm happy, really happy. Funny, isn't it?'

This was Omar Baradinsky, who owned a game farm only three miles away from mine. So far, he hadn't even prospered in his adopted profession, but he was breaking even by selling trios and stags to other cockers. His game cocks usually lost when he fought them in Southern pits. He must have been hard enough to succeed in the business world, but the stubborn streak of tenderness in his makeup didn't give him enough discipline to make Aces out of his pit fowl. He overfed them, and he didn't work them hard enough to last.

Turning away from the poem, Omar turned his huge brown orbs on me and jerked a thumb at the wall.

'Did you write that, Frank?'

I shook my head and pulled out a chair for him to sit down.

'Then what about your new cock, Icky? If that chicken wasn't bred purely for color I've never seen one.'

I shrugged. Icky had been bred for color, certainly, but from a pure game strain, and his conformation was ideal for fighting. In a few days I'd see whether he could fight or not when I gave him a workout with sparring muffs in my training pit.

'Anyway, I like the look of those Mellhorn Blacks, and especially your two Middleton Grays.'

So did I. Buford, my part-time Negro helper, had gone downtown to the depot with me the night before when I picked up my shipment of Mellhorn Blacks. After helping me put the dozen cocks away in their separate stalls in the cockhouse, he had driven by Omar's place and told him about them. Omar had arrived early that morning for a look at the Mellhorns and a long admiring examination of Icky. Buford had undoubtedly given Icky a big buildup, but Omar hadn't been impressed until he saw the cock for himself.

'Tell me something, Frank, if you will,' Omar said, when he finished pouring some condensed milk into his coffee. 'Did you get an invitation to the Southern Conference Tourney at Milledgeville?'

In reply, I got up from the table, rummaged in the top drawer of my dresser until I found the invitation and the schedule for the S.C. pit battles, and passed them to Omar. He glanced at the forms, pulled on his shaggy beard a couple of times, and returned the papers.

'I just don't understand you people down here,' he said. 'It may be partly my fault, because I wrote Senator Foxhall a personal letter asking for an invitation and enclosed a two-hundred-dollar forfeit. Three days later I got the check back in the mail and no invitation. Not a damned word of explanation. What in the hell's the matter with me? I've got more than fifty birds under keep, and last season my showings hit fifty-fifty. Maybe I'm not in the same class with the S.C. regulars, but if I'm willing to lose my entry fee why should Senator Foxhall care? And here you are — I saw the date on your invitation — you didn't own a single gamecock when you got that invite! I'm not belittling your ability, Frank. I know you're a top cocker and all that, but how did the senator know you'd be able to attend? How did you receive an invitation without asking for one when I couldn't get one when I did?

'I've never attended the Milledgeville meet, and I want to go, even as a spectator. But after fighting at all the other S.C. pits this season, I'd be embarrassed to attend the tournament without an entry. Do you know what I mean?'

I knew what he meant, all right. Omar had done the normal, logical thing, and the turndown had hurt his feelings. Most of the U.S. derbies and tourneys get their entries through fees. The man who sends in a two- or three-hundred-dollar forfeit either shows up or he loses his money. A contract is returned to him by mail. When the list is filled, no more entries are accepted. I didn't really know why Omar had been turned down by Senator Foxhall. It wasn't because he was a Pole or a New Yorker.

Members of the cockfighting fraternity are from all walks of life. There are men like myself, from good Southern families, sharecroppers, businessmen, loafers on the county relief rolls, Jews, and Holy Rollers. If there is one single thing in the world, more than all the others, preserving the tradition of the sport of cocking for thousands of years, it's the spirit of democracy. In a letter to General Lafayette, George Washington wrote, 'It will be worth coming back to the United States, if only to be present at an election and a cocking main at which is displayed a spirit of anarchy and confusion, which no countryman of yours can understand.' I carried a clipping of this letter, which had been reprinted in a game fowl magazine, in my wallet. I had told Mary Elizabeth once that George Washington and Alexander Hamilton had both been cockfighters during the colonial period, but she had been unimpressed. Nonetheless, cockfighters are still the most democratic group of men in the United States.

But the Milledgeville Tourney was unlike other U.S. meets. Senator Foxhall had his own rules, and he made his own decisions about whom to invite. I had earned my right to fight there, and I suppose the old man knew that I would be there if it was physically possible to be there. Maybe he didn't think Omar was ready yet. I didn't know. Surely Omar's fifty-fifty showing didn't put him into the top cocker's class. He still had a lot to learn about game fowl if he wanted to be a consistent winner.

I looked at Omar and smiled. There wasn't any use to write a note for him telling him what I thought was the reason for his turndown. His feelings would be hurt more than they were already. By writing to the senator, he had made a grave error, a social error. It was like calling a host of a party you were not invited to and asking point blank for an invitation!

I had finished my coffee, and I had work to do. I got up from the table and clapped Omar on the shoulder. Before leaving the shack, I took a can of lighter fluid off the dresser and slipped it into my hip pocket. Omar sighed audibly and decided to follow me out.

When we got to the cockhouse, I removed the Mellhorn Blacks one at a time from their separate coops, showing off the good and bad points to Omar as well as I could before putting them back. For a shipment of a dozen, they were a beautiful lot. As Jake had promised in his letter, six were full brothers, a few months past staghood, and the other six were Aces, two to three years old, with one or more winning fights behind them. Each cock was identifiable by its web-marking, and the cardboard record sheet of each bird had been enclosed in its shipping crate when Jake had expressed them down from North Carolina. Before putting them away the night before, I had purged them with a mild plain-phosphate mixture, and they were feeling fine as a consequence.

As a conditioning bench, I used a foam-rubber double mattress stretched flat on a wooden, waist-high platform Buford and I had knocked together out of scrap lumber when I had first leased the farm. I had one of the older Mellhorn cocks on the bench showing it to Omar. The cock was a one-time winner, but he must have won by an accident. His conformation was fair, but the bird was high-stationed, with his spurs jutting out just below the knee joint. He would miss as often as he hit. A low-stationed cock would have greater leverage and fight best in long heels, but a high-stationed cock like this one would never make a first-class fighter. Jake Mellhorn hadn't gypped me on the sale. He was truly bred, and in small-time competition against strainers, the cock could often win. It had weight in its favor and was close to the shake class, but the chicken couldn't really compete in S.C. competition unless it got lucky. Luck is not for the birds. The element of chance must be reduced to the minimum if a cocker wants to win the prize money. In a six-entry derby, for instance, when the man winning the most fights takes home the purse put up by all the entries, the odd fight often provides the verdict. I couldn't take a chance with this one.

After pointing out the high spurs to show Omar what was wrong with the Black, I picked up my hatchet and chopped off the rooster's head on the block outside the doorway.

'I see,' Omar said thoughtfully, as he watched the decapitated chicken flop about in the dusty yard. 'You don't like to pit high-stationed cocks.'

I clipped the hatchet into the block so it stuck.

'Some cockers prefer high-stationed birds,' Omar said argumentatively. 'And a seventy-five dollar chicken is damned expensive eating.'

True, the plateful of fried chicken I would eat that night would be a costly meal, but it would have been much more expensive to pit the cock when he would probably lose. And an owner should only bet on his own gamecock — not against it. I shrugged indifferently.

'I suppose you know what you're doing,' Omar said. 'But he was a purebred Mellhorn and could have been kept as a brood cock.'

Except on a small scale, I've never done much breeding. I prefer to buy my gamecocks. Conditioning and fighting them are what I do best, but I would never have bred the high-stationed Black. Like begets like, and the majority of the chicks sired would have been high-stationed.

I shook my head and grinned at Omar. He was well aware of the heredity factor — his head was crammed with breeding knowledge he had learned through reading and four years' experience. Omar was still sore about the Milledgeville Tourney.

'What about the six brothers? How do you know they're game? The Aces have been pit-tested, but if one of the brothers is a runner they all may be runners.'

Unfortunately, there is no true test for gameness. Only a pit battle can decide gameness. There are various tests, however, a cocker can try which will give him an indication of a cock's gameness. In the case of the six brothers, I was stymied by a lack of knowledge concerning the father and mother. If the father had been a champion, Jake Mellhorn would have said so, and charged a higher price for them. The six cocks were obviously Mellhorn Blacks. I could tell that by looking at them. But only one drop of cold blood from a dunghill will sometimes cause a cock to run when it is hurt. One of the young cocks had to be tested for gameness, and I had planned on doing it this morning before Omar came over. If the cock I tested proved to be game, I could then assume that the others were equally game. But in the testing I would lose the gamecock. Another seventy-five bucks shot.

One rigid test for gameness is to puncture a cock all over his body with an ice pick, digging it in for a quarter to half an inch. If the injured cock will still attempt to fight another cock the next morning, even if all he can do is lie on his back and peck, it is considered game. The ice-pick method of testing is fairly popular with cockers because they can usually salvage their bird after it recovers from its injuries. I don't consider this test severe enough. The Roman method I use is more realistic than a halfhearted jabbing with an ice pick, even though the cock is lost during the process.

For the test, I selected one of the brothers with the poorest conformation. The choice was difficult because all of the brothers were fine Mellhorn Blacks. For an opponent, I used the largest of the two Middleton Grays. Omar held the Gray when I heeled it with sparring muffs. The Black would be practically helpless, and I didn't want him killed until he had suffered sufficiently to determine his gameness.

My homemade pit is crudely put together with scrap lumber, but it meets the general specifications. I've also strung electric lights above it in order to work my birds at night, and it's good enough for training purposes. Omar put the Gray under one arm, after I completed the heel-tying of the muffs, and headed for the training pit in front of my shack.

The young Black was a man fighter and pecked my wrist twice before I could get a good grip around his upper legs with my left hand. A moment later I had his body held firmly against my leg where he couldn't peck at me anymore. In this awkward position, I stretched his legs out on the block outside the cockhouse and chopped them off at the knee with the hatchet.

When I joined Omar at the pit, his brown eyes bulged until they resembled oil-soaked target agates. 'Good God, Frank! You don't expect him to fight without any legs, do you?'

I nodded and stepped over the pit wall. I cradled the Black over my left arm, holding the stumps with my right hand, and raised my chin to indicate that we should bill them. Omar brought the Gray in close and the Black tore out a beakful of feathers.

We billed the cocks until their ingrained natural combativeness was aroused, and then I set the Black down on the floor of the pit and took the Gray away from Omar. The Gray was anxious to get to his legless opponent, but I held him tightly by the tail and only let him approach to within pecking range. When the Black struggled toward him, I pulled him back by his tail. Without his feet, the Black was unable to get enough balance or leverage to fly, and his wildly fluttering wings couldn't support him in an upright position. He kept falling forward on his chest, and

after a short valiant period of struggling, he gave up altogether. I let the Gray scratch into range, still holding him
by the tail. The Black pecked every time, although he no
longer tried to stand on his stumps. Finally, I let the Gray
go, and he described a short arc in the air and landed,
shuffling, in the center of the Black's back. Getting a good
bill hold on the prostrate cock, the Gray shuffled methodically in place, hitting the padded muffs hard enough to
make solid thumping sounds on the Black's body. This
was the first time I had seen the Gray in action. I realized
that Ed Middleton had really done me a favor when he
gave me the once-battered fighter. Any cock that could
shuffle with the deadly accuracy displayed by the
Middleton Gray would win a lot of pit battles.

The Black was too helpless to fight off the Gray, so I
picked up the muff-armed bird and gave him to Omar to
hold for a moment. I took the can of lighter fluid out of
my hip pocket, and sprinkled the liquid liberally over the
Mellhorn Black. Flipping my lighter into action, I applied
the lighter to the cock, and his feathers blazed into oily
flames.

When Omar returned the Gray I pitted him against the
burning bird from the score on the opposite side of the pit.
He walked stiff-winged toward the downed Black with his
long neck outstretched, holding his head low above the
ground. The fire worried and puzzled him, and he was
afraid to hit with his padded spurs. The Gray pecked
savagely at the Black's head, however, even though it was
on fire, and managed to pluck out an eye on his first bill
thrust.

The Black tried to stand again, fluttering his smoldering
wings, but his impassioned struggles only succeeded in
increasing the flames. The smell of scorching feathers
filled the air with a pungent, acid stench. As I grabbed the
Gray's tail with my right hand, I held my nose with my
left. As the flames puffed out altogether, the Black lay
quietly. The charred quills resembled matchheads or
cloves dotting his undressed body, and for a moment I
thought he was dead. But as I allowed the straining Gray

to close the gap between them, the dying Mellhorn raised his head and pecked blindly in the general direction of the approaching Gray. With that last peck, a feeble peck that barely raised his head an inch above the ground, he died.

I put the Gray under my arm and turned around to see what Omar thought of this remarkable display of game-ness. But Omar had gone inside the shack. I cut the sparring muffs away from the Gray's spurs and returned him to his coop.

Omar sat at the table, staring at his open hands, when I joined him inside the shack. I opened a pint of gin I had stashed away behind the dresser — because of Buford — and put the bottle on the table. Omar took a long pull, set the bottle down, and I took a long one myself. I needed that drink and felt a little sick at my stomach. And I knew that Omar felt as badly as I did. But what else could I do? I had lost a wonderful game cock, but I could now assume that his five brothers would be as game as he had been. The unfortunate part of the testing was that I didn't really know if the brothers were equally game. But I could now *assume* they were.

'I couldn't treat a gamecock like that, Frank,' Omar said, without looking at me, keeping his eyes on his open hands. 'Sure, I know. A chicken is supposed to be an insensitive animal and all that crap. But *I* couldn't do it! I could no more set a cock on fire than I could —' His mind searched for something he could no more do, and then he shrugged his heavy shoulders and took another shot of gin.

I took another short one myself.

'Was he game, Frank? It was too much for me. I couldn't stick around to see.'

I nodded glumly and lit a cigarette.

'Unbelievable, isn't it! Burning like a damned torch and still trying to fight! A man couldn't take that kind of punishment and still fight. Not a man in this world could do it.'

I stubbed out the cigarette. It tasted like scorched feathers, despite the menthol and filter tip.

'Well, Frank,' Omar said pensively, 'there're a lot of things I don't like about cockfighting, but a cocker's got to take the bad with the good.'

I nodded in agreement and pushed the bottle toward him.

Omar studied my face and, ignoring the bottle, leaned forward.

'You and I need each other, Frank,' he said suddenly. 'Why don't we form a partnership for the season?'

For some reason his suggestion startled me, and I shook my head automatically.

'Don't decide so hastily,' he continued earnestly, leaning over the table. 'I've picked up twenty cocks already, and I've still got better birds to pick up on walks in Alabama. Between the two of us, if you conditioned and handled, and I took charge of the business end, we could have one hell of a season. I know how tough it's been since you lost your voice. I still remember how you used to holler and argue and knock down the odds before the fights. What do you say, Frank?'

I was tempted. Two of my cocks were gone before I started. I only had thirteen birds left for the season, and my cash was low. If we combined our game cocks we could enter every money main and derby on the circuit, and if Omar didn't interfere with my conditioning —

'Let it go for now,' Omar said carelessly, getting to his feet. 'Just think about it for a while. I don't like to mention my money, but I'm lousy with capital. I've got a lot more than you have, and if you had a partner putting up the forfeits, entry fees, and doing all the betting, you could concentrate on conditioning and handling. And on a partnership we can split everything we take in right down the middle.'

He turned in the doorway and his shadow fell across my face. 'No matter what you decide,' he said cheerfully, 'come over to my place for dinner tonight. I'll take that high-stationed Mellhorn home with me. I've always wanted to eat a Mellhorn Black with dumplings.' He laughed. 'Chicken and dumplings for two! That's about thirty-seven fifty a plate, isn't it?' Omar waved from the door and disappeared from sight.

I remained seated at the table. A few minutes later I heard the engine of his new Pontiac station wagon turn over, and listened to the sounds as he drove out of the yard. The pot of coffee on the hot plate burbled petulantly. I poured another cup, and a cock crowed outside, reminding me of all the work still to be done that morning. I couldn't put off the dubbing of Icky any longer.

Ordinarily, the deaf ears, wattles and comb are trimmed away when the bird is a young stag of six or seven months. Ed Middleton, for reasons known only to himself, had failed to dub Icky. He probably meant to keep Icky as a pet and brood cock and had never intended to pit him. But I was going to pit him, and he had to be dubbed for safety in battle. With his lovely free-flowing comb and dangling wattles, an opposing cock could get a billhold and shuffle him to death in the first pitting. I had been putting off the dubbing, afraid that he might bleed to death. With a stag the danger is slight, but Icky was fully matured, more than a year-and-a-half old. And it had to be done.

I got my shears, both the straight and the curved pairs, and went outside to Icky's coop room.

He was a friendly chicken, used to kindness and handling, and ran toward me when I opened the gate. I picked him up, sat on the bench in front of the shack, and went to work on his comb. With my experience I don't need a man to hold a chicken for me. I've dubbed as many as fifty stags in a single morning, all by myself, and I've never had one die from loss of blood yet. But I was extra careful with Icky.

Gripping his body firmly between my knees, and holding his head with my left hand, I clipped his comb with the straight shears as close to the head as possible. Many cockers leave about an eighth of an inch, believing erroneously that the slight padding will give the head protection from an opponent's pecking. But I've never known a cock to be *pecked* to death. I trim right down to the bone because the veins are larger close to the head and there isn't as much bleeding. I cut sharply, and with solid, quick snips, so the large veins were closed by the force of the shears. Luckily, Icky's head bled very little. I then cut away the wattles and deaf ears with the curved shears, again taking my time, and did a clean job. As an afterthought I pulled a few short feathers out of the hackle and planted them in Icky's comb. The little blue feathers would grow there and ornament his head, until they were billed out by an irate adversary.

When I completed the dubbing I turned him loose in his coop. He had held still nicely, and because he had been so good about it, I caught the Middleton Gray game hen running loose in the yard, and put her into his coop. The dubbing hadn't bothered him. He mounted the hen before she had taken two steps. A moment later he flew to his roosting pole and crowed. Within a week his head would be healed completely, and he would be ready for conditioning.

Omar had taken the decapitated Ace Black with him, but the charred Mellhorn was still in the pit. I buried the dead chicken and the other cock's severed head in the sand before eating lunch.

If I had been completely broke, or without any game cocks of my own, I wouldn't have considered a partnership with Omar. But I had enough Ace chickens to hold up my end. Omar had excellent, purebred game cocks. All he needed was a man like me to work the hell out of them. The idea of forming a partnership with anybody had never occurred to me before, although partnerships were common enough in cockfighting circles. Besides, I had a good deal of affection for Omar, almost a paternal feeling toward him, despite the fact that he was more than twenty years older than me. He wanted success very much, and there were many things he had to learn. And there was a lot that I could teach him.

After feeding the chickens that evening, I drove to Omar's farm for supper. His farm was on the state road, and his house was a two bedroom-den structure with asphalt-tile floors. It was a luxurious house compared to my one-and-a-half room shack. There was an arch above the entrance gate, and a sign painted with red letters on a white background stated:

THE O.B. GAME FARM
'Our Chickens Lay Every Night!'

Omar had been in advertising too many years to pass up a good slogan. In addition to the arch sign, there was a smaller sign nailed to the post of the gate at the eye level of passing motorists.

EGGS. $15 PER DOZEN

At least once a week, some tourist driving down the highway toward Santos or Belleview would stop and attempt to buy eggs from Omar, thinking that the sign was in error and that the eggs were fifteen cents a dozen. Omar enjoyed the look of surprise on their faces when he told them that there was indeed no mistake. Of course the eggs were fifteen dollars a dozen and worth a hell of a lot more! And of course, Allen Roundhead and Claret setting eggs were a bargain indeed at fifteen dollars a dozen.

Smiling at the sign, I turned into Omar's farm. A man like Omar Baradinsky would be a good partner for me. Why not? I couldn't think of a single valid objection.

That evening after supper, when Omar brought out the bottle of John Jameson, a partnership was formed.

Chapter Eleven

For the next three days Omar and I lived out of his station wagon, driving through southern Alabama and picking up his country-walked roosters from various farmers. The back of the station wagon had been filled with young stags before we left, each of them in a separate coop. Every time we picked up a mature cock we left a stag to replace it.

Omar paid these Alabama farmers ten dollars a year for the privilege of leaving one of his game cocks with the farmer's flock of hens. In addition to the board bill, he also had to buy up and kill all the farmer's stags each year. Selecting the right farm walk for a fighting cock is an art, and Omar had done a careful, thorough job. All his Alabama walks were more than adequate.

A game cock is a bird that loves freedom of movement. With his harem at his heels, a cock will search for food all day long, getting as far as three or more miles away from his chicken house on the farm. The more difficult his search for food, the greater his stamina becomes. At night, of course, once the chickens are asleep, the farmer must sneak out and scatter enough corn in the yard to supplement the diet. But he must never put out enough feed to completely satisfy the chickens. Like members of a welfare state, chickens who don't have to get the hell out and scratch for their living will soon learn to stand around waiting for a free handout, getting fat and useless.

The hillier the farmland, the better it is for the cock's legs. Trees to roost in at night, green fields, and, whenever possible, a fast-flowing brook for fresh water are the requisites for a good walk. Florida is too flat for good walks, and Omar had been wise to put his roosters out in southern Alabama.

To assist us in picking up the half-wild, country-walked game cocks, I had brought along my big Middleton Gray. He had a deep, strong voice and an exceptionally aggressive disposition. We had little difficulty in getting the half-wild cocks to come back to the farmyards.

First, we drove into a farmer's yard, and Omar told him we were there to pick up the rooster, and that we had another to replace him.

'Well, now, Mr. Baradinsky,' the farmer said, invariably scratching his head, 'I ain't seen your rooster for two or three days now.'

'Don't worry,' Omar would laugh. 'He'll be here in a minute.'

By that time, I would have the big Gray heeled with a pair of soft sparring muffs. As soon as I dropped the Gray in the yard, he would begin to look for hens, crowing deep from his throat. Within seconds, an answering crow would echo from the fields or woods a mile away. As we watched, the cock we came for would be running toward us as fast as his strong legs could carry him, his harem scattered and trailing out behind him. He often crowed angrily as he ran — *Who is this threat to my kingdom? This interloper who would steal my hens?* — he seemed to say. When he reached the yard, he attacked immediately, and the Gray, seeing all those pretty hens, piled right into him with the sparring muffs. Omar would catch the wild country-walked cock, and I'd put the Gray back into his coop.

After closely examining the wild game cock, I'd saw off his natural spurs a half inch from the leg, and arm him with the other pair of sparring muffs. We pitted the two cocks then and there to see how the bird fought. It is very difficult to spot a runner on his own domain — often a useless dunghill rooster will fight to protect his own hens — but I could always get a fair idea of the bird's fighting ability. If the cock was satisfactory, we left a young stag to take over the harem and placed the cock in the stag's coop. Before leaving, Omar would pay the farmer ten dollars in advance for the next year's board and warn the man against clipping the new stag's wings. We never took the farmer's word either. Before leaving we always checked personally to see that there weren't any other full-grown roosters, turkeys, or guinea fowl around. A stag must be in complete control of the yard. If there was a mature rooster on the farm, dunghill or otherwise, the stag might have been intimidated and gone into hack, submitting to the dunghill's rule.

Omar had developed a firm, gruff manner with these farmers who loaned their farms for walks. Despite his strong New York accent, which rural Southerners distrust instinctively, he had won them over completely during four years of contact. He didn't merely leave a stag and forget about it until the following season. He wrote letters periodically during the year, asking how his rooster was getting along, enclosing a stamped, self-addressed post-card to make sure he would get a reply. The farmers responded cheerfully to Omar's active interest, and, if nothing else, they were awed by his impressive jet-black beard.

Most farmers, once they accept the idea of having a game cock instead of a dunghill ruling their hens, are well pleased by the setup. Why shouldn't they be? The eggs they obtain are bigger and better-tasting, the offspring of a game cock have more meat, and the small payment of ten dollars a year is money from an unexpected source. And any farmer who keeps a few hens has to have a rooster. Why not a game rooster?

Every time we picked up another country-walked rooster my heart swelled with pleasure. Their feathers were tight and their yellow eyes were bright and alert. Their exercised bodies were firm to the touch, and their dubbed combs usually had the dark red color of health. Out of the twenty-eight cocks Omar had on country walks, we picked up twenty-one. The other seven, in my considered opinion, needed another full year of exercise in the country.

*

I was happy to get back to Ocala and anxious to get to work. The little town of Ocala has always been my favorite Florida city, combining, as it does, the best aspects of Georgia and the worst side of Florida. A small city, of about twenty thousand permanent residents, and some one hundred miles below the Georgia state line, Ocala is where the state of Florida really begins.

As a driver enters town on the wide island-divided highway, the first sight that hits his eyes is the banner above the road: OCALA — BIRTHPLACE OF NEEDLES! This famous racehorse will be remembered by the Ocala townspeople forever.

To his left, six miles away, is Silver Springs, one of the most publicized tourist attractions in the world. On either side of the highway there are weird attractions, displays and souvenir shops. Commercial Florida also begins at Ocala. But the town itself is like a small Georgia town. Decent, respectable and God-fearing. The townspeople are good Southerners — they provide their services to the rural residents and to themselves, and take only from the vacationing tourists with cameras dangling from their rubber necks.

Two miles outside the city limits in gently swelling country is my small leased farm of twenty-three acres, a small house to live in, an outhouse and outside shower, a well-constructed concrete brick cockhouse and some thirty-odd coop walks. My shack, as I called it, was unpainted but comfortable. The man who built it had started with concrete bricks, but ran short before the walls had reached shoulder height. The remainder of the house had been completed with rough, unfinished pine, and roofed over with two welded sheets of corrugated iron. In a downpour, the heavy pounding of raindrops on the corrugated iron had often driven me out of the shack.

Omar dropped me off first and then drove to his own farm. He had much better facilities to take care of the cocks than I had, and, upon his suggestion, I had agreed to alternate between our farms for conditioning purposes.

Buford ran out of the cockhouse as I entered the yard, a big white smile shining in the middle of his ebony face.

'Mr. Frank,' he said happily, taking my bag. 'I sure is happy to see you! My curiosity's been drivin' me near crazy for two days. Just wait till you see them big packages I put in the house!'

I entered the shack, followed closely by Buford, and the first thing I did was reach behind the dresser for my pint of gin. As I had suspected, the bottle contained less than two ounces, and it had been almost half full when Omar had picked me up three days before. I looked sternly at Buford, but he was pointing innocently to the two large cardboard boxes on my bed.

'I don' know what they is, Mr. Frank,' he said quickly. 'The man from the express brought 'em out day before yesterday, and I signed your name. What do you reckon's in there?'

I finished the gin, and handed the empty to Buford. Buford had had his share while I was gone — the man had an unerring instinct for discovering where I hid my bottle. He thought that finding my bottle was some kind of game.

I took out my knife and slit open the two cardboard boxes. One box contained a speaker, and the long box held an electric guitar. But *what* a guitar! The instrument was fashioned out of some kind of light metal, painted a bright lemon yellow and trimmed in Chinese red. On the box, above the strings, there were two sets of initials, encircled by an outline of a heart.

If I thought I had made the grand gesture when I sent Bernice a dozen yellow roses, she had certainly topped me. The electric guitar and its matching yellow amplifying speaker must have set her back four or five hundred dollars. I searched through the excelsior in both cartons for a note of some kind, but there wasn't even a receipt for the instrument. The initials inside the heart contained her message.

Buford looked admiringly at the guitar, shaking his

head with feigned amazement. As soon as I looked at him he laughed the professional laugh of the American Negro.

'Whooee!' he exploded with false amusement. 'You got yourself a guitar now for sure, Mr. Frank!'

I pointed to the door. Out in the yard I gave Buford a ten-dollar bill in payment for looking after the place for three days. Buford had his own farm, a wife and four children, but he spent more time with me than he did with his family. When I happened to think about it, I'd slip him a five or a ten, but I didn't keep him on a regular salary because I didn't need him around in the first place. He knew as much about the raising and handling of game cocks as any Negro in the United States, if not more. Unfortunately, because of his color, he was barred from almost every white cockpit in the South. He would have been an invaluable assistant for me on my trips to circuit cockpits, but I couldn't take him along. However, he helped me out around the place, handled opposing cocks in my own training pit and made himself fairly useful during conditioning periods. He loved game cocks. That much I knew about him. And I believe he would have sacrificed an arm or a leg for the opportunity to fight them. Because I knew this much about the man, I was well aware that his rich and easy laughter was insincere.

What in the hell did Buford have to laugh about?

'I fixed up all them sun coops the way you showed me, Mr. Frank,' Buford said. 'And I put some new slats in the cockhouse stalls. But they ain't much else to do, so I won't be back around till Saturday.'

I nodded, and Buford climbed into his car.

'Whooee!' he laughed through his nose. 'You got you a git-fiddle now, sure enough! Will you play some for me come Saturday?'

Again I nodded. As Buford made a U-turn onto the gravel road toward the highway, I entered the shack.

The wonderful and unexpected gift had made my heart sing with delight, although I had controlled my inner excitement from Buford. As soon as he was gone, I connected the various electrical cords, following the directions in the illustrated instruction booklet. I plugged the cord into the wall outlet and tuned the strings. The full tones, amplified by the speaker set at full volume, reverberated in the small room and added a new dimension to my playing. After experimenting with several chords, banging them hard and listening to them echo metallically against the iron ceiling, I tried a song.

Halfway through the song I stopped playing and placed the guitar gently on the floor. Unconsciously, I had played 'Georgia Girl' first. The rich amplified tones brought suppressed visions of Mary Elizabeth flooding into my mind, and I dropped the plastic pick.

In the sharp silence, following so closely on the sound of the echoing song, I pictured Mary Elizabeth in my mind, still in the same position where I had left her at The Place. She sat quietly, feet below the surface of the pool, and with dancing dappled sunlight reflecting on her pale nude body. Her blue-green eyes looked at me reproachfully, and her ordinarily full lips were set in a tight grim line.

To make her disappear I shook my head.

This was a recurrent vision of Mary Elizabeth. Whenever I happened to think of the woman, a guilty, sinking feeling accompanied the thought. She was always nude, always at The Place. I never thought of her as fully clothed — that was a Mary Elizabeth I didn't want to think about — the spinsterish, school-teacherish, Methodist kind, with a reproving expression on her face. As a rule, when I hadn't seen Mary Elizabeth for several months, her features became indistinct, except for her hurt blue? green? eyes. But her body was always as clear in my mind as a Kodachrome color print. I remembered every anatomical detail, the way her right shoulder dipped a quarter of an inch lower than her left, the round, three-eyed shape of her button navel, and every golden pubic hair.

I loved her and I had always loved her and I always would love her, and the dark guilty shadows erased her pink-and-white body from my mind. No man had ever treated a woman any shabbier than I had Mary Elizabeth!

Suppose, I thought blackly, she just says the hell with you, Frank Mansfield, and marries a nice stay-at-home Georgia boy ... a bloated bastard like Ducky Winters, for instance, the manager of the Purina Feed Store? Why not? He's single and over thirty. What if his bald head does look like a freshly washed peach and the roll of fat around his waistline resembles a rubber inner tube half filled with water? He's got a good job, and he's a member of the Board of Stewards of the Methodist church ... well, isn't he? His mother can't live forever, and he did pinch Mary Elizabeth on the ass at the box social that time ... remember? You wanted to take him outside, but Mary Elizabeth wouldn't let you.

How many good prospects does she have? Ducky Winters, no matter what you may think, is one of the *better* prospects. Suppose she marries one of those red-necked woolhat cronies of her brother's? Wright doesn't want her to get married, but he would approve of some farmer who would keep her close to home, just so he would be assured of seeing her every day. What if she married Virgil Dietch, whose farm is only three miles down the road? Virgil's only forty, a widower with two half-grown boys, and he'd be damned happy to marry a woman like Mary Elizabeth. With his growling German accent — despite three generations in Georgia — and his lower lip packed chock-full of Copenhagen snuff, she wouldn't be able to understand half of what he said, but Wright liked Virgil and ran around with him. And Wright wouldn't object to a marriage between them.

For more than an hour I tortured myself, mulling over the list of eligible suitors in the county Mary Elizabeth could marry if she wanted to spite me. There weren't many left. Most of the men in rural Georgia get married young, and divorces are rare. The remaining eligibles were a sorry lot, especially when I considered the widowers who had worked their wives into an early grave.

It was exquisite torture to consider these ignorant wool-hatters who shaved only on Saturday, who wore a single suit of long johns from October to May, and who didn't take a bath until the Fourth of July. And yet, as far as husbands were concerned, every one of these men would make a better husband than I would. As a woman, she was entitled to a home and children and a husband who stayed with her at all times.

I had provided Mary Elizabeth with eight years of nothing. A quickly scrawled line on the back of a picture postcard, and on one of my rare, unscheduled visits, a quick jump in a woodland glen. To make matters worse, I hadn't even talked to her on my last two visits. But I had never been able to talk to her anyway. She had consistently resisted every explanation I had tried to give her concerning my way of life and had never consented to share it with me. Perhaps I could write her a letter, a really *good* letter this time, a letter that would make her think?

This year was going to be my year. I could sense it, and my new partnership with Omar was the turning point in my run of ill fortune. I knew this. My prospects had been as good before, but they had never been any better. I couldn't continue through life silent and alone, and I couldn't keep Mary Elizabeth dangling on a thread — the thread would break, and both of us would be lost. If there was to be a break, it would have to be now — Her way or My way — and *she* could make the choice!

I sat down at the table to write Mary Elizabeth a letter:

Dearest Darling,

I love you! How inadequate are written words to tell you of my feelings! To be with you and yet to be unable to speak, to tell you again and again that I love you is unbearable. To leave without saying good-bye, as I did, hurt me more than you can ever know. And yet, I had to leave silently, like a thief in the night. If I had written you a note with a bare 'Good-bye', you would have rightfully demanded an explanation I couldn't give because I couldn't speak! But an explanation is due, my love, and on the blankness of this

*page I shall attempt the impossible. Never, never doubt
my love!*

*First, I was home to obtain my rightfully owned
property. You know this now, of course, because your
brother bought my farmhouse and land from me.
What you don't know is that Judge Powell was
instructed to sell only to Wright. Whether I was right
or wrong in turning Randall out of his home depends
upon how you want to look at it. In the Holy Bible the
eldest son gets the inheritance of his father, as you
know. In the eyes of the Lord, and I recognize no other
Master, I was right. But even so, I only sold my land
because I had to.*

*For ten years my goal has been to be the best cock-
fighter in the United States. Several, not many, times
I've tried to explain cockfighting and my ambitions to
you, but you have never listened. Read this, now, and
then decide. Our future happiness, yours and mine,
depends upon your decision. Closing your ears to all
rational argument, you have always said that cockfighting was cruel and therefore wrong. But you have
never SEEN a cockfight, and you said that you never
intended to. At last I say you must!*

*The only way that you can find out that cock-
fighting is not a cruel sport is to see for yourself. I am
now engaged in my very last try to reach the top. To
continue fighting year after year without success is no
longer possible. If I don't win the two-day Milledgeville Tourney this year, I promise you that I'll quit
forever! We will be married immediately, and I'll enter
any profession or endeavor YOU decide upon!*

*However, if I do win, and I want you physically
present at the Milledgeville pit, win or lose, I intend to
follow cockfighting as a full-time profession for the
rest of my natural life. If you can accept this way of
life, we will get married immediately and go to Puerto
Rico on our honeymoon.*

*The remaining alternative, of course, is to tear this
letter to bits and put me out of your mind forever. If*

this latter course is your decision, I'll abide by it, and I'll never, I promise, write or see you again, but my heart will be completely broken!

Don't write and tell me what your decision is. If you do write, I won't open your letters. Two seats will be reserved in your name at the Milledgeville Tourney (bring your brother if you like) from March 15 to March 16. I won't write again, and will pray daily to the good Lord above that you will TRY — and please let your heart decide — to be there at Milledgeville.

I love you. I always have and always will!

Frank

I read the letter twice before sealing it into an envelope, and I thought it was a damned good letter. The little religious touches were particularly well done, and so was the part about going to Puerto Rico for our honeymoon. There are many luxury hotels in San Juan, and March is a good time to see slasher fights at the Valla Piedros. The pit opens daily at two p.m. and the cockfights are continuous until the cocktail hour. After dinner we could hit the casinos, shoot craps or even play a little black-jack.

Of course, there was always the chance that Omar and I wouldn't win the tourney. With ten entries scheduled, a lot of things could happen, but the main idea of the letter was to ensure Mary Elizabeth's physical presence at the pit. Once she saw for herself how well organized the tourney was, and how fair the pit decisions were, I was positive she would like the sport. A lot of ministers follow cockfighting zealously without conflict with their religious beliefs. After all, the cock that crowed after Peter denied Jesus Christ thrice was a game cock! That was right in the Bible and a damned good point.

I considered rewriting the letter and mentioning this fact to Mary Elizabeth, but it was too late. I had already sealed the envelope. A better idea, perhaps, would be to introduce her to a couple of the ministers who attended the Milledgeville Tourney every year and let them talk to her. I knew little about the Bible and hadn't read any scripture in fifteen years, maybe more.

Suppose she didn't show up? My stomach tightened at the thought. I had to risk it. If she couldn't see my side of things after reading a letter like that, there was no hope left for the two of us anyway. Feeling better about our relationship than I had in months, I picked up the guitar again and strummed it gently, enjoying the amplified sounds.

The tablet was still on the table, and I decided to write Bernice Hungerford a letter. She was entitled to a thank-you note after giving me such an expensive gift. A letter was the least I could do. Perhaps Bernice would like to see the tournament? She thought I was some kind of modern-day minstrel. What a terrific surprise it would be for her to learn that I was a professional cockfighter!

Dear Bernice:

What a wonderful surprise, what a wonderful guitar! There is only ONE way you could have pleased me more, and I intend to get into that later. This may come as a shock to you, but I'm a professional cock-fighter, not a musician. For the next few months I'll be out on the circuit and won't be able to see you, but two seats will be reserved for you at the Milledgeville, Georgia, S.C.T., March 15–16. Please come. Bring your nephew, Tommy, along to keep you company, because I'll be too busy during the meet to sit with you. I know it's a long time off and I don't know how I'll be able to wait that long without seeing you again, but I must.

I have reason to hope that my voice will come back within the next few months. A letter is not the best way to tell you how I feel about you — I would prefer to tell you in person, whispering in your pretty ear! Perhaps I've written too much already, but you should have a

*FAIR idea of how I feel about you. All my love — till
March 15.*

Frank

*P.S. The Milledgeville pit is north of town. Check at
any gas station in town for directions.*

After sealing and addressing the envelope to Bernice, it
occurred to me that she might not know anything about
cockfighting or what the initials S.C.T. stood for — most
of the people in the U.S. thought that because cockfighting was illegal it had been abolished. I should have
spelled it out in detail, I supposed. But if she made any
inquiries at all, she could find out about it easily enough.
Her nephew could do the investigating for her, and my
name was certainly well known in cockfighting circles.
The letter was better this way. If she attended the
Milledgeville meet, I'd be able to determine if she was as
interested in me as she appeared to be.

I walked down the gravel road to the highway and put
the two letters and some change for stamps into my
R.F.D. mailbox. The night was warm and soft for late
September, and a gentle breeze blew steadily across the
fields. There was a steady hum from a million insects
communicating with each other in their own little ways.

When I switched on the overhead lights in the cockhouse to check the chickens, the Mellhorn Blacks jumped
up and down nervously in their coops, clucking and
crowing almost in unison. They were all hungry, and I
intended to keep them that way. I filled the water dips
with water and returned to my shack. Without turning on
the lights again, I sat in the dark strumming away on my
new guitar until way past midnight.

This was one of the most pleasant evenings I have ever
spent by myself. Although I was tired after three hectic
days on the road with Omar, I was much too happy to
sleep.

Chapter Twelve

We were unable to make the first Southern Conference meet, October 15, at Greenville, Mississippi, but there was ample time to prepare our game cocks for the six-cock, November 10 derby in Tifton, Georgia.

During the interim, Omar wrote to Pete Chocolate at Pahokee and arranged a hack match at the Ocala cockpit to be held on a Sunday afternoon in two weeks. Pete Chocolate was a worthy opponent, although he was eccentric in many ways. He was a top cockfighter and a longtime Southern Conference regular and usually fought Spanish game fowl and Spanish crosses. He also had the distinction of being the first Seminole Indian to graduate from the University of Florida with a master's degree in Asian Studies. I don't know why he wanted a degree in Asian Studies, but I know how he got it. A rich Chinese pawnbroker who had made all his money in Miami left an annual scholarship to the university in Asian Studies for any Seminole who wanted to take it. The Chinaman had been dead for more than fifteen years, and Pete Chocolate had been the first and only Seminole to take advantage of the free degree.

Another peculiarity about Pete was his habit of wearing a black tuxedo suit at all times, even when he handled in the pit. He didn't always wear a white shirt and black tie with the tuxedo. Sometimes he did, but he occasionally wore a sport shirt, a blue work shirt, or, as often as not, no shirt at all.

His master's degree and tuxedo had nothing to do with his ability as a cockfighter. He was a top handler and feeder, and a tough opponent to face in the pit.

The check weights for the hacks were 4:02, 5:00, 5:06 and 5:10. This early in the season, Pete only wanted to fight these weights, and we had to meet them in order to get the match. Each hack was to be a separate pit battle, and we were to put up fifty dollars a fight. With the wide selection of cocks we had, it was easy to meet the weights. I selected two of Omar's Roundheads, one Ace Mellhorn Black, and my 5:00 Middleton Gray. Although Icky's weight was only 4:02, I put him on the conditioning program too, in case I could get an extra hack for him. Before I could enter Icky in the Milledgeville Tourney against my old rival Jack Burke, he had to win at least four fights. In my opinion, Icky was the cock to beat Burke's Little David. With this eventual goal in mind, I intended to select Icky's four preliminary matches with care.

For the first few days of our partnership, Omar was often sullen, but he gradually came around to my way of conditioning. To prepare a game cock for the pit is tough enough if he is in good feather already, but if the conditioner has to work off excess fat at the same time, his task is doubly difficult. When I worked out a regular diet for Omar's flock of Roundheads and Clarets, he objected bitterly.

'Damn it, Frank,' he said, shoving my list of feeding instructions back into my hand, 'I feed my cocks three times as much as that!'

We were looking over Omar's chickens at the runs on his farm, so I tried to show him why the new feeding schedule was necessary. I picked one of his Claret roosters out of a nearby coop, felt his meaty thighs with a dour expression on my face, handed him to Omar, and nodded for him to do the same.

'He's hard as a brick,' Omar said defensively, squeezing the Claret's legs.

I shook my head, picked up a stick and printed FAT! on the ground with the point of it. Omar rubbed out the word with his toe, returned the cock to the coop, and pawed through his beard.

'All right. If you say so, Frank. But he doesn't feel fat to me!'

Although Omar had been fighting cocks for four years, it was evident that he had never 'felt' a truly conditioned game cock. The right *feel* of a game cock is indescribable. Maybe it is an instinct of some kind, but if a man ever gets the right feel of a perfectly conditioned game cock in his fingers, his fingers never forget. The exact right *feel* is an incorporeal knowledge, and once the fingers memorize it, they are never satisfied until they find it again. When a game cock has the right feel, it is ready for the pit. Omar thought my regular diet was drastic, but I had to get the excess fat off his birds before I could put them on my special conditioning diet.

I checked the list again: *1 tablespoon of ²/₃ cracked corn and ¹/₃ whole oats, once a day, tossed into scratch pen. One-fourth of an apple every four days. Two ounces of hamburger every ten days. Plenty of grit and oyster shells available at all times. Keep the water cups full.*

This was a good diet, a practical feed I had learned through long apprenticeship. The chickens wouldn't starve, and they wouldn't get fat. If they had any fat when they were put on it, they would lose it in a hurry. And as long as this diet was maintained, any cock could be switched to a battle-conditioning diet and be ready to fight within ten days. By weighing them daily, any sudden, dangerous weight loss would be detected, and the feed could be increased slightly. But Omar had to begin some-where, and the new diet was the first step forward in his professional education. I returned the list to my unhappy partner and this time he accepted it. The Claret crowed deeply, anxious to get some more attention.

'You'd better crow now,' Omar shouted at the game cock. 'By this time next week you'll be too damned hungry to crow!'

The conditioning of game fowl is not a job for a lazy man. To condition five game cocks for the hack coming up was easy for me, but I don't think Omar had ever worked as hard in his life. The way he groaned and complained was downright funny. Just wait, I thought, until we start conditioning twenty or thirty at a time. In order to get six cocks ready for the Tifton derby, we would have to condition at least twenty.

After I rousted Omar out of bed at his farm at four thirty two mornings in a row, he brought a cot and his sheets over to my shack and bunked there. There was an old Negro couple, Leroy and Mary Bondwell, who looked after Omar at his farmhouse. During the two weeks Omar lived with me, Leroy fed Omar's cocks with the new diet. Every afternoon Omar drove home to check and weigh his birds, returning to my place for the evening conditioning sessions.

Buford dropped by for an hour or so every day, and I would put him to work changing straw in the coops, painting coop walks with creosote, or give him some other kind of odd job. But Omar and I, on a strict time schedule, did everything else.

I wakened Omar daily at five. I shaved and Omar fixed breakfast. By five thirty, at the latest, we were in the cockhouse.

During the entire conditioning period, the cocks were each kept in a separate stall in the cockhouse. The wooden slats on each door were close enough together so the chicken couldn't stick his neck between them and jump up and down. They were so hungry, they thought they were going to be fed every time a man entered the cockhouse. If they were allowed to bounce up and down, with their necks between the slats, they would bruise the top of their dubbed heads.

While Omar crushed two hard-boiled eggs, shells and all, into the feed pan, I measured out cracked Flint corn and pinhead oats. When the mixture was blended, each of the five cocks got one heaping teaspoonful. We never mixed more than enough for one feeding, and they all got a second feeding that night. Every other morning I tossed three or four large chunks of marble grit on the floor of their stalls.

When the chickens finished eating, and they ate fast, a cup of water was put in each coop. As long as they were drinking they were left strictly alone, but the moment they quit drinking or lost interest in the water, the cup was removed.

By six thirty they were ready for the foam-rubber mattress workbench. It was firm and only slightly springy, and it was covered with an Army surplus shelter half. I ran the cocks first, one at a time, of course, from one end to the other, and then back again, twenty times the first day, thirty the second day, increasing the number of runs each day until they reached a hundred. A cock fights fast so I ran them as fast as I could up and down the workbench.

Following the runs, the cocks were flirted. Flirting forces a cock to flap his wings to maintain his balance, and his wing muscles are strengthened. Like the runs, they started with twenty flirts the first day, and were increased ten flirts every day until they reached a hundred. Once a man gets the hang of it, flirting isn't really difficult. A conditioner must remember to always be as careful as he can so the cock won't get bruised. If a cock is flirted roughly, he will soon get stiff, even if he doesn't get bruised. Omar was good at flirting so I usually took the runs and let him fly them back and forth between his big hands. It was a pleasure to relax with a cigarette and watch Omar work.

With his left hand on the cock's breast, he would toss the bird deftly back for about a foot and a half, catch him with his right hand, and then toss him back. Omar started slowly, but once he caught the rhythm the cock was flying back and forth from one hand to the other so fast it looked like the cock was running in place. He had a definite flair for careful flirting, and he was proud of his ability.

Every other day, following the flirting period, we heeled a pair of the cocks undergoing conditioning with sparring muffs, and let them fight each other in the pit for about a minute and a half.

If one of the cocks appeared to be too tired, I didn't

spar him. There is always risk involved in sparring. Even when a bird is armed with soft chamois muffs he can get hurt. But by watching two sparring cocks closely, I can observe how well their stamina is building up.

After the sparring period, the cocks were allowed to rest for fifteen minutes, and then we washed them with warm soapy water. To help relieve soreness, I rubbed their legs down gently with a sponge dipped in rubbing alcohol. When the birds were all washed and rubbed down, they were placed in separate sun coops for twenty minutes. There was a roosting pole in each sun coop, and if the cocks were still active enough to have a fine old time jumping up to the pole and then down again with animated eagerness, I made a note to increase their runs and flirting for the next day.

The drying-off period gave Omar and me enough time to have a coffee-break.

Before we returned the cocks to the cockhouse for the day, each bird was given two flies. Two daily flies not only bring out the aggressive spirit of a gamecock, they get him used to the idea that the best way to reach his opponent is to use his wings and fly to him. For the fly, Omar held out one of the cocks with his arm extended, with the tail of the bird facing me. I held the flying cock on the ground until Omar was ready, and then I'd let him go. When I released his tail he would take to the air, but before he could reach the bird Omar was holding out toward him, Omar would twist slightly to one side, causing the flying bird to extend himself to fly higher. After a few days of flying, a mature cock could rise eight or ten feet into the air from a standing position. If a cock could remember that he knew how to fly this well, it could save his life when pitted.

The flies completed the morning conditioning. A record sheet was kept on a clipboard beside each coop, and I filled in the cock's weight, number of runs, flirts, flies, and made a note of his color. The well-conditioned cock has a dark red face and comb. When the color turns pinkish something is wrong. In the space for comments I jotted down any observed weaknesses, or changes to be made in the diet due to gains or losses that were unexpected.

Like people, every game cock has to be handled a little differently. A chicken's brain is about the size of a BB, but within those tiny brains there is an infinite variety of character and personality traits. I've seen personalities that ranged from lassitude to zealousness, from anarchy to obedience, from friendliness to indifference. Luckily, a chicken can't count. If they could count, they would have resented the daily rising of the number of flirts and runs we gave them.

A game cock is the most stupid creature on earth and, paradoxically, the most intelligent fighter.

When my chart notations were completed, I dropped a canvas cover over the slatted doorway of each coop, and the darkness kept the birds quiet until it was time for the evening training periods.

The other cocks, not under conditioning, were fed, watered, examined and weighed, and I was through for the morning. Omar and I would then play chess until time for lunch. When Buford was around, I drove to Omar's farm for lunch, and inspected his game cocks before returning home. If Buford failed to drop by, I would cook either a potful of canned beef stew or pork and beans and fix a pan of hoecakes.

'How come you've never gotten married, Frank?' Omar asked me one day, as he looked unhappily at his heaping platter of hot pork and beans. 'By God, if I didn't eat something else besides stew or beans every day, I'd marry the first woman who came along!'

Omar was so used to my silence by now that he answered his own questions. 'I don't suppose many women would want to marry a professional cockfighter, though. Most of the women I've known want their husband home every night, whether they like him or not, just so they can have somebody to complain to. But canned beans — ugh!'

In the afternoon, after Omar went home, I took a walk with one of my gamecocks that wasn't undergoing conditioning. When taken out of their runs, some of the cocks would follow me around. They liked attention, but they also hoped that I would drop a grain of corn on the ground now and then. And sometimes I did.

Mary Bondwell either fixed supper for us at four thirty at Omar's farm, or we drove into Ocala for a steak or barbecued ribs. By five thirty, we were ready to start the conditioning all over again — the feeding, weighing, flies, flirts, runs and recording. Not many game strains can stand up to the hard conditioning I give them, but my two cocks — the Mellhorn and the Gray — came along fast, and Icky thrived on it. Omar's Roundheads had a tough time for the first three days, but as soon as their excess fat disappeared, they came up nicely.

At night, to get our game cocks used to lights and noise, because they would be fighting at night later on in the season, I turned on the overhead lights of the cockpit, and played sound-effects records on a portable phonograph. The records weren't loud enough to suit Omar. He charged around the outside of the pit, shouting out bets at the top of his voice.

'Hey! Who'll give me an eight to ten! I got a blinker here, half dead already! Who'll lay twenty to ten!'

He then accepted preposterous bets in a mincing falsetto, managing to make enough noise for a major cockpit. It was comical to watch his wild antics, charging around the pit, flopping his big bare arms loosely, his black beard glistening under the lights. I could never picture Omar in a homburg and gray flannel suit walking down Madison Avenue. He fitted in with a cocker's life as though he had been born to it.

After only a few nights of noise and lights, every one of the cocks could stand quietly and patiently in the center of the pit, and pay no mind either to the records or Omar.

And of course, we had a bottle every night, either gin or bourbon, and we passed it back and forth. Omar would tell me stories about New York, the advertising business, or anecdotes about radio and television people he had known.

Quite suddenly he would stop relating a story in midsentence — 'Frank, do you want to know something?

You and I, you big, dumb, silent son-of-a-bitch, we've got the best life in the entire world! I wouldn't trade my life now if I was given every filter-tip account in the United States and fifty percent of the stock!'

He would reach for the bottle, take a healthy swig and pass it to me.

'I know you're tired of listening to me ramble on. Why don't you get out that electronic monster of yours and play us something?'

I had rigged an extension cord from the shack, and I would play for an hour or so, sitting on the bench beside the lighted cockpit. I never played songs, I more or less played with the guitar instead, trying out chord progressions, or attempting to express a mood of some kind. Omar never said whether he liked my music or not, but he listened attentively.

One night Buford drove over with a big pot of greens his wife had cooked for me. Omar told Buford to get his enamel cup from the hook above the faucet where he kept it, and then filled it with whiskey. Before Buford had finished the cupful of whiskey he got mellow and sang for us — old-time blues and field hollers. When he held a note long enough for me to catch it, I would hit the corresponding chord on my guitar. I might have been a little drunk, but I thought Buford had the greatest voice I had ever heard.

These were all pleasant evenings for me. I have always guarded my aloneness jealously. But Omar didn't encroach on my solitude, he complemented it. For the first time in my life, I realized that companionship between two kindred spirits is not impossible — as long as each man respects the other's rights.

On the eighth day of conditioning, the exercising of each cock was cut in half. On the morning of the ninth day my Mellhorn Black got moody and refused to eat. He wasn't sick, he was mean and sulky. I put the Gray game hen in his coop with him for a couple of hours and he snapped out of his lethargy. When I removed the hen and dumped a spoonful of feed on the floor of his coop, he gobbled it up in no time.

Omar thought this was funny. 'Maybe that's what's wrong with me, Frank,' he laughed. 'If somebody dropped a blonde into my bed for two hours every night, I could probably eat those beans of yours and like them.'

On the twelfth day, the cocks were taken off exercise and food together. They weren't given any water, but they didn't want water. This was a good sign, and meant they were ready for the pit. They would fast right up until pit time. All five cocks were in the peak of condition. I made Omar 'feel' every one of them, and his fingers learned the difference.

'If I didn't know better, Frank,' he said, 'I'd think these cocks were made out of stone.'

Sunday afternoon we put the cocks into traveling coops and drove to the cockpit in Omar's station wagon. The Ocala Game Club wasn't really in Ocala — it was closer to Martel, eight miles west of the city. But it was called the Ocala pit because out-of-town cockfighters stayed in Ocala motels when the February 24 S.C. derby was held. During the entire season, the pit operator, an old retired farmer named Bandy Taylor, held hack matches almost every Sunday.

Bandy Taylor was in his late sixties, with brown leathery skin and enough deep wrinkles on his face to resemble a relief map. His legs were so bowed, he couldn't have caught a pig in a trench.

Although Bandy's pit was not an elaborate setup, all of the Lownes County cockfighters liked to meet there. His wife maintained a small stand outside the pit area, where she sold coffee, Coca-Colas and hamburgers, and Bandy charged a reasonable, one-dollar admission fee. The old man, an authorized S.C.T. referee, never bet on the fights, but he made enough money on admission fees and the food his wife sold to get by. Any wins I had there could be signed by Bandy on the official records, and they would be acceptable by the Milledgeville judges for qualifying purposes.

The crowd was small, considering that four hacks between Pete Chocolate and our new partnership had been scheduled. There were thirty some-odd spectators, including a nervous Yankee tourist from Silver Springs. There were only a half dozen other cockers, looking for extra hacks. I wanted to get an extra hack for Icky, but the prospects weren't too good. I wrote my name and Icky's weight on the blackboard and hoped for the best.

Pete Chocolate won the toss and decided to fight from bottom weights up. His fighters were all Spanish crosses, and they were in fine feather. Omar held for me while I heeled the 4:02 Roundhead, and then he tried to rustle up a few bets in the bleachers. I considered fighting Icky against the other 4:02 opponent, but the Spanish Ace looked too formidable. I had made a good decision. Omar was also lucky in the stands, because the only bet he could get was a ten-dollar even money wager.

The Spanish cock uncoupled my Roundhead, breaking his spine, in the first pitting. He was counted out, paralyzed and unable to move a feather. Omar paid Pete Chocolate the fifty-dollar loss, and paid off the fan in the stands. Because of our quick loss in the first fight, Omar was able to lay a thirty-dollar bet on the outcome of the second hack.

In the second fight, I showed the 5:00 Middleton Gray, and he finished his opponent in the fourth pitting. My Gray shuffler got above the Spanish every time.

The third battle was one of those fights that never appear to get anywhere. The two cocks were evenly matched, and very little damage was done until the eighteenth pitting. By the twenty-third pitting we were alternating on calling for the count. On my count, however, the Spanish developed a rattle from an earlier wound, refused to face, and the hack was mine. Our Roundhead was well battered and wouldn't be able to fight again for at least two months.

The fourth hack was a miracle win. My 5:10 Mellhorn Black had been in fights before, and he smothered the Spanish in the first two pittings. In the third pitting, the

Black attacked furiously the moment I released his tail. The Spanish was bowled over and fell back close to the wall. He leaped high into the air, and landed on the ground outside the pit. The Spanish was game — he wasn't a runner by any means — but he was outside the pit and my Black was still inside.

It was a tense moment. I held my breath, and none of the spectators made a sound. If Pete's Spanish had jumped back into the pit, the fight would have been continued. He didn't. Confused, twisting his head about in search of my game cock, the Spanish darted under the bleachers in bewildered retreat. The hack was mine by default.

I had known Pete Chocolate for several years, but this was the first time I ever saw him get really angry. He caught his game cock, removed the heels, and swung the cock's neck against an upright post. He then jerked off the cock's head. This isn't easy. It takes a strong man to pull a chicken's head off with his bare hands. He tossed the dead chicken on the ground and came back to the pit.

'That's the first runner I ever had, Frank,' Pete said blackly. 'A Spanish don't run! That same cock won two fights before. Is that a runner? D'you ever hear of me showing a runner?'

I shook my head solemnly. Blood had dripped from the dead chicken's neck onto the white polo shirt Pete was wearing with his tuxedo, and his white tennis shoes were splashed with blood.

'He didn't run, Pete,' Omar said. 'He was confused and didn't remember where the pit was, that's all.'

'He won't get confused again!' Pete said with satisfaction. He whipped out his wallet and paid Omar off. We were ahead one hundred dollars from Pete Chocolate, and Omar had won eighty dollars more in side bets. We had lost one cock, and our Roundhead had been battered so badly he might not ever win another fight. We were just about even.

A good first day, I thought, as Omar joined me at the lunch stand.

'Frank,' he said, 'there's a kid at the cockhouse with a

Gray cross of some kind who wants to fight Icky. His name is Junior Hollenbeck. D'you know him?'

I nodded and finished my Coke. I didn't actually know Junior, but his father, Rex Hollenbeck, was a real-estate man in Ocala. He had introduced himself to me one day in town. Mr Hollenbeck was a fan, he said, and he had seen me handling at the Orlando International Tourney.

'Do you want to fight him, Frank? The kid's only about nineteen, and his Gray shades Icky two full ounces.'

I started toward the cockhouse to see whether I did or not. Junior was waiting in front of Icky's coop, cradling his Gray game cock in his arms. He was a well-dressed young man, wearing buckled shoes, charcoal-flannel Daks, and a gaily colored body shirt. His tangled chestnut hair was worn long, all the way to his shoulders, and his face was sunburned. He had a sparse straggly moustache, and the pointed chin whiskers of a young ram goat. Evidently his nose had peeled, because it was smeared with a thick covering of white salve.

'This is Mr. Mansfield, Junior,' Omar introduced us.

'I know. I saw the 4:02 weight on the blackboard, Mr. Mansfield,' Junior said, all business, 'and thought I'd challenge you. My cock's won two fights this year and has a couple of ounces over yours, but I'm willing to cut away some feathers for the chance to fight you.'

I stared impassively at the kid, and he blushed through his sunburn.

'That is,' he added, 'the man I bought him from *said* he won two fights in Tallahassee.'

I took the Gray out of Junior's arms and felt him. The bird went in and out like an accordion. I turned to Omar, winked, and moved my chin down a fraction of an inch.

'You've got a hack, Junior,' Omar said. 'And you don't have to cut any feathers. The Southern Conference allows a two-ounce leeway either way on hacks. But you'll have to fight short heels. Got any?'

'No, sir. I don't have any heels at all. I thought I might borrow a set. And I want to bet twenty-five dollars, even money.'

'Fair enough. I'll lend you a pair. D'you want me to heel him for you?'

'I know how to heel him,' Junior said defensively. 'I've heeled cocks plenty of times. Just lend me the heels and hold him for me.'

Omar laughed good-naturedly. 'Sure. Wait'll I tell Bandy there's an extra hack, before his crowd gets away.'

There had been two hacks held before the four between Pete Chocolate and me. After our last hack, a few of the spectators had departed, including the nervous tourist, but there were still a dozen or more standing around discussing the fights. When Bandy announced that there was going to be another hack, they scrambled hurriedly into the bleachers and began making bets.

We heeled with inch-and-a-quarter gaffs. To my surprise, Junior did a good job of heeling his Gray. By the way he handled his chicken, I could see he knew his way around the pit, and I felt a little better about the fight coming up.

While Bandy examined both cocks prior to the fight, I listened to the bettors. Although the Gray was announced as a two-time winner, and the Blue — as Icky was called — was announced as a short-heel novice in his first fight, most of the bettors were taking Icky and offering five to one. The odds were caused, in part, by my reputation, but they really preferred my game cock because of his color. This kind of thinking was like betting on the color of a jockey's eyes instead of on the record of the horse at a racetrack. At any rate, Omar had a hard time getting bets. Even with the high odds, only a few men were willing to back the Gray. But Omar finally managed to lay three ten-dollar wagers.

Junior was nervous during the billing, but he handled fairly well.

When Bandy told us to 'get ready' in his reedy old man's voice, Junior squatted behind his score, and held the Gray's tail like a professional.

'Pit!'

Icky took two short steps forward and then flew six feet into the air. The Gray ran forward on the ground at the same time, and Icky landed behind him. They wheeled simultaneously and mushed, breast against breast, engaged in a shoving contest. The Gray backed off, and then tried a short rushing feint that didn't work. Icky got above him, shuffled, and the two went down with Icky's right gaff through the Gray's left wing.

'Handle!'

Junior disengaged the heel from the Gray's wing bone, and we retreated to our respective scores for a thirty-second rest. The boy worked so furiously over the Gray I had to grin. He blew on the cock's back, stretched and jerked the neck, spat into its mouth, rubbed the thighs vigorously between his hands, and licked the head feathers and hackles with his tongue.

These were all legitimate nursing techniques, but to use them, any of them, after the first pitting was ridiculous. Over-nursing does more harm than good. Unless a game cock is in drastic need of help, the handler can help him best by letting him rest between pittings. I laced Icky away from the Gray and let him stand quietly so he could get the maximum benefit from the rest period.

'Get ready,' Bandy said, watching his wristwatch sweep-hand.

'Pit!'

We dropped them on their scores. Because of rough over-nursing, more than for any other reason, the Gray was slow in getting started. Icky made a forward dash with raised hackles, took off in a low, soaring flight, fanning in midair, and cut deeply into the Gray's neck with blurred gaffs. The left heel stuck, and the two cocks tumbled over, coupled.

'Handle!' Bandy said quickly.

The instant Junior moved Icky's gaff from the Gray's neck, his game cock strangled. When a cock's neck fills with blood, the strangling sound is unmistakable. Except for going through the motions in accordance with the rules, the fight was over. Until the Gray actually died, or refused to fight through three twenty-second counts, or unless his handler picked him up and carried him out, we still had to go through the routine pittings and counts.

Junior had heard the strangle, but he nursed the Gray furiously. He sucked blood out of the Gray's throat and rubbed its chest hard enough to dislodge the tight feathers. He held the feet, placed the cock on its chest and pressed his mouth against the back, blowing his breath noisily into the feathers to warm the Gray's circulation. The Gray was down, his neck stretched flat, and his eyes were glazed. Blood bubbled from his open beak, but he wasn't dead. And then, right before my astonished eyes, Junior inserted his right forefinger into the downed Gray's vent and massaged the cock's testicles!

I snapped my fingers in Bandy's direction, but he had witnessed the foul as soon as I had.

'Foul!' Bandy yelled. 'The Blue wins in the second pitting!'

I picked Icky up and held him tail first toward Bandy so he could cut the tie strings away from the heels with his penknife. None of the spectators complained about the ruling. The Gray had obviously lost before the foul was called anyway. With his sunburned face redder than it had been before, Junior pushed between us.

'What do you mean, foul!' he shouted at Bandy.

'Mr. Mansfield and I both saw you put your finger in the vent, son,' Bandy said quietly. 'And so did everybody else, if they had any eyes.' Omar joined me in the pit and I handed Icky over to him.

'That's no foul,' Junior protested. 'Nursing's allowed, ain't it?'

'Legitimate nursing, yes. Not that kind!'

'I was told if you rubbed the balls with your finger you could put new life in your chicken —' Junior argued futilely.

'Who told you that, son?' Bandy cut him off.

'My dad told me,' Junior replied. We were all three staring at him now, and he looked at us worriedly. 'Is that considered a foul?'

'Your daddy told you wrong, Junior,' Bandy said quietly.

'You rub a cock's balls and you take every speck of fight right out of him. It's a deliberate way of throwing a fight.'

'Well, I didn't know it,' Junior said. 'I want to apologize, Mr. Mansfield,' he said, with evident sincerity.

'Too late for that now,' Bandy told him. 'You're through. I got to send in a report on this to the Southern Conference. As of now, you're blacklisted at every cockpit in the S.C. I reckon that's what your daddy wanted or he wouldn't have told you no lie. But you've pitted your last gamecock at this game club, Junior.'

Junior's sun-reddened face was reduced to a pink glow. 'How long's the blacklist last, Mr. Taylor?' he asked.

'Forever. Whether you knew what you were doing or not don't make no difference. You threw the fight and there was people with bets on your Gray. I don't want you comin' out here no more, and you tell your daddy that he ain't welcome out here neither!'

Bandy turned away, his speech over, but Omar took a grip on his arm. 'Now, just a minute, Bandy,' Omar said good-humouredly, 'aren't you carrying this thing too far? The kid said he didn't know about the rule, and he apologized. Isn't that enough? The Gray had strangled anyway.'

'Are you arguing with me, Mr. Baradinsky?' Bandy said testily. 'You'd better read up on the rules before you try! My decision's final, and if you want to argue you just try it! I'll suspend you from this pit for thirty days so fast your head'll spin!'

Omar started to say something else. I managed to catch his eye, and put a finger to my lips. Bandy turned away and headed for the cockhouse, walking as dignified as a bandy-legged man is capable of walking. I took out my notebook and pencil, scribbled the word *Apologize!* and handed the open notebook to Omar.

'The hell with that crusty old bastard,' he said, returning my notebook. 'Why should I apologize?'

'Please don't get into trouble on my account, Mr. Baradinsky,' Junior said humbly. 'I've learned a lesson today I'll remember all my life.'

'I agree. But it's a hard lesson. Bandy meant what he said, you know. You're washed up when it comes to cock-fighting.'

'I know it, sir. But I still want to apologize to you both.' Junior hung his head, and started to leave the pit. I snapped my fingers, and held out my hand, palm up.

'Oh, that's right!' Junior smiled winningly. 'I owe you twenty-five dollars, don't I? Well, to tell you the truth, Mr. Mansfield, I don't have any cash with me. I was so sure I'd win I didn't think I'd need any. But I've got some money at home, and just as soon —'

I grabbed Junior's wrist, twisted his arm behind his back and put some leverage on it. He bent over with a sharp cry of pain, and then whimpered. I took his wallet out of his right hip pocket with my left hand and passed it to Omar who promptly put Icky on the ground. Omar opened the wallet and counted seventy-eight dollars. After taking twenty-five dollars from the sheaf of bills, he returned the remainder and threw the wallet disgustedly on the floor of the pit.

As I released Junior's wrist, I coordinated nicely and booted him with the pointed toe of my jodhpur boot. He sprawled awkwardly on the hard ground, and his head made a solid 'thunk' when it bounced against the low pine wall of the cockpit. Without a word of protest, Junior picked up his wallet and broke for his car in the parking lot at a dead run. I picked Icky up and grinned.

For a moment, Omar stared at the bills in his hand, and then cleared his throat. 'Well, Frank,' he said, 'I guess I'd better find old Bandy Taylor and apologize. If anybody learned a lesson today, it was me.'

Omar headed reluctantly toward the cockhouse, his hands shoved deep in his pockets. Omar might have been a big shot in the advertising business, but he certainly had a lot to learn about people if he wanted to make a name for himself in cockfighting.

Chapter Thirteen

To prepare our cocks for the six-cock Tifton derby, I found it more practical to move myself and my game cocks to Omar's farm. I was made comfortable there. I had my own bedroom, there was an inside shower and bathroom, and the meals prepared by Mary Bondwell were a lot tastier than the bachelor meals I had been cooking for myself.

I was so anxious to win the Tifton meet, I put thirty cocks into conditioning just to shape up six top fighters. Working thirty cocks daily rarely gave me a free hour to myself during the day, and I was usually asleep by eight thirty. Sunday is not a holiday for a cockfighter when he has birds to condition for a derby. There were too many things I had to do on Sunday to fight at the Ocala pit, but I sent Omar to the pit to fight some of the cocks that peaked fast. He didn't lose a single hack out of the eight battles he fought.

Our wallets were growing fatter.

On the morning of November 9, we left for Tifton, Georgia, at five, and arrived at the Tifton game club at three the same afternoon. We signed the derby contracts and were assigned to a cockhouse and given a padlock for the door.

Jack Burke was an entry in the Tifton derby, and he looked me up that evening after supper. Omar had stayed in our motel room to watch television, but I was edgy and drove out to the pit to take a final look at the twelve cocks we had brought along. The birds were roosting all right. As I locked the door and lit a cigarette, Jack Burke approached me through the dusk.

'Evenin', Frank,' he greeted me cordially. 'It's nice to see you again.' Jack looked prosperous in a double-breasted blue worsted suit, a wide paisley necktie, and black-and-white shoes.

I shook hands with the man. Jack rubbed his chin nervously, and I could sense that something was on his mind. He fixed his eyes on an imaginary point to the left of my head.

'I don't suppose you heard the good news,' he said, smiling bleakly.

I waited patiently for him to tell it.

'I got married!' He laughed. 'Bet that surprises you, don't it? Yes, sir! Sooner or later they catch up with the best of us, Frank!' He hesitated. 'I married Dody White, Frank,' he added softly.

I felt sorry for Jack, but I shook hands with him again anyway. So White was Dody's last name. I had wondered about that. And now she was Mrs. Dody Burke.

'I wanted to bring Dody along to the derby, Frank, but she wouldn't come because you were here. I tried to tell her you weren't the kind who would rake up the past, but she wouldn't believe me. She seems to have the idea that you can talk, and she's afraid you'll say something about her. I know you can't talk, but I couldn't convince Dody.' He hesitated. '*Can* you use your voice, Frank?'

I smiled and flipped the butt of my cigarette in an arc to the ground. The idea that I would ever say anything about Burke's wife whether I could talk or not was patently ridiculous. And Burke knew it. Dody had undoubtedly forced him to ask me to keep quiet about our former alliance. For an instant I felt sorry for him, and then despised him for being so damned weak and pussy-whipped.

'I feel like a fool!' Burke blushed. For a man in his mid-forties, the ability to blush is quite a feat.

'Well,' Burke said, 'I'll bring her along to the Plant City derby, and introduce you all just like you'd never seen each other before. That way, Dody's mind'll be at ease. All right?'

I nodded and looked away. I could almost smell the rancorous acid burning Jack's insides. What a comedown for Jack Burke, to let a little tramp like Dody humiliate him this way.

'Now to business!' Jack said briskly, in his regular voice. 'D'you think you and that new partner of yours can show enough cocks after the Plant City meet to fight me in an old-fashioned main?'

The decision was up to me. I was positive Omar wouldn't object to the challenge. Burke fed almost twice as many cocks as we did, but I had a fierce hankering to beat him in a two-entry main. I lowered my chin a fraction and spat between his feet.

'Good! I'll make the necessary arrangements to get the pit on the thirty-first, the day after the derby. How does two hundred dollars a fight sound, with a thousand on the odd fight?'

For the third time in as many minutes, I shook hands with Burke.

He started to say something else, changed his mind, and walked away through the deepening dusk toward the parking lot. Burke was still a damned good man. In time he would learn how to handle Dody. But the memory of this humiliating episode would rankle him forever. I knew this, and I knew just as well that he would eventually blame me instead of himself. That's the way men are.

The next day we lost only one fight in the six-cock derby, but it was one fight too many. Jack Burke didn't lose a single fight, and picked up the thousand-dollar purse. Getting close only means something when it comes to pitching horseshoes. But despite the lost fight, Omar had placed enough judicious bets to add nine hundred dollars to our bankroll.

The money was welcome, of course, but the Tifton loss was made even more depressing by the sad news that Martha Middleton, Ed Middleton's wife, had died of a heart attack. Her obituary appeared in the same issue of *The Southern Cockfighter* that carried the announcement of Ed Middleton's retirement from the sport.

542   CHARLES WILLEFORD

I had liked the old lady, and I tried to write Ed a letter
of condolence. But after a futile attempt to write a decent
letter that didn't sound banal or morbid, I gave up on the
idea and sent him a commercial condolence card by
special delivery. Not much of a writer himself, Ed
Middleton acknowledged receipt of my condolences by
thanking me on the back of a picture postcard of Disney
World. His card was waiting for me when I returned to
Ocala.

There was also a letter waiting for me in my mailbox
from Frances, my fat sister-in-law. Frances was the last
person I ever expected to hear from. After two stiff drinks
and a wait of one hour, I made myself open the letter.

Dear Frank,

*Only a few short weeks ago I hated you and would
have been glad to shoot you. But now I see your
wisdom in getting Randall out of the terrible rut he
was in. He won't write you, because he's too proud. But
he loves you and he's your very own brother and I want
you to write him soon.*

*It was an awful shock to move out of what I consid-
ered my home for life, especially knowing that
wreckers were going to tear it down the next day.*

But I forgive you, Frank, for what it did for Randy.

*We could have moved in with Daddy in Macon, but
Randy wouldn't do it. We rented a room in a boarding-
house in Macon instead — and Frank, Randy hasn't
had a single drink since the morning we left the farm!*

*He found a position right away. You remember how
he used to dig through those law books day after day?
Well, he took some of his findings down to the White
Citizen's Council and they were actually amazed at
some of the loopholes he found in the new bussing
laws. Anyway, they hired him as a full-time WCC
counselor with a retainer of eight thousand dollars a
year! And it's all been so wonderful for me, too.
Randy takes me to all the meetings and I've met ever
so many nice new people! His speeches are just*

wonderful, Frank, and he gets one hundred dollars and expenses every time he talks. Next Monday, we're going to the WCC rally in Atlanta and Randy is going to talk about the black-power movement. I'm proud enough to bust and his picture will be in the paper! Next Monday, in the Constitution, *but I'll cut it out and send you a copy.*

I can't tell you how happy I am about Randy's success. Make up with your brother, Frank. Please?

He loves you and so do I!

All my love, Frances

I had no intention of writing Randall and making up with him. But I appreciated the news from Frances. I had feared that the two of them would appear at my Ocala farm some morning, begging to be taken in — and I would have been forced to shelter them. Now that Randall was finally on his own, he could go his way and I would go mine. I didn't answer Frances either, but I saved the envelope because it had their Macon address.

When Christmastime came, I would send them a card. *Peace on Earth. Good Will toward Men!* Anytime Randall really wanted to make up with me, all he had to do was to send me the three hundred dollars he owed me.

It was my fault that we lost the Plant City derby, although no one can win them all, no matter how good his game cocks are. But I had concentrated on the selection and the conditioning of the cocks for the post-derby main with Jack Burke, and Omar had done most of the conditioning for the derby. I can't blame Omar for the loss. He did a good conscientious job. I did feel, however, that if I had helped him more we would have come out better than third place. There was some consolation in the fact that Jack Burke finished fourth. Like me, Jack had undoubtedly concentrated his efforts on preparing for our main.

The Texas entry of Johnny McCoy and Colonel Bob Moore were the winners of the derby, and it was no disgrace to lose to them. These partners are two of the biggest names in U.S. cockfighting.

Like a bridge player, who can remember every important hand he held in a rubber of bridge five or ten years back, a cockfighter can remember the details of every pitting in an important cockfight. The details of the two-entry main between Jack Burke and myself are still as vivid in my mind as if it were held ten minutes ago. But I like the way Tex Higdon reported the event in *The American Gamefowl Quarterly.*

Tex had been reporting cockfights for game fowl magazines for twenty years or more, and he's a topflight pit reporter. And yet, hardly a season goes by when Tex doesn't get into one or two fistfights for his pains. His way of writing rubs a lot of high-strung cockfighters the wrong way, especially when they are on the receiving end of his sarcasm. But his reporting is conscientious when it comes to accuracy. It takes a damned good eye to catch fast action in the pit. The following is a tear sheet of his article from *The American Gamefowl Quarterly*:

Red Heels At Plant City?
by Tex Higdon

Plant City Florida, November 31 — if you're looking for the results of the Southern Conference Plant City Derby, held November 30th, you'd better look elsewhere in these pages. This Texan is reporting the Main between the two master cockers, Jack Burke and silent Frank Mansfield. By the way, folks, Frank has gone out and got himself a partner after all these years, a New York country boy with the worst looking black beard your reporter has seen in a month of Sundays. It's a good thing Frank don't talk anymore. His new sidekick, Omar Baradinsky, does enough talking for *three* cockfighters!

The Main was a real old-fashioned-type event, well worth staying over for in Plant City another day. I wish we had more mains like this one, or at least more mains. This is an old cockpit, but there's plenty of room for three hundred people. The main pit is below ground, the way they ought to be; there are plenty of cockhouses, and clean latrines for visitors, plus a drag pit that's better than most regular pits I've seen at supposedly high-class game clubs. Pit operator-referee Tom Doyle sells toasted cheese sandwiches for a dollar apiece, and that's an outrage, but as long as people buy them, he'll probably keep the same price. Next time I visit Plant City, this Texas boy will bring his own lunch!

Referee Tom Doyle announced right off: 'If you people violate our rules, have yourself a few too many drinks and get tough, you're just right for me to handle!' Tom Doyle is big enough for the crowd to believe him. They were downright cowed, and hip pints were well hidden.

There were three checkweights, 5:00, 6:05, and shake, as set up by Jack Burke. Mansfield won the toss and decided to fight from bottom weights up. Twenty-six cocks were shown by both cockers and thirteen fell in.

No. One. Both show 5:00 cocks, Burke a Brady Roundhead, Mansfield an Allen Roundhead. Mansfield broke through early and then slowed up about the 12th pitting. He was blinded in the 20th right after they went to breast on the time call. The Brady was a hardhead that kept trying, took plenty of punishment, and broke counts as fast as the Allen Roundhead took them. In the 48th pitting Jack Burke won with a down cock that got the count and kept it while his opponent breathed gently down his neck but quit pecking.

No. Two. Burke a 5:01 Claret cross; Mansfield a 5:02 Mellhorn Black. This was a bang-up 1st pitting, followed by a dozen dirty buckles in the 2nd. Mansfield had the best cutter, and in the 18th Burke stayed put on his score. When they went to breast in the 25th the Mellhorn Black kicked like a taxpayer and won in the 30th when Burke carried his bird out.

No. Three. Burke showed an Alabama Pumpkin (if I ever saw one) bred by his brother Freddy in Vero Beach. 5:08. Mansfield a Middleton Gray, 5:06. Mansfield had a great shuffler that wasn't even touched. He was over the Burke chicken in the 1st pitting like a short-circuited electric blanket, uncoupled him in the 2nd, and won in the 5th when Burke carried out a dead one. This made the Gray a five-time winner, according to Mr. Baradinsky — who made a special trip to the press box to relieve me of fifty dollars — and I could very well believe it.

No. Four. Burke showed a 5:08 Blackwell Roundhead, Mansfield a 5:07 Claret. This was the most even and best match so far. The two cocks mixed like sand and cement every time they met until the 10th when Burke got tired. The Roundhead was down on his score in the 18th, and taken out in the 19th unable to face.

No. Five. Burke a Blue-Spangle cross, Mansfield a green-legged Allen Roundhead with the widest wing-spread I've seen outside of Texas. Both scaled 5:09. Two ring-wise roosters met in this battle and it was truly the best fight of the whole Main. Mansfield rattled in the 6th and then came back strong after I don't know how many changed bets. Burke was killed in the 19th after the Roundhead regained vigor and shuffled all over the Cross a dozen times. Folks, there was *money* lost on this fight!

No. Six. Both showed 5:10 cocks. Burke a Tulsa Red and Mansfield a Claret cross. The light-footed Tulsa Red was truly a great cutter that uncoupled the Claret in the 2nd pitting. Mansfield carried him out in the 3rd.

No. Seven. Both showed 5:12 cocks. Burke an O'Neal Red. Mansfield a low-stationed Mellhorn Black. Burke was rattled in the 3rd and down on his score in the 14th. The Mellhorn Black who spiked the steel with unerring accuracy in every pitting won for

Mansfield in the 20th.

No. Eight. Both showed 5:13 cocks. Burke a Butcher Boy and Mansfield an Allen Roundhead. The steel was tossed from every angle in the 1st and 2nd pittings as sudden squalls hit Middle Florida. The Butcher Boy weakened in the 3rd but grew stronger in the 7th and hurt the Roundhead in the next two pittings. In the 9th the Roundhead slowed and the Butcher Boy put him out of the running. Mansfield carried him out after the 10th.

No. Nine. Both showed 5:14 cocks. Burke a battle-wise Whitehackle, Mansfield a fine-colored Claret. Mansfield was smiling all over the place up to the 8th pitting when the Whitehackle got down to business and changed his smile to a frown. His Claret was counted out in the 12th.

No. Ten. Both showed six-pounders. Mansfield a side-stepping Mellhorn Black that skipped constantly to the right, and Burke a black-and-white Spangle. The Black broke the Spangle's leg in the 3rd and Burke carried his cock out. Mansfield had a real Ace here, and his way of fighting bewildered the Spangle. This was the sidestepper's fourth win this season.

No. Eleven. Two more six-pound cocks, Burke with an Ace Kansas Cutter, and Mansfield with a three-year-old Alabama-walked Claret. The Kansas chicken hung every time he got close to the Claret, and Mansfield had to take him out in the 9th.

No. Twelve. Burke showed a 6:02 Sawyers Roundhead and Mansfield gave him two ounces with the Claret he showed. These cocks came out with plenty of gas, and buckled hard for the first five pittings. An even match, one in and then the other. Mansfield was cut down on his score in the 13th. A few fast shuffles by the Sawyers Roundhead and the blood-sodden Claret was carried out helpless.

The score was tied six to six!

Odd fight. Shakes. No weights were given, of course. Burke looked determined to win the odd fight when he showed an enormous Shawlneck. My educated guess gave the Shawlneck at least ten ounces over Mansfield's oversized Roundhead. But Jack needed more than weight. In Mansfield's hands the Roundhead showed a furious style of fighting that befuddled the heavier bird. Burke was down in the 18th with a broken leg and Mansfield won in the 23rd.

But there was an even better fight to come!

As Jack Burke, great sportsman that he is, was counting out the greenbacks into Mansfield's eager hand, Mrs. Dody Burke, Jack's beauteous young bride, decided to put on a hack of her own! Weighing approximately 125 pounds, and armed with red shoes (with three-inch heels), she flew across the pit and gaffed silent Mansfield in the shins. She also tried a right-cross to Mansfield's jaw with a free-swinging red leather purse, but was blocked by her handler, Jack Burke, and carried out of the pit screaming. A fine ending to a fine main! We wonder what kind of conditioning Mr. Burke is giving his new bride?

Chapter Fourteen

'When the pressure's on, a promoter's got to do the best he can,' Fred Reed said petulantly for the fourth time during his sales talk. He ought to make a recording, I thought to myself.

Fred Reed had done the best he could all right, but I didn't like the setup, not any part of it. Including Mr. Reed, there were nine of us sitting around in the plush pink-and-white bridal suite of the new Southerner Hotel in Chattanooga. Johnny Norris, Roy Whipple, Omar and myself were all Southern Conference regulars, but the other entries were not, although they had paid their fees for the Chattanooga derby.

Except for promoter Fred Reed, who wore a suit and necktie, the rest of us were either in sports clothes or blue jeans, and we looked as out of place in the mid-Victorian decor of the bridal suite as a honeymoon couple would have looked bedded down in a cockpit. My picturesque partner, with his wild beard and bib overalls, sat uneasily on a fragile gilded chair by the door to the bathroom. I was sharing a blue velvet love seat with Old Man Whipple, a gray-stubbled cockfighter from North Carolina whose odor would have been improved by a couple of quick runs through a sheep-dip.

Mr. Reed wiped his sweaty brow with a white linen handkerchief and continued: 'Boys, when the S.P.C.A. really puts their foot down, the sheriff has to go along with 'em, that's all there is to it!

'Elections are coming up, and I just couldn't pay nobody off. But I did get to the city officials and we can stage the derby right here in this suite without interference. I know you men have all fought cocks in hotel rooms before, but you've never had a better one than this! Just take a look at this wonderful floor.' Mr. Reed bent down with a broad smile on his face and rubbed the blue nylon carpet with his fingers. 'Why, a carpet like this makes a perfect pit flooring for chickens! And don't worry about damages. The manager has been tipped plenty, and I promised him I'd pay any cleaning charges on the carpets. You've all got reserved rooms on this floor, and we've got the exclusive use of the service elevator to bring the cocks straight up from the basement garage.

'Frankly, boys, I think the Chattanooga derby is better off here than it is at my pit outside of town. There won't be as many spectators because of the space limitations, but I've invited some big money men, and you'll be able to place bets as high as you want to on your birds.'

Old Roy Whipple, sitting beside me on the love seat, spat a stream of black tobacco juice onto the nylon carpet and then cleared his throat. 'Where're we goin' to put the dead chickens, Mr. Reed?'

'That's an excellent question, Mr. Whipple,' Reed replied pompously. 'I'm glad you asked it. The dead cocks will be stacked in the bathtub. Are there any other questions?'

'Yes, sir. I have one,' Johnny Norris said politely. 'The action will be slowed down considerably, won't it, if we have to bring the cocks up from the basement before every fight? It'll take forever to finish the derby. And what do we use for a drag pit?'

'That's another good question, Mr. Norris,' Reed replied, with the deference in his voice that Johnny Norris usually received. 'But these matters have all been taken into account. Except for the traveling pit, the rest of the furniture in here will be removed, and folding chairs will be set up. You'll heel the cocks in the bedroom, and the weights'll be announced far enough in advance so that there'll always be another pair waiting to pit. There's another connecting door through the bedroom to the next suite — the V.I.P. suite, the hotel calls it — and the living room of the next suite'll be used as a drag pit. With two referees, I can assure you, gentleman, that the fighting will be as fast here as anywhere else. Are there any more questions, anything at all?'

There were no more questions.

'All right then, gentlemen. The fighting starts at ten a.m. tomorrow morning. Mimeographed schedules will be run off tonight and will be slipped under the doors to your rooms. If you'll all give me a list of your weights, I'll get started on the matching right away. By the way, gentlemen, if you don't want to dress up for dinner, you can have your meals served in your rooms. Otherwise, the hotel's got a rule about wearing coats and ties in the dining room. Your meals have been paid for, too, including tips.'

Discussions began among the other cockfighters, and they started to work on their weight lists. I caught Omar's eye and jerked my head for him to follow me out into the hall. When Omar joined me in the corridor, I led the way to our room. I wrote a short note to my partner on a sheet of hotel stationary:

No good, partner. Deputies understand agrarian people and cockfighters, but city cops have a bad habit of not staying bought. There'll be a lot of drinking and a lot of money changing hands. That means women present and women mean trouble. We've got thirty of our best cocks in the basement and a confiscation raid would ruin us for the season. Get our entry fee back from Mr. Reed.

Omar read the note and then stared at me morosely with his large brown eyes. The corners of his mouth were probably turned down as well, but I couldn't see his mouth beneath his heavy moustache. 'Damn it, Frank,' he said, 'I'm inclined to go along with you, but we'll be passing up a whole lot of easy money. Fred Reed told me personally that there were two big-money gamblers flying in from Nashville tonight, and we get fat. Really *fat*! The only entry we really have to worry about is Johnny Norris from Birmingham.'

I took the note out of his hands and ran a double line under every word in it to emphasize the meaning, and passed it back.

'I'm with you, all right. Don't worry,' he said earnestly. 'But don't forget those eight cocks we selected to enter. They're trimmed mighty fine. If we don't fight them tomorrow they're likely to go under hack.'

I nodded, thinking about the problem.

If we didn't fight our eight conditioned game cocks, we would have to put them back on a regular maintenance diet and then recondition them all over again for the January 10 Biloxi meet. Even if they were reconditioned, they would be stale. And stale, listless cocks aren't winners.

I opened my suitcase, remembering the four-cock derby scheduled at Cook's Hollow, Tennessee. I flipped through the pages of my current *Southern Cockfighter* magazine until I found Vern Packard's advertisement for the meet. As I recalled, the derby was scheduled for the next day, December 15, at the Cook's Hollow Game Club. Vern Packard was a friend of mine, although I hadn't fought at his pit for more than four years. I circled Vern's telephone number in the advertisement, and wrote on the margin of the magazine:

Call Packard. We're too late for the derby, but I can fight our cocks in post- and pre-derby hacks. Vern's a friend of mine. You take the truck and the rest of the cocks on to Biloxi like we planned.

Omar, cheered considerably, laughed and said: 'I'll buy that, Frank. And raid or no raid, the idea of fighting cocks in a bridal suite doesn't appeal to me anyway.'

Omar picked up the telephone and called Vern Packard. As I thought, I was too late to enter Vern's derby, but there were only three entries instead of four, and Vern planned 'feathering the pit' hacks as well as post-derby hacks. He was happy to have me, and told Omar that he would put me up in his spare bedroom and have some coops readied for my eight cocks.

While Omar looked for Fred Reed to get our entry money back, I packed both our bags. Ordinarily, we would have had to forfeit the two hundred dollars we put up, because we had already signed the contracts and mailed them in from Ocala. But we had contracted to fight at the Chattanooga Game Club, five miles out of the city, not in a hotel suite. It was Fred Reed's hard luck that the sheriff had padlocked his pit, not ours. I repacked our bags, and by the time Omar returned to the room we were ready to leave.

As we entered the elevator, Omar said: 'Fred was mighty unhappy about our withdrawal, Frank. We were the only entry to pull out. He tried his damndest to talk me out of it. There's going to be a bar with free drinks and sandwiches all day, he said, which only proves that we're doing the right thing. By one tomorrow afternoon that suite'll be so full of smoke and drunks you won't be able to see the chickens.'

Although I couldn't have agreed with Omar more, I hated to leave. There was something exciting about fighting cocks in a hotel and the prospect of winning large sums of money. It's almost impossible to resist free drinks, and there would be some beautiful women around to spend some money on. And when it comes to good-looking women, Chattanooga has got prettier girls than Dallas, Texas.

I had written to Dirty Jacques Bonin in Biloxi and arranged a deal to put Omar and me and our game cocks up at his game farm. When he came to fight his chickens at the Ocala derby in February, we would fix him up with like facilities either at my place or Omar's.

We shook hands and parted in the basement garage of the hotel. Omar headed for Biloxi in the pickup with twenty-two game cocks, and I drove to Cook's Hollow with Icky and the derby-conditioned birds in the station wagon.

In the heat of the fighting the next day at Vern

Packard's pit, I realized how much I had depended upon
Omar to look after things during the season so far. If Omar
hadn't done a good portion of my talking for me, I would
have had a rough time getting matches. But thanks to
Omar's efforts, I managed to fight five of my eight cocks,
and I won every hack. By picking the winning derby entry,
and laying even money with a local gambler, I won four
hundred dollars. My five hack wins added two hundred
and fifty dollars more to my roll, and I was well satisfied
with the outcome of the side trip to Cook's Hollow. This
was a small sum compared to what we might have won at
Chattanooga, but it was enormous compared to winning
nothing at all.

By four that afternoon the fighting was over, and I
hadn't been able to get a match for Icky. Icky scaled now
at a steady 4:02 and was too light for derby fighting in the
Southern Conference. All of the S.C. derby weights began
at 5:00, and the only way I could fight Icky was in hack
battles. In New York and Pennsylvania, where the use of
short heels is preferred and smaller game cocks are
favored, I could have had all the fights I wanted. So far,
Icky had only had two fights. Before he met Jack Burke's
Little David at Milledgeville, I wanted him to win at least
three more. He would need all of the pit experience he
could get to win over Burke's Ace.

The Cook's Hollow Game Club was similar to a
hundred other small Southern cockpits. The pit was on
Vern Packard's rocky farm, adjacent to his barn, and
covered with a corrugated iron roof. There were three-tier
bleachers on three sides, and the fourth side was the barn
wall. A double door in the barrier provided an
entranceway inside, and two-by-two coops were nailed to
the interior walls of the barn to serve as cockhouses for
visitors.

There was a large blackboard nailed to the outside of
the barn. The fans could follow the running results of the
derby as they were chalked up by the referee following
each battle. Cockfighters looking for individual hacks also
used the blackboard. I had written my name and the

weights of all my cocks in square letters, hoping for a challenge. When three-quarters of the crowd had left, I
decided to quit myself.

I was inside the barn, transferring my birds into my
traveling coops, when Vern Packard introduced me to an
old farmer and his son.

'Frank,' Vern said, 'this is Milam Peeples, and his son,
Tom.'

I shook hands with both men. Milam Peeples was in his
late fifties, tanned and well weathered by his years of
outside labor. The yellow teeth on the left side of his
mouth, I noticed, were worn down almost to the gum line
from chewing on a pipe. The son was a full head taller
than his father, with long thick arms and big raw-looking
hands. He had a lopsided smile, a thick shock of wheat-
colored hair, and he wore a gauze pad over his left eye.
His right eye was blue. A thin trickle of spit ran down his
chin from the left corner of his slack mouth. Either it
didn't bother him or he didn't notice it. I noticed it, and it
bothered me.

'Glad to meet you, Mr. Mansfield,' Tom Peeples said.

'I saw on the blackboard out there' — his father made a
sweeping gesture with his malodorous briar pipe — 'that
you got a 4:02 lookin' for a fight. If you don't mind givin'
me an ounce, I got a 4:03 out to my place that can take
him.'

'He's my cock, Mr. Mansfield,' Tom broke in. 'Little
Joe. You ever hear of him?'

'Mr. Mansfield hasn't fought in this neck of the woods
for some years, Tom,' Vern answered for me. 'I doubt if he
has.'

'Little Joe's a six-time winner, Mr. Mansfield,' the old
man continued, 'but I've never fought him here in Vern's
pit. He's crowd shy and can't be conditioned to people or
noise. But if you want to drive on out to my farm, maybe
we could have us a little private hack.'

I nodded sympathetically. Often a game cock is crowd
shy. But I wasn't too anxious to pit Icky against a six-time
winner.

'I'll tell you what,' Milam Peeples said generously, 'I'll give you two-to-one odds, and you can name the amount. After all, you got to fight at my place instead of here, and I want to be fair.'

I agreed, holding up five fingers.

'Nope,' Milam Peeples shook his head. 'I ain't fightin' Little Joe for no fifty dollars. Ain't worth the risk.'

I had meant five hundred dollars. I grinned and opened and closed my fist five times, as rapidly as I could.

'Five hundred dollars?' Mr. Peeples took the pipe out of his mouth.

When I nodded, he hesitated.

'Now that's getting mighty steep. If I lose, you win yourself a thousand dollars.'

'You offered Frank two to one,' Vern Packard reminded the old man.

'Little Joe can take him, Daddy!' Tom said eagerly.

'All right.' Peeples agreed to the bet and we shook hands. 'When you're ready to go you can follow us on out in your car.'

'Why don't you load Mr. Mansfield's coops in his station wagon, Tom,' Vern suggested. 'And I'll take him up to the house to get his suitcase.'

'Yes, sir,' Tom said.

As soon as Vern and I entered the back door of his house into the kitchen, he dropped into a chair beside the table where we had eaten breakfast. There was an amused smile on his friendly, open face. Vern was a short, wiry little man with a sparse gray moustache, and he had been a good host.

'Just a second, Frank,' Vern's voice stopped me as I started for the bedroom. 'It's a trick. Old Man Peeples has never heard of you, Frank, and he's taken you for a sucker. I've seen him take itinerant cockers before, and I've never said anything. Why not? Peeples is a local cocker, and most of the drifters who fight here don't come back anyway. But I don't feel that way about you. Because the local gamblers didn't know your reputation I won six hundred bucks today on your hacks.' Vern laughed with genuine amusement.

'You wouldn't fight the old man anyway, once you saw his setup. He's got a square chunk of waxed linoleum in his barn for the floor of his cockpit. And that cock of his hasn't won six fights, he's won at least *eighteen* fights! He rubs rosin on Little Joe's feet, and on that slick waxed floor the opposing cock doesn't have a chance. But if you really think your cock can take him, now that you know their game, I'll give you a chunk of rosin. That way, you'll both start even.'

I got my suitcase out of the bedroom. Vern rummaged through the drawers of the sideboard.

'Here,' he handed me an amber chunk of rosin the size of a dime-store eraser. 'You don't need very much, Frank. But don't fight him on that waxed linoleum unless you use it. If you want my advice, you're a damned fool to fight him at all!'

I winked, shook hands with Vern and crossed the yard toward the station wagon. These two peckerwoods had a lesson coming, and I had made up my mind to teach it to them. Icky was in peak condition, as sharp as a needle. They would be counting on their trick to win. With the rosin safe in my pocket, the odds were in my favor. I couldn't believe that Little Joe, despite his eighteen wins, was in proper condition to beat Icky in an even fight.

I put my suitcase in the back, checked Tom's loading of my coops, climbed into the front seat, and honked my horn to let Peeples know that I was ready to go. I followed his vintage black car out of the parking lot. The Peeples farm was some six miles out in the country, and to get there I had to follow the lurching car over a twisting, rock-strewn, spring-breaking dirt road. When the old cock-fighter stopped at the entrance to his dilapidated barn, I parked beside him.

I could see the cockpit without getting out of the station wagon. The linoleum floor was a shiny, glistening design in blue-and-white checkered squares. The glassy floor was such a flagrant violation of pit regulations — anywhere — that I began to wonder if there wasn't more going on here

than Vern Packard had told me. But Vern had advised me
not to fight, so I decided to go ahead with it and see what
happened.

When I leaned over the seat to pull out Icky's coop,
Tom opened the front door and offered his help.

'I'll hold him for you, Mr. Mansfield.'

I took my blue chicken out of the coop and passed him
to Tom Peeples. He smiled, hefting Icky gently with his
big raw hands.

'He feels jes' like a baseball!' Tom said, as I opened my
gaff case. 'Sure does seem a shame to see Little Joe kill a
pretty chicken like this one.'

I cleared Icky's spur stumps with typewriter-cleaning
fluid, and heeled him low with a set of silver one-and-a-
quarter-inch gaffs. Holding the cock under the chest with
one hand, Tom passed him back to me.

'By the way,' he said, snapping his fingers, 'Little Joe
always fights in three-inch heels, if you want to change.'
Tom had waited patiently until I had finished heeling
before providing me with this essential information.
Another violation of form. Of course, he had no way of
knowing that I wouldn't have changed to long heels
anyway.

I shook my head indifferently, and he ran to meet his
father who was rounding the corner of the barn. Mr
Peeples had gone to the rows of chicken runs behind the
barn to get Icky's opponent while Tom had helped me
heel. I took a good look at Little Joe from the front seat.

The cock had been so badly battered I couldn't determine his game strain. His comb and wattles were closely
cropped for fighting, and most of his head feathers were
missing, pecked out in earlier battles. Instead of the usual
graceful sweep of arching tail feathers, the Peeples cock
had only three broken quills straggling from his stern.
Both wings were ragged, shredded, in fact. Both wings had
been broken in fighting, and although they had knitted,
they had bumpy leading edges. As Milam Peeples sat
down on a sawhorse beside the pit and turned the cock on
its back for Tom to heel him, I noticed that Little Joe's left

eye was missing. A blinker on top of everything else. If Little Joe had won eighteen fights, and from his appearance he had been in many battles, Icky was in for the toughest fight of his life.

Maybe his last.

Under cover from Milam and Tom Peeples, I sat in the front seat of the station wagon holding Icky in my lap and briskly rosined the bottom of his feet. I was still rubbing the feet when the old man called out that he was ready. There was only a sliver of rosin left, but I put it in my shirt pocket and joined Milam and his son at the pit.

'I'm goin' to handle,' the old man said. 'And if you don't have no objections, Tom here can referee.'

I nodded, stepped over the low wooden wall of the pit, and took my position on the opposite score. The waxed floor was so slick my leather heels slipped on it slightly before I got to the other side. Although I figured Mr. Peeples was expecting an argument of some kind about the illegal flooring, I kept a straight face. I wondered, though, what kind of an explanation he used to counter arguments about the pit. It must have been a good one.

'Better bill 'em, Mr. Mansfield,' Tom said.

We billed in the center, and Icky got the worst of the prefight session. The bald head of Little Joe and shortage of neck feathers didn't give him a mouthful of anything. The Peeples cock was the meanest and most aggressive biller I'd seen in some time. I dropped back to my score. Both sets of scores, the eight and the two feet, had been straightedged onto the linoleum with black paint. As I squatted behind my back score, Tom asked me if I was ready, and I pointed to his father.

'Get ready, then,' Tom said to the old man.

Milam was forced to hold the straining Little Joe under the body with both hands. There weren't enough tail feathers for a good tail hold — and I watched Tom's lips.

'Pit!'

The fight was over.

The battle ended so quickly, all three of us were stunned. I've seen hundreds of cockfights end in the first pitting, a great many of them in fewer than fifteen seconds. But the fight between Icky and Little Joe didn't last two seconds.

I was aware that Little Joe's feet were rosined as well as Icky's. Mr. Peeples had coated them surreptitiously when he got the chicken from its coop run behind the barn. So the only way I can account for the quick ending is by crediting Icky's superior speed and conditioning and my long-time practice of releasing him first. The old man was hampered when the time came to let go, because of the manner in which he had to hold the Ace cock.

Tom's sharp order to pit was still echoing in the rafters of the barn when I released my Blue. Icky, with his sticky feet firmly planted, didn't take the two or three customary steps forward like he usually did. He flew straight into the air from a standing takeoff. Old Man Peeples scarcely had time to pull his hands away from beneath Little Joe's body when Icky clipped twice and cut the veteran fighter down on its score. It happened that fast. *Click! Click!* One heel pierced Little Joe's head, and the other heel broke his neck.

As the three of us watched in silent stupefaction, Icky strutted proudly to the center of the pit, leaving white gummy footprints in his wake, and issued a deep-throated crow of victory. The expressions on the faces of Milam Peeples & Son were truly delightful to see. And then Tom Peeple's face changed from milky white to angry crimson.

'You killed my Little Joe!' he shouted.

I was still squatting on my heels when he yelled, and I was totally unprepared for the enormous fist that appeared from nowhere and caught me on the temple. I crashed sideways into the left pit wall and it was smashed flat under the weight of my body. My eyes blurred with tears. All I could see were dark red dots unevenly spaced and dancing upon a shimmering pink background. I must have sensed the darker shadow of Tom's heavy work shoe hurtling toward my head. I rolled over quickly, and his kick missed my head. Two more twisting evasive turns, and I was in the empty horse stall next to the pit. As I scrambled to my knees, my fingers touched the handle of a heavy grooming brush. I regained my feet and swung it in an arcing loop from the floor. Tom saw the edge of the weighted brush ascending, tried to halt his rushing lunge, and half turned away. The brass-studded edge caught him on his blind side, on the bump behind his left ear. As Tom fell, his arms held limply at his sides, the opposite wall of the pit collapsed under him. He was out cold.

I could see all right now, but I kept a firm grip on the brush handle as I watched Milam Peeples to see what his reaction was going to be. The old man shook his head sadly, and removed an old-fashioned snap-clasp pocket book from his front pocket.

'You didn't have no call to hit the boy that hard, Mr. Mansfield,' he said. 'Little Joe was Tom's pet. He was bound to feel bad about losin' him so quick.'

I tossed the brush back into the empty horse stall and rubbed my sore side. My bruised ribs felt like they were on fire. My head was still ringing, and I probed my throbbing temple gingerly with a forefinger. There was a marble-sized knot beneath the skin, and it was swelling even more as I touched it.

'Now, I'm a little short of a thousand dollars in cash, Mr. Mansfield,' Milam Peeples said plaintively, standing on the other side of Tom's felled body, 'but here's three hundred and fifty-two dollars in bills. You're goin' to have to take the rest of the debt out in game fowl. We'd best go on down to the runs and you can pick 'em out. I figure six game cocks'll make us even.'

I didn't. I counted the bills he handed me, shoved the wad into my hip pocket, and then held up ten fingers.

'Most of these cocks are Law Grays, Mr. Mansfield,' Peeples protested. 'And three are purebred Palmetto Muffs. You know yourself there ain't no better cocks than Palmetto Muffs! Take a look first, and you'll see what they're worth. I only got ten game cocks altogether.'

I followed the old man out of the barn.

Professional cockers frequently pay off their gambling debts with game cocks instead of cash. But this kind of payoff is normally agreed upon before a fight — not afterward. I had no objection to taking game cocks instead of money this late in the season. Some hard-hitting replacements would be useful before we entered the Milledgeville Tourney, and I was on the high side of the hog when it came to settling up with Peeples.

On the way to the coop walks, Peeples stopped at the watering trough to light his pipe and to do some preliminary dickering.

'Now you seen them three Grays I fit this afternoon, Mr. Mansfield. Aces every one. You take them, and any five more of the lot and we'll be fair and square. Countin' the cash I gave you already, you're gettin' the best end and you know it.'

Giving Peeples more credit than he probably deserved, I figured his game cocks were worth about fifty dollars a head. According to my arithmetic I would be short about two hundred and fifty dollars if I only took eight cocks. Even if I took all of them I would be one hundred and fifty dollars short of the thousand dollars he had bet me. I shook my head with a positive-negative waggle.

Feet pounded on the hard-packed ground behind me. I turned. Less than twenty feet away Tom Peeples was charging toward me with a hatchet brandished in his upraised right hand. His red face was contorted and his angry blue eye was focused on infinity.

Without taking time to think I jumped toward him instead of trying to dodge his rush, twisted my body to the left, and kicked hard at his right shinbone. Tripped neatly, he sprawled headlong in the dirt. The hatchet flew out of his hand and skittered for a dozen yards across the bare ground. Before he could recover himself I had a handgrip in his thick hair and another hold on his leather belt. With one jerk as far as my knees, followed by a short heave, Tom Peeples was in the water trough. I shifted my left hand from his belt to his hair and held him beneath the water with both hands. His legs thrashed the scummy water into green foaming milk, but he couldn't get his head up. I watched the popping bubbles break at my wrists and held him under until his feet stopped churning.

'You'd best not hold his head under too long, Mr. Mansfield,' his father said anxiously. 'He'll be drownded!'

That was true enough. I didn't want to drown the man. I only wanted to cool him off so I could complete my business with Mr. Peeples and get back to Cook's Hollow. When I let go of Tom's head, he broke free to the surface, blubbering. He had lost the bandage in the water, but both eyes were closed. He took handholds on both sides of the tin-lined trough and brought his body up to a crouched position. He stayed that way, half in the water, and half out, his chin on his chest, weeping like a child. But he wasn't a child. He was at least twenty-two years old, and he had tried to kill me.

Mr. Peeples and I continued our walk toward his chicken runs. Although the old cockfighter complained, he helped me put the seven mature cocks into narrow traveling coops that were in the runs, and brought the three Grays that were already in coops over to my station wagon from his old car. It was easy to catch Icky, who was scratching in a horse stall. After cutting off the heels, I put him back in his coop.

'I suppose you're goin' to tell Vern Packard how you beat me,' Mr. Peeples said, as I slipped behind the wheel and slammed the door.

Looking him directly in the eyes, I nodded my head.

'If you do, Mr. Mansfield,' he begged, 'me or Tom neither'll be ashamed to show our faces down to the pit for two or three years.'

I shrugged, and let out the clutch.

As I drove out of the barn lot, Tom Peeples was still hunkered down dejectedly in the water trough like an old man washing his privates in a bathtub.

On the return drive to Vern Packard's house I missed one of the turns and had to redouble twice before I found the way back to the main road. It was dark when I wheeled into his driveway. Vern switched on the yard lights and came outside to meet me.

'Who won?' he asked excitedly, as I got out of the station wagon.

I handed him the fragment of rosin, took the wad of bills out of my pocket and counted off one hundred dollars. Grinning, I pushed the hundred dollars into his hand. He kissed the bills, and returned the sliver of rosin.

'You keep it, Frank,' he said happily. 'You paid me enough for it. Come on inside and eat. I was looking for you to get back an hour ago, but I've been waiting supper on you. It's still warm though.'

As soon as I was seated at the kitchen table, Vern served the plates and turned the burner up higher under the coffee to reheat it. There were rolls, baked ham and candied sweet potatoes. Vern put enough food on my plate for three men, but I dug into it.

As he poured the coffee, Vern said jokingly, 'What do you carry, Frank? A rabbit's foot, a lucky magnet or do you wear a bag of juju bones around your neck?'

I stopped eating and looked at him.

Vern laughed. 'Your partner telephoned about twenty minutes after you left. Mr. Baradinsky. First, he wanted to know how you made out, and I told him. Then he had some news for you about the Chattanooga derby in the Southerner Hotel.'

I put my knife and fork down and waited, trying to hide my impatience at the way he was dragging out the story.

Again Vern laughed. 'No,' he said, 'it isn't what you're thinking, Frank. They weren't raided. The pit was hijacked, and the thieves got away with about twenty-five thousand bucks, according to your partner. He got the information secondhand, and it won't be in the papers. No chickens were lost, but everybody there — cockers, gamblers and even Mr. Reed himself — lost their pants. There were three holdup men, all with shotguns, and they knew exactly what they were doing. They made everybody take off their pants and throw them in the middle of the pit. Then one of them filled up a mattress cover with all the pants and they left the hotel suite. They didn't fool with rings or watches. Just the pants' — Vern laughed heartily — 'but the *money* was in the pants! That closed the Chattanooga meet. I'll bet Fred Reed has a tough time getting an okay from Senator Foxhall for a S.C. derby next year!'

I pursed my lips thoughtfully, nodded my head, and started eating again. My swollen temple was throbbing, and I wanted to put an ice pack on it.

The next morning I left Cook's Hollow to join Omar in Biloxi, with a standing invitation to fight at Vern Packard's game club any time I felt like it. I had added $902 to my bankroll and ten purebred fighting cocks to our stake in the S.C. Tourney. But no matter what Vern Packard thought, I wasn't lucky.

At long last, my experience and knowledge of cock-fighting were beginning to pay off. That, and the fact that I was using the good sense God gave me.

Chapter Fifteen

I have back issues of all five game fowl magazines covering the Southern Conference derbies held at Biloxi, Auburn and Ocala, but I don't have to dig through them to find the results. I remember them, all of them, perfectly.

In Biloxi, we fought in the cockpit established in a warehouse near the waterfront, and we won the derby 6-3, plus three thousand five hundred dollars in cash. Icky also won his fourth hack at Biloxi over a Hulsey two-time winner entered by Baldy Allen from Columbus, Georgia. Omar, who was spelling me on handling in the pit from time to time, was awarded a wristwatch by the pit officials as the Most Sportsmanlike Handler in the Biloxi derby. My partner was as pleased with this award as I was, but he wouldn't admit it. I knew that Omar was proud of the award because he put his Rolex away, and, from that day forward, wore the wristwatch he was given at Biloxi — a cheap, $16.50 Timex.

My partner didn't attend the Alabama meet with me. The meet at Auburn on January 29 coincided with his wife's annual visit to Florida. I never met the woman, but I had seen a half-dozen snapshots she had mailed to him that had been taken at Fire Island. In the photos, all six of them taken in a crocheted bikini, she looked brittle, thin and febrile-eyed. She didn't look particularly sexy to me, but inasmuch as it was costing my partner more than twelve thousand a year to keep her in New York City, I couldn't begrudge him a week in bed with her. He was entitled to that much, I figured.

Johnny Norris of Birmingham won the Auburn derby,

and I came in third. Four of my Allen Roundheads were killed during the meet, but I won two thousand five hundred dollars. A carload of arsenal employees drove over from Huntsville, Alabama, and I won most of my money from them. When it came to cockfighting, these rocket makers didn't know which way was up. In a post-derby hack, I pitted Icky against an Arkansas Traveler that ran like a gazelle in the second pitting.

Our veterans took every fight in February 24 Ocala derby. They fought in the familiar pit as though they were defending their home territory and hens against invaders from outer space. Out of fourteen pit battles, I only carried out one bird. In order to get bets, Omar was forced to give three-to-one odds on every fight, but we still made eighteen hundred dollars on the Ocala derby and hacks.

As the weeks passed, I kept as busy as possible. My personal life, perhaps, may have seemed dull, but I loved the way I lived. On my way home at night, after a day of conditioning at Omar's farm, I often selected a book out of my partner's library. Like a lot of businessmen in New York, he had always wanted to read books, but never had enough time. When he moved permanently to Florida, he ordered a complete set of the Modern Library, including the Giants. Starting at the lowest number, I was gradually working my way through them. By March, I was up to *The Plays of Henrik Ibsen.*

Not only did I get up with the chickens, I went to bed with them as well, but I still had time for reading and for playing my guitar. My partner had asked me to stay at his house, but I declined. I liked Omar, everybody did, but we were together all day, and that was enough. Both of us were entitled to privacy, and I think he was relieved when I decided to sleep at my own farm.

Omar Baradinsky, like any man who has strong opinions, liked to talk about the things he was interested in. This was understandable, and most of the time I enjoyed the insight he revealed on many subjects.

However, to listen to him every night, especially when he got a little high on John Jameson, was too much. Unable to talk back, I had to grit my teeth sometimes to prevent myself from setting him straight when he got off the track.

Against the day when my vow was over and I could talk again, I made little entries in a notebook. Someday, Old Boy, I thought, I'm going to set you straight on every one of these topics. If we hadn't separated every evening, our partnership probably wouldn't have lasted the entire season. As it happened, we were still friends after more than five months. Because we were friends, I was worried. We were leaving the next morning and I didn't want to hurt my partner's feelings or interfere in any way with his individuality. But when it came to the Milledgeville Tourney, Omar had a serious problem, and it was up to me to explain it to him.

On the afternoon of March 13 we sat across from each other at the big oak table in Omar's living room going over the ledger and our accumulated records in preparation for the tourney. We had received a telegram the week before from Senator Foxhall reconfirming our joint entry in the tournament and acknowledging receipt of our five-hundred-dollar entry fee. The wire also told us that there would be only eight entries instead of the ten originally scheduled. Two entries had forfeited.

'It's going to make a big difference, Frank,' Omar said, rereading the telegram for the tenth time that day. His initial delight over our joint acceptance — which in my mind had never been in doubt — had gradually turned to concern about whether we would win the tourney or not.

'I know we won't need as many cocks as we figured on,' he continued, 'but neither will the other seven entries. Every cock in the tourney will be a topflight Ace.'

I nodded understandingly. Omar's concern was justified. With only eight entries instead of ten the competition would be a lot stiffer. In comparison with a derby, a major tournament is a complicated ordeal. The matchmaker for a tourney has a compounded headache. In setting up the matches for a derby, the matchmaker only has to match the cocks to be shown at the closest possible weights.

In a tournament, every entry must meet each other at least once. Not only is the matchmaking more complicated, each tourney entry must have an Ace for every weight — that is, if he expects to win.

I wanted to win the tourney just as much as Omar did, but this was my fifth try against my partner's first, and I refused to worry about winning. There was nothing more either one of us could do except pray. We had to fight the game cocks we had, and they were in the peak of condition. To worry needlessly about winning was foolhardy.

'Do you think we've selected the right cocks?'

I nodded.

'That's it, then.' Omar closed the ledger. 'I'm not taking our entire bankroll, Frank. Four thousand is in the bank, and I'm leaving it there. That way, if we lose, we'll still have two thousand apiece to show for the season. I'm taking eight thousand in cash to the tourney, and I'm going to lay it fight by fight instead of putting it all down on the outcome. No matter what happens, we'll still have a fifty-fifty chance of coming home with a bundle. Now, just in case we win the tourney, how much do we stand to win?'

I wrote the information on a tablet, and shoved it across the polished table.

Not counting our separate bets —

8 entries @ $500 each	*$4,000*
Sen. Foxhall purse	*$2,000*
Total	*$6,000*

If I win the Cockfighter of the Year Award, that'll be another $1,000 —

Omar dragged a hand through his beard as he looked at the figures. 'Doesn't Senator Foxhall take a percentage of the entry fees like the derby promoters?' he asked.

I shook my head and smiled. The senator wasn't interested in money. He had more money than he knew what to do with, but he would still come out even and probably ahead. There would be at least four hundred spectators at the two-day tourney paying a ten-dollar admission fee each day. And the senator would make a profit from his restaurant, too. The Milledgeville cockpit was seven miles out in the country. Where else could the visitors eat?

'Do you have to win the tourney to get the Cockfighter of the Year Award, Frank?' Omar asked me.

I spread my arms wide and shrugged my shoulders.

I didn't really know. Senator Foxhall hadn't given the award to anybody in three years, and it was possible that he wouldn't give the medal again this year. All I knew was that the senator awarded the medal to the man he thought deserved it. I didn't want to think about it.

I studied my partner across the table. If anything, his beard was blacker and more unkempt than it had been at the beginning of the season. He still wore his bib overalls, short-sleeved work shirt and high-topped work shoes. During our association, I had never seen him dress differently. He was a free American and entitled to dress any way he pleased. Once a week, when he took a bath, he changed his overalls, but he wore them everywhere he went, to dinner when we ate in Ocala, and downtown when we had fought in Biloxi. Everywhere. This was my problem, and I had to tell him. I pulled the tablet toward me and began to write.

Here are some things about the tourney I have to tell you. As official entries, we'll be put up in Senator Foxhall's home, and eat our meals there. We don't have to wear tuxes for dinner, but we do have to wear coats and ties. Entries and spectators alike are not admitted to the pit unless they wear suits and ties. This is a custom of the tourney out of respect to Senator Foxhall. But he's really a good man. He was never a real senator, I mean in Congress. He was a Georgia state senator in the late twenties. But for whatever it means, he's a gentleman of the old school and we have to abide by the customs. I don't mind wearing a suit and tie in the pit and you shouldn't either, because it's an honor to fight at Milledgeville.

I also have a personal problem, two of them. I've made seat reservations for four people. My fiancée and her brother, and for Mrs. Bernice Hungerford and her nephew. This was several months ago. I don't know if they're coming — neither woman has written or wired me. I don't care. Well, I won't lie. I DO care. If they come, help me entertain them. I'll be handling most of the time, and you'll have to give them some attention for me. Neither woman has seen a cock-fight before. My fiancée's name is Mary Elizabeth Gaylord...

I looked over the message, which had taken two sheets of tablet paper, and then passed it to Omar. He scanned it slowly, folded the two sheets, put them carefully in his shirt pocket and entered his bedroom.

He slammed the door behind him.

I wanted to damn Omar's sensitive soul, but I couldn't. The custom of the cockpit wasn't my doing, but I felt ashamed. To dictate a person's wearing apparel is a violation of every human right, but I had been forced to tell my partner about the custom or he wouldn't have been allowed through the gate.

After fifteen minutes had passed, and Omar still didn't reappear, I got out of my chair and knocked softly on his door.

'I'll be out in a minute,' he called out. 'Fix yourself a drink!'

I measured three ounces of bourbon into a six-ounce glass. Every time I wrote a note of any kind, I always felt that I was circumventing my vow in an underhanded way, but I was sorry I hadn't written a more detailed explanation about the suit business. But I needn't have worried.

Two drinks later the bedroom door opened. I set my glass on the table, grinned at my partner and shook my head in disbelief.

Omar had cut his beard off square at the bottom with a pair of scissors, and evenly trimmed the sides. His newly cropped beard was as stiff as the spade it resembled. His heavy black moustache had been combed to both sides, and the ends were twisted into sharp points. The white smiling teeth in the dark nest of his inky beard were like a glint of lightning in a dark cloud. He wore a pearl-gray homburg over his bushy black hair, a dark gray double-knit suit, a white shirt and cordovan shoes. Hanging out for two or three inches below his beard, a shimmering gray silk necktie was clipped to his shirt by a black onyx tie bar. He looked like a wealthy Greek undertaker.

'I was saving this costume as a surprise for you tomorrow,' Omar said with a pleased laugh. 'My new suit arrived from my New York tailor three days ago. How do I look?'

I clasped my hands over my head like a boxer, and shook them.

'Do you know what makes my beard so stiff?' Omar said, as he mixed a drink at the table. 'Pommade Hong-roise. And just in case you don't know what that means, it's imported moustache wax from France.'

Omar added more whiskey to my glass.

'You Southerners don't have a cartel on manners, Frank. It may come as a shock to you, partner, but I even know the correct tools to use at a formal dinner.' He raised his glass. 'A toast, Mr. Mansfield!'

I grinned and clinked my glass against his.

'To the All-American cockfighters, the English-Polish team of Mansfield and Baradinsky! Gentlemen, gamblers, dudes and cocksmen, each and every one!'

We drank to that.

We left Ocala at three o'clock, but it was almost two in the afternoon before we reached Milledgeville. I should have traded my old pickup in for a newer truck, but I had never gotten around to it. For Omar, trailing me all the way, the slow rate of speed on the highway must have been maddening.

When we reached Milledgeville, I waved for Omar to follow me out, and drove on through without stopping.

Milledgeville isn't much of a city — a boy's military academy, a girl's college and a female insane asylum — but it's a pretty little town with red cobblestoned streets lined with shade trees.

Once we were out of town and drawing closer to the cockpit, I didn't mind driving so slowly because I liked the familiar scenery. During the summer, the highway would be bordered on both sides with solid masses of blackberry bushes draped over the barbed-wire fences. In the middle of March, the fields were iron-colored and bare. The tall Georgia slash pines were deep in rust-colored needles. The sky was a watercolor blue, and tiny tufts of white clouds were arranged on this background like a dotted-swiss design. The sun was smaller in March, but the weather wasn't cold. The clear air was sharp, tangy and stimulating, without being breezy.

Like Omar, in his new double-knit suit, I was dressed up, and we both had a place to go. I wore a blue gaberdine suit that I had had for two years, but it was fresh from the cleaners. Well in advance of the tourney, I had ordered a white cattleman's Town and Country snap-brim hat from Dallas, and a new pair of black jodhpur boots from the Navarro Brothers, in El Paso. For the past seven nights I had shined and buffed the new boots until they gleamed like crystal. I wore yellow socks with my suit, and I had paid forty dollars in Miami Beach for my favorite yellow silk necktie, with its pattern of royal blue, hand-painted game cocks.

I wasn't dressed conservatively, but a lot of my fans would be at the tourney, and they expected me to look dashing and colorful. Press representatives from all five game fowl magazines would be present, and Omar and I were bound to get our photos printed in two or three magazines whether we won the tourney or not.

A Georgia state highway patrolman waved us through the gate to the senator's plantation without getting off his motorcycle. Seeing the back of the pickup and the station wagon both loaded with chicken coops, he didn't need to check our identification cards. A mile down the yellow-graveled road, I took the fork toward the cockpit and cockhouses to weigh in and put our game cocks away before signing in at the senator's house.

Peach Owen met us in the yards, assigned us to a cockhouse, and gave us our numbers to wear on the back of our coats. We were No. 5, and before we did anything else we pinned on our numbers.

Mr. Owen was the weight-and-time official for the tourney, and president of the Southern Conference Cockfighting Association. He was a well-liked, friendly man in his mid-thirties who had given up a promising career in cockfighting to work full time for the senator and the Southern Conference. Senator Foxhall, who was getting too old now to do much of anything, paid Peach ten thousand dollars a year to breed and take care of his flock of fancy game fowl.

'Do you want to weigh in now or wait till morning?' Peach asked.

'Let's get it over with,' Omar said, handing Peach our record sheets.

'I don't need both of you,' Peach winked at me. 'There's a fellow up at the house who wants to see you, Mr. Mansfield.'

He didn't say who it was so I stayed for the weighing-in, an almost useless precaution at a professional meet like the S.C. Tourney.

At the majority of U.S. tournaments, cocks are weighed and banded upon checking in. This banding procedure is supposed to ensure that each entry will fight only the cocks he has entered. Before each fight, weight slips are called out, and the entrants heel the cock from their assigned cockhouse according to the exact weight on the slip. If they fail to show a cock making the weight within the check margin, that fight is forfeited to the other cocker who can. The metal band on the leg of the heeled cock is checked by the weight-and-time official immediately prior to the fight and then removed. If the cock wasn't banded by one of the tourney officials upon arrival, the cock is a ringer. In theory, banding upon arrival at a tourney appears to be a sound practice, but bands can be purchased from a dozen or more manufacturers of cocking supplies by anybody who wants to pay for them. The man who wants to cheat by entering a sure loser, for instance, instead of a legitimate fighter, can buy all the metal leg bands he wants to, and clamp one on a ringer in a couple of seconds.

Banding had been eliminated at the S.C. Tourney. Every cock pitted at the S.C. Tourney was a four-time winner at an authorized cockpit or game club. And all the wins were entered upon an official record sheet and initialed by the pit operator. Weighing-in at the tourney consisted of checking each game cock against his record sheet and description and weighing the game cock itself. Minor weight variations were taken into account by the official.

The system wasn't foolproof. It was still possible to substitute a runner for one of the checked-in fighters, but a man would be a fool to try it. Among the spectators were most of the S.C. pit operators who could recognize at sight the game cocks that had fought in their pits earlier in the season. If one of them or one of the other entries spotted a ringer, the man who tried to pull a fast one was through with cockfighting. His name went out on a blacklist to every U.S. pit operator, and the blacklist of crooked cockfighters was published annually in the April issue of every U.S. game fowl magazine.

The four-win stipulation was a tough rule, but I was all for it because it separated the amateurs from the professionals and raised the breeding standards of game fowl. This single rule had been the biggest advance in U.S. cockfighting since the late Sol P. McCall had originated the modern tournament. Many of the fans and gamblers who attended the two-day event traveled thousands of miles to see it, but they knew they would get their money's worth. The fighting would be fast, and every cock shown had proven himself to be dead game.

After completing the weighing-in, which took about an hour, our thirty-one game cocks were transferred to their stalls inside the cockhouse. We gave each bird a half dip of water, and I scattered a very small portion of grain on the moss-packed floor of each coop to give them some exercise after the long trip. We dropped the canvas covers over the coops to keep the birds quiet, locked the door, and drove the short distance to the senator's home to sign the guest register.

I believe that Omar was impressed by the senator's home. I had been the first time I stayed there, and it still gave me a warm feeling to see the big house as we topped the rise and parked in front of the wide veranda. The mansion was one of the better Southern examples of modified English Georgian. There are many great homes like it in the southern states, but not many of them are as well tended as they should be. It takes a lot of money. Good craftsmanship had been insisted upon when the house had been constructed. All the doors, and even the windows, had ornate, carved designs. The great balustrade that led from the downstairs hall to the upstairs bedrooms had been formed and curved for the purpose from a single tree. There was enough room to sleep thirty guests, but except for the official entries, their wives, and pit officials, spectators attending the meet had to find accommodations in a hotel or motel in Milledgeville.

As we climbed the steps to the veranda, the front door opened and Ed Middleton came out and grabbed my hand. He laughed at my expression and said fondly in his deep, booming voice: 'You didn't expect to see me here, did you? How's my pretty blue chicken getting along?'

In a lightweight gray linen suit, with a pink-and-gray striped tie, Ed didn't look like a sick man to me, but the brown circles under his eyes were a little darker on his pale face. He looked happy, however, and he hadn't been happy when I last saw him in Orlando. Despite his appearance of well-being, he was still liable to have a heart attack at any moment.

Still gripping Ed's hand, I jerked my head for Omar to come forward and introduce himself.

'How do you do?' Omar said. 'I've seen you referee,

Mr. Middleton, but I've never had the pleasure of meeting you.'

'Glad to meet you at last then, Mr. Baradinsky. Evidently you've been a settling influence on my boy here. When I heard about the holdup in Chattanooga, I checked right away, and don't think I wasn't surprised when I learned that you two had pulled out before the meet! The *old* Frank Mansfield I knew would've been right in there, reaching for the ceiling with the rest of 'em.'

Omar laughed. 'If there's any influencing going on, Mr. Middleton, it's Frank working on me, not the other way around.'

'Well, come on in,' Ed entered the hall ahead of us. 'I'm not the official greeter here, Mr. Baradinsky, I'm only filling in for Mrs. Pierce. She had to go downtown for something or other.' Ed snapped his fingers at a grinning Negro boy of fourteen or fifteen in a white short jacket. 'Take the bags out of the station wagon to Number Five upstairs.'

'Yes, sir!' the boy said quickly. He had been eager enough to get our luggage, but the three of us had blocked his way.

While Omar and I signed the guest register, Ed Middleton surprised me again.

'I'm not here as a spectator, Frank,' he explained. 'I'm the referee, and don't think I won't be watching every move you make in the pits.' He turned to my partner. 'I retired a while back from active cockfighting, Mr. Baradinsky, but I decided later that I was too young to quit.'

Ed laughed, and then he looked at me, staring directly into my eyes. 'I promised Martha I'd quit, as you know, Frank' — he shrugged — 'but now the promise doesn't mean anything — now that she's passed away. And I know damned well she wouldn't want me sitting around all by myself.'

I nodded sympathetically and smiled. Two full and active days on his feet could very well kill Ed Middleton. And yet, I was still glad to see him and delighted to learn that he was the Number One pit official. Suppose he did

keel over dead? That was a much better way to go than
eating his guts out with boredom while he stared at a
grove of orange trees.

'Say, Frank,' Ed snapped his fingers as we started to go
upstairs, 'did your partner ever see the senator's flock of
fancy chickens?'

'No, I haven't, Mr. Middleton,' Omar said, 'although
I've heard enough about them.'

'Good! Mrs. Pierce'll be back soon, and I'll take you on
the ten-cent guided tour.'

We climbed the stairs to the second floor to where the
Negro boy held the door open. I gave him a five-dollar
bill, which was plenty, but Omar gave him a five as well.
The boy was so astonished by the size of the two
gratuities, he returned to our room in less than three
minutes with four additional bath towels, a bowlful of
icecubes and a pitcher of orange juice.

Omar glanced critically around the room and eyed the
cut-glass chandelier in the high ceiling. 'I'll say this much,
Frank,' Omar said, 'the rag rug on the floor isn't made of
rags, the furniture wasn't made in Grand Rapids, and that
calendar on the wall above my bed wasn't placed there by
any Baptist.'

I opened my suitcase on my bed and unpacked, putting
my extra black button-down shirts and white socks into
the high walnut dresser between our beds. Omar pushed
open the double French windows and looked out, his
hands clasped behind his back.

'There's a good view of the cockpit from here, Frank,'
he said. 'The dome has turned rose in the afternoon sun.
Take a look at it.'

I joined him at the window. A half mile away, the dome
was pink on one side, and on the other side, away from
the sun, the shadows were a dark purple. The twenty
separated concrete cockhouses formed a U on the
southern side of the circular pit. The Atlanta architect who
had built the cockpit had settled for concrete blocks, but
had incorporated many of the features of the Royal
Cockpit at Whitehall Palace into the structure. The long

narrow windows, recessed deeply into the walls, were traditional, but they didn't let in enough light. The five strong electric lights over the pit had to be turned on for both day and night fighting.

The square squat ugly restaurant, with a white asbestos tile roof, had been added ten years after the cockpit had been finished and was connected to the pit by a screened-in breezeway. The restaurant was entirely out of keeping with the general design, and I had always thought it a pity that it hadn't been built in the first place by the original architect.

The interior of the two-story pit held circular tiers rising steeply to the rim of the dome, and seated four hundred people. The judge's box was to the right of the connecting hall to the drag pit, and the press box was directly above this exit. Including the new doorway that had been cut through the wall leading to the restaurant, there were five arched doorways to the pit.

I finished my unpacking, and slipped on my jacket again in preparation to go out. Omar turned away from the windows, and poured a glass of orange juice.

'I want to tell you something, Frank.' The husky tone of his voice stopped me before I reached the door. 'Whether we win the tourney or not, I want you to know that I'll always be grateful to you for getting me this far. This is truly the greatest experience of my life.'

He said this so warmly that I hit him fondly on the arm with my fist. I was tempted to tell my partner about my vow of silence, but this wasn't the time to tell him. If he knew that my voice was riding on the prospect of being awarded the Cockfighter of the Year award, he would have gotten more nervous about the outcome than he was already.

'Well,' he said cheerfully, clearing his throat, 'isn't it about time to take a look at those fancy chickens?'

I wagged my chin and pointed to his chest. I couldn't go with him, but I knew he would enjoy seeing them. Senator Foxhall had one of the finest collections of fancy game fowl in the world. He had turned fancier, after getting too old to fight chickens in the pit. He raised purebred Gallus Bankivas, the original wild jungle fowl from which all game fowl are descended, Javanese cocks, with tails ten feet long, miniature bantams from Japan — beautiful little creatures not much larger than quail — and many other exotic breeds. If Mary Elizabeth came to the meet, I intended to show them to her. But I couldn't go with Ed and Omar right then. I had to drive into Milledgeville.

I had wired the Sealbach Hotel and reserved four rooms, but with the crowd of visitors expected the next day I knew the manager wouldn't hold them for me unless I paid for them in advance. I wrote a short note for Omar, telling him where I was going and why.

'If you want me to, I'll go with you.'

I shook my head.

'Okay. But rest easy about your guests, Frank. I'll see that they're well taken care of, don't worry. Didn't I ever tell you that I was once a vice-president in charge of public relations?'

I waved a hand in his direction, and drove into town.

By seven thirty that evening all the official entries had signed in, and the great downstairs hall was crowded as we waited for Senator Foxhall to come downstairs to lead the way into the dining room. On time, the old man came down the wide stairs, clutching his housekeeper's arm tightly for support. A slight, spare man, not much taller than a fifteen-year-old boy, he still managed to hold himself rigidly erect. In his old-fashioned, broad-lapeled dinner jacket and white piqué vest, he had an almost regal appearance. His pale blue eyes, deeply recessed now in his old age, were still alert and friendly behind his gold-rimmed glasses as he passed through the crowd. Somehow, he had preserved his hair, and his ivory mane was combed straight back from his high forehead in a well-groomed pompadour.

Ed Middleton, my partner and I were standing together. When the senator reached us, Ed introduced the old man to Omar.

'Oh, yes. Baradinsky? You're a Russian, aren't you?'

'No, sir,' Omar replied. 'Polish.'

'You look like a Russian.'

'It's probably the beard,' Omar said self-consciously.

'Maybe so. Anyway, you're in good hands with Frank Mansfield.' The senator smiled in my direction, exposing his blue-gray false teeth. 'You'll teach him our American ways, won't you, son?'

Smiling in return, I nodded my head. Omar's great-great-grandfather had emigrated to the United States, but it would have been useless to explain this fact to the senator.

Senator Foxhall nodded his head thoughtfully about twenty times before speaking again.

'Frank is a good man, Mr. Baradinsky. I knew his grand-daddy. You listen to Frank and you'll learn something about game cocks. Did you ever hear of Polish poultry?'

'Yes, sir.'

'Well, they don't come from Poland! I'll bet you didn't know that, did you?'

'No, sir, I didn't.'

'I didn't think you did,' the old man said gleefully. 'Not many people do. Did you know that, Ed?'

'I sure did, Senator,' Ed said, with a rueful laugh. 'I once tried to cross some frizzle-haired Polish cocks, and after losing three in the pit, I found out that they wouldn't face when they were hurt.'

'You should've come to me,' the old man said. 'I could've told you that and saved you some money.' He turned back to Omar. 'Cockfighting in Poland has never been up to standard, Mr. Baradinsky. They don't feed them right. Same thing with Ireland. Gamecocks can't fight on raw potatoes, Mr. Baradinsky.'

'I'll remember that,' Omar said blandly.

Mrs. Pierce, the senator's housekeeper for more than thirty years, tugged on the old man's arm. 'We'd better go in to dinner now,' she reminded him. As the old couple turned away from us to lead the way into the dining room,

Omar shrugged his shoulders helplessly, and winked at me. I grinned and nodded my head. Actually, my partner had shown considerable restraint. The senator had been correct in everything he said. If Omar had tried to argue with him, the old man would have cut him to shreds.

Except for Omar and myself, the guests seated around the dinner table were a rather eccentric group. I had known most of them for years, but even to me it seemed like an unusual gathering of people. All of us wore our entry numbers on the back of our coats. We needed these numbers in the pit as identification for the benefit of the spectators. But we also had to wear them at all times for Senator Foxhall. He knew our names, and he knew them well, but sometimes he had a tendency to forget them. When he did forget, he checked his typewritten list of entries against our numbers so he could address any one of us by name without embarrassment.

Senator Foxhall sat at the head of the long table, and Mrs. Pierce was seated at the opposite end. Ed Middleton and Peach Owen were seated on either side of the senator. Next to Ed was Buddy Waggoner, the second referee, who would preside over the drag pit.

By their entry numbers, the remaining guests were seated around the table, clockwise from Buddy Waggoner.

No. 1. Johnny McCoy and Colonel Bob Moore, USAF (Retired). Johnny McCoy and his partner, Colonel Bob, flew to meets all over the U.S. from their fifty-thousand-acre ranch near Dan's Derrick, Texas, in a Lear jet. Colonel Bob, although he had been retired for at least ten years, still wore his Air Force blue uniform at all times. Only two days before, this Texas partnership had fought in the Northwest Cockfighting Tourney in Seattle, Washington. From there, they had flown back to Dan's Derrick and picked up fresh, newly conditioned game cocks. They then had flown in to Macon. The senator's limousine and private game-fowl trailer had brought them from Macon to Milledgeville.

No. 2. Pete Chocolate, Pahokee, Florida. Except for the senator, Pete Chocolate was the only male guest wearing dinner clothes. He had spoiled the effect, however, by wearing a blue-and-white T-shirt under his black tuxedo jacket. And around his neck he wore an immaculate cream-colored ascot scarf.

No. 3. Dirty Jacques Bonin, Biloxi, Mississippi. There was nothing 'dirty' about Jacques Bonin's appearance. His suit was flawlessly tailored, and his spatulate nails were freshly manicured. Clean shaven and soberly attired, he looked like, and was, a church deacon. He had earned the appellation of Dirty Jacques during World War II when he had organized the gang of strikebreakers who killed or maimed eighty striking long-shoremen on the Mobile docks. He had never lived the name down, although his full-time occupation was now the breeding and fighting of Louisiana Mugs.

No. 4. Jack Burke. Dody sat beside her husband, and I sat next to her — one of Mrs. Pierce's ideas. Dody spoke to me once, and only once, during dinner.

'Jack told me to apologize for kicking you at Plant City,' she whispered.

I waited politely for her to continue, but that was all she said.

Jack Burke also spoke to me during dinner, leaning forward in his chair and twisting his head in my direction.

'Let's make it an even thousand bet between Little David and your chicken, Frank. I've okayed it with Ed and Peach to have the hack immediately after the last tourney fight while the judges tote up the final scores. All right?'

When I nodded in agreement, he sat back in his chair.

No. 5. The English-Polish team of Mansfield and Baradinsky.

No. 6 Roy Whipple and his son, Roy, Jr. Mr Whipple was the old cockfighter who had shared the velvet love seat with me in the bridal suite of the Southerner Hotel in Chattanooga. He had lost a bundle in the holdup, but it hadn't dented his bankroll. The man owned three Asheville, North Carolina, resort hotels. Roy, Jr., was a senior at the University of North Carolina, Chapel Hill, and had obtained special permission from the dean of men to assist his father at the meet.

No. 7 Baldy Allen, of Columbus, Georgia, was the owner of several liquor stores. Breeding and fighting milk-white Doms was not only a sideline for Baldy, it was a profitable enterprise. His gregarious wife, Jean Ellen, who did his betting for him, accompanied Baldy everywhere.

No. 8. Johnny Norris, Birmingham, Alabama. Johnny was famous as a conditioner of game fowl, but I didn't consider him a first-rate handler. For fifteen years he had conditioned cocks for the late Ironclaw Burnstead. When Mr. Burnstead died, he left Johnny three hundred thousand in cash and his entire flock of game fowl. In the past three years, Johnny had gained a reputation as an all-around cocker, and this was his first entry in the S.C. Tourney.

During dinner, I listened attentively to the conversation. All I heard was 'chicken talk.' The only subject that any of us had in common was cockfighting, and the love of cock-fighting was the distinguishing feature of every entry. Every man present had the game fowl, the knowledge, the ability and the determination to win the tourney, but only one of us could win.

I intended to be that one.

Chapter Sixteen

Out of long habit more than anything else, I drank a quick cup of coffee in the dining-room the next morning and was in the cockhouse by five thirty. Game cocks cooped for long periods in a small two-by-two stall have a tendency to get sleepy and bored. Too much lassitude makes a cock sluggish when pitted. To wake them up, I took each cock out of its coop and washed its head with a damp sponge dipped in cheap whiskey. By the time I finished the sponging at seven thirty, our gamecocks were skipping up and down inside their stalls with rejuvenated animation and crowing and clucking with happiness.

Omar joined me at eight, and a few minutes later Doc Riordan showed up at the cockhouse to wish me luck in the tourney. The pharmacist and my partner hit it off well together from the moment they met.

'I never miss the Southern Conference Tourney,' Doc told Omar, 'but all season long I've been chained to my desk. I'm the president of the Dixie Pharmaceutical Company, as Frank may have told you, and this year our firm is launching a new product.' He reached into his coat pocket and handed Omar a small white packet. 'Licarbo!' he said proudly. 'Advertising is our biggest headache, although the raising of capital isn't the simple matter it used to be.'

'Who handles your advertising?' Omar asked, tearing open the sample and cautiously tasting the product with the tip of his tongue.

'Unfortunately,' Doc sighed, 'I have to handle it myself. That's been my main trouble. But I'm a registered pharmacist, and most of the drugstores in Jax have allowed me to put my posters in their windows.'

'I think you've got a good idea here in Licarbo,' Omar said sincerely. 'After the tourney I won't have too much to do until April, and maybe you and I can get together on this product. I used to be in advertising in New York. Perhaps Frank told you?'

'No, he didn't.' Doc looked at me reproachfully. 'I didn't know Frank had himself a partner until I read the account of the Plant City Main between you-all and Jack Burke. Now, that was a main I wish I'd seen! That reminds me, Frank —' Doc took a small bottle of black-and-gray capsules out of his pocket and placed it on the workbench. 'These are energy capsules. I made 'em up for Mr. Burke from a formula he gave me, and they should be good. They take about an hour for the best results, but when I made 'em up for Mr. Burke's chickens, I said to myself: "While I'm at it, I'll just make up a batch for Frank Mansfield."'

'We appreciate it, Doctor,' Omar said — and then to me, 'The restaurant should be open by now. Let's get some breakfast.'

Shaking my head, I opened my gaff case on the workbench and started to polish gaffs with my conical grinding stone.

'I'll have some coffee with you, Mr. Baradinsky,' Doc offered.

'Fine, I'd like to find out more about Licarbo.'

'Right now,' Doc said, 'advertising isn't quite as important as raising a little capital. However, I'd appreciate any advice you'd —'

'I'll bring you some coffee, Frank,' Omar said over his shoulder. 'Capital, Doctor, is simply a matter of devious stratagems worked out through a mathematical process known as pressure patterns peculiar to pecuniary people.'

As soon as they were out of earshot I opened the small bottle of energy capsules Doc had given me, dumped them on the floor, and crushed them into powder with my heel. The capsules might have been wonderful, but I wouldn't take any chances with them. Jack Burke knew that Doc Riordan was a friend of mine, and that fact alone was enough to make me distrust the medicine. Perhaps Jack Burke didn't have enough brains to plan anything so devious, but I wouldn't have used a strange product on my chickens whether Burke's name had been mentioned or not. A major tournament is not the place for experimentation.

As the parking lot filled slowly, I leaned against the locked door of our cockhouse and watched the arriving cars as they pulled in and parked under the directions of the attendants. By nine a.m., when the time came for Omar and me to go over to the pit for the opening of the tourney, there was still no sign of either Bernice or Mary Elizabeth.

Tension was building up inside me, as it always does just before a meet, and I was happy when Peach Owen disengaged the mike, and handed it to Senator Foxhall. Peach played out the extra cord behind the senator as the old man marched stiffly to the center of the pit. The senator waited for silence, which didn't take very long. This early in the morning, there were only about two hundred spectators, but by two in the afternoon, the place would be jammed.

'Ladies and gentlemen,' Senator Foxhall said in his high reedy voice, 'welcome to the Southern Conference Tourney! We sincerely hope that all of you will have a good time. There is only one rule that you must observe during the meet.' He paused. 'Conduct yourselves like ladies and gentlemen.'

(Applause.)

'Before the tourney is over,' he said wryly, licking his thin lips, 'some of you may desire to place a small wager or two —'

(Laughter.)

'If you do, make certain you know the man you're betting with — there *may* be Internal Revenue agents in the crowd!'

(Laughter.)

The old man turned the hand microphone over to

Peach Owen and returned to his chair beside the judge's box. For the remainder of the tourney he would sit there quietly, watching everything that went on with his deep-set, cold blue eyes. With those experienced eyes watching me, I knew I couldn't make a single mistake when I was in the pit.

I was elated when Peach Owen called over the PA system for entry Number Two and entry Number Five to report to the judge's box to pick up their weight slips. My tension disappeared. Now I could be busy.

The first match was 5:00 cocks. After getting our weight-slip, Omar and I double-timed back to the cock-house to heel our chicken. Time was going on from the second we received our weight slip, and only fifteen minutes were allowed to heel and be ready for the pitting. If an entry failed to make it on time, he forfeited that fight, and the next waiting, heeled pair was called. The fifteen-minute time limit kept the fights moving along fast. Where a match was even, or after ten minutes of fighting in the main pit, the two cocks were sent to the drag pit and a new pair was started in the center pit.

From the first pitting, I knew that the fight was going to be a long-drawn-out battle. Pete Chocolate matched a Spanish cross against my Mellhorn Black, and both birds were wary and overcautious. They did little damage to each other by the fourth pitting, and just before the fifth, when Ed Middleton saw that Roy Whipple and Baldy Allen were heeled and ready, he signaled for second referee Buddy Waggoner to start the next match and ordered us to follow him into the drag pit.

In the thirty-first pitting we went to breast after the third count of twenty, one hand under the bird only, at the center score.

'Get ready,' Ed Middleton said.

Pete and I faced each other across the two-foot score, both holding weary fighters with our right hand, and one foot above the ground. That's when the Indian made his first mistake.

'Pit!'

I dropped on signal and so did Pete, but Pete pushed, causing his Spanish to peck first because of the added impetus. I saw him plainly, but Ed missed it. Snapping my fingers I made a pushing gesture with my right palm and pointed to the straight-faced Seminole.

'I'm refereeing this fight, Mr. Mansfield!' Ed snapped angrily. 'Handle!'

We picked up the cocks for the short rest period. I couldn't argue, but Ed had been alerted and he watched Pete closely during the next actionless pittings. There are no draws at the S.C.T., and I was beginning to think the fight was going to last all day when Pete just barely pushed his bird on the forty-fifth pitting. This time, Ed caught him at it.

'Foul! The winner is Number Five!'

'Foul?' Pete asked innocently. 'I committed a foul of some kind?'

'Pushing on the breast score. Are you trying to argue, Mr. Chocolate?'

'I'm afraid I must, Mr. Middleton,' Pete said with feigned bewilderment. Spreading his arms widely, Pete turned to the crowd of a dozen or so spectators who had followed the first fight into the drag pit. 'Did any of you gentlemen see me pushing?'

'That's a fifty-dollar fine for arguing. Anything else to say, Pete?'

Pete glowered at Ed for about ten seconds, and then shook his head. We carried our birds out, returning to our respective cockhouses. The door was open and my partner was attempting frantically to heel a 5:02 Roundhead by himself when I entered.

'Take over, Frank!' Omar said excitedly. 'Your drag lasted almost an hour, and we've got less than five minutes to meet Roy Whipple with a 5:02!'

I put the battered Mellhorn away, and while Omar held, I finished heeling the Roundhead. We made it to the weighing scales with two minutes to spare. During the long drag battle with Pete, three fights had been held in the main pit.

From the word 'Pit!' my Allen Roundhead lasted exactly twenty-five seconds with the Whipple cock before it was cut down in midair and killed.

The fighting was just as fast for the rest of the morning. If I didn't lose during the first three or four pittings I usually won the battle. My tough, relentless conditioning methods paid off with stamina. In a long go, my rock-hard game cocks invariably outlasted their opponents. Every fight at Milledgeville was a battle between two Aces, however, and during the first three to five pittings, when both cocks were daisy fresh, it was anybody's fight. At one p.m., when a one-hour break for lunch was called, I had lost two and won three.

Omar and I left the pit together, planning to eat at the senator's house rather than wait for service in the crowded restaurant. As we left by the side entrance, a parking attendant came running over and caught up with us.

'Mr. Mansfield, there's a lady down in the lot who asked me to find you.'

'Shall I go with you, Frank?' Omar said.

I nodded, and we followed the attendant into the parking lot.

It was Bernice Hungerford. As we approached her car, she got out, slammed the door and waited. Bernice looked much prettier than I remembered. Either she wore a tight girdle, or she had lost fifteen pounds. A perky, wheat-straw, off-the-face hat was perched atop a brand new permanent, and her dark hair gleamed with some kind of spray. She wore a mustard-colored tweed suit, softened at the throat by a lemon-yellow silk scarf. The air was chilly, but it wasn't cold enough for the full-length sheared beaver coat she held draped over her left arm.

When I accepted her white-gloved extended right hand, I noticed that it was trembling.

'I had to send for you, Frank,' she apologized, lifting her face to be kissed. I brushed her lips with mine, and she stepped back a pace, blushing like a girl. 'I've been here for more than an hour,' she said with a shy laugh. 'But when I went up to the entrance and saw all those men standing around — and no women — I was afraid to go inside!'

'You'll find a lot of ladies here, once you get inside, Miss —'

'Mrs. Hungerford,' Bernice said self-consciously.

'Mrs. Hungerford,' Omar said, 'I'm Frank's partner, Omar Baradinsky. And I'm glad the boy caught us in time. We were just leaving for lunch, and now you can join us.'

'I feel better already.' Bernice smiled. 'I started not to come, Frank.' She took my arm, and Omar relieved her of her heavy coat. 'Tommy couldn't get away, and I dreaded coming by myself, but now ... Mr. Baradinsky,' she turned impulsively to Omar on her left. 'Is there such a thing as a powder room around here?'

Omar laughed. 'If you can hold out for about five hundred more yards, Mrs. Hungerford, you'll be made comfortable at the house.'

'Thank you. How do I look, Frank? How *does* a lady dress for a cockfight?'

'A woman as beautiful as you,' Omar said, 'could wear a sackcloth and still look like a queen.'

'Now I do feel better!' Bernice laughed gaily. 'What does one *do* at a cockfight!'

'At first, I'd advise you merely to watch. But if you decide to place a wager, let me know. Frank and I will be busy, but one of us will look after you when we're free.'

Thanks to my partner, the luncheon was a success. He was gracious and paternal toward Bernice, without being patronizing, and before we returned to the pit, she was no longer ill-at-ease or prattling with nervousness. When the fighting began, I rarely sat with her. Most of Omar's time was taken up with the placing of bets, payoffs and collections, but he joined her as often as he could.

There was another one-hour break at seven, and then the fights were to continue until midnight. According to the schedule — if everything went according to plan — the tourney would be completed by three p.m. the following afternoon. After the prizes and purses were awarded, the senator always held a free barbecue for everybody on the park-like lawn between his house and the cockpit.

We ate dinner, all three of us, in the restaurant. After dinner, Bernice begged off as a spectator from the evening fights. She was tired and bored from watching them. Without a basic understanding or knowledge of what to look for, Bernice's boredom was not unreasonable. Women rarely find cockfighting as exciting as men do.

Although I missed her friendly white-gloved wave and cheery cry of 'good luck' each time I entered the pit, I wasn't sorry to send her to the hotel in town. She promised to meet us at noon the following day, and I was relieved that I didn't have to entertain her until then.

The night fighting got bungled up.

There were two forfeits in the 5:12 weights, when Dirty Jacques Bonin and Jack Burke weren't heeled and ready on time, plus long technical arguments on both sides. To return to the cockpit after heeling, it was necessary to cross through the parking lot. Jack Burke claimed — and I think he had a reasonable point — that automobiles leaving the area after the ten-thirty fight had held him up. He failed to see why he should be penalized for a parking attendant's failure to control the traffic properly. Peach Owen brought out the rules and read them aloud. The rules stated clearly that the handler was to be ready for pitting within fifteen minutes after receiving his weight slip. No provisions had been written concerning interference, so Jack forfeited the fight after being promised by Peach Owen that this provision would be discussed by the S.C.T. committee before the next season.

Due to these delays, it was after one o'clock before Omar and I got back to our room in the mansion. I had lost four fights out of twelve, but my partner, who had placed shrewd bets on every match held during the day, had added two thousand eight hundred dollars to our bankroll.

'Are we going to win the tourney, Frank?' Omar said, as we undressed for bed.

Down to my underwear, I sat on the edge of my bed and checked over the official scorecard. Jack Burke, Roy Whipple and Johnny Norris were ahead of us, but they weren't so far ahead that we couldn't catch up with them the next day. I drew a large question mark on the blank side of the scorecard, sailed the square of cardboard in Omar's general direction and got wearily into bed. With a full day of fighting to go, the top three could just as easily be the bottom three when the points were tallied at the end of the meet.

Before Omar finished counting and stacking the money into neat piles on top of the dresser and switched off the overhead chandelier, I was sound asleep.

The next morning at eleven — during my third match of the second day — soft-spoken Johnny Norris was no longer a contender. His name was stricken from the lists, and he was barred forever from Southern Conference competition for ungentlemanly conduct.

At most Southern pits, the sidewalls are constructed of wood, but the sunken pit at Milledgeville has concrete walls. At a wooden-walled pit, when two cocks are fighting close to the barrier, it isn't unusual for one of the fighters to jab one of his gaffs into a board and get stuck.

Because of this possibility, cockpits with sixteen-inch wooden walls have a ground rule to 'handle' when an accident like this happens. The handler then pulls the gaff loose from the wall and, following a thirty-second rest period, the birds are pitted again.

There was no such rule at Milledgeville.

With a concrete pit, this ground rule was considered unnecessary. Unfortunately for Johnny Norris, after many years of operation, there were hairline cracks in the concrete wall. In the sixth pitting, my Claret drove Johnny's spangled Shuffler into the wall. During a quick flurry, the Shuffler hung a gaff into one of the narrow cracks. The long three-inch heel was wedged tight. The Shuffler was immobilized, with his head dangling down, about ten inches above the dirt floor of the pit.

Johnny looked angrily at Buddy and said: 'Handle, for Christ's sake!'

'No such rule at this pit.' Buddy shook his head stubbornly.

My Claret had backed away and was eyeing the upsidedown bird, judging the distance. Advancing three short steps, he flew fiercely into the helpless Shuffler with both heels fanning. The fight was mine.

Johnny swung a roundhouse right and broke Buddy Waggoner's jaw.

After a near riot, order was restored when Senator Foxhall announced that he would stop the tourney and clear the pit if everybody didn't quiet down. Johnny Norris was taken off the S.C.T. rolls and banished back to Birmingham. Because of Johnny's forced withdrawal, the remaining seven entries had to be reshuffled and rematched by the officials. This administrative work took more than an hour.

At one o'clock, when the lunch break was called, Mary Elizabeth still hadn't put in an appearance. I had made a nuisance out of myself by writing notes and checking periodically with the box office and parking attendants, but by one p.m. I had resigned myself that she wouldn't come.

I took Bernice to the house for lunch.

The rematching delay ruined the planned schedule. The last match between Roy Whipple and Colonel Bob Moore didn't start until three thirty. The moment the two cockfighters entered the pit, Omar and I raced for our cockhouse to heel Icky for the last hack between my bird and Burke's Little David.

When we returned to the pit, Jack Burke was already heeled and waiting. As the three of us stood in the doorway, watching the fight in progress, Jack looked contemptuously at Icky and said, 'Let's raise the bet to two thousand, Frank.'

Omar bridled. 'One thousand is the bet, Mr. Burke. You've had Little David on a country walk all season, and Icky's had to fight to qualify. If there's any bet-changing to be done, you should give us some odds.'

'Are you asking for odds, Frank?' Burke challenged, ignoring my partner.

I shook my head. Holding Icky under my left arm, I pointed to the pit with my free hand. Colonel Bob was carrying out a dead chicken, and Ed Middleton was cutting the gaff tie strings away from Whipple's winner with his knife.

We reported to the judge's booth and weighed in. Icky was at fighting weight, an even 4:02. The freedom of the long rest on a farm walk had brought Little David's weight up from four pounds to 4:03. Omar protested the one-ounce overweight immediately, and Peach Owen ordered Burke to cut away feathers until his cock matched Icky exactly.

'While the results of the tourney are being tabulated and rechecked,' Peach drawled into the microphone with his deep southern voice, 'there'll be an extra hack for your pleasure. The weight is 4:02, short heels, between entries four and five!'

A murmur of approval and a scattering of applause encircled the packed tiers. The majority of the people in the audience were aware of the extra hack before the announcement. Omar had laughingly told me about some of the rumors he had heard. Some people thought that the hack was a simple grudge match, while others claimed that several thousand dollars had been bet between us. The reported incident at Plant City, when Dody had kicked me in the shins, had also caused a great many rumors. Supposedly, I had made a pass at Jack's wife, or Jack Burke had taken Dody away from me, and — wildest of all — Dody had been my childhood sweetheart. How man of thirty-three could possibly have had a childhood sweetheart of only sixteen didn't prevent the rumors. What Jack had spread about himself, or what people said about me, didn't matter. My only concern was to win the hack.

Ed Middleton examined both cocks, returned them to us, and told us to get ready.

'I've *been* ready!' Jack said.

I bobbed my head, and Ed said, 'Bill 'em!'

We billed the cocks on the center score.

'That's enough,' Ed said, when he saw how quickly the combativeness of both cocks was aroused. 'Pass 'em once and get ready.'

Holding our gamecocks at arm's length, we passed them in the air with a circling movement and retreated to our respective eight-foot scores.

'Pit!'

As usual, by watching the referee's lips, I let Icky go first, beating Burke off the score. I needed the split second. The O'Neal Red, with its dark red comb, and fresh from a country walk, was faster than Icky. Despite his superb condition, the days and nights in a narrow coop walk had slowed my Blue chicken down. Icky missed with both spurs as Little David side-stepped, and my cock wound up on his back with a spur in his chest.

'Handle!'

The second I disengaged the spur from Icky's breast, I retreated to my side of the pit and examined the wound. It wasn't fatal. Using the cellulose sponge and pan of clean water furnished by the pit, I wiped away the flowing blood, and pressed my thumb against the hole to stop the bleeding until the order came to get ready.

'Pit!'

Little David was overconfident and Icky was vigilant. The Red tried three aerial attacks and failed to get above my pitwise Blue. With mutual respect, they circled in tight patterns, heads low above the floor, hackles raised, glaring at each other with bright, angry eyes. Icky tried a tricky rushing feint that worked. As Little David wheeled and dodged instead of sidestepping, Icky walked up his spine like a lineman climbing a telephone pole. There was an audible thump as Icky struck a gaff home beneath Little David's right wing.

'Handle!'

Burke removed the gaff with gentle hands. The O'Neal Red had been hurt in the second pitting. The wound in Icky's chest no longer bled, but I held my thumb over the hole anyway, and made him stand quietly, facing him toward the wall where he couldn't see his opponent.

The third, fourth and fifth pittings were dance contests that could have been set to music. The two colorful gamecocks maneuvered, wheeled, sidestepped, feinted and leaped high into the air as they clashed. When one of them did manage to hang a heel, first one and then the other, the blow was punishing.

Prior to the sixth pitting, I held Icky's legs tight under his body to rest them, facing him toward the wall. I raised my eyes for a moment, and there sat Mary Elizabeth, not six feet away from me. I almost didn't recognize her at first. She was wearing a light blue coat with raglan sleeves, and she had a pastel-blue scarf over her blonde hair, tied beneath her chin. She sat in the second row — not in the seat I had reserved for her. Her skin was pale, and her expression was strained. As I smiled in recognition, Ed called for us to get ready, and I had to turn my back.

'Pit!'

For the first time in months I was second best in releasing my gamecock's tail. Little David outflew my Blue and fanned him down. On his back, Icky shuffled his feet like a cat. Both birds fell over, pronged together with all four gaffs, like knitting needles stuck into two balls of colored yarn.

'Handle!'

It took Burke and me almost a full minute to disengage the heels. Both cocks were severely injured and my hands were red with blood as I sponged my battered bird down gingerly with cold water. During the short rest period I didn't have time to exchange any love glances with my fiancée in the stands. Thirty seconds passed like magic.

'Get ready ... Pit!'

Both gamecocks remained on their scores as we released them.

'Count!' Burke ordered.

'One, two, three, four, five, six, seven, eight, nine and one for Mr. Burke. Handle!' Ed said, looking up from his wrist-watch.

Both of us needed the additional thirty-second rest

period. I sucked Icky's comb to warm his head, held his beak open wide and spat into his open throat to refresh him. I was massaging his tired legs gently when Ed told us to get ready.

'Pit!'

Stiff-winged, the two cocks advanced toward each other from their scores and clashed wearily in the center. Too sick and too tired for aerial fighting they buckled again and again with weakened fury. Little David fell over limply, breathing hard, and stayed there. Grateful for this respite, Icky also stopped fighting, standing quietly with his head down, bill touching the dirt.

'The count is going on,' Ed announced, watching his wrist-watch and the two cocks at the same time. At the silent count of twenty seconds, when neither bird had tried to fight, Ed ordered us to handle.

I wanted to work feverishly, but I was unable to do the nursing needed to help my fighter. Rough nursing could put Icky out of the fight for good. I sponged him gently and let him rest. Icky had recovered considerably by himself from the twenty-second count.

When the order to pit was given again, he crossed the dirt floor toward his enemy on shaky legs. Little David squatted on his score like a broody hen on eggs, with his beak wide open, and his neck jerking in and out.

Icky pecked savagely at the downed cock's weaving head. An instant later, the maddened Little David bounced into the air as though driven by a compressed spring and came down on Icky's back with blurring, hard-hitting heels. My cock was uncoupled by a spine blow, paralyzed, and unable to move from the neck down. Little David's right one-and-a-quarter inch heel had passed cleanly through Icky's kidney and the point was down as far as the caeca. On the order to handle, I disengaged the gaff and returned to my score.

I didn't dare to sponge him. There was very little I could do. Water would make him bleed more rapidly than he was bleeding already. I held him loosely between my hands, pressing my fingers lightly into his hot body, afraid he would come apart in my hands. Fortunately, Little David was as badly injured as Icky. His last desperate attack had taken every ounce of energy he had left.

After three futile counts of twenty, Ed Middleton ordered us to breast on the center score, one hand only beneath the bird.

Which gamecock would peck first?

Which gamecock would die first?

It was an endurance test. Little David had been the last chicken to fight. If Icky died first, Little David would be declared the winner by virtue of throwing the last blow. On the third breast pitting, Icky stretched out his limp neck and pecked feebly. The order to handle was given. Again we pitted, and again Icky pecked, and this time he got a billhold on the other cock's stubby dubbed comb. Little David didn't feel or notice the billhold. Little David was dead. And so was Icky, his beak clamped to the Red's comb to the last.

'I'll carry my bird out,' Jack Burke said.

'You're entitled to three more twenty-second counts,' Ed reminded him, going by the book.

'What's the use?' Burke said indifferently. 'They're *both* dead, now.'

'Dead or not,' Ed said officially, 'you're entitled by the rules to three counts of twenty after the other cock pecks.'

Without another word Jack Burke picked up his dead gamecock and left the pit. I picked up the Blue and held him to my chest. His long neck dangled limply over my left arm. My eyes were suddenly, irrationally, humid with tears.

'That's what I call a dead-game chicken, Frank!' Senator Foxhall called out from the judge's box.

I nodded blindly in his general direction and then turned my back on the old man to look for Mary Elizabeth. She wasn't in her seat. I caught a glimpse of her blue topcoat as she hurried out through the side entrance to the parking lot. I ran after her and caught up with her running figure just beyond the closed, shuttered box office.

'Mary Elizabeth!' I said aloud. My voice sounded rusty,

strangled, different, nothing at all like I remembered it.

She stopped running, turned and faced me, her face like a mask. Her lips were as bloodless as her face.

'You've decided to talk again? Is that it? It's too late now, Frank. And I know now that it was always too late for us. You aren't the man I fell in love with, but you *never* were! If I'd seen you in the cockpit ten years ago, I would've known then. I didn't watch those poor chickens fight, Frank, I watched your face. It was awful. No pity, no love, no understanding, nothing! Hate! You hate everything, yourself, me, the world, everybody!'

She closed her eyes to halt the tears. A moment later she opened her purse and wiped her eyes with a small white handkerchief.

'And I gave myself to you, Frank,' she said, as though she were speaking to herself. 'I gave you everything I had to offer, everything, to a man who doesn't even have a heart!'

I didn't know this woman. I had never seen her before. This was a Mary Elizabeth I had hidden from myself all these years.

I dropped my dead Blue chicken to the ground, put my left heel on its neck, reached down, and jerked off his head with my right hand. I held the beaten, bloody, but never, never bowed head out to Mary Elizabeth in my palm. I had nothing else to say to the woman.

Mary Elizabeth licked her pale lips. She took Icky's head from my hand and wrapped it in her white handkerchief. Tucking the wrapped head away in her purse, she nodded.

'Thank you. Thank you very much, Frank Mansfield. I'll accept your gift. When I get home, I'll preserve it in a jar of alcohol. I might even work out some kind of ritual, to remind myself what a damned fool I've been.'

Her emerald eyes burned into mine for a moment.

'My brother's been right about you all along, but I had to drive up here to find out for myself. You're everything he said you were, Frank Mansfield. A mean, selfish sonofabitch!'

Turning abruptly, she headed toward the rows of parked cars. After only a few steps, she broke into a wobbling, feminine run. I don't know how long I stood there, looking after her retreating figure, even after she had passed from sight. A minute, two minutes, I don't know.

A voice blared over the outside speakers of the PA system: 'MR. ROY WHIPPLE AND MR. FRANK MANSFIELD. REPORT TO THE JUDGE'S BOX, PLEASE!' The announcement was repeated twice, and I heard it, but I didn't pay any attention to the amplified voice. I was immobilized by thought. I've grown up, I reflected. After thirty-three years, I was a mature individual. I had never needed Mary Elizabeth, and she had never needed me. Finally, it was all over between us — whatever it was we thought we had. My last tie with the past and Mansfield, Georgia, was broken. From now on I could look toward the future, and it had never been any brighter —

He must have made some noise, but I didn't hear Omar's feet crunching on the gravel until he grabbed my arm.

'For God's sake, Frank,' Omar said excitedly. 'What the hell are you standing out here for? Senator Foxhall's awarding you the Cockfighter of the Year award! Let's go inside, man! As your partner, I'm entitled to a little reflected glory, you know.'

Now that he had my attention, he smiled broadly, his white teeth gleaming through his black moustache. 'Of course,' he shrugged, 'Old Man Whipple won the tourney, but what do we care? Thanks to Icky's victory, we're loaded!' He patted his bulging jacket pockets. 'We've got so damned much money, I'm almost afraid to count it.'

Smiling, I gestured for him to go on ahead of me. Omar turned toward the entrance and trotted down the short hallway to the pit.

When I reached the doorway, I paused. After the barbecue was over, I would ask Bernice to go to Puerto Rico with me for a month or so. If it got dull in Puerto Rico, we could swing on down to Caracas, and I might be able to pick up some Spanish Aces for next season. Omar could put our proven birds out on their Alabama walks without any assistance from me. And then, if I returned from South America by the middle of April, I would be back in plenty of time to start working with the spring stags.

Across the pit, standing behind the referee's table in front of the judge's box, the two greatest game fowl men in the world were waiting for me. Senator Foxhall and Ed Middleton. To the left of the table, Peach Owen was holding the leather box that contained my award.

Well, they could wait a little longer.

As I neared her seat in the front row, Bernice smiled and said, 'Congratulations, Frank!'

'Thanks,' I replied.

'Oh!' she said, her eyes widening with astonishment. 'You — you've got your voice back!'

'Yeah,' I said, grinning at her expression, 'and you'll probably wish I hadn't.'

'I — I don't know what you mean.'

'You'll find out that I'm quite a talker, Bernice, once I get wound up. How'd you like to go to Puerto Rico for a few weeks?'

'Right now,' she said, 'I'm so confused that the only answer I can think of on the spur of the moment is "Yes."'

I laughed and turned away, joy burbling out of my throat. How good to talk again, to *laugh* again!

I jerked my jacket down in back and pushed my white hat back on my head at a careless angle. Then, squaring my shoulders, I crossed the empty pit to get my goddamned medal.

No Beast So Fierce - Eddie Bunker

An angry and mercilessly suspenseful novel about an ex-con's attempt to negotiate the "straight world" and his swan dive back into the paradoxical security of crime. It is airtight in its construction, almost photorealistic in its portrayal of L.A. lowlife and utterly knowledgeable about the terrors of liberty, the high of the quick score and the rage that makes the finger tighten on the trigger of the gun.

"Integrity, craftsmanship and moral passion...an artist with a unique and compelling voice" - *William Styron*

"The best first person crime novel I have ever read" - *Quentin Tarantino*

"Quite simply, one of the great crime novels of the past 30 years" - *James Ellroy*

No Beast So Fierce - £5.99. Please add £0.75 P&P. Cheques/P.O's payable to Oldcastle Books Ltd. Credit cards welcome. Also available from Eddie Bunker - The Animal Factory (£5.99) and Little Boy Blue (£5.99)

NO EXIT PRESS, (CWO), 18 Coleswood Rd, Harpenden, Herts, AL5 1EQ, England